THE TOWN

BY THE SAME AUTHOR

The Blood Artists
The Standoff
The Killing Moon
Devils in Exile
The Strain (with Guillermo del Toro)

THE TOWN

CHUCK HOGAN

BLOOMSBURY

LONDON · BERLIN · NEW YORK · SYDNEY

First published in Great Britain 2005 under the title *Prince of Thieves*
This paperback edition published 2010

First published in USA by Scribner, an imprint of Simon & Schuster Inc.

Bloomsbury Publishing Plc, 36 Soho Square, London W1D 3QY

A CIP catalogue record for this book is available from the British Library

FSC
www.fsc.org

MIX

Paper from
responsible sources

FSC® C018072

ISBN 9781408815694

10 9 8 7 6 5 4

Typeset by RefineCatch Ltd, Bungay, Suffolk
Printed in Great Britain by Clays Ltd, St Ives plc

www.bloomsbury.com/chuckhogan

To my mother:
How great the darkness.

For where your treasure is, there will your heart be also.

—Matthew 6: 21

Charlestown, Massachusetts's reputation as a breeding ground for bank and armored-car robbers is authentic. Although faithful to the Town's geography and its landmarks, this novel all but ignores the great majority of its residents, past and present, who are the same good and true people found most anywhere.

While Charlestown is home to some of the most decent people in the city, it has, like no other neighborhood, a hoodlum subculture that is preoccupied with sticking up banks and armored cars.

—*The Boston Globe*, March 3, 1995

... a community to which more armored-car robbers are traced than any other in the country, according to FBI statistics.

—*The Boston Globe*, March 19, 1995

This self-described Townie spoke . . . on condition of anonymity, describing what it was like to grow up in Charlestown. "I'm mighty proud of where I come from. It's ruined my life, literally, but I'm proud."

—*The Boston Globe*, March 19, 1995

First, a toast. Raise a glass. Solemn now:

To the Town.

To Charlestown, our one square mile of brick and cobblestone. Neighborhood of Boston, yet lopped off every map of the city like a bastard cropped out of a happy family portrait.

This is the heart of the "Old Eleventh", the district that first sent the Kennedy kid to Congress. The one square mile of America that shipped more boys off to World War II than any other. Site of the Battle of Bunker Hill, the blood of revolution sprinkled like holy water over our soil and our souls. Turf and Tribe and Townie Pride—our sacred trinity.

But now look at these outsiders snapping up our brownstones and triple-deckers. Pricing us out of our own mother's houses. Yuppies with their Volvos and their Asian cuisine, their disposable incomes and contempt for the church—succeeding where the British army failed, driving us off our land.

But sure, we don't go away so easy. "Don't fire until you see the whites of their eyes!"—that was us, remember. This carnation here may be a bit brown at the edges—but see it still pinned to the tweed lapel over my beating Townie heart.

Be a hero now, reach me that jar. We'll have a hard-boiled egg with this last one, see how she goes down. It's caps off, gents. Here's to that towering spike on a hill, the granite battle monument that'll outlast us all: the biggest feckin' middle finger in the world, aimed right at good brother Boston and the twenty-first century beyond.

To the Town. Here's how.

PART I
PRIDE

1
THE BANK JOB

DOUG MACRAY STOOD INSIDE the rear door of the bank, breathing deeply through his mask. Yawning, that was a good sign. Getting oxygen. He was trying to get amped up. Breaking in overnight had left them with plenty of downtime to sit and eat their sandwiches and goof on each other and get comfortable, and that wasn't good for the job. Doug had lost his buzz—the action, fear, and momentum that was the cocktail of banditry. *Get in, get the money, get out.* His father talking, but fuck it, on this subject the old crook was right. Doug was ready for this thing to fall.

He swung his head side to side but could not crack his neck. He looked at the black .38 in his hand, but gripping a loaded pistol had long since lost its porn. He wasn't there for thrills. He wasn't even there for money, though he wouldn't leave without it. He was there for the job. The *job* of the job, like the *thing* of the thing. Him and Jem and Dez and Gloansy pulling pranks together, same as when they were kids—only now it was their livelihood. Heisting was what they did and who they were.

His blood warmed to that, the broad muscles of his back tingling. He rapped the hard plastic forehead of his goalie mask with his pistol barrel and shook out the cobwebs as he turned toward the door. A pro, an athlete at the top of his game. He was at the height of his powers.

Jem stood across from him like a mirror image: the dusty navy blue jumpsuit zipped over the armored vest, the gun in his gloved hand, and the white goalie mask marked up with black stitch scars, his eyes two dark sockets.

Happy voices approaching, muffled. Keys turning in reinforced locks, strongbars releasing.

A spear of daylight. A woman's hand on the knob and the kick of a chunky black shoe—and the swish of a black floral skirt walking into Doug's life.

He seized the branch manager's arm and spun her around in front of him, showing her the pistol without jamming it in her face. Her eyes were green and bright and full, but it was his mask that scared short her scream, not the Colt.

Jem kicked the door shut behind the assistant manager, smacking the cardboard caddy out of the guy's hand. Two steaming cups of coffee splattered against the wall, leaving a runny brown stain.

Doug took the bank keys from the manager's hand and felt her going weak. He walked her down the short hallway to the tellers' row behind the front counter, where Gloansy—identically dressed, masked, and Kevlar-bulked—waited. The bank manager startled at the sight of him, but she had no breath left for screaming. Doug passed her off to Gloansy, who laid her and the gray-suited assistant manager face-first on the carpeting behind the cages. Gloansy started yanking off their shoes, his voice deepened and filtered by the mask.

Lie still. Shut your eyes. Nobody gets hurt.

Doug moved with Jem through the open security door into the lobby. Dez stood beside the front door, hidden from Kenmore Square by the drawn blinds. He checked the window before flashing a blue-gloved thumb, and Doug and Jem crossed the only portion of the lobby visible from the ATM vestibule.

Jem unfolded a deep canvas hockey bag on the floor. Doug turned the stubbiest key on the manager's ring in the night-deposit cabinet lock, and silver plastic deposit bags spilled to the floor like salmon from a cut net. A holiday weekend's worth. Doug gathered them up five and six at a time, soft bags of cash and checks bundled in deposit slips, dumping the catch into Jem's open duffel.

After raiding the night drop, Doug went on alone to the access door behind the ATM. He matched key to lock, then looked over to the tellers' cages where Jem had the branch manager on her feet. She looked small without shoes, head down, hair slipping over her face.

"Again," Jem commanded her. "Louder."

She said, staring at the floor, "Four. Five. Seven. Eight."

Doug ignored the choke in her voice and punched the code into the mechanical dial over the key. The door swung open on the ATM closet, and Doug unlatched the feeder and pulled the cash cassette. After the long weekend it was less than half full. He scooped out the sheets of postage stamps as an afterthought and dumped them with the tens and twenties into the bag. Then he flipped the service switch, reloaded the empty cassette, and hustled back past the check-writing counter, running the bag through the open security door to the tellers' cages.

There, he retrieved a small strongbox from a drawer at the head teller's station. Beneath some dummy forms and a leftover stack of flimsy giveaway 1996 desk calendars was a brown coin envelope containing the cylindrical vault key.

THEY COULD HAVE BEEN a couple waiting for an elevator, except for the gun: Jem and the manager standing together before the wide vault door. Jem was holding her close, exploring the curve of her ass through her skirt with the muzzle of his .45 as he whispered something in her ear. Doug made noise coming up behind them and Jem's gun moved to her hip.

Jem said, "She says the time lock's set for eight eighteen."

The digital clock built into the vault door said 8:17. They stood for that one minute in silence, Doug behind the manager, listening to her breathing, watching the hands of her self-hugging arms grip her sides.

The clock changed to 8:18. Doug inserted the key over the thick black dial.

"We know all about panic codes," Jem told the manager. "Now open it clean."

Her hand came out stiffly, steadying itself against the cool steel door and leaving a brief, steamy palm print there before starting in on the dial. When she hesitated after the second turn, Doug knew she had made a mistake.

"No fucking stalling," said Jem.

She dried her quivering hand on her skirt. The second time, she made it past the third number of the combination before her nerves betrayed her, her fingers twisting the dial too far.

"For *Christ*!" said Jem.

"I'm sorry!" she wailed, half in anger, half in terror.

Jem put the gun to her ear. "You have kids?"

She veered away from him, her voice strangled. "No."

"A husband? Boyfriend?"

"*No.*"

"Christ! Parents, then. Do you have parents? Who the fuck can I threaten?"

Doug stepped in, easing Jem's gun away from her face. "How many attempts before the lock triggers a duress delay?"

She swallowed. "Three."

Doug said, "And how long until it can be opened again after that?"

"I think—fifteen minutes."

"Write it *down*," said Jem. "Write out the combination, I will fucking do it myself."

Doug looked at her grimacing face in profile, feeling her fear. "You don't want us here another fifteen minutes."

She considered that a second, then reached fast for the dial, her hand darting like a bird from a cage. Doug caught her wrist, held it firm.

"Slow," he said. "Take your time. Once you start, do not stop."

She wrapped a fist around her thumb. When he released her, her hand went cautiously to the dial. Her fingers obeyed her this time, shaking again only as she approached the final number. The interior *clack* was audible.

Jem spun the locking wheel and the door released, opening on massive hinges, the vault emitting a cool, cottony yawn after a long weekend's sleep.

Doug grabbed the manager's arm and walked her away. She paused in sight of her office, their entry point, where they had brought the ceiling down on top of her desk.

"It's my birthday," she whispered.

Doug walked her fast out to Gloansy, who put her back with the assistant manager, facedown on the floor. Dez stood near with his scarred mask cocked at a quizzical angle. A radio check, him listening to the unseen wire rising up from inside his jumpsuit collar.

"Nothing," Dez said. The police frequencies were all clear.

AS A CONQUEST, VAULT interiors always disappointed Doug. The public access areas such as the safe-deposit rooms were kept polished and showroom clean, but the actual money rooms were no more impressive than utility closets.

This vault was no exception. The main cabinet door containing the cash reserves was made of thin metal and fastened with a flimsy desk lock, which Doug busted open in one stroke. Despite the vault's hard-target exterior, once you were in, you were in. He ignored the heavy racks of rolled coins and instead pulled down stacked bundles of circulated paper currency. The color-coded paper straps that banded the bills told him the denominations at a glance: red for $5s, yellow for $10s, violet for $20s, brown for $50s, and beautiful mustard for $100s. He snapped them off as he went, fanning the wads of cash, spot-checking for dye packs and tracers.

Four cash-on-wheels teller trucks lined the back of the vault. The top drawers held about $2,500 each, and Doug cleared out all of it except the bait bills, the thin, paper-clipped bundles of twenties laid out at the bottom of each slot. The first drawer was the one tellers drew from during routine transactions, the one they emptied in the event of a stickup.

The second drawers were deeper than the first, containing higher denominations for commercial transactions and account closings, more than four times as much money as the first drawers. Doug again emptied each one down to the bait bills.

They ignored the safe-deposit room altogether. Opening boxes would have meant drilling each door individually, ten minutes per lock, two locks per box. And even if they did have all day, the Kenmore Square BayBanks branch served a transient community of Boston University students and apartment renters, so there was no point. In an upscale-neighborhood bank, the safe boxes would have been the primary target, since branches in wealthier zip codes usually carry less operating cash, their customers relying on direct deposit rather than paycheck cashing, purchasing things with plastic rather than paper.

Dez's blue palm halted them on the way back. "Asshole at the ATM."

Through the blinds, Doug made out a college kid in sweats playing the machine for allowance money. His card was rejected twice before he bothered to read the service message on the screen. He looked to the door, checking the bank hours printed there, then lifted the customer service phone off the receiver.

"Nope," said Dez.

In the middle of this, Doug looked at the manager lying behind the second teller's cage. He knew things about her. Her name was Claire Keesey. She drove a plum-colored Saturn coupe with a useless rear spoiler and a happy-face bumper sticker that said *Breathe!* She lived alone, and when it was warm enough, she spent her lunch hours in the community gardens along the nearby Back Bay Fens. He knew these things because he had been following her, off and on, for weeks.

Now, up close, Doug could see the faintly darker roots of her hair, the pale brown she treated honey blond. Her long, black linen skirt outlined her legs to the lacy white feet of her stockings, where jagged stitching across the left heel betrayed a thrifty mending never meant to be seen.

She rolled her head along her bent arm, just enough for a peek up at Gloansy, who was hunched over and watching the kid on the ATM phone. Her left leg began to creep toward the teller's chair. Her foot slipped underneath the counter and out of Doug's sight, poking around under there, then gliding swiftly back into position, her eyes returning to the crook of her elbow.

Doug exhaled slowly. Now he had a problem.

The kid in the ATM gave up on the dead telephone and kicked the wall before shoving bitchily through the doors out into the early morning.

Jem dropped the loot bag next to the tool bag and the work bag. "Let's blow," he said, exactly what Doug wanted to hear. As Gloansy pulled plastic ties from his pockets, and Jem and Dez lifted jugs of Ultra Clorox from the work bag, Doug turned and walked fast down the rear hall into the employee break room. The security equipment sat on wooden shelves there, and the system had tripped, the cameras switched on and recording, a small red light pulsing over the door. Doug stopped all three VCRs and ejected the tapes, then unplugged the system for good measure.

He brought the tapes back out to the front and dumped them into the work bag without anyone else seeing. Gloansy had the assistant manager in one of the teller's chairs, binding the guy's wrists behind the chair back. Bloody snot painted the assistant manager's lips and chin. Jem must have flat-nosed him on their way in.

Doug lifted the heavy tool bag to his shoulder just as he saw Dez quit splashing bleach, setting his jugs down on the floor.

"Hold it!" Dez called out.

Dez's finger went to his ear as Jem emerged from the vault, jugs in hand. Gloansy stopped with the manager seated behind the assistant manager now, back-to-back, a tie for her wrists ready in his free hand. Everyone looked at Dez—except Doug, who was looking at the manager staring at the floor.

Dez said, "Silent alarm call, this address."

Jem looked for Doug. "What the fuck?" he said, setting down his bleach.

"We're done here anyway," said Doug. "We're gone. Let's go."

Jem drew his pistol, keeping it low at his hip as he approached the seated bankers. "Who did it?"

The manager kept staring at the floor. The assistant manager stared at Jem, a black forelock of hair hanging ragged and sullen over his eyes.

"We were gone," said Jem, pointing at the back hallway with his gun. "We were out that fucking door."

The assistant manager winced at Jem through his hair, eyes watering from the bleach fumes, still sore from his cuffing at the door.

Jem locked on him. Wounded defiance was the worst possible play the assistant manager could make.

Dez picked up his bleach, hurriedly finishing splashing it around. "Let's go," he said.

"We've gotta move," Doug told Jem.

Another few seconds of staring, and the spell was broken. Jem stepped off, relaxing his gun hand, slipping the piece back inside his belt. He was already turning away when the assistant manager said, "Look, no one did any—"

Jem flew at the man in a blur. The sound of knuckles against temple was like a tray of ice being cracked, Jem holding back nothing.

The assistant manager whipped left and slumped over the armrest, the chair tipping and falling onto its side.

The assistant manager sagged, still bound to the chair by his wrists. Jem dropped to one knee and hammered away again and again at the defenseless guy's cheek and jaw. Then Jem stopped and went back for his bleach. Only Doug's hooking his arm stopped Jem from emptying the jug over the man's shattered face.

That close, Doug could see the pale, nearly white-blue of Jem's irises within the recesses of the goalie mask, glowing like snow at night. Doug twisted the bleach out of Jem's hand and told him to load the bags. To Doug's surprise, Jem did just that.

Doug soaked the night drop in the lobby. He soaked the carpet where they had filled the loot bag, jumpy near the windows, expecting sirens. He shook out the jug over the ATM cassette, then returned to the counter.

The assistant manager remained hanging off the overturned chair. Only his wheezing told Doug the guy was still alive.

The bags were gone. So was the manager.

Doug walked to the back, bleach fumes swamping his vision. The bags were stacked and waiting, and Dez and Jem both had their masks off, standing at the rear door, Jem's hand clamped on the back of the manager's neck, keeping her from seeing their faces. Dez picked up her brown leather handbag where it had fallen upon entry, shooting Doug a hard look of warning.

Doug whipped off his goalie mask, his ski mask still on underneath. "Fuck is this?"

"What if they already got us walled in?" said Jem, wild. "We need her."

Wheels skidding on alley grit, the work van pulling up outside, and Gloansy, unmasked now, jumping from the wheel to throw the side doors open.

Dez started out, two-handing the first duffel bag, swinging it aboard.

"Leave her," Doug commanded. But Jem was already rushing her out to the van.

Doug's ski mask came off, crackling with electricity. Seconds mattered. He carried the work bag into the glaring sunlight and dumped it into the van with a crash. Jem was next to him, trying to load the manager into the van without her glimpsing his face. Doug took her by the waist, boosted her up, then cut in front of Jem, leaving Jem the third bag.

Doug pushed her down the length of the soft bench seat to the windowless wall. "Eyes shut," he told her, stuffing her head down to her knees. "No noise."

The last bag thudded and the doors slammed and the van lurched up the sharp, ramplike incline, bouncing off the curb and onto the street. Doug pulled his Leatherman from its belt pouch. He opened up the largest blade and tugged the hem of her black jacket taut, cutting into the fabric, then collapsing the blade and tearing off a long strip. She flinched at the noise, shaking but not struggling beneath him.

He looked up and they were headed around into Kenmore Square, the red light at the end of Brookline Avenue. The bank was on their right. Doug kept his weight on the manager's upper back, watching. No cruisers yet in the square, nothing.

Gloansy said, "What about the switch?"

"Later," Doug said, through his teeth, sliding the Leatherman back onto his belt.

The light turned green and the traffic started forward. Gloansy went easy, bearing east on Commonwealth Avenue.

A cruiser was coming, no lights, rolling west toward them, around the bus station in the center island of the square. The cruiser lit up its rack to slow traffic, making a wide U-turn and cutting across behind them, pulling up curbside at the bank.

They rolled past the bus station toward the Storrow Drive overpasses. Doug wrapped the fabric twice around the manager's head, tying it tight in a blindfold. He pulled her halfway up, waving his hand in front of her face, then made a fist and drove it at her, stopping just short of her nose. When she didn't flinch, he let her sit up the rest of the way, then slid to the far end of the bench, as far away from her as he could get, tearing off his jumpsuit as if he were trying to shed his own criminal skin.

2
CRIME SCENE

ADAM FRAWLEY PARKED HIS Bureau car in the slanting shadow of Fenway Park's Green Monster, jogging across the short bridge over the Massachusetts Turnpike with his folder and notebook trapped under his elbow, pulling on a pair of latex gloves. The fence along the side of the bridge was high and curved at the top to keep Red Sox fans from hurling themselves off it every September. At the tail end of Newbury Street, two windbreakers from the Boston Police crime lab were crouching inside yellow tape, dusting a graffiti-tagged metal door and bagging loose alley trash near a plum Saturn coupe.

Newbury Street was the tony promenade listed in every Boston guidebook, beginning downtown at the Public Garden and riding out in orderly alphabetical blocks, Arlington to Berkeley to Clarendon, all the way to Hereford before skipping impatiently to *M,* the broad Massachusetts Avenue that formed the unofficial western border of the Back Bay. Newbury Street continued beyond that dividing line, but with its spirit broken, forced to run alongside the ugly turnpike more or less as a back alley for Commonwealth Avenue, its humiliation ending at the suicide bridge.

Frawley rounded the corner to the front of the bank, at the tail end of a block of brick-front apartment buildings topping street-level retail stores and bars. Kenmore Square was a bottleneck fed by three major inbound roads, Brookline, Beacon, and Commonwealth, converging at a bus station where Comm boulevarded into two lanes split by a proper grass mall. Curbside clots of police cruisers, fire engines, and news vans were squeezing traffic down to one lane.

An industrial-sized fan blocked the bank's open front door, broadcasting pungent bleach out onto the sidewalk. A handwritten sign on the window said the branch was closed for the day and directed customers to area ATMs or the next nearest branch at the corner of Boylston and Mass.

Frawley opened his credentials holder, pressing his FBI ID card and his small gold badge against the window near the FDIC sticker that was his ticket inside. The Federal Deposit Insurance Corporation guaranteed all deposit accounts up to $100,000, making any bank crime committed on U.S. soil a federal offense. A Boston cop holding a handkerchief to his mouth stepped into the ATM vestibule and switched off the big fan in order to let Frawley inside.

"Here he is," said Dino, greeting him beside the check-writing counter, clipboard in hand. The smell of violation was not so strong there as at the door.

Frawley said, "I was fine until I hit the expressway coming back."

The Boston Bank Robbery Task Force operated not out of the field office downtown but out of a resident agency in Lakeville, a small bedroom community thirty miles south of the city. Frawley had been pulling into the industrial park there when he got this call.

Dino had a pair of paper bootees for him. Dean Drysler was Boston Police, twenty-seven years, a lieutenant detective on permanent assignment to the task force. He was local product, tall, long-boned, sure. Boston saw more per capita bank jobs and armored-car heists than anywhere else in the country, and Dino was indispensable to Frawley as someone who knew the terrain.

Frawley was thirty-three, compact, laser-sighted, a runner. He had less than two years with the Boston office, eight overall with the FBI following rapid-fire assignments in Miami, Seattle, and New York. He was the youngest bank robbery agent in the country, one of a platoon of five Boston agents assigned to the BRTF, investigating bank crimes throughout Massachusetts, Rhode Island, New Hampshire, and Maine. The working partnership he and Dino had formed was of the teacher-student variety, though the roles of teacher and student flip-flopped day to day, sometimes hour to hour.

Frawley pulled the bootees on over his size-eight-and-a-halfs and organized his rape kit: paperwork folder, notebook, tape recorder. He scanned the various uniforms and acronym-proud windbreakers. "Where is she now?"

"Break room in back. They let her go at Orient Heights, north of the airport. She walked to a corner market, they called it in. We already had a cruiser here on the silent bell."

"From?"

"Teller cage number two." They walked through the security door behind the counter, where the vapors were stronger, the industrial carpeting already blanching in spots. Dino pointed his clipboard at a floor button. "Panic bell. The assistant manager is down the street at Beth Israel, he caught a pretty good beating."

"Beat him, then took her for a ride, let her go?"

Dino's eyebrows arched satanically. "Unharmed."

Frawley set his suspicion aside, trying to go in order. "Anything on the vehicle?"

"Van, seems like. I put a BOLO out for car fires."

"You talk to her?"

"I set her up with a female officer first."

Frawley looked at the open vault door behind Dino, its round piston locks disengaged. Two techs in jumpsuits and bootees were going over the inside walls with blue lasers. Print dust on the outer door showed a beautiful handprint over the dial, but small, likely the manager's. "Morning Glory?"

"Morning Glory and a Jack-in-the-Box. Worked a bypass and busted in overnight. Phones here are all dead. BayBanks central security tried a callback on the silent and got no answer, dispatched the patrolman. Security chief's on his way over with the codes and specs, but I'm figuring two hard lines and a cellular backup. They tricked out the cell and one of the Nynex lines."

"Only one?"

"Waiting on a Nynex truck to confirm. I'm guessing the vault is hardwired, bank-to-station, same as the teller panics. Our guys let the time lock expire and had the manager open sesame."

"Under duress."

"That is my understanding."

Frawley jotted this down. "Easier than humping in SLICE packs and oxy tanks and burning through the vault walls."

Dino shrugged his pointy shoulders. "Whether they could have jumped the vault bell or not."

Frawley considered that. "Neutralizing the vault might have tipped their hand too much."

"Though with some of these guys—you know it—burglary is pussy."

Frawley nodded. "It's not a payday unless they're robbing someone face-to-face."

"Bottom line is, they know phone lines and Baby Bell tech."

Frawley nodded, surveying the fouled bank from the perspective of teller station number two, his cop eyes starting to sting. "These are the same guys, Dino."

"Throwing us curveballs now. Look at this."

THE TREND IN "COMMUNITY BANKING" was to feature the branch manager's office up front, prominent behind glass walls, playing up accessibility and putting a friendly, local face on a corporation that charges you fees for the privilege of handing you back your own money. Kenmore Square was a prime location—high foot traffic with the student population, the nightclubs, the nearby ballpark—but the space itself was an odd fit for a bank, deeper than it was wide, owing to the ending curve of the road. The manager's office was tucked away behind the tellers, along the back hallway near the break room and bathrooms.

A police photographer was inside, his flash throwing shadows off the chunk of ceiling concrete atop the desk. It had crushed a telephone and a computer monitor, cords and keyboard dangling to the floor like entrails. Neatly sheared rebar and steel mesh lay among rubble of plaster, ceiling corkboard, concrete dust, and mottled gray chips.

Frawley looked up at the layers of flooring visible in the square ceiling hole, seeing an eye chart above an examining-room sink. The robbers had broken into the second-floor optometry shop and cut through overnight. This was the hidden cost of doing business in an older city like Boston, and why banks preferred to open branches in freestanding buildings.

A red helmet appeared in the hole, a fireman doing a pretend startle. "Thought you guys were bank robbers!"

Dino nodded upward with a smile. "Off your break already, Spack?"

He said it old-city style, *Spack* instead of *Spark*. Dino could turn the hometown accent on and off like charm.

"Just getting my eyes checked. This your whiz kid?"

"Special Agent Frawley, meet Captain Jimmy here."

Frawley waved at the ceiling with his free hand.

"A perfect square, two by two," said Captain Jimmy. "Nice work."

Dino nodded. "If you can get it."

"Hope you two catch these geniuses before the cancer does." He pointed down through the hole. "Those gray chips there, that's asbestos."

Frawley said, "Any tools up top?"

"Nope. Nothing."

Frawley eyed the smooth cut, turned to Dino. "Industrial concrete saw."

"Yeah, and a torch for the rebar. Nothing very fancy. Our boys are blue-collar bandits. Real salt-of-the-earth numskulls."

Frawley said, "Numskulls who can bypass alarms."

"Spack's gonna cut out this hole for us," said Dino, turning to leave. "Hey, careful up there, Spacky, you don't pull any muscles, have to take a year's disability vacation on my account."

Chuckles from firemen above, and Captain Jimmy saying, "Dean, you know there's only one muscle I'd pull for you."

OUTSIDE THE BACK DOOR Frawley heard the cars on the nearby turnpike, speeding into and out of the city. The small parking spaces and chained Dumpsters sat lower than the street, a culvert gathering sand, grit, and trash.

A Morning Glory score was typically the most successful and lucrative type of bank robbery. Ambushing employees before the bank opened meant fewer people to control. The branch's cash stores were still centralized in the vault, not yet disbursed to tellers or spread around in secondary safes or backup drawers, and therefore easy to find and carry with speed. The typical Morning Glory involved a distracted branch opener getting waylaid in the parking lot at gunpoint. Breaking in overnight and lying in wait for the manager to arrive— the Jack-in-the-Box—showed a deeper level of preparation and, among notoriously lazy bank robbers, an aberrant affinity for hard work.

Frawley saw a photographer laying a ruler next to the tire treads in the road sand. He almost told her not to bother. The stolen getaway van would turn up in a few hours, in a vacant lot somewhere, torched.

He envisioned them loading the van, hustling but not panicked, the silent alarm ringing only in their heads. Why take the time to beat the assistant manager? The vault was empty, and they were already on their way out. Taking the manager was schizo. It was a piece that didn't fit, and as such, something for Frawley to key on.

THE SHAPE OF THE bloodstain soaked into the carpet behind the tellers' cages resembled the continent of Africa. A lab technician was sampling it and depositing fibers into a brown, coin-sized envelope.

"He was cuffed to the chair." Dino held up an evidence bag containing a snipped plastic bundling tie, the kind with locking teeth.

"Cracked his jaw, maybe his cheekbone, the bones around the eye."

Frawley nodded, the odor at its most pungent there. Bleach effectively fragged DNA. Criminalists at the FBI lab used it to blitz their work surfaces clean, to avoid any evidentiary cross-contamination. Pouring bleach was something he had heard of rapists doing, fouling genetic matter left on the victim, but never bank robbers. "Bleach, huh?"

"A little extreme. But camping out here overnight, you can never be too careful."

"They sure don't want to get caught. These guys must be facing a long fall." Frawley slid his beeper to his hip and crouched behind the third teller's cage, noticing blond crumbs on the paling carpet, partially melted by the bleach. "They sat here and had a picnic."

Dino crouched with him, his mechanical pencil tucked behind a hairy ear. "Gets hungry on a job, Frawl. I told you, these are blue-collar bandits. Boiled eggs and thermos coffee. The Brown Bag Bandits."

Dino stood again while Frawley remained on his haunches, imagining the bandits hanging out there as the sun came up, the bank theirs. He rose and looked through the teller's cage to the windows along the front of the building, the square outside. He had a vague memory of passing through it the day before—a sense of entering the home stretch, his legs burning, the crowd cheering him on. "Marathon runs right by here?"

"Holy shit, Frawl, I forgot. Look at you. Twenty-six point two miles and you're up and around like nothing happened."

Frawley returned his beeper to the front of his belt. "Broke three and a half hours," he said. "I'm happy with that."

"Well, congratulations, you loose screw. That is one lonely sport you got there. What is it you think about the whole time?"

"Finishing," Frawley said, now looking at the lockbox open on the back counter. "So the eye doctor was closed all day."

"Top-floor gym was too, but some employees got together to watch the race—picture windows, good view up there. They were out by six. Traffic control ends around eight at night outside, even with runners still stumbling in. Our guys didn't need more than a few hours to load in, punch their hole, and drop down."

"Young guys. Lowering themselves through a two-by-two hole in the ceiling."

"Not the old masters, no. The older generation—lockpicks, plumbers—they'd need a bed to land on."

"How'd they access the building?"

"Another rear door. Separate entrance for the shops upstairs."

"Exterior security cameras?"

"Not for the bank. But we'll check. Though if it's our guys—"

"Yeah, they'll already have been busted." Frawley put his hands on his hips, his thighs and calves still stinging. "So what's your call?"

"Early call?" Dino sucked in a breath and joined Frawley in looking around. "It's a good pick here. The holiday, the hundredth running of the marathon. Nice weather, a square full of hungry race fans. The bookstore, clothing stores across the street—though they're mostly credit-card transactions. But the convenience store, the McDonald's, that Espresso Royale coffee thing. Plus the Sox are in town, that ups the neighborhood restaurant and bar cash big time, over three days. Plus—Jesus—the nightclubs on Landsdowne Street. Their combined Saturday-Sunday takes?" Dino worked his tongue around the inside of his cheek. "I'm gonna go large here. With the vault, the night deposits, the ATM? Put me down for three and a quarter. Plus or minus ten percent, yeah, I'd say a good three and a quarter."

"I'm going three-five," said Frawley, turning toward the open vault. "*Fuck*, I want these guys."

FRAWLEY NEEDED THE VAULT. The vault was his vic. Not the corporation that owned the bank, not the federal government that insured it and employed him. The vault: emptied and plaintive and violated. He needed the vault in the same way that homicide detectives generate sympathy for the corpse to fuel their hunt.

The safe-deposit room had not been touched. Drilling each individual box demanded a blind man's patience and a lottery player's devotion, a hundred-to-one gamble on finding anything of value that wasn't insured and traceable.

He moved through the open interior door into a well-maintained cash hold. Frawley sometimes found tellers' jackets and umbrellas hanging inside vaults. He had seen vaults used as break rooms.

Fingerprint dust coated the cabinets and doors. Only traveler's checks, scores of torn, color-coded paper straps, and the manager's tally sheets remained inside the forced cabinet. Frawley tried to shut the bent door with his elbow, the hinges whining as it crept open again.

Six rigid bundles of cash had been set aside, left behind in a small, neat pile over the cash drawers. Frawley cracked open one of the short stacks of retired bills, finding a dye pack nestled in the hollow. He recognized the SecurityPac brand. Dye packs worked when removed from the bank's premises, triggered by electronic transmitters hidden near the doors. The device was timed to delay detonation for twenty or more seconds, the pack burning at 400° Fahrenheit, too hot for the thief to grab and throw. It released an aerosol cloud of indelible red dye powder that turned note-passers into human smoke bombs, voiding currency and staining human skin for days. Less well-known was that many dye packs also emitted a small burst of incapacitating tear gas.

He examined the drawers without touching them, empty but for the bait bills clipped together in the bottom of each slot. Bait bills were $10 or $20 notes whose denominations, series years, and serial numbers were recorded and kept on file by the bank, per federal deposit insurance regulations. This established a paper trail linking a suspect and the cash in his pocket to the crime scene.

Many bait bills also contained a tracer in the form of a thin magnetic strip that, once removed from the drawer, triggered a silent alarm signal to police dispatch. Known as B-packs, these particular bait bills acted like tracking bugs, the same way a LoJack device works in a stolen automobile. Many counter-jumpers, arrested at their home hours after what seemed to be a successful $1,200 job, never learned until their court date how it was that the FBI fingered them.

With no carpet to absorb it, the bleach odor was dizzyingly potent, but Frawley remained inside as long as he could. He wished that the vault could beg him for justice. That it was someone whose hand he could take in a gesture of reassurance, offering a covenant, cop to vic. Then he wouldn't have to bring so much to these empty repositories himself.

THE TECHNICIAN SWABBED THE insides of the branch manager's cheeks, collecting elimination DNA along with her fingerprints while Frawley made a copy of the manager's contact sheet on the bank's Xerox machine.

Claire G. Keesey. DOB 4/16/66. Frawley looked again and realized that today was her thirtieth birthday.

Dino wanted a look upstairs, leaving Frawley to do the interview solo. She was wiping ink from her fingers as Frawley introduced himself, making their perfunctory handshake awkward. He had snagged her a Poland Spring, which she thanked him for, uncapping it and sipping a little before setting the bottle down on the table beside them, next to an empty Diet Coke.

Frawley sat in the corner with her facing him, so that the police passing outside the door would not distract her. The bleach odor was only mild here. She shifted in her seat, making herself ready for the interview, smiling a little, uncertain. She rubbed her stained hands together in her lap as though chilled. Her arms were long and bare.

"No jacket today?" said Frawley.

"Someone took it," she said, looking back at the door. "For evidence. They . . . they cut my blindfold out of it."

"Would you like . . . ?" He opened his own jacket, and she nodded. He stood and draped it over her shoulders, though as he sat back down, she slipped her arms into the sleeves. The cuffs hung just an inch too long. If he had known a woman would be wearing his jacket that day, he would have chosen a newer one. "And you're sure you're okay, you don't want to go get checked out?"

"Just stiff," she said.

"No bumps, bruises?"

"No," she said, realizing only then how odd that was.

Frawley showed her his microcassette recorder, then turned it on and set it on the table. "Ms. Keesey, I want to start with your abduction, then take you back through the robbery itself."

The word *abduction* brought a blink and a deep swallow. This trauma had many layers and she was in only two or three deep.

"It's unusual to see a bank employee kidnapped during an otherwise successful robbery. But it means you spent a fair amount of time in the company of the bandits and perhaps possess some information that can benefit our investigation. I am the local bank robbery coordinator for the FBI, and this is all I do, work bank crimes, so nothing you can tell me is too trivial. Let me also say that if I don't ask a question you want asked, go right ahead and answer it anyway."

"Then, if I could . . . no one's been able to tell me about Davis."

"The assistant manager?" said Frawley. "He's being checked out at the hospital, but he's going to be okay. He's hurt, but he's going to make it. That's what you wanted to know?"

She nodded and rubbed her cheek with her hand, the dried stain leaving no exchange.

"You saw them beat him?" said Frawley.

She looked down and nodded.

"It was brutal," he said.

"I didn't . . . I looked away."

"Now I'm assuming these bandits threatened you upon your release. Told you not to cooperate in any way with the police, the FBI, correct?"

"Yes."

"Okay. And could you detail the exact nature of that threat for me?"

"It was after they stopped. One of the ones in front—he was the same one with me at the vault—he had my handbag."

"Okay, hold on. Now, you were blindfolded for the entire ride, no?"

"Oh—yes, he shook it. My big Coach bag—I know the sound of my things. He unsnapped my purse, told me he was pulling out my driver's license. He read it to me. Said he was keeping it."

"In his words, if you can remember them?"

She crooked her head, looking down, repeating them quietly. "'If you tell the FBI anything about us, we will come back for you and fuck you and kill you.'"

"Okay," said Frawley, pretending to write that down, coming back up with a neutral smile. "Of course, intimidation is a bank bandit's stock-in-trade. What I can tell you is, they have their money, they think they have gotten away, and I can assure you they want no more involvement in this investigation. No way they would risk exposing themselves now."

"I . . . all right."

He had her take him slowly from the bank into the getaway vehicle. "You're sure it was a van?"

"Yes. That van-sound of the doors. The bouncing as it drove."

"Do you remember seeing a van outside when you arrived at work this morning?"

She winced, shaking her head. "I don't know. A white one, maybe?"

She took him through the drive. "You couldn't see anything out of the blindfold? Not even at the very bottom?"

"Sometimes a narrow strip of light. My lap against the seat. The seat was white, or cream."

"Any sensation of light passing? Windows in the back where you were?"

"I . . . no. I can't say. I don't remember."

"It was a passenger van."

"I guess. Yes."

"You're not certain."

"I don't know what a 'passenger van' is. If that's a minivan, then, yes, I'm certain. We went skiing up in Maine last winter—myself, some friends—and I rented the van. It was a Villager, I remember, because that's a strange name for a car, and we called ourselves the Villager People. I don't know if this was that, but it was like that."

"Okay, good. Like that how?"

"Two separate seats up front. The middle bench I was in. Another bench behind." She winced again. "I'm bringing too much to it, maybe. At least, this is how I see it in my mind."

"That's fine." He wanted to encourage her without flattering her, keeping her account honest. "Where were you sitting?"

"The middle bench. Yes, the middle."

"How many sat there with you?"

"Just one."

"To your . . . ?"

"My right."

"On the door side. You were against the wall. And you don't think there were any windows there. How many in front?"

"Two men in front."

"Anyone behind?"

"Yes."

"Two men in front, one next to you, and one behind."

"I think . . . yes."

"And they didn't have their masks on in the van."

"But I don't know how I know that for sure. Maybe I don't know that."

Frawley chided himself for focusing on the van. The van was going to turn up torched. "How did they communicate? Did they speak much?"

"Very little. 'Right.' 'Left.' 'No.' 'Yes.' Like that." She looked up at him. "That's how I know they didn't have their masks on."

"By their voices."

"They were so *beastly* in the bank, with them on. So distorted and . . . not even human. Like monsters. Can I . . . should I talk about the masks?"

"Go ahead."

"They were all the same. Like Jason, like *Friday the 13th*."

"You mean hockey masks."

"Yes, but—with these scars drawn all over them. Black stitches."

"Stitches?" said Frawley.

"Like hash marks. Sutures." There was fear in her distant gaze. "Why do that? Why *scars*?"

Frawley shook his head. It was a strange detail and his investigation welcomed strange details. "So they didn't speak much in the van."

She was reluctant to return there. "No."

"Did they seem to know where they were going?"

"Maybe, yes."

"Did they tell you where you were going?"

"No."

"Did they tell you you were going to be released?"

"No."

"Did you think you were going to be released?"

"I . . ." She stared into the middle distance, almost in a trance. "No."

"Did the van make stops?"

"It did."

"What for?"

"Traffic, I guess."

"Okay. No doors opened, no one in or out?"

"No."

"And you never tried to escape?"

A blink. "No."

"Were you ever on a highway?"

"Yes. For a while."

"Were you wearing a seat belt?"

She touched her lap, aiding her memory. "Yes." Then, green eyes focusing on him: "I didn't try to escape because they had guns."

"Okay." Wanting not to break the spell. "You asked them no questions?"

She shook her head.

"And they never addressed you?"

"No."

"Nothing was said. Basically they left you alone in the backseat."

"The middle seat."

"Right."

"Yes. Except . . ."

"Go ahead."

She was far away again. "The one who was sitting next to me. Not *next* to me . . . but in the same seat, the same bench, the two of us. The one who blindfolded me. I could tell somehow . . . he was looking at me."

"Looking at you."

"Not like that. I mean . . . I don't know. Maybe it was just a feeling."

"Not like what?"

"Not like, you know, *looking*. Just, I don't know. Just *there*."

"You had his full attention. And then what?"

Her eyes swelled in the recalling. "They just drove and drove. Seemed like hours. I guess I have a sort of . . . it seemed like it went on forever, but now it's like there were whole blocks of time . . . I'm just blank. I know that at some point I realized we were off the highway, making lots of turns. I was praying they would stop, praying it would be over—and then all of a sudden they did stop, and all I wanted to do was keep on driving. The engine was still running but I could tell the ride was over. That's when they shook my Coach bag." She found Frawley's face. "My credit cards, my car keys . . . ?"

"If they turn up, you'll get them back. The one in the seat next to you, he made the threat?"

"No. No, the voice came from in front of me, the angry one. The one who took me to the vault." She pulled at her stained fingers. "I had trouble with the combination."

"Was he the driver?"

"I don't . . . no, I don't think he was. He wasn't—because I was on the left, and his voice came from the right front."

"Would you say he was in charge?"

"I don't know. I know he did the talking then."

"What about the one next to you?"

She lifted the lap of her skirt to cross her legs, and Frawley noticed that her shoes were gone, just dirty stockinged feet. "I think there might have been tension."

"Between them? How so?"

"The angry one, he was the one who wanted to take me."

"From the bank. And the others?"

"One of them questioned him—I'm not sure, it happened so fast. I think it was the one who sat next to me."

"So the angry one, as you call him, he takes your license."

"And then the side door opened. The one next to me helped me out."

"Door slid open or opened out?"

"I . . . I don't remember."

"And the one next to you—you say he 'helped you out'?"

"Just that—I was afraid of falling. I was afraid of *everything*. But he didn't let me fall."

"So he didn't pull you from the van?"

"No. He grabbed my arm and I went. It didn't feel like I had a choice."

"Did he lift you down, walk you down?"

"I wasn't—I mean, of *course* I was scared, I was very scared, *terrified*." She uncrossed her legs, sitting still. "But it wasn't, like . . . I didn't think he was . . . maybe I was naive. If it was the angry one taking me, I would never have left the van on my own. I wouldn't have been able to *walk*."

"Okay, slow down. Did you get a sense of his size?"

"Yes. He was big."

"Big as in strong?"

"As in strong, tall."

"Would you say he was friendly?"

She picked up on Frawley's implication. "No. Impersonal. Just, not angry."

"Okay. So you're out of the van."

"I'm out of the van, and we're walking fast. He's got me by the arm. The ocean stunk, really foul, and the wind was hard. I thought I was at the airport—I heard planes—but it wasn't a runway because the ground was sand around my feet. It was a beach. And basically he told me to walk to the water until I felt it on my toes, and not to take off the blindfold until then. It was so windy, and the sand was blowing up, airplanes screaming overhead—I could barely hear him. But then suddenly my arm was free and I was on my own. I know I stood there for like a minute, idiotically, until I realized I had to be walking. I took very short steps—not even steps really, dragging my feet through the cold sand, arms out in front of me, because I had this image of myself stepping off a cliff. It took, literally, forever. The longest walk of my life. Another plane roared overhead, a rising roaring, a terrible noise, like pulling all the air up with it—and then the sand was different and I felt water washing around my heels. I pushed off the blindfold and I was alone. And I had only walked maybe, thirty feet." The toes of one foot rubbed the heel of the other as she looked at her ruined stockings. "Why did they take away my shoes in the first place?"

"To keep you from kicking or running, don't you think?"

She reached for the water and swallowed some down, her hand shaking more now. "My first day of kindergarten, I pitched a fit when my mother tried to leave, and Mrs. Webly took away my new patent leather shoes as punishment. And just like that, I stopped crying." She rubbed at her stained fingers.

Frawley let her burn off more residual adrenaline, then focused her on the robbery itself. She took him through it with mixed results, returning again and again to the garish black stitches on their masks. Tears pushed to her eyes but did not spill as she recounted Davis Bearns's beating at the hands of the "angry" bandit. "He had fallen . . . he was just sagging off the chair . . . and that one just kept hitting him . . ."

"Did you see Mr. Bearns activate the alarm?"

She reached for her Poland Spring again but held the bottle without opening it, watching water slosh around inside. Car-wreck eyes. Something was up, but he couldn't tell if it was her account or just trauma bleeding through.

"No," she answered softly.

The foot traffic outside the break-room door had quieted. "Ms. Keesey, are you sure you don't want to go somewhere and get checked out?"

"I'm sure. I'm fine."

"It was a long ride. And you said yourself, you can't really account for the entire trip."

"I just . . . spaced. I shut down, that's all."

"It's available to you now. It couldn't hurt."

Her eyes came up on him, cooler, assertive. "Nothing happened." Frawley nodded. "Okay."

"But that's what everyone's going to think, isn't it?"

He tried to distract her. "Is someone coming here to—"

"He rubbed his gun against my butt." She blinked a few times, fighting back tears and exhaustion. "The angry one. While we were standing at the vault. He said some things, told me what he wanted to do to me. That is *all*."

Frawley started off shaking his head, shrugging, searching for something to say, then ended up just nodding. "Do you want to tell me what he said?"

Her smile was fierce and cutting. "Not particularly."

"Okay," said Frawley. "Okay."

"Now you're looking at me like I'm some stupid . . ."

"No, no, no."

"Like I'd jump in a van with *anybody*."

"No. Look—"

He reached over for his tape recorder. In fact he had nothing to say to her. He only hoped the act of pressing STOP would provide a distraction.

She sat there breathing deeply, thinking deeply. "When I was walking to the ocean . . . I thought of nothing. Nothing, no one. But in the van, driving, blindfolded like that—I saw my life. I saw myself as I was, as I am, my life up until this day. Today—it's my birthday."

"I see," said Frawley.

"Sounds crazy. Just another day, I know. I don't know why it matters." She crossed her arms, her stockinged foot bobbing. "It doesn't matter."

A quick thank-you and a handshake could have ended it there if she weren't still wearing his coat.

"Look," Frawley said. "I've seen people—bank customers standing in line to cash their check when a two-time loser comes through the door and announces a robbery—who come away never looking at life the same. People think of bank robbing as a victimless crime, an insured crime, but when a teller gets a gun pointed in her face—that can change a person's life forever. I'm only telling you this so you can prepare yourself."

"I haven't even cried yet—"

"The adrenaline's fading, you're probably going to feel a little depressed for a while. Sort of like mourning—just let it happen. It's normal. Some people bottom out all at once, others just gradually get better until one day they don't wake up thinking about it. For a little while, you'll see these guys behind every closed door. But you will get better."

She was staring at him, rapt, as though he were turning over tarot cards. He knew he had to watch himself here. A pretty girl, hurt, vulnerable. Taking advantage of that would have been like pocketing the bait bills from the vault. She was his vault now, his vic.

"And stay off the Diet Coke," he added. "No caffeine or alcohol, that's key. Stick with water. In the breast pocket of my jacket, you'll find my card."

She fished one out as he stood. "What about my car?"

"You should be able to pick it up whenever. It'll take a hand-washing to get all the fingerprint dust off. If you don't have spare keys, you should be able to get them from your dealer."

She curled her toes. "And my shoes?"

"Those, we'll have to hold on to for a while. Crime lab people, that's how they are. If they could wrap you up in a paper bag and put you on a shelf for a few weeks, they would."

"Might not be such a bad idea." She slipped out of his jacket as she stood, smoothing the sleeves before returning it to him. "Thank you." She read his card. "Agent Frawley."

"No problem." He dropped it over his arm, its tempting warmth.

"And don't worry about those threats. Just focus on yourself."

She nodded, looking at the door, not yet moving. "Actually, my license—it had my old address anyway."

No point in telling her that the bandits had likely been following her for weeks before that morning. Frawley felt up his jacket for a pen. "Let me get your current."

FRAWLEY WATCHED HER HUG a pink-faced, white-haired man in a pin-striped suit inside the door fan.

"Seemed like a good wit," said Dino. "You want to handle the summary narrative?"

Frawley shook his head, still watching her. "Gotta do my 430 case-initiation form for D.C."

"Uh-oh," said Dino, coming up closer to Frawley. "That look in his eyes."

Frawley shook his head, watching daughter and father walk past the front windows and away. "I was ready to write her off complete-ly, except . . ."

"C'mon. I can take it."

"Except that she moved about a year ago. The address we had is out-of-date."

"So she has a new address. And?"

Frawley turned back, watching the wise smile dawn on Dino's seen-it-all face.

"Nah," Dino said, playing at disbelief. "Can't be."

Frawley nodded. "Charlestown."

3
THE SPLIT

DOUG CARRIED A HAM and cheese sub from the Foodmaster out across Austin Street and up Old Rutherford Avenue to the O'Neil Memorial Ice Skating Rink.

"Hey, hon," said the oaken woman smoking behind the rentals counter, and Doug waved hello with a genial smile that belied his down mood. Nailed to the wall behind her was a yellowed newspaper photo of Doug in his Charlestown High hockey uniform, which he took care to ignore.

The rink inside was only half-lit, Boston Bruins and Charlestown Youth Hockey rafter flags hanging high over the day-care kids leaning on milk crates and chop-stepping their way around the overweight instructor in a slow parade. Two teachers stood outside the boards, sloppy, elephant-legged neighborhood girls in long shirts and stretch pants who checked out Doug as he passed them for the skate-scored bleachers.

Jem and Gloansy were halfway up the risers where the bleachers ended at center ice, splitting a sausage-and-burger pizza and drinking out of paper-bagged bottles of beer the shape of artillery shells.

"What are you two pedophiles up to?" said Doug, rapping their fists and sitting one row above them.

Freddy "Gloansy" Magloan of the Mead Street Magloans wore the same splotchy freckles that were the birthright of his seven brothers and sisters. His face was jaw-heavy, jocular and dumb, his ears so mottled they were tan. His pale hands were tarnished with the same sun rust.

Jimmy "Jem" Coughlin of the Pearl Street Coughlins was all shoulders and arms, his head a small squash under swept-back hair that was thick and old-penny brown. The pronounced ridge beneath his nose didn't help, and then there were those blue-white snowflake eyes. The Jem machine operated at two speeds: Mirth or Menace. The gang of knuckles around his emerald-studded gold Claddagh ring were still purple and swollen from his tune-up of the assistant manager.

"Here's the criminal mastermind now," said Jem. "Where's the Monsignor?"

"Coming," said Doug, setting his bag down over some ancient racist knife-scratchings.

"Cheryl, man," said Gloansy, crooking his head at the teacher with the dark, frizzy hair squeezed off in a leopard-print scrunchy. "Ever I see her, I think of third-grade class picture—Duggy, right? Front row and center. *Little House on the Prairie* dress with ruffles, pink plastic shoes. Hands folded, legs crossed tight at the ankles."

"Last time that happened," chewed Jem.

Doug remembered one day in fourth grade, coming out of school to find Cheryl waiting. To kiss him, she said, which she did—before shoving him backward off a curb and running home laughing, leaving him scratching his head about girls for the next few years. Home for her, then as now, was the town-within-a-town of the Bunker Hill Projects, a brick maze of boxy welfare apartments whose architects had taken the word *bunker* to heart. A couple of years ago her younger brother, known around Town as Dingo, got dusted and leaped off the Mystic River Bridge, catching a good shore breeze and only missing his mother's gravel roof by two buildings. One of the black kids tripping over the ice out there now was Cheryl's.

"Think about her mouth and where it's been," said Jem.

"Don't," said Gloansy, his own mouth full.

"That girl could give a plastic soup spoon gonorrhea."

Gloansy said, garbled, "Let me swallow first, for fuck's sake."

"You know she had to take a Breathalyzer once, came back blue-line pregnant?" Jem took a mouthful of beer and gargled it. "Think of Gloansy's shower drain trap, all gooey and hairy—that's Cheryl's tonsils."

"For Christ!" protested Gloansy, choking down his food.

Desmond Elden entered the rink, muscled though not to the extent of Jem or Doug, but with an added bookishness, thanks to his thick-rimmed Buddy Holly eyeglasses. He wore lineman's boots, fading jeans, and a denim work shirt with the Nynex logo over the pocket, his fair hair matted down from wearing a phone company helmet all morning.

Dez gave Cheryl and her posse the courtesy of a *Howzitgoin'* before mounting the bleachers, his insulated lunch sack in hand.

Jem said, "I should dock you just for being polite."

Dez sat down one riser below them. "What, you didn't even say hello?"

"Fuckin' softie," said Jem. "Anything with chicks."

Doug said, "Where'd you put the truck?"

"Foodmaster parking lot. Cruiser there, so I walked the long way around, just in case." Dez unzipped the nylon bag between his knees and pulled out a thick sandwich wrapped in wax paper, smiling. "Ma made meat loaf last night," he said, then bit in big. "Gotta snap to. I'm due in Belmont in like forty minutes, install a ISDN line."

Jem took a long pull on his beer and pointed at Dez. "That's why I hadda swear off work. Too many commitments."

Gloansy toasted that. "Amen, brother."

Doug cracked open his Mountain Dew. "So let's do this."

Jem ripped a burp and none of the kids on the ice even turned their heads. Doug liked the rink for its awful acoustics. He was worried more and more about surveillance around Town, but no bug could outwit those rumbling refrigerators.

"Not much to say," said Jem. "Looks like we're out clean. Newspapers got everything wrong, as usual. Nothing went sour until the end, when everything did."

Gloansy said, "Duggy, man, you said banks train their people not to hit any alarms until after."

"They do. It's a safety issue. Plus banks carry kidnap and extortion insurance, and shit like that voids it."

Jem shrugged. "So the homo pissed himself. Thing is, it shouldn't of happened. Could of been real fucking bad. Time to settle up now, and these things get counted. Gloansy, my friend, it's time to pay the piper. You're docked."

Gloansy's face fell, his open mouth full, looking at Jem. "What the fuck?"

"It was your watch. You knew Monsignor Dez had to leave the vault and teller bells hardwired."

"*I'm* getting fucking docked? *Me?*"

"All you had to do. Keep the citizens down on the floor and away from the bells."

"Fuck you." Gloansy was teary, he was so shocked. "Fuck you, all I had to do? Who boosted the work van? You think you fuckin' . . . think you *walked* to and from this job? And who torched the rides after the delayed switch?"

"Who was watching that kid at the ATM instead of the bankers at his feet?"

"Fuckin' . . . so who delayed the switch? You're the one that brought the manager along. Why'n't you dock yourself?"

"Plan to. Same as you. A hundred-dollar whack to the each of us."

"A hundred—" Gloansy's face relaxed, pulling back into a fuck-you frown. He punched Jem's left triceps hard, saying, "Fuckin' ass munch."

Jem smiled tongue-out and slapped Gloansy's cheek. "Fuckin' *this* close to bawling, Shirley Temple."

"Fuck you," said Gloansy, shaking it off, all better now, taco-ing another sloppy slice into his freckled mouth.

Doug took a bite out of his sandwich, so fucking tired of the whole fucking thing.

"So, the magic number," said Jem, tearing open packets of salt over the closed pizza box. "This is per, now, and net expenses." With his finger he traced out a five-digit sum: 76750.

Gloansy worked on the upside-down figure until his eyes grew big.

Dez nodded, a smile flickering before he checked on Doug.

Doug finished chewing, then leaned down and blew the salt figure away.

Jem went on, "That's minus a chunk I dropped into the kitty for the next one, replace the tools I dumped. And some short bundles of new consecutives, I incinerated, not worth worrying over. And then ten percent off the top for the Florist. Overall, a fucking dynamite haul. Oh—yeah." He reached into his back pocket. "From the ATM. Stamps for all."

Doug said, "What's this with the Florist?"

Jem passed out the stamp sheets. "His tribute."

"And why you involving him?"

"It's not like he doesn't already know about it. It's the right thing to do."

"How'd he know?" Doug let his sandwich drop back onto the wrapper on the bench. "I didn't tell him. I didn't tell anybody. Unless someone here told someone, he didn't know."

"Duggy. People know. People in the Town."

"Tell me how they know."

"They just know."

"What do they know? What? Yeah, maybe they *think* they know something. But *thinking* you know something, and actually *knowing* something—that's two different things. The cops and the G, maybe they *think* they know something. But not *knowing* it is exactly what keeps us on the street, keeps us in the game."

"Fergie knows a lot of secrets, Duggy."

"And now he's got one more on us. I don't see the point of putting it out there."

"We don't duke him, there could be trouble down the road."

"How?" Doug felt himself getting carried away and not caring. "Trouble how? What trouble, explain that to me. This 'Code of Silence' trial now, everybody in town is an opera star. Clutching their hankies and belting it out for the cops and the papers. The fat lady, she's singing. Just tell me you didn't visit him in his shop."

"I saw him out on the pier. He's my mother's cousin, Duggy."

"We're not Italian, Jem. Third or fourth cousin means maybe a nice Christmas card, not 'Here's my kidney, you should need one.' The G is all over his shop, that is guaran-fucking-teed."

"It's so. But you think *he* don't know that?"

Dez piped up, "That thirty-five grand or so you gave him—he gonna wash that clean before sending it out to the IRA?"

Jem scoffed and said, "All that's rumor. That's just for street cred."

Doug said, "Dez *thinks* he knows that Fergie fronts for the IRA. He doesn't *know* it—not like he *knows* that Fergie puts dust out on the street, not to mention has a taste for it himself. This is a sixty-year-old man on angel dust you're meeting out there on the pier, Jem kid. Chatting with, handing bank money to."

"Look, Fergie's always putting things into motion. You're working on our next, sure, but he said, and in not so many words, that he's got some big things that would suit us nice. That we could buy from him."

Doug thought he was going to levitate out of his seat. "Why the fuck would we want to work for someone else? *One* good reason."

"These are marquee scores."

"Marquee scores!" Doug waved at the vanished salt. "You got kids in braces or something, that's not enough? We got more than we can conveniently wash as it is. Marquee scores mean marquee busts, Jem boy. Fergie's got room on his roster exactly because Boozo's crew got lazy up in New Hampshire and Boozo's tweak-freak son, Jackie the Jackal, shot up that armored guard. And the heat from that is *still* out all over the Town. Jackie's what, he's our age? Younger? And he's gonna die in prison. He'd fucking die there anyway, for being stupid and running his mouth, but eighty years is not something he's gonna

survive. And that's without a murder charge ever being brought—that's the racketeering thing, interstate, plus the firearms mandatories. This isn't kid stuff anymore. We all of us, except the Monsignor, got strikes against us. We take a fall now, with twenty-year gun mandies, we're never gonna land. Got it? I gotta spell this out in salt for you?"

Gloansy said, "I ain't taking no more falls."

Doug said, "And I ain't taking any falls before you. The only thing the law likes less than pro outlaws are reckless outlaws. The G—they don't like it when you rob banks, that's fine, fair. Honest heat is honest heat. Toss in kidnapping and assault, their fucking palms start getting sweaty. They take that personal. Suddenly they got jobs on the line—reassignment, whatever. They need results. And we can't win going up against them nose-to-nose. This crazy Cagney shit you pull, it draws them out. Things go wrong on every job. Trick is, keep moving, don't fix one fucking mistake with another."

In the silence that followed, Doug realized he had gone on what was for him a tirade. He was the only one who could talk to Jem like this, and even he was pushing it. Gloansy, or especially Dez, they would have been on the floor with Jem's knee in their throat.

Jem was making a show of fishing food out of his teeth with his tongue. Doug had been sitting on this stuff too long. He didn't even know specifically why he was so pissy himself. It was the jokes, it was the beer on their breath and the hour of the day. It was all of their youth going round and round in circles on the ice down there.

"Fuck it," Doug said with a wave. "You want to duke the Florist, fine, duke the Florist. Keep him happy? Fine. But I won't work for him. We are pros here, not cowboys in a Wild West show. We're different. That's what keeps us ahead in this cat-and-rat game. Free agents, we gotta stay smart, full-time, else we'll get beat. I will walk away before I became some gangster's personal fucking ATM machine. If I even *thought* that was coming, I'd walk away right now."

Jem put on a grin. "Bullshit. You could never walk away."

Doug said, "Have to, someday."

"You'd make a real good old woman, you didn't have such a fucking nose for crime. Only you could be raggy about this score."

Doug chewed and watched the kids make their way off the ice, skate-walking to the doors.

"Duggy's share is back at my place," said Jem, proceeding as if nothing had happened. To Gloansy and Dez, he handed over orange-headed locker keys. "Your pieces are out front. Remember, it's all dirty linen and's got to be washed. Now, last thing—bank manager."

Looking at Doug. Doug shrugged and said, "Yeah?"

"You grabbed her license from me. What's the scoop?"

"Nothing."

"Thought you said she lives in the Town."

"Hasn't been back home yet. I think we can forget about her. So long as you ditched the masks, she's got nothing."

"Course I ditched the masks."

"Well, you seemed pretty fond of your artwork, I want to be sure."

"Masks, tools, everything ditched."

Doug shrugged. "Then whatever."

Gloansy said, "I saw her on the news, being walked away, her father. She's too shaken up to tell them shit anyway."

"Yeah," said Doug, swiping his nose like the manufactured cold was getting to him.

"Done, then," said Jem. "We're clear. With that, this investment club meeting is officially adjourned."

Dez packed up his trash. "Gotta rock."

"I'm behind you," said Doug, bagging his.

"Whoa, where you running off to?" said Jem. "What clock you on?"

"I got some stuff," said Doug.

"Blow it off. Free ice now. Me and Gloansy gonna skate."

"Can't," said Doug, rising, Dez already smacking fists and starting out.

Jem frowned and said to Gloansy, "Guy lives in my house, I never see him."

Doug said, "I gotta breeze. You know how I get, between things."

"So stay. Have a few tall boys with us, relax. Gloansy brought his goalie pads, he's gonna let us take shots at him."

"Fuck you," sang Gloansy, lifting out the last skinny slice.

"I'm walking," said Doug, starting down the scarred planks. "Besides, you're wrong. I do got a job. Keeping you homos in line."

"Ho, shit," said Jem, their little tiff passing like a storm cloud. "That's some full-time work right there."

DOUG CAME OUT THROUGH the doors as Dez was pulling his cut from the rink lobby lockers, the size of two thick phone books wrapped in butcher paper. Jem had left a Filene's shopping bag folded in there and Dez dumped the package inside, rolling the bag into a bundle and tucking it up under his arm, football-style. They walked together through the doors out into the hard, white daylight.

Dez said, "Ma's been after me to get you over for dinner again."

"Yeah, we'll do that soon." The high sun summoned up in him a tremendous, satisfying sneeze.

"God bless," said Monsignor Dez.

Doug squinted. "You going up to drop half that in the collection box right now?"

"No time. Later."

"St. Frank's gonna put a hot tub in the confessional before you're done."

Dez looked at Doug without a smile. "The split's light," he said. "Isn't it."

Doug rubbed his eyes. "Ah, fuck it."

"Why? Why let him be in charge? You know you run things. And that whole dock thing, that was a charade."

Doug shrugged, truly uninterested. "Hey, what's a IDSN line?"

"ISDN," Dez corrected. "Data streaming, high-speed Internet. Like if I was a plumber bringing you your water, this'd be a much wider pipe. Fiber optics. Makes World Wide Web surfing like changing channels."

"Yeah? That the future?"

"Today it is. Tomorrow, who knows? Someday there'll be no wires, I know that. Someday there'll be no linemen."

"Maybe you oughta think about getting something going on the side."

Dez smiled in the direction of the highway. "I gotta roll." They rapped fists, Dez taking off down the incline with the bundle of cash under his arm.

Doug turned and went the other way, up Old Rutherford, habitually scanning the parked cars for snoops as he went. He turned right on Devens and followed it around to Packard, a one-way street, one of the few in the tightly packed Town with a back alley. The narrow alley showed bow windows and Juliet balconies over brick walls separating tiny parking spaces. Empty trash cans stood at every cobblestoned parking court except Claire Keesey's, the plum Saturn still gone. A poker hand of takeout menus was fanned inside her back screen door.

Keep moving, he told himself, jamming his fists inside the pockets of his warm-up jacket, pretending he was satisfied. All he had done was save her from a beating. He lowered his head like a regular citizen and walked on.

4
PLAYSTATION

THE BACK OF THE hill was Charlestown without the gas street-
lamps. It was wooden row houses with stepped roofs and front
doors that opened onto sidewalks sloping at forty-five-degree
angles to the sea. During the Blizzard of 1978, on plastic Super
Saucers and collapsed cardboard box "project sleds," neighborhood
kids got up over twenty miles an hour bombing down the sheer faces
of Mystic, Belmont, and North Mead before bottoming out hard
onto Medford Street below.

The gentrification that had made new virgins out of other Town
fiefdoms such as Monument Square, City Square, and the Heights,
had embraced but not yet transformed the uncapitalized old lady
known simply as "the back of the hill." Its curbs saw a few Audis and
Acuras, designer water bottles lay in some recycling bins, and most
exteriors had been power-washed and painted smooth. But Irish lace
still fluttered in a few windows, a handful of Boston firefighters and
city employees still calling it home.

Doug ate two buttered corn muffins out of a wax paper bag at the
crest of Sackville Street. His large tea, thick with milk and sugar, steamed
out of the tall Lori-Ann's cardboard cup set on the roof of his rust-
pocked 1986 Caprice Classic.

Breakfast there was for him a regular thing. The house he was
looking at across the street, with its rich red siding and nurse-white
trim—formerly dove gray over flaking charcoal—was the home of his
youth. He still considered it his mother's house even though she had
abandoned it, and him, when he was six years old. His father managed to hold on to it for ten more years, meaning, and this seemed
impossible, that Doug had lived half his life away from it now. It still
ruled his dreams: the monster oil tank in the stone basement; the dark
wood parlor with cabinet radiators and custard wallpaper; his corner

bedroom on the first floor, swept by passing headlights.

This was the place he went to get his head together. A bungled job—this one had netted them plenty, but he would forever think of the caper as failed—always left him in a sour mood, but never with the mental mono like this one had. He returned to the heist over and over in his head, trying to untangle its faults, only to get caught up again in the image of the branch manager blindfolded next to him in the van. This image possessed him, how fragile she had appeared, yet also how composed. How she had wept tearlessly beside him—he had felt her shaking, her hands limp and empty in her lap—like a statue of a blindfolded woman crying. Having followed this stranger around, he now felt himself getting sucked into the mystery of her existence.

He was breaking out of that rut today. It was April and the sidewalks of the Town were teeming with Claire Keeseys, drawn to the neighborhood by its cheap rents and safe streets, baring their shoulders and legs after a long winter's hibernation. The Town was a stocked lake and fishing was back in season. This fog, whatever it was that had descended on him at the beginning of the bank job and lingered in the days that followed—it was finally lifting.

He shook his head and crumpled up the muffin bag. His not telling the others about her triggering the alarm: that was not going to haunt him anymore. It was over with. In the past. Time to move on.

"CHECK THIS OUT," said Jem.

Doug set down his liter slam of Mountain Dew and accepted the wrinkled Victoria's Secret spring catalog. On page after page, Jem had applied a drop of water to each of the lingerie models' breasts, puckering the thin paper and raising persuasive nipples.

Doug nodded, turning the pages. "And you say this project only took you half the morning?"

"Some days, you know? You just wake up horny. I have all this fucking energy, I already worked out twice today, shoulders and calves. What do you do, days when you can't focus on anything because your mind keeps running back to your dick?"

"Some call it 'applying the pine tar.'"

"No, no," said Jem, shaking his head. "No, I don't do that anymore."

"Excuse me, what?" Doug smiled. "You don't do that anymore?"

"They say weed saps your ambition? I say, yanking it does. Saps your drive. Makes you soft, more ways than one. Always leaves me tired, dopey. I'm serious."

"You'll be down in the basement *three* times a day, working out, and all that's gonna happen is, spume's gonna back up into your system, turn you gay. I seen it happen, man. It's tragic."

"Voice of experience here."

"Radical idea just came to me out of the blue. How about going easy on yourself, getting a regular girlfriend?"

"I think I do awright. And I'm gonna start doing even better. Abstinence makes the dick grow fonder. Hey, you're the last person should be giving shit. Mister fucking life change already."

Doug dragged the remote off the glass-topped coffee table and opened up the cable menu over the soft-core pool-table scene playing on Jem's black box Spice Channel. He found a kung fu movie on pirated pay-per-view, put it on the huge TV. "Your eyesight improves, maybe you can get a smaller screen."

"Hey, how about this. Tonight, right? They say yanking it also gives you hairy palms, right? Okay, we get that spirit gum like we used for the Watertown job, the stuff that gave us fake chins and cheeks? Slop it on our hands instead, then shred up a wig, stick fur on there. Walk in the door at the Tap with all the yuppies, give the place a big wave. High-five the bartender with our furry mitts."

Doug grinned. "You walk in reading your catalog?"

"I will spill water on my *crotch* before I walk in, a nice round little cum stain." He mimed walking into the bar for Doug, open hand raised, hips thrust forward, big Irish smile. "Evening, friends!"

Doug said, "This, right here, is why we don't have regular girlfriends."

"*For Christ*, then it's working." Jem hopped down Fonzie-style onto his green leather couch and grabbed a PlayStation controller. "Bruins," he called.

They played NHL '96 on Jem's Trinitron, first a couple of straight games with the crowd noise roaring in stereo, then they ignored the puck and skated their players around the ice looking for trouble, doling out hard checks until helmets popped off and the view zoomed in and the computer men threw down their gloves, the announcer bellowing in sim surround, *FIGHT!*

At one point, Jem turned to Doug, eyes bleary with game glee. "Like old times, kid! Can you tell me why we don't do this every fucking day?"

Eventually Doug had to step out past the tower speakers to take a piss. The worn checkerboard bathroom tile, the rotten shower curtain, the foam-coated pipes running up through the ceiling into his own third-floor bathroom: it all seemed virtual to him, flickering, pixilated. At that moment the computerized rink with its frictionless ice was more real to him than Jem's mother's house.

He stepped back into the narrow hallway with its undulating walls and twitching corners, a world with seams, the framed photograph of Cardinal Cushing hanging over the long-dry holy-water bowl looking poor-graphics fuzzy.

The sound of the glass rattling on the downstairs door sent a dead feeling through Doug, the caffeine and carbonation draining from his alter world, his game buzz gone flat.

"Krista's home," he said, returning to Jem.

"It's cool, man, she won't bug us."

"Let me get my take, get it squared away."

Jem smiled icily. "You're gonna breeze."

"No. Just get my shit squared away, then come right back down."

Jem stood, unconvinced, going to the frame of the doorway between the parlor and the neglected second-floor kitchen. He yanked on the molding and brought it loose in one long piece, revealing plywood shelves nailed in between the old walls like a row of mail slots. Jem withdrew Doug's bundle, leaving many smaller newspaper-wrapped parcels behind, many ripped open and spilling cash.

"You stash here?" said Doug.

"Why not?"

Doug nodded at Jem's room full of toys. "You take a search warrant and they see all this hardware against your tax return, then the electricity you steal, the cable you pirate—you don't think they're gonna tap on the walls?"

Jem shrugged and fit the molding back over the wall edge, hammering it in tight with the heel of his hand. "Always so fucking panicked. What, where you keep yours? You don't spend it, I know that."

"Not upstairs." Doug weighed the bundle in his hand. "Speaking of, how you fixed for clean linen?"

"Could always wash some."

Doug nodded, feeling residual good humor from the game. "We could go native tonight."

"Native it is. But only if we eat down there. Make a night of it this time, Duggy, do it right, not just up and back like going to the cash machine."

Doug nodded, cool with that. "I'll run this upstairs. You call the two homos."

* * *

DOUG RETURNED DOWNSTAIRS CARRYING a suede Timberland jacket with eight thousand dollars in twenties and fifties tucked inside the quilted lining.

Jem's mother's house was a classic Charlestown triple-decker of stacked, identical apartments. Diabetes had claimed Jem's mother's body in pieces, toes and feet first, then fingers, knees, kidney, and finally her heart. The disease had since spread to her house, rotting it room by room.

Doug's rent for the entire third floor was a couple of grand a year in real estate taxes. Jem, on the second floor, took care of all stolen utilities. The first floor was Krista's.

Kristina Coughlin was Jem's Irish twin, exactly eleven months and eleven days his junior. They bickered like husband and wife, she doing his laundry and occasionally cooking a meal—her mother's gooey chicken à la king her specialty—while he handed her money and generally laid around watching TV.

Krista shared her brother's wild streak. She had smoked her twenties down to the filter, the wear and tear just now starting to show, though she had snapped back from her pregnancy like a fresh rubber band. Merit Longs kept her in fighting trim. She had the Coughlin white-blue eyes, not so bad as her brother's, but when she drank, which was often, they glowed like demon jewels. Something she did to her hair with a razor kept the layers jagged and sharp. Like her partying soul, her dirty-blond hair lay flat and useless during the day, only to be teased into action every night. Her chest was criminally small, her long legs usually done out in stonewashed denim and heels in order to show off her proud, heart-shaped ass.

The three of them had grown up together, Doug spending so much time at the Coughlins' house as a kid that, when Doug's father went away, Jem's mother's taking him in presented little change. Krista and Doug had been a longtime, on-and-off couple, bad for each other in every way except carousing and sex. But now she couldn't let go. She had even tried to get clean with Doug after his release from prison, just weeks after her mother's death, but after a few months of sobriety fell out rather dramatically. For Doug, this had been a source of secret relief. She had been the heaviest of many stones roped around his neck. A couple of months later she was a couple of months pregnant and going around Town telling everybody that Doug was the father.

Now Krista sat at the table, watching Jem down half a High Life at a gulp. "And you wonder why he don't come down no more?" she said with smoke in her voice.

"Fuckin' Duggy doesn't mind—do you, kid? His will is *strong*." Douche-bag grin as he killed the bottle. "Maybe too strong." The dinged-up cordless phone trilled and he snapped it off the table, answering, "Gloansy, you fatherless prick," rising and wandering away down the narrow hall.

Almost nothing had changed on the first two floors in the three years since Jem's mother's passing. They were sitting now in the first-floor back parlor, directly below Jem's game room. A maple chair-rail border ran between velvety milk-white parchment wallpaper stained nicotine yellow and scuffed white wood. The only new addition was an empty walker sticky with old juice, and the padded plastic high chair with the nineteen-month-old girl strapped into it.

Shyne gripped a gnawed graham cracker in one hand, the pink ribbon of a sagging Mylar heart balloon in the other. Despite the name and its inventive spelling, Shyne was a white child, an alabaster doll with fine, threadlike copper hair and sad, small, Coughlin-white eyes. She looked nothing at all like Doug, eliminating any sliver of doubt remaining in anyone's mind—even his own—as to Krista's paternity claim.

Shyne chewed on her cookie and stared across the table at him. The little girl was like a clock running slow. At a glance, you might not notice that anything was off, but spend any amount of time with her and you'd see she wasn't ticking with the rest of the world. The few times Doug had brought this up with Jem, Jem always countered with some pap he had heard on television, about children developing at different paces. And he could never bring it up with Krista, who was always reading him for signs that he was ready again to care.

Alone with him now, Krista shook out her ash-blond hair and sat back from the table, looking small and tired in the old armless chair. "I don't ask him to do that."

Doug watched the perfectly still, half-inflated red balloon, wanting the year-and-a-half-old to bounce it, something. "Do what?"

"Leave us alone together like this. It's fucked-up, his pushing. Sometimes I swear he wants it more than I do. Like it's you and his friendship he wants to save."

"Where are you getting all this?"

She shrugged as though it were obvious. "You don't come around. I mean, he's an asshole, but you guys are like brothers." She combed up her hair with her fingers, lifting it high off her ears, then letting it fall. "Or maybe it's me. Like I'm so radioactive now you can't come around."

Doug sat back and sighed.

"It's you who's radioactive," she said. "Your X-rays got inside me young, altered me permanently." She picked at a waffled, clover-shaped place mat, the old food dried into it. "You came home late from your meeting last night."

"Jesus," he said. "That fucking glass rattling in the door."

Jem blew back into the room. "Gloaner's in," he said, dropping down in front of Shyne and plucking at her balloon string, trying to grab her attention. She gazed up at the sagging, slow-drifting heart. "Talking about your meetings again?" Jem said. "Like fucking church with you."

Doug said, "It's in a church."

Jem gave up on his niece and turned to the gored table, rolling an Irish-flag Zippo lighter over and over in his hand. "Hey, I go dry. Days at a time. Good to step back now and then, reset the clock. Healthy. But this is, what, you're on like a year or more? That's fucking hitting pause, kid."

"Two years next month."

"Key-reist almighty. Real comfortable up there in the front seat of that wagon. I'm remembering one time you fell off—Dearden's wedding."

Krista smiled at the memory. Doug wondered why this always came up. "That was a mistake."

"A mistake where you rocked the house, buddy. That was a night."

"I had almost a year in, until that slip."

"Slip? Yo, a *slip*? That was a high-dive, Rodney Dangerfield. A *Back to School* Triple Lindy belly flop. My point is, Duggy—you went right back. Look at you. Unshakable. Better, stronger, faster. So what's the fucking harm now and then, breaking down and getting a little wet with your poor, misguided, dry-throated friends?"

The phone rang and Jem snapped it up, answering, "Monsignor Kid-Toucher, what's the word?" again jumping to his feet and wandering away.

Krista sat there with her arms crossed, watching her daughter, lost in thought. "You're no priest," she said.

Doug turned to stare at her. "The hell are you talking about?"

"Even the Monsignor, Desmond the Nearsighted—the Pope of the

Forgotten Village—even he lowers himself to drink with the boys."

"Because he can handle it. I can't."

"'Cause you're an *alcoholic*."

"Right. 'Cause I'm an *alcoholic*."

"So proud, though. Proud of your disease."

"Jesus, Kris," said Doug. "You were asking why I don't come down anymore?"

"So what's your high now? Just banks? Being the prince of these thieves?"

Doug frowned, done. He never talked about this with her, and she knew he didn't like her talking about it at all. "Any more shots you want to take before I go?"

Krista wiped some cracker mush from her daughter's mouth before turning on him. "Yeah. What's it gonna take to wake you up from whatever dream it is you're dreaming?"

When he didn't answer, she stood and carried her crossed arms into the kitchen, leaving him alone with Shyne's staring eyes.

THEY DROVE SOUTH THROUGH Rhode Island into Connecticut in Gloansy's tricked-out '84 Monte SS, black with orange trim. With three convicted felons on board and riding with a lot of cash, Gloansy couldn't be trusted to keep his Halloween-mobile under the speed limit, so Dez had the wheel. Doug sat up front with him, working the radio and using his side mirror now and then, idly checking for tails, while Jem and Gloansy split a six in back.

Two hours to Foxwoods, door to door. Careful as they were on the job, even a circulated bill could be marked, and washing the money was one of Doug's rituals. Insisting on it had the added benefit of slowing Jem's and Gloansy's spending.

Jem liked the roulette wheel and usually ended up dropping half of what he came to wash, drinking Seven and Sevens on the house and overtipping like a fifteen-year-old out on a date.

Gloansy bought a $12 cigar and set out to lose at high-min poker.

Dez floated back and forth between rooms, paranoid about pit bosses and floor managers with their cop eyes.

Doug worked steadily at the blackjack tables. He started by laying out sixty twenties on the felt of a $50 table and watched the dirty bills get dunked, forty-eight $25 chips pushed over to him. He drank Cokes without ice and played not to win but *to not lose,* which is different. Not losing means staying in every hand as long as possible, sitting on fifteens and sixteens and letting the dealer do all the busting. When he cashed in thirty minutes later, he was down only six chips. He folded the clean $1,050 into his zippered pocket and moved on to a $100 table, washing another quick $1,300 there before cashing out and rotating again.

It took him less than three hours to roll over the entire eight grand, ending hot, dropping a total of $320 in play and tips, a minuscule 4 percent commission to what the papers said was the most profitable casino in the country.

He met up with Dez again by a revolving red Infiniti. They made two complete circuits of the floor before an Indian war cry brought them to Jem, finding him doing a rain dance around the $50 roulette table, having finally scored on double zero. They cashed him in and steered him away.

Jem wanted to stop for a quarter-hour massage at one of the jack shacks near the casino, but Gloansy refused. "The red man just jerked me off for nineteen hundred dollars, I'm not going to pay some greasy geisha half a yard to do the same."

Instead, Doug drove them a few exits north to a steak house, where they filled a booth by the window in sight of the back-finned Monte. Soon the table was cluttered with steaks, High Lifes, and Doug's large no-ice Mountain Dew.

"So what's next, Duggy?" asked Gloansy.

"Strip club," chewed Jem.

"I mean, for us. For the team."

"I don't know," said Doug. "Think we need to mix it up a bit. I'm looking at a few things."

Jem said, "You talked about hitting a can."

"Maybe. Might be looking at something softer first."

Jem waved that off. "Fuck softer."

"Hitting a can means daylight. Armed guards, crowds, traffic. Going in strong like that, I don't know. We need a win."

Jem pointed his steak knife. "You're losing your edge, DigDug. Startin' to worry about you. Used to be you were the first one to throw down gloves and go."

"Used to be I got a hard-on every morning, homeroom. But now it's 1996 and I'm thirty-two, and I got that shit together."

Gloansy said, "Whatever it is, I'm ready. Anytime you say, Duggy."

Jem speared one of Gloansy's pinkest morsels and pushed it into his own mouth. "Anytime *I* say, corn hole."

Gloansy watched his steak get swallowed, poured ketchup on more. "I'm sure that's what I meant."

They ate and drank and got loud and stupid as usual. Doug tried to hustle them along like children, like he was running a fucking field trip outside the Town.

Gloansy said, "If I had to go one hundred percent legit? One of those batting cages things. Indoor/outdoor. Snacks and shit. Town needs something like that. What about you, Jem?"

"Liquor store, man. Also sell smokes, lottery, and porn. That's one-stop vice shopping."

Gloansy said, "That was Duggy's brainchild once upon a time."

"Duggy don't drink anymore. So that million-dollar idea goes to me."

Dez said to Jem, "Maybe put in a photo-developing booth too?"

Jem stared at him, Dez holding the look for another few seconds before cracking, Doug too, both of them falling into snorts of laughter.

"What is that?" said Jem. "The fuck is that, 'photo-developing booth'? It's not funny. He's not funny. It makes no fuckin' sense."

Jem's fury only made them laugh harder, the nearby tables starting to get annoyed. Doug went to use the head, and on his way back he saw what the other diners saw sitting there at the side booth: Gloansy and Dez playing goalposts with a packet of butter, Jem draining another longneck and staring out the window, bobbing his head to some interior tune. The glamorous life of the outlaw; the majesty of being the prince of these thieves.

The waitress delivered the check as he returned. "Let's split," Doug said.

"Got a stop to make on the way back," said Gloansy, grinning. "In Providence."

Doug was tired, he wanted to get back to Dodge. "Losers."

"No," Gloansy corrected him. "*Horny* losers."

The munching sound next to Doug was Jem eating the food bill.

DOUG RECEIVED A BEAUTIFUL lap dance from a long-haired Portuguese girl with teardrop-shaped breasts. He succumbed to the hypnotizing power of cleavage, the pendulousness of femininity, as she ran her small hands over the muscles of his shoulders and leaned boldly into his face. When she turned and ground herself into his lap, waist and hips undulating, the swelling in Doug's jeans reminded him that he was already four months in to going 0-for-1996.

Afterward, as she dressed in the seat next to him, Doug felt shitty and alone. Even a guy without a girlfriend had to admit that patronizing a strip club was like cheating on womankind in general, and with this vague sense of guilt came a philandering husband's determination to repair and repent. She relieved him of his $20 wad with a wink and a smile, then paused, giving his face a pursed-lipped look of concern. She reached out and explored, gently, the sliver of skin where Doug's left eyebrow was split, planting a soft kiss on the old scar there before walking off in search of her next dance.

The free kiss threw him. Twenty doughnuts for tits and friction, and then a gratis moment of actual intimacy? She could have saved the dance and charged him twenty just for the compassion.

Hitting the sidewalk outside the Foxy Lady was like quitting PlayStation, gravity reclaiming Doug, the night air a chilly hand cupping the back of his neck. Laughter gave way to honking snores at the Massachusetts border, the Monte reeking of spicy Drakkar Noir and stripper sweat as Doug sped back toward Dodge, his orphan mind once again returning to the image of Claire Keesey sitting blindfolded in the van. He crossed the bridge back into Town, turning toward Packard Street for a quick detour—just one look, her door, her dark windows—before shuttling his slumbering Townies back home.

5
INTERVIEW

"I N A WAY," said Claire Keesey, shrugging, "nothing since that morning's really seemed real to me."

She was curled up on the maroon cushions of a college rocking chair, the Boston College seal emblazoned over her head like a small sun. Her father's home office took up half of the living room, a desk-and-shelf unit of austere mahogany behind brass-handled French doors. Claire's mother—tight smile, anxious hands—had tucked a quilted paper towel beneath the tin BC coaster supporting Frawley's glass of water, as an extra layer of protection. Her father—gull-white hair over a rare-meat complexion—had taken the early Friday train to be there to answer the door and eyeball this agent of the FBI.

Frawley glanced at his Olympus Pearlcorder on the bookshelf near the head of the rocker. The handheld tape recorder had been a gift from his mother on the day of his graduation from Quantico, and every Christmas since, along with the sweater or turtleneck or pants from L.L. Bean—one year she mailed him bongo drums—she included a four-pack of Panasonic MC-60 blank microcassettes, *For your stocking!*

It clicked over, the tiny spools reversing, thirty minutes gone by. Claire sat with her legs tucked beneath her, arms folded, hands lost inside the cuffs. Her eggshell sweatpants announced *BOSTON COLLEGE* in a maroon and gold banner down one leg, her loose, green sweatshirt whispering *BayBanks* over her breast. It looked like a sick-day outfit, though her hair was brushed and smelled faintly of vanilla, and her face was scrubbed.

"My mother doesn't want me to work at the bank anymore. She doesn't want me to leave the *house* anymore. Last night, after three or so vodka tonics, she informed me that she had always known something bad was going to happen to me. Oh, and my father? He wants me to get a gun permit. Says a cop friend told him pepper spray is useless, only good on scrambled eggs. It's like, I'm *watching* them take care of me. Like the thirty-year-old me has gone back in time but is still a child in their eyes. And the scary thing? Sometimes I like it. Sometimes, God help me, I *want* it." She shuddered. "By the way, they don't believe me either."

"Don't believe what? *Who* either?"

"About nothing happening to me out there. My mother treats me like the ghost of her daughter, back from the dead. And my father's all '*Brrrhrrrhrrr*, business as usual, let's rent a movie . . .' "

Frawley's first impulse always was to counsel. He reminded himself that he wasn't there to help or to heal, he was there to learn. "Why do you think I don't believe you?"

"Everyone handling me like I'm porcelain. If people want me to be fragile, watch out, because I can be *very* fragile, no problemo." She threw up her handless cuffs in surrender. "So stupid, getting into that van. Right? Like a six-year-old on a pink bike, pulled into a van, and not even screaming or kicking. Such a *victim*."

"I thought you had no choice."

"I could have struggled," she argued. "I could have let them, I don't know, *shoot* me instead."

"Or ended up like your assistant manager."

She shook her head, wanting to relax but emotionally unable.

Frawley said, "I went out to visit Mr. Bearns. He said you haven't been by yet."

She nodded at the floor. "I know. I need to go."

"What's holding you up?"

She shrugged hard inside the baglike sweatshirt, avoiding the answer. "We're trained to help robbers," she said. "You know that, right? To actually *help* the criminals, and not to resist. Even to repeat their commands back to them, so they know that we're following their orders *to the letter*."

"To put the bandit at ease. To get him out of the bank more quickly, away from customers, away from yourself."

"Fine, okay, but—*helping* the thief? Like, rolling over for him? You don't think that's a little whacked?"

"The vast majority of bank theft is drug addicts looking to score. Their desperation, their fear of being sick, makes them unpredictable."

"But everything is like, *Do what the robber says*. Like—*Don't give him dye packs if he tells you not to.* Hello? So why do we have them? And—*Be courteous.* What other business do they say that in? 'Thank you, bank robber, have a nice day.' "

Through the side window, Frawley watched two boys tossing around a tennis ball a few backyards away, making showtime catches on a late Friday afternoon. "Speaking of training," he said. "It's written policy at BayBanks for the openers to enter one at a time, the first one confirming that the bank is secure, then safe-signaling to the second."

She nodded contritely. "Right. I know."

"And yet this was not your usual practice."

"Nope."

"Why not?"

Shrug. "Laziness? Complacency? We had an all-clear for the tellers."

"Right, the window shades. But the tellers don't arrive until a half hour after you two. And setting off the silent alarm—you're trained to wait until it is safe to do so."

"Again—what is the point of sounding an alarm *after* a robbery? Can you tell me that? What is the *point*?"

"Mr. Bearns put you both at risk."

"But you couldn't *know* that while it was going on," she said, angry suddenly, tearing into him with her eyes. "They were inside the bank, *waiting* for us when we walked in—outnumbering us, scaring the *shit* out of us. I didn't think I was ever walking out of that bank again."

"I'm not placing blame, I'm only trying to get at—"

"So why haven't I gone to visit Davis? Because I couldn't stand to let myself fall to pieces on him. *Me,* little suburban *me,* not a scratch on her, safe and fine and hiding out—at her *parents?*" She pushed hair off her forehead where there was no hair and looked away. "Why, he asked about me?"

"He did."

Her shoulders drooped. "The hospital won't tell me anything over the phone."

"He's going to lose most of the sight out of one eye."

Her handless sleeve went to her face. She turned to the window, toward the boys playing catch. He pushed it here, needing to be sure.

"Broken jaw. Busted teeth. And, unfortunately for me, no memory of that day. Not even of getting out of bed that morning."

She kept her face hidden. "I'm the only one?"

"The only witness, yes. That's why I'm sort of counting on you here."

She watched outside for a while, without actually watching anything.

"The rest of your staff," Frawley went on. "Anyone there you might consider disgruntled, or whom you could imagine providing someone else with inside information about bank practices, vault procedures—"

Already shaking her head.

"Even unwittingly? Someone who likes to talk. Someone with low self-esteem, who has a need to be liked, or to please others."

Still shaking *no*.

"What about someone who could have been blackmailed or otherwise coerced into providing information?"

Her face came away from her sleeve—sad but tearless, squinting at him. "Are you asking me about Davis?"

"I'm asking about everyone."

"Davis thinks that being gay—he's crazy, but he thinks it will hold him back. I told him, look around, half the men in banking live in the South End. This Valentine's Day, he asked what I was doing, and I said, you know, renting *Dying Young* and watching it alone, what else? And he had no one, so we went out together instead, for Cosmos at The Good Life, had a great time. We've only been real friends that long."

"Was there anyone new in Mr. Bearns's life? Maybe a relationship gone bad?"

"I wouldn't know. I never met his friends. He didn't talk about that with me. He was just fun. It was nice having a guy around who noticed when I got my hair cut."

"So you don't know if he was promiscuous?"

"Look . . . they *beat* him, remember? He's *innocent*."

He absorbed her disappointment in him, wondering if there wasn't something behind her flash of anger. The way Bearns was *innocent*. "So he was ambitious, he was looking to move up?"

"He was going to business school nights." Defensive now, firmly in Bearns's corner.

"Not you, though."

"Me? Nooo."

"Why not?"

"Business school?" she said, like he was crazy.

"Why not? Promotions. Advancement. Four other assistant

managers you trained have leapfrogged over you to corporate. Why stay on the customer end?"

"It's been offered." A little pinch of pride here. "The Leadership and Management Development program."

"And?"

Claire shrugged.

Frawley said, "You can't tell me you love being a branch manager."

"Most weeks I hate it."

"Well?"

She was bewildered. "It's a *job*. It pays well, really well, more than any of my friends make. No nights, no Sundays. Nothing to take home. My father—*he's* a banker. I'm not a banker. I never saw banking as my career. I just—my career was being young. Young and uncomplicated."

"And that's over now?"

She sank a little in the chair. "Like my friends, right? They were supposed to be taking me out that night. My birthday, the big three-oh, whoo-hoo. They rented a limo—cheesy, right? So I wind up bailing because I'm still in shock from this, and I tell them, you already got the limo, go ahead without me. So they call the next day, going on and on about dinner and the cute waiter with tattooed knuckles and the guys who bought them drinks, and driving up Tremont Street singing Alanis Morissette out of the roof, and Gretchen making out with an off-duty cop outside the Mercury Bar—and I'm like, my God. Is this who I am? Is that who I *was*?"

Frawley smiled to himself. He found her vulnerability attractive, this confused girl with her soul laid bare, struggling with newfound introspection. But he resolved to keep his pursuit pure. He was after these Brown Bag Bandits, not a date with Claire Keesey.

"I should feel worse, shouldn't I," she said. "People I tell, they give me these looks like, *Oh my God*. Like I should be in intensive therapy or something."

He stood and snapped off his tape recorder. It felt like they were done. "It was a robbery. You were an unwilling participant. Don't search for any meaning beyond that."

She sat up, anxious now that he was preparing to leave. "So weird, my life suddenly. FBI agents showing up at my door. Do you know, I barely recognized you when you walked in today? I only mean that—I was so out of it when I talked to you last time. It's all a blur."

"I told you, it's normal. Robbery hangover. Sleep okay?"

"Except for these dreams, my God. My grandmother, she died three years ago? Sitting on the edge of my bed with a gun in her lap, crying."

Frawley said, "That's the caffeine. I told you, leave it alone."

"So you haven't made any arrests yet?"

He stopped by the doors. Was she stalling him because she wanted information? Or was she interested in him? Or was it simply that she didn't want to be left alone with her folks? "No arrests yet."

"Any leads?"

"Nothing I can really talk about at this time."

"I read about the burning van."

Frawley nodded. "We did impound a torched van, yes."

"No money inside?"

"Sorry—I really can't say."

She smiled and nodded, giving up. "I just—I want answers, you know? I want to know why. But there is no why, is there?"

"Money. That's the why. Pure and simple. Nothing to do with you." He tucked his kit under his arm. "You staying here a few more days?"

"Are you kidding me? It's like, if I don't get out of here now, I never will."

"You're going back to Charlestown?"

"Tonight. I'm counting the minutes."

Frawley wanted to remark on the irony of her moving back to bank bandit central, but decided that would only spook her.

FRAWLEY STEERED HIS BUREAU car, a dull red Chevy Cavalier, past mini-mansions with landscaped lawns swollen like proud chests, looking for a road out of Round Table Estates.

"Everything about her says squeaky-clean," Frawley said into his car phone. "Except for the fact that she's lying about something."

"Uh-huh," said Dino. "That the only reason you're buzzing around her?"

"I'm not buzzing," said Frawley, thinking back to her stalling him.

"Then what are you doing out there, Friday after six?"

"Canton is on my way home."

"Every single town on the South Shore of Massachusetts is on your way home, Frawl. You waste three hours a day driving back and forth between Charlestown and Lakeville. I like your devotion to living among the bandits, but this is getting to be an addiction. Frawl."

"Yeah, Dean?"

"Spring is in bloom. Know what that means?"

"A young man's fancy turns to . . . ?"

"Bank robbing. And buzzing around pretty flowers. You've got approximately sixty hours off ahead of you. That's your weekend, federally mandated and enforced. Take off the tie and get yourself laid. No more running ten miles, stopping to yawn, running ten more. For my sake."

Frawley hung a left at the end of Excalibur Street. "Copy that. Over and out."

6
THE SPONSOR

THEY HUDDLED AT THE back of Sacred Heart like father and confessor: the middle-aged man sitting relaxed, his left hand gripping the pew in front of him, gold band glowing brassy in the candlelight; and the younger man, half-turned in the row before him, watching bodies rise from the basement like ghosts wearing the raincoats they died in. The coffeepot downstairs had been emptied and rinsed, all the munchkins eaten, the stirrers and sugars boxed away, the trash bagged and pulled.

"Good meeting," said Frank G., the middle-aged man, fingers drumming the dark wood. "Crowded tonight."

"Weekends," agreed Doug M., as he was known here.

Frank G. was a Malden firefighter, father of two young boys, on his second marriage. In three years, that was the sum total of personal information Doug's sponsor had let slip. Nine years dry, Frank G. was devoted to the program, especially the *Anonymous* part, even though—or maybe because—Sacred Heart was apparently his neighborhood parish. Doug drove fifteen minutes north from Charlestown for every meeting, specifically to avoid having to pour out his soul to familiar faces, which seemed to him very much like taking a nightly dump out on his own front porch.

"So what's the word here, studly, how's things going?"

Doug nodded. "Going good."

"You spoke well down there. Always do."

Doug shrugged it off. "Got a lot to talk about, I guess."

"You have a tale to tell," agreed Frank G. "Don't we all."

"Every time, I say to myself—just stand up, speak your piece, two or three sentences, sit right down again. And I always end up doing five minutes. I think the problem is, meeting's one of the few places where I make sense to myself."

Frank G. nodded in his way, meaning *I agree*, and *I've been there*, as well as *It's all been said before*, and at times, *Go on*. He had the sort of dour, everyman face you find on the can't-sleep guy in a cold-remedy commercial, or the beleaguered car-pool dad suffering from occasional acid indigestion. "It's a gift, having a place like this to go. To sort it all out, keep focused. Some people, it's addictive. Too generous a gift."

"You noticed," said Doug.

"Sad-eyed Billy T. Getting off on the shame like that. It's opening night every night with him, rising to sing his song and spill his tears until they drop that curtain. That's his drunk now."

"Gotta feel that shame, though. Someone like me—I got nobody to let down, except myself. Nobody at home keeping me honest. Back in the Town"—in meeting, Frank G. had once mentioned growing up in Charlestown, though with Doug he never acknowledged their common background—"I don't feel it."

"The stigma."

"I talk about going to prison for beating someone up in a bar, there it's like, 'Hey, it happens. Some guy needed fine-tuning, but you did your time, you got out'—like something I hadda endure. Like I been in the army two years. People downstairs here? I mention prison and their eyes bug out, they pull their purses closer. And this is Malden, not some soft suburb—but it reminds me I'm not always living in the real world, where I am."

"Nobody's here looking for friends," said Frank G. "This here, you and I, this isn't friends. This is a partnership. What we have is a pact. That said, I don't know what all this is exactly about your being out there on your own."

"Okay. You're right."

"I'm your wife in this. Me, I'm your kids. I'm your parents and I'm your priest. You let yourself down, you let us all down, the whole system crumbles. And as to the others listening to you—hey, so they're not asking you for a ride back to the T. They respect the work. You're doing it. Coming up on two years? That's getting it *done*. I'd take respect over back pats, any day."

An old man came shuffling up the center aisle, shrugging on his raincoat, saluting them before hitting the door. "Billy T.," said Frank G., waving good-bye, watching the church door close. "Wonder what he goes home to, huh? If he's got anybody but himself to answer to." He shook his head at the character of the guy, then shook him all the way off. "But one thing I don't get about you, and it's a big one. Why you're still doing your two the hard way. After all you learned here—why you don't know you can't be around people who drink."

Doug made an impatient noise, knowing Frank G. was right and also knowing Doug wasn't about to change. "You choose your friends, right? But not your family? Well, my friends—they are my family. I'm stuck with them, they're stuck with me."

"People grow up and leave their families, guy. They move on."

"Yeah, but the thing with that is—they actually keep me sober. That's how this works. By their example. Seeing them fuck up over and over—that works for me."

"Okay. So hanging around with knuckleheads makes you feel smarter."

"It's like lifting weights. Resistance training. The temptation is to give in, to skip that last rep, short the weight, arms burning. I ignore all that, finish out my set. Being with them reminds me that I'm strong. Reminds me I'm doing this. Without that, I could get lazy."

"Okay, Doug. And I hear you, right? And I still think you're packed full of crap. This uncle of mine, right? His wife died, he's getting ready to go to a nursing home, and I'm helping get him set up there. Decent attitude, all things considered. Month or so ago, we're sitting in Friendly's over grilled cheeses. All-around good guy, telling me how now he looks back over his life and thinks, *Hey, if only I knew then what I know now*. Not regrets necessarily, just his perspective now, you know? That whole, *Youth is wasted on the young* thing. And I was polite and all, sucking my Fribble through a straw. But I'm looking at him, this uncle of mine, struggling to get that flat yellow sandwich into his mouth, and I'm thinking—no way. He'd do things *exactly* the same way he did them before, even knowing what he knows now. Drop him back into his life at twenty-one, twenty-five? He'd slip right back into the moment, make all those same mistakes. Because that's *who he is*." Frank G. leaned closer to the back of Doug's pew, resting his forearms on the top and lacing his fingers. "So who are you?"

"Me?"

"What makes Doug M. think he's different from everyone else."

"I guess—only because I *am* different from everyone else."

"Fine, good. We got a problem here, let's address it." Frank G.'s hands grappled with the air. "You don't seem to realize that you *are* your friends. That's who you are—the people you attract, who you keep around you. Now, I'm a part of you, right? Just a little taste, maybe—lucky dog, you. A bigger part is this goddamn cancer tumor part, I'm talking about your knucklehead friends. Seeing them tonight?"

"Yeah."

"Okay. Do this for me. Take a good long look around. Because those faces you see staring back—that's you."

Doug wanted to answer that, wanted to lodge his protest. He wanted Frank G. to know he was more than the sum of his friends.

The priest was out in his black suit and Roman collar, cupping his hand around the candles on the altar, blowing flames into smoke. "Looks like last call," said Frank G.

Doug said, "I think I might've met someone."

Frank G. was quiet awhile, a silence more meaningful than a simple pause. Doug suffered through it, alternately sickened by his desire to please Frank G. and hoping he had succeeded.

"She in the program?"

"No," said Doug, surprised.

Frank G. nodded like that was a good thing. "What does it mean when you *think* you meet someone?"

"I don't even know. I don't know what that means."

Frank G. rapped a knuckle on the back of Doug's pew, like a blackjack dealer knocking a push. "Take things slow, that's all. Take care picking who you hook up with. Attraction does not equal destiny, the thirst teaches you that too. Not to break your tender heart here, kid, but nine times out of ten, romance is a problem, not a solution." Frank G.'s brows remained high over long-sober eyes. "Aside from not walking into a bar alone, my friend, this is the most important choice you're ever gonna make."

7
SATURDAY NIGHT FEVER

DOUG CONTINUED ON TO the Tap that night because he had told them all he would. Upstairs was filled with warm bodies arranged around a glass bar underneath some nouveau lighting, lots of laughter and clinking and the general hubbub of people working on their weekend buzz. Whiny guitar chords warned drinkers away from the doorway leading to the smaller rear room and its one-light, one-stool stage. All the young professionals who couldn't get into the Warren Tavern on a Saturday night, this place was their Plan B.

Doug turned down into the narrow stairway just inside the front door, descending into the haze of smoke. Downstairs was old-Town style, brick-walled and low-ceilinged, a dungeon of piss and beer. A glass bar here wouldn't last one night without shattering. Cases of empties formed benches along the walls, and a CD jukebox pumped in the corner like a beating heart. The bathrooms were grim but never crowded, drawing buzz-emboldened ladies from Upstairs, picking their way through the hometown crowd like debutantes at a sewerage convention with minced *Excuse me* faces, French-tipped nails pointed toward the His and Hers.

"MacRaaay!" hailed Gloansy from the bar, jumping up on the iron-pipe foot rail. He had that crazed, this-night-will-last-forever burn in his army-green eyes.

Doug made his way there, letting maniacal Gloansy hug him and slap his back. "'S'up?"

"I'm getting there, man. You good?"

Splash, the wet-handed barman, saw Doug and shouted something along the lines of *Long time, no see,* then slapped down an automatic soda-water lime. Splash spilled every drink he served. Doug answered Gloansy by taking a slurp of soda water, then looked around the room.

Gloansy had already signaled Jem, who detached himself from two sour-looking kids Doug didn't know and made his way toward the bar, a lane opening up for him. Jem, in turn, thinking Doug couldn't see him, gestured to the corner to hail Krista, and like half-drunk chessmen on a crowded, sticky board, the pieces made their moves. Krista stopped stirring her bourbon and Coke and placed a hand on Joanie Lawler's forearm, starting away from their conversation, and Joanie—a sturdy, frog-faced girl from the projects, the mother of Gloansy's boy, Nicky, and Gloansy's longtime bride-to-be—shooed her on, mouthing something encouraging.

Dez fed the corner juke a dollar bill and The Cranberries' "Linger" came on, a recent favorite on the all-Irish Downstairs playing list. Another hour or so and Dez would be firmly installed there for the night, the self-declared DJ, enforcing the mood, clearing out any malingering yuppies with a barrage of Clancy Brothers and accordion jigs before getting serious with a late-night set of U2.

Jem came up and telegraphed a roundhouse right, following through at half-speed, Doug playing along, snapping his head back in mock contact. Doug returned a sharp, *Star Trek* jab to the face that back-stepped Jem, who in his zeal for Hollywood splashed a pair of idle, hoop-earringed girls with foam out of his High Life longneck.

"The mastermind," greeted Jem.

"The masturbator," said Doug, smacking Jem's fists.

"Not anymore," Jem reminded him, killing his beer with a muscular flourish and pointing hard at Splash. "Four Highs."

Gloansy smiled, never tiring of the horseplay. "Jem kid, I think you shot a little beer cum on those ladies there."

Jem turned, the neighborhood girls glaring at their blouses like they'd been bled on. They were sore but receptive, and any politeness at all—an apology, a napkin, the offer of a free drink—might have opened the door to opening their legs. But Jem dismissed them with a nasty grin. He'd only be kissing beer bottles tonight.

"Fuckin' packed Upstairs, huh?" he said, under a belch. "We should open a bar. *I* should. Front somebody the liquor license. Drinking and money, combine my two loves."

Doug said, "Not so sure how well a gay bar would do here."

Gloansy howled, stamping the floor, Jem smiling like he had the secret murder of a thousand men on his mind. Doug turned, seeing himself in the bar mirror, Krista having arrived at his side without a word.

"Bully's was fucking hoppin'," said Jem. "We started there. Pitchers, he serves. And no cock-ass tourists."

"Bully's clears maybe twenty cents a beer," said Doug. "And no ladies show up there without they wheel in their own oxygen."

Splash was yelling at them from the end of the bar, pointing upstairs, disappearing.

"Old McDonough chased us outta there," said Jem. "Weaving around the place, waving his fucking walking stick, offering up laments for the Town. Weepy, bandy-legged old fraud."

"Lived all his life three streets down from me," said Gloansy, swiping at his nose with glee. "So how's it his brogue gets thicker every year?"

"It's the fucking brain damage," said Jem. "This guy needs to be put down humanely. Bumming pitcher hits off everybody, singing his songs. Making his toasts. How the old Town is gone, gone, gone . . ."

Doug felt Krista lean into him, making *Hi, I'm here* hip contact. Of all the associations the Tap Downstairs held for him, hers was the strongest. Once upon a time they had ruled this cellar together, back when Doug's nights never ended. Downstairs was old territory and so was she. Old habits he had kicked but kept close. The only difference being, beer bottles couldn't jump down off the shelf and rub against him.

Doug started a little trouble to distract himself. "Isn't it, though? Isn't it all gone now?"

Jem smacked the air with a grandiose backhand. "Fuck that."

"So it's not gone? It's just hibernating? Taking a little break?"

"These things're cyclical," said Jem, the last word rising up on him like a curb.

"Sickle-lickle," said Doug. "You think those bananas upstairs're going to drop all this money on real estate here, and someday just walk away from it?"

"Run, not walk," said Jem. "I got a plan."

"You got a plan," said Doug. He looked to Gloansy. "He's got a plan."

"I do have a plan," said Jem. "You know sometimes I feel like the last fuckin' sentry on the watch here. The only one who fuckin' cares about the auld Town at all."

Dez came up on them then, rapping knuckles with Doug and singing, "Here he is among us!"

Doug slowed him down with mock-seriousness. "Jem has a plan."

"Ah," said Dez, draining his High Life, eyes shining behind his eyeglasses. "About blowing up synagogues again?"

Jem horselaughed, then punched Dez in the left tit.

"Taking back the town," said Doug. "Turning back time. Being Marty McFly and all."

"Ho, yeah, great idea," said Dez, rubbing his chest, but not backing down. "I'm all nostalgic for those busing riots and street-corner stabbings."

Jem feigned at Dez again, then let it go, confident enough in his drunken scheme to proceed, showing them a scarred-knuckle peace sign. "Two options."

Doug repeated this for the benefit of the others. "Two options."

"F'r'instance, lookit these twats right here." They came off the rubber-carpeted stairs together—safety in numbers—like candle-holding virgins entering a horror-movie cave. One wore a shapeless black blouse, the other a mint green cashmere sweater hanging over her shoulders, sleeves knotted into a tit-covering bow. "The papers're right—it's single women overrunning the Town. Neighborhoods're safe, there's street spaces for their fuckin' Hondas and Volkswagens, and so on. Now I ask you, are we seeing any of this action?" He pointed up. "I think not. We gonna go sit Upstairs with the turtle-necks, sipping Chablis, fuckin' sweaters tied around our waists?"

"Sipping Chablis." Gloansy appreciated that one.

"Gotta scare them all out of Town. How? Okay. First thing would be, a chemical spill. The environment, bad air. Fumes. They start worrying about their ovaries, all that. So fucking health-conscious it makes *me* sick. Then? Like, a serial rapist."

Doug nodded at his reasoning. "You planning on handling that work yourself?"

"Just rumors, that's all you need. Put it out there. This 'safe neighborhood' rap—that's what's bringing them in by the carload. Make it unsafe. Put a little fear in them, and—*fffft!* The sound of housing prices falling all over Town."

"So basically," said Dez, upon a moment's reflection, "you'd shit in your own backyard just to keep people away."

Doug said, "I think it's foolproof."

"Fucking *genius* is what it is," said Gloansy.

Splash reappeared with four uncapped High Lifes tangled in his fingers. "You guys're onna tear tonight. Hadda hit Upstairs for more cold ones."

"And four more again," said Jem, dealing out the brews, setting one down on the bar in front of Doug.

Miller High Life had always been their weapon of choice. A tawny brew, cold gold in a crystal-clear, long-neck bottle. The Champagne of Beers. Something about the label always reminded Doug of a bill of currency, the easy-twist cap a serrated silver coin.

Jem had laid a loaded gun down in front of him—the bottle waiting, misting.

Krista leaned around Doug. "Jesus, Jimmy."

Jem guzzled his, coming back angry. "Fuck's your problem?"

"You."

"*I'm* your problem? Think I'm more like your freeloadin' fuckin' solution."

"Don't be a drunk prick. Pick one, be a drunk or a prick, but don't be both."

"So long as you're drinking on my dollar, why don't you just *shut the fuck*."

She squinted at him like he was so far away. "What's wrong with you? This is like the same thing with you bringing Ma all those fucking pastries."

Jem's eyes went dead white. If he reached around to smack Krista, Doug would get dragged into it, and the last thing he wanted to do was rescue her from anything. The truth was that Krista preferred Doug drunk and pliable too, but right now her brother was a convenient, common enemy.

And then, just as suddenly, some blue leaked back into Jem's eyes and he smiled, if only to himself. He leaned in close to Doug's elbow. "You understand me, right?"

"Well as anyone," said Doug.

"We always said, did we not—one of us takes a fall, the others keep the split going four ways, hold his cut. That's what this is. I buy a round? I buy four, always four. You die tomorrow, and I buy a round tomorrow night? I buy four. You're always in for a quarter. Even in this jail of yours, serving your own self-sworn sentence. In my head I been count-culating your share these past two years—"

"*Count-culating?*"

"I—fuck you—been *calculating* your share, and you're in for a motherfucking bitchload. When the floodgates open, brother, you drink free and long—on me. This is my *brother* right here!" he announced to the bar, standing up on the foot pipe as four more beers arrived. "This is my *sister* here, and this is my fuckin' *brother*!"

Heads turned, but there were no cheers, nothing like that, the Downstairs accustomed to his outbursts. Jem killed his beer, then traded his empty for a new one, his sudden affection carrying him away into the room. Dez extracted from Doug the promise of an ass-kicking later at the bubble hockey table, and then Gloansy disappeared, Doug finding himself alone with Krista at the bar.

She pushed aside her half-empty bourbon and Coke and took up Doug's untouched beer. He tried not to watch as she drank half of it. "Proud of you," she said.

"Yeah." Flat smile.

"I mean it. Strongest guy I've ever known. Stronger than any of these—"

"Yeah, okay." Doug got Splash's attention, pointed for another soda.

Krista took another pull, running her knee along the outside of Doug's thigh. "What was it that happened to us? Haven't we come through all that bullshit now? I mean—here we are, the two of us. Still."

"Still."

"If you think about it honestly," she said, choppy, dirty-blond hair falling off her ears in daggers, "is there anyone else for either of us? All this history that we have."

The tilted bar mirror gave Doug a good scope on the room. Dez had retreated to his jukebox confessional. Joanie sat on a stack of Beck's cases, one hand gripping a Bud bottle, the other hooked in Gloansy's back pocket while her drunken fiancé tossed off a nasty compliment at a woman walking past. Jem was back with the two unknowns—Townie kids, young and eager—regaling them with his stories, hands out like he was revving a Harley, getting laughs. The kids listened like bright-eyed disciples, and Doug felt an immediate distaste.

Frank G. saying, *Those faces you see staring back*. The haze of the room and Krista's closeness was working on him like déjà vu.

"I don't want to spend the rest of my life down here," said Krista. "I really don't."

Doug didn't quite believe that. He didn't quite believe anything Krista said, even the stuff he knew to be true.

"Can I tell you a secret no woman should ever tell a man?" She leaned in close, her warm breath tickling his ear. "I'm starting to feel old here."

She hung on Doug's reaction. "I'm feeling like I'm a hundred fucking years old," he admitted.

"I think we're being replaced."

Doug nodded and shrugged, dunking the lime wedge in his soda water. "Maybe that's not such a bad thing."

Her beer was gone. "Not if you got someplace else to move on to. Someone else to be."

So routine was the sensation of Krista's hand inside his thigh that Doug only registered the touch when her fingers started to creep along his inseam.

"How long has it been for you?" she said.

They say drowning men feel the water get warm before they slip under. The pull of familiarity here was like the tepid bath of sleep. *That's who you are—the people you attract, who you keep around you.*

"It's been too long for me." She had a magician's ability to keep talking into his ear while her trained hand worked. She was all over him now like the humidity of the room. "You know what I miss? Your high-mileage sofa. The grip I used to get on that armrest. I like thinking that every day you walk by it and see my nail marks there."

Doug stayed focused on her forgotten bourbon and Coke, the stirrer standing in melting ice, its tip nibbled. He felt a stirring himself.

He smelled her foxy grin along with the High Life on her breath and lips. "The strongest man I know. . . ."

As the first chords of "Mother Macree" reached him, Doug stood, her hand sliding off his leg. "Be right back," he told her. He set out in the direction of the john, but once in the crowd of merrymakers he cut back, slipping through the doorway and moving up the rubberized steps two at a time.

SURFACING UPSTAIRS WAS LIKE climbing out of a subway station into a cocktail party. A room full of pleated pants and necklace-twiddlers and roving, impatient eyes. Kids with drinks in their hands, aping their parents, trying to outshine one another. Guys pretending they cared, girls pretending they didn't. The big charade.

The hand-stamper at the door asked if everything was all right, making Doug wonder what the look on his face said. An alcoholic's rage, his apartness. The line waiting to get inside stretched almost to the corner, and Doug walked fast, stuffing his hands deep inside his pockets so he wouldn't hit anybody, heading south on Main.

Closer to Thompson Square, the sidewalk beneath his feet changed from cement to Colonial brick. He noticed a pale light inside the hazed glass of Fergie's flower shop across the street, glowing faintly like the withered power of the old mobs that, until just a few years ago, ruled the Town like royalty. Fergie, Doug figured, knew about as much about flowers as Doug did, which is zilch. The light winked out as he passed, the front door opened by a big white-haired mick in a tracksuit: Rusty, a supposed ex-IRA gunner who was Fergie's guy. Rusty scanned both sides of the street, warily tracking Doug's shadowed form—then Fergie appeared behind him, a head shorter, his boxer's hands tucked into his sweatshirt pouch, the tight hood stretched like a cowl over his head. The old mobster filled out the zip-up pretty well, though Doug could recall his father telling him long ago that Fergie wore women's sweatshirts because the female cut accentuated his size.

Doug took only that one brief glance before switching his focus to the lit point of the monument. Best not to gaze curiously at a gang-ster, especially not on a dark street at night, and especially not at one so paranoid and tweaked as Fergie. Triple especially if you're already feeling pissed off: true killers can read that shit and turn it back on you, and next thing you know there's rounds whistling into your chest. He heard the car doors close and the engine rumble as the liv-ing ghost of the old Town sank into his black, hearselike Continental and cruised away.

If the Bunker Hill Monument was the needle of the Charlestown sundial—the Town an irregular circle bleeding yolklike to the north-west—Doug had left the Tap at about nine o'clock, now headed for eight. His mother's house on Sackville stood at just after eleven, Jem's mother's house on Pearl ticking closer to midnight.

Packard Street, Claire Keesey's address, stood at about six thirty.

That previous night, he had found her plum Saturn returned to its brick-walled space. The no-haggle, sporty-cute coupe had been parked nose-in, the wasted spoiler and happy-face *Breathe!* sticker turned to the alley. It was while sitting there in his car looking at her dimly lit, second-floor windows that the question *Now what?* had occurred to him. He was wasting his time cruising a stranger's house, looking for . . . yeah, for what?

Pride had finally made him peel out of there, racing the Caprice up narrow Monument Avenue—a tunnel of brick row houses rising to the stage-lit granite dick. He returned home and slid her driver's license out of its hiding place behind the sill of his kitchen window. The ID had seen a lot of action, its plastic laminate curled at the edges, creased from long nights in tight pockets. In the unflattering photograph she looked startled, like someone bumped from behind in mid-smile.

The plastic blackened and sagged before it burned, her image melting, crying, the license suffering in his ashtray before curling up and surrendering oily black smoke. A simple ceremony to put an end to his wrongheaded infatuation.

Then this very evening, on his way out to Malden for his meeting, as he pulled into the Bunker Hill Mall to grab a Mountain Dew— there it was, pulled up to the curb outside the Foodmaster like a bomb waiting to go off, the bumper sticker screaming at him, *Breathe!*

He parked one row away, sitting there, his hands relaxed on the steering wheel, watching the ticking Saturn in his rearview mirror. Then, cursing himself, he was out of the Caprice and cutting across the parking lot, guessing CVS and moving inside, checking the store aisle by aisle.

He spotted her halfway down in Hair Care. She wore a red sweat-shirt, gray sweatpants, Avia ballcap, running shoes, and amber sun-glasses. It was a familiar look around Town, the frumpy weekend girl, yuppies doing their errands behind hats and glasses and baggy clothes, no one in the Town much worth impressing.

He fooled with packs of playing cards at the end of the aisle while she weighed conditioners. Some ballcaps on women looked wrong, joyless, severe—but Doug could see her running out a slow grounder up the first-base line, her sunny blond ponytail flying. She chose a tube the color of butterscotch, and Doug tailed her across two aisles to the magazine racks, where she pulled down *People*. She sidetracked into the wide central aisle, looking watchful all of a sudden, grabbing a quart-sized carton of Whoppers malted-milk balls and folding the magazine around it before walking to the front.

Doug pulled a Cadbury crème egg out of the clearance bin and fell into line behind her. He smelled the vanilla that was maybe the last of her old conditioner and eyed the faintly freckled slope of her neck. He worried that she would pick up on his presence with some self-protec-tive sixth sense of fear, but she looked only at her small, red key-chain purse, its plastic driver's license window empty.

Doug stepped back for her as she left, then spilled some coins for his candy while she helped an old woman tug a handcart full of no-name toilet paper through the folding doors to the sidewalk outside. Doug exited after her, feeling like a ghost, watching her climb into her car and check her mirror before backing up and pulling away.

See? Nothing special, said the class-conscious part of himself—the thirty-two-year-old bachelor in him answering back, *Yeah, right.*

Why he went on to tell Frank G. he might have met someone, he still didn't know.

And now here he was, back again, on foot this time, gazing up at her window. Mornings outside his mother's house, nights outside hers: Since when had he become such a sad sack? Was this what he had kicked the juice for? To spend his Saturday nights standing in alleyways like a bashful thief?

This was all he had ahead of him. You couldn't even call it a dream. It was the opposite of a dream, and the opposite of a dream is not a nightmare but nothingness. Dead sleep. The Town was one big walk-in cooler, and her window up there, its yellow light, was the last cold one sitting on the shelf. The bottle he could not open; the one he was never to touch.

HE WAS FLIPPING DROWSILY through *Vette* magazine and watching the cable rebroadcast of that afternoon's Sox game when his door tapped sometime after 1 A.M. He walked barefoot in boxers and a T-shirt through the parlor that, one floor below, was Jem's playroom, and below that, Jem's mother's old dining room, now the ground floor domain of Krista and Shyne.

Prison time had left Doug with a meticulous, almost military appreciation for order—Jem called it fussiness—and his place reflected this. Clean house, clean life, clean mind. By choice, he never had visitors anymore.

He stopped before the locked hall door and the shadow in the stripe of light beneath it.

"Duggy."

Krista, her voice bar-hoarse and bourbon-hushed. The tapping became a fine scratching, and he could almost see her body leaning against the door, her ear pressed to it the same way she used to listen to his heart through his chest. Her hand would be close to her mouth, telling the door a secret.

"I know you're in there."

All the drinks he didn't drink that night, all the mistakes he could have made but didn't—coming back for him now. Picking at his door, one last chance.

"Tell me what you want me to do," she said. "Tell me why wanting you isn't enough."

He lay his palm flat against the door, in the hope that some sort of current of understanding might pass between them. Then he turned off all the lights, passing by his sofa with her nail marks in the armrest, going to bed.

8
FRAWLEY AT THE TAP

"**W**HERE'D YOU GO?" asked Frawley.

"Bathroom downstairs," said June, hanging her bag on the stool back and easing his knee aside with her hand as she returned to her seat. "No line."

They sat together at a black Formica tabletop the size of a small steering wheel. The same people kept walking past.

"There's a downstairs?"

"Sure. All the girls know it."

She had a lot invested in that word, *girls,* did June, a thirty-six-year-old Realtor whom Frawley had met one night at Store 24, she buying cream cheese, him size AA tape recorder batteries. They both lived in the navy yard, she in a water-view condo with glass furniture and indirect lighting, he in a highway-view, two-window sublet with milk-crate bookshelves and most of his clothes still in cardboard boxes. For some reason, being and remaining a *girl* was inordinately important to her, with streaked blond hair crowding both sides of her face, hiding—like a terrible family secret—the margins where lines and creases were starting to form.

"You've never been here before," she said twinklingly, ever amused.

Frawley shook his head, still looking for the stairs.

"But you've been to the Warren," she said.

"Nope."

"Olives? Come on, you've at least been to Figs."

"I've walked past both."

"My God, Adam." She put her hand on his wrist, like offering a prayer for his speedy recovery. "Do you know that I had reservations at Olives last weekend, nine o'clock—and it was *still* a forty-minute wait? When I moved here, in '92—way ahead of the curve, by the way—there were only two restaurants I would even think of setting foot in, the Warren and the Tavern on the Water. Now look." She gestured proprietarily at the room. "All this you see here—this is happening *right now*. This is *the* hot neighborhood, the South End of a few years ago. Only instead of gay men, now it's single girls leading the charge." *Girls* again, thought Frawley. "The only drawback is the negative stigma, with the gangsters and dockworkers and all that—which by the way is fading every week. This is boomtown right now, I'm fielding a dozen calls a day from girls looking for apartments." She sipped a fresh margarita, cleaning the salt off her lip with a small tongue, Frawley hearing Motley Crüe's "Girls, Girls, Girls" in his head. "Even Thai food now. That says all you need to know right there. Thai food in Charlestown? Run up the white flag."

Frawley nodding, still wondering where those stairs were.

"There's a new bistro and wine bar opening up next month—where the old Comella's was? The space was vacant for almost a year. We'll have to try it."

"Great," he said, thinking, *Uh, no*.

"And you have to take me running with you sometime. They say it's great training for cardio-boxing."

Training for a workout class, that was something new. Frawley touched the "fun" margarita she had talked him into ordering. A bad experience in his freshman year at Syracuse—he had never before or again since vomited purple—had taught him never, ever to trust tequila. "So," he said, "what was it that made you move here in '92?"

"Honestly? The parking. And now this whole neighborhood has exploded around me. My first place, before I bought in the yard, was over on Adams, this rickety condo with a girl who answered phones for Harvard Health. She lived in her pajamas all weekend and cried every Monday morning before work. Utterly manic, and I mean up until three in the morning painting walls. She had this absolutely dreadful, hopeless affair with one of the jerks who lived over us—got herself *pregnant* and was lucky that was all she got from him—then wanted me to go with her, you know, to get it taken care of, and I had to cross the protest lines with her, outside the clinic through all these crazy—what are you looking for?"

"Oh. Nothing. Our server."

"He'll be back," she said, grabbing a strand of her streaked hair and twirling it. "But why do *you* live here, *Special Agent Frawley*?" She loved that. "Your commute sounds insane. It's not really about the bank robbers, is it?"

"I guess it is."

"You're like some Sigourney Weaver observing the apes by living among them?"

He deserved this for trying way too hard to impress her on their first date. "Just like that," he said.

"Because that's all fading away. That meteor that killed off all the old dinosaurs? Coming down on this town like thigh-high boots with a thirty-foot heel. That's girl power." A shrill tone rang between them, barely audible. "Ah," she said, a smiling frown, tugging her bag off the stool back and sliding out a flip phone, pulling up the antenna. "I was afraid this might happen." She answered it, covering her opposite ear. "Hi, Marie." Eye roll. "I can barely—hold on—" She covered the mouthpiece. "A client, signed a purchase-and-sale today, a two-bed with roof deck on Harvard, court parking, my exclusive. Needs some hand-holding." She unfolded a pair of flat-framed specs and slid them on. "Two minutes, cross my heart." She resumed the phone call. "Okay, Marie, June's here . . ."

Frawley excused himself and wandered through the crowd until he found the stairs near the entrance, a downward flight of beer-slicked, rubber steps without a sign. It looked like he was headed into the Tap's storage basement until a twist cut off the clatter Upstairs, blending in laughter, yells, and music below.

He came off the steps into a catacomb of brick walls and sticky stone floor. There was a short, dirty-mirrored bar, a jukebox pumping in the far corner, stacks of empty cases, a plastic-domed foosball table, and plenty of hothouse sweat. The music beat a blood pulse through the crowd, Frawley recognizing "Bullet the Blue Sky," placing it somewhere around law school: faculty-student cocktail hours, driving his guacamole green diesel Rabbit to his FBI interview. The *Joshua Tree* album? Or *Rattle and Hum*?

A fair-haired type in comically thick-rimmed eyeglasses was grooving at the jukebox, mimicking Bono's midsong rap, "Peelin' off those dollar bills / Slappin' 'em down . . ." Then every voice in the room cheered as one:

> *One hundred!*
> *Two hundred!*

Frawley noticed the tequila in his system now, tasting it in the sweat along his upper lip. This was where Frawley needed to be, not Upstairs with the smart set but underground, in the furnace room where the beast was nightly fed—the real Charlestown, the authentic Charlestown—Bono growling, "Outside it's America . . ."

The bump shocked him back into himself. It was a professional bump, almost a cop's bump, making out Frawley's service piece on the shoulder rig beneath his jacket.

Frawley looked up, met the bumper's eyes. They were bloodshot, the pupils a misty, near-white blue, close set. Those and the pronounced ridges beneath the bumper's nose stuck out in Frawley's mind: the memory of a face with a number board beneath it. A mug shot from the thick Charlestown files back at Lakeville.

The stare went on, Frawley still digesting the pro bump as well as the mug, too stunned by it all even to begin competing with the bigger guy's prison-yard stare. Downstairs not a full two minutes, and already he was made.

"Jem, you're up!" yelled someone—the bartender, turning the bumper's head.

The bumper grinned hard and angry. "Bathroom's that way," he said, shouldering hard past Frawley toward a quartet of beers opened and waiting on the bar.

9
THE GARDEN IN THE FENS

AFTER BREAKFAST OUTSIDE HIS mother's house on Sackville Street, Doug crossed the bridge into the city, bought a *Herald* and a *Globe* from a shaking, grizzled hawker outside the veteran's shelter on Causeway, then piloted the Caprice up onto the expressway, riding south against the morning traffic.

He spent much of the morning cruising suburban banks, trying to work up some enthusiasm for a low-margin score. He was looking for something he could control, something he could get them into and out of quickly and that would show a decent payday for their efforts—which was to say, the same thing any thief went looking for. Taking down scores was a game of momentum, and the Kenmore Square job had thrown them off their winning ways. They needed a nice medium-weight take to get back their confidence, and city banks were getting too complicated.

He eyeballed a co-op in East Milton Square, a Bank of Boston on the Braintree–Quincy line, a credit union in Randolph—but nothing that lit up his switchboard. He tried to figure out if it was the size of the scores or his mood that was putting him off. Cash was out there, everywhere he looked: the trick was finding enough of it concentrated in one place, however briefly, to make a job worth the risk.

ATM machines were cropping up all over, in bars, gas stations, even all-night convenience stores. These droids were fed by armored-car couriers making as many as fifty stops per day, sowing cash around metro Boston like uniformed Johnny Appleseeds. Unlike bank runs, ATM couriers never picked up cash, they only distributed, starting at the beginning of the day with a full whack and dropping between fifty and eighty grand at each jump, returning at end of day with only printouts and receipts. These couriers therefore had to be hit early, within their first few stops, and this had worked for Doug before, but now contractors were getting hip to the routine. They were showing more care early in their daily runs—using two-man deliveries, maintaining constant radio contact, even hiring out the occasional police escort—then easing off coverage after lunch.

Convenience stores and the like took only twenties, usually from commercial armored trucks like Loomis, Fargo, & Co. or Dunbar—but their delivery times and routes varied due to demand, and there was no outside way for Doug to track that. Banks required tens as well as twenties—some of the downtown machines even took neat stacks of hundreds—distributed separately from branch deliveries, generally by unmarked armored vans with specially plated exteriors and bulletproof windows. But the bank bills were usually new and serialized—and therefore highly traceable.

It had gotten to the point where Doug was willing to look beyond banks, but businesses doing even half their sales in hard cash were getting harder and harder to find. There were nightclubs, but that was often goombah money, and stealing from the government was a lot safer than getting tangled up in a lot of spaghetti. Fenway Park had caught his eye during prep for the Kenmore job, but though he had enjoyed working out a scheme in his head, it was too much of a name job, "a marquee score" as Jem termed it, and good only for unending scrutiny and heat. Never mind being sacrilegious. Sometimes just knowing you can pull off a job is enough.

What he had been looking at more and more were movie theaters. The big ones, the multiscreens. Only a portion of the ticket sales were done by credit card, and all the concessions remained strictly cash. As with ballparks, theater profits weren't in their ticket prices. Food and drink were their main action. Theaters made most of their coin on the appetites of captive audiences, and big summer movies meant row after row of shiftless kids with nothing better to do than spend. The multiscreens lived off these opening weekends, and Monday mornings found them sitting as fat as a bank on Friday. Jump a can making a pickup, and maybe they'd have themselves something.

But possibilities and probabilities, that was all he had. He scoped out a few movie houses on his way back into the city, just drive-bys, him trying to get his head together. Whether by accident or intent, his return route took him in past Fenway and over the turnpike bridge toward Kenmore Square.

The Saturn was there in its regular space behind the bank, jumping out at him like something thrown at his windshield. The spike he felt in his chest was the same charge he got as a kid whenever he thought he spotted his mother in a crowd. For a year or more after she had disappeared, he'd faithfully cataloged his daily activities in a Scribble Pad, so that when she returned, he would be able to catch her up on everything about him she had missed.

He banged a one-eighty around the bus station and cruised into the parking lot beneath the landmark Citgo sign, the same spot he had used to case the bank from, all the time wondering if there was a name for this virus he had. He thought he might just sit there awhile, watch the bank across the square.

A minute later he was slamming the door of the Caprice and crossing the street. From Uno's, he told himself, he could get a better look. Then the Walk sign stayed white, and his feet carried him all the way across Brookline Avenue to the sidewalk outside the bank.

One quick pass by the windows was all he could afford. The bank door opened as he approached it, him reaching out to hold the door for a black lady in a wheelchair—and the next thing he knew, he was inside, telling himself to scrawl something on a deposit slip and get the fuck out.

Then he was in line for a teller, smacking himself on the thigh with his rolled-up *Herald*. This was something a sweaty-eyed arsonist did, returning to the scene of the crime. A whiff of bleach hit him, even if it was present only in his mind.

"Oh, hi." She made him right away, Jesus Christ, this skinny-necked black teller with her hair flour-sacked on top of her head, smiling. "Haven't seen you for a while. Meter change, right?"

"Yeah, thanks." He pried a dollar bill off his damp fingers and pushed it through. He had the slimmest of angles on the hallway to the door of the manager's office from there. Someone was moving around.

The teller leaned toward the perforated bulletproof partition. "Did you hear we got robbed?"

"Yeah, was that this branch?" Cameras perched on the wall behind her like little one-eyed birds, him keeping his head down, making himself watch her hands. "Everybody okay?"

"I'm fine, I wasn't here." She made a four-quarter stack with dry, delicate brown fingers and pushed them forward like casino chips, speaking low. "But our assistant manager was beaten. Badly—he's still in the hospital. The manager was supposed to be back today—you know the blond girl, carries her keys on a strap?"

"Okay, maybe."

"Not to open, just to be here—her first day back. She never showed."

The words actually rose in his throat, Doug almost informing her that the plum Saturn was parked out in back. A brain virus, it had to be. He choked on his swallowed words, scooping up his quarters and walking away, half-blind, not even trusting his mouth with a cordial *Thank you.*

DOUG WAS SAFELY BACK inside the Caprice when it hit him, his theory, and he would not sleep again unless he proved it right or wrong. That was what he told himself as he drove back over the short bridge toward Fenway, parking there and jogging a block under the warming sun to Boylston, across Park Drive into the Back Bay Fens.

The Fens was a park laid out around a dead-river pond, a city oasis glowing hormonally emerald in the full-on puberty of spring. Inside the bike paths along Park Drive were the Fenway Gardens, five hundred fenced lots staked along meandering dirt-and-pebble lanes. A couple of times in early April he had followed Claire Keesey here on her lunch hour, watching from a distance as she sat on a crumbling stone bench, picking through a Tupperware salad under the pale green fingers of a willow tree. She had sat with perfect posture, as though posed for one of the pictures in the thick fashion magazine open at her side. She usually embezzled a few extra minutes of lunch hour beyond her allotted sixty.

His landmark for locating her plot was a rain-hatted scarecrow dwarf at the end of the row, fashioned out of basket wicker and tilted on a crucifix of broken ladder. Nothing else anywhere looked familiar to him. Spring had sprung and the gardens were completely transformed.

He saw her kneeling on the ground, going at it hard with a hand fork, clawing the soil as though it were a memory that would not die. When she stopped and got to her feet for a water break, Doug saw that she was dressed not for gardening but for work—a soft pink sweater-blouse over a long, muddied skirt, both ruined. She reached for a spading fork and pushed up her dirtied sleeves, resuming her all-out assault on the earth.

People on bicycles or walking their dogs slowed as they passed her, one feisty little gay pug yapping at her with concern. Claire Keesey never looked up. A shirtless man eyed Doug from three plots down, and Doug bashed him with a look, starting back quickly to his car, the mystery of Claire Keesey clouding his mind.

10
STAINED

DUE TO A QUIRK OF either geography or city planning, the C branch of the MBTA Green Line subway made twelve stops along a three-mile straightaway between Boston's Kenmore Square and Boston's Cleveland Circle—all of them in the town of Brookline. The old-fashioned trolleys ran aboveground there, on tracks that cleaved the length of Beacon Street. At the St. Paul stop stood a half-block-long, three-story Holiday Inn hotel with a glassy corporate atrium, where on four Tuesday mornings each year the Boston Bank Robbery Task Force and associated agencies assembled for a breakfast meeting.

The BRTF was formed in late 1985, at a time when alliances of federal, state, and local law enforcement agencies routinely failed due to conflicting mandates and general bad blood. It was a shotgun marriage: the Massachusetts region had seen fifteen of the nation's sixty-five total armored-car robberies in that year. By the early 1990s, the task force had halved that number—significant progress, but not enough to shake Boston's title as the Armored Car Robbery Capital of America. Gains had also been made in reducing the number of bank robberies, pushing the regional total below two hundred per year, and showing a whopping 73 percent clearance rate, as compared to 49 percent nationwide.

The full-time investigative arm of the BRTF, headquartered at Lakeville, was composed of five FBI agents, two Boston police detectives, and three Massachusetts state troopers. Today's informational meeting included associated members of the Massachusetts Department of Corrections, the Cambridge Police Department, a guest speaker from the Drug Enforcement Administration, liaisons from every major area bank chain and armored-transport company, and a representative from the Federal Reserve Bank of Boston—all sharing information and identifying trends over croissants and cranberry juice.

That morning found Frawley unusually impatient. He had spent the entire day before in his Cavalier with Dino, shadowing a Northeast Armored Transport truck on a tip from the Organized Crime section. Fifty-four stops at supermarkets, convenience stores, and nightclubs throughout Saugus and Revere, and they'd be back at it again tomorrow—leaving him little time to pursue the Brown Bag Bandits from the Kenmore Square heist.

Frawley was a doodler and a good one. As the suit from the Federal Reserve Bank outlined concerns regarding the Big Dig—the Central Artery reconstruction project that included, as part of its ten-year overhaul of the city's crumbling highways and fallen arches, a major tunnel within a few dozen yards of his institution's gold bullion vaults—Frawley added hash-mark scarring to the egg-eyed hockey masks lining the margins of his schedule memo. He did them mug-shot style, full-face and profile: two small bean holes for the nostrils, a flat, expressionless slot for the mouth, and the twin tribal triangles at the pits of the cheeks. Tracing the masks was a dead end: a visit to a Chinatown costume store showed him dozens of easily adaptable *Friday the 13th* party masks staring down from the walls.

Hunting a disciplined crew was most difficult because it eliminated Frawley's two greatest advantages over bank robbers: their stupidity, and their greed. He could not rely on their compulsion to pull reckless jobs, leaving him fewer opportunites to capture them.

He wandered back to the raided vault in his mind. The yawning cabinet, the plundered cash drawers: he tried to let that feeling of violation wash over him again. He remembered the bait bills and dye packs left behind, untouched. Pro bank bandits, like practitioners of any arcane craft, were a superstitious bunch. Frawley hadn't touched them either, being superstitious in his own way, himself the student of a dying art. He was the last in the long line of bank detectives. The bloodline traced directly from the first stagecoach Pinkertons to himself. If he couldn't be there at the beginning, he figured the second-best place to be was right where he was, at the tail end. Credit cards, debit cards, smart cards, the Internet: the dawn of the cashless society meant the twilight of the modern bank bandit, and the coming of a new breed. Identity theft and electronic embezzlement were the future of financial crime. The next Adam Frawley would be a pale, deskbound Net-head hunting cyber-thieves with a mouse and a keyboard instead of an Olympus Pearlcorder and a blue Form FD-430. Adam Frawley would soon become obsolete. The techniques, the tradecraft, everything he knew about banks and vaults and the men who robbed them, and all he had yet to learn—it would die with him, the last bank robbery agent.

Below the cartoon masks, he sketched the handset of a telephone and connected the two by a coiled wire. This wire was his only tangible lead now. It was the phone company tech the Brown Bag Bandits exhibited, in the Kenmore Square job as well as the others the task force now suspected them of: credit unions in Winchester and Dedham; the Milk Street Pawn cut-in; ATM jobs in Cambridge and Burlington; a co-op in Watertown; two banks just over the New Hampshire border; last September's weekend spree of three Providence storage facilities, for which they had disabled the ADT Security System network across most of eastern Rhode Island; and the nontech armored-car heists Frawley hunched them for, in Melrose, Weymouth, and Braintree. All three- and four-man crew jobs, all of them spread out over the past thirty months.

Frawley had found fresh wounds running up a telephone pole around the corner from the BayBanks, left there by a lineman's spikes. A Nynex crew in a cherry picker worked for three hours to diagnose and repair the junction-box reroute.

No one Frawley had talked to inside the Monopoly game that was the booming telecom industry could satisfactorily explain how a thief could locate the particular cellular antenna—disabled one and a half miles away, on the roof of a Veterans Administration Hospital on Roxbury's Mission Hill—responsible for bouncing the bank's backup alarm signal to the Area D-4 police station.

He sketched a cell tower with suturelike antennas, then fleshed out the tower, letting it grow into the Bunker Hill Monument.

The bleached crime scene, stolen surveillance tapes, and torched work van left them with no physical evidence at all. Frawley's only hope now was that the subpoena would prove out, this one seeking not just Nynex service logs but employee records and home addresses. He would run down any leads involving phone company employees residing in the Town—possibly opening up the case to a "Charlestown witch hunt" defense at trial, but right now it was all he had.

On top of all this was the phone call he had received just prior to the start of this meeting, informing him that Claire Keesey had yet again failed to return to work.

His felt pen moved incessantly, all these things playing inside his head, finding expression here and there in automatic writing: gloved hands aiming BANG! cartoon guns; fat moonshine jugs labeled BLEACH; dollar signs hash-marked with stitching scars.

He willed himself not to check his wristwatch again as an enormously pregnant DEA agent outlined the positive impact that falling heroin prices might have on note-passers. Apparently a price-and-purity war was raging between the Colombian cartels and the traditional Asian heroin producers, the Colombians gaining East Coast market share by wooing needle-wary smokers and snorters. At $5 per thumbnail-sized bag, street H was now stronger than coke and cheaper than beer.

Heroin use was also rising in Charlestown, but along with the institutional anachronism of the neighborhood, Townie drug addicts retained their affinity for the bad-boy drug of the late 1970s, angel dust. Dust came sold in small packets, or "tea bags," the powder acting as an anesthetic, a stimulant, a depressant, and a hallucinogen—all at the same time. Its status as the outlaw drug of all drugs surely accounted for its special appeal within the Town.

But his mind was wandering again. He focused on the tablecloths, their bright coral pinkness reflected in the water glasses like floating lilies. Outside the right-hand wall of windows, the dreary street was drawn in charcoal pencil, smudged by the all-morning drizzle.

Frawley's and Dino's pagers went off at the same time. Frawley sat back to read the display on his hip, showing the Lakeville office phone number, followed by the code 91A. The FBI offense code for bank robbery was 091. *A* was shorthand for "armed."

Dino had his phone, Frawley rising with him, both of them in suits for the meeting, moving away from the tables. Dino held his phone elbow high, as though cell-phone use required a more formal technique than regular telephones.

"Ginny," he said. "Dean Drysler. . . . Uh-huh. . . . Okay. When was that?" He stepped to the wall, looking out the weeping windows to the western end of Beacon. "Got it." He hung up, turned to Frawley. "Note-passer. Just happened. Claimed gun but didn't show."

"Okay." Hardly anything to shake them out of a meeting for. "So?"

"Coolidge Corner BayBanks, intersection of Beacon and Harvard." He pointed out the window. "Two blocks that way, across the street."

Frawley tensed, then looked for the door to the lobby. "I'm gonna run."

Frawley was out of the room fast, new-shoe-running over a slippery carpet into the lobby, blowing past the doorman in his silly vest and out into the gray mist. Down a steep, turnaround driveway, across busy Beacon against the light, then following a low fence along the trolley tracks until he could cross the slick inbound lane of Beacon ahead of onrushing traffic, up the rising sidewalk past a Kinko's and a post office and a whole-foods market.

He covered the quarter-mile in no time, arriving outside the corner bank with his hand on his shoulder piece. The sight of a dapper man dancing back and forth there with keys in his hand, searching hooded faces, told Frawley the thief was already gone. Frawley drew his creds out of his jacket, flapped it open.

"My *God,* you got here fast," said the branch manager, silver eyeglasses perched ornamentally on his face.

"How long?" said Frawley.

"One, two minutes. I came almost right out after him."

Frawley scanned in all four directions, the intersection calm in the rain, no one reacting to a man running, no cars tearing out of handicapped parking spaces. "You don't see him?"

The manager craned his neck until the rain specks on his glasses made him draw back under the overhang. "Nowhere."

"What'd he have, a hat? Sunglasses?"

"Yes. Scarf around his neck, tucked into his jacket, to his chin. A caramel brown chenille."

"Gloves?"

"I don't know. Can we go back inside?"

Frawley saw blue cruiser lights about a half mile up the inbound lane, cars pulling over for them. "After you," said Frawley.

It was a handsome old bank, well-appointed, underlit. Customer service was corralled in the center by a low, wood-railed office gate with a thigh-high swinging door. Green-shade banker lamps illuminated boxy computer monitors. The teller booths and a currency-exchange window lined the rear.

The customers and service reps stopped their buzzing, all eyes turning to the manager and the overdressed FBI agent. In back, the tellers had left their windows to huddle with their co-worker in the rightmost window.

"Make the announcement," said Frawley.

"Yes," said the manager. "Umm—everyone? I'm sorry to say that there's been a robbery here just now, and—"

A collective gasp.

"Yes, I'm afraid so, and we're going to have to suspend our transactions for at least an hour"—a confirming glance at Frawley—"or two, perhaps even just a bit more, so please, if you would, bear with us for a few minutes, and we'll have you on your way."

Frawley's call for a show of hands of anyone who'd seen the bandit leave the bank got him nowhere. Customers are usually never aware that a note job is going down until afterward when the manager locks the front door.

Dino arrived at the same time the police did, shaking their hands and generally keeping them out of the way while the manager let Frawley in back with the tellers.

"CCTV or stills?"

"What?" said the manager.

"Close circuit cameras or—" Frawley looked up and answered his own question. The video cameras were placed too high on the wall. "Those aren't even going to get under his hat brim," Frawley said, pointing. "Seven and a half feet high, max—make sure those get lowered. Do they slow to sixty frames after the alarm is punched?"

"I—I don't know."

The others remained huddled around the rightmost teller, hands of support on her shoulders and back. She was an Asian woman in her midthirties, Vietnamese perhaps, tears dripping off her round chin and spotting her salmon silk shirt, her nude nylon knees chunky and trembling.

Her top drawer was open, its slots still full of cash. "How much did he get?" asked Frawley.

A woman wearing a long hair braid of gray and silver answered, "Nothing."

"Nothing?" said Frawley.

"She froze. She's a trainee, this is her second day. I saw she was in trouble, and I saw the note. I hit my hand alarm."

The note lay just inside the window slot, scribbled on a white paper napkin, wrinkled like a love letter held too long in a sweaty hand. "Did you touch this?"

"No," said the Vietnamese teller. "Yes—when he first pass it to me."

"Was he wearing gloves?"

The head teller answered for her. "No."

"Anybody see the gun?"

The Vietnamese teller shook her head. "He said bomb."

"Bomb?" said Frawley.

"Bomb," said the head teller. "He was carrying a satchel on his shoulder."

The note read, in a shaky, frightened slant, "I have a <u>BOMB</u>! Put ALL MONEY in bag." Then, larger, bolder: "PLEASE NO ALARMS OR ELSE!!!"

The word *please* jumped out at Frawley. "A satchel?"

The head teller said, "Like half a backpack. Not businessy. Gray."

Frawley lifted out his capped felt pen and used it to flip the note. On the back was the familiar pink and orange Dunkin' Donuts logo. Dino appeared on the other side of the teller window like a customer. "Still smell the coffee," said Dino. "There's one across the street here—right, ladies? And you can see the bank from the window, correct?"

Yes, mm-hmm, they all nodded.

Frawley said, "He sat there and wrote out the note, crossed the street with it in his hand inside his pocket. . . ."

"Impulse, maybe," said Dino. "Not a hypo."

"Not a bomber either." Frawley turned back to the Vietnamese teller. "The note mentions a bag. The same bag the bomb was in?"

She was sniffling now. "No, a white bag, trash bag. He took with him."

"And just left? Walked right out?"

She turned to the head teller then. "I need the lady room now."

The head teller said to Frawley, "He got nervous. I think it was me noticing him. He turned right on his heels."

Frawley looked back at Dino. "Guy needs money, like now."

Dino nodded. "Trolley's free outbound from here."

Frawley said to the head teller, "What's the next bank down the line?"

"A . . . another BayBanks branch. Washington Square."

Dino said, "Ladies, I need their telephone number, pronto."

Frawley was moving past the head teller toward the opened security door. "Hat? Jacket?" he said over his shoulder.

"Bucket hat," she answered. "Some kind of golf thing on the crest. Jacket was short, tight. Heavy for spring, but not cheap. Hunter green—he dressed nice."

"Dino?" said Frawley, moving fast.

Dino waved him on, picking up a phone, "Go, go."

Frawley stopped on the wet curb outside. Dino's Taurus was pulled up there, his grille blues and headlamps flashing. Double-parked cruisers had jammed up traffic in all four directions.

A trolley came clanging up the rise, the only thing moving. Frawley crossed the street and ran to intercept it, darting inside the opened doors. "I need you to go straight through to Washington Square," he told the toothpick-chewing conductor.

The guy squinted doubtfully at Frawley's creds. "Small badge."

"It's real enough." This was Frawley's first commandeered vehicle. "Let's go."

The driver thought a moment, then shrugged and closed the doors. "Fine by me."

The trolley nosed through the honking cars, gaining speed past the intersection, passing boutiques, a high-end pastry shop, a RadioShack, apartment houses.

"So what kinda money you people make?" the driver asked.

"Huh?" said Frawley, standing next to him, heart pounding, creds still in hand. "Less than you probably."

"Any overtime?"

"Mandatory ten-hour day."

"Thought you guys supposed to be smart."

The driver sounded his horn as they failed to slow for waiting raincoats and umbrellas at the next stop. "Hello, excuse me!" said a woman behind Frawley, grocery bags sagging at her feet like sleepy dogs.

"FBI's driving the car now, ma'am," said the driver.

They blew another stop to a chorus of middle fingers. Then, suddenly, the roadside on Frawley's right separated from the track, rising on a hill above them. "Hey! Where's that going?"

"It'll be back, don't worry," said the driver. "Listen. You people gotta unionize. It's every American's right."

"Yeah, noted," said Frawley, looking for the road. "Where the hell is Washington Square?"

"Washington Square, next stop!" sang out the driver.

The roadside plummeted back down to realign with them, the joined road opening into another intersection. Frawley saw the green and white BayBanks sign on the near right corner. The trolley braked, wheels squealing, turning every head in the square—but none so dramatically as that of the man in the green jacket, tan scarf, and bucket hat exiting the bank door with a travel satchel on his shoulder, a white plastic trash bag in his hand.

The nature of his work dictated that Frawley dealt almost exclusively with crime scenes. In his eight years of chasing bank bandits, he had never once witnessed one in action.

"Open!" said Frawley, banging on the door. The driver opened it before he stopped, and Frawley jumped out and hit the ground running, sprinting into the intersection, suit jacket flapping, darting around cars.

The suspect strode across the side street as though unaware of this man yelling, *"Hey!"* and running after him. A car in Frawley's way forced him to go wide and intercept the suspect at the far curb.

Up close, the guy looked like a blank, not at all menacing, a nose and a mouth under a gray rain hat, big sunglasses, and the coiled caramel scarf. The L.L. Bean walking shoes, mossy corduroys, and gray travel bag—those did not compute. Not your standard note-passing outfit. Frawley was close enough to him now to see loose fifties static-pressed against the white, one-ply trash bag hanging limp in his left hand.

"Hold it!" said Frawley, one hand opened toward the man, his other up on the butt of his holstered gun. The suspect's jacket was zipped to the collar; any move he made would have to be a clumsy one. "FBI," announced Frawley, feeling good as he said it, the suspect stopped before him in the light, misting rain.

There was a crackling sound that was almost fuselike, coming from somewhere on the suspect. Frawley remembered the guy's bomb threat—then the sidewalk went blind red.

Frawley reeled backward, certain the guy had exploded into pieces in front of him. Something struck him hard—the pavement—and his throat began to burn, eyes stinging and tearing. He brought one hand in front of his face and saw it painted red.

Frawley tried to right himself on the sidewalk, his respiratory system closing up on him. Through slitted eyes he saw the suspect on the move, stumbling backward, tripping off the curb. Something fluttered up into Frawley's face like a bloody bird and he fought it off—then another, and another, one sticking to his hand. Gray-green and red. He held it before his swelling eyes, trying to focus.

It was a fifty-dollar bill, stained and burned.

A dye pack. Not a bomb but half an ounce of red dye and tear gas bursting from a tiny, pressurized CO_2 canister sandwiched inside a hollowed-out stack of retired bills.

Frawley turned on his knee, forcing open his bleary eyes and seeing the dappled bills fluttering across the square like fall leaves off a money tree. The red-splashed trash bag tumbled empty and dream-like toward the stalled Green Line trolley.

Frawley got to his feet. He found his way off the curb. His pace grew more certain with every step, and he yelled both to stop the suspect and to keep his airway open.

The form before him trailed a long scarf. Something small lay in the road—the dropped satchel—and Frawley followed the vague shape between two parked cars. It turned right at the end of a fence, the fringed scarf slithering away.

A chorus of high-pitched screams as Frawley reached the corner. An elementary-school playground, Frawley's appearance sending them squealing toward the school.

The sight of the children slowed the suspect just enough for Frawley to dive for the end of the scarf, clotheslining the guy, bringing him down. Frawley got on him fast, wrestling the guy's flailing arms behind him and kneeing his face into the turf.

Frawley carried no handcuffs. He hadn't collared anyone without an arrest warrant since his first office assignment. He whipped off the perp's gloves and squeezed the guy's thumbs together, pulling up hard on his arms, immobilizing him with pain.

The guy spat something into the dirt. "What?" said Frawley, adrenalized to the max, ears ringing, nose running.

"Shoot me," the guy said. Frawley realized then that the guy wasn't fighting him, only sobbing.

Sirens coming now. Kids still dropping off the monkey bars, Frawley yelling at teachers to get them indoors. He eased up on the guy, unwinding the muddy scarf from his neck. The guy looked maybe forty, despairing, already ashamed.

"Mortgage or sick kid?" said Frawley.

"Huh?" the guy sniffed.

"Mortgage or sick kid?"

A defeated, wincing sigh between sobs: "Mortgage."

Frawley fished out his creds yet again, holding the gold badge high for the screaming cruisers. "Should have refinanced."

The cops came up all loaded for bear, weapons drawn, and Frawley shielded the bandit with his body, bellowing at them, *"It's okay, back off!"*

They finally holstered, Frawley so furious by then that he snatched a pair of handcuffs out of one of the patrolmen's hands and hooked up the bandit himself. Then he stalked off toward the now vacant playground, stopping at the short fence, wiping his draining eyes and nose on his suit sleeve and checking himself out. The suit was ruined, his shoes, belt, and tie, all stained. He rubbed at his left hand, his palm a bright red, the clinging aerosol powder already adhered to his skin. He looked up to clear his vision and found rows of little faces at the classroom windows, teachers trying to pull them away. He touched his own face, cringing, fearing the worst.

Dino was climbing out of his Taurus, hustling across the sidewalk toward Frawley, then seeing Frawley was okay, slowing down. "Now this," he said, baring dentures perfect and white, "is a definite first."

Frawley held his arms out from his sides as though he were soaking wet. "You okay there, Dean?" Frawley said, congested. "All that getting in and out of the car, I was worried."

Dino took in the full view. "Everything but the paint can over the head. Do me a favor? Hold out your gold badge like this, say, 'Jerry Lewis, FBI.'"

Frawley showed him a brilliant red middle finger instead. He looked back to the bandit, now bent over a cruiser for a pat-down, his ear to the hood like it was whispering his children's future. Then they straightened him up, folding him sobbing into a cruiser.

Dino said, coming up next to Frawley, "Fun job, innit?"

11
JAY'S ON THE CORNER

NEW DRY CLEANERS WERE popping up all over the Town. The modern career woman required first and foremost a dependable local launderer. So much so, even old-style wash-'n'-drys such as Jay's on the Corner were putting in lacquered black counters, advertising overnight send-out service, playing "continuous soft hits" inside, and prettifying themselves in general: squeegeeing the windows clean every morning, hosing off the sidewalk, repainting signs, power-washing stubborn brick.

The message there was that the renewing power of capitalism was a lot like falling in love. No other force in the universe could have moved old man Charlestown to run a new razor over his cheeks, close his collar with a necktie, check his manners, splash on a little cologne. Springtime was in bloom all over the Town, and free-market commerce was a pretty girl in a sundress and heels.

Jay's was narrow like a tobacconist's, new-Town up front— chrome fixtures on the counter, free coffee—while still old-Town in back—corkboard walls stuck with business cards and guitar lesson flyers, the ancient soap machine, and a broken wooden-bead maze table for the kids. The washing machines were lined up in back-to-back rows under a high center shelf, double-decker dryers facing them along both long walls. The newer dollar-accepting washers were up front; the older, thudding, coin-tray jalopies rattling in back.

Doug was positioned halfway down the left lane of washers, sitting atop the last clean machine before the dials got crusty. He was feigning interest in the free *Boston Phoenix,* riding out his churning clothes, with Claire Keesey's loads tumbling almost directly behind him. She had been there a while now—long enough for Doug to book home to grab up some dirty clothes, get back, follow her inside. His hamper bag lay empty on the floor now, one of the few things of his father's that Doug had held on to: a strap-tie army sack with faded black stenciling, MACRAY, D.

Now what? He had acted on instinct, or else simple insanity, sensing opportunity but now not knowing how to follow through. He was just a few yards away from her, and they were basically alone—the guy behind the counter rubbing his bald head and talking Greek into the phone—yet he could think of no good way to bridge that final gap. Borrow some soap? Be that obvious? *Hey, you wash your clothes here often?* Sure, why not just scare her off for good?

Even if she did happen to look over at him now and didn't immediately turn away—even if some small smile were to appear on her face—it was the middle of the morning: no matter what, he looked like an out-of-work Townie making a clumsy play.

Hey, haven't I seen you at the Foodmaster?

A brilliant, foolproof plan. Except for his clothes getting clean, this whole thing was a colossal waste of time. He imagined the others walking in and seeing him there trying to work up the courage to bump into the manager of the bank they had robbed.

Her first load finished while he sat there berating himself. She started pulling out warm clothes one by one, folding and packing them into a custard-yellow laundry basket. Her other dryer load was nearly done, along with a pair of tennis sneakers rumbling alone in a third machine, going *pum-pum-pum-pum* like the drumbeat of battle.

He closed the newspaper and threw it down, determined now, stand or fall. His boots hit the floor, hands vigorously rubbing his face to rouse himself from wussyland. What could he say here that didn't make him seem like a panty-cruising creep?

A relevant question. Something about separating colors from whites. No—any fucking idiot knows that. Just ask, What do I wash in cold, what do I wash in hot? Simple. Like, Feed a fever, or starve a cold?

He quickly examined this gambit for offensiveness: Maybe there was something somehow antifeminist about assuming that women knew more than men about laundry? Then he realized that, hey, that was exactly what he assumed, and if steam blew out of the top of her head when he asked, then good, he had his answer, he could head on home.

He shook his fists loose and cracked his neck—even as he felt himself pussying out again. *Fuck you!* Thinking about the hours of agony his backing out here would cause him—that was the only thing that started him toward her.

He crossed the break in the rows of washers, hands stuffed unthreateningly into his pockets. She had paused in her folding, her back to him, a white blouse in her hands.

"Uh, hey, excuse me?"

She turned fast, startled to find him there.

"Hi, uh, I was wondering if you knew . . ."

So focused was he on his delivery that it took him until then to register the tears in her eyes. She swiped at them, fast and guilty, dismayed at having been discovered—then tried to brush off the whole thing with a fake smile.

Doug said, "I . . . oh."

The tears reappeared and she tried to smile him off again, then gave up, turning away. She tipped her head up to the ceiling fans in an *Oh, God* type of gesture, then resumed her folding, faster now, as though he weren't there.

"You okay?" said Doug, though it came out sounding wrong.

She turned her head in profile, blinking, waiting for peace. Then she turned all the way, glaring, her quick, harsh look imploring him, *Please go away.*

Which he should have done. His presence was only making her more upset. But he was stuck. If he stepped away now, it would be forever.

She scooped out the rest of her load with him hovering at her back, dumping her clothes unfolded into her laundry basket, a tennis sock and a pair of lilac panties dropping softly to the floor. She wanted to be done, to leave. She dragged her basket of warm clothes off the washing machine and started past him, head down, rushing toward the front door—her other load still going around the next dryer.

"Hey," he said after her, "you forgot . . ."

But she had turned out onto the sidewalk and was gone. The bald guy behind the counter craned his neck, holding the phone to his chest. A male customer balancing his checkbook looked to the door too, his girlfriend staring accusingly down the row at Doug.

Doug turned back to the spinning dryers and the sneakers bouncing *pum-pum-pum*, wondering what the hell had just happened.

NORTH OF THE TOWN, the Malden Bridge crossed the Mystic into Everett, the sky opening up over a dire patch of industry lit like a Batman movie, road signs reading Factory Street and Chemical Lane. Main Street in West Everett drew tired multifamily homes to the sidewalks like spectators waiting half a century for a promised parade.

Doug parked the Caprice outside a darkened funeral home and walked three blocks to a side street, a D'Angelo sandwich and a True Value Hardware plastic bag in one hand, a Valvoline carton the size of two VCRs under his arm.

The houses at the end of the side street were single-family, post-war Capes and cottages with square yards front and back. The door he went to was unlit, and he set his things down on the step. He knocked gently before going to work on the lamp over the door, unscrewing the glass cap, brushing out the dead bugs.

"Here I am, Douglas," sang Mrs. Seavey, unlocking the door and pulling it wide of her walker. She wore an Irish sweater buttoned over a red flannel housecoat, her gray face smiling moon-bright. She had seemed old to Doug back when she was his third-grade teacher.

"I'm a little late," said Doug, hearing the *Wheel of Fortune* theme song behind her. "How's that leg? Nurse come today?"

"Oh, yes. I think so."

"Getting around okay?"

With a mischievous, half-dreaming smile, she released the walker and shuffled back and forth in her foam slippers, arms out for balance, singing, "Da-daa-dee-da . . ."

Doug's class had been Mrs. Seavey's last before retirement. She cleaned everything out of her legendary coatroom closet during their last week of school, offering the contents to whoever wished to carry them home. Doug claimed as many workbooks, activity packs, phonics flash cards, and dried-up markers as he could get his little hands on, so anxious was he to take home pieces of her. But the Forneys—the foster family he was living with at the time—had hardly any room for him and made him throw out most of it anyway. His mother had been gone two years by then, his father away on a twenty-one-month tour at MCI Concord.

Doug opened the hardware-store bag and pulled out a package of coiled lightbulbs. "Now I bought you these fancy ones instead of the regular bulbs because they reminded me of you."

"Aha," she tee-heed. "Screwy?"

"Definitely that." He read from the package. "'Low-wattage, energy-saving, extended life.' Says right here, 'Years of continuous illumination.'"

She tittered again, then watched from inside the screen door as he traded the dead, tinkling bulb for the new coiled one. She hit the switch inside, and the light was soft but fast, riding the gas inside the tube.

"Anything else you need done tonight?" he said.

"No, bless you, Douglas. I'm all set, thanks be to God."

He opened the screen door, removing a thick roll of bills from his pocket. Nana Seavey liked fives and tens, small bills she could use at the corner store. "There's nine hundred," he said. "My next three months' rent."

She grasped his hand over the bills, shaking it softly. "God bless you, boy," she said, the bills disappearing into her sweater pocket.

"Now, I'll probably be out there late tonight."

"You stay as long as you want." She waved him on like he was being bad, and he saw the sore on her wrist, brown and blue, still unhealed. "I'm off to bed."

She gripped his fingers again, her skin papery and cool, the bones of her hand like small pencils in a bag. Doug leaned down to kiss her forehead. "You stay well, now. Be good."

"If not," she said, shuffling backward from the door with a smile, "I'll be careful."

He listened for the lock and waited until the light winked out, then started across the walkway to her garage. Mr. Seavey had worked and died making rubber for Goodyear, but on nights and weekends he and his brother had operated a private taxi and limousine service. Doug could still recall his last day of third grade, watching from the sidewalk outside school, Mrs. Seavey blowing him a small kiss from the backseat of a jewel-black Oldsmobile with silver window curtains.

Mr. Seavey had an Irishman's fondness for automobiles, like a hunter's love for his dogs, and he had built himself, with help from a few drinking buddies, a barnlike, two-car garage with swing-out doors. Doug had since, with Mrs. Seavey's blessing, knocked off the outside handles so that the broad front doors could only be opened from the inside. Entry now was through a small side door just inside the low picket fence marking the edge of Mrs. Seavey's property. By the scant blue light of a plastic Virgin Mother glowing in the next backyard, Doug unlocked the padlock and threw open the top and bottom bolts, closing the door behind him before hitting the wall switch inside.

Halogen work lights clamped to the rafters illuminated the emerald green Corvette ZR-1 in the center of the cement floor. The jewel of the price-doubling ZR-1 performance option package was its all-aluminum, 405-horse Lotus LT5 engine. Doug's was one of the last of the 448 ZR-1s built in 1995, their final production year. The car stickered at $69,553, paid in cash, papered in Krista's name in order to avoid federal tax scrutiny.

The custom emerald finish was so creamy that running a hand along the long, sloping prow, from the solar windshield down to the retractable headlamps, was like swiping frosting off cake. The car was jacked up on blocks, Doug nearly finished installing a new stainless-steel exhaust system.

He set his sandwich down next to the *Chilton's* repair manual on the workbench beneath a broad array of Mr. Seavey's old tools. The garage had been built deep to accommodate the Olds, and there was a four-foot drop in back: a dirt-floored, stone-sided storage area cluttered with ancient three-speed bicycles, push-powered grass clippers, and a monstrous electric snowblower, its rusted blades like gnashing teeth stained with dry blood.

Doug left the Valvoline box on the edge and hopped down, lifting the heavy snowblower by its handles and boosting it away from the stone wall. The rock he wanted was ostrich-egg-sized and loose, coming away from the chipped mortar and exposing a cavity. Originally Doug had found in there, behind a row of empty Dewar's flasks, a dusty airmail letter with a 1973 postmark, written in jerky English by a Frenchwoman searching for an American soldier named Seavey who had passed through her mother's village in the winter of 1945.

Doug lifted the newspaper-wrapped parcels out of the Valvoline box and added his cut from the BayBanks job to the rest of the odd-sized stacks of cash, then stared at his ditch-cold treasure. In the hole its value was zilch: a collection of numbered strips of fabric made up of 75 percent cotton and 25 percent linen, printed with green and black ink. Little rectangular rags whose unbankable mass was becoming a problem. Doug was running out of both space—the hole had been dug as wide as it could go—and time—Nana Seavey being just one stumble away from a nursing home. His garage rent payment was an offering meant to bring them both three more months of good luck, because Doug had no contingency plan, either for his stash or his Vette.

He withdrew a cold, inch-thick wad from a neat pile of already washed bills, then folded up the thick plastic wrap and fit the stone back into place, repositioning the blower and climbing back up top. The heat from the lamps was starting to warm the garage, and he unwrapped his roast beef sub and pulled a Dew out of the minifridge he kept there, switching on the portable radio. Normally the thought of grabbing tools and getting greasy underneath the ZR-1 was enough to make the anxieties of the outside world disappear. He lay back on Mr. Seavey's old "Jeepers" creeper—"Immigrant Song" on

'ZLX following him in underneath the jacked-up car—and though Doug never totally lost himself under there, at least for a few hours he got far enough away.

FROM THE STREET, DOUG heard music slamming out of Jem's. Inside, climbing the stairs, he felt the heat from the second-floor door as he passed. Inside his own apartment, the weak walls shuddered and the sagging floor thumped like drum skins. Doug's spoon quivered on his kitchen counter and one of his cabinet doors swung open on its own. That was Jem: all bass, no treble.

Doug pulled his bed out of the sofa and sat on the end, eating a bowl of Apple Jacks, debating whether to fight this barrage with his own TV noise or just ride it out. He was too tired to go pounding on Jem's door, and more than that, too wary of getting pulled inside. He figured there was an even chance the roof was going to come down on top of them all anyway.

Who is Doug MacRay? These are the questions sober people ask themselves over bowls of cereal at three in the morning.

Folding her laundry for her and leaving it at the counter: big mistake. Too feminine, too puppyish and nuzzling, tail-wagging, hand-licking, proudly-pissing-on-the-newspaper eager-to-please. It was pussy.

He lay back flat on the mattress and waited for the ceiling to fall in on him.

DOUG ENTERED JAY'S ON the Corner briskly, knocking on the counter—"Hey, Virgil"—and nodding to the bald clerk in the Rolling Stones red-tongue T-shirt, whose acquaintance Doug had since made, and whose confederacy he had purchased with a fifty-dollar bill.

Doug moved down the left lane of washers, aware of her gaze but ignoring it. He sensed her surprise at seeing him again—she was about a third of the way down on the right—and then her suspicion at the coincidence.

He opened a dryer door and lifted out a load of cool laundry. The clothes had been sitting in that machine for two days, awaiting his return, but only Virgil knew that.

Doug went about folding the clothes like he had a lot of important things on his mind, jeans first, then shirts, beginning to think she wasn't coming over—until he heard the voice, soft like a hand on his shoulder, turning him around.

"Excuse me? Hi?" A nervous smile across the central double-lane of washing machines. "Hi."

He looked blank, then let his face come to life. "Oh, hey—how are *you*?"

"Mortified." She clasped her hands together, twisting them. "In fact, I was almost too embarrassed even to come over here, but my conscience, it marched me right over to tell you thank you—"

"No no no."

"I was, I guess, having a really bad . . . well, month, actually. I don't know why, but it all kind of hit me at once. Here, unfortunately." A forced, guilty smile, as in *My bad*.

"Don't worry about it. So long as you're feeling better."

"Much, yes," she said, still mock-formal, maybe even talking down to him a bit, putting her good manners on display. "Anyway—thanks for pulling my clothes out. I can't believe I just abandoned them like that. And your folding them, Virgil told me you did that."

"Oh, yeah, Virgil. Well . . ." As though it were supposed to have been a secret between two men. "That was nothing. So long as it was all right with you, I mean. Kind of weird, you know, folding a stranger's laundry."

"Yeah." Smiling, but there was tension in her neck. "I guess so." She patted her flat hand against the washing machine lid, glancing away. "So anyway—it was really nice of you to do that, you're a nice person. And I'm sorry I ran off like that, sorry I wasn't as polite to you in return." Trailing away now, an abrupt nod punctuating her halting gratitude. "Anyway, thanks again. Thanks."

Doug watched her retreat to her machine, nodding, wanting to say something.

Nothing came out. He turned back to his open dryer with a harsh face. He had pushed it too far, scaring her off with *folding a stranger's laundry*—idiot panty-sniffer. What was he doing here anyway, taking advantage of this emotionally confused person? *Fuck*. He wanted to smack himself on the head but maybe she was watching.

He looked over and she was reading a paperback. It occurred to him then that he had *forgotten to ask her name!* Or offer his! That was some quick thinking there. No wonder she walked away.

He had blown it. He'd had his chance, and now he was in an awkward no-man's-land with her: not strangers anymore, but not acquaintances either. Running into her again somewhere else would only raise her antenna, make her skittish.

Maybe it was better this way. Over before it began. Where had he expected to go with it anyway? Ask her to drinks Upstairs at the Tap? Dinner at Olives, then on to the fucking opera?

No sparks. There it was in a nutshell. *No fireworks.*

Then he remembered her smiling. Twisting her hands anxiously. Looking at him longer than she had to. The suspense in her eyes, shining beyond politeness. This summoned the counterbalancing image of her wearing a blindfold, and Doug remembered how much he wanted that image out of his mind.

She sensed him coming, looking up from her book as he approached her across the washing machines. "Hi," he said. "Slightly creepy Laundromat guy here again."

"No-o," she laughed.

He pressed his fingertips atop the machine before him like a pianist about to launch into a solo. "I was back over there pairing off socks, and you were over here—and I knew I would never forgive myself if I didn't come over and take a shot."

Her eyebrows flinched at his poor choice of words, making him talk faster.

"Because if I don't take a shot," he said, repeating the offending phrase, pretending that it was not in fact unfortunate, "it's going to wind up haunting me for like the next four weeks at least."

She smiled, changing direction, showing lighthearted concern. "Are you really that hard on yourself?"

"You don't even know," he said, relaxing just a fraction. "It would progress from, say, smacking myself repeatedly on the forehead, to, like, stopping in here a couple of times each day, doing my laundry one sock at a time, hoping you'd come back in alone and that you'd remember me, and we'd get to talking again, and I'd have something incredibly devious to say about the weather. . . ."

She was smiling by the end of it, until some sort of protective instinct closed her lips. "Well," she said, "now that you've taken your *shot*"—she kicked the word playfully—"is that enough? Enough to keep you from hurting yourself, I mean, and spending all your quarters here?"

"No way. Not anymore. See—now we've talked. Now it's a character issue. If you were to say no to me now, then it's like—then there's something wrong with *me,* and this whole haunting thing continues, only much, much worse. Because now what it means is, I'm not fit to attract a quality person like yourself."

She squinted, still smiling but mulling this over, not knowing what to make of him. Which was okay: Doug didn't quite know what to make of him himself.

"Quality?" she said, liking the ring of it, and he felt her giving in.

"For sure," he said, dazzled by his success. "Quality."

12
CHECKING IN

H ER MESSAGE ON HIS voice mail went:

"Hi—Agent Frawley? This is Claire Keesey, um, the branch manager from the robbery—the one, the BayBanks in Kenmore Square? Hi. I don't have any, this isn't—I have no pertinent information regarding the robbers or anything like that. I'm just calling to let you know that I'm normal—that I finally had a little mini-episode, my junior breakdown, and I'm feeling better now, I really am. It was at a Laundromat, and . . . I guess something made me think of my jacket, the one they cut? And it all came crashing down on me at once. I actually ran off and left my clothes there and now have to get up the nerve to go back and claim them. A total case. Anyway—I know this is a strange message and I'm probably taking up valuable crime-fighting time, but who else would understand? And I really wanted to thank you, because if you hadn't warned me that something like this might happen, well—I would think I was headed for Prozac and a group home. So—thanks. That's all. Bye."

Frawley didn't get the voice mail until a day and a half later. He tried her at the bank first, then reached her at home.

"Oh, hi. Hold on, okay?"

The call-waiting blip.

She came back in a few seconds. "Sorry about that. My overbearing mother."

"No problem, how're you doing?"

Music being turned down. "Good. Doing better. I'm doing well, actually."

"Good. I just got your message."

"Oh, God. Rambling, right? I just—after feeling so blah for so long, so walking-dead, getting that little bit of relief—it was almost the same as feeling great."

"I tried to reach you at work."

"Yeah, no, I haven't—I finally went back today. For the first time, just to look around. They redid my office. Desk, chair, ceiling. It was a little bit of a haunted house, but I'll get there. I start back full-time tomorrow."

"That's good. It's time."

"No, it is good. Otherwise I'm just sitting around here, watching way too much TV."

"You might experience a rush of anxiety or even adrenaline, seeing someone enter the bank with the same body type as the bandits', or a similar demeanor. If so, you might try to remember what it is about them that triggered that, and let me know."

A pause. "Okay. Wow, I hope not."

"Don't stress out about it. Get your clothes back?"

"Oh—from the Laundromat?" she realized. "God, it was so humiliating. Yes, I got my clothes back. Cleaned and folded."

"Nice. A little service they provide weepy customers?"

"That's right. As advertised in the window."

He could hear her smile in her voice. "You had a coupon or something?"

"A competitor's coupon, for emotional distress, which they honored. But seriously—the weirdest thing?"

"What?"

"Some guy there asked me out on a date. Another customer, the guy who pulled my clothes out. He's actually the one who folded them. It was funny—he definitely seemed not the type for folding women's clothes."

"Really," said Frawley, intrigued by the competitiveness this news triggered in him. "What did you say?"

"I actually said yes, because it was sort of in-the-moment. But I think he's like a furniture mover or something. I mean, I don't think my head's quite right yet. A guy I met in a Laundromat? I'm sure I'll just end up blowing him off."

Frawley smiled, feeling oddly energized. "You would laugh out loud if you could see me right now."

"Why? Are you undercover or something?"

"My neck and cheek, and my left hand—they're all stained red. A dye pack exploded on me."

"A *dye* pack? Get out."

"A robbery in Brookline, I chased the guy down and it went off. And of course it takes a lot longer to fade than the three days they claim. So I'm sort of out of commission here for a while, at least socially. But maybe next time we see each other I'll tell you my tale."

"Sure. That sounds good."

"Good," he said, buzzed. "And, hey, good luck tomorrow."

"Oh, yeah. Yuck. I'll be fine."

As Frawley hung up, Dino's voice surprised him from behind. "What was that?"

Dino was sitting on the edge of Flott's desk inside the Lakeville bull pen. "Branch manager from the Morning Glory."

"What's she got?"

"Nothing. Just checking in."

"Checking in, huh? Thought you cleared her."

"I did."

"Uh-huh." Dino smiled. "Okay. Just watch yourself there."

"No, no."

"They love cops in their life after something goes wrong."

Frawley shook that off. Dino was holding a legal-sized manila envelope in his hairy hands. "What's that? Congress Street subpoena already? The Nynex records?"

Dino danced it out of Frawley's grasp. "Like a kid on Christmas morning. Say *please*."

Frawley pulled his hand down contritely—then lunged and swiped the envelope out of Dino's hands, sitting back again and smiling and ripping it open. "Please."

13
AM GOLD

DOUG PLAYED A RARE street-hockey matinee up where Washington Street dead-ended beside the rink on a paved bluff. In terms of the neighborhood, this was an *event*, like if native son Howie Long had come back to play touch football over at the Barry Playground. Doug didn't skate much anymore, and never out on the streets, because the game to him was freighted now with too many negative connotations: his youth, faded dreams, his father. Pulling on the skates and pads was like climbing inside his younger self again, and that kid was a royal screwup. Doug had to be feeling good to want to play—and today he felt really, really good.

A kid from Chappie Street who fancied himself a street Gretzky faced off against Doug, and got schooled. Doug put on a clinic. Jem, who lived for this shit, was a conspicuous no-show, leaving Gloansy to dust off Doug's old high school handle, hooting, "Stick came to *play*!" as Doug finished the third game with a rising slap shot that nicked the crotch of the goalie's droopy jeans—a wannabe-black white kid from the Mishawum houses—the orange-ball puck finding a tear in the net and arcing away down the slope to the streets below. Doug skated a victory lap backward, pumping his fist under the wide blue sky.

Fast-forward to a quarter after eight that evening, Doug MacRay rearranging the appetizer card, the glass salt and pepper shakers, the purple petunia in the tiny black vase. He had sent the aproned server away twice and now felt the other Tap diners looking his way, entertaining themselves, watching some Townie bozo get stood up but good.

He tried hard to appear relaxed, not pissed, like everything was cool and going according to plan. But first of all: Why the Tap? Why pick a place where he might get made? Secondly: Why Upstairs? Who the fuck was he trying to be? These frauds he despised?

Bottom line was, he'd panicked at the Laundromat. She said yes and he blanked, because he had no strategy beyond that, the Tap Upstairs the first thing that jumped into his head.

Like a teenager, he had been idealizing their date. *She'll sit there, I'll sit here. I'll say this, she'll laugh.* A fucking little boy. And this "oatmeal"-colored pullover tugging tight across his shoulders, that he had bought off a headless mannequin on a last-minute run to the Galleria—after spending half an hour going through his closet? Fucking God—*look at yourself.* Black pants with the crotch cut too high. A braided leather belt, soft black shoes.

Huge mistake, this whole thing. Hiding in the back of the place, taking this table because he couldn't risk being seen up front. He scanned the appetizer menu for the eighth fucking time. He watched the glass doors, the color bleeding out of his vision.

He deserved this humiliation. He deserved to be stood up. A mistake from the word go.

Five more minutes he waited. Then another five beyond that—his punishment, sticking his nose in it, forcing himself to soak in his own shame. *Learn from this.* What was it Frank G. had said? *Aside from not walking into a bar alone, this is the most important decision you're ever gonna make.* Nice work. Fucked up on both counts.

Two choices: either resume drinking, hard, and right now—piss away two goddamn years for a stuck-up yuppie bitch—or get up, walk to the door—*Maybe stop at the ladies' room on your way out*—and walk his tight-crotch pants back home.

As always, Doug fell back to the one thing he knew he could count on. The one thing Doug had that no one could take away from him. His criminal eye. Others—maybe it was a wife or kids they took shelter in. Someone or something to run to where they could feel like a success no matter how often the rest of the world humiliated them.

Double up on the armored-car surveillance. Focus on the big multiscreen movie theaters, Revere, Fresh Pond, Braintree. With the "summer" releases starting in early May, all he needed to do was zero in on a place and a time.

The front windows were darkening with night, headlights finding their way along Main. Dim enough for Doug to make a clean escape and drag his sorry ass back up the hill. He waited for his server to get busy at another table, then stood and started heavy-legged for the door, head down, his exit slowed by two chicks picking through the basket of mints at the hostess station.

That's where he was when Claire Keesey came rushing in. She gave the tight-skirted hostess a quick once-over, then looked right past Doug to the central bar.

The chicks in front of him exited, and he could smell the street and the night, and he started to follow them out, wanting to be done with it. He had already torn her down beyond repair in his mind—himself too—and the moment had passed.

"My God! You're right here!" She reached out and squeezed his elbow. "I am so late, I know. Were you leaving? My God, I'm so sorry. I don't even—but you're still here, I can't believe it."

Believe it. Or, maybe, *Hey, I don't believe it either,* cutting her dead—and then walk out on her, take his anger on home.

But she was looking up at him and smiling, catching her breath. "It's Doug, right?"

"Right."

"I didn't, when I came in . . . you look different."

"Do I, yeah."

Sizing him up. "I didn't . . . hmm." Concerned about her own clothes now, a white cotton button-up blouse fitted nicely at the waist, distressed jeans, black shoe boots. "I was running late. I thought more casual . . ."

"Doesn't matter. I think I folded those jeans."

She checked them out with a smile. "I think you did."

He started to feel good again, despite himself. "Searched the pockets for loose change and everything."

She smiled brightly, her eyes fully involved. He realized he was standing inside the entrance to the Tap, the door to the Downstairs five steps behind him. He nodded to the back of the room. "Maybe I haven't lost our table yet."

They threaded through the tabletops to the back wall. She tucked her little red key-chain purse in next to the flower vase, Doug sitting across from her on a cushioned, bar-height chair, his back to the wall. The low-watt overhead lamp sprayed soft light onto her honeyed hair, the rest of the lounge room fading from view behind her.

Doug patted the table, smiling, exhaling.

"Well," she said. She leaned forward a moment, the overhead lamp creating a mask of shadow around her eyes. Doug leaned back reflexively, not wanting her to see any masks on him. "So why am I thirty minutes late?" She looked away for the answer, but became distracted. "I'm still shocked you waited. I mean—I'm glad. And I'm sorry. But I'm also amazed."

"Well, really only about fifteen minutes of it was me waiting for you. The other fifteen was me pouting, knocking myself in the head."

"Oh, no! You warned me about that."

"It's a problem I have."

"You don't—I think I tried to tell you this at the Laundromat—but you don't strike me as the type to be so, I guess, tough on yourself."

"I'm a fragile sort."

She smiled at his arms, his shoulders. "Right. You bruise easy."

"I put too much pressure on myself, I guess. Some things I take too seriously."

"Please, you're sitting across from the original life-or-death, agonizing-over-everything girl."

She went off searching for that answer again as their server arrived, a short-haired platinum blonde with one ear rimmed with copper clips. She smiled at Claire. "You made it."

"I made it," said Claire, pleasant, appraising.

"He looked very worried," she said, hugging her leather order pad, nodding cheerily at Doug. "Actually, he looked pissed off."

Doug said, "Thought I was hiding it."

Claire said, "Was he really hitting himself in the head?"

"Close to it. My name is Drea, what can I get you?"

Claire asked for a wine recommendation and settled on something Italian called a valpolicella.

"Glass or bottle?" said Drea, looking at them both.

"Bottle," said Doug.

"Terrific." Drea started to leave.

"And I'll have a soda water, lime," said Doug.

Drea paused a second before nodding and flipping her pad back open and scribbling that in. "I'll be right back." And she was gone.

Claire looked at the table, wondering about his order.

"I'm driving," Doug told her.

She looked up at him. "Okay."

"For the rest of my life."

Claire nodding, then gesturing after Drea. "I don't even have to . . ."

"Nope," he said, rocking gently. "It's cool. Really."

"Why did you get a bottle then?"

"I don't even know," he said, his head pounding. She was looking at him differently now. Questions popping in her mind like flashbulbs. "You were saying . . ."

"I was?"

"About being . . ."

"Right, yes. About being late." She crossed her arms on the table and leaned on them, damning body language. "Well . . . the truth is, I wasn't even going to come at all."

"Ah. Okay."

"I was going to blow this off. I had decided not to come. That's why I was late."

Doug nodded, waiting. "So what was it that changed your mind?"

She took a deep breath, held it, smiled. "I guess, in a weird way—the decision *not* to come. In other words, deciding that I didn't *have* to come here tonight. Realizing that I don't *have* to do *anything* . . . sort of relieved me of any obligation. The longer part of the story is that . . . I've been through a lot of crap recently, and I'll spare you all that—but my thinking's been strange. Thinking and rethinking everything, examining my life to death, driving myself absolutely nuts. More so than usual, that is. So, fine—I'm not going to go, right? Okay, that's decided. Then eight o'clock rolls around and I'm sitting at home, deliberately doing nothing, watching eight o'clock roll around, and I was like—'Well, Claire, you don't have to *not* go either.' These are the conversations I have with myself. But it seemed like I was setting these rules, these arbitrary rules, putting up fences around my days, my nights. Following rules instead of following . . . the flow, you know? Doing what I want. Being me. So I decided—why the hell not? This is two people meeting for a drink, not life-or-death. Right?"

"Sure," he said. "No."

"People meet for drinks all the time, it's not that mind-bending. I know I'm rambling. This happens a lot."

"It's good. Saves me from coming up with a bunch of clever things to say."

"Long story short—I yanked my head out of my butt, and here I am."

The wine arrived and she grew quiet again, circumspect, Drea opening the bottle at her hip with professional flourish, pouring a taste into Claire's glass with that drip-saving twist of the wrist. Claire sipped and nodded that it was fine, and Doug drank some soda while Drea poured Claire a deep glass and said she'd be back for their food order.

At the end of this, in the background of Doug's vision, two guys entered the Tap, saluted the doorman, and disappeared downstairs. Doug had made out an oversized Bruins jersey on one of them and, with a jab of anxiety, believed it to be Jem.

"Leave the iron on?" she said.

"Huh?"

"You had this look."

"Oh." Reading her smile. "Yeah. I think I left the milk out on the counter. Hey—are you even hungry?"

"Well, considering I didn't plan on coming, I already ate."

He checked the door to the stairs again, thinking, thinking. "How about getting out of here?"

"I—what?" She looked at her glass. "And going where?"

Good question. "Someplace with a view maybe. Of the city. Unless—I don't know, your place, does it have a view?"

"I—" She stopped fast. "*My* place?"

"Whoa, no, hold up, I don't mean—I only meant, I don't want to be showing you the city if it's something you see every morning when you wake up."

"Oh." Suspicious now. He was losing her, and fast.

"See," he said with a glance at the surrounding tables, "I picked this place—I wasn't ready for you to say yes, and so I went with here because it seemed like maybe the sort of place you'd like. You, who I don't even know, right? And—*do* you even like it?"

She smiled through her confusion. "You don't even drink."

"Exactly. I lost my head. So what do you say?"

She looked at her glass again. "But what about . . . ?"

"Bring it with you." He was pulling his cash roll from his pocket.

"Bring it?"

"I'm paying for it. Take the glass too."

"I can't—the glass?"

Doug unfolded his roll, discreetly but making sure she got a look at its heft, winding the thin red rubber band around his fingers and stripping a century off the top, standing it in front of the vase, Franklin out, then snapping the band back around the roll and tucking it away.

"Just smile at the doorman," he said, lifting the bottle as she stood. "I guarantee you, he won't see a thing."

THEY MADE SMALL TALK going up the hill, walking slow, she with her arms folded, the wineglass in one hand. Their date had spilled out into the Town at large, potential complications on every block. An undercurrent of self-interrogation went on like radio chatter inside his head. *What the fuck are you doing?* And his answer became a mantra: *Just one date. Just one date.*

"So what about you?" she asked. "You've lived here—"

"All my life, yeah. You, before this?"

"I've lived all over the city, since college. Grew up in Canton."

"Canton. That's Blue Hills, right? There's a rink there, off the highway. Skated there a few times."

"Right, Ponkapoag, I think."

"So, the suburbs, huh?"

"Oh, yeah. The suburbs."

Doug plucked an overturned recycling bin out of the street, returned it to a doorway. Working hard to be smooth. "What do you do for a job?"

"I'm in banking," she said. Then: "Wow."

"What?" Doug looked around for *wow*.

"No, just that phrase. 'I'm in banking.' Not sure if that was meant to impress you or bore you. I manage a BayBanks branch. It's a lot like running a convenience store, except I move money instead of calling cards and snacks. You?"

"What do I do? Well, that depends. We still trying to impress each other?"

"Sure, go for it."

"I'm a sky-maker."

"Wow," she said again. "You win."

"I'm in demolition. Blasting rock, bringing down buildings. *Making sky,* that's from when you level a big building, opening up views. Suddenly you've made some sky."

"I like it," she decided. "Do you do those old hotels and stadiums they always show on TV, that detonate inward into their own pile of rubble?"

"No, I'm more hands-on. Basically, if you've seen *The Flintstones,* that's me. When the whistle blows, I'm surfing down the neck of a brontosaurus and outta there."

They crested on Bunker Hill Street, having climbed from about nine to almost eleven on the ticking Charlestown clock. He led her across the gas-lit thoroughfare to the mouth of Pearl Street, the outline of a plan starting to form.

Any thoughts he had of changing his clothes were dashed with one glance at Jem's mother's demo-worthy house halfway down the plunging street. The Flamer, Jem's banged-up Trans Am, blue on blue with blue flames detailed on the sides and hood, was parked there like a flare in the road warning Doug away.

His own Caprice Classic was three cars down. "Just a sec," said

Doug, pulling out his keys, opening the driver's-side door.

She stayed back on the curb, looking at the dingy white four-door and its fading blue, soft-top roof. "Is this your car?"

"Oh, no," he said, reaching under the velour passenger seat, rocking the musky orange Hooters deodorizer dangling from the cigarette lighter. "I loaned this jerk I know some CDs." He felt around the blue carpeting for them, then straightened, waving two jewel cases, too fast for her to read them.

He walked her back across Bunker, hiking up three blocks west under the gas lamps to the Heights, stopping before St. Frank's steeple at the top of the hill. "Here we are."

It was a clean brownstone triple with bowfront windows and blooming flower boxes painted fireball red. The double doors were black with buffed brass knockers, handles, and kickplates. Doug stepped inside the faux-marble entrance, nudging aside a couple of FedEx boxes with his new shoes.

"You live here?" she said, cautious, remaining on the sidewalk.

"No way." He reached up, feeling along the top of the frame of the interior door. "No, friend of mine manages it." He came down with the key, showed it to her, turned it in the door. "We're just gonna use the stairs to get up top. What do you say?"

After a glance of concern up and down the sidewalk, she followed him inside.

The roof was rubber-sealed and lumpy, hedged on all four sides by two-foot brick crenellations. An abandoned wire-and-wood pigeon coop did not obstruct their postcard view of the city, Boston laid out against a silk screen of blue-black, from the financial towers to the mirrored Hancock to the dominant Prudential building, with the busy interstate a twinkling ribbon wrapping it all.

Claire stood at the southern edge, the city side, looking down at the rest of the Town like a woman on a high bridge, the now empty glass in her hand. "Wow."

"That is the word of the night," said Doug. He unfolded two lawn chairs from inside the coop, their blue-and-white nylon webbing frayed, the hollow aluminum frames predating cup holders. "Drops off pretty good down the hill, don't it."

The rooftops on either side were graded steps climbing to the sky, many with cedar decks, patio furniture, grills. Old, thorny TV antennas mixed with satellite dishes turned like hopeful faces to the southwest. To the left, looking east above Flagship Wharf in the navy yard, jet lights slid out of the sky, stars on a string. Other

planes circled overhead in defined holding patterns, a swirling con-
stellation.

The sounds of the Town rose to them as she walked back to the
chair next to the wine bottle, her free hand in her pocket. "This sky—
is it one of yours?"

Doug took a careful look around. "Yep, it's mine."

"I especially like what you did with these stars over here."

"We get those imported. Hey—ever ordered anything off TV? You
know, late night, infomercials?"

"No. But if I did, it would be a Flowbee."

Doug held up the two CDs. "*AM Gold*. Time-Life stuff, you
know, try it for thirty days, we'll send another every four to six weeks,
you can cancel at any time?" The boom box, an old Sanyo missing its
cassette drawer, was bike-chained to the doorpost of the coop. Doug
dropped in the first CD, let it spin.

"Oh my," she said. It was the Carpenters.

"You gotta give it a little time to work on you. This is a big step
for me."

"What is, coming out of the closet as a Carpenters fan?"

"Let me correct you right there. Definitely not a Carpenters *fan*.
This is about the total effect of the music, the predisco seventies. I
don't sanction every single track, and some of them are pretty bad.
'Muskrat Love' is on here somewhere. What I like is the radio station
aspect of it, like receiving a signal time-delayed twenty years."

She took the jewel case from him and sat down to look it over.
"Wow," she said, amused. "My mom used to have these songs on all
day."

"Sure, WHDH, right?" He sat down a respectable three feet away
from her, both of them facing the city like it was the ocean.

"Every morning, getting ready for school."

"Jess Cain."

"*Yes*. Wow." The uniting power of nostalgia. "And Officer Bill in
the traffic copter."

Doug's mother had kept the kitchen radio going day and night. It
was one of his clearest memories of her. But sharing this fact with
Claire would have invited other questions, and his past was a minefield. He had to be careful not to blow himself up here.

She handed him back the CD case. "You come up here often?"

"No. Almost never."

"This isn't where you take all your dates?"

"In fact, I should admit it now, what I said downstairs was sort of a fib. I don't actually know who manages this building. I just know where the key is."

"Oh." She thought about that, looking out at the city winking back at her.

"I wanted to get us up above the Town, you know, try to show you something."

She settled back into her chair, good for a little mischief. "Okay."

Lou Rawls started up with "Lady Love," and Doug mustered all the bass he had to say, *"Oh, yeah . . ."*

She smiled, stretching out her legs, flexing her ankles like she was lifting them dripping out of a light surf. "So where do you live?"

"Back of the hill." He thumbed behind them. "I rent. You own your place?"

"I got a great rate from my bank. Actually cheaper for me to own. Are you going to live here forever?"

"You mean, like most Townies? I can admit, until maybe a couple of years ago, I never even considered it a choice."

"Okay, you see now—I could *not* imagine living in my parents' same town. There's just no way. So what is it about this place that keeps such a tight hold on people?"

"Comfort-level thing, probably. Knowing what's around every corner."

"Okay. But even when what's around that next corner maybe isn't all that . . . good?"

"I'm giving you how it *was* more than how it *is,* because honestly, I can't say for certain how it is right now. I feel sort of apart from it, these past couple of years. But growing up, yeah, it was easy. You were known. You had a role in the Town and you played it."

"Like a big family."

"And families can be good or bad. Good *and* bad. Me, my role around Town, I was Mac's kid. Mac was what they called my father. Everywhere I went, every corner I passed, everybody knew me. *There goes Mac's kid*—like father, like son. And you wear that around long enough, it becomes part of you. But now things are getting different. Everybody's not related to everybody else anymore. New faces on the corner, strangers, people who can't recite your entire family history, generation by generation. And there's freedom in that, at least there is for me. What you give up in comfort, in familiarity—for me it's nice not to be reminded on *every* block, 'This is who I am, I'm Mac's kid.' "

"But I would think that sort of thing would inspire people to want to get out more. To go on their own, make a clean break."

Doug shrugged. "That what you did?"

"What I tried to do. What I'm *still* trying to do."

"I think suburbs are like that. Launching pads. The Town, it's more like a factory. We're local product here, banging it out every day. There's pollution, but it's *our* damn pollution, know what I'm saying?" That didn't come out as clever as he had hoped. "It's a box, I'll give you that. It's like an island that's tough to swim off of."

She sipped her wine, having poured herself some more without his noticing. The song changed. "'Wildfire,'" she said, gazing back at the radio. "My God, I used to love this song. The horse?"

"You see?" he said, getting jazzed again.

They listened awhile, under the orbiting plane lights. "You mentioned your dad," she said.

Shit. Minefields. "Yeah."

"Your whole family live here?"

"No, actually, none of them, not anymore."

"They all left and you stayed?"

"Sort of. My parents, they're split up."

"Oh. But they live close by?"

"Not really."

"'Not really.' What does that mean?"

Boom! His leg below the knee. "My mother, she left my dad and me when I was six."

"Oh, sorry. I mean, gosh, sorry I asked."

"No, she got out while the getting was good. For her own sanity, I'd say. My father."

"You're not close with him?"

"Not anymore." Skirted that one—still hopping along one-leggedly.

"I hope I'm not asking too many questions."

"First date," said Doug. "What else are you gonna do?"

"Right, I know. Usually, guys I meet for the first time, they go on and on, packaging and selling themselves. Either that or they try to wear you down with questions, like proving how *interested* they are. Like, if I'm so involved recounting my own life story, maybe I'll lose track of how many Stoli and Sprites I've had."

As the song faded out, there was a spray of bullying laughter from the street below, then the pop and smash of a glass bottle shattering, followed by cursing, laughing, footsteps running away. "Nice," grumbled Doug.

Then the Little River Band came on, making it all right.

"I know this one," she said. "I'm realizing I've been listening to some really depressing music recently."

"Yeah? Like how bad?"

"Like college-radio bad. Like, old Cure. Smashing Pumpkins."

"Yikes. The Pumpkins. Sounds serious."

She nodded.

He went easy. "This something you want to talk about?"

She held up her glass, empty again, twirling it by the stem, examining her lipstick on the rim, the finger smudges. "I don't know. Kind of nice to get away from it."

"Good, then. We're away."

She lowered the glass. "Do you have any questions you want to ask me?"

"Oh, only about a couple of hundred or so. But like you say, this is a nice vibe right now. I figure there's time. Least, I hope there is."

That was good. Saying that did something to her—even as his mind reminded him, *Just one date*.

"Can I ask you another question then?" she said.

Doug cut her off at the pass. "I had a very misspent youth. When I drink I become a jerk, so I just don't drink anymore."

She smiled gently, almost embarrassedly. "That wasn't what I was going to ask."

"I haven't had a drink in two years. I go to meetings regularly, a few each week. I like them. I consider what I have an allergy. Someone's allergic to nuts or something, people don't hold that against them. Me, I'm allergic to alcohol. I break out in jerk hives. And this whole thing, it makes for a very bad first impression, but that's what I have to live with." He breathed. "Okay. Sorry. What were you gonna ask?"

"Whew." She undercut that with a smile. "I was going to ask why you wanted to take out someone you saw crying in a Laundromat?"

Doug nodded thoughtfully. "This is a good question."

"I know it."

Police lights crawled along the interstate, bright, pinpoint blues. "I don't have a good answer for you. I guess, sure, I am curious about that. A pretty girl with problems—that's not something you see every day."

This time he heard the wine trickling almost guiltily into her glass. "Miracles" was starting now, Jefferson Airplane, or maybe Jefferson Starship. He closed his eyes a moment and saw his mother's old black-and-silver RCA singing from the top of the refrigerator.

"Honestly," Claire said after a sip, "how much of this did you plan?"

"Not a second of it, I swear to God."

"Well, it's perfect. I mean, you can't even know how. If I could stop time right now, keep that sun from coming up tomorrow morning . . ."

"Yeah? What's the sun got on you?"

"Tomorrow morning I start back at work."

"Start back?" said Doug, mustering innocence.

The wine slowed her words down a little. "I've had sort of an extended vacation."

"That's nice."

"Not really." Another sip and she turned to him. "You've lived here all your life, right?"

"Right."

"So what do you know about bank robbers?"

He cleared his throat, letting out a long, silent exhale. "What's to know?"

"There's supposed to be a lot from here. I figured maybe you grew up with some."

"I guess—maybe I did, yeah, I guess."

"My bank, where I work . . . a couple of weeks ago, we were robbed."

"Oh. I see."

"They were hiding, waiting for us inside."

Stunning, how immediately shitty he felt. "And what, they tied you up?"

"Held us at gunpoint. Made us lie down. Took our shoes off." She looked at him again. "Isn't that the weirdest? Our *shoes.* I'm stuck on that, I don't know why. Belittling, you know? I have all these dreams now where I'm barefoot." She looked at her shoe boots against the rubber-coated roof. "Anyway."

"But you weren't hurt."

"Davis was—my assistant manager. They beat him. A silent alarm went off."

He had to keep it up now. "But if it was silent, then . . . ?"

"One of them had a radio wire in his ear. A police radio."

"Right. They beat this guy up because he set off the alarm."

She stared at the city as though the correct answer were out there somewhere. She never answered him. Doug pondered that.

"Police catch these guys yet?" he said.

"No."

"They're on them, though."

"I don't know. They didn't say."

"You probably had to go through, what, a whole interrogation?"

"It wasn't too bad."

He let it go. Best not to push. "And you haven't been back at work since?"

She shook her head, frowning, pensive. "They took me with them when they left."

Doug couldn't play along with her here. He couldn't say anything.

"They were worried about the alarm." She followed the jet lights in the sky to the airport off to their left. "Somewhere over there, they let me out. I was blindfolded."

It was all there in her voice, everything he never wanted to hear. "Scary?"

She took a long time to answer, so long that Doug started to wonder if he hadn't given himself away somehow. "Nothing else happened," she said.

She stared at him now, eerily intense. Doug stumbled over his words. "No, I didn't—"

"They just let me go. That's all. Once they knew they weren't being followed, they just pulled over and let me out."

"Sure," he said, nodding. "Of course."

She folded her arms against the creeping cool. "I've been in such a funk since. The FBI agent, he told me it would be like being in mourning."

Doug said, as evenly as he could, "FBI agent?"

"But I don't know. When my grandparents died, I was sad, very sad. But did I truly *mourn* . . . ?"

Doug kept nodding. "And you're working with them?"

"The FBI? Just this one agent I talk to. He's been great."

"Yeah? That's good." Waiting a patient beat. "What does he ask you, like, 'What'd they look like? What'd they say?' "

"No. At first, yes. Not anymore."

"Now what, he, like, calls you up, checks in?"

"I guess." Her little side glance informed Doug that she had noticed he was asking a lot of questions. "What?"

"No, I'm just wondering. From his point of view. Maybe he's thinking, 'Hey, inside job.' "

She stared. "Why would he think that?"

"Only because, this other guy was beat up, you were taken for a ride, let go unhurt."

"You're saying he *suspects* me?"

"How would I know? It's just a thought. You never thought that?"

She sat perfectly still, like someone hearing a strange noise at night and waiting to hear it again. "You're freaking me out a little."

"You know what? Maybe I should stick to talking about things I know something about."

"No," she decided. "No, it's impossible."

"They're probably just casting a wide net."

But he had thrown a little monkey wrench of uncertainty her way, and that was enough. Her shoulders were bunched now, arms crossed high on her chest.

"Getting cold?" he said.

"I am."

"I think 'Muskrat Love' is coming up next anyway. That's our cue."

She said she was done with the wine, so he poured the rest into the roof gutter, stowing the chairs and switching off the CD player in the middle of "Poetry Man." The wine formed a bloody stain on the sidewalk as they left the building, walking back down Bunker Hill Street to Monument Square. A handful of skateboarders hanging out around the stairs at the base of the granite obelisk put Doug in the mind of his crew, making him itchy. They came to a five-street junction in the heart of the remade section of Charlestown.

"Okay," said Doug, bringing her up short on the brick sidewalk, her door only a hundred yards around the bend.

She was surprised. "Okay . . ."

Ask for her number. It would be rude to do otherwise. Then fade away forever. For her sake as much as yours.

"So," she said, waiting.

He swiped a mustache of sweat off his upper lip. *You had your date, your flirtation with danger, you got that out of your system.* She was looking up at him, her empty glass catching some of the lamplight, holding it there.

"Look," he said. "I probably shouldn't even be here with you."

She reacted like he was making up his own language. "Why do you say that? What do you mean?"

"I don't even know." He shuffled his feet, needing to leave. "I'm all messed up recently, my mind. I'm used to order, clarity, things a certain way. Not this. Not doing things I don't understand."

"But that's—me too." A revelation, a bright smile of communion.

"I'm exactly the same way right now."

"And I need to . . . I'm trying to be good in my life, you know?"

"Hey." She stepped up to him, examining his face in the light of the gas lamp. She reached for his forehead, and when he did not protest, touched the scar that split his left eyebrow. "I wanted to ask at the restaurant."

"Hockey scar. An old injury. You—you like hockey?"

Her finger came away from his face. "I hate it."

Doug nodded fast. "So what are you doing tomorrow night?"

She said, surprised, "What—tomorrow?"

"Probably have a busy day, right? Back to work, you'll be tired. How about the night after?"

"I don't . . ." She looked amazed. "I don't even know."

Doug felt like someone was trying to open up an umbrella in his chest. "Okay, here it is right here. Whatever it takes to see you again, I'll do. Would you want to see me again?"

"I . . ." Looking up at his face. "Sure."

"Great. Okay. So we're both crazy, that's good. Your turn this time. You pick the place—somewhere outside C-town. I'll pick you up right here. Give me your last four digits."

She did, and he gave her no time to ask for his, forsaking all thoughts of a parting kiss, just trying to tear himself away from her. He was acting drunker now than he ever had before.

"Good luck," he said, backing off. "With tomorrow."

"Thanks." She held up the glass as though it were a gift. "Good night, Doug."

"Wow. Hey, could you say that for me again?"

"Good night, Doug."

"Good night, Claire." He said it, and there was no lightning striking him dead in the street.

14
THE POPE OF THE
FORGOTTEN VILLAGE

DEZ LIVED IN THE NECK.

As Charlestown was the orphan of Boston, so was the Neck the orphan of Charlestown. Getting there meant heading out past the Schrafft's tower at the western gate of the Town, banging a one-eighty by the MBTA rail shop in the Flat, ducking under two crumbling highway elevations, then turning past the all-cement salute to urban blight that was the Sullivan Square Station. Tucked behind there was the six-street patch of old railroad houses also known as the Forgotten Village, an outpost teetering on the edge of Charlestown and of Boston itself, the last settlement before the Brazilian food markets of Somerville's Cobble Hill.

The Neck embodied the Town's siege mentality. Dez's mother still hissed about the traitors who'd accepted the city's relo money, making way for planners and engineers to carve up the Neck. Whole streets had been bulldozed—Haverhill, Perkins Place, Sever—chopped off like arms and legs, and yet, proud old veteran that it was, the Neck survived.

Dez's mother's aluminum-sided two-story on Brighton Street was shouldered between two taller houses, its square front yard fenced with child's-height chain-link. Growing up beneath a major highway had made Desmond Elden feel isolated and marginalized—and proud. Looking up at the rusting struts—the corroding Central Artery and its crumbling chunks of concrete—Dez often thought of the view fish had, looking up at a pier.

Dez earned enough—legitimately, from his other mother, dear old Ma Bell—to move them both out of there, though he knew better than to even bring up the subject. Ma would never give up the land

she had been bitching about for years. Certainly there was no leaving
the parish. Dez's mother didn't drive, and her daily walks to mass
were a hike: a dreary quarter mile over hot asphalt in summer, battered by whipping river winds in winter, always taking her life into her
hands crossing the highway rotary. And this was just to reach the
Schrafft's tower—from there she had to march all the way up Bunker
Hill to the steeple at the crest of the Heights. But you'd just as soon
ask her to trade in Dez for another son as leave St. Frank's. This daily
odyssey was part of her experience of mass, as it was part of the experience of living in the Neck, of being Catholic, of being Irish, of being
an aging widow. It was suffering made proud. There were only two
ways she would leave the Neck, Ma always said, and one of them was
by being bulldozed.

Dez understood her view of the world, though he no longer
embraced it. Wire work had taken him high above much of Greater
Boston, in a cherry picker over leafy towns like Belmont, Brookline,
Arlington, neighborhoods with grass and parks and unobstructed sky,
even some elbow room between houses. But the Neck was all she
knew. It was like smoking to her now—gone beyond habit and addiction, a way of life.

The smoking, pursued vigorously over four decades, was finally
and forever drying Ma out. Her hair—the wavy red mane she had
been known for—was thinning into wisps of brown. Her skin was stiff
and going gray like an old sink sponge, her eyes marbling, her lips
shriveling along with her beauty, all that was supple and yielding
about her evaporating away. Her wrinkled hands trembled without a
butt or a soft pack or a lighter to busy them, and more and more
nights she spent alone at the kitchen table under the fruit-glass lamp,
listening to talk radio and filling the house with exhaust.

She put the smokes away long enough to sit down and eat the
meal she had prepared. Doug's visit had brought her to life, which
was nice to see. At least she could still snap-to for company: fussing
about the old kitchen with a dishrag on her shoulder, humming the
way she used to. Both she and Dez had needed this lift.

"Meat loaf's better than ever, Mrs. Elden," said Doug, bent over
his plate, scooping it in.

Her secret was to bake a small loaf of spice bread first, then shred
that and work it into the meat. Her cooking was getting spicier and
spicier, the cigarettes snuffing out her taste buds one by one.

"Potatoes, too, Ma," said Dez. She whipped them with a mixer,
melting in four sticks of butter.

"Yeah," said Doug. "This is a meal."

"Such manners on you two," she said, pleased. "My Desmond, of course, I expect it. Raised him that way. But, Douglas, the way you were brought up? The bad luck you seen?"

He helped himself to a little more ketchup. "Just so as I get asked back."

"Don't give me that now. You know you're welcome here, any day of the week."

Dez ate happily with his father's photograph at his elbow. It had been moved there from its customary position across the table in order to make room for their dinner guest. The picture showed two blurry nuns and most of the word *Hospital* behind a happy, surprised-looking man in shirtsleeves and thick-rimmed, black eyeglasses, holding a thin-banded summer hat. The picture had been taken on July 4, 1967, the day of Dez's birth, and the resemblance between father and son was made extraordinary by their shared pair of eyeglasses. The specs in the picture were the same ones Dez wore now. In the sixteen years since Desmond senior's murder, neither Dez nor Ma had taken a home-cooked meal without his portrait joining them at the table.

The linoleum floor was warped, and when Doug rested his arms on the table, all three glasses of Pepsi jumped. Dez said, "I gotta get that shimmed."

"How's your father doing?" Ma asked Doug. "See him much?"

"Not that often," said Doug.

"Jem says he's doing good, Ma," said Dez. "Jimmy Coughlin goes up and sees him more than Doug does."

Doug wiped his mouth, nodded. "His old man and mine ran around together, and Jem, I think he likes to hear the tales. Stories about his old man, because that's all he's got."

"Those Coughlin kids," said Ma, shaking her head—Dez tensing. "How you became who you are today, Douglas, living in that household, I'll never know. Any trouble you ever got into, I blamed that family."

"No," said Doug, aiming his fork at his own chest. "You can place all that blame right here."

"That woman and her tirades. *Mother of God.* Get herself loaded and start calling around town, ranting at her enemies. I know she took you in, Douglas, and God bless her for that. Her one and only ticket upstairs. I do wish we coulda taken you at the time, given you a proper home."

"That's beautiful of you to say, Mrs. Elden. But Jimmy's ma, you know, she did her best. Truthfully, I think she liked me better than her own kids. I know she treated me that way."

"And that daughter of hers . . ."

"Ma," said Dez.

"Desmond don't like me talking about it, but"—she put out a hand to keep Dez from cutting her off—"I am just over the moon that you two are no more."

"*Jesus,* Ma," said Dez, "I didn't tell you that so you could—"

"No, no, no," said Doug, putting out his own hand. "It's fine, really. Krista's all right, Mrs. E. She'll land on her feet. She's doing good."

His respectful lie hung in the air as the three of them chewed.

"I know the four a you were all friends in school, but that's not the kind of boy I let Desmond hang around at night." She looked over at her Dez. "But he's a man now, and he can pick his own friends. He knows right from wrong. Knows enough to stay out of trouble."

Dez kept his head down, chewing over his plate.

Doug said, "Everybody we meet, Mrs. Elden, I tell them Dez is the best of us."

Dez frowned, looking up, pleased. "Come on."

"College-educated," said Ma, needing no encouragement, "good phone company job. Clean boy. Manners. Such a help to me all these years. And look how handsome. So why isn't he married then? The both of you's."

Dez pointed at Doug. "You walked right into that one."

"Your pal there, what's his name." She snapped her fingers dryly. "The Mead Street Magloans. Freckled kids, like a litter of toads."

"Gloansy," said Dez, sharing a grin with Doug.

"Alfred Magloan," she said, nodding. "Desmond tells me he has a boy with this girlfriend of his now. I don't know her."

"Joanie Lawler. From the houses."

"Okay, the houses, that explains some of it. But ask me and she is damn lucky to be getting *anything* out of him now, after already giving away the store. My day, we wouldn't have let a pair like you get past twenty-three. We'd've grabbed hold and held on. Those days, girls knew how to." She sat back, done with her meal though she had hardly touched it, lighting up. "I used to think the problem was you very modern men. Now, the more I see, the more I realize it's the women of the species. Too soft."

* * *

THE ODOR OF SMOKE clung to everything in the house, including Dez's bedroom upstairs. The comforter on the twin bed, the dumbbells on the floor, his work gear. All his U2 imports, rarities, and bootlegs stacked on top of the bureau. Dez put on The Alarm's *Strength,* just loud enough to give them some privacy. The Alarm had been on the same socially conscious, Catholic, protest-punk track as U2 and Simple Minds in the eighties, and Dez was doing his part to keep the music alive.

A bus moaned into Sully Square. All day and night they arrived, the subway cars and the squealing wheels of the commuter rail— never mind the trucks pounding the highway overhead. But to Dez it was all lullabies. God forbid it should ever stop some night, how would he ever get to sleep without it?

Doug sat big in the small chair at Dez's computer, his hand clumsy over the mouse, reminding Dez of old men at the library trying to work the microfilm. Dez was showing Doug the speed of his ISDN line, and how to use a search engine called Alta Vista.

Doug had entered *Corvette* and was surfing the Web pages it gave him. "All right, now what?"

"Any of those words that are a different color interest you, click on them."

The screen jumped to a site named Borla, something about exhaust systems. "Your Ma really likes Jem, huh?"

"Loves him," said Dez. "You want to know what that's about? Specifically?"

"I bet I don't."

"All these years, Jem's been inside my house exactly once, okay? Maybe a year ago now. Not ten minutes total, he's here—and he takes the biggest fucking smash of his life."

Doug cracked up laughing. "He did not."

"Doesn't even flush, just leaves it there. Kid has no respect."

Doug swiped his face with his hand, trying to control his laughter.

"Scented candles, my mother lit," said Dez. "They burned for three days straight, trying to exorcise the spirit of that kid. And this is a one-bathroom house!"

"Hey, don't tell me, I live above him."

"He should of just lit the bathroom on fire when he was done with it, saved us the trouble."

"Remind me to flush, if and when."

"Hey—you could piss on the curtains and dry-hump the sofa,

Ma'd find some redeeming aspect in it."

"Well, the kid's a maniac. Always has been."

"Yeah. But getting worse. Every time he hands me a piece before a job, he says, 'I know you won't use this.'"

Doug nodded. "He says that about you. 'He'll never shoot.'"

"But if you have to shoot a gun on a job, it's because you've blown it. Right? You screwed it up. The gun is your emergency backup plan."

"You don't open up your parachute while you're still standing inside the plane."

"But to Jem—you *don't* shoot a gun on the job, you've blown it."

Doug was onto another page. "Kid's warped."

"So what are you doing about this wedding?"

"Don't know. I fucking hate weddings."

It was to be a double ceremony, Gloansy and Joanie's nuptials as well as the christening of their little freckle, Nicky. Jem was Gloansy's best man, Doug the boy's godfather. Dez was just a groomsman. He was never the type to be first or second in any group—but Gloansy rating third out of the four of them irked him. Dumb-guy Gloansy, the car booster—whereas, without Dez, they'd be pulling low-percentage strong-arm heists, risky in-through-the-front-door jobs. Dez wondered if other people spent as much time as he did worrying about his place in the hearts and minds of his friends.

They had all come up through school together, Jem joining them after being kept back a grade. Good friends right up through middle school, when Dez started drifting away. Or they drifted away from him: part of it was his college-track classes, and part of it was Ma keeping him in nights to study. Doug never became a stranger, but he wasn't exactly a buddy either. Dez followed his career the same as everyone else in Town: hockey star, destined for glory, drafted by the Bruins out of high school—then bounced out of the AHL under murky circumstances, returning to the Town, and after a few months getting pinched for armed robbery. "High School Hockey Star Arrested," sang the papers. Then back to the Town after his release, drinking and brawling, a wrong-way hood maturing into full-time criminal. Then a second short prison sentence, and back out on the streets again.

Dez played in a couple of street hockey games with him after his return, with not much more than a *Hey, what's doing?* between them. Doug's circle had always been a tough group who lived like they played—rough, loud, and cheap—and openly mocked working guys like Dez. But the Doug MacRay who had returned from prison was like a soldier home from combat overseas: a changed man, newly sober, more concerned with security and survival than being a punk.

Hockey was never Dez's game, not like baseball. But one day over on Washington Street, choosing up teams, Doug picked Dez first. Week after that, same thing—Doug even feeding him some easy assists at the net, shots Doug MacRay could have put in eyes shut, and chatting him up between points. Dez started coming around more regularly, and after one game they had a talk about their fathers, on a long walk down Main Street, which came as a revelation to Dez. As part of the old neighborhood Code of Silence, no one had ever talked to Dez about his father. All he knew was that, one night in January 1980, some three years after losing his Edison job, the man was found shirtless in the snow in the middle of Ferrin Street, shot twice in the chest at close range, once through each nipple.

No witnesses had ever come forward, and no one was ever charged. Before the casket was closed that final time, twelve-year-old Dez lifted the eyeglasses off his father's sagging face and slipped them into his pocket.

His mother only spoke of the pain of his passing, and even the priests who helped her raise Dez, keeping him on track to college, discouraged Dez's inquiries. It was Doug who told him that Dez's father had been killed on his way to deliver a "package" to one Fergus Coln: then an ex–professional wrestler doing low-level mob enforcement; now the head of the PCP ring in Town, the notorious Fergie the Florist. Whatever had happened to his father after losing his Edison job, Dez realized that this package he was delivering on Ferrin Street in the middle of a winter night—it wasn't doughnuts.

In time, as Dez and Doug's renewed friendship evolved, Doug began to ask questions about Dez's work at the phone company. Pole work and junction boxes; alarm procedures and switching stations. Doug's motivation was transparent, but rather than being disappointed, Dez was thrilled to bring something of value to their relationship.

He started on the setup end of things: half-blind advance work like line rerouting, plug-pulling, cable cutting, all the while earning Doug's trust. Doug kicked him a decent percentage, but it wasn't the money that kept Dez coming back. Half always went into St. Frank's collection box anyway, in Ma's name. It was the attention Doug paid him, this neighborhood legend, and the dividends that paid Dez around Town.

Dez started to think like a criminal, keeping his eyes open at work, feeding Doug new schemes. When Doug needed a fourth pair of hands for a job in Watertown, Dez insisted on jumping in. They wore disguises and carried guns, and Dez threw up when he got home afterward, but then he looked at himself in the mirror over the sink, righting his father's thick, black rims on his face, and it was like a switch had been thrown.

Most of all, it was the belonging: the intensity of the crew during the Watertown heist, their brotherhood, like rocking in a great band. Friendship was by nature a thing that could never be consummated— could never rise to an ultimate point of perfection—but pulling these jobs together, that was when it came closest. That was the high he kept chasing. The rest of the time, he never felt as tight with them as they seemed to be with each other. They called him the Monsignor, a tease on his devotion and his strict upbringing, but also using the elitism of the clergy as another way to set him apart.

Dez's lot in life was to be the guy behind the guy, and as such, his side friendship with Doug not only continued, but flourished, and for that he was grateful—it was worth everything—though at its root, theirs was a partnership founded upon need: Doug needing Dez's phone company knowledge, and Dez needing Doug as a friend. This particular evening was one he had been looking forward to longer than he cared to admit.

"Elisabeth Shue," said Doug. "What is that, *u, e*?"

"I think." Dez started his $275 set of four U2 bobbing-head dolls—a recent purchase via mail order from Japan—nodding. "That's who you're bringing to Gloansy's wedding?"

Doug tapped in her name two-fingeredly, results filling the screen. "Either her or Uma Thurman, I can't decide." Then he sat back, shaking his head. "Some fucking inconsiderate shit, him getting married."

Dez nodded along with his bobble heads. Screen caps from *Cocktail* came up, showing Elisabeth Shue topless under a waterfall.

"That's it," said Doug. "I gotta get me a computer."

All evening Dez had the sense that Doug had wanted to tell him something. Anything personal, besides the radio static of shit-shooting guy talk, they only discussed when they were alone like this.

"I gotta get you married now," said Doug. "Mother's orders."

"Yeah," said Dez. "Well, good luck."

An outsider watching then might have thought Doug's facial expression a goof on seriousness, his brow knit, his eyes somehow sad. But Dez knew that this was as close as the guy ever came to baring his soul.

"You ever meet somebody, Dez, and, like—you *knew* something was there, beyond the boy-girl, man-woman stuff? Something almost touchable?"

"Honestly?" said Dez. "I fall in love, like, two or three times a day. I see women all the time on the job, everywhere. Even moms are starting to look good to me now."

"I could see that. You fitting in with a ready-made family. Single mom, you move right in. . . ."

"A *hot* single mom," added Dez, throwing in a little guy talk to keep them centered.

"You're not still, you know, for Krista though, are you?"

"Nah," said Dez.

"'Cause that would be trouble."

"She's outta my league, I know that."

"No, no, no. Not what I'm saying. I'm saying you're outta hers."

Dez didn't understand that; that would not compute. "Know what she calls me? The Pope of the Forgotten Village."

"And you love it. But she's like a whirlpool, Desmond. Know anything about whirlpools?"

"Sure."

"They don't just drown you. They swallow you. They hold you down there in that swirl, going round and round, days at a time, even weeks—the force of the water sucking away your clothes, your hair, your face."

"Hey," said Dez, "Jem would never go for it anyway."

"He would freak. And your ma."

"Ho, she'd be racing around the house, hiding the silver, stashing the Hummels." Dez grinned at that image, enjoying it maybe a little too much. "Krista never came clean about who's Shyne's father, did she? After admitting it wasn't you?"

"She never even admitted that, least not to me."

Dez remembered her at the Tap the other night, coming up to him after Doug had breezed, touching his shoulder like it was made out of mink, requesting that Cranberries song again—and the dollar bill she had pulled from her jeans, the way she offered it to him clipped between two fingers. *My treat,* he had told her, then watched the seat of her jeans as she walked back to the bar.

Doug turned in his chair. "What do you say we hit a movie theater?"

"All right," said Dez. "What's playing?"

"No, I mean—*hit* a movie theater. What would you say?"

Dez got it then. "Yeah, whatever. You think?"

"Let's go see something, take a look around."

Dez nodded, excited, reaching for his coat. They had a mission.

DOWNSTAIRS, DOUG SAID GOOD-BYE to Ma, who held her cigarette away to receive his kiss on her cheek. "Watch out for my Dezi, now."

"Always do, Mrs. E."

And so Dez had to pop in for a kiss too, still tasting the smoke on his lips as he moved to the door. "We're gonna catch a flick."

"Meet some girls," she called after them. "Preferably Catholic ones."

Dez patted his pockets as they moved through the low gate onto the sidewalk, ritually checking for his wallet. The night was cloudless and cool. He scanned the street on which he had lived his entire life, a car parked a few houses down catching his eye. Dez continued forward a few steps with Doug before tugging his leather jacket sleeve, turning him around.

"Look, this is maybe stupid, but . . . today I was out in Chestnut Hill, this neighborhood set off the parkway, family area, lotsa money? I'm up on a pole checking a reading, and I could see the whole street from up there—and I notice this red sedan, like a Chevy Cavalier, keeps cruising past. Like it's circling the block or something, every couple of minutes. As I said, it's a family area, kids roaming around. So I keep an eye out. I know he can't see me with the trees up there, my truck's parked around the corner. Then, just as I'm thinking maybe something needs to be done about this, the Cavalier stops coming around. I finish up, climb down, move on."

"Beautiful story, Desmond."

Dez pointed to his own sternum, indicating the street behind them. "Couple of houses down. Red Cavalier parked across the street. Or else I'm just paranoid."

Doug's eyes going dead gave Dez a chill.

"We can head up this way," said Dez, pointing up at Perkins Street. "Loop around, take the shortcut back to—"

Doug was out in the street, striding right out toward the dark Cavalier.

Dez hesitated, surprised, then went after him, but staying on the near sidewalk.

When Doug was more than halfway there, the Cavalier's engine gunned to life. Headlights came on and it swung out into the one-way road.

Doug stopped where he was in the street and the Cavalier had to brake, stopping just a few inches from Doug's knees. It was beaten and dull-looking, its sour headlights throwing Doug's shadow over the street.

As Doug moved around to the driver's-side window, the car peeled out, Doug thumping the side with his fist before watching it go. Brake lights reddened the intersection with Perkins, the Cavalier veering hard left.

Doug took off the other way, running fast toward Cambridge Street, and Dez followed, adrenaline surging now. They reached the corner just in time to see the Cavalier empty out one street over and rev past them, speeding under the interstate, lifting over the rise before plummeting toward Spice Street, back to the Town.

"The fuck was *that*?" said Dez, out of breath.

Doug stared after the disappeared car.

"A cop?" said Dez.

"Cop would have gotten out, badged me. Not hid. Not run."

"Then what?"

"Fuck," spat Doug, kicking at the sidewalk.

A bus hissed past them, turning into Sully Square, gassing them with a lead-colored cloud of exhaust. "But if it's the G, how'd they . . . wait, through *me*?"

"Maybe we pushed the phone stuff too hard. Mother*fuck*."

"You get a good look? I didn't."

"Birthmark," said Doug, waving at the side of his face. "Like a rash."

"What, one of those, a port-wine stain?"

"Yeah. His hand too." Doug squeezed his own hand into a fist. "Fuck it, Dez. I gotta pass on the movies."

"Right," said Dez. Then: "You sure?"

Doug was looking toward home, the old candy-factory tower, the hilltop steeple of St. Frank's.

"What do I do?" said Dez. "Am I made? What's it mean?"

A gleaming black Mercedes wheeled past them into Somerville, pumping bass-heavy rap. "We gotta huddle up," said Doug. "Let me talk to the others. You just keep your eyes open like you did. Making him—that was good work."

Doug held out his fist for a smack, then jogged across the street back toward the Town. Dez watched him go, wanting to run after him and help him piece this thing together, but maybe Dez was too hot now.

The G parked there on his mother's street. Dez jammed his hands deep into his pockets, spooked, watching for red Cavaliers as he walked back home.

PART II
WHEN LOVE COMES TO TOWN

15
THE MEET

THE FREEDOM TRAIL WAS a tourist thing, an inlaid-brick sidewalk trail retracing the "birth of America." It started downtown at the Boston Common training field and snaked north through the city, past the site of the Boston Massacre, past Paul Revere's House in the North End, all the way across the Charlestown Bridge to end at the 221-foot granite obelisk marking the site of the Battle of Bunker Hill.

The second-to-last stop along the trail was the oldest commissioned floating warship in the world, the USS *Constitution,* also known as *Old Ironsides* for her thick, cannonball-repelling hull. In the warming of early May, the pavilion at the southern edge of the old navy yard saw a surge in attendance from school field trips: teachers in sun visors and knee-length shorts, parent chaperones gripping huge cups of iced coffee, and fifth-graders with lunch bags and foil-wrapped cans of soda, all squinting up at the flags tracing the sail outline along the ship's three tall masts.

Doug, Jem, and Gloansy wandered around the dry dock between the ship and its museum, mixing with the school groups and the knee-socked foreign tourists, Doug hoping to confound any parabolic microphones that might be aimed their way. Jem worked the brim curve of his lucky blue Red Sox cap, which not coincidentally had the added effect of flexing his arms. He wore small, smirking, syrup-tinted sunglasses too expensive and European-looking for his bargain-bin American face. Gloansy wore yellow-tinted sport shades that made his toad eyes bulge, his freckled forearms looking like two logs of Hickory Farms cheese.

Jem spit into the ocean and said, "Fucking cunt."

Doug turned on him fast, too fast. *"What?"*

"What *what?* Fucking branch manager, who else?"

"What are you talking about?"

"It's fucking gotta be."

"How? What could she have told them?"

"I dunno. Something."

"You tell me. What could she have told them?"

Jem flipped his cap back on top of his head, the brim newly horse-shoed. "Easy, kid. How would I know?"

Doug should have stopped himself, didn't. "I don't want to be throwing stuff around like it doesn't matter. Because this matters. This is important—fucking critical—and I want to be dealing in certainties. She could tell them what? That there were four of us? What, we drove a *van*?"

"Okay. Then how?"

Doug looked off across the harbor at the Coast Guard piers jutting off the North End. "Could be any number of things. Anything."

"We took a lot of precautions on that job. Fucking drove me nuts, but we did them, and it all went smooth, until the bell."

"I'm saying I don't have any answers yet, and neither do you."

"We bleached it up. I did the tool count, there was nothing left behind."

"Could be an accumulation of things. Could be they put someone on us special. We been pulling a lot recently."

Gloansy said, a one-hand-in-his-pocket shrug, "How do we even know it's anything? Could've been some guy parked on the street."

"Yeah," said Jem, pointing at Gloansy, "Banjo Boy is right. Some Peeping Tom. A Somerville hypo, shooting up. How come you're so sure of yourself here, Duggy?"

"I don't know anything," said Doug. "Except what I know."

A class shuffled past, boys smiling and pointing out Jem's *Yankees Suck!* T-shirt. When they were gone, Jem said, "Sniffing around the Monsignor, that I don't like."

"I talked to him," said Doug. "He knows how to handle it."

"*You* know how to handle it. Gloansy here, *he* knows how to handle it. The Monsignor, I don't have that kinda faith in."

"Here's the thing," said Doug, facing them. "Boozo's crew running wild—that was our cover. They took every ounce of heat that was out there because they were so fucking Cagney and greedy all the time. It was a vacation in Tahiti working in their shadow. Couldn't *buy* that kind of protection. But now they're good and gone, and the G still sees jobs being pulled. See, that machinery's all still in place. I think they're turning it on us now."

Gloansy said, "The G?"

Doug looked at him, *duh,* and went on, "It's not like they weren't *aware* of us before, but not this close. Maybe they're more focused now, because they can be. What bothers me is—why Dez? The only one of us with no record?"

Jem set one unlaced high-top sneaker on top of a piling, facing the harbor as though he owned it. "So we're the top dogs now."

Doug threw him a *duh* look too. "That's not a vacancy I'm looking to fill. We don't want to be out there in front, attracting attention. I like us running second, riding the wake of the high-stepping idiot in first place."

"Second place?" snarled Jem, as though Doug had insulted him.

"There is no finish line, kid. The trophy is this, right here, us walking around, money in our pockets, free as the breeze. This is breaking news to you?"

"I'm saying, number one is number one." Big shrug. "Sucks being the best—but there it is."

A foreign tourist with a crazy accent and his safari-hat-wearing wife approached them with a guidebook, looking for Faneuil Hall, and Jem played his favorite game, kindly directing them to Chelsea Street, up toward the projects.

Gloansy turned to Doug in private. "How bad do you think they have us?"

"Maybe not at all. Maybe they just have Dez right now. Or maybe they have all our houses and our cars, I don't know. Maybe they're up on one of these rooftops right now, watching."

"That means court orders and everything?"

"They don't need anything to start snooping on their own. No probable cause or subpoenas, they can just start tapping into us first, figuring out who's who and what's what, then once they know where to look and what to look for—then they go legal, get their papers in order, come marching into Town."

Gloansy was lost in thought a moment, a scary thing to see. He leaned closer to Doug. "What about, like, cameras in the bedroom, shit like that?"

Doug was forced to entertain a split-second image of Gloansy and Joanie grinding. "I would say, kid, these guys' jobs are tough enough."

Jem came back to them still muttering about Dez. "Fuckin' near-sighted Pope. Walking around out there with all our fates in his pockets. Makes me fucking nuts."

"I told you I talked to him," said Doug. "He's the one who made this guy in the first place."

Jem said, "This is why the movie thing is good. Changing our whole MO, if they're onto that."

Doug shrugged. "Good, maybe."

"Whoa," said Jem, protesting. "Douglas. C'mon, kid. Don't let these fuckers get you down."

"I think we gotta pull back a while."

"Fuckin'—no way."

"We gotta coast a bit."

"Why? We'll work around the Monsignor. Hijacking a can means no black-box phone shit, no tech. We'll go in the original Three Musketeers."

Gloansy said to Duggy, "For how long?"

"Listen," said Doug, "if you two've got nothing tucked away in the back of your sock drawers, I got this much sympathy for you."

"It ain't greed," said Jem. "It's knowing a good thing when I see one."

What do you see except what I show you? "Why you always in such a rush?"

A tour guide dressed as Paul Revere nodded to them as he passed.

"Why? Because I been on the losing end of things, and the one thing I promised myself when I was there was to make hay while the sun shines. Sun's shining bright here, Duggy."

"Too bright. That's not sunlight you're feeling, that's heat, that's the G, and I gotta know what we have here first."

"How you gonna do that? How you ever gonna know?"

"*And* we gotta keep our distance, starting now. Gotta stay separate, case they haven't made all of us yet. Even if they do. Avoid any criminal-conspiracy rap."

Jem shook his head like he was going to have to punch somebody. *"It was a fucking guy in a car!"*

Gloansy said, "My wedding, Duggy. Joanie will go apeshit."

Doug said, "Wedding's fine. Big group thing. So long as we skip the photos, it's fine. I'm talking about the four of us getting together for some ice cream, going out gallivanting. No."

"Fucking *cunt*," sang Jem under his breath.

Doug turned on him again. "You're making me fucking crazy with this."

"Why? What's it to you?"

Doug didn't know if what he said next was meant to put them at ease, or just to cover his own ass. "I'm going to do some looking into that."

"Looking into what? How? Tail her again?"

"Let me worry about it. I'll do my thing, you two go off and do yours. And quietlike. Be citizens. Assume they got eyes on you whenever you step out the door. Don't cross against the light and don't litter. Use the streets, use the neighborhood—they can't hide there. None of us sees anything more in a week or two, we'll get back together, think about moving ahead again."

"A week or two?" said Jem. "Jesus *fuck*."

"It's a vacation, kid. Enjoy it."

"Vacation? I'm fucking *always* on vacation."

"Duggy's right," said Gloansy, probably still worried about cameras in his bedroom. "Maybe we should cool it a whi—"

Jem flat-handed Gloansy in the chest. "That's for thinking, dumb shit. Fuck you, 'cool it.' *I* decide when to cool it."

"Fine, whatever," said Gloansy, rubbing his pec. "Jesus."

"Two fucking weeks, Duggy," pronounced Jem. "Then we'll see."

16
THE GIRL WHO GOT ROBBED

HE SAW HER WAITING for him in the lamplight of the five-street junction, wearing a shimmering black top that was either velvet or silk, a slim turquoise skirt ending in a ruffle at the knee—her legs were as blond as her hair—and low black heels, a black sweater in one hand, a small black handbag dangling on a string in the other. The taxi ahead of him slowed, trawling for an early evening fare, and she smiled and shook her head no, waving it along—and already Doug felt his reserve melting away.

He eased the Corvette's prow in along the stone curb at her knees. He was wearing Girbaud jeans, the same toe-pinching black shoes, and a white shirt under a black jacket. He stood out of the car—he always felt good rising out of the Vette—and walked around to get her door.

Her eyes broadened at the sight of the emerald green machine. "Wa-*how*," she said, her hand going to her chest. At first he thought she had expected a dusty pickup with tools rattling around in back and a pissing-Calvin sticker on the window. But as she sank into the low passenger seat, he recognized the look on her face as one of amusement. He felt a sting of foolishness then, that he wasn't prepared for. She swung her legs inside and he closed the wide door on a whiff of butterscotch, rounding the flat rear of the car, seeing himself and the city block reflected and elongated in the glassy green finish, not liking his hurt-little-boy feelings.

"So," he said, closing his door, trying to stay positive. "What do you think? Too much muscle?"

She turned to look in back. "I can't believe how clean it is."

"It's a collector's car, but not a fetish with me. Some guys, forget it. Working under the hood, that's what I like. Taking it apart and putting it back together again. I don't even drive it that much." She was exploring the upholstery with a light hand, the instrument panel with curious eyes. His plans for being so tough and crafty and inscrutable—like a magic trick, one glance from her had turned all his face cards blank. "I had it painted custom. Most collectors, stripping down and painting the exterior an off-stock color, that's ruining a collector's item like this. Me, I kind of liked making it mine. A one-of-a-kind." She touched the soft trim, and he couldn't take her silence any longer. "So, what? Is it ridiculous?"

"*Yes,*" she said—but with a smile, not catching his meaning. "Do you race this?"

"I've taken it around a speedway in New Hampshire once or twice on my own, just to open her up."

"How fast?"

"One-sixty, sustained. I topped out at one-eighty."

"Gulp," she said. He shifted into first and pulled away from the curb, clutching into second, the engine lifting them toward City Square like a speedboat over calm water. "I feel like I'm lying down."

Doug eyed her legs extended into the deep foot well. "I think it looks good on you."

She rubbed the leather seat hips with her palms and shook out her hair a little, getting comfortable. "I think my car's going to be jealous."

"Yeah, well. Corvettes and Saturns, that's like dogs and cats."

He slowed into the traffic light onto Rutherford, feeling a little better. "Hey," she said, turning to him curiously after the stop, "how did you know I drove a Saturn?"

Doug kept his eyes hard on the red light. "Didn't you mention it? You must have mentioned it."

"Did I?" Green light, Doug gripped the wheel and gunned it out toward the bridge, and she looked ahead again. "I guess I probably did."

Shithead. "Where we going?"

"I was thinking about the Chart House? It's nice but not too nice, you know? By the Aquarium on Long Wharf, overlooking the harbor? What do you think?"

"Let's do it."

"You thought I was going to pick some place on Newbury Street, right? Sonsie, or something."

"Yeah, maybe," he said. Newbury Street, he knew of only as an avenue of art galleries and shopping boutiques; Sonsie, he had no clue.

"But—before that." She turned to him again. "I was wondering if I could ask you a huge favor."

"Sure," he said, trying to read her as they crossed the rusted bridge into the city. "Anything, what?"

"I know it's not much of a way to start the night . . . but I have a friend who's having an operation tomorrow morning, and I promised him I'd stop by and visit."

Doug nodded, thinking, *Him*. "And you wanted some company?"

"I promise it won't take too long. Cross my heart."

"No problem at all." *Him*. "Just tell me where."

When she said, "Mass. Eye and Ear," Doug realized who the friend was.

SHE WAS SOMEWHERE OTHER than inside the elevator with him, and Doug realized that she was more anxious than he was. "You seem worried about something."

She stopped nibbling her lips and switched to pulling invisible thimbles off her fingers. "Just hospitals," she said. "Give me the creeps." She watched the numbers blink. "My brother died in a hospital."

"You had a brother?"

"He had a tumor in his bladder. It wrecked my parents." She shook it off, turning to him for distraction. "You cut your hair." She reached up and rubbed the stiff bristle over the nape of his neck. Her hand was gentle, cupping, cool. "What is it about a new haircut on a man?"

He thought that nothing had ever felt so good. "I might start purring here."

The floor dinged and the doors opened, her hand falling away. Signs pointed them to a circular hospital wing where they followed the numbers to the correct room.

Doug said, "I'll wait out here."

"No," she said, thinking he was jealous. "Meet him."

She took his hand, and before he knew it she was leading him into the room.

The patient was propped up against an avalanche of pillows. He turned toward them, head and shoulders moving as one. Gauze and bandaging masked half his face, bulging thick over his right eye, but Doug saw enough to recognize the assistant branch manager of the Kenmore Square BayBanks, Davis Bearns.

Claire released Doug and crossed to Bearns, Doug remaining just a few steps inside the private room.

Bearns held out his johnny-bare arms and Claire bent into them, a gentle kiss against his unbandaged cheek. "Hey there," said Bearns, his throat and lips doing most of the work, his fixed chin giving him a Harvard lockjaw. When she was slow to pull away, he said, "I'm getting some action here."

Claire straightened and smiled, whisking away a tear. She looked back at Doug and made introductions, and Doug nodded, giving Bearns a flat wave and a *Hey*.

"Are you comfortable?" she asked. "I wish you had let me bring you something."

"I just want to be done with it—this operation, this place."

"You said they're hopeful."

"They better be. I am. If I recover fifty percent sight in this eye, it will be a roaring success. I just want to get on with it, get home, get back to work."

"Really?" she said. "Back to work?"

"Anything, God, yes. Something to focus on instead of large-print crossword puzzles. But it won't be for a while. They'll have me on this dim-light-only diet for a few weeks, at least."

She nodded, tugging on a sheet wrinkle. "I'm having trouble at work."

"Well, see, you have memories. The one inconvenience I was spared." He turned his face farther toward her for inspection. "Which would you rather?"

She shook her head at his halfhearted joke, looking away. "Someday I'll go through it all with you. I promise. But not now."

"Of course not now. Tell me your plans for tonight. Vicarious living is all I have."

Doug cut in, "I'm gonna step outside. Nice meeting you, good luck."

"I won't keep her long," said Bearns. "But we will talk about you."

"Fair enough," said Doug, turning away, remembering Jem standing over bloody Bearns with the open jug of bleach.

BEING AT THE CHART HOUSE with Claire felt nice and clean and free of deception—until Doug remembered that, in fact, their entire relationship was founded on deception. But then the conversation would continue and he would again lose himself in the flickering candle of temporary innocence. What amazed him was his sincerity. Within the overarching lie—maybe because of it—he talked freely and was more honest and open with her than he had ever been with anyone else.

She ordered a single glass of white wine without comment. They worked out three Boston College football games they had separately attended. His steak arrived, her scallops. She talked about work at the bank and how unmotivated she was, killing two-hour lunches in her garden in the Fens and then suffering from pangs of guilt. "BayBanks does this community service thing, you know, masquerading as a small bank that cares? It's mostly bullshit, but they do pay you a couple of hours each week to volunteer somewhere. I started a year ago, at the Charlestown Boys and Girls Club?"

"Sure, yeah."

"Working with kids who were about the age my brother was. Whatever that means, right?" She smiled self-consciously, shrugged. "I just chaperone trips and stuff. They're delinquents, but they're good delinquents. Funny kids. Probably like you were, I'm guessing, right?"

"Nice that you do that."

"Thing is, it's supposed to be like three hours a week, and I'm spending more time there than I am at the bank."

"They're gonna catch up with you."

She nodded. "Part of me hopes they do."

The waiter wasn't used to being paid in cash. Outside, they followed low, black iron chains slung post-to-post along the waterfront, the night surf knocking boats into docks, groaning the piers, slapping wood. Doug was hit up by a skinny extortionist hand-selling roses out of a mop bucket, and Claire stripped away the cellophane and tissue down to the dethorned stem, raising the petals to her nose, then slipping her hand around the crook of his elbow.

In Columbus Park, at a sprawling, vacant play structure, they crossed the soft wood chips to still rubber swings. She sat and twisted in circles, letting the chains twirl apart and then twisting them again. She stuck her legs straight out as she spun, flexing her smooth calves, and Doug imagined that every flight of stairs she had ever climbed was mere training for that moment in that light, in his eyes.

"Okay, getting dizzy," she said, swiveling to a rest. Doug stood near her like a bodyguard, toeing at the tamped-down mulch. She looked out at the airport, the planes coming in. "Weird, isn't it? Here we are, two people, enjoying the night—and then Davis, sitting alone in a hospital room, waiting."

Doug watched her eyes. Something was happening in them. "He got a tough break."

She tracked a seagull flying over the docks. "One little thing—that's all it takes. You turn the wrong corner one morning and suddenly—you're Davis, you're on the outside of life, looking in."

"Some terrible luck."

"No," she said, looking down now. "It's worse than that." Her arms were inside the swing chains, worrying the stem of the rose in her lap. "It's actually my fault."

Doug followed this through. "How is it your fault?"

"I was the one who set off the alarm at the robbery. Not him. They beat up the wrong person." She sighed to forestall tears. "And I watched them do it. I could have spared him, I could have told them it was me. But I just stood there and let it happen. I took the easy way out, because that's what I always do."

"But come on. You were scared."

"He's marked for life now, and he did nothing wrong—nothing to deserve it. *I* did this to him."

"Look," said Doug, dropping into the swing next to her. "You gotta find a way to stop thinking about this. Is it the FBI? They still coming around?"

"The agent, he assumed that it was Davis who hit the alarm. And of course I let him. Admitting otherwise wouldn't have been the easy way out." She looked up into the sky over the water. "Why am I this way? You wouldn't have lied."

"Me?" said Doug, going for it. "I wouldn't have told them anything."

"What do you mean? Anything like what?"

"Nothing beyond the basics."

She turned, confused. "Because you think the agent suspects me?"

"This is one of the differences between growing up in Canton and Charlestown, I think. People who don't deal with cops that much, such as yourself, you probably tend to believe all that stuff about the Search for the Truth. Forgetting that cops, FBI, anybody with a badge who has a lot of power—they're just people like anyone else. They have lives, they have jobs to protect. And how they do that is by clearing arrests. Getting results. Which also means, if they can't catch the one who did it, sometimes they'll settle for the one who fits. And that person is usually the one who talked the most."

She stared. "You're serious."

"How often do you hear about convictions overturned, confessions coerced? We learn early where I'm from, don't talk to the cops. Or if you do, get a lawyer present."

"You're saying I should hire a lawyer?"

"No, too late. Don't do it now. You lawyer up now, you better believe they're going to start taking an interest in your story, a very close interest."

She nodded, assailed by his logic.

"You did your civic duty," Doug told her. "And that's great. You don't know anything, right?" He pressed her. "Right?"

"No, I don't."

Doug nodded, relieved, easing off. "So leave it at that. Personally? It seems to me like you're hanging on to this robbery too tight. I think you know this. It's bad, what happened to your friend. And bad, sure, what happened to you."

She was eager to cut him off. "I know, it doesn't seem . . . a robbery, okay. Masked men, guns, the van. Other people have been through so much worse—I *know* this. But it's like I'm stuck. I thought I was going to be murdered, I was going to die on the floor of the bank . . . and my life seemed wasted." She winced, frustrated that this sounded like whining. "If only I could get that morning back. Or like Davis, have it wiped away forever."

"Here's the thing," said Doug. He had put this pain into her face, maybe he could take it away again. "I'm outta my league here, I know. But I can tell you this. For a long time in my life, I was The Kid Whose Mother Left Him. That's all I was, the sum total of my existence. And it led me into a world of trouble. Right now, I think you're The Girl Who Got Robbed."

She stared, listening hard.

"Now," he went on, "I happen to like The Girl Who Got Robbed. I don't mind her at all, she looks pretty good to me. But I think she's not all that thrilled with herself."

"You're right," she said, thinking, nodding. "You're really right."

"You can get past this."

"I have to. I know." She sat up, squaring her shoulders, a harbor breeze lifting her honey-colored hair with its fingers. "I'm sorry for getting into this with you, bringing you down. I'm going to cheer up now, I promise. Grow up too. Count to three."

"One, two, three."

"Ta-da." She smiled. "Happy face."

They sat there in swaying silence, drifting away from and back toward each other.

"You know what you are, Doug?" she said. "I just figured it out. You're decent."

"Oh." Doug gripped the swing chains. "Christ, no."

"You are, and more than that—a lot of people who are decent, they were *raised* to be decent, you know? Like me—good parenting, good manners, blah, blah, blah—which is all fine and good until a little pressure comes into your life, and then you crumble like stale bread. But you—you've made mistakes, you've said as much. You're not a saint or anything, but you know how to be good. Your decency is earned, not learned."

Doug said, "I don't know how well you know me," but she mistook his discomfort for modesty.

"Can you tell I've been thinking about you?" she said.

"Oh yeah?"

She swayed a little more, bumping her seat gently against his, eyes bright, grateful, and deep. "Yeah."

17
DEMO

T HE CHARGES CRACKED LIKE a volley of gunshots from the head of the cliff, wind whisking away the smoke tails, sheets of rock dropping like a hand had opened up and let them go, sliding off the stratified face into rubble and dust.

Doug and Jem squinted at the rip and crumble, feeling the earth shudder in complaint, watching the gray dust arise. They stood near the silver-sided break wagon and the hard hats lining up for Winstons and coffees, Doug wearing a loose, long-sleeved shirt reading *Mike's Roast Beef*, Jem a white sweatshirt bearing a peeling green shamrock under the arched word *T O W N I E S*. The hood was snug over Jem's head and ears, emphasizing his small skull. Both carried their old yellow helmets under their arms, like blue-collar jet pilots.

"Look at you," Jem said.

Doug watched a hard hat cup a blue pill into his mouth like it was his morning vitamin. The break wagon also sold speed at $3 a pop. Doug remembered the jolt of a blue with a beer back, ten or ten thirty in the morning, kicking the workday into gear. "What?"

"You."

"What?"

"All the way up here, you're in fucking La-La Land. You get laid last night?"

"Yeah. I wish."

"Anybody I know? He do you right?"

Doug smiled in spite of himself, watching the dust spreading in the distance.

"What is it, then?" said Jem. "You found Jesus or something?"

"I did. In a condo over on Eden Street. Nice place."

"Yeah, I hear he's a good carpenter. I would of thought maybe you ran into him at the Tap."

Doug went cold under the white sun. "What are you talking about?"

"Splash the bartender said he thought he saw you in there, few nights before."

"That Saturday night, all of us?"

"No, fuckhead. Recent."

A dismissive shrug, a good one. "Different Doug MacRay."

"I see. Maybe the *old* Doug MacRay, come back to us like Jesus on Eden Street. All I can say is, you *better* not be drinking on the side. I been waiting too fucking long. Your first drink back, I'm there at your elbow, or else."

Relief seeping in. "Speaking of abstinence—how's that going for you?"

"I remain pure."

"Get the fuck."

"My mother's grave."

"Yikes, that's where you do it?"

"I'm pulling two full workouts a day. Check these guns."

"Hey, cowboy—all the same to you, I'm gonna take a pass on standing here, checking out your shoulder hard-ons."

Jem studied him one-eyed in the sun. "You got laid, motherfuck. Come clean."

Doug smiled big. "I always do."

The whistle blew the all clear and Jem found his hat under his arm. "Let's go see Boner and get this shit over with."

In the distance, a demo crew in hard hats, goggles, and face masks advanced on the settling dust. Doug could smell the grit from where he was, remembering the feeling of it stopping up his pores. "You ever miss this?"

Jem twirled his helmet like he used to, the *J. Coughlin* fading on the back, the head strap inside worn to the foam. "You fucking kidding me?"

"I miss it a little. Not the commute, the bullshit, eating lunch out of a truck, fucking dust in my hair."

"You like blowing shit up."

"No. I just like watching it fall."

"Well, second thought, going at a wall with a crowbar, that wasn't so bad either. The old wrecking crew, right? Hammers, sledges, and pickaxes. Walking into some condemned building in our dusted overalls like, '*Warriors, come out to play-ayy . . .*' "

Doug shrugged. "I just liked watching it fall."

Inside the construction trailer, they waited for Billy Bona, Billy saying, "Yup . . . yeah . . . sure . . . ," into the phone and strangling the cord in his hands. Ten years before, while tearing out a condemned building alongside Doug, a falling cinder block claimed the nails of the last three fingers of his left hand. Doctors told him they would grow back twice as thick, but they never grew back at all. Now Billy was the demo foreman in his father's company and only used his helmet-less fingers for pointing at guys and signing things.

He hung up and came across to shake hands. "The original thick-dick micks."

Doug said, "Billy Boner."

Jem said, "'S'up, Little Italy?"

"You know how it is," said Boner, sliding a clipboard off his desk, "this and that, that and this. I got two minutes here, literally. What's the squeal?"

Doug said, "Highway project, huh?"

Jem was twiddling Boner's Rolodex like a kid on a visit to his dad's office. "This economy, I take it where it comes," said Boner, distracted, not liking his cluttered desk touched. "What you got? Potato famine suddenly? Coming back to do some real work?"

"Never, man," said Jem. "Just wanted to go over terms of our deal."

Boner frowned, looked at Doug, concerned. "Fuck's wrong with the deal?"

Jem held up a *Bonafide Demo* paperweight showing the Leaning Tower of Pisa. "Know what I'd like to see on this instead?" he said. "That chef from the pizza boxes, twiddling his Rollie Fingers mustache, you know? That would be good."

Boner said to Doug, "What's going on here, MacRay?"

Doug had forgotten Jem's sourness toward Boner, it had been that long. "It's all good, Billy," said Doug, dropping *Boner* for the moment. "Nothing wrong with the deal. Everything's cool."

"'Cause your guard dog here is slobbering all over my desk."

Jem smiled his smile, challenge accepted, and went around to sit in Boner's big chair, putting his mud-caked boots up on the desk. "Seat's a little hard, Boner. Your ass is much more accommodating than mine."

Boner gripped his clipboard two-handedly. "If this is some fuckin' poor man's shakedown, you can both—"

"Whoa, whoa," said Doug. "Hold on. How well you know me?"

"*Used* to know you good, Duggy. Going way back. So what the fuck?"

Doug said to Jem, "Get out from behind the man's desk," just to be polite, not really expecting Jem to move, which he didn't. Doug said to Boner, "Everything with the arrangement is going great, everything's fine. We just think we might be hearing hoofbeats, so to speak, so we wanted to come up here, make sure all our bases are covered."

"A reminder," said Jem, picking up a pad of pink phone-message slips, flipping it at Boner. Boner made no move to catch it and the pad bounced off his arm, falling to the floor.

"Not a reminder," said Doug. "A courtesy call, let you know you might have visitors coming up here with badges, questions. Or maybe not, we don't know."

"Jesus," sighed Boner, not needing this hassle.

"You been making a tiny little mint off us," said Jem, sitting up behind Boner's desk. "Keeping us on the books, paying us full sal, us kicking half back to you."

"Keeping you outta *jail,* sounds like, giving you taxable income for the IRS." He looked back at Doug. "And what, an alibi?"

"Maybe," said Doug. "But mostly just gainful employ. Our good citizenship. They got nothing pinned on us, 'cept their own ambitions. So you don't have to worry about a thing. We just didn't want anyone coming up here and throwing you, catching you off guard. All you need to do is pledge us as two of your contract guys."

"Your very best contract guys," said Jem. "Good workers and nice fellows, handsome guys. Only out sick that day."

"And then let us know. That cool, Billy?"

Boner nodded. His glance at the wall clock told Doug that Boner was busy and this was no big thing to him, which was all Doug wanted to know.

Jem said, "Boner's cool. 'Course, he's got no fucking other choice anyway."

Boner wheeled and pointed with a finger off his clipboard, sputtering. "Why you so fuckin' hot all the time, Jimmy? I mean, what the *fuck*?"

Doug explained, "He gave up jerking off."

"Yeah? Traded it for *being* a jerkoff," said Boner, having had all he could stand. "You never showed my dad any respect, you fucking hump."

"Respect?" said Jem, hands folded, still seated, too calm and comfortable. "That's all you ever showed him, fuckin' daddy's little girl. Taking over the business so he can head off down to Florida."

"Seems like you inherited your daddy's business too."

Jem bounded up and around the desk, up into Boner's face with the chair back still rocking. Doug stayed where he was, so fucking tired of it all.

"You think I'm afraid of you?" said Boner, the clipboard at his hip now. "Huh? Yeah? Well you're goddamn fucking right I'm afraid of you, you half-a-psycho." Boner backed off and picked his message pad off the floor—then whipped it at the papers on his desk, slapping down his clipboard and bouncing a pen off his phone.

He stopped, facing his vacant chair, shoulders riding his anger. "You two came here to tell me something, and now you told me, and now I've got some real fucking work to do. Guys under me who actually work for their paychecks, guys with families to feed, *earning* their salaries."

He turned back looking for some trace of shame in their faces and, failing that, banged out of the thin trailer door empty-handed.

BACK INSIDE THE FLAMER, Jem's beat-up Trans Am, driving south from Billerica to the Wendy's parking lot off the highway where Doug had left his Caprice. No tail either way, and they had been super-fucking-careful—but instead of relief, this only increased Doug's paranoia. He made a mental note to recheck his wheel wells and firewalls and poke around under the hood for tracking beacons.

Jem drove eager-eyed, tearing up the road. He tried the radio and a *Sesame Street* tune blasted out of the speakers. "Jesus *fuck*," he said, hitting Eject and tossing the tape into the backseat like it was on fire. "See that? That's why I don't fucking let her use my car. She wanted me to put a *baby* seat in back there, full-time? Yeah, like Jem's cruising around Town with that chick magnet."

He wheeled onto the highway, the white sun glaring off the gaudy blue-on-blue flame work on the hood, bouncing into Doug's eyes. Their helmets rolled around the piles of crap in back like the aggravation rattling inside Doug's head.

"So what about the Dez situation?" said Jem.

"What about it?"

"I don't like it."

"Okay."

"Of all of us, he's the weak link."

"Dez is fine, I told you."

"When's he been proven? A fucking *candy* store, even—the kid's never put gum in his pocket without paying for it. How's he gonna stand up under a grilling, told to turn us over or else? Where's his track record on that?"

Doug wasn't so annoyed that he couldn't find some truth in this.

"And what about the manager?"

"The bank manager?" said Jem.

"No, Don Zimmer. Yes, the bank manager. Said you'd have something there."

"There's nothing there. A dead end. Done."

"You think so."

"I know so. I can fucking guarantee so."

"How?"

"She checks out. Don't worry about it."

Jem switched lanes, slicing between two cars with maybe six inches to spare on either end. "So there's no need to remove her from the equation, then."

Doug turned to him, Jem's stupidity as blinding as the sun. "Are you fucking *kidding* me?"

"I'm just saying."

"You're just saying what? What are you just saying? You're a fucking contract killer now?"

Jem shrugged, playing tough guy. "I don't like loose ends."

Doug had to take a breath and remind himself that this was all just talk, part of the movie playing twenty-four hours a day on the cable channel in Jem's head. "Listen, De Niro. You need to start jerking off again. And I mean fucking pronto, like right now, pull over, I'll wait. Fuck's gotten into you? The music all night—"

"What, is it too loud?"

"Is it too *loud*?"

"Awright, whatever, what the fuck."

"Turn down the volume in your head, kid. What is it? Vampire bite you or something?"

"Just trying to be careful."

"Let me be the paranoid one, all right? Let me do the worrying. Cool it."

"Fuckin' . . . it's cool, man. It's cool."

They were quiet for a while, Doug's head ringing, Jem rolling down his window to spit.

"So, Gloansy's wedding, huh?"

"Yeah," said Doug.

"Who you taking? Got anything set up?"

Doug shook his head. "I'm nowhere on that one."

"Yeah." Then: "Krista has no date neither."

Doug stared ahead, letting it pass.

"What else're you doing with your time?"

"Why, what the fuck? What are you poking at me for?"

"Poking at you?" said Jem. "What are you talking about?"

"I don't know—what are *you* talking about?"

"See—this is you between jobs." Jem nodded like one of them was crazy and it wasn't him. "Time off for you is no fucking good, time off for *any* of us." He palmed the wheel, pushing the car ahead. "Speaking of time. Mac, last weekend—he was asking for you."

"Yeah?" said Doug, wondering where the hell this was suddenly coming from. "Yeah, how's he been?"

"Good, good. Says he wants you to come by sometime."

"Yeah. I been meaning to."

"Says he don't like to ask, but he wants to see your face. Wants to know what's up, I guess. I said I'd tell you."

"Sure," said Doug, already angling to duck it. There was a latent smudge on his side window, brought out by the sun: a little round handprint, dead center, and Doug wondered what the fuck Shyne was doing riding around in the front seat with no belt on.

Jem said, "You know I get the fuckin' biggest kick outta your dad."

"Yeah," said Doug, thinking, *You're the only one*—his eyes staying trained on the oily ghost of a tiny little uncreased palm.

18
DATING THE VIC

"**B**UT HOW DID YOU KNOW?" asked Claire.

"Know what?" said Frawley.

"'Mortgage or sick kid,' how would you know that?"

"Ah." Frawley rubbed his cheek, a ruminative habit he had adopted since getting stained. The dye had faded to a coppery orange, like misapplied self-tanner. "The smell of coffee on the note. The way his first, failed attempt went down. And then just looking at him there, facedown in the playground. A kind of desperation I've seen before."

They were seated away from the bar inside the Warren Tavern, over low-key drinks and apps. The place was crowded on a weeknight, and Frawley wondered how a colonial-era pub suddenly got so tony.

Claire wore a cream top with the sleeves shrugged up. She sipped her white wine, concerned for the robber. "And that's five years in jail?"

"Federal sentencing guidelines are pretty strict. Between forty and fifty months for a first-time offender, then add on maybe a year and a half for the bomb threat. But I spoke with the assistant district attorney and recommended that only state charges be brought. It's not up to me, but that would be less of a smack. This yo-yo might even be able to put his life back together after that."

She said, "That's because you're a nice guy."

"No, it's because he's not the kind of bad guy I'm after. Note-passing is the dumbest of crimes. Broad daylight, plenty of witnesses, and you're photographed in the act. Hello. Fifteen hundred dollars against four or five years in prison. Banks attract dumb, desperate people." An excuse to reach across the table and touch her forearm. "Bandits, not employees."

She smiled. "Thanks for clarifying."

"A professional crew that's ready to hurt people, put them in the hospital—that's what I'm here for. Not the sad case sitting in a Dunkin' Donuts one morning, thinking his life is ending."

She noticed him rubbing his cheek again. "Does that itch?"

"Only psychologically. I'm like half-cop, half-criminal. You should see the looks I get."

She smiled and Frawley thought he was doing well. "So, why banks?" she said. "What is it about banks and you?"

"Have you seen those ads for the tornado movie coming out, *Twister*?"

"Sure, with the cow flying across the screen?"

"I grew up—well, I grew up all over. My mother had this knack for meeting men just as they were about to move out of state, and she would move with them, only to split up a few months later, leaving us out on our own again. We didn't have much and kept losing things in the breakups. She carried around with her a couple of items she called her 'treasure.' Some photographs of her as a girl, her grandmother's Bible, letters she had saved, my birth certificate, her wedding ring. So every new town we pitched a tent in, the first thing she'd do would be to go down to the bank and rent a safe-deposit box, store her treasure there. It became a routine—new town, new bank, new box. When I was eight or maybe nine, we were living in Trembull, South Dakota, and a tornado hit. Flattened the town, killed eight. We rode it out on the floor of a fruit cellar—my mother blanketing me, screaming the Lord's Prayer—and when it was over, we climbed back upstairs, and the upstairs was gone. Roof, walls, everything. The entire neighborhood, people crawling out of their cellars like worms after a hard rain. Everything gone or moved and tipped over on its side. We all just followed the path of destruction into the center of town. Only, the center was gone too. Just a war zone of cracked lumber and debris—except for one thing. The bank vault. The bank building itself was gone, but that silver vault remained standing. Like a door to another dimension."

Her frown had a smile behind it. "I hate people who know exactly who they are, and why they want what they want."

"The next day the manager came and opened it up, and there was my mother's treasure, safe and sound."

"And where's your mother now?"

"Arizona. Fourth husband, a cattle auctioneer. The guy answers the phone, I can't understand a word he says. But of the thirty-four states she's resided in, Arizona's the first she's lived in twice. So I'm thinking, this guy, maybe he's finally the one."

Claire smiled. "Explains why you're not married yet."

"I don't know. I think it's more because I've moved around so much with the Bureau. And hope to be moving again soon."

"To?"

"The top job for a bank robbery agent is Los Angeles. Boston may be the armored-car-robbery capital of the world, but L.A. is the bank-robbery capital, no contest. One out of every four bank jobs in the country goes down there. And with the freeway system, they have to do a lot more with tracking devices, gadgets, gizmos. Charlestown here, their methods are quaint compared to those out West."

Claire nodded, swirling the last sip of wine around the bottom of her glass. He wanted her to have another. "So funny to me that you live here too."

"It's a great town. And I've lived all over. Great neighborhood, great people. It's just that there happens to be this ultrasmall faction, this subculture of banditry." He finished his Sam Adams. "Do we need another round?"

She looked from her glass to him. "I'm not clear on something. Is this work, or is this a date?"

He shrugged. "It's not work."

"So it's a date."

"It's a pre-date. It's appetizers, drinks."

"Because," she said, "and maybe this sounds crazy, but someone warned me that I shouldn't speak to you again without a lawyer."

"Wait—someone from Charlestown, right?"

"How'd you know?"

He dropped his voice a little. "Well, that's the other thing here, this 'Code of Silence.' Born out on the docks, I guess, with bootlegging and longshoremen. Something like fifty murders committed in this town over the past twenty years, many of them with witnesses, and yet only twelve have been solved. The code was, 'Talk to the cops, you're dead, your entire family is dead.' But it's all unraveling now. People testifying against each other, rushing to cut deals. Ugly."

She nodded, only half-listening. "Do you consider me a suspect?"

Who was feeding her this? "What makes you say that?"

"I don't know. The questions you asked me at my parents' house. It never occurred to me that you might think . . ."

"Well, early on, I had a kidnapping that resulted in the bank manager being released unharmed. Add to that the fact that she lived in Charlestown, and—where are you getting all this?"

"Nowhere."

Nowhere? "Would I have asked you out here if I suspected you?"

"I don't know. Maybe."

"Not if I'd wanted a conviction, evidence that would hold up in court."

That seemed to satisfy her. She sat back, distracted. "Honestly, at this point? I almost hope you never catch them. In terms of testifying and all that. I just want to put this thing behind me and move on."

"Well," Frawley told her, "I am going to catch them. Don't sweat the testimony. Even if I bagged them tomorrow, court's easily a year or two down the line. And with twenty-year federal mandies for repeat offenders using firearms in the commission of a violent felony, on top of whatever they draw for the crimes—those are tantamount to life sentences. And believe me, once you see these bozos in court, see their faces—oh, yeah, shit." He searched his jacket pockets. "Almost forgot. Just a moment of investigatory stuff here."

He handed her the color copy he had made from a beat-up library book about the history of the Boston Bruins. It showed a pair of melancholy eyes inside a goalie mask covered with hand-drawn scars.

Frawley said, "That's Gerry Cheevers. Bruins goalie from the Bobby Orr era."

She stared as though he had handed her a photograph of the bandits themselves. "Why those scars?"

Dino's explanation became his own. "Every puck shot Cheevers took off his face mask, he drew the stitch scar over the resulting dent. His trademark."

She looked a moment longer before handing it back, not relaxing until he had returned it to his pocket. "Hate hockey," she said.

"Not so loud," he joked. "Ice hockey and bank robbing are the two year-round sports here in Charlestown."

Their server returned. Claire said, "I'll take a coffee. Decaf."

Frawley held up two fingers, masking his disappointment. "So what do you say we try a real date? Go see *Twister* or something?"

She nodded agreeably. "That might be great."

"Okay." He ran that around his head again. "Might be?"

"Could be. Would be."

"Uh-huh. But?"

"But I'm seeing someone else too."

"Okay."

"I just thought it would be fair to let you know." She smiled then, looking a little giddy and perplexed. "Why am I so popular all of a sudden? It's like getting boobs again. Two interesting guys I meet, after this robbery—what happened? What changed?"

"Is this the piano mover?"

Her surprised look said that she had forgotten telling him about that.

"The guy you met in a Laundromat." Frawley smiled. "I thought you stood him up."

"What's so funny?"

"Nothing."

"You don't want to hear this, but he's helping me."

"Good. That's good."

"He's not a piano mover."

"What's wrong with piano movers?" Their coffees came, and the check. Frawley wasn't worried. "Competition's good. Raises the bar."

She smiled at him, uncertain. "So there aren't any FBI rules about this?"

"Against dating the vic? No. Just a personal rule I abide by."

"Which is?"

"Never, ever do it," he said, laying down his credit card and a smile.

DINO DROVE A COP'D-OUT 1993 Ford Taurus, the police blues under the grille only noticeable if you were looking for them or if the sun hit them just right. It wasn't an undercover car like Frawley's staid Bureau Cavalier, but other than the whip antenna curling off the trunk, it was good enough for cruising the Town incognito.

The police radio squawked an "odor of gas" call—the attending patrolman acknowledging the 911 dispatcher not with *Affirmative* or *Roger* or the military *Over,* but rather with the distinctly Boston *I have it*—as Dino and Frawley rolled out from under the Tobin Bridge, passing two Housing Authority sedans idling driver-to-driver at the end of Bunker Hill Street.

"I've told them," said Frawley. "I've said, you know, just get me an apartment here, set it up. Nothing fancy—just let me work this square mile exclusively, give me the *time,* give me the *space.* Let me play the *part.* I'd be a yuppie Serpico, you know? A yuppie Donnie Brasco. This town, the way it is—the streets are so narrow, so tight. Any change is noticed, any deviation from the norm. You can't surv a house here, even if you have the manpower—even if there's a vacant apartment right across the street and your target's religion forbids window shades—because the people here, they're too *involved.* Crack open a beer and a guy three doors down gets thirsty. You gotta be part of the landscape."

"But they won't do it."

"Boston would okay it. The SAC could be persuaded, but not D.C. People not from around here have a hard time understanding what a fountain of banditry this zip code is."

"Fountain of banditry," chuckled Dino. "You got a way."

The markets on lower Bunker Hill Street advertised their welfare-friendliness with window signs stating EBT Accepted, WIC Accepted. Above and to the left, the tapered spike of the monument rotated as they passed, the Town slow-roasting on an enormous granite spit.

"So what do you got on this phone company guy?" said Dino.

"Elden. Desmond Elden. What have I got? I've got nothing, that's what I've got. Guy lives with his mother, holds down a steady job, pays his taxes in full and on time, and has never spent a minute of his life in a jail cell. Goes to mass three, four times a week."

"And yet you're convinced—"

"Oh, I'm absolutely fucking positive."

"No record," said Dino. "No time in double-A ball. Jumps right into the majors."

"I don't know the backstory, but it is what it is. As for getting into it later in life, I'd offer this guy's father as Exhibit A."

"Okay, go."

"He was clean too, no record, nothing, when they found him on one of those streets we just passed, early 1980, two bullet holes in the chest. Don't have the full read, but it looks like he was a bagman, not an enforcer, more like a buffer between the street and the guys he was collecting for. Arrest bait, this guy with a clean record. Fourteen years with Edison before that."

"Gotcha."

"This guy, Elden, he'd be their tech. Spotless work record, including attendance, except for a few important dates. Such as the sick day he took the Tuesday after the marathon. Your next right."

Dino flipped on the blinker. "Okay, so it's starting to come into focus."

"Thus far, I've only made him with one other guy, ID'd from the Lakeville mugs. One Douglas MacRay."

"MacRay?" said Dino.

"Yeah, ringing a bell?"

"My age, more like plinking a triangle. Bear with me. Mac MacRay's son?"

"Bingo."

Dino licked his lips, smelling something cooking. "Okay. Big Mac's gotta be a good ten or fifteen in. Walpole, I think."

"MacRay junior last saw twenty months for ag assault. Jumped a guy in a bar, no provocation, nearly killed him. *Would* have killed him if they hadn't pulled him off. Shod foot was the deadly weapon, public intox, resisting arrest. Got out about three years ago. Note that this string we're looking at now started up about six months later."

"Hockey star, wasn't he?"

"Something like that."

"Yeah, yeah, high school hockey star, Charlestown. MacRay. Drafted, I think. Christ—was it the Bruins?"

"This is Pearl Street, where he lives now."

It was a one-way street, the one way being straight down. Frawley pointed out the worst-looking house halfway down the suicide slope. With the cars parked along the right, there was barely enough room for the midsized Taurus to squeeze through.

"See what I mean about surveillance?"

Dino watched his spacing and tried to take in the house at the same time. "Least he keeps it nice."

"Oh, it's not even his. He rents, or shares, I can't tell. The house is in two names, a sister and a brother, Kristina Coughlin and James Coughlin."

"Coughlin."

"Heard the bells that time?"

"Like Christmas morning at the Vatican. Fathers and sons, huh? What a piece of work Jackie Coughlin Sr. was. I think—I *think*—he bought it falling out of a fourth-floor window or something, a B and E. Wouldn't surprise me if he was pushed by his own partners."

Frawley remembered the bumping he had received in the cellar bar of the Tap, having matched Coughlin's foggy, more-white-than-blue eyes to his card in the Lakeville mugs. "Young Coughlin started with DUIs and race crimes in his teens and got more adventurous from there. By some miracle he's stayed clean for the past thirty months. No arrests, even served out his parole. He and MacRay went down on a bank job together in 1983, still juvees. Amateur hour, Coughlin vaulting the counter, MacRay brandishing a nail gun."

"Oh, that's nice."

"A .22-caliber construction gun loaded with staples. Guy's got a temper. Couple of months before that, he'd gotten himself drummed out of the AHL for putting another player in the hospital."

"In hockey you usually earn a bonus for that."

"Guy he fought was on his own team."

Dino snickered. "The happy-go-lucky type. What about Coughlin's sister?"

"Sister? I don't know. Haven't even looked at her."

They bottomed out on Medford and turned left. Dino said, "That makes three."

"The fourth I'm doing a little conjecture on. We know—or almost know—at least we think that they don't farm out their car jobs, because if they did, it's a good bet we'd have had a snitch by now, or at least some whispering on the wind. Coughlin was picked up on a joyriding bid in '90 or '91 with an Alfred Magloan. On his own, Magloan is a convicted car thief and a member of Local 25, does some film-crew work as a driver."

"That's pretty comprehensive work for file-checking and part-time eyeballing there, Frawl."

"I'm on them. My sense here is, they smell something. That's why they're staying clear of Elden. But I'm having enough trouble watching one, never mind all four. That's why we're in your car today."

"You think you got made?"

Frawley was reluctant to admit it. "Just being real careful. I put in for a new Bureau vehicle, but that's going to take some time."

"You want me for some weekend duty."

"Elden is the only one we've got the subpoena for, so I'm all for sticking with him. Build up some paperwork, make a case, grow it out from there."

"What about this bank Elden's been cruising? In Chestnut Hill."

"I don't know."

"Come on. Speak."

The Schrafft's building came around the corner, the firehouse, Local 25's headquarters. "Small neighborhood branch. Two exits—a busy parking lot and narrow Route 9. A small-time bank, ATM. I don't see it."

Dino signaled and turned back onto Bunker Hill Street, the opposite end, starting up toward the Heights. "So what's he doing there then?"

"I hope not distracting us."

19
SANDMAN

"**M**Y GOD!" SHE SAID, spinning around from the purple flowers she was planting in the ground.

"Hey," said Doug.

"You *scared* me! Where did you come from?" She looked around like he might have brought a surprise party with him. "What are you doing here?"

Her smile made Doug forget who and what he was, made him forget everything. "I was in the area, thought I'd take a chance."

She brushed at the browned knees of her jeans, as though he cared that they were dirty. "You spying on me?"

"Maybe just a little."

"Well, stop it and come on in here."

The gate catch was a simple wire loop. Inside, he stuck to the neat, S-shaped path of small, crunchy stones. A hello kiss would have come off too forced and awkward, too formal even. She stayed close to him as he looked around. A weathered wooden chest was open behind the bench, stocked with hand tools, fertilizer, Miracle Grow. "This is nice," he said.

"Yeah, well. . . ." She surveyed it with the backs of her wrists curled against her hips. "My perennials are perennially frustrating, and my annuals are a semiannual disappointment. Oh, and the spearmint is strangling my phlox."

"I thought I smelled gum."

"Other than that—welcome to my little patch of heaven. I was just putting in some impatiens for color. If you want to wait, I'm almost done."

"I'll sit."

His shoulders rustled some weeping-willow tendrils—and just like that he was sitting on her stone garden bench. He was in. He tried to see across to where he used to watch her from, but couldn't make it out now.

She knelt on a foam pad, facing away from him, planting and patting the rest of the flowers in a bed of overturned dirt. The lilac band of her panties showed over the stressed belt of her jeans, panties he had once picked up off the Laundromat floor.

"This is a surprise," she said.

"Time on my hands. I was in the area, and I remembered you raving about this place at dinner."

"Right. Now—were you really in the area? Or did you sort of *put* yourself in the area?"

"I put myself here, definitely."

She looked back at him over her shoulder with a smile. "Good."

"Plus I'm a big fan of flowers."

"I could tell." She returned to them. "What's your favorite kind?"

"Oh, lilac."

She reached forward, patting the soil around a short stem in the manner of one tucking in a blanket around a baby. "You can see my underwear from there, can't you."

"It's all right. I don't mind."

She didn't straighten, didn't cover up, a very simple, sexy thing, just letting it be. She finished and splashed some hose water on the beds and her own dirty hands, then packed away her tools, smoothed her hair back into a scrunchy, and took him for a stroll through the gardens.

"I have to tell you," she said, twirling a green leaf by the stem as they walked, "I did a terrible thing yesterday."

"What was that?"

"I watched a soap opera. Used to schedule my college classes around them. Anyway, there was this typically ridiculous scene where two people stand across the room from each other and talk, talk, talk, until the woman turns to the window, gazing off for her big close-up, sighing, 'Why am I falling for you?' It was so crazy and overblown, I was smiling when I turned it off. But then I got to thinking." She glanced at him. "Why *am* I falling for you?"

"Wow," he said, the words hitting him like booze.

"You're not at all my type. My girlfriends, I've told them about you, and they think it's just, like, big rebound. And I'm like—rebound from what? The robbery? I mean—are we that different? Really? I think we have more in common than we have differences."

"Agreed."

"We both love flowers."

He laughed. "Right."

"Anyway, my friends." She shook her hands like she couldn't express herself clearly. "I feel sort of estranged from them, I think maybe that's what they're picking up on. I have changed. I can feel it. They still have this, like, carelessness about them—which I sort of envy, but at the same time, I don't really understand anymore. It's scary to think that I might be, you know, leaving them behind."

"Yeah," Doug said, following this closely. "I think I know exactly what you mean."

They turned the corner at a double-wide plot with pebble paths and a big bonsai tree. A barefoot Asian woman was practicing slow-motion, invisible-wall-pushing tai chi.

"But this, you and me—it's happening too fast," said Claire. "I don't trust it. I think about you and I feel like . . . I can picture you in my mind for a second, but then you're gone. It's like I know you really well, but almost not at all. Like you're not real—like I invented you, or you invented me, some Zen thing like that. Are you real, Doug?"

"I think so."

"Because I can't root you in anything. Charlestown, I guess, but that's too vague. I don't even have your phone number. I can't call you. Or your address—no house to drive by and torment myself and wonder, 'Is he home? Is he thinking about me?' "

"You mean you want references?"

"Yes! And a look at your driver's license and another valid form of ID. I want to stand in your bathroom. I want five minutes alone in your closet. I want to know that you're not just going to turn to smoke on me someday."

"I'm not."

"And fine, I know this is stupid, it's only been two dates. I *know* that I'm crazy, okay? But I can't help this feeling that there's something . . ." She shook her head, throwing the leaf to the dirt path. "Are you married?"

Doug sputtered. "You said *married*?"

"Can't you see—you're making me ask! *Making* me embarrass myself here."

"*Married?*" he said, wanting to scoff and laugh at the same time.

"I need to know that there's water in the pool. Even if—okay, fine, even if I've already jumped, I still want to know whether or not there's water in the pool."

"There's—there's water in the pool," he said, confused.

"We could go to your apartment. You could show me where you live."

He started to say no.

"Five minutes." She showed him that many fingers, growing frantic. "So I can *plant* you somewhere in my mind, so you're not this, this sandman. I met you in a *Laundromat*, Doug MacRay. It is Doug MacRay—right?"

He couldn't give in here, and she slowed along the path, hands falling to her sides. "See, this is—now my mind is filling with possibilities."

"Whoa, what? Like centerfolds all over the walls or something? Dirty laundry hanging from the ceiling fan?"

"That's . . . *minimum*."

"I am not married." That time he did laugh, angering her.

"Neither am I," she said. "So far as you know."

"My place—" He stopped himself. "I was going to blame it on my neighbors, but that's not true, it's me, all me. See, I'm making some changes in my life"—Doug was hearing this himself for the first time—"and my place—that's the old me. Something I'm trying to fix."

She jumped on that. "But I want to see—"

"The old me? No, you don't. Would you want me poking around your college dorm room to find out about you now?"

"But, wait—"

"Listen. I just grew up. Just a little while ago. The day I met you, maybe. Already, I've turned over so many bad cards for you."

"And I'm still here."

"And you're still here. So what I'm asking for now is, please—let me work on trying to impress you for a change. Please."

She nodded, unconvinced.

Doug made a pretend move for his wallet. "I have a license and a Blockbuster card."

"Just tell me, Doug." She reached out and gripped his wrists. "Tell me if I'm making a mistake. I will still make the mistake. That's no problem. I just want to know now."

"I'm saying there is no—"

"*Aaah!*" Her tiny scream startled a nearby family of ducks. She pulled on his arms, staring into his eyes. "Yes or no. Am I making a mistake here, or not?"

Doug looked down at her hands manacling his wrists. He knew

what he wanted to say, and he knew what she was waiting for him to say. All he had to do was say it.

"No."

She stared hard, then let go of him, pointing a finger at his chest. "You promised."

Doug nodded. "Okay."

A bird fluttering to a nearby trellis caught her eye, and she watched it peck at some vines, softening her mood a bit. "So much agitation around me these days," she said. "Stuff swirling. But with you, when I'm alone with you—there's a silence, there's peace. You make all that other stuff go away." The bird disappeared to a high branch. "But again—whether any of this is real or not, I have no idea."

"Maybe if we just stop talking about it. Maybe if we just let it be."

"I'm not looking for a guarantee. Just good faith."

Doug nodded, feeling better about it now himself. "And that's what I gave you."

She relented then, turning to start back, one hand finding its way to the pocket of her jeans, the other into his hand. "Do you think that was our first fight?"

"Was it?"

"Maybe just my first freak-out."

Relief filled him like breath. "Our first *discussion,* maybe."

"That's it, a *discussion.*" She swung their joined hands a little. "I don't even think true fights are possible between a couple until sex enters the equation."

"Yeah," said Doug at first. "Wait. Is that a vote for fighting, or . . . ?"

"A relationship filled only with firsts. Wouldn't that be the best? No past, no history to worry about, things moving too fast. You and me up on the rooftop, over and over again. Everything light and new."

"We could do that."

"Could we? Every date our first?"

"Why not?" He let go of her hand. "Hey, I'm Doug."

She smiled. "Claire. Nice to meet you."

They shook hands, then Doug looked at his empty palm, shrugging. "Nah. No chemistry."

She pushed him away, laughing, then grabbed his hand again, hooking her arm around his, pulling him close.

* * *

CANESTARO'S WAS A PIZZERIA and bistro with café seating on the park end of Peterborough Street. Nice without the Chart House finery, no table linen, butter with the bread instead of oil. He was comfortable here. With the sun still peeking over the high wall of apartment buildings lining the other side of the street, they claimed one of the sidewalk tables and split a pizza, half 'roni, half chicken and broccoli. Echoes of Fenway Park reached them from two streets away, the announcer droning, "Vaughn. First base, Vaughn."

Claire was better by the time the food came, and the meal passed as the best ones do, offering few great revelations but constant little connections, two people dining on each other's character, curious and gentle as nibbling fish. Then she said something about his mother that threw him. "Just that, how, whenever you talk about your mother leaving, it's like she *escaped* from you and your father. As opposed to, well—deserting you."

"Yeah," he said, surprised both by the change in topic and the observation itself, never having thought of it that way. "Guess you're right."

"Why?"

"I guess," he said, "because it's true."

"But you were six years old. How can you blame yourself?"

"No, I hear you."

"No one ever told you what she was going through? There must have been some signs. . . ."

"No one told me anything about my mother. Not my father, that's for sure. But that's also because, pretty much, he was the problem."

"How so?"

Cars rolled past while he deliberated. "Well," he said, "you're not gonna like it."

"What do you mean, *I'm* not gonna like it?"

The strangest thing was, he wanted to tell her this. It amazed him how honest he wanted to be, how dry he felt under the broad umbrella of the lie. "You know how you asked me one time about Charlestown, bank robbers?"

She just looked at him, waiting for him to say something other than what she was thinking.

"Yeah," said Doug, unable to spare her. "I didn't say anything because . . . well, because."

"My God. I never thought . . . I'm so sorry—"

"No, no." Doug grunted a harsh laugh. "*You're* not the sorry one.

Doesn't matter to me, I'm used to it. I didn't say anything because of you."

She looked off down the street, grappling with this.

"Two years after my mother left us, he drew a twenty-one-month prison sentence, meaning I drew twenty-one months in a foster home. I was eight. I'll never forget when he got out, how he made out like he was the hero, rescuing me. I was sixteen when he went up again, and that time the bank took our house. I moved in with a friend's mother who was basically raising me anyway." He shrugged and took a deep breath, looking at his pizza. "That's my tale of woe. No one ever tells me about my mother. But between my father, being who he was, living like an outlaw, and me there, a little hydrant-sized version of him—I think it was probably too much for her. Probably her or us, you know? In her mind, I think she had no choice. I always assume she went off and started up another family somewhere, and she's happier there. I don't blame her. But—I wouldn't mind talking about something else either."

It was dizzying to speak of such things. Dizzying and freeing at the same time.

"So many of my friends," said Claire, after a respectful silence. "They pick the wrong guy, again and again." A cheer from the ball-park crowd reached them like a cry of attack from a distant battlefield. "I wonder why so many girls seem dead set on picking out a guy who's bound to make them unhappy."

"I don't know," said Doug, careful here. "Is it that, or are they picking out someone they think they can help? Maybe someone they can save?"

She poked around her side salad, considering a tomato wedge. "But how often does that happen, right? What's the success rate there?" She declined the tomato, laying it back on her dish. "And why aren't there more *guys* out there looking for *women* to save?"

Doug shrugged. "Maybe there are."

Claire looked him over, his face, and she smiled. "You are helping me, you know. It's so bizarre, the random way we met. Almost like you were *sent* here to help me."

Doug nodded, sincere. "I want to help you." Then he opened his hands to indicate the pizza, the restaurant, the fading day. "I'm having a good time. A really good time."

She pulled her napkin from her lap and dropped it on the table, pushing back her chair. "Good. Then you'll miss me while I'm gone."

After some confusion at the door with an exiting waitress, Claire disappeared inside to the bathroom and Doug sat back. The sun was just slipping behind the apartment row, a wall of shadow reaching across the street. Organ music played from the ballpark, distorted and warbling with echo. He tipped his chair back until it hit the pointy tips of the wrought-iron fencing and looked up at the sky, the smoky contrail of a jet plane. He ruffled his hair with his hand and his mind unwound, following one of those hopscotching strings of reason, wondering what they would do next, anticipating the bill, thinking about how much clean cash he had left, remembering Foxwoods and how long he had to drive every time he needed to wash currency. If only there were an Indian casino someplace where he could go and wash his soul.

He set the front two feet of his chair back down on the sidewalk terrace and pulled his money roll from his jeans pocket. As he was counting it, something jabbed into the back of his neck, and at first he grinned, thinking it was Claire. Then he remembered the short fence and realized it had to be someone off the street.

"Gimme all ya money," said a low voice.

Doug tensed, his adrenaline response delayed by the friendly street setting, the other diners eating calmly, the cars rolling past.

The stickup man appeared next to him in a white nylon Red Sox jersey untucked over jeans, and small, stupid, syrup-lens sunglasses: Jem with a white-lipped smirk.

"I froze you, fothermucker."

Doug sat up with a hard glance at the pizzeria door. The adrenaline arrived and he started to stand out of his chair before stopping himself.

"What're you doing here?" said Jem, pulling off his shades to scan up and down Peterborough, then hanging them on the top button of his shirt and stepping over the fence, dropping into Claire's seat across from Doug.

"What?" said Doug, lost, another cheat at the door.

"Chicken and broccoli?" Jem scooped up the slice Claire had been eating, bit into it. "Fuck is *this*? Who you here with?" Smiling, having fun.

"No one," said Doug—the strangest, most feeble lie.

"No one, huh?" said Jem, reaching for her lemonade glass. He put his lips on her straw and sucked, and Doug's insides went icy. "'S'up with you?"

Jem looked straight enough, his eyes lacking their doomsday blur, maybe only three or four beers in. The door was still closed. Doug peeled off two twenties and spilled them on the table, making to stand. He'd explain it to her later. "Wanna get outta here?"

But Jem stayed hunkered over his slice, waving him back down. "I'm cool, take your time." He gobbled the slice up to the crust. "But who puts fuckin' broccoli on a pizza?"

The door opened and Claire stepped back outside, and Doug went deaf.

Claire slowing, strange. Smiling at Doug, but odd, walking up to the man sitting in her chair.

Jem gnawing on crust, oblivious. Looking up. Standing, not shocked.

Hi, Claire's lips say.

Hey, say Jem's, still chewing. Not much taller than her, but broad, all shoulders and arms and neck. Guess I'm in your seat.

Surrendering the chair with his jerk-gentleman flourish. Standing behind her now, grinning at Doug. The jaw of his small head, chewing.

This was no chance meeting. Suddenly Doug was no longer intimidated, only angry. The same adrenaline surge, a different state of mind.

Claire also looking at Doug, awkward. She gave up waiting for him and turned to Jem to introduce herself, offering her hand, sound roaring back into Doug's head.

"I'm Claire. Claire Keesey."

"Jem." He took her hand, a perfunctory up-and-down shake.

"Jim?"

"Jem," he said. "Just Jem."

She nodded, turning again to Doug for help.

"I'm a friend of this loser right here," Jem told her. "He lives with me. Not *with me,* domestic partners, but above me, my house."

"Oh?" she said.

A snake's grin as Jem held her chair for her. Claire sat as offered, staring across the wire table at mute Doug.

Jem retreated to a chair at the end of the table. "Yeah, I came down here to catch the ball game, and what do I see but the Shamrock parked around the corner. Thought I'd walk the block, you know, check up on this guy." Grin. "Gotta keep tabs, always."

Claire said, "The Shamrock?"

"His machine. Scoundrel, this guy is. Never breathed a word. The secrets he can keep."

Claire took them in together. "You two have been friends a long time?"

"No, only since second grade," said Jem. "Like brothers, everyone says. Huh, Duggy?"

Worlds colliding. Doug sat still, there and not there at the same time.

"I'm sorry," said Claire, "did you say your name was Jim, or Gem?"

"Ah, both actually. A combination. You might think it's because of the family jewels. These ones up here." He pointed out the grinning blue-white marbles of his eyes. "But the truth is—Duggy knows this—truth is, that's what the teachers would say when they passed me off to each other, shuttling me around by the scruff of my neck. 'Here's this one, he's a real gem.' And Jimmy, Gem, it kinda sticked."

She wore that distant smile people get when they're evaluating someone. "A troublemaker, huh?"

"Oh, the worst. What do you do for yourself there, Claire?"

It was like watching a movie—Claire taking a slow-mo sip of lemonade through the straw Jem had just sucked on.

"I work in a bank," she told him. "Just around the corner from here, one street over. Kenmore Square."

"Hey, wait. The BayBanks?" Jem pointed at Doug, then back at Claire. He even snapped his fingers. "Wasn't that the one . . . ?"

"Yes," she said. "The robbery."

"Ha. I don't know what made me remember that." He glanced at Doug. "So how'd you two kids meet?"

Claire looked to Doug to tell the tale—to say something, anything—but he could not. "A Laundromat," she said, concerned.

"Laundromat, huh? This guy stealing bras again? Seriously, your socks get mixed up? Love among the bleach, huh?"

Doug dead-staring at Jem now. Not a crack anywhere in Jem's grinning facade.

"Like I said, I was gonna go pick up some cheap seats off a scalper, root-root-root for the home team. Guys interested? Duggy? What do you say?"

Claire looked at Doug, but Doug's eyes stayed on Jem.

"No?" said Jem. "That's awright anyway. Hate being the third wheel, you know?" He smiled at them both, then formed a gun with his fingers, shooting it at Doug. "Don't trust a word he says, Claire. What kinda lies he been telling you?"

Claire watching Doug now. "Wait," she said. "Do you mean he's not really an astronaut?"

Jem pointed her out to Doug. "Hey, that's quick, that's spunk. Very good. No, but, yeah, we are both in the space program, so if you got any friends interested in that stuff, who also happen to be red-heads and a little bit on the easy side . . ."

"I will let them know."

"You do that, cool. She's awright, Duggy. Oh, hey." He patted the table before he stood. "Don't get too used to this here, your leisure, loverboy. We got some more work coming our way."

Claire said, "You two work together, too?"

"Told you, we're tighter than tight. Used to tell each other *every*-thing."

"You're a sky-maker too?"

"That's us. Another takedown job. My Duggy here, he loves to watch 'em fall."

The smile vanished a moment under his dead eyes, and then just as fleetly reemerged. He stepped over the fence onto the sidewalk. "You watch out for this one now, Claire. Remember what I said— pure trouble."

Jem slapped Doug hard on the shoulder and took off down the street in a bobbing saunter, replacing the shades on his face. Claire watched him go, her eyes falling to Doug, who was still staring at the empty chair.

"He seems nice," she said flatly.

"That's being polite."

"What is wrong, Doug? You were scaring me."

"I wasn't ready for you to meet him yet."

"Is that what you were talking about—the old you?"

"Yeah." Doug still staring at the empty chair. "That was some of it."

"What's up with his eyes?"

Doug could think of no way to answer that question.

"Are you okay?" she said. "Going to be?"

"Sure," he said, surfacing, looking around, seeing his twenties still on the table. Claire reached for her lemonade again, but this time Doug took the glass from her hand. She stiffened, watching him.

"You want to be alone?" she said.

He was alone. Jem had just seen to that.

20
WORKOUT

T HE MORNING WAS WET, the rising sun burning off shadows and dampness, raising street steam. Through the cat's cradle of power and phone wires, falling to eye level as Sackville Street plunged headlong into the Mystic, a barge was being unloaded by tall, pecking cranes. Gulls coasted overhead, dipping and swirling around Doug's mother's house, threatening to shit.

When his father had first lost the house, Doug was so pissed he didn't come around for years, avoiding Sackville Street altogether. The life he was leading then, that of a drinking man, offered little solace, his mind stewing in boyhood memories and associations, rather than drawing on their strength. But during his stay at MCI Norfolk, all thoughts of home, of the Town, centered around his mother's house. Not the Monument, not Pearl Street, not the rink. Her house was the first place he visited after his release. The Town was his mother. The Town had raised him. This house was her face, watching over him. These streets were her arms, holding him close.

Acting impulsively had been the hallmark of Doug's drinking years, and never had it come to any good. He always wound up hurting people. How had he thought this was going to end any differently?

It was the lottery mentality. Something he had been working so hard to suppress these past three years: the all-or-nothing play, going after that "marquee score." It was something else he had inherited from the Town, like his eyes and his face: a gambler's dream of that one sweet score that would change everything forever.

He preached this to the others about banks: Don't be greedy. Don't overstep, don't overreach. *Get in, get the money, get out.* Now he had to take his own advice.

The thought of Jem standing behind her at the pizzeria—like a flickering image-echo of the two of them at the Kenmore Square vault, a couple waiting for the elevator—gripped his heart like a fist. It crystallized the danger Doug had invited into her life, as well as his own. Staying away meant keeping Jem away from her and the G away from him. No more daydreams about healing Claire Keesey, or magically absolving himself. The best thing he could do for her now, the only thing, as well as for himself, was to let her go.

THE GLASS PANE RATTLED in the front door as Doug entered, heading upstairs to Jem's before realizing the music he heard was pounding in the basement, not on the second floor. He turned and went outside, walking along a weedy stripe of cracked cement to the backyard bulkhead.

The stone cellar was dank, the floor moist and brown, tears of condensation glistening in the corners. The clank of steel on steel—Jem always smacked the weight plates together, he was there to make some noise—died against the damp walls, a discordant counterpoint to the soar and crash of Zep's "Kashmir."

Jem was on his back, doing presses on the old, overweighted machine. The cables squealed, the bottom rails rusty and fuzzed with mildew from cellar floodings.

He finished and sat up, fire-faced, the long veins in his forearms like blue snakes feeding under his skin. "Hey," he said, hopping off the bench, "check it out, I just picked these up." Three thumping speakers were set on shoulder-high stands around the machine like cameras on tripods. "Wireless," he said, moving his hands around one like a magician demonstrating a levitation trick. "Receives from my stereo upstairs. Three bills each, but *damn*." He cranked the volume to demonstrate, head jerking to the beat atop his thickened neck, forgetting or simply not caring that any metal inside the speakers would be oxidized within a matter of weeks. "Fuckin' *rocks,* man."

Unlike his speakers, Jem was wired. It was the buzz of lifting and maybe something more. He turned the music back down and boosted a curling bar, balancing two wide, fifty-pound plates and a couple of twenties. "Get changed and come back down, we'll hit it serious." He started a set of preacher curls, his face filling with blood.

This was not the welcome Doug had expected. Jem coming off friendly and pretending nothing was wrong was scarier than him taking a sledge to the weeping walls.

"Last night," said Doug.

"Was that a fucking outrage or what?" said Jem, breaking off his reps, bouncing the bar on the floor. "Motherfuckin' Wakefield, I hate knuckleballers. Straight-ball pitcher starts to lose his stuff in the sixth, you can see it, his speed, his control. Funny-ball pitchers lose their stuff? It's like a trapdoor opened. Ball stops moving, and now they're serving up fucking gopher balls to free-agent millionaires."

"Who you following, Jem? Me or her?"

Still the poker face. "Told you, kid, I made the Shamrock out on Boylston, parked outside 'BCN. Which is fucked-up, by the way. Somebody take that primo shit off your hands, leave a thank-you note taped to the meter."

"You got something to say, say it now."

Jem smiled past him to the near speaker. "Don't know, kid," he said, turning down the tunes. "See—I think that's *my* line here."

Doug sniffed, shifted his weight. "Told you I was working on things. Making sure we were clear."

"Yeah. And maybe it started out that way." Jem tightened the wrist straps on his lifting gloves. "Then again, you grabbed her license from me pretty fast."

"That's bullshit."

"Is it, yeah? I mean, she's awright, don't get me wrong. I had my hand on her ass too, at the vault." He looked up. "Though I guess you broke that up too, didn't you."

"The fuck are you talking about?"

"You tell me you're workin' a scam here, I'll say, 'Cool.' 'Cause that's something I *get*. That's something makes *sense* to me. But anything else, and I'd say we got us a problem here."

Doug tried going on the attack. "That was stupid, you coming around like that. A stupid play. What'd you think—you were embarrassing me or something? You could of come to talk to me alone. I was keeping her separate from you guys—but especially you, assgrabber. She remembers anyone, it's gonna be the guy who took her for a ride."

"You always talk about Boozo's crew and how reckless they were, like maniacs, crazy for action. Then you go off making googly eyes at the one person—the *one*—who could give the G anything on us. Oh, but I'm a fucking moron." A Jem smile to go along with the Jem shrug. "Hey, thanks for your protection."

"You're welcome."

"And no, I didn't tell the others yet. Only because it would flip them the fuck out, and they're skittish enough already. Plus your boyfriend, the Monsignor, he'd be so brokenhearted jealous. Besides—there's nothing to tell, right?"

"I told you, I got from her what I wanted."

"Yeah? It any good?"

Doug frowned. "I'm saying, it's done. Over."

Jem squinted to see him better. "Hey, guess what? By the way, me and that assistant manager? We went out hankie shopping together last week. Yeah, I didn't think it was all that important to tell you."

"If that's your fucking point, then you made it."

"I'm a fucking porcupine with points. You worry me, kid. Seeing her on the side, away from us? That's like a move, brother. Says that to me. Us or her."

"Bullshit."

"I don't see any room for overlap there. Tell me I'm wrong."

Doug had always been the only one able to handle Jem. When things got tight, he could pull that brother-withholding-love shit on him and Jem would always come around, settle down. Now everything was out of balance. Now Jem was sitting on all the power.

"Awright," Jem said, flexing out his lumpy arms, nodding. "Then we can get started on this movie caper."

Too soon, but now Doug couldn't say no.

Jem read his silence with a jacked, hungry smile. "You made anybody on your tail? I haven't."

"Somebody was watching Dez's house."

"*Was*. I think we're ready to put ourselves back in play."

"Then Dez has to sit this one out."

"Fine. And actually dandy too."

"But he still gets his quarter take."

Jem eyed Doug, taking his measure. The shrug and the smile arrived together. "Fuckin' whatever. All ends up in the collection box at St. Frank's anyhow, right? Catholic charity, bring us some luck. So long as this gig comes together *quick*. That means no fucking stalling. And don't tell me you ain't been rolling this around your mind, 'cause I won't believe it. I bet you got a mark already picked out. Hell—you maybe even got a plan floating around in there."

Maybe Doug did. Maybe this was exactly what he needed right now, something to occupy his mind. Something to bring them all back together, to the way things used to be.

21
CLOCKING IT

BRAINTREE IS A SUBURB south of Boston where the Southeast Expressway out of the city splits in two: west toward the Maine-to-Florida Interstate 95, and east along Route 3, a state highway riding south to the flexed arm of Cape Cod. Braintree's draw for city kids of the late 1970s and 1980s was the South Shore Plaza, one of the first enclosed shopping malls in the region, a quick bus trip via the MBTA Red Line stop at Quincy Adams. A hobby shop that sold exploding rockets, a B. Dalton that stored overstock *Playboy*s under tables in the back of the store, the tobacconist C. B. Perkins that also sold lighters and knives, Recordtown, and the suburban girls that roamed the mall in packs and pairs—plus a movie theater, a detached two-screen job next to a Howard Johnson, known as the Braintree Cinema.

Across the street from the mall, Forbes Road was a thin thoroughfare curling wide around the castlelike Sheraton Tara Hotel and the South Shore Executive Park. The road came into view of the highway there, tailing off along the bottom of a blasted rock cliff. A narrow, two-lane offshoot named Grandview Road climbed steeply to the summit of the mount where, surrounded by a few acres of blacktop parking, the old Braintree Cinema had reopened in 1993 as a brand-new multiscreen General Cinemas complex known as The Braintree 10.

Across an eight-lane highway gorge was another cliff road, set on the edge of the Blue Hills Reservation, studded with industrial parks and office buildings. From there the big-signed movie theater looked like a temple above a ravine of automobiles.

An isolated mark. Easy highway access. Secluded vantage points.

The second most important part of the job, after the getaway, is target selection. Once you commit to a target, the details that follow shape themselves to the task at hand.

* * *

You PARK WITH THE other nine-to-fivers in front of the faceless office building next to the movie theater at the top of Grandview. Behind the building is a wood that descends into a residential area across from the shopping plaza, and there is a neglected fire road there, its entrance blocked by two craggy boulders. This will be your emergency escape route. If everything else goes to hell, you know that you can take to the trees on foot, dump your weapons and strip down to street clothes, and cross to a car parked at the mall before K-9 units and State Police helicopters hunt you down.

Your Bearcat 210 scanner crackles underneath the newspaper, jammed between the two front seats. Field glasses wait in the glove, with the bird-watching guide as their excuse, but you won't need the nocs today. Your position is too good: a side view of the movie-theater parking lot between low shrubs, the morning crows picking at pretzel bites and Raisinets.

The only two cars in the lot appear empty. A navy blue Cressida putters in after 10 A.M., parking on the side near the trash cage. The manager locks his car, uses his key in the side entrance door under swooping, popcorn-loving seagulls, and you clock it.

Seagulls and crows, that's all you have until 11:15, when a couple of rattling imports pull in: the weekday crew, mostly older people, part-timers. You clock it.

First showing of any movie that day will be at 12:20. Late-Monday-morning pickup time means no crowd control, no citizen heroes, minimal witnesses.

At 11:29, a white Plymouth Neon rolls in, parking at the wood railing along the front edge of the lot. A guy wearing sneakers and a ponytail gets out, climbs onto the roof of his car, and sits there cross-legged. He opens a sandwich and a yogurt, eating lunch while looking across the highway at the serene Blue Hills.

At 11:32, the can rolls in. You clock it, committing the time to memory but nothing to paper—no evidence in case you get pulled over.

The armored truck rumbles in steady on oversized wheels. You recognize it as a Pinnacle truck. Pinnacle's colors are blue and green.

The can rolls right up to the front and parks in the fire lane at the stairs to the lobby. Its lone rear door faces you as the truck idles.

Nothing happens for one minute.

The passenger door opens and the courier guard, also known as the messenger or hopper, steps out with the heel of his hand on the butt of his belt-holstered sidearm. He wears an open-collared, police-blue shirt with his identification hanging alligator-clipped to one of the collar points, the Pinnacle patch sewn onto his right shoulder, an oversized silver badge pinned to his breast pocket.

He is middle-aged, portly but strong, sporting a thick, white brush mustache and walking determinedly around to the rear doors. The brim of his police-style cap sits low over his eyes. No bulletproof vest. Vests are expensive and Pinnacle neither supplies nor requires them.

You pay close attention to his movements. You absorb the routine.

The courier knocks twice on the right rear door. The driver inside unlocks it with the push of a button, and the courier pulls on the handle.

Your Bearcat is silent. No radio traffic on Pinnacle's radio frequencies. This is normal.

From the cargo area, the courier pulls out a two-wheeled dolly pasted with Pinnacle stickers and stands it next to the can's broad steel bumper. He reaches into the truck again and lifts out a long-handled, blue-and-green, canvas Pinnacle delivery bag.

This is the theater's change order. You note that it looks small. He sets the bag down on the bottom of the dolly and shuts the rear door.

The courier's hand returns to the butt of his gun as he pushes the dolly up the handicap ramp along the perimeter of the outside stairs. He goes to the center doors, which are unlocked, opens them, and disappears inside.

You clock it. 11:35.

You cannot see them, yet you know that the second set of doors, the ones past the ticket windows, are certainly locked, and that the manager waits behind them with a key.

Yogurt Man finishes his lunch and lies against his windshield, his face turned to the sun, oblivious to the cash pickup far at his back. A white paper bag tumbles across the lot where the empty cars wait.

The armored truck sits tight, locked and idling.

THE TRUCK HAS FOUR doors—one driver, one passenger, two rear—and a small sixteen-by-eighteen-inch package door on the left side. An additional jump seat is in the cargo area, separated from the cab by a locked door, which sits empty on this two-man run. The doors all have special Medeco high-security key cylinders, as do the interior safes or lockboxes. The ignition key is not a special key, but a kill switch is concealed somewhere inside the front cabin, or else a series of random actions (for instance, switching on the defrost, then depressing the brake pedal, then switching on the defrost again) must be performed in sequence before the engine will turn over.

When the ignition key is turned, all doors automatically lock. When the driver's door is opened, the back doors automatically lock. If any door is unlocked, a red warning light shines over the dash and the wheels on the vehicle lock to prevent the can from moving. In addition, manual dead bolts are installed inside each door.

In a siege situation, the driver is trained to lock down and radio for help. The twelve-ton truck is a mobile bunker impervious to outside attack, its stainless steel armor designed to preserve structural integrity. Due to weight-load restrictions, the cargo area is usually armored one level lower than the cabin; for example, the cargo area might be certified to withstand an AK-47 or M14 assault, whereas the cabin could handle M16 fire. The weakest section of the cargo area, the rear door, is still three inches thick.

Windshield and window glass is a glass-clad polycarbonate, less dense than but equally effective as heavier bulletproof glass.

There is a roof-mounted beacon, a siren, and a public address system. Four eyehole gun ports are cut into the body of the truck. The heavy-duty bumpers are built to withstand a ram attack, and the tractor-size tires are puncture-resistant. The undercarriage would resemble that of any normal two-ton truck, but reinforced to carry six times that load; for example, the fifteen-inch differential unit is easily three times that of a standard vehicle.

The security and liquidity of the world's leading economy rides on these trucks, tens of thousands of them out on the streets at any hour, billions of dollars in notes and coin perpetually in transit. You know and accept that there is no practical way to compromise the hulk of an armored bank vehicle without also destroying its contents. The can is only vulnerable through its human operators.

AT 11:44, THE COURIER reappears on the front ramp, rolling the stacked dolly ahead of him, having spent nine minutes inside. You clock it.

The courier wheels the dolly to the rear of the truck. The handcart is stacked halfway up with three white canvas sacks of cash. The plastic trays below the white sacks contain rolled coins. The original blue-and-green Pinnacle canvas bag rides on top.

Inside the sacks are deposit bags containing cash and receipts. The clear plastic bags are supplied by Pinnacle and each one bears a tracking bar code. Much of the courier's nine minutes inside was spent inspecting the bags for tears, testing the seals, and reconciling the amounts printed on the deposit slips inside with the amounts on the manager's manifest.

The driver has spent this nine minutes watching the exterior perimeter. Security mirrors around the truck are specifically trained on the rear-door ambush area.

Courier and driver remain in constant audio contact, both wearing small, black wire earphones and microphones. The driver monitors the courier's conversations for warning signs and responds to his reports, such as *I'm on my way out*.

As the courier approaches the can, a small playing-card-sized parabolic mirror mounted near the door handle gives him an eye line on anyone behind him moving into the ambush zone. Two knocks and the right rear door is unlocked. He pulls it open and promptly loads the white sacks into the hold. He stows the empty dolly and shuts the door.

He walks to the passenger door, plucking out his ear wires. The side door is unlocked by the driver and the courier climbs inside. 11:46.

The truck sits for four more minutes while the driver double-checks the deposit receipts, entering bar codes into Pinnacle's tracking system.

You pull away during this time. Armored-truck guards are vigilant for tails, and a well-trained driver will spot your car driving away and make a mental note of its color and make.

You drive to the bottom of Grandview and back along Forbes to the parking lot of the Sheraton Tara. There, you and your partner switch into a work car and wait.

The can comes rolling along Forbes Road past you toward the mall. You see that the driver is a black man in his fifties. With no vehicle following him out of the parking lot of The Braintree 10, he starts to relax, falling in with the traffic, maintaining a safe and reasonable distance from the other vehicles. You pull out a few cars behind him.

The interior of the armored-truck cab is wide but unremarkable, a cross between a police cruiser and a long-haul truck. Aside from the hypnotizing drone of the engine and the occasional radio chatter, the cab is essentially soundproof. Armoring and special glass make it like driving inside a vacuum. For such a boxy, bulky, dense vehicle— armored trucks average between three and four miles to the gallon— the suspension is exceptionally smooth, and driver and courier feel no bumps.

Guards are often retirees from the MBTA or the Turnpike Authority, usually with a military background, earning between 65K and 90K per year. The shuttle between deliveries and pickups, or jumps, is the safest and least stressful part of their workday.

You remain two or three car lengths back from the truck, in a different lane when possible. When the can pulls into a parking lot for another pickup, you radio your freckled friend, who has been circling you in another stolen work car, and who then enters the lot and eyeballs the can. One of his talents is pretending to be asleep.

Then it is your turn to circle and wait. Your other partner, the one riding with you, unscrews the cap on the empty mayonnaise jar you brought for such eventualities and relieves himself into it. Part of you can't help but think how pleased he is at any excuse to whip out his dick in public, and how proud he must be at the duration of his piss, the singing sound it makes against the jar glass. You tolerate his satisfied sigh.

Your remote friend radios you in code, giving you the direction of the can, and you resume the tail as before.

Five more jumps. Some of them quick change orders, some pickups.

Another dozen jumps. Working your way through Holbrook, into Brockton.

Ten more. Almost four o'clock now. After a supermarket jump in downtown Brockton, the can rides west for a while, ten minutes without a stop, twenty. You know, because it is your job to know, that the Pinnacle armored-car facility is hidden behind double security fences in rural Easton up ahead. Your day's work is done. You pull off when the can gets close.

DEZ WASHED HIMSELF LIKE a marked bill in order to get free. He took a taxi from Sully Square out to Harvard Square in Cambridge, bought a ticket to a late-afternoon matinee at the Brattle Theater, sat for first fifteen minutes of a subtitled Hong Kong action movie, then carried his popcorn out through the curtained doorway at the front of the theater and exited into the side alley off Mifflin Place, sliding into Doug's waiting Caprice.

Doug had tailed Dez's taxi over from Charlestown himself. No one else followed. He kept his eye on his mirrors now, making switchbacks and U-turns just in case.

"Either they're off me," said Dez, "or they've got powers of invisibility."

"You just keep cruising that bank in Chestnut Hill," Doug told him. "Go in whenever you can and make change."

"I've eaten lunch in my truck across the street every day this week. How's the other thing coming?"

"Good. Trying to figure out what weekend now, pick a movie. Going over *Premiere* magazine's 'Summer Movie Preview' issue like it's the *Racing Form,* trying to pick a winner."

"Striptease," said Dez.

"I know. Demi Moore. My dick already bought a ticket. But June twenty-eighth, that's not soon enough."

"Mission: Impossible. Theme song remade by Adam Clayton and Larry Mullen."

"Yeah, Tom Cruise got my vote. But that's Memorial Day weekend. Jem wants it now, now, now."

"You don't need to rush it."

"No. But it's coming together fast on its own."

"As good as you thought?"

"Check my math. Theater's main screens seat, say, five hundred capacity. Two good afternoon matinees, plus the seven and ten p.m. shows, that's two thousand Saturday and two thousand Sunday, plus another thou Friday night. Five thousand numb asses per theater, say there's four outta ten screens running the newest movies. Just four out of the ten screens—twenty thousand asses and mouths. Eight bucks per ass at night, five seventy-five per in the day, and then there's the food. A popcorn, Pepsi, and Goobers alone will take you up over ten dollars, but then there's a Pizzeria Uno and Taco Bell in the lobby—with no restaurants nearby. Half a mil, easy, that's our floor, Dez. With a quarter to you for just playing decoy."

JEM'S PART WAS THE supply: weapons, vests, clothes, masks.

Gloansy's was the vehicles, the work cars and the switch cars.

Doug was the planner, the architect, the author. He was also the worrier, the perfectionist, and the cautious one. The sober one, trusted for his sense of self-preservation.

The next few days found him being super careful, spying the can guards on different routes, unrelated to the movie theater, just getting the nuances of their routine down. Also, he needed to satisfy himself that they were not plants, not FBI agents playing guards, paranoid as he was that the G was onto them. He needed to be certain that these were real wage earners with families to go home to at night. So he cooped down the road from Pinnacle's vault facility—at a safe distance from their cameras and fences; it was not unknown for these depots to hold eight figures on an overnight—and eyeballed the passing cars, looking for the guards heading home. A plum Saturn coupe stopped his heart once, but it wore no *Breathe!* bumper sticker.

He spotted the guard with the white brush mustache behind the wheel of a blue Jeep Cherokee and fell in behind him, trailing the Jeep to Randolph, to a modest split-level near an elementary school. He watched the uniformed guard leaf through his mail in the driveway as a Toyota Camry pulled in behind, the wife returning home from work.

Doug watched the guy with his happy, broad-hipped wife, walking to his aging house and overgrown lawn, and saw all the things this guy had to lose. Casing a life was different now, post–Claire Keesey. But these same pangs of guilt gave him an idea, and suddenly he knew exactly how they were going to pull this job.

He got lost trying to get back out to I-93 and found himself stuck in downtown Canton, Claire Keesey's hometown. He drove past the high school, past leafy trees and widely spaced houses with pampered lawns, the evening becoming too pregnant with associations. He felt chased as he steered out fast for the highway, antsy about returning home. Instead, he detoured to The Braintree 10.

He circled the bottom of the hill first, below the complex. The twin screens of an old drive-in theater remained there, decomposing, the property now split between a driving range and the parking lot for park-and-fly shuttle service to Logan Airport. Near a row of batting cages was a road barred by steel swing gates, secured by a key lock and chain. Doug drove back up to the theater parking lot, finding the outlet there, also gated and locked, the unused road winding down the weedy hillside to the batting cages in an S. Both Forbes and Grandview were narrow, twin-lane roads, the parking lot a nightmare to get into or out of during weekend prime time, making the emergency road necessary. Its direct access set Doug's mind jumping again.

He went inside and bought a ticket like a citizen, then laid out another fin for a personal pan pizza. He killed time wandering around the wide lobby, spotting an office door marked No Admittance half-hidden behind a three-part *Independence Day* cardboard display showing the White House being blown to smithereens. On one wall was a framed portrait of the young manager, Mr. Cidro Kosario, thin-necked and smiling in an ill-fitting suit, alongside his welcome message and his signature endorsing General Cinemas' "Commitment to Theater Excellence."

An advance poster for *The Rock*—an action movie about an old man who escaped from prison—worked on Doug like an omen, scaring him into his theater. The last preview before *Mulholland Falls* was for *Twister*. When the audience cheered a cow flying across the screen and continued to chatter about it over the feature's opening credits, Doug saw a big opening weekend coming and smiled there in the dark.

NEW HAMPSHIRE WAS THE state where Massachusetts residents shopped to avoid paying a sales tax. It was also the state where Massachusetts car thieves went to steal cars.

The reason for this was LoJack, the vehicle-recovery service, a transponder unit installed inside cars that pinged its location to police once the tracking service was activated. Not a problem for joyriders and chop shops with a couple of hours' turnover time, but if you needed work vehicles for anything longer than an overnight, no good. LoJack used no window decals to warn thieves, and the transponder and its battery backup together were about the size of a sardine tin, small enough to be hidden anywhere inside the car.

Massachusetts, Rhode Island, and Connecticut all used LoJack, but not New Hampshire or Vermont. So: boost the car in nearby New Hampshire, then slap on a pair of stolen Massachusetts plates.

Doug drove Gloansy up-country. They needed three vehicles total for the job, and today's target was the work car. They were looking for a minivan with tinted windows, Gloansy favoring the Dodge Caravan, though he would settle for a Plymouth Voyager or similar. Even a Ford Windstar, though not the new 1996 model. Ford had begun embedding transponders in the plastic heads of ignition keys, meaning that, even with the steering wheel column punched, the starting system remained disabled without a corresponding key. Gloansy carried a volt meter to defeat the system, but measuring the resistance between wires under the dash and joining the matching resistors cost him an extra thirty seconds, a lifetime in daylight car theft.

"Fucking with my livelihood," said Gloansy, working the Caprice's factory radio, the stations dying one by one as they pushed farther north. "Like when robots put guys out of work at the factory—trying to make me obsolete."

Doug said, "What's a car thief with a young family to support gonna do?"

"Start *hijacking*, I guess. Keep the keys and roll the driver into the trunk. Then car owners'll be *begging* to get rid of these immobilizer systems."

"All of us," said Doug, "getting outmoded. These wires." Old telegraph poles spaced the country road, phone wires running taut. "Money juicing through them as we speak, right there over our heads. Credit card money, dollar signs flowing like electricity. Gotta be some way to tap into that. Turn all this one-zero-zero bullshit into actual cash."

Gloansy had bought a couple of sour pickles at a country store and was chomping them like bananas, wiping his fingers on the Caprice's blue velour seats. "Like how?"

"You got me. When it comes to that, then I'll know I'm done."

They found what they needed in a parking lot outside a stadium-sized Wal-Mart. A dull green Caravan with tinted back windows, parked a quarter mile from the store. The new Caravans had sliding doors on both sides, as well as removable rear seats, which was better than perfect.

A child's car seat in back was considered bad luck by many boosters, but not Gloansy. He whistled his way across the lot to the Caravan's door, working with dried Krazy Glue on his fingers to queer his prints. It was too warm for gloves. A baseball jacket in early May was suspect enough, but he needed the bulky sleeves for his tools.

Gloansy was at the door only a few seconds before popping the handle. He was a good minute behind the wheel before the engine started up, long for Gloansy, but then Doug saw him toss a red Club steering-wheel lock in back and understood. The Club itself was basically impervious, but the steering wheel owners clamped it to was made of soft rubber tubing, so Gloansy left the Club intact and cut through the wheel around it. Then he punched the ignition barrel on the steering with a slide hammer, started up the Caravan, and rolled past Doug without a wave, only the merest hint of a froglike smile.

Gloansy: A good enough guy, and yet there was something slick and sweaty about him that threatened to rub off, his surface eagerness masking something cold and reptilian beneath, an interior life just smart enough to keep itself hidden from view. It was no surprise to Doug that Gloansy had been the first of them to father a kid, but Monsignor Dez would have been Doug's money pick as the first one to get married.

* * *

DOUG STOOD TWISTED OFF the curb, leaning across Shyne's doll legs, trying to get the frayed blue Caprice seat-belt strap fed through the back of the car seat so that he could secure the clasp. He tried hard not to curse, ignoring the little girl's unwavering gaze and her sour breath, ignoring even her hand rubbing his cheek, his neck, his hair—all of it infuriating as he tried to make this fucking thing fit.

Krista turned around in the front seat. "Sometimes you gotta kneel on the thing. Kneel on it."

He was a fucking centimeter away from catching the lock when Shyne slipped her finger inside his ear, and in shaking her off, he whacked his head on the car ceiling and roared like he was going to explode. She didn't cry, nothing, her face still, her skin waxy like pesticide-glazed fruit. There was a slight odor of spoil about her, of sour juice, of urine.

Not his child. Not his problem.

He dropped all his weight on the sides of the seat and with one final effort made the clasp bite, then ducked out fast and arched his back, feeling those red arrows of pain from the TV commercials. Shyne looked at him the same way she looked at everything: as though for the first time. He swung the car door shut on her and she didn't jump.

"Hell is Jem?"

Krista looked out her open window. "No idea."

Doug went around to his side, scanning the street as he went, then climbed in, slowly rebending his back.

"I really appreciate this, Duggy," Krista said, sitting next to him like she belonged there. "Shyne's had this cough, and the only appointment they could give me was right away. I felt funny asking."

Right. "How's she doing on those other things?" he ventured, starting up the engine. "You were going to get her checked out."

"She's doing great now, she's really starting to come along. Out of her shell. She's just shy. Like her mother, right?"

Doug nodded at the attempted joke, pulling out past Jem's blue Flamer parked curbside. "There's his car."

"Yeah," she said. "I don't know. He's probably hungover anyway."

"I thought you said he wasn't home."

"If he was, I mean." She looked out her window, close-bitten fingers at her worm-thin lips. "He's not reliable. Not like you."

Doug dropped fast to Medford Street, still hoping to sit out the morning in the parking lot of The Braintree 10. Shyne watched him through his rearview with that same passive, sad-eyed gaze.

"Gloansy's wedding's coming up, huh?" said Krista.

Doug understood now the nature of this medical emergency. He turned out along the wharves, pissed, pushing the Caprice.

"Nice, you being Nicky's godfather." She flicked at the musky orange Hooters deodorizer swaying from the cigarette lighter. "Jem says you might be going alone."

"Did he."

"Joanie said we bridesmaids can wear whatever we want, except white. So I bought this new dress I saw downtown, dripping off a mannequin. Backless, black. Comes down like this." Her hands were moving low over her chest, but he didn't turn to look. "Rides up high on the sides of each leg. Like a dancing dress, but formal. Sexy."

He rolled under the highway past the Neck, crossing into Somerville toward the free clinic, trying to be impervious. *There is no way to compromise the hulk of an armored vehicle without at the same time destroying its contents.*

"A cocktail dress," she went on. "Which is funny, because I won't be drinking any cocktails in it. I gave up drinking, Duggy." She was watching him, her body shuddering with the potholes. "This time for good."

Doug thinking, *The can is only vulnerable through its human operators . . .*

22
THE VISIT

MALDEN CENTER SMELLED LIKE a village set on the shore of an ocean of hot coffee. With the coffee bean warehouse so close, sitting in Dunkin' Donuts was a little redundant, like chewing nicotine gum in a tobacco field. But that's what they were doing, Frank G. in a soft black sweatshirt, nursing a decaf, and Doug M. looking rumpled in a gray shirt with blue baseball-length sleeves, rolling a bottle of Mountain Dew between his hands.

"So," Frank G. said, "what's up, Sport? Let's have it."

Doug shrugged. "You know how it is."

"I know that I get nervous whenever a guy strings together a bunch of no-shows."

"Yeah," said Doug, admitting it, settling back into his chair. "Work's been a bitch."

"You should take on a wife, studly. And a house to keep up, and two kids who never wanna go to bed. And yet and still, I find the time to make it down here three or four nights a week."

"Right," said Doug, nodding, agreeing.

"It the romance?"

"Nah, no."

"She have a problem with you not drinking?"

"What? No, nothing like that."

Frank nodded. "So it's over already."

"Over?" Doug had blabbed way too much last time. "It's not *over* over."

"What is it then?"

"Guess it's on hold."

"She's done with it, but you're still into her."

"No." Doug shook his head. "Wrong-o. Other way around."

"Okay. My concern is you trading one addiction for another. Like an even exchange, going up to the counter at Jordan Marsh with your receipt. *This booze thing isn't working out for me so well. I want to trade it in for a pretty girl.* And they initial your receipt and off you go. Then the new one—the *positive* one, right? 'Cause it's *love,* man. This *new* one up and dumps you, and what you're left with then is a garage-sized hole in your daily life."

"Christ, Frank—I skipped a couple of meetings. My bad. I been real busy."

"Busy, bullshit. This is the heart and soul of your week right here. This is the oil that greases the engine. Without this you have nothing, and you should know that by now. Everything else will just go away."

"This is like friggin' high school. You show up on Tuesday, they yell at you for skipping Monday."

"This isn't anything like school." Frank G.'s anger surprised Doug. "I look like your truant officer? You don't go to meetings— that means I get to bust you up about it. That's how this works."

Doug looked at the table and nodded. He waited.

And waited.

"Fine." Frank G. checked his watch. "Let's cut this short then."

Doug looked up. "What?"

"You come and make time for me at meetings, I'll make time for you. As it is, if I hustle, I can make it home for my kids' bedtime, read them a story for a change."

Doug shrugged, hands high. "Frank, I missed some fucking meetings here and there—"

"Do the work, then you get the perks."

"Perks? Did you say perks? Sitting in a Dunkin' Donuts in Malden Center at eight thirty at night, this is a perk?"

Which was stupid, stupid. Frank G. stared at Doug, then reached for his yellow windbreaker, starting to stand.

"Frank," said Doug. "Frank, look, man, I was kidding. That didn't come out the way it sounded."

"See you in church." Frank G. was checking his pockets for keys. "Maybe."

Frank was walking past him. Doug had fucked up. "I'm going to see my old man tomorrow," he blurted.

Frank G. weighed his keys in his hand as though they were Doug himself, a fish he might throw back. All Frank knew about Mac was that he was in jail. "How long's it been?"

"Good long time. He asked me to come in, see him about something."

"Uh-huh. And how's it gonna go?"

"Power of positive thinking, right?"

"A lot of it's up to you."

"Then it's gonna go splendid. And he'll go back into his cell, and I'm good for another year or so. That's how it's gonna go."

Frank G. nodded and started for the door. "See you 'round."

THE NAME MCI CEDAR JUNCTION sounded like one of those corporate-brand stadiums, with naming rights purchased by a long distance phone company or a logging concern. MCI stood for Massachusetts Correctional Institution. When Doug's father started his tour there, the place was called MCI Walpole, after its host town, but at some point during the mid-1980s, Walpole's residents realized that sharing their name with the state's toughest prison—it was also home to the DDU, the Departmental Disciplinary Unit, known as The Pit—placed a slight drag on property values and sued successfully to have it renamed after a long-abandoned railroad station.

The complex was originally constructed in the 1950s to replace the old Charlestown Prison. Entering it brought all sorts of associations flooding into Doug's mind, first and foremost his stay at MCI Norfolk, a prison still named after its host town just a couple of miles away. Norfolk was medium security, Level 4, with 80 percent of its inmates serving time for violent crimes. Cedar Junction was Level 6.

He paced in the waiting room ahead of his scheduled meet, the only male in a group of six visitors. The combined smell of their perfumes reminded him of the Haymarket on a hot, late Saturday, produce fallen between the carts, spoiling and trampled underfoot. Three black women sat heavily, depressedly, with blood-threaded eyes and bruised stares. The two white women looked hard, worn down to the core. Blue denim, sweatshirts, and bralessness were on the Prohibited Clothing List. Evidently stretch pants and cleavage-canoeing knit tops were not.

Wall postings warned against physical contact, and a brand-new sign on the door, UNDERPANTS MUST BE WORN, made Doug's arms itch.

Only one person visited Doug while he was in stir, and that had been Krista, every third weekend. How grateful he had been—though he never admitted it—for those brief conversations, at least at first. But once he started getting into AA inside and taking the program seriously—how she had changed in his eyes.

They were called inside and Doug sat alone in his partition, getting his head together. It was almost worth the visit just for the leaving, being able to walk back out of the prison again, getting into his car, driving away. Stopping at a gas station for a soda on the way home: simple freedom, an impossible dream within these walls.

Visiting Mac was like a dentist appointment and license renewal at the RMV all wrapped up in one. A trial. Something to dread, something to endure. Though in truth Doug had a good setup here, and he knew it. He controlled the contact, having Mac brought to him like a damaged library book pulled from general circulation.

Mac's shadow fell over him, and there was always that little kick when Doug saw the old crook again, always a ripple in his fabric of the hero he once knew, the strong man who used to call him Little Partner. Not the selfish *me* machine who had gone down sixteen years ago and lived mainly as a voice in Doug's head ever since.

Mac sat in his chair with a smart smile, a rooster sucking all his strength into his chest. But things were settling in him, Doug noticed: the middle getting thicker, the neck loosening up, his face sinking deeper into his skull. The casino-dice eyes that dared you to trust them, telling you straight out, *Play with me long enough and you'll lose.* The smile that was always more for him than for you. And his big Irish gourd, the shiny scalp oranged with freckles, now scored with pink treatment scars.

Mac straddled the chair, his proud, strawberry arm hair lighter now, nearly invisible. He always acted as though they were meeting on equal terms—as though their relationship had some balance—and Doug felt as sorry for him as he did for any trapped thing, having been there himself. Seeing Mac once a year was like flipping through a scrapbook, watching hair go, the features fading, blemishes rising. The resemblance between father and son, always remarkable, haunted Doug now more than ever. Looking into that partition was like looking into a mirror twenty years deep. The traces of his mother that Doug used to find in himself—that he once took great pains to seek out—were long disappeared.

"Look at you." This was what Mac always said.

"Dad," said Doug, that word he got to use for about twenty minutes each year. "How's it going?"

"How ya been?"

Doug nodded. "Good. You?"

Mac shrugged. "Still here."

"Looks that way. Been getting the money?"

"Money's good. Makes things easier. Though it ain't that bad in here neither. You know how we got things arranged."

The hive of Cedar Junction was home to a colony of Townies who, with the assistance of a few friendly guards, got most of what they needed. There were good and bad assignments in the prison industries program, like laundry or making license plates, whatever they did for their seventy-three cents an hour.

Doug nodded to him, pointed to his own head. "That it?"

Mac touched it like it was hot. "The skin cancer, yeah. They just keep burning off bits of it. Gets me into the infirmary now and then, which is good. Passes the time."

"Where you getting all this sun?"

"This is pre-1980 damage. Shoulda worn my scally cap more, I guess. It's not the bad cancer, now. This is just freckles on a mutiny. I'm still as strong as the stink in Chelsea." He inhaled like he could smell it now. "So, Jem talked to you?"

"Jem told me this, yeah."

"Never get lonely with him around. In here all the time. Funny kid when he gets going. Excitable like his dad. What you gotta do with a Coughlin is, you gotta keep that carrot hanging out in front of his beady eyes. 'Cause the stick in back, it don't register."

"Got it," said Doug.

Mac pretended to work on some food in his teeth, studying Doug, his only child. Whatever he saw, he kept his observations to himself.

"I should have come to see you more," Doug said, having to say something.

"Well, it's a long trip, coming out here to the country."

"Been doing things, you know. This and that. Time goes by."

"Hey. You're talking to a clock here." Still looking at Doug, one year older. "I didn't blow it with you, Duggy. What I hear, you're doing awright."

Doug shrugged. "Day to day."

"Older I get, the more I think about the years I missed. Fuckin' shame."

"Yeah." Doug tugged at the shelf, wondering how much longer.

"I think I know why you're pissed at me all the time."

Doug sat up a little. "Yeah? Am I?"

Mac crossed his arms over his blue scrub shirt, his chest now sagged back into his midsection. "Me losing your mother's house."

Doug rubbed the back of his head. "Nah. I don't care about that no more."

"Those legal bills, Duggy. Fuck. I had a shot at staying out—some nervous witnesses, a few changed stories—but you know no court-assigned PD could do it. You claim indigence, you might as well drive yourself to prison the day the trial starts."

"It's just that—you never had anything solid put away. With all you took. It's like you never imagined a rainy day."

Mac absorbed this criticism along with whatever else he was drawing off Doug. "I heard some knucklehead crew took a hostage in that Kenmore Square thing."

Doug said, "Yeah. I read that too."

"Bonehead play. Hostages bring a lot of heat. Better to take the pinch, should it come. Less of a bill to pay, and you earn your stripes, you come out stronger."

Doug looked at the patches taken out of Mac's head, thinking, *Are you coming out stronger?* "Well," Doug said, vigilant for guards within listening range, "like I said, I read about it."

"Seemed like a good haul, though."

"I suppose it might have been."

"And how's about old Boozo and his crew?"

"Gone away forever. Boozo's on a shelf in some federal pen in Kentucky or somewheres. Not like here. No connections. No home away from home."

"His kid, what's his name?"

"Jackie."

"There's a fuckup. Not like my boy."

"Jackie's gone too, and he's not missed."

"RICO, huh? That racketeering stuff?"

"RICO was twenty years ago. G's got a bigger stick now, a much heavier stick. Called the Hobbs Act. Anything interstate, interfering with any commerce like that. They don't need to prove conspiracy now."

"Getting tough out there."

"I guess. But when was it easy, right?"

Mac smiled. He was trying to read Doug's face like words might appear. "Jem says he's worried about you."

Doug was beginning to understand the eyeballing. "Is he."

"Says you're doing some things, acting some ways . . . he's concerned."

"Uh-huh. Was it his idea for us to meet again, or yours?"

"Both."

Doug crossed his arms, unused to getting played by Jem. "So here

I am then. Presenting myself for inspection to show you everything's fine, thanks for asking. Next topic?"

"He's worried about you not having your eye on the ball."

"I'm gonna tell you something. Him looking after me? That's like you looking after me, okay? You wanna push it, that's what you're gonna hear. You mentioned something, I think, about a hostage, earlier? Who do you think was *solely* responsible for that little fiasco?"

"You still keeping dry?"

"Fuckin' . . . next topic. How was your Christmas?"

Mac scratched the back of his neck, looking lazily at the guards on either end, then leaning closer to the glass. "Sixteen months."

Doug nodded, waiting for more. "And? What? Sixteen months, what?"

"Sixteen more months for me, here. I'm getting out."

"Out? Out of what?" Doug was sitting up now. "What do you mean, *out*?"

"Out, Little Partner." Mac nodding, smiling. "Gonna be you and me again."

All feeling flushed from Doug's face. "What are you talking about?"

Big, satisfied shrug. "Been in the works for a while. Parole board's under pressure to free up room for all the young shoot-firsts coming up. Either that or build a new prison, you know? Old outta-step bank robber, never even seen an ATM—what's he gonna do, right?" Big grin. "Hey, I didn't even tell Jem. Didn't want to jinx it. Would of kept you updated, I'd seen you more."

He was getting out. Mac was getting out.

"The neighborhood, Dad—it's all gone. The Town. There's nothing left."

"You trying to talk me into staying? We'll get it back."

"Get back what? There's nothing . . . it's all changed, understand? It's *gone*."

"You've been doing good, I can see that. Some bumps in the road, but okay. Now we're gonna take things to the next level."

Doug's chair was no good for him anymore. He needed to stand, to move, but the room rules kept him low and squirming—panicking like the old man was walking out *right now*.

"I'm gonna get back your mother's house, Duggy."

Doug shook his head, hot. "You don't even know, Dad. You couldn't even begin to afford it."

Mac smiled his smile. "I'll get it back."

"What you think, you're gonna walk in, have one of your famous sit-downs? Like you're still the king thief? Nobody's afraid of you there, Dad. Nobody even knows you anymore. A few old guys, sitting outside the Foodmaster—they might shake your hand. They might doff the cap. It's not like it was. The code is gone. The old ways, all of it. Gone."

"Ain't gonna be just like it was, Duggy," said Mac, the old *ka-ching* returning to his eyes, popping up like dollar-sign tabs on an old-fashioned cash register. "Gonna be better. Let the G bring their big sticks. You two, you and Jem, working under me . . . ?"

Doug stared. Mac was getting out.

DOUG DROVE HARD INTO the night, turning out the ZR-1 along the 95-to-93 interstate circuit, doing ninety-mile-an-hour doughnuts around the city. Sometimes he imagined he had taken all the bad energy of his youth and harnessed it in that 405-horse, all-aluminum V-8. He watched the lights in his rearview mirror, thinking about the G following him, or even Jem, when in reality it was the ghost of his father. The old crook had been chasing him all along.

Mac and all the old-school armored-car guys and stickup men— they were the neighborhood Evel Knievels. Daredevils who went after cans instead of strapping rocket packs to their backs. Winding up short of the mark was just another part of the job—a prison hitch their equivalent of a hospital stay. That was what was coming Doug's way: Mac's jailbird disease. The years being burned off him like cancer. Doug's father was hard time incarnate.

Sixteen months. For Doug, it might as well have been sixteen days.

HE RETURNED TO THE city in the Caprice, parking it illegally in the alley behind Peterborough. Streetlights and the glow of the city were just enough to help him find his way to Claire Keesey's garden, hop her fence, open her unlocked wooden chest.

With a short-handled spade he dug into the overturned soil. Four feet deep seemed good enough for short-term storage.

The walk back from the trunk of the Caprice with the few hundred thou packed in auto parts boxes inside thick plastic sheeting—that was the only really chancy part. The Fens was home to a lot of unsavories on warm nights, and his digging had made noise. But the traffic on Boylston Street provided adequate cover, masking the thump of the heavy boxes at the bottom of the hole. He looked at his small fortune a moment before covering it over with dirt and felt like he should be saying a prayer. He couldn't see the one-to-one between visiting his father and moving his stash from Nana Seavey's garage to Claire Keesey's garden, but where money was concerned, Doug listened to his instincts. Things were changing. That was all he knew for sure.

Call her.

He longed to. This, here—the treasure he was stashing in her garden—seemed like a commitment. He patted his pockets for coins, even thinking what he might say into a pay phone, inviting her to the wedding tomorrow. Showing up with her on his arm. It was pleasing to think about as he drove away. Almost like he could go through with it.

23
RECEPTION

DOUG SAT HUNCHED OVER his soda water lime, his bow tie undone, watching Gloansy and Joanie, groom and bride, work the far end of the VFW hall together. The new Mrs. Joanie Magloan was squeezing and smooching everyone in sight, a Bud Light in her hand, while Gloansy got his palm pumped by every wisecracking husband and father in the place, laughing too empty, too hard. Meanwhile, little Nicky Magloan was over at his grandma's table, his freckled face and nonstop hands coated with wedding-slash-baptism cake frosting.

The Monsignor yanked out a chair next to Doug and dropped into it. "Well," he said, "the music sucks."

"Desmond," welcomed Doug, rousing out of his pissy mood.

Monkey-suited Dez looked bleary behind his trademark rims. Jem had been treating the rest of the wedding party to rounds of Car Bombs: a half-pint of Guinness with a shot of Baileys and Jameson dropped in.

The girl Dez had brought with him, Denise or Patrice or something, a thin-faced but flabby-armed 411 operator, rose from her seat across the dance floor and started toward the bathroom. Doug said, "You left her alone over there."

"Because she won't mix! She doesn't know anybody, and this group—how can you introduce outsiders? And fucking Jem—thinks he's funny, working 'bat wings' into the conversation, like she doesn't already know she has heavy arms. Asshole." Dez wrapped himself in the flaps of his tuxedo jacket like a cold boy inside a black blanket. "It's my own fault for trying to bring someone. I see *you* came stag."

Doug shrugged and sat back. He tried to imagine himself there with Claire—huddled together at the rear of the room, happily making fun of other people.

"Smarter than I am anyway," said Dez. "She's miserable, I'm miserable. I already called her a cab."

Doug said, "Here comes the happy couple."

"Yeah, how about that dress?"

"Nice. If you like mosquito netting."

"I was talking about the neckline, the lack thereof."

Joanie was the type of girl who never missed a chance to show off the twins. "She's sturdy," Doug said, "and this is her big day."

She bustled over and Doug stood for a kiss, going cheek to cheek against her red-veined rosacea and getting a generous chest press for his trouble. One or two beers in, Joanie was always good for a ten-dollar hello. He received a chin squeeze on top of that, as thanks for being Nicky's godfather.

"Joanie, I don't know," said Doug, nodding over at the cake-smeared kid. "I'm not sure that baptism took. Little freckle's still got the devil in him."

She pretended to smack him, then put Dez on the receiving end of another friendly tit rub. "Great dress," he said, fixing his glasses as though they were steamed. "Lots of fluff on there."

"Itches like a fuckin' disease," she confided, scanning the room as she shimmied up the twins before taking another swallow and hustling on. "Don't you guys lose those jackets or wander off nowheres. Pictures in a little while."

Gloansy stepped up in her place, rapping fists, looking foggy and dazed. "Fuckin' shoot me now," he said.

Doug said, "She mentioned pictures."

"I know, I know. But it's her wedding, man. I'm already ducking out on my own honeymoon, ain't I? Your wife gonna let you do that?"

Dez set him straight. "Elisabeth Shue will have absolutely no say in the matter."

Doug said, "Okay, Dez is blotto, but you better not be. Where's Jem?"

"Fuck knows. Lighting fires somewhere."

"Try to keep him cool too, all right?"

Doug smacked fists with Gloansy and watched him slink away after his wife. He never liked that Joanie knew about their exploits—assuming she knew at least as much as Krista learned from Jem, which was much too much. Doug never understood that, telling your girl-friend, your wife, your Irish twin. At times he wondered how much his mother must have known—how much had been enough for her to leave. This was another reason they were so tough on outsiders. Heisting was the sort of thing you had to be born into.

Dez said, "I better go check on Patrice," and started toward the doors, walking chair back to chair back. Doug sat down again and watched an old couple dancing alone out on the parquet floor, cheek to cheek, the photographer shadowing them, flashing away. The shutterbug wore a cheap magician's tux, his gold hair slicked back, something iffy about him in general. He was also the videographer, whose prying lens Doug had spent half the afternoon avoiding.

"This seat taken?"

Another prying lens he had been avoiding. Krista sat down and Doug focused on the clumsy dancers, clapping politely when the swing tune ended.

She sipped her soda water lime, making certain he saw her do so. "Any idea why Dez's date is crying in the bathroom?"

Doug shook his head. "I don't think she feels welcome."

"You haven't said anything about my dress."

"It's nice," he said, not having looked at her since she sat down. He was in a cruel mood. That usually warned people away, but not Krista.

"They say it's good luck at a wedding if a bridesmaid and a groomsman hook up."

A new tune started quietly, the annoying DJ saying something about a special request. "Well, your girl Joanie needs all the good luck she can get."

She toasted that, drinking again, then leaning closer. "You know, I don't think we ever did it straight. Sober, I mean. Think about it. Even once, all those years, I don't think we just looked each other in the eye and went at it."

He heard, from the direction of the bar, voices cheering his name now and saw bottles and pint glasses going up in salute. He recognized the song then, "With or Without You," the tune Doug had sung at Dearden's wedding.

More cheers and catcalls followed, and Doug nodded through his anger, glowering at the crumbs and gravy stains on the tablecloth.

Krista touched his elbow with hers. "Dance with me?"

"I don't think I'm in a dancing mood."

"It's a slow one. I bet I could change your mood. We don't even have to *dance* dance, just stand together."

He looked up halfway, saw a few couples out there moving slow. He felt sluggish, like a candle burning down, the flame winking out.

She laid her hand over his, rubbing the raised veins there. "You know you sang this song to me?"

She turned his hand over, revealing its softer palm, nestling hers inside. Doug went blank for a while, determinedly so, until her hand slipped away again. She sat back.

"Maybe I should ask Dez then."

Doug shrugged, feeling snuffed out. "Maybe you should."

Dez was cutting back across the room now, as though summoned by the music. He smiled their way, then in response to some motion of Krista's, pointed to his own ruffled chest and changed course, heading over.

"Hey," he said, checking Doug, uncertain of what he was stepping into.

"She leave?" asked Krista.

"Yep," Dez sighed. "She's gone."

Krista swung her legs out from beneath the table, the dress falling off them. "Doug won't dance with me. I need to dance."

It took Dez a moment to realize he was being asked. He checked Doug to see if it was okay. All Doug did was drink his drink.

"Don't look at him like he's your boss," she said, getting to her feet. "If you want to dance with me, take me out there."

"Sure," said Dez, emboldened, seizing her offered hand. She finished her drink, pointedly setting the empty glass back down next to Doug's. He was certain she had a look for him as she started away, but Doug wouldn't give her the satisfaction of a glance. This was what happened when people break up but don't leave each other, he thought. Scars itch and get picked at. Scabs form but never heal.

Jem came up along the edge of the dance floor—he the solar center of this never-leaving, the rest of them spinning in his orbit of nostalgia, his scarred-knuckle sentimentality, his bullying and unweaned devotion to the old ways of the Town. He was jacketless, half his shirttail hanging out, a High Life tangled in his fingers. Psycho glee in his face, white fire in his eyes. "Hey, to the bar. Toast to Gloansy."

Dez and Krista hadn't gotten far, and Doug saw Dez let go of her hand. "You already made your toast," said Doug.

"That was for the corpses here, you know." He came around and pulled Doug's underarm, lifting him out of the chair, Doug smelling adrenaline on him as they moved. "How we lookin', huh? Everything cool?"

"Everything's cool."

"I got the pieces, I got the vests." He was close, talking in Doug's ear as he pulled him along. "Got jumpsuits from this air-conditioning repair company outta Arlington—fucking perfect."

"We got a lot of work to do tonight. Cutting the fence, finding a truck to boost. Said you'd go easy, right?"

"Ah, sleep—fuck needs it?"

Alarming, the blue-white snap in Jem's naturally fucked-up eyes. It was raining outside, but there was no mist in Jem's penny-brown hair. "Where you been? What you been doing?"

The grin. "It's a party, man. Great occasion." He pointed out the World War II medals under glass behind the bar. "Ever tell you my gramps was a war hero?"

"Only every time you drink Car Bombs."

The laugh. "Hey—am I fuckin' crazy, or what the hell was the Monsignor doing holding my sister's hand?"

The others assembled around Gloansy now, the commotion drawing in more guests and even a few ladies. "Just cool it," said Doug, "all right?"

Jem snarled a laugh—then broke from Doug's side to rush up on Gloansy, fist cocked, following through with a fake sucker punch in slow, hard motion. Gloansy's head snapped back, his toad lips spraying beer over their audience, with Jem's cackle leading the dowsed guys' laughter, the routine succeeding in scattering all the ladies except Krista. She remained close to Dez, trying to throw Doug looks.

"Here we go," said Jem, parting the group, revealing a cluster of a dozen or so High Life longnecks, uncapped and waiting.

They went fast in the confusion, passed around like rifles during an ambush. Doug found one in his hand, cold and smooth. Jem said into his ear, "Gloansy's big day, don't be a fag."

Doug looked at the bottle in his hand, its grip familiar and icily sure. He missed most of the ribald toast, the bottle sweating cold into his hand—Jem saying something to the effect that while marriage and fatherhood were known to change a man, he was confident that Gloansy would always remain faithfully, resolutely, 100 percent gay. It ended with another explosion of drunken laughter and the old Irish salute: *Here's how.*

Doug's bottle got clinked hard by Jem, who then turned his up to the ceiling and opened his throat to drain it at a swallow. Every bottle went up and empty around him.

Doug's life now: a drink he couldn't swallow; a fortune he couldn't spend; a girl he couldn't date.

It wasn't the thirst that shook loose the first few boulders of the cave-in: it was this self-disgust. This worthlessness. And the feverishness of his friends, the box they had him trapped and suffocating in.

Then the bottle was gone from his hand—Dez at his elbow, draining Doug's beer with a wet-eyed wink of confederacy. Krista wiped her lips behind him, an empty in her hand. When she was drunk, she wanted to be sober; sober, she wanted to be drunk.

Doug was halfway across School Street outside when Jem's voice turned him around. "Yo!" he heard through the rain, Jem holding the door to the VFW post open at the top of the brick steps. "'S'up? Where you headed?"

"Nowhere," Doug told him, moving on. "That's my problem. See you at midnight."

THE NAME NEXT TO the doorbell, hand-printed in all capitals, read KEESEY, C. The door opened wide, and her eyes followed suit.

"Hey," Doug said, breathing mist into the rain. "Wanna go for a walk?"

She looked him over, his soaked tuxedo. She was barefoot with rosy pink toenails, wearing loose, maroon shorts and a soft gray T-shirt, warm and dry. She checked the street behind him, as though for an idling limousine. "What are you doing?"

"I was just in the neighborhood."

She stepped aside. "Come in here."

He moved onto her white-tile landing, arms held away from his trunk like sopping branches. "Kick off the shoes," she said, all business, pointing him ahead. "Hang your jacket in the shower."

In damp socks he padded over a lemon-carpeted living room to a bathroom of old black tile. He peeled off his jacket and draped it over the curtain rod, the pale pink shower curtain billowing, the sash of the frosted-glass window raised a few inches on the rain-swept back alley.

Back out in the living room, clothes clinging, he took a good look around. Prints on the wall, the Maxell-tape guy being blown back into his chair, a couple kissing on a street in Paris. Her diplomas, high school and college. She had a decent Sony stereo set on a steel-wire hardware-store shelf unit, some CDs spilled around it. A cozy breakfast table stood outside the kitchenette, half of it taken up by mail, a checkbook, and statements in sliced envelopes, banded together. The centerpiece was a large wineglass with a small pink flower floating in it, which Doug looked at twice, believing it to be the glass from their night in and out of the Tap.

She returned from her bedroom and made to toss him a clean, mocha towel—then pulled it back, holding it hostage. "Why haven't you called me?"

He was seeping into her carpet. "Because I'm an idiot. Because I'm a jerk."

"You *are* a jerk." She tossed him the towel.

He buried his face in it, hiding a moment, then went to work on his hair. He blotted uselessly at his pants, water running off him. "I probably shouldn't have come."

"Unannounced? Dripping rain all over my place? No, probably not. Now sit down."

"You sure?"

"Sit."

He eased down into the soft tan leather sofa, trying to minimize the damage. She sat on the coffee table opposite him, gripping its edge, bare knees facing him.

"Are you coming from a wedding or something?"

"I am."

"Yours?"

He smiled only at the thought of it. "No."

"Your date dumped you?"

"She sure would have, if I'd've brought one."

She studied his eyes, finding no lie in them, then wondering about the accuracy of her own internal polygraph. "Look at my hectic Sunday afternoon. What are you doing going to weddings alone? Why haven't you *called*?"

But before he could answer, she got to her feet and thrust out her hands, stopping everything. "You know what? Don't even answer. It doesn't matter. Because I'm past all this. I am past the dating games, the waiting games."

"I'm not playing games—"

"I finally figured out that the reason my life feels so out of my control is because I haven't *taken* control. Of it. And that is something I have to change."

"Look, don't—can I tell you something? This is how messed up I am. Waiting outside your door just now—every time I'm about to see you, I tell myself, 'She's not going to be as pretty as you remember her. She's not going to be as sweet. She's not going to be as great.' And every time I'm wrong."

She looked at the floor and blew a strand of hair out of her eyes. "I guess you're entitled to your opinion," she said, showing some game.

"I try to tear you down in my head. Nothing against you—just reducing my expectations. Suffering through the breakup without even . . . is that crazy?"

"No," she said. "No, I know all about that."

He felt himself puddling on the sofa. "I'm sorry for showing up like this. It's stupid. I'll leave whenever you want me to."

She thought about that, then held out her hand for the towel as though the time to go was now—then threw the towel over his head and went at his hair vigorously with both hands. When she was done, she dropped down onto the sofa next to him, him pulling the towel down around his neck.

She said, "I saw your picture yesterday."

That stopped him cold. The light smile on her face baffled him.

"God, you look stricken," she said. "It wasn't *that* bad of a picture. On the wall at the Boys and Girls Club. You playing hockey."

Doug had imagined mug shots, surveillance photos. "Jesus. Right."

"A local hall of fame they have there."

Now he was squirming. "Please."

"It was a Bruins uniform you had on."

"Providence Bruins. Like minor leagues."

"You were drafted? You played professional hockey?"

"There was a time, yes."

She waited. "And?"

He was feeling her air-conditioning now, his shirt and pants going cold. "It didn't work out."

She read the disappointment on his face. "Well—you gave it your all, right?"

"Actually, it was worse than that. I got kicked out. I got into a fight with another guy on my own team."

She was almost smiling. "On your own team?"

"This guy was better than me. I can say that now. Not much better . . . but I had never faced that before, someone with stronger natural skills. He was a shooter, all finesse, and sort of expected me to run interference for him. Me to take the hits and the penalties, him to get the shots on goal and the glory. And the coach supported this, everything about the team geared toward grooming this guy for his pro debut. What ignited me that day, I don't remember. An accumulation of things. Both teams tried to pull me off him. I don't even think he'd ever been in a hockey fight before in his life. The only shot he got in on me was as they were dragging me back. Kicked me with his skate."

She reached for the scar that split his left eyebrow. "Is that how you got . . . ?"

"Yeah. Marked for life."

He remembered showing up hungover for practice the next day, and the coach coming up to him in the locker room, telling him not to lace up. Then the long walk upstairs to the general manager's office, his agent waiting inside. The office windows looked down over the ice, and Doug watched the team practice as the GM waved around an unlit Tiparillo and berated him. Dollars and sense—how much Doug had cost the franchise, how little sense he had shown. And still, they weren't shit-canning him completely. *Take some time off, get your fucking head on straight, kid. Keep up with your workouts and stay out of trouble.* They would have taken him back in a couple of months. But Doug returned home pissed off, back in the Town with a will to self-destruct. Getting loaded with Jem, pulling the nail-gun job. His agent wrote him a letter, something about the possibility of starting over in Hungary or Poland or somewhere. Doug never even called the guy back.

Good, he thought, all this flashing through his head with Claire sitting right there next to him. *Remember it all.* Don't blow this shot too.

"You know," she said, "when I first opened the door, I thought you'd been drinking."

Doug smiled, sad but determined, thinking of the wedding toast near-miss and shaking his head. "Not drinking. Thinking."

"I thought maybe you thought you were showing up here for a booty call."

"Ha!" he snorted. "How could you even . . . oh, man. No. I mean, unless you're into it."

Not even a courtesy chuckle. He was only 70 percent joking, but her eyes effectively told the other 30 percent to take a hike. "What *did* you come here for?" she asked.

The difficulty of that question sat Doug back. "This wedding reception I left? It was more like a farewell party. My own."

She nodded without understanding, needing more.

"Let me ask you this," he said. "Am I your boyfriend?"

She smiled at the word. "'Boyfriend?' I haven't had a boyfriend since sixth grade."

"Am I your guy? Could I be?"

"I don't know." She didn't flinch, eyes near and unblinking. "Could you?"

The question hung in the air between them, her eyes inviting him to close the gap. He did—kissing her for as long as he could hold his breath—then he sat back, his question answered. "That's what I came here for."

24
THE SURV

O N A SURV, MURPHY'S LAW reigns: forgetting your camera is the only way to guarantee that something photo-worthy will happen.

Tailing Desmond Elden that drizzling Sunday afternoon brought them to St. Francis de Sales at the top of the real Bunker Hill (the famous monument actually stood atop Breed's Hill; Dino assured Frawley it was a long story) for a May wedding, with Magloan, the car thief, apparently the groom. Frawley decided against risking entry, waiting curbside with Dino until it was over, then falling in with the attendees making their way down to the Joseph P. Kennedy Post of the Veterans of Foreign Wars, a stand-alone brick building located at the foot of the hill, behind the Foodmaster.

Dino stayed parked out on School Street until the last of the stragglers arrived, then crept into the parking lot, tucking his Taurus in deep next to a pale blue Escort with a photographer's name spelled out in gold stickers on the side window. From there they had a decent side view of the entrance, wipers clearing away the drizzle once every fifteen seconds or so. Beyond the VFW post, the city stood high and wide, looming like a wall.

Dino said, "They say rain is good luck for a wedding."

"You had hail, I take it."

"Worst drought in fifty years. When are you gonna get busy, get yourself some wedded bliss?"

"When I can afford it."

Frawley had spoken to Claire Keesey a few times since their pre-date, once setting plans, to meet for drinks at the Rattlesnake, but the late-afternoon robbing of an Abington bank—a crackhead counter-jumper so junkie-sick and nervous he'd puked on his own gun—forced Frawley to cancel on her at the last minute. Judging by her remarks, it seemed that the piano mover was out of the picture.

The wipers slicked the rain-smeared windshield clean, Frawley watching a guy in black exit the post, jogging down the front steps to the street without umbrella or coat.

"Your generation," said Dino, smiling. "So cautious. So afraid of marriage. But then somebody suggests skydiving, and everyone's fighting over parachutes."

Frawley said, "Dean, hit these wipers again."

Dino did. Frawley saw the guy in the tuxedo, now halfway across the street, turned and talking to a jacketless guy standing outside the door.

"That's MacRay," said Frawley.

"Which? On the road?"

"I think. And the other one, that's Coughlin."

Dino rolled down his window but the rain drowned out the conversation. It didn't look like an argument, but it didn't look like *See ya soon* either. MacRay continued away across the street, Coughlin watching him a few moments before ducking back inside.

"What do you think?" said Dino.

Frawley watched MacRay cut into the mall parking lot outside the 99 Restaurant, shoulders hunched against the rain. "Don't know. Home is that way." He pointed to the hill behind them.

"Could be just ducking out for a Certs. What are we doing here, anyway? It's not like they're gonna knock over their own wedding reception."

Frawley was pulling on his red rain shell. "You take off, Dean. I'll jump here."

"Sure now?"

"Navy yard's in that general direction anyway, so I'll see where he goes, then get home myself."

"No argument from me," said Dino.

Frawley stood out of the Taurus—rain always looks harder than it feels—and jogged toward the mall parking lot, wishing it was Coughlin he was following, reading the pale-eyed bumper as the likely ringleader. MacRay was hard to miss in his tuxedo, and Frawley stayed well back, following him across the lot to the next street, climbing a side road past the skating rink.

Near the five-street junction, Frawley felt something happening. He sensed a convergence but pushed it aside until he neared Packard Street and alarms started ringing in his head. Still it was too much to accept, even as MacRay stopped outside one of the doors. Frawley watched from the corner, unable to tell from that angle which building was Claire Keesey's.

He felt a lift when MacRay changed his mind, starting away—but MacRay was only pacing, and Frawley watched from the corner, standing under a downspout, roof runoff pattering his shoulders.

MacRay ran up the stoop again and pressed the bell. The door opened. Words were exchanged, MacRay was invited inside, and the door closed.

Frawley splashed up the sidewalk and climbed the same three stone steps, finding the bell buttons, noticing immediately the one that was wet. The name next to it read KEESEY, C.

He went blind for a minute, standing there. She had invited MacRay inside—one of the thieves who had knocked over her bank and taken her for a ride. And Frawley had cleared her. He had excluded her, beyond a doubt. He had been trying to *date* her.

Had they scammed him? Was he being outfoxed by these scumbags? Had she—of all of them—fucked him over good?

The piano mover.

If the door opened now, they would see him there, standing before them. And he wanted that. He wanted them to see him, wanted them to know that *he knew,* that he had seen them together. And then—

And then he didn't want that at all.

THE GOLD ALPHABET STICKERS applied to the second-story window of the Brighton row-house apartment read GARY GEORGE PHOTOGRAPHY, and below that, smaller, PROFESSIONAL PORTRAITS—HEADSHOTS—GLAMOUR.

Frawley reached inside the wrought-iron cage over the basement apartment window to rap on the glass. Through it, he had an odd, God's-eye perspective looking down into a living room, where an Indian guy was curled up on a sofa in lounging pants and a T-shirt, cuddling with his lady friend in front of a soccer match on TV. They spooked at Frawley's badge, the guy leaping off the sofa and buzzing Frawley inside.

The tile floor of the lobby was cracked but clean. The soccer fan padded up the stairs alone, barefoot, nervous. "You're all set, I just needed a buzz in," Frawley told him, displaying the creds again and shooing him back downstairs.

Frawley climbed to the second floor, finding the door with the business name on it, again in mailbox letter stickers unevenly spaced. He knocked and heard soft footsteps coming up on the other side.

Frawley held his credentials over the peephole. "FBI, open up."

The door yielded two inches, the length of a security chain. The photographer's skin was shiny and buffed, like he'd been scrubbing it all evening. "Is this a joke—"

Frawley shoved open the door, shoulder lowered, the chain snapping, the doorknob banging, the links *ching*ing across hardwood like spilled dimes.

The photographer staggered backward, stunned. He wore a short, blue, terry-cloth bathrobe with nothing underneath it. Frawley knew there was nothing underneath it because the shock of jerking back from the door had caused the robe to fall open.

Frawley straightened, the door having suffered for his anger. "Close your robe, Gary."

Gary George closed his robe. "You can't come in here without a search warrant."

"I can't collect evidence without a search warrant," said Frawley, closing the door. "But generally all I need to get in anywhere is this"—he showed him his creds—"and this"—he flapped open his jacket to show him the SIG-Sauer shoulder piece. "That's usually enough."

Gold hair slicked back with mousse during the day now flopped dryly around Gary George's face, drooping weedily to his cheeks. He double-knotted his robe. Frawley smelled incense.

"I'm having a bad day today, Gary," Frawley told him, "a real bad day. I'm warning you in advance so that you know not to make it any worse. You worked a wedding in Charlestown this afternoon. How did you know those people?"

"I don't."

"Who hired you?"

"I came with the flowers."

"You came with the flowers."

"Mainly as a favor to someone."

Frawley's realization nearly made him step back. "Fergie the Florist?"

Gary George's silence was a yes.

"Fergus Coln, Charlestown gangster and drug dealer? Hell of a guy to be doing favors for, Gary." Frawley stepped close, checking Gary George's pupils. "You loaded right now?"

He was too stoned to be properly defiant. "I might be."

"The photographs you took today—I want them. Group shots of the wedding party. Anybody in a tuxedo. I will pay you for the prints, maybe even throw in a buck or two for the busted door chain if things go smoothly. Do we have a deal?"

Gary George thought about it, nodded.

"Excellent decision, Gary. So far, so good. What do you have, one of those bathroom darkrooms?"

Frawley paced among the mood lighting and beaded doorways and velvet slipcovers, waiting while Gary George worked. On one wall was a giant studio portrait of a model wearing a bobbed black wig, long beads, and a flapper dress, and, of course, the model was Gary George himself. Frawley found four sticks of incense smoldering in the kitchen and threw one after another out of the window into the rain. His anger built again as he thought of MacRay lounging at Claire Keesey's, while Frawley waited on a doped cross-dresser in a ladies' beach cover-up.

"What?" asked Frawley, when Gary George emerged from the bathroom at the half-hour mark, empty-handed.

"Taking a little cigarette break."

Frawley shoved him back inside the bathroom and shut the door.

When it opened again, Gary George held dripping prints with rubber-thumbed tongs. Frawley studied one group shot posed around a table, the bride and groom in back, the wedding party in chairs before them. He recognized Elden on the far right, and beady-eyed Coughlin near the middle, a beer bottle half-hidden next to his leg. But no MacRay. Nor was he in any of the others.

"The big guy," said Frawley. "Kind of thick-nosed, buzzed hair."

"This is it for tuxedos. They weren't very into the whole portrait thing."

Frawley checked the image again. The woman in a slinky black dress, darkly blond, bad-girl hot, had to be Coughlin's sister, the one living in the house with him and MacRay. She had Coughlin eyes.

"Maybe he's on the video," suggested Gary George.

Frawley turned and stared until Gary George started moving.

Back through the doorway beads, out in the main room, Frawley snatched the videocamera out of Gary George's hand, ejecting the unlabeled VHS tape himself.

"I'll need that back," said Gary George.

Frawley kept a twenty and threw down the rest of his wallet money on a lace-draped sewing table. "Tell anyone about this, Gary, and I will return with a narcotics warrant and a thick pair of gloves and tear this place apart. Understood?"

Gary George picked through the bills. "This is only like thirty-seven dollars."

But Frawley was already through the door and moving down the hall to the cracked stairs, thinking only, *MacRay, MacRay, MacRay . . .*

PART III
BAD

25
POPCORN

THE MANAGER, CIDRO KOSARIO, drove a dusty blue Cressida with a failing muffler. He parked in his usual spot on the west side of The Braintree 10, unfolding reflective silver sun shields over his dash and rear ledge before locking the car and twirling his keys around his finger as he ambled to the side door. He slid the key into the lock, and Doug stepped out from behind the trash pen.

"Morning, Cidro."

Cidro startled. He saw their fucked-up faces and the guns pointed at him and his Monday-morning eyes died like stabbed yolks.

Jem was at Doug's elbow. "We're here for the popcorn."

Doug told Cidro, "Inside."

Cidro unlocked the door, Doug's gloved hand pushing him through. The warning tone was shrill, the alarm keypad flashing on the wall. Jem shut the door on the daylight behind them and got right up in Cidro's face. "Bet you couldn't even *remember* the panic code right now, if you wanted to."

Doug said, "And you don't."

Cidro looked incapable of much of anything at the moment. He took one more quick glance at their faces—*yes*, this was happening—then turned his eyes to the geometric pattern of the dark carpet, barely looking up again for the next two hours.

Growing up, Halloween had always been Doug's and his friends' number one holiday. Christmas brought presents, Independence Day bottle rockets and cherry bombs, but only Halloween allowed them to be criminals: wearing masks, roaming the night, marauding.

Gloansy, in his legit life as a sometime union driver for local movie productions, was always nicking stuff off sets. Props, cable, snacks—anything he could eat or move. Off an Alec Baldwin movie called *Malice* he had taken a makeup kit that looked like a big fishing tackle box, to which Doug had since added clearance rack Halloween disguises.

Doug and Jem had used the mirrors inside the stolen Caravan to apply their faces in the hour before Cidro pulled up. The point was to intimidate as well as disguise. Jem wore a gargoyle application over his nose and cheeks, an old man's chin, some Frankenstein-style ridging over his eyebrows, and a clown's red mustache. He looked like sort of a dog-man, a human mutt, and when he had turned to Doug for a quick check, Doug said from the backseat, "Christ, that's fugly. Take my money too."

Doug had made himself look like a cross between a burn victim and an ugly man with a creeping skin disease. They wore vests underneath the blue repairman jumpsuits and matching service caps, with pale blue latex gloves and wide, mirrored sunglasses. Doug carried a Beretta, Jem a Glock 9.

"Key in the disarm," said Doug, his hand squeezing Cidro's shoulder. "Go."

The theater manager did, five digits, the aliens' tune from *Close Encounters of the Third Kind*. The warning tone ended on two beeps, the keypad lights blinking out.

Cidro Kosario was a mix of Portuguese and black, a dark-eyed, mournful young man with short, kinky hair and an eagle beak, his flesh nearly silver. The two types of citizens who got hurt in heists were assholes and superhero-in-waiting movie fans. Accordingly, Doug had tailed Cidro. "What's your baby, Cidro, boy or girl?"

"She's a . . . huh?" He almost looked up at them again.

After seeing Cidro and his short wife walking their baby stroller outside a Quincy apartment building, Doug knew the manager would give them no trouble. "A girl, that's nice." Doug kept his hand heavy on the skinny man's shoulder. "So this is a robbery, okay? Everything's gonna go smooth, and then we're out of your life for good. Nothing's gonna happen to you—*or* them—so long as you follow along and do as you're told."

Doug felt the guy starting to shake.

Jem took Cidro's keys from him and said, into the crew's walkie-talkie, "We're in."

"*Yah,*" came back Gloansy's voice.

They started past the individual theater doors toward the brighter light of the central lobby. Being in a quiet theater in daytime reminded Doug of matinees, and how going to them had always felt like playing hooky—before he went into playing hooky full-time.

Doug asked, "How long until the armored truck comes for the money?"

Cidro was sagging, twisting a little, buckling into a standing squat.

Doug said, "About an hour and a half or so, am I right?"

Cidro tried to nod, breathing funny.

Doug said, "You're gonna take a shit, aren't you."

Cidro froze, his face a mask of pain.

"Lucky for you, we got time. Can you still walk?"

DOUG WAITED AGAINST THE wall across the handicapped stall, his gun on Cidro, the guy's pants around his ankles, hugging his bare knees as he exploded himself into the toilet. "Yeah, go ahead, wipe," said Doug. The humiliation on Cidro's face was genuine, boylike. "Okay? Let's see the office."

Jem staggered away from the draft caused by the opening restroom door. "Ho! Armed robbery *enema*."

They walked Cidro behind the triple-wide *Independence Day* cardboard display into the locked manager's office. It was a drop safe, a small manhole in the floor with twin locks like eyes over the flat grin of a one-way deposit slot.

Doug said, "Why don't we get your safe key now, so we're ready."

Cidro pulled it from a cash box full of stamps and gift certificates at the back of a desk drawer. That weekend's deposit receipts were paper-clipped to a cash sheet on the calendar blotter, waiting to be tallied and phoned in. Doug glanced at the slips and liked what he saw.

Jem yanked the phone lines out of the wall, cutting them while Doug scanned the room for potential weapons. "What time does your day shift arrive?"

Cidro glanced at the wall clock, stalling. Doug decided not to give him the opportunity to lie.

"About eleven fifteen, right?" said Doug, collecting *Edward Scissorhands* scissors, an *American Me* letter-opener shiv, and a heavy *Jurassic Park* paperweight. "All right, back out. Lie down here on the carpet, on your stomach. We're gonna chill for a while."

Cidro did as he was told, lying on the floor of the lobby with his face turned away from them, his wrists bound with a plastic tie.

Jem's impatience allowed Doug to hang cool at the end of the candy counter, watching him pace. Jem wandered around the lobby inspecting the posters and the freestanding cardboard displays, studying the stars' faces up close as though trying to see what they had that he hadn't. Later he opened up a $2.50 box of Goobers on the glass counter, popping one after another into his mouth.

Gloansy's voice squawked on the radio, "First one's on the way."

Doug's watch read 11:12. "Cidro," he said, using his Leatherman to cut the manager's hands free. "You're gonna stand up now and let in the first of your day shift. You've had a lot of time to think, lying there, and I hope it was all about your family, your home in unit eleven on the fourth floor of the Livermore Arms, and not about alerting your employees or trying to bolt on us once you open up that side door."

Cidro let in the first worker, the second, the third, fourth, and fifth—all without incident. The old projectionist held his chest after seeing mutt-face Jem, but he seemed okay once they laid him down and cuffed him with the others. Jem yelled out, "Stop fucking trying to look over here!" every few minutes, just to keep them properly terrorized. Doug brought Cidro to the front to unlock the outside doors as usual, then re-locked the inside ones and brought him back to the lobby, laying him down to wait.

Jem was popping Sour Patch Kids now. *"Too fucking easy, man,"* he hissed, resuming his pacing. He didn't mean that something seemed wrong. He meant that he wasn't having any fun. It was all going too smoothly and he wasn't enjoying himself.

The radio squawked again at 11:27. "Yogurt Man."

Doug stepped to the tinted lobby doors and saw, way out at the far edge of the parking lot, the white Neon, Yogurt Man climbing onto the hood with his lunch.

Gloansy's voice: "It's on. Heading your way."

Doug yawned, pulling oxygen into his lungs, enriching the blood feed to his heart, his brain. The old fear rising nicely. Jem waited back with the prone workers as Doug pulled Cidro to his feet and at gunpoint told him how it was going to go.

They heard the can pull up outside, the squawk of the heavy brakes, a fartlike sigh.

Gloansy's voice was different now: juiced, in motion. "Road's set. Good to go."

This meant that Gloansy had blocked off Forbes Road, the only way in, with the boxy green *Boston Globe* delivery truck he had boosted from South Boston that morning—in the early hours of what was supposed to be the frogman's honeymoon.

Doug returned the keys to Cidro, then stood behind a *Striptease* standee.

A shadow moved to the doors. The click-clack of a key tapping against glass.

"Go," whispered Doug, and Cidro went, fumbling the key into the lock and admitting the white-brush-mustached courier, pulling the handcart behind him. ID card on the collar, patch on the shoulder, big badge on the pocket, gun in holster, black wire earphones.

"And how're you today, sir?" said the courier, blustery, efficient.

"Good," said Cidro, a blank.

"Good, good."

Cidro stared at him a moment, then the courier moved to the side, waiting for Cidro to lock the door. Cidro did.

"Inside, and all clear," said the courier aloud. Then, less automatedly, he said to Cidro, "Rough weekend?"

Cidro was staring at him again.

"Or is that new baby of yours keeping you up? Yep—*been* there, *done* that."

Cidro nodded. "Okay," he said, then started them toward the office.

Doug stepped out from behind the cardboard Demi Moore with his Beretta up, moving straight at the courier. The courier halted, seeing everything at once, the gun, the cap, the shades, the face—his mind waking up to *ROBBERY!*—but before he could speak or even let go of the cart, the Beretta's muzzle was in his face like a bee on his nose.

Doug unsnapped the guard's sidearm, tugging the .38 free of his belt. Jem appeared and pulled Cidro away, then Doug traded Jem the guard's gun for the walkie-talkie and Cidro's keys.

Adrenaline made Doug's voice loud and strange. "Arnold Washton," he said in the direction of the microphone in the courier's chest, "driver of the truck. You have a wife named Linda. You live at 311 Hazer Street, Quincy, with three small dogs. *Do not* make the distress call. I repeat—do *not* make that call. Morton, tell him."

The courier stared, dumbfounded.

Doug said, "Morton Harford, 27 Counting Lane, Randolph. Wife also named Linda. Two grown children. Tell him, Morton."

"There's . . . two of them," said Morton, the good-natured bluster evaporated from his voice. "Two I see, Arnie. Masks. Guns."

Doug said, "Arnold, do not make that call. The two Lindas join me in telling you that you are to sit tight in the truck and do nothing. There is a van pulling up next to you now, the driver wearing a dinosaur mask. He is monitoring a police radio and will overhear any dispatches. If you understand and agree with me, raise both hands off the wheel now so that the driver of the van can see them."

They waited, Doug holding up his radio. Gloansy's voice squawked, mask-distorted. "Hands are up."

"Good." Doug took one step back from Morton the courier. "Open your shirt, Morton. I want your radio and earphones."

Morton did, but slowly, as though stalling were the same as resisting. He lifted the microphone off the V-neck collar of his undershirt and, with Jem holding Morton's own gun on him, surrendered the wires and the black box to Doug.

Jem patted Morton down for an ankle holster while Doug miked himself, hanging the wires inside his ears. "Arnold," he said, "say something to me."

No static over the two-way channel, Arnold's voice entering his head crystal clear. "Look here, no money's worth anybody getting—"

"That's fine. Turn off the engine using one hand, then raise them both up again."

Jem was getting goosey, holding the guard's gun on him palm-down like they do in gang movies. It occurred to Doug only then that maybe he hadn't given Jem enough to do.

Outside, the rumble died. Gloansy said, "It's off."

Doug told him, via radio, "We're good." Then to the truck, via the microphone now clipped to his jumpsuit collar, Doug said, "Sit tight, Arnold. We won't be long."

He motioned Cidro and the open-shirted courier toward the office. Cidro entered first, then Morton pushing his hand truck. Doug remained in the doorway.

"Empty the bag on the desk."

The courier lifted the blue-and-green canvas bag off the tray of rolled coins at the bottom of the dolly. He opened the bag and pulled out a standard-sized bundle of currency, ten packs of one hundred fresh-cut one-dollar bills banded in blue Federal Reserve Bank straps. Then he lowered the handles of the sagging bag, facing Doug with an *If it weren't for that gun* expression.

"Is that it?" said Doug.

Morton did not respond. Doug cocked his head at Morton, then pulled the first safe key from his pocket. He tossed it to Cidro.

Cidro caught it and looked at Morton. "C'mon, man, just do what they say."

The mustached courier's scowl intensified. He reached back into the canvas sack and pulled out Pinnacle's safe key.

"Down on your knees," Doug said. "Take the coin tray off the cart, open the safe, and start stacking bags."

They were bringing deposit bags out of the floor well when gunshots cracked in the lobby. Doug ducked automatically, wheeling and pointing his Beretta out the office door, seeing nothing. He didn't know where Jem was—stopping himself from calling out his name. He turned back the other way and put his gun on Morton and Cidro, who had both dropped facedown onto the floor.

Then another smattering of gunshots. Doug was wild with incomprehension, yelling *"Fuck!"* as Arnold's voice in his head said, "Dear God, *no*."

Doug backed through the doorframe, low, still seeing nothing. Glass cracked and tinkled, the employees screaming, Arnold yelling in Doug's head, "Morty? *Mort!*"

Doug backed straight out of the office, crouching, keeping Morton and Cidro in sight as he scanned the lobby, smelling cordite, searching for Jem. Then another crack and thump—this time followed by Jem's voice: "Goddamn! That's a pretty fuckin' good milk shake!"

"THE FUCK!" bellowed Doug at him, backing into a fake ficus tree.

Jem moved into view, the guard's .38 at his side. He spun and brought the gun around fast, firing twice, *crack-crack,* shootout-style, shuddering Bruce Willis on a cardboard standee for *Last Man Standing,* singing, "Yippee-ki-yay, motherfucker!" Then a shot— "Ain't gonna *be* no rematch!"—into Stallone's chin, on a standee for *Daylight.* "Say hello to my leettle—" Pacino got one in the gut, a promo for *City Hall.*

The gun clicked twice, finally dry, sparing the animated stars of *Beavis and Butt-head Do America.* Jem tossed the piece aside, slipping his Glock back into his right hand and then seeing Doug crouched beneath the plastic tree. Jem's vested chest was heaving, his face a slicing, fucked-up smile.

Arnold screaming, *"Morty!"*

Gloansy shouting from Doug's hip radio, *"Fuck is that?"*

"Arnold!" Doug said, rising to full height, elbowing the tree out of his way and checking Morton and Cidro again. "Arnold, everything is fine."

"What in fucking hell—!"

"Do not make that call, Arnold. Your partner is fine, everyone is

fine—no one has been hurt. Here—" His body pounding, Doug returned to the office and pulled the mustached courier to his knees. "Talk to him, Morton. Speak, tell him."

Morton said slowly, "I'm okay, Arnie. I think."

"He's not hurt," said Doug.

"I'm not hurt," said Morton, checking himself over, making sure it was true.

"Mort, what they shooting at?" said Arnold—confused, thinking his partner could still hear him.

"Do not make that call, Arnold," said Doug, getting his breath back now, grabbing Cidro by his shoulder and hauling him to his feet. "Here is the manager." Doug pulled Cidro out of the office and showed him his employees: still lying on the carpet, hands covering their heads. "Tell him, Cidro."

Cidro looked around at the target practice Jem had made of the lobby. "I don't—"

"Just tell him!"

"No one is hurt!"

"No one is hurt, Arnold," said Doug, shoving Cidro back into the office.

Gloansy said from his hip, *"Fuck is going on, man?"*

Doug grabbed the radio. "We're cool, everything's cool."

Gloansy said, *"Everything's cool?"*

"Yogurt Man, what's he doing?"

"Nothing. No movement."

"All right. Sit tight. Almost fucking there."

WHEN THE SAFE WAS empty, Doug had Morton wheel the cart out into the smoke-hazed lobby. Jem got the employees up, hustling them into the windowless office—"Let's *go*, fucking *move* it, *go*, *go!*"—putting them in there with Cidro. "Now if you're thinking about opening this door, I am going to be standing right fucking here." He slammed it shut and hustled away.

Morton pushed the hand truck ahead of him to the lobby doors, looking a little hinky, his head not moving as he walked, his mind working hard. Doug came up abreast of him and caught Morton's eyes searching the lobby for something, anything.

"You're thinking too much, Morton."

Morton stiffened, slowing down even more. His mustache rippled as he said, "No one calls me Morton."

"I do, Morton," said Doug, reacquainting him with the Beretta.

"You're ripshit at me right now, Morton, I understand that. Because I brought your family into this thing, you're super-fucking-pissed." *Reservoir Dogs* suddenly coming out of Doug. "Remember this isn't your money, Morton, and how nice it will be tonight to get home. You too, Arnold," continued Doug, into his own collar. "We're coming out now and you're not gonna do a damn thing but sit tight and still. Tell me you will, Arnold."

Arnold's voice in his ears said, "This ain't right."

"Tell me you will, Arnold."

"Lord Jesus been listening in on you just like I have."

"Arnold, tell me you fucking will."

"I will," said Arnold. "I have done my job here. I will leave the rest to Him."

Into his hip radio, Doug told Gloansy, "We're coming out."

Doug unlocked the glass door with Cidro's keys. They passed the imitation velvet rope and the ticket booths on either side, Doug stopping at the unlocked outside doors.

"Okay, Morton?" said Doug.

Morton just started straight ahead.

They exited onto the cement landing atop the stairs, Arnold sitting inside the driver's window of the Pinnacle can, hands above the steering wheel, watching them.

Doug and Jem followed Morton and the cash cart down the ramp to the sidewalk, then over the fire lane markings and around the rear of the can to where the Caravan was idling. Gloansy sat there in his dinosaur mask, eyes trained on Arnold.

Jem threw open the rear hatch of the van and tossed the bags inside, Morton standing there, his unbuttoned shirt flapping in the breeze. Doug stood behind Morton, scanning the sunny sky for helicopters.

"Arnold," said Doug, "the dinosaur's gonna keep monitoring the police radio, and I'm gonna stay in touch with you until we're outside broadcast range, understand? You don't make a call until then."

Doug yanked down his earphones without waiting for Arnold's answer. Jem slammed the hatchback shut and Doug walked Morton around to the passenger side of the van where Jem pulled open the sliding door for Doug, then climbed into the front passenger seat. Jem covered Morton from the open window while Doug backed inside and shut the sliding door on Morton's scowling eyes.

Gloansy floored it. They screeched through the empty parking lot toward the cliff edge. As Doug pulled a seat belt across his chest,

Jem stuck his gun arm out his window, drawing a bead on sun-worshipping Yogurt Man.

Jem did not shoot. Gloansy turned hard toward the emergency access road, banging through the gate—they had cut the lock and chain overnight—and plunging down the road. It was no steeper than Pearl Street, and Gloansy banked hard at the end, slapping through the second cut gate and bottoming out hard next to the batting cages and the driving range.

Gloansy yanked off his mask and pushed the van for all it had, driving hard across the cracked parking lot and straight at the chain fence separating lower Forbes Road from the broad, busy highway. The fence had also been precut overnight, links snipped up the middle so that when the van bumped the curb, it smashed clean through.

They rattled over a stripe of high grass before jumping out onto 93 at the mouth of Exit 6, cutting off another minivan and veering across the breakdown lane into the traffic flow, throwing off a pair of hubcaps like wheeling quarters. Other cars braked and honked their disapproval, Gloansy punching the horn to scare off the panicked midday commuters, zooming ahead, falling in with the traffic and running south through the highway split, toward the rail station and the switch—with the cash-filled deposit bags sliding around in back, Jem howling like a madman in front, and Doug furiously stripping off his face.

26
INSIDE THE TAPE

FRAWLEY STOOD AND WATCHED the highway traffic zipping past him as though the green minivan might come around again, hours after the fact, MacRay and his crew in their ugly-face masks hooting at him out of the windows, waving fistfuls of cash.

The tire tracks, twin stripes of churned soil cut into the high grass, drove right through the precut six-foot chain-link fence and out onto the highway. The highway split offered them a variety of escape routes . . . and blah blah blah blah blah.

Thwock! Behind Frawley, the lone driving-range employee teed off again, eyeing the cops and the evidence van as he reloaded between drives. Frawley envied the guy's bystander status, tired of cop-think, and nearly on autopilot here, having trouble finding a reason to care about this particular crime—while at the same time feeling a mounting sense of fury toward the bandits.

The photographer was done, the tire tracks measured and cast, a fireman now cutting out that section of fence for crime lab comparison, in the event the offending tool were to be found. But it would not be found. It had certainly been chopped into several pieces and disposed of in various trash receptacles between here and Charlestown.

Dino was saying something about estimating the time of the fence snip and the cut gate chains. He was still working the crime; Frawley was working the criminals.

The van offered a glimmer of hope. Frawley had a BOLO out on suspicious green vans, with special attention to handicapped plates. None of the witnesses had said anything about handicapped plates, but Frawley and Dino both knew that armored-car guys loved the tags for their access, letting them park closest to business doors without attracting attention.

None of the highway drivers who dialed 911 could pinpoint where the getaway van had pulled off the highway. Frawley guessed they had skipped the split in order to put some distance between them and the looky-loos who saw them bang through the fence—but they wouldn't have gone too far before making their switch, not with the new highway-overpass traffic cameras.

Now the TV news helicopter was making another pass overhead. A hot, muggy June afternoon, thunderstorms due to crack the heat. Frawley's boxers clung to him like wet swim trunks he had pulled pants on over. Leaving his necktie on in this humidity had been a form of self-punishment, but now he ripped open the knot and yanked it out of his collar, stuffing it into his pocket as, with Dino, he turned back toward the access road. The heat was one more obstacle the robbers had left him in their wake, one more taunting F.U.

"It's them," Frawley said.

Dino nodded, saying, "Okay," not doubting or disbelieving Frawley, only wanting to make him work for it. Dino's shirtsleeves were sopping, rolled up past his hairy gray forearms. "The guards, the manager, everyone says only three doers."

"Could have been one more in the back of the van. Or maybe one of them was an extra pair of eyeballs out on the mall side, watching for cop patrols."

"But no tech whatsoever. Not one clipped wire. All manpower and coercion."

"None of the armored-car jobs have used tech. There can *be* no tech on an armored. This is them shaking it up. Knowing they're being sniffed at."

"Okay. But Magloan—he goes out robbing the morning after his wedding?"

"That's the first thing their lawyers will proclaim in court. It's perfect."

"And if it turns out Elden's been at work all day?"

Frawley shook his head, adamant. "It's *them*."

A Braintree cop stood by the dented gates, waiting for someone to collect the green-van-paint transfer. The cut chain lay there like a dead snake. Frawley and Dino walked the hooked road back up to the parking lot. "Some big movie, I guess, this weekend?" said Dino. "*Twister*? That the movie of the game?" He was trying to pull Frawley out of his funk. "'*Huge* opening,' said the manager. What my last partner used to say about his wife, '*Huge* opening.'"

Frawley nodded, stubborn, nursing his bad mood. The wind up at the top was the stale gust of heat that comes at you when you open an oven. The broken chain there was being bagged, print dust smoking off it like gray pollen. The *Globe* truck stolen out of South Boston, which they had used to block off the roads leading in, sat on slashed tires atop a flatbed trailer, its green sides dusted as though it had been driven through a sandstorm.

Frawley stood at the knee-high wooden railing around the parking lot and looked across the highway canyon to the facing road of industry set atop a cliff of blasted stone. A dozen different angles for casing the theater from there.

They crossed the lot to the armored truck, still parked in the fire lane outside the theater entrance. Something about the yellow police tape offended Frawley and he tore it down himself, saying, "They never even touched the truck."

"Went backdoor. Like at Kenmore."

"Going out of their way to get the drop on the mark. They could have come at the truck head-on. It's isolated enough up here— doesn't get much more isolated. Doable, though messy."

Dino patted the can's side reassuringly as he might a spooked elephant. "They knew better."

Frawley watched the police tape slithering across the baking lot. "These guys knew there was more money in the can, had complete control of the situation, *and they let it go*. Add in the days and weeks of prep, casing the job, following all the players? Decidedly risk-averse. Being super careful."

Dino said, "That's another kind of good for us. They get too careful, too tricky, they'll screw themselves up."

"Yeah," said Frawley, starting up the stairs to the lobby. "Except, I am through waiting for them to screw up."

Entering the theater lobby was a jump from the oven into a refrigerator. The manager had set out bottled water and tubs of popcorn for the cops. They were hoping to reopen in time for the seven-o'clock shows.

"That older guy, the projectionist, he okay?" asked Frawley.

"No chest pains," said Dino. "Just gas."

The two guards were sitting on folding chairs with their caps in their hands, going over forms with a rep from Pinnacle. Their fuzzy descriptions told Frawley that the bandits' intimidation—their knowledge of the men's home lives—was still working. Neither Harford, who had spent time in both gunmen's company, nor Washton, into whose ears the radio gunman had issued his instructions, said they would be able to identify the bad guys. The only useful thing Frawley had gleaned from their accounts was the fright makeup, similar to an earlier job he suspected these Brown Bag Bandits of, a co-op bank in Watertown.

The guards acted like they knew their interview with the boss from Pinnacle was a formality. Both men had allowed themselves to be tailed on the job and followed home after work, enough to get them fired for cause.

The smell of gunfire lingered in the chilled air. Little numbered orange evidence triangles stood on the carpeted floor, marking where brass cartridge casings from Harford's gun had been collected. Frawley stood by a *Barb Wire* cardboard display, looking at the bullet-hole nipples in Pamela Anderson Lee's vinyl-corseted tits, contrasting that act with the discipline of leaving $1,000 in new, traceable bills sitting on the manager's desk. It was like the kidnapping after the Morning Glory job: schizo.

Maybe they'd start spending their money now. Their take was all clean, circulated cash. Frawley turned to remind Dino of this, but Dino was gone. Frawley wondered how long he had been standing there alone, ruminating.

He saw the manager down by the side door where the robbers had first jumped him. Mr. Kosario was rocking a baby, his wife's arms tight around his waist. She was a small Latina with straightened, blond hair, wearing a silky blouse and a red leather skirt with a tight hem. A skinny movie-theater manager with a hot little wife, and there stood Special Agent Adam Frawley, still trying to pimp his gold shield to get laid.

He ducked into one of the empty theaters and took a seat in the dark back row. When he first received the call that afternoon, he hadn't wanted to report. He wanted to ignore it altogether. *I am tired,* he told himself, *of chasing bank robbers and bad men.*

Now this heist vexed him. Viewed one way, it was a step forward for this crew: a takeover robbery, a broad move beyond banks. Viewed another way, it was a step back: a safe play, shying away from financial institutions. He feared it might be evidence of them cycling down—until he remembered that bad guys like these almost never quit until they're caught.

Either way, Frawley needed to move fast.

He kept going back and forth on Claire Keesey, between raging contempt and white-knight longing. Was she knowingly sleeping with the enemy, or just an unwitting damsel in distress? He stood and faced the blank screen, but try as he might to make a blank screen of his mind, the movie that kept playing there was Claire Keesey inviting MacRay into her home, into her bedroom, in between her legs.

In the lobby he found Dino looking for him, pointing with his clipboard. "Van on fire, about a mile away. Hosing it off now. Might not be a total loss."

FRAWLEY RAN OFF HIS excess adrenaline that night, doing intervals through Charlestown, down the suspects' streets and past their doors—even all the way out to Elden's house, in the area they called the Neck. The black-and-orange Monte Carlo SS outside Magloan's wooden row house on the downslope of Auburn Street still had beer cans tied to the bumper, JUST MARRY'D spelled out in Silly String on the rear window.

He needed to remind himself how close he was to them. He ran past the Tap on Main Street and thought about getting cleaned up and dropping back Downstairs for a beer. Instead he turned onto Packard Street, past Claire Keesey's and through the alley behind, looking for inspiration and also MacRay's beat-to-shit Caprice.

At home he made a protein shake and microwaved some chicken, eating in front of the Bulls-Sonics NBA Finals. Then he showered, put away some laundry he had stacked up, opened his mail. All of which was a prelude to the night's main event.

A pot stash, junkie works, porn mags, fishnets and garters—the sneaker box on the floor of his closet could have held any old shameful fetish, but Frawley's kick was minicassette-tape dubs of old crime-scene interviews. He wired his Olympus recorder through his stereo receiver, first warming up with a few older teller debriefings from past cases, some Greatest Hits—tellers weeping, reaching out to him for answers, *Why me?*—just to get his mind in that place. Then with the lights off and the shades down, he lay on the floor and listened as Claire Keesey's voice filled his room, transporting him back to the Kenmore vault and his desire for justice for her on that day . . .

. . . The one who was sitting next to me. Not next to me . . . but in the same seat, the same bench, the two of us. The one who blindfolded me. I could tell somehow . . . he was looking at me . . .

27
NEXT MORNING

HE HAD PUT UP with the blaring music all night. On his way out of the house, pissed-off first thing in the morning, Doug came down banging on Jem's door like a cop.

Nothing. No response. Doug's pounding was just more bass in the mix.

He was near the bottom of the stairs when two guys unlocked the inside door. Young guys with clipper haircuts, thick with new muscle, sporting different T-shirts but matching fatigue pants and paratrooper boots. Camo kids who looked like they'd walked straight off the rack of the Somerville Army/Navy Surplus store.

They entered like they belonged there, the loose pane of glass rattling in the door. Doug thought he recognized them, maybe just from around the Town. Then he remembered—the Tap that night, the two younger guys Jem was talking to in the corner.

They nodded at him—not friendly, more out of respect of Doug's size coming off the steps. "Hey, man, 's'up?" Something like that.

Said Doug, "Who're you?"

"Aw, we're going up to see—"

"How the hell'd you get a key?" He was on the landing now, facing them.

"Jem, man. He gave it to us." They said it as though Jem's magic name solved everything.

"What's that mean? You live here or something?"

"Naw, man." Now they looked at each other like cats, sensing trouble, wondering what to do. "Yo, we got some business with him."

"Yo, no you don't. Not in this house."

Another look between them. "Look, man," said one, coming on confidential, "hey, we know who you are. We know—"

Doug was on him fast, grabbing him by his T-shirt collar and driving him back up against the door. "Who am I? Huh? What do you know?"

The loose pane of door glass popped out, shattering on the floor of the dingy vestibule. Doug hadn't meant to do it, but he didn't care much either. He shoved the camo kid halfway through the empty frame.

"Take it easy, man, we just—"

Krista's door flew open behind Doug. She came out barefoot in a short black silk Victoria's Secret robe that was familiar to him. "What the—?" she started to say, but seeing Doug there with the camo kid silenced her.

Dez appeared behind Krista, rushing to the noise, pulling on a shirt. He saw Doug and paused a moment—then stepped out onto the threshold, ready to back him up.

The music grew suddenly louder upstairs. "Hey!" Jem was over the railing, looking down at the broken door. He turned and came down a step, wearing a ratty white hotel bathrobe open over smiley-face boxers and sweat socks, coffee mug in hand.

Krista's hand pressed against Dez's chest, and he stepped back against her door.

"Duggy," said Jem, coming down two more steps, "what the fuck?"

Doug released the glaring kid. They went around him to the stairs, seething, starting up toward Jem.

Doug looked for some explanation, but Jem made a *Later* face and waved him on with his coffee mug. He started up ahead of the camo kids, then turned and came back down a few steps, seeing the light coming out of Krista's door. "If that's my sister, tell her I'm out of underwear here, she could throw in a wash."

He turned and followed his pets up onto the landing, the door closing on the music.

Krista sulked, Dez looking apologetically at Doug.

Doug turned and walked out the front door, boots crunching glass, getting the fuck away.

28
LEADS

NSIDE THE HANGAR GARAGE of the South Quincy wreck yard, Frawley and Dino examined the charred corpse of a 1995 Dodge Caravan. The heat had blown out all the glass. The rear and middle were hopelessly charred, the front hood buckled up over the fused metal of the engine, but the dash had survived. The steering wheel was warped silly but remained whole.

"They made some mods to the vehicle," said Dino, pointing out a blackened strap attached to a clip soldered to the frame along the driver's door. "Racing harness, in case of a chase. They also replaced the steering wheel—the original had a Club on it and must have got cut. The accelerants were in freezer bags duct-taped to the floor in the rear, which is why the bad burn there."

Frawley leaned inside the driver's window frame. The melted upholstery gave the stinking heap its extra-toxic stench. The steering wheel was plain black with grip grooves and an illegal "suicide" knob clamped on for fast steering.

"No prints," said Dino. "The driver guard, Washton, said he saw driving gloves on dinosaur man."

Magloan. Frawley fit Coughlin for the quiet one with the clown mustache who shot up the inside of the lobby, MacRay for the talker, the earphone man with the cosmetic burns. "Stolen out of New Hampshire?"

"Wal-Mart parking lot, week ago Monday."

"Handicap plates?"

"Off a customized Astrovan outside a medical building in Concord, the day after."

Frawley went around to the blackened rear of the still-warm car.

"Little spots of latex there from the disguises, and some shreds of incinerated clothing," said Dino. "That would be the uniforms, stolen out of a dry cleaner's in Arlington. That melted box there, that's the guard's radio unit."

Frawley returned to the front. Something about the warped steering wheel bugged him. "Wheel wasn't stolen though."

"No. Probably new. Pick up a wheel at any auto store anywhere."

"You say the dinosaur wore driving gloves?"

"Right."

"The kind with the holes in the knuckles?"

"Probably so."

Frawley pointed. "They print the entire wheel, or just the grips?"

Dino shrugged. "Long shot, with the flame heat—but good question."

"One of the 911 callers from the highway—you remember?"

"She said they were hitting the horn, getting stragglers out of their way."

Frawley mimed it. "He's fired up, strapped in with a racing harness and a suicide knob, just pulled off a big job, speeding down the highway, hitting his horn . . ."

Frawley punched the center of his pretend steering wheel with his fist.

THEY TURNED IN THEIR loaner hard hats and stood in conference outside the Billerica work site, having just been lied to, lavishly, by Billy Bona. The double whistle went off, which, according to warning signs on the fence, meant a blast was imminent.

"These guys used a shape charge in the Weymouth armored job, one of the early ones."

Dino nodded, crossing his arms and sitting back against the Taurus's trunk. "Wonder what the arrangement is here. Maybe they got something on this Bona."

Frawley squinted up into the sun, promising himself that when this all came down, he would personally deliver Bona his subpoena for aiding and abetting.

"Problem is," said Dino, "on paper they were here yesterday."

"Yeah. He happened to have their time cards right there with him."

"We could go man-to-man here, break down every hard hat on this job, waste a day or two trying to find one who's ever worked with these two goofs—"

"Funny how they're not here today. 'First day they've missed, I can remember,' Bona says. Lying to a federal agent. The *balls* on that guy."

"Then there's Elden too, at work all day yesterday, and that one's verified—"

"Yup. Boss says yesterday Elden checks in with him before getting in his truck—says he remembers this because the guy's never *once* before stopped in to shoot the shit, ask how the kids are, the whole production."

"Means he knew it was going down. Maybe there was no falling-out. Not if he's part of their alibi. And Magloan—let's face it, he'll have somebody swearing up and down he was otherwise occupied the whole day. Bottom line is, bogus or not—we got nothing. Not enough to bring anybody in on."

"I'm not talking about putting them in a lineup."

"It's not even enough to go around shaking trees," said Dino. "We start turning the Town upside down over this—even if we ignore Elden and his squeaky-clean record—lawyers will be leaping out of their wing tips crying witch hunt. We don't have it."

"We can get it."

"Not enough to haul in these jokers. DA's office would ball this up and throw it right back at us, and we'd be poisoned for the next time. Where'd you get the authority to check their tax returns for employment anyway?"

"This MacRay has no credit cards, nothing in his name. His ride, this '86 Caprice Classic piece of crap, it's registered to the Coughlin sister who lives on the first floor of their house. I run her—it turns out she's got seven different cars reg'd to her name, her insurance. One of them's a high-line Corvette. Fifty dollars says she doesn't know about any of them."

There was a hot crack of thunder, a cannon shot, and Frawley felt the pulse in the ground like a shudder. They could not see the blast but heard the echo riding out, fading away.

Dino said, "I think we need to go full-court press on this. Bring on some assistance."

Frawley watched for rising dust. "No need."

"If these tea-pissers are feeling our heat, then we need to go broader, push them harder. Farm out some of this work."

"We can push them ourselves."

Dino said nothing, meaning Frawley had to turn back to face him. "Okay," said Dino. "Now tell me what the hell is going on here."

"What's going on is, I'm trying to catch some bad guys."

"No, I think what's happening is, you're taking this thing person-ally. I can't figure why, but that is the numskull approach and you're too clever for that. This is how mistakes get made."

"I want to bring this one home ourselves."

"Look, Frawl—I can play hard. I've been a detective seventeen years, I know how. I don't particularly mind going to war. All I need is a good reason."

"This is no war," said Frawley, backing off. "Boozo and his crew, they were like a big rock we flipped over, all these other little bottom-feeders wriggling out into the light. MacRay and company, we know who they are and we know where they are. Them squeaking by has gone on long enough."

"MacRay?" said Dino. "I thought you liked Coughlin as honcho."

"I'm thinking now it's MacRay."

Dino frowned impatiently. "And this is based on?"

"Call it a hunch."

Which Frawley regretted saying as soon as it left his lips. Dino slow-crossed his arms, leaning against his car, Frawley waiting for it. "What is this you're giving me now? Bullshit *hunches?*"

"Dino, look. These guys, they're an insult, an affront. Laughing at us. Now it's our turn to make them sweat a little. Let's take a bite out of *their* day for a change, just to let *them* know *we* are but a matter of time."

Dino's cell phone rang. "We get one chance," he told Frawley. "One." He went into his car for the phone and stood there with his elbow high, talking fast. He hung up and turned back to Frawley almost disappointed. "Your steering wheel," he said. "It's dirty."

29
ROUNDUP

DOUG STEPPED OUT OF Lori-Ann's coffee shop and saw two uniformed patrolmen waiting at the curb. Only a split-second reluctance to spill the large tea in his hand saved him from obeying his first, immediate, and not entirely irrational impulse, which was to take off running. Illness rose in his chest, a gut reaction to these two uniforms and the death of freedom they represented. But running would have been a huge mistake, and this near catastrophe was a second cup of ice water down his back.

Everything else looked normal for 7:30 A.M. on lower Bunker Hill Street: cars moving, civilians waiting for the 93 bus into the city, two project kids sitting on basketballs at the corner. For the arrest of an armed-robbery suspect, the G would have shut down the street like it was parade day, or else dispatched plainclothes federal marshals to serve the warrant.

The cops stepped up to him. "Douglas MacRay?"

He elected to go with them rather than follow in his own car. That they gave him the choice after patting him down was another good sign. The backseat of the cruiser was torn up and cramped, with the usual foot or so of legroom. Nice to be in there without handcuffs for a change.

He set his copy of the subpoena down on the duct-taped vinyl next to him and pulled out a glazed doughnut and bit in, relaxing. "Might want to go Prison Point instead of the C-town bridge," he told them through the plastic partition, "unless you're gonna light up your roof."

Instead they sat for minutes on the groaning iron skeleton of the Charlestown Bridge. Doug finished his second doughnut, a Boston crème, while reading through his subpoena.

United States District Court, it headlined. *SUBPOENA TO*

TESTIFY BEFORE GRAND JURY, below that. Under *SUBPOENA FOR,* there were check boxes, and an X was drawn through the box next to *DOCUMENTS OR OBJECT(S),* leaving the box for *PERSON* unchecked.

Area A-1 was the police district that covered Downtown Boston and Charlestown. The station was a big brick box around the corner from City Hall Plaza. They parked between two other blue-and-whites angled along Sudbury Street and led Doug down the steps to the glass doors and the lobby. It was a shift change, the halls crowded as they moved left past the women's detention room to the booking area, in sight of the holding cells and the slumbering prisoners.

The cop opened the ink pad and Doug licked sugar off his fingers. "What happened, you guys lose the prints you had?"

They printed his palm also, and the soft side of his hand opposite his thumb, then they had him make fists and printed each of his bottom knuckles before handing him a tissue. This was strange and worrisome, though Doug went along like he was enjoying the tour.

They took photographs with the height marker, front and profile, no booking number around his neck. Doug didn't smile, but he didn't not smile either, going for a borderline-amused *Sure, why not?*

They took a DNA swab from the pockets of his cheeks with a double-sized Q-tip that screwed into a plastic tube. Then they plucked eleven strands of hair from his scalp. "You want some piss too, I drank a large tea on the way over."

They declined his offer, handing him a script instead and making him recite witness-remembered sentences into a digital recorder:

Arnold Washton, 311 Hazer Street, Quincy.

Morton Harford, 27 Counting Lane, Randolph.

Take the coin tray off the cart, open up the safe, and start stacking bags.

Remember this ain't your money and how nice it's gonna be to get back home.

Ain't gonna be no rematch. Say hello to my little friend.

We're here for the popcorn, Mugsy. Yeaaahh, see?

They made him do the last line three times over until he read it straight, then allowed him into the bathroom for his unwanted piss before shutting him inside an interrogation room and leaving him alone for the better part of an hour. Soft carpeting covered the soundproof walls. Doug got up once to check the thermostat—he had heard this was how interrogators turned on hidden microphones—but couldn't tell anything without lifting off the box.

Instead he dropped a little whistling on his imagined audience, "The Rose of Tralee," and hoped they liked it.

The one who came in introduced himself as a detective lieutenant assigned to the Bank Robbery Task Force, name of Drysler. He was long-armed and walked with the stoop of a tall man getting older. He set down a clipboard with Doug's print card on top and pulled off a pair of reading glasses, folding his long arms like someone collapsing the legs of a card table.

"One chance," he told Doug. "I'm giving you one shot, and this is it."

Doug nodded like he was interested.

"You're the first one brought in," said Drysler. "So lucky you gets first crack at setting up a deal."

Doug nodded and leaned close to him. "Okay, I did it," he confessed. "Tell O.J. the search is over. I killed Nicole Brown Simpson and Ron Goldman."

Drysler stared, too old and too pro to get pissy. "Did you like prison, MacRay?"

"To that I'd have to answer no."

"They say life is full of choices, MacRay, but it's not. Life is lived choice by choice by choice. What you eat, what you wear, when you sleep, who you sleep with. You choose wrong here, MacRay, and you may never get the opportunity to choose anything again. That's what life in prison means—the death of choice."

Doug swallowed, the older detective's words going down like razors, but he smiled through his pain. "If you got that printed on a bumper sticker or something, I'll take one home with me."

Drysler nodded after a long moment of consideration. "Okay, you can go."

On his way out to the lobby, Doug passed a guy standing near the watercooler, jacketless like Drysler, a simple blue tie on a long-sleeved white shirt tucked deep into tan dress pants, shoulder rig prominent beneath his left arm. He was drinking water from a cone paper cup, watching Doug over the rim, and Doug found something in the guy's eyes that was familiar.

The cup came down and the guy looked at Doug as he swallowed, showing attitude. Doug was past him before he realized who it was and stopped, turning back.

"Hey," said Doug with a nod. "Rash cleared up, huh?"

The G-man just kept looking, wearing the same I'm-smarter-than-you face as do all the true believers in the Cult of the Gold Badge.

The only thing different about this one was his hair, not straight and tight like a boy's regular but a tawny morass of rings and tangles. Doug had two or three good inches on him, and at least forty pounds.

Doug said, "What, a little penicillin from the clinic took care of that?"

The look became a stare. Drysler came up on them to shoo Doug along, and Doug should probably have kept going to the lobby and out the door, but he couldn't resist. He stopped again and snapped his fingers, pointing back at the G-man and his professionally insolent face.

"Red Cavalier, right?"

No answer, the G's hand a tight fist at his side, trying to compress the paper cup into a diamond. Doug grinned, then turned and walked through the lobby, though by the time he hit the outside steps rising to the sidewalk, his grin was well gone.

SPENCER GIFTS SOLD ASS-SHAPED beer mugs that farted when tipped to drink. The mall store was deep, dark, and disorientingly loud, the clerk behind the counter—looking like a cross between an Orthodox rabbi and the Red Hot Chili Peppers' Flea—mouthing the anguished lyrics of a screeching Nine Inch Nails song like a man mumbling prayers at work.

Doug felt ridiculous himself, having outgrown this place ten years ago, but the store was G-proof and the music made it virtually unsnoopable.

Dez arrived late, his black eyeglass rims achieving a kind of retro rightness as he passed a jewelry counter of body art and skull rings. He was all worked up, Doug holding out a hand to slow him down, giving him a quick fist-rap of reassurance.

"They picked me up in the parking lot at work," said Dez. "This is after paying my boss a visit, checking on my story."

Doug nodded, keeping an eye on the store entrance. "Easy, kid. Take a breath."

"Trying to make me lose my *job*." Dez brought his voice down. "This is a *federal grand jury*."

"Relax. All that means is a roomful of citizens sitting around deciding if evidence is evidence."

"Oh? That's all?" Wild sarcasm didn't look good on Dez.

"The cops. What'd you tell them?"

"What'd I tell them? I didn't tell them anything! They didn't even *ask* me anything, just, 'Smile for the camera, open your mouth.' I don't even know if it was for the"—Dez looked back cautiously at two kids looking through Tupac and marijuana-leaf posters—"the most recent thing, or what. They didn't say *anything*."

"And neither did you."

"*Christ,* of course not. *Jesus.* They take that swab thing of your mouth?"

"Yep. Your palm, knuckles?"

"Sure. That's not normal?"

Maybe the van didn't burn right. Maybe Jem did something asinine, like taking off a glove while eating candy at the glass counter. Or maybe it was nothing. "They're just shaking the trees, trying to get lucky. Stirring us up."

"Well—it fucking worked!"

Doug nodded, shushing him. "Newspaper said they brought in some fifteen other Town guys. A dragnet, all of them players—except you. Calling you in with no armed-robbery record, that shows they're onto the other capers."

"But how? How do they know?"

"*Knowing* means nothing more than a hassle. It's what they can or cannot *prove*."

Dez looked at a disco ball twirling on the ceiling. "Trying to make me lose my *job*. . . ."

Doug shook his head, amazed that Dez was worried about his job here. Two people walked in the front, just girls, not thirty years between them, with skunked hair and pierced ears more metal than flesh.

"Jem thinks it's the branch manager from the Kenmore thing," said Dez.

Doug looked hard at him. "Where's that coming from? You talk to him?"

"No, not recently. This is from before."

"When before? What'd he say?"

Dez shrugged. "Just that. That she told them something, or she knew something—I couldn't really follow him. She's bad luck anyway, you gotta admit."

"How's that?"

"Ever since then, you know? It's been one thing after another."

Doug looked away to hide his annoyance, his eyes falling on a Jenny McCarthy poster, the topless blonde clutching her tits like she was going to rip them off her chest and chuck them at his head.

"Jem's fucking up all over the place," said Doug. "He went *Full Metal Jacket* in the movie theater lobby. Shot it up with one of the guard's guns—for no sane reason."

"He say anything about me?"

"About you? What, like you blabbed?"

"No. Wait—he thinks that?"

"Whoa, I don't know what the hell Jem thinks, I haven't seen him. What are you talking about?"

Dez tried to say it once, failed, exhaled, tried again. "Krista."

Doug stared. With everything else he had completely forgotten about that. "Aw, for Christ," he said in semidisgust.

"I ran into her at the Tap, the night of you guys' thing." Dez assessed Doug, wondering whether he should say anything more. "We hung out awhile, then she wanted to go back, watch the robbery coverage on the late news."

Doug knew how Krista got when she drank. So did a lot of other guys. And so, now, did Dez.

"Kid, I'm gonna say this just once. You're being played. She's putting you in the middle of what she thinks is this epic tug-of-war battle between her and me, not understanding that that's a rope I let go of a long time ago."

"Duggy—"

"On top of that . . ." A guy in a polo shirt and a ballcap passed the entrance without looking in, Doug getting antsy, starting to feel trapped. "On top of all that, she's running all over town doing errands for the guy who killed your dad."

"Her uncle. She works for him, does his books."

"A distant, *distant* cousin at best. And Krista's not known for her algebra, Dezi."

"What are you saying? About what she does for him?"

So idiotic, Dez getting all twisted up over Krista with these bombs going off around them. "Christ, will you cool it? What I'm saying is, she helps out Fergie the Florist from time to time, and I know what the Florist peddles and so do you. Clean those specs of yours."

"My specs are clean, Doug."

"Fucking fantastic for you. Oh, and one last little thing."

Sour now, pissed. "What?"

"That guy in the Cavalier outside your ma's house? He was at the police station when I was there."

Dez's face breaking, getting nervous again. "No."

"And no rash disguise this time. He is the G, and he's coming after all of us." Doug thumped Dez in the chest with his finger. "You want something to worry about, kid, start worrying about that."

30
BUY YOU SOMETHING

HE WATCHED HER THERE a moment, kneeling and working in her garden, before making his presence known. The riot of color and life that surrounded her was at its peak, this long late week in June. Though gardening in general struck Doug as the ultimate in futility—bringing a plot of land to life only to watch it die again, a chore doomed from the beginning—something in the way she threw everything she had into it, regardless of the outcome, was lovable.

All this passed through him in the instant before she saw him: Doug watching her kneeling on the dark rug of soil that held his treasure, in the thin, sidelong light of the setting sun, her shadow reaching across her garden sanctuary.

"I WANT TO BUY you something," he said.

They were in the plaza outside Trinity Church, part of an early-evening crowd surrounding a street performer juggling two bowling pins, a bowling ball, and a pair of bowling shoes. Only Claire watched the juggler—Doug watched the amusement in her face. The act ended to applause, Claire clapping prayer-handed under her chin.

"What do you want to buy me?"

"What do you want?"

"Hmm." She retook his hand, twisting slightly on her heels. "How about a new car?"

"What kind?"

"I was kidding. I don't want a car."

He said nothing, waiting.

"You're serious," she said.

"It's the first thing that came into your mind."

"That's because I was *joking*."

"If we trade in your Saturn on top of it, you could do pretty well."

She smiled, mystified by him. "I don't. Want. A new car."

"What do you want then?"

She laughed. "I don't want anything."

"Think. Something you wouldn't buy for yourself."

She made a thinking face, playing along. "Got it. Frozen yogurt at Emack's."

"Not bad. But I was thinking more along the lines of jewelry."

"Oh?" She smiled at the sidewalk ahead of them. "Yogurt or jewelry. I could be up all night wrestling with *that* choice."

Earrings didn't excite him. He looked at her neck: graceful, bare. "How about a chain? Where would we go to look for something like that?"

She put her free hand to her throat. "Why—Tiffany, of course."

"Okay. Tiffany it is."

"You know I'm still joking."

"I know you were joking before, when we were talking about a car. But once the topic of jewelry came up—I think you got a tiny bit serious."

She laughed like she should have been insulted and hit him lightly in the chest. Then she looked at him more closely. "What's gotten into you tonight?"

"I want to do this," he said. "Let me."

THE BROAD-HIPPED SALESWOMAN with the jailer's ring of cabinet keys waited as Claire turned and gathered up her hair. The woman worked the clasp and Claire turned to the framed mirror on the counter, opening her eyes and fixing on the diamond pebble glittering in the freckled scoop of her neck. Ringed in gold, the solitaire rode out a deep swallow.

"This is crazy," she breathed.

"It looks good on you."

"How can you . . . you can't afford this."

"It's cheaper than a car."

"Lasts longer too," said the saleswoman, smiling.

Claire's eyes never left the diamond. "I almost wish you wouldn't." She turned her head and watched it sparkle. "I did say *almost*, didn't I?"

The saleswoman nodded. "Will that be credit, or do you need to finance?"

"Cash," said Doug, reaching for his pocket.

CLAIRE STOPPED BEFORE A window a few shops away, checking her reflection again, this time over a display of fountain pens and sport knives. She touched her collarbone in exactly the same manner as the women in diamond advertisements. "I have to buy a whole new wardrobe now, just based around this."

Doug noticed her bare wrist. "There was a matching bracelet too, you play your cards right."

She admired it a few more moments before her hand fell away. "I should never have let you buy me this."

"Why not?"

"Because. Because the intent on your part was enough. The impulse you felt—I love it, whatever prompted it. That was the magic. A stronger person maybe, she would have told you that—and meant it—and let it go right there. A more secure person, maybe. But you didn't have to do this."

"The guilt," marveled Doug. "It's immediate."

"It is, isn't it?" she admitted, smiling a moment. Then she turned toward him, the smile gone. "Doug—I did something today, I have news."

A little heat came into his forehead. "What's that?"

"I quit my job."

Doug nodded slowly. "The bank."

"I had to. And really it was only a matter of time before they fired my ass." A flash of a smile at her slang, again quickly replaced by earnestness. "I was slacking off so much, I was no use to them anyway. Ever since the robbery . . . I won't bore you with that again, but I just couldn't do it anymore. Not because of what happened there. Because of me. I needed to make a clean break. I just—I can't believe I actually did it."

"It's sort of sudden, though, isn't it?"

"I guess. Why?"

"I'm just thinking about the police. A few weeks after the robbery . . . and now you're quitting the bank."

Her hand went to her open mouth. "Oh."

"I mean, maybe they won't . . ."

"That never even occurred to me. You don't think . . . ."

He did. This was sure to bring renewed attention from the FBI. And if they started watching her, how could he keep seeing her and stay out of their crosshairs? And then, if they ever put him and Claire together . . .

That made him think. "You still talk to that FBI agent?"

Her hand came away from her mouth. "You think he'll be talking to me again?"

Doug felt icy suddenly. He wondered why he hadn't thought of this before. "What's he look like? Anything like on TV?"

They were moving again, through the Copley Mall toward the escalators, the Tiffany & Company bag dangling in Claire's hand. "He said he's a bank robbery agent, that's all he does."

"What's he like, a haircut in a suit?"

"Not hardly. He actually lives in the navy yard somewhere."

"The yard, huh?"

"Like my height, maybe an inch taller. Thick brown hair, kind of wavy-curly, all over the place. In fact—it's probably gone now, but he had this reddish sort of stain on his skin from this guy he was chasing, a bank robber who got a dye pack. Do you know what a dye pack is?"

They were on an elevator going down, which was lucky, because Doug could barely move.

Too convoluted, the whole thing. Too massive, he couldn't break it down. Had he fucked up? Had this bank sleuth somehow been feeding off him through Claire?

He watched her at the revolving doors, pausing in her story about the bank robbery agent getting stained in order to eye her necklace again in the reflective chrome.

She knew nothing. Maybe the sleuth knew nothing either. Maybe.

Outside, they crossed a brick-and-stone plaza, commuters flooding the street from the Back Bay station, jumping curbs and chasing down taxis. Claire took his hand. "Delayed sticker shock?"

"No," he said, coming back around. "What are you going to do now?"

"Right now? I don't—"

"No, I mean—now that you're out of a job."

"Oh. I've got some money saved, I have a cushion. What do I *want* to do?" She looked up at the tops of the skyscrapers. "Stay out of banking, that's for sure. My parents are going to freak out. I thought about teaching, but—what I do with the kids at the Boys and Girls Club, that's not really teaching. It's not social work either. It's nothing you can make a living at. Though I did talk to the director over there, in case a paid position opens up."

Thoughts came to him as fast as the commuters swarming around them. "What would you think," said Doug, "if I quit my job too?"

She laughed a little. "I guess then I'd have company. But why?"

"I got some money saved too. My own cushion. Hell, I got a whole sofa stashed away."

They walked a few more steps against the crowd, then she looked up at him, remembering the necklace. "A whole sofa, huh?"

"Matching love seat, even."

Everything seemed threatened now, everything converging. Like his old life had suddenly been condemned, explosive charges being laid on all the load-bearing beams, a crew of badass demo hard hats advancing on it with crowbars and sledges.

"You know how everybody's always got that place they want to go—their *if-only* place? You know, *If only I had the money,* or, *If only I had the chance.*"

Claire nodded. "Sure."

"I never had a place like that. I bet you do."

"Only about half a dozen."

"The problem is—no one ever goes to their if-only place."

"No, they never do."

"Well, why not? Why couldn't we be the first?"

She smiled, finding a different angle on his face, discovering something there. "Know what, Doug? You're a romantic. I think I knew it all along, only you hide it so well."

"Things are changing for me, Claire. Changing fast, like hour to hour."

"There's one small problem I foresee with your if-only plan."

"What's that?"

She smiled. "There's no Charlestown anywhere else in the world."

"Yeah," he said. "Yeah, that is a snag."

And he left it floating there like that: mere talk. Twenty-six years ago his mother had walked away from the Town. Maybe now it was his time to follow.

31
KEYED

CLARK MAYORS WAS A locksmith with a small key-making shop on Bromfield Street, one of the narrow lanes off the cobblestone boulevard of Downtown Crossing. The night-duty agent had given Frawley Clark's pager number, the Boston FO being without a good lockpick and contracting the sixty-year-old keymaker for side gigs, both on and off paper. Clark was a careful, square-faced, solidly built black man with a pleasant, home-cooked smell and half-glasses over snowy cheek stubble. His no-questions fee of a hundred an hour was coming straight out of Frawley's own linty pocket.

Just a few hours before, Frawley had been sitting in the backseat of his new Bureau car, a banged-up, navy blue Ford Tempo, trying to stay awake half a block down from Claire Keesey's door. The muscular growl of a Corvette engine roused him in time to see the two of them nuzzling in the front seat, then her getting out and going into her place alone. Frawley put off his plan to drop in on her then, instead rolling out after MacRay.

The bold green sports car seemed headed for the interstate, in which case Frawley wouldn't bother trying to keep up, but then MacRay cut sharply toward the Schrafft's tower at the last moment, crossing the Mystic north into Everett. He turned off Main Street down a dim residential road, Frawley thinking MacRay had made him, only to see the Corvette's round brake lights turn into a driveway. Frawley backed off and waited, parked up on Main trying to figure out his next move, when just in time he recognized MacRay's second car, the dumpy white Caprice Classic, parked right in front of him. Frawley took off and made a slow loop past a funeral home, and by the time he returned, the Caprice was gone.

Frawley's adrenaline had hardly subsided from then until now, watching Clark work on the side door of a broad garage. The only light source was a pale blue spritz coming off the next-door neighbor's backyard Madonna.

Clark first snaked a worm scope under the door, previewing the interior bolts and checking for alarms. His handheld, gray-and-white monitor showed no booby traps, nothing tricky. Then he hiked up his pants and knelt before the padlock, a folded rag under his knee, an old black curtain draped over his shoulders and head to swallow his working light. Frawley kept an eye on the street—the neighborhood struck him as one likely to mete out swift street justice to housebreakers—listening to Clark's patient click-scratches.

The cloak was whisked away and Clark straightened with a soft grunt, lifting his Klein Tools bag off the ground and nodding to Frawley. Frawley gripped the knob with his break-in gloves and it turned easily, no creaks or whines to worry the night. Clark followed him inside, Frawley quickly shutting the door.

Clark turned his flashlight back on—a white spray off a wire hooked to his half-glasses—and found a wall switch screwed to an unfinished beam by the door. He gave the exposed box the once-over, fingering each electrical connection, and then with the aid of Frawley's stronger Maglite, followed the stapled wires up to the ceiling rafters and the lamps clamped overhead.

Clark hit the switch and the lamps came on loud, the halogens blazing up the old garage. The muscle car glowed dead center, emerald against cement, a long, low, lustrous jewel resting on five-spoke, star-rimmed wheels.

Against the near wall was a red tool cart on casters and a built-in workbench under particleboard shelves of small parts, accessories, and tools ancient and new.

"Pretty thing," said Clark, snapping off his spy light.

Frawley walked to the car and rested his gloved hand on the glass-smooth hood, expecting a pulse. It must have had half a dozen coats of paint. He slipped his fingers underneath the handle of the driver's-side door and opened it wide.

The interior was black leather, still smelling like a new baseball glove. He lowered himself into the driver's seat, the upholstery moaning but not protesting. He reached for the stick and toed the pedals, touching the leather-wrapped wheel. He would have needed to inch the seat forward to operate it comfortably.

"Dope dealer, huh?" said Clark, eyeing the finish, tool bag in hand.

Armor All slicked the dash. Frawley reached across the passenger seat for the glove compartment, and suddenly smelled Claire Keesey there, that butterscotch hair product she used. The car was registered to Kristina Coughlin of Pearl Street, Charlestown, Massachusetts. Underneath the registration card was a CD jewel case labeled *AM Gold*.

Frawley climbed out, shut the door. He moved to the workbench, sliding open each drawer of the tool cart, then checked the minifridge, pulling out a one-liter bottle of Mountain Dew. He cracked the cap and drank down half of it at a gulp. He peered into a cardboard-box trash can, but it was just empty Dew bottles and shop rags.

In the rear of the garage, the cement floor ended over the old wood framing, dropping down four feet or so to packed dirt. Frawley trained his flashlight on the yard tools rotting there, the bicycles and sleds, a limp tetherball game. The soil looked hard and unlikely to preserve his shoe tread, so he hopped down, exciting dust in his flashlight beam. Decades of oxidation gave the dark trench a metallic tang. He looked around but it was all just junk, and Frawley wondered what the homeowner's relationship was to MacRay, making a mental note to run the address in the morning.

He was on his way back up when his beam found a head-sized stone loose from the rocky subfoundation. Its shadow moved when he did, betraying a hollow inside. Frawley shoved an ancient snowblower out of the way and crouched down before the stone and the scooped-smooth hole, like an eyeball tumbled out of its socket. The cavity was empty but for a few silica-gel packets, the Do Not Eat kind packed inside sneaker boxes to absorb moisture. Frawley put his face to the opening. The smell he got was the unmistakable old-linen odor of stored cash.

He stood, downing more Mountain Dew. MacRay had just recently moved his stash. If only he knew how close on his heels Frawley was.

Clark yawned up top, reminding Frawley that the meter was running. He climbed back to the cement floor, the Corvette gleaming proud. He tried to envision it torched. "You can lock it back up again from the outside?" asked Frawley. "Make it look like no one's been in here?"

Clark nodded, his voice rug-soft and shag-smooth. "No time at all."

"Go ahead and kill the light then, get set up outside. I'll be right there."

Clark switched off the rafter lamps and exited, leaving Frawley with his Maglite beam and the car. Frawley dug out his ring of keys, comparing them in the heat of his flashlight, the new Tempo key having the sharpest teeth. He walked to the long front fender of the Corvette and dug the key into the soft finish, gouging it across the driver's-side door and all the way to the rear, then stepped back to admire his work.

THERE WERE SOME EXCEPTIONALLY handsome front doors in Charlestown, but Claire Keesey's was not one of them. Around Monument Square and the nearby John Harvard Mall, the European-style entrances compared favorably to those in Beacon Hill and the lower Back Bay, but hers was entirely ordinary: no brass, no stained glass, no bold color, just a drab brown door, the weathered varnish flaking off the grain.

She opened it wearing gray gym shorts and a ribbed, black tank shirt, braless and barefoot, her hair wet but combed out, falling straight. Surprise in her eyes when she recognized him behind the sunglasses—though Frawley noted disappointment as well.

"Hi," she said, as in *What are you doing here?*

"This a bad time? Were you expecting someone else?"

"No. No—come in."

He moved past her across the white-tile threshold, down the short hallway into the living room. Against the widest wall, a wire shelving unit and a bamboo hutch were paired off in a feng shui tug-of-war. The leather sofa was a plump, safe tan straight out of Jennifer Convertibles. There were other staples—the rattan CD tower from Pier One, the Pottery Barn slab rug—as well as some out-of-place wall prints left over since college. It was all mishmash, the product of a decade of gradual accumulation.

The coffee table was cluttered with clothing catalogs and issues of *Shape* and *Marie Claire*. He peeked into her bedroom, the comforter rumpled, the bed unmade, then cut back to the kitchen, looking out the window to the buildings across the alley.

"You want to blow-dry, I can wait."

"No," she said, put off by his wandering around. "That's okay."

He looked at her a long moment. He carried MacRay's mug shots in a manila envelope tucked under his arm. "So you quit the bank."

A tiny bloom of panic in her eyes. "Yes, it just—it got to be too much."

He had tried to give her the benefit of the doubt. To view her as an unsuspecting pawn, as the victim of an ex-con's con. Along with needing to determine how much she knew about MacRay, Frawley had gone there that morning in the hope of working up some sympathy for her.

But any chance of that went away when he saw the flat-shell jewelry case on her kitchenette table, classic Tiffany & Company blue. He laid the manila envelope down on the table and opened the hinged case, lifting out a thread-thin necklace, dangling it between his hands, the solitaire quivering like a tiny crystal eye.

"Lovely," he said.

"That—it was a gift."

"Not from the piano mover?"

She did not answer. Frawley kept himself in check. He was holding a chunk of MacRay's movie money in his hand. The crook was buying her jewelry with it. "May I see it on you?"

Her hand went protectively to her neck. "I'm not really dressed for . . ."

He was already bringing it to her, undoing the delicate clasp and waiting for her to turn. She did so, reluctantly, sweeping the hair off the back of her neck, and Frawley clasped the necklace beneath her darker roots, waiting for her to turn back around.

She kept her eyes low, self-conscious, trying not to be. The diamond winked above the scoop neck of her tank top, her breasts pressing against the black fabric. Her nipples were erect and she crossed her arms guiltily.

Frawley said, "Did you hear about that movie theater in Braintree?"

She blinked at this abrupt change of subject. "Yes, sure, the holdup."

Frawley nodded, backing away. "The same guys. We're pretty certain."

"The same?" Her surprise was authentic.

"It was an armored-car pickup. We also now know they're all Charlestown guys."

Again, her shock. "For sure?"

"In fact we're watching a couple of jokers now. Getting close."

She looked down, nodding like she was trying to figure out something. Maybe some ghostly concern that had been tugging at the edge of her consciousness for a while. Frawley talked to keep her off-balance.

"These Townie guys, they love armoreds. Banks and armoreds,

that's always been their thing. Rite-of-passage stuff, them getting dusted and pulling stickups. Boston cops used to respond to bank alarms by shutting down the Charlestown Bridge and waiting for the dopes to try to cross back over with their loot. Especially in winter—they love the snow, the havoc it wreaks, pulling on ski masks and going robbing. But some of these kids, a select few, after bouncing around the system a little—something kicks in and they start getting smart. Those are the ones who grow into professionals. The ones for whom robbing banks becomes a career, a vocation, their life's work. See, the prison theory, that's always seemed a little too pat to me."

She shook her head, trying to follow him. "Prison theory?"

"The community college, under the highway? Used to be *the* prison in Boston. Sacco and Vanzetti, Malcolm X. Theory goes that the inmates' families settled here to be near them, breeding successive generations of crooks and bandits. But I think it's simpler than that. My own theory is that bank robbing is just a trade here, the way villages in old America and Europe used to be known for a particular craft. Like glassblowing or bootmaking or silversmithing. Here it's bank robbing and armored-car heists. Techniques developed and refined over time, talents passed down through generations. You know, father to son."

Claire looked pale now, staring into the middle distance, reaching for the sofa corner with one hand and absently touching her necklace with the other.

"And then there's this Revolutionary War mentality," Frawley went on. "They've taken that mythology and perverted it. The fuck-the-invaders tradition—appropriated it for their own criminal means. The bank robber as folk hero, all that nonsense. Like I'm the enemy here, right? The law is the bad guy." He picked up a CD from the top of her stereo, turned to her. "Huh. *AM Gold*. Any good?"

She didn't hear him. She was somewhere else now.

Frawley replaced the case and moved on. "But, no, don't worry. These guys always find a way to screw up, even the smart ones. Things like talking too much about banks. Or asking too many questions of people, trying to learn things about the FBI. Or flashing lots of cash around. These are things people notice."

Claire's hand came away from her necklace.

"And on top of all that," said Frawley, returning to the table to pick up his manila envelope, "on top of all that, we've got ourselves a partial handprint."

This roused her from her trance. "I thought you weren't able to talk about things like that."

"Well . . ." He showed her a big smile and a shrug. "Who are you going to tell, right?"

She nodded without meeting his eye. The necklace was starting to choke her now, and Frawley found that he could pity her ignorance, but not her fate: she had invited aboard this shipwreck of her life the very pirate who had scuttled and looted it in the first place. Frawley could have protected her if she had let him. He could have spared her all this. But now she was his advantage over MacRay, and as such, a thing to exploit. He tucked the sealed envelope back under his arm. Catching bank robbers was his job, not rescuing branch managers from themselves.

"Sure you're okay?" he said.

She crossed her arms again, nodding, standing almost on one leg. She could see dark clouds massing on the horizon, but refused to acknowledge the storm they forecast.

"Yeah," said Frawley. She was waiting for him to leave now, and he let her wait. "Yeah," he said again. "Well." Then he fit his sunglasses back on his face and started for the door, stopping next to her, again struck by the necklace. He pressed the tip of his forefinger lightly against the pocket of flesh between her clavicles, touching the starry little pill, absorbing her discomfort, her distress. "Okay," he said, and left.

32
RINK

FOUR GUYS IN KNEE-LENGTH denim shorts and T-shirts, black skates over heavy cotton socks pushed down under meaty calves, eating lunch on the indoor ice in the middle of June. They had the rink to themselves, refrigerator fans rattle-roaring like truck engines outside the boards as they circled around two Papa Gino's pizza cartons set upon milk-crate pedestals.

"So," Jem said, swigging a Heineken, calling the summit to order. "Somebody fucked up somewhere."

Doug dropped his crust into the open box, curling effortlessly around Jem's back and plucking his bottle of Dew off the ice floor, gliding backward.

"And we still don't know how," said Jem. "I don't even know yet who the fuck to dock."

Dez drifted away from the pizza without meaning to, better on Rollerblades than he was on ice.

Jem said, "That ride better have burned."

Gloansy finished a Heineken and stooped to return the bottle to the six-pack carton, saying, "Fuck you, you were there."

Doug looked up at the rafters. He remembered the cheering and the bleacher-stomping and the way his last name rhymed with *Hurray!* and also how it always seemed that a win for the home team was never enough—how it seemed that nothing short of the entire building going up in a ball of flame would satisfy the bloodlust of that crowd.

He could still see the Bruins scout, the guy in the Bear Bryant hat and fingerless wool gloves sitting in the last spot on the fifth riser, center ice, making frantic marks in his spiral notebook as the Martin sisters next to him kept screaming Doug's name. His summary report, showed to Doug after the draft, described MacRay as "a thug player with a touch of class," a high-scoring, high-potential defenseman blending the goon tradition of the seventies with the new eighties finesse.

But it was all just echoes now. He found himself touching his split eyebrow and pulled his hand away, angry. This was why he didn't like being out on this ice anymore.

"There were no obvious problems on the job," Jem continued, "least none nobody admits to. So how come we each spent half our morning making sure we were clean of the G, getting here? How come all of a sudden we're earning so much heat?"

No cops were waiting for Doug when he carried his tea out of Lori-Ann's that morning—yet everything seemed changed. It was like a protective seal on the Town had been broken, and now there could be cops waiting for him anywhere: his car, his home, his mother's house.

"Simple," said Doug, coming back around for another slice, spraying some shavings against the stacked crates with a sharp stop. "They were onto us from before. And we went ahead and rushed it anyway."

"Rushed, nothing," said Jem. "But we didn't sit around neither, let 'em shut us down."

"No," said Doug. "No, that would have been foolhardy."

"Aha, a little attitude from the mastermind here. Okay, genius. Tell us, then. Where and when did all this shit go wrong?"

"For that I'd have to take us all back to a bitter-cold day in early December 1963."

Jem frowned off the reference to his birthday. He turned to Dez, the only one of them who hadn't been at the movie theater. "Duggy's pissed 'cause I went and had a little fun."

"That what that was?" said Doug. "That was fun?"

Jem smiled his angry smile. "That job was the driest fucking job. It was *nothing*."

"Nothing," said Doug.

"Truth be told, Douglas—it was pansy-ass. It was pussy. Hadda be said."

Doug slowed and drifted back toward the crates. "So let me get this straight. The job went *too* smooth for you. Not enough fucking up, far as you're concerned, your usual quotient."

"It wasn't no heist. It was a friggin' lemonade stand we knocked over. We could of been three *girls* in there, pulling that off."

"It was a sweet score, and it fell like a feather."

"Awright, assholes, enough," said Gloansy, looking to douse the flames.

But Jem wasn't interested. "It's not the paycheck, kid," he said, gliding away from the pizza podium to engage Doug. "It's how you bring it home."

"It's *that* you bring it home—*period*," said Doug. "You're too old to die young, Jemmer. That time is passed."

"Fuckin' Johnny Philosopher here. What've you got to lose all of a sudden?"

The leer in Jem's face was for Claire Keesey, but Doug was in no mood. "This is about being a pro and acting like one. About doing it good and right. That's the thing."

"No, Duggy, see, that's *your* thing. *You* plan it, no one else. And then what—I gotta follow your rules and regulations? I'm your employee here?" Jem's slow trajectory brought him closer to Doug, his hands resting on his hips. "See, my thing is getting into it on the job, mixing it up. 'Cause I'm a motherfucking *outlaw*."

Doug let Jem drift past, the smell of beer trailing him like a cloud of flies.

Dez and Gloansy had stopped chewing, waiting on opposite sides of the pizza pedestal like kids watching their parents fight. Doug said to them, "You guys on board with that? You want me keeping you *out* of danger, or putting you *in* some?"

Jem circled back, speedy but measured, lifting skate over skate. "And what is this with playing it safe? We are *bank robbers,* man. Stickup men, we go in packing, balls to the wall. It's a gun in our hand, not a fuckin' briefcase. There is nothing *safe* about this." He spun around so he could face them all, gliding backward. "The hell happened to you, Duggy?"

Gloansy said, "Can we all fucking forget this, please?"

Dez said, "Yeah. Frigging boring."

Gloansy put down his beer. "Give us our magic number and let's call it a day."

Jem started back at a decent clip, looking to do a breeze-by. "Like your trick there with the guards. Holding their families over them, immobilizing them with that. So *safe*. So fucking *clever*. Know what?" He zipped past Doug, spinning, heavy-legged but clean. "I fucking *hate* safe and clever."

Doug said, "This is why you beat on the assistant manager at the Kenmore thing. Why you had to go and grab the bank manager. Stealing's not enough for you anymore. That won't get you caught fast enough."

"This is what I'm talking about," Jem said, talking to Doug but playing to the jury. "Since when did you let the people in our way *get* in our way?"

"You tuned up that guy for no reason. Other than to bring the heat down on us, which we are now enjoying this very fucking day."

"Did you forget that that motherfucking brown hound hit the bell?"

"No, he didn't."

"No, he didn't," scoffed Jem. "Yes, he very well fucking—"

"He didn't," said Doug. "She did."

Jem just drifted past, staring.

Gloansy checked Dez, then Doug. "How do you know, Duggy?"

"How do I know?" Doug watched Jem curling around them, Doug saying, *Shall I?*

You don't have the onions, said Jem's white-eyed challenge.

Doug said, "I know this because she told me."

Jem still stared, trying to figure Doug out, Doug saying, *You got nothing on me now.*

Dez said, "What do you mean, she told you?"

"Checking her out after the job—I met her. We talked a couple of times."

Jem said, "He's fucking going steady with her."

Doug kept talking. "And now Jem has her as an undercover FBI agent or something. All sorts of conspiracy theories, probably. When she's just someone trying to put her life back together, simple as that. There. Now everybody's caught up."

Jem said, "You're still seeing her."

"Am I? What, you gonna follow me some more? Follow the G following me? We'll do the motherfucking parade down Bunker Hill Street, how about that? Streamers, silly hats, everything." Doug kicked away then, rounding the three of them in a tight, slow circle.

Gloansy turned, tracking Doug. "Who's following *who*? Fuck's going on?"

Jem said, "What is it you're not getting? Our Duggy here's been dating that cooze from the Kenmore job. The one who rode with us. Oh, wait—but *I'm* the one that wants to get caught."

Dez said, stunned, "How long, Duggy?"

"Not long."

"Well—you still seeing her?"

Jem said, "How about it, Romeo? When you gonna bring her around, meet your buds?"

Doug said, "She doesn't know anything."

Gloansy said, "Well, Duggy, for Christ—she *better* not."

"She doesn't."

Jem said, "And I bet he hasn't even lit her lamp yet." He mimed a slap-shot goal. "Hasn't slipped one in between the pads."

Doug threw Jem a look saying, *Enough*.

"You know," said Jem, blowing through that stop sign, "me and the assistant manager, we danced that one time. Whyn't I call him up, we'll double-date? Go out for milk shakes or something. Can he drink through a straw yet? Or wait—what kind of milk shake did I mean?"

"All right, Jem," said Doug, throwing down the gloves. "Here's the deal. And this is as un*safe* and as un*clever* as I can make it. Okay? You ready?"

Jem's waiting smile was full of dragon steam.

Doug said, "I am not with your sister anymore. And I won't be, and I never will be, and that's the end of that. Krista and me—we are not getting married. Never. We are not all going to live in your house, the three of us and Shyne, happily ever after. Not gonna happen."

Jem's wild smile became a hot, dark slice in his face. A Jem-o'-lantern with the candle blown out, smoking. He stood perfectly still on the ice. "She's got you wrapped so motherfucking tight."

"That's right," said Doug.

"You fucking whip-ass pussy."

"Man," said Doug, swinging at the chilled air, amazed that it had gone this far, and at the same time not surprised. They were grappling on the edge of a cliff here, this close to going over together for good.

"You're turning into fucking tapioca right in front of me. What's she got on you, man? Or are you so fucking blind you can't see?"

"What is it I can't see, Jem?"

"You can't see what she's doing."

"Tell me, Jem. Tell me what she's doing."

Jem's head shook in disgust. "If we can't trust her, kid—how we gonna trust you?"

Doug smiled. So much coming out of him, a riot of pent-up thought and anger. "You are so fucked in the head, Jem boy. You don't trust me? No? Then find yourself someone else to set your scores. No—better than that, *you* do it. Yourself. *You* map it out. And I'll sit back until game time, then show up and shoot the place up from under you, just for fucking *fun*."

"There's always Fergie, man."

Doug's head jerked back like Jem had taken a jab at him. "Don't fucking even."

Jem's eyes were bright and daring. "He's got some real scores lined up. Big hits for big hitters. He's said as much."

"Excellent. Then you're all set, kid. You don't even need me here. 'Cause I will *never* work for that psycho piece of shit." Doug glided backward on the strength of his own outburst. He looked to Dez. "How about you, Monsignor? Wanna go work for the guy who gunned down your dad?"

Dez exhaled a stream of determination and shook his head.

Doug shrugged back at Jem. They were paired off now, Doug and Dez versus Jem and Gloansy. A lot of silence, everyone's breath billowing out fast.

Doug said finally, "So is this how it ends?"

Gloansy put out his hands as though elevator doors were closing. "Hey, okay, hold on, just hold on."

Jem shook his little head. "Nothing's ending, man."

"No?" said Doug. "Only because you don't have the *sense*. Gloansy too, the both of you—you're gonna keep taking jobs until you get grabbed."

Fury twisted at Jem, his frown warping, jumping. "I ain't never getting grabbed."

"Always, I knew this, but I never saw it as clear as right now. The movie theater score—that was our biggest ever. Not enough. Nothing ever will be."

Jem looked at him in white-eyed amazement, slow-drifting toward him. "You talking about money? When's it ever been about money? This has always been about *us*. The four musketeers here, taking on the fucking world. About being outlaws, man. I don't know when you forgot that, Duggy. I don't know when you forgot that."

"All right then. For kicks, since no one here really cares—what's our split?"

Jem still drifting forward, eyes locked on Doug, a collision course. "One-fourteen, three oh two. Per."

Dez said, next to Doug, "Holy shit."

Gloansy laughed out a tension-breaking gasp. "And that's all clean? Spendable, like right fucking *now*?"

Dez said, "Holy fucking *shit*."

Jem remained staring at Doug, Doug at him.

Gloansy said, "Lemonade stand, whatever—that's fucking *genius*!" Cackling now, shouting at the ceiling. *"Aaawooo!"*

Doug said evenly, "The split is light."

Jem stopped drifting.

Doug angled his blades on the ice, setting himself. "Even with your ten percent ass-kiss to Uncle Fergus, it's light. That's a soft split."

Gloansy stopped his celebrating. Dez looked at Jem. No breath came from anyone's mouth now.

"I saw the receipts," said Doug. "But, hey, right? I mean—it's not about the *money*."

Jem started for Doug, and Doug started for Jem, Gloansy and Dez lunging after their respective teammates, wrapping them up to prevent a brawl. Gloansy was just strong enough to keep Jem off Doug, and though Dez was overmatched by Doug, Doug didn't really want a fight here. He wanted to win the argument, then leave.

"Every split you ever did was soft," said Doug. "And why did we let you handle the cash? Because we trusted you? No—because you're Jem. Because that's the cost of being fucking friends with you."

Jem lunged again, Gloansy digging his skates into the ice and fighting hard to hold him, swinging Jem around, taking some of his blows.

Doug went on, shouting, "'Cause you're a thief with a petty fucking heart. Little rip-offs, ever since I known you. A Wiffle bat here, a comic book there. Things of mine that would vanish."

Another swipe missed, Jem getting closer, saliva slicking his chin. Doug kept himself back just enough to deny Jem contact.

"That Phil Esposito photo card you needed to complete your set, that I wouldn't trade you? What—you thought I never knew? But that's the kid you were, and that's the kid you are still. Funny-guy Jem, the cutup—that's what's carried you through. But it's not funny anymore. This is the last split of mine you are gonna handle, and I mean *ever*. Always gotta have more than the rest, always gotta be in charge."

"I *am* in charge, you mother—"

"No." Doug used his skating advantage to muscle Dez off him. "You keep your skim, and when you're using it to buy your next pair of fucking speakers or whatever, just remember how, yeah, it did all used to be all about us, four kids from the Town. How, yeah, we did have something once."

He looped around past Jem, just beyond his reach, bringing Jem tumbling down on top of Gloansy. Doug curled to scoop his Dew back up off the ice, then skated for the doors, Jem's vulgarities bouncing off his back like boos.

His skates were off, socks stuffed inside them, by the time Dez came out, looking more anguished than usual, a guy full of questions, forever quizzing the world about himself and his place in it. Doug stopped him before he could say word one. "You cut loose of Krista, you understand me? Now you know for sure that I got no stake in it. You had your thing with her, now get out. These Coughlins'll kill you. You hear me?"

Dez nodded, shocked.

Gloansy came out skate-walking over the hard rubber flooring to where Doug sat lacing his Vans. It surprised Doug that Gloansy, of all of them, was the one most desperate to keep the crew together. "Duggy, hey—you're gonna cool this down, right? And so's he? You guys, huh?"

Doug could already hear the dominoes clicking, tiles spilling from the end all the way back to the beginning, spelling out his flight. But there was no point trying to explain this to Gloansy. Doug stood and carried his skates to the door.

33
BILLY T.

FRANK G. LOOKED GRAY under the yellow doughnut-shop lights. He hadn't shaved in two or three days, and kept running his hand across his bristly lips like a rummy. His eyes were tea-bagged and his shoulders flat under a *Malden Little League Coach* shirt.

"Well, that's good to hear," said Frank G., distracted. "Yeah, you been needing to break with them for a long time."

Doug waited, shrugged. "That's all I get? No trumpets, no angels singing?"

Frank G. squirmed in his seat. "So—we get this call at the station last week."

Doug was startled. Mr. Anonymous made a point of never talking about himself or his work. "The station," said Doug, alerting Frank G. to his slip.

"Guy's hit by a truck on the Fellsway. Okay, no big deal, we suit up and head out to assist EMS, it's routine. Then, big commotion as we arrive on the scene. Something's up. Middle of the road is this huge dump truck with a haul full of sand, engine still running. They tell us there's an elderly man pinned underneath it. Truck's got four twin sets of wheels, big mothers, and I'm thinking, mashed foot, some poor jaywalker's looking at a wheelchair for the rest of his days. So my guys are getting out the equipment, and I go round this truck, find the driver sitting on the curb median, bawling into his hands. A big guy, and he's falling apart, sobbing, asking for a priest. So I know it's gonna be bad.

"I go round to look, and my eyes, it takes a second to process this. The tire, the outside one, is right on top of this guy's pelvis. Flattening it. Inside tire has his legs crushed at the knees. EMTs and a young lady cop are crouching by this guy, attending to him, and my mind's telling me it's fake, it's a movie, guy lying in a hole in the road, dummy legs set on the other side of the tires.

"And then the old guy's head turns. I can't even believe he's still moving. His head turns and his eyes find me, his mouth open like a baby's. And now I *really* can't believe it. Because I fucking know this guy. It's Billy T."

Doug said, "Whoa, whoa. Billy T.? Sad-sack Billy T.?"

"From the meetings. The scally cap he always wore, that moth-bitten thing, it's lying next to the EMT's medical case. And then I see in his eyes, his wet, little wooden eyes—he recognizes me. He's trying to place me—I'm in uniform, red helmet, jacket, reflective stripes—but he knows the face. Probably thought I was an angel or something, you know? The body like that, the brain releasing those, whatever they're called, hormones, opiates, whatever. Least I hope that's what it does, when you wake up under a dump truck."

Frank G. watched steam escape from the triangle torn out of his cup cover.

" 'Billy,' I says to him. The people attending to him, they look up at me like he's my dad or something, I know this guy's name. One EMT jumps up, takes my arm, handles me like I'm next of kin, tells me Billy was crossing the street against the traffic, truck knocked him down, rolled over him, stopped. Billy T. should be dead, he tells me. Any other way this had happened, he would be gone already. But the truck was like a giant tourniquet, cutting off the bleeding, keeping him alive.

"Meantime, my crew is scrambling to slide a twenty-five-ton hydraulic jack under the dumper, setting up these two big seventy-ton air bags. They see me huddled with the EMT and think Billy's my wife's uncle or something, so they're working double-time for me, and I'm like, Whoa, whoa, *whoa!* We raise this thing off him and Billy dies. We leave it where it is, Billy dies too—only more slowly.

"So now I've got the EMT in my face, he's flipping out on me, talking about surgeons and field amputations and such, and I'm no doctor, but I can see there's nothing to amputate here. A magician, maybe, could saw Billy T. in two, pull him out, then wave his hand and put him back together again. So I become the point guy on this. I want to go off, sit down with the truck driver, wait for the priest—but I'm the guy now. I have to make the call.

"So I kneel in the road next to Billy. They'd cut his shirt off and I can see his little heart beating through his old dishrag of a chest, but real slow. He moves his arm—guy's moving still—reaching for me, so

I take his hand. His little fingers are hot, he's burning up. And the look on his face. But I see his lips are working, so I get down low. Both feet in the grave and he's still able to whisper to me. 'Frank,' he's says. I yell back to someone to turn off the truck so I can hear, and then the engine goes silent, the whole world goes silent.

" 'Billy,' I says to him. 'My friend.' All of a sudden this weepy old man's my friend, like we're soldiers on a battlefield somewhere, the same unit. I take off my helmet. 'We gotta lift this truck, Billy. We gotta get it off you. Anything you want to say?' I don't know if he's got kids, what. 'Any message for anybody, something I can do for you, my friend?' I keep calling him my friend, over and over. 'Anything you want to tell me, Billy, anything to say?'

"And his hand, there's like this little squeeze of pressure, and I get in tight. I'm right there, him breathing on me, this half-ghost, looking me square in the eye. 'Frank,' he whispers. 'Frank.'

"I say, 'What is it, Billy, anything at all.'

" 'A drink, Frank. Get me a drink.'

"The EMT next to me, he jumps up again, calling for bottled water, a dying man's last request. Me, I'm kneeling there as cold as a fish on ice. Because I know Billy T. I know this weepy old, bandy-legged Irish punter with bologna on his breath. He didn't want any *water* to drink just then. He didn't want fucking *water*."

Doug shared Frank G.'s chill, but not his anger. Frank left it hanging there, until Doug finally had to ask, "So what happened?"

Frank G. looked at him like Doug hadn't heard a word he'd said. "*That's* what happened. *That's* the story."

"No, what happened to Billy T.?"

Frank shrugged, pissed. "My guys did the best they could for him. We shimmed some timber cribbing around the wheels to cut down on the vibration, we raised the truck. What happened to Billy T.? They put a sheet over his face and took him away. We hosed off the road and went back to the station."

A gust of laughter from the clerk and an Indian customer at the counter—Doug and Frank G. sitting there like two guys who had just donated blood.

"Okay," Doug said.

Frank G. looked up from the study he was making of his coffee cup. "Okay, what?"

"Okay, so I'm waiting for you to drop some wisdom on me."

"Wisdom? I got nothing for you, buddy. I'm fresh out here. Billy T., he was a royal pain in the ass at meeting—but the guy did good work. He was dry some twelve fucking years. I can't get my mind around this thing."

"What, that he—"

"That with all the work he did, *twelve long years*—every single day of it he was just marking time until he could take a drink again. Waiting for that day. Like someday he'd hit all nines on the odometer and it would roll over to zero again and he'd get to start fresh. A life with no restrictions on it. And what *I* want to know is—is that all of us? Just marking time here, waiting? Thinking someday, some miracle's gonna happen, and we're going to be free again?"

Doug nodded. "Maybe, yeah."

"Christ, don't agree with me, Doug. I'm fighting for my life here. What was he thinking, what? That heaven is an open bar? Jesus wiping out pint glasses, setting out a coaster, *What'll you have?* That's what we're being good for here?"

"The guy was dying, Frank."

"Fuck him." Frank sat back. "Fuck Billy T."

"All right, Frank. Hey."

"Fuck you, *hey*. You weren't there. How would you like it if I was going down, you holding my hand, and I asked you for a quick pop? Huh? I *begged* you?"

"I wouldn't like it at all."

"You'd be sick. Fucking repulsed. All my words here? You'd tell me I was full of shit, and you'd be right." He dropped his hands on the table. "I am, anyway."

"Frank, man," said Doug, looking around for something to say to him. "I don't wanna see you like this."

"Listen, Doug, you're still my obligation, you got my number. But I can't do this anymore. Least not right now."

"Whoa, hold up. What are you—"

"I'm saying maybe you ought to be in the market for another sponsor."

"Frank—no fucking way, Frank. No way. You can't."

"Can. Am."

Doug stared. "Frank—you would never let me."

"No? How would I stop you? Huh? How you gonna stop me?"

Doug rubbed his face hard in a panic. Up popped a memory from a long-ago meeting, one Jem had appeared at—uninvited, twenty minutes late, and stinking drunk. He had dropped into a folding chair two rows behind Doug and, in the middle of Billy T.'s lament, started humming "The Star-Spangled Banner." When someone finally asked him to leave, Jem burst out crying and started talking about his father and how he never really knew the guy, and all he ever wanted was his love. Two people slid down the row to comfort him, at which point Jem jumped up and cackled, *Suckaz!*—knocking over chairs and lurching toward the door. *Duggy,* he had said, *c'mon, man, lezz go!* And it was Frank who came over to Doug later, telling him, *Your friends are afraid of you getting healthy. They want to keep you sick.*

"Frank," said Doug, still searching for some angle to play, some lever to pull—but all he could summon was unreasonable anger. "Don't walk out on me now. I *need* this."

"Hey. Sorry if my little crisis of faith is inconvenient for you. Sorry if I'm the one maybe needs a little counseling now."

"I—I can't fucking counsel you. I wouldn't know the first—"

"Then respect my decision and leave it at that, for Christ's sake." Frank picked up his keys and started to stand, then sat back down again. Something else was tugging at him. "I wasn't going to tell you this. But this guy came to see me about you."

Doug froze. "What guy?"

"Other day, over at the station house. Showed me an FBI badge, asked if I knew someone named Doug MacRay. We went back and forth on that one a little while, me trying to go the priest-doctor-lawyer route, confidentiality. He wouldn't have it. Kind of a prick. So I basically told him what I knew. That this Doug M. reminded me of myself some fifteen years ago, and that I was trying to be a sort of priest to him, the way I wish someone'd been a priest to me. I asked this guy, I said to him, 'You got a priest?' And he says, 'Yeah. Me.' So I tell him, 'No, then you're lost. Gotta answer to someone.' He says, 'I do answer to someone. The archdiocese of the FBI.'"

Frawley. What had he told Frank G.? Frank, who had always praised him. Frank, who thought Doug was something.

"You probably . . . maybe you heard some things," Doug said. "About me—did you hear some things?"

Frank ignored that like he hadn't heard Doug. "So then this guy, he says to me, 'Priests don't hit their wives.'"

Doug got lost on that one.

"Yeah," said Frank, nodding his way through this. "I hope you're hearing this first from me. I am a shitbag wife-beater. That was my drunk, getting pissed off and slapping around my first wife. Great guy, huh? Good sponsor. Finally she had me arrested one night, but jail time would have meant no firefighting job, no salary, and as she was now fixing to divorce me, no alimony. So she dropped the

charges. I have her greed to thank for my life now." Frank smiled bit-
terly, blowing out a long breath. "So much pride I had. That I'd
turned everything around since then. That I'd put down this asshole
living inside me." He shook his head. "Fucking Billy T.," he mumbled, pulling himself to his feet. "You got my pager if you need it."

Doug stood with him, in shock. "Frank . . ."

Frank shook his head, unable to look Doug in the face. "Careful
crossing that street," he said, and then he was out the door.

34
DEFINITELY GOOD NIGHT

DOUG TURNED IN HIS seat again, scanning the faces behind him, fans carrying beer caddies up the aisles behind home plate, leaning on the back rail with their scorecards and their ballpark food. The wires in their ears were just radio earphones, and Doug told himself to relax.

"What are you looking for?" asked Claire, next to him.

"Nothing," he said, turning back. He had bought her an official Red Sox dugout jacket after the weather turned chilly in the fifth inning. The cuffs were empty, her hands tucked inside the leather sleeves. Her necklace hung below her throat. "Just taking in the crowd. The Fenway experience. Getting my money's worth."

He looked out past the plate umpire's broad back to Roger Clemens on the mound, the ace, ten years off his rookie season. Clemens hid his grip behind his glove and stared in, shaking off a sign. He went into his motion, delivered, and the pitch sliced flat off the bat, fouled straight back against the screen—the first ten rows jumping like heads on springs.

"Are we hiding?" she said.

Doug turned to her. "What?"

She shrugged under the bulky jacket, curious. "I don't know."

She had picked up on his sleuth paranoia. A yellow-shirted hawker appeared in the aisle and Doug waved him up, as though a box of Cracker Jack was what he had been looking for all along. "Here we go."

"I guess I thought the secretive stuff would go away after a while," she said, softening her words with a smile. "You being so hard to get hold of. I mean—it's romantic and all, you leaving me a Red Sox ticket on my garden seat. Just not normal."

"It bothers you, yeah? I can give you my phone number, no

problem. Just that I'm never home, and I don't have an answering machine."

She shook her head, denying making any demands on him. The kid with the $2.25 price button on his cap came with a rack of over-sized Cracker Jack boxes, and Doug busied himself paying for one. The kid was slow making change, his leafy roll of cash drawing Doug's roving criminal eye. Maybe someday that would go away, he thought. Maybe he could train himself not to watch for these things, not to compulsively puzzle out ways to relieve cash businesses of their profits.

For the first time in a long time, certainly since he got sober, Doug had nothing lined up. Nothing else he was working on, no jobs, nothing in prep. Frank G.'s defection weighed on him as one more reason to move on. All he had to do now was devise some sort of graceful exit strategy from the Town, some way to tell the others good-bye.

Claire eyed him as he rose half out of his seat to stuff his cash roll back into his jeans. He remembered how she had fallen silent when he'd pulled it out to pay for her jacket.

He ripped open the box of caramel popcorn and offered her some, which she declined. "Do you ever see your father much?" she asked.

Doug looked out to the left-field wall, which was where this question seemed to come from. "I see him once in a while. Why?"

"What sort of things do you two talk about?"

"I don't know. Not much." He dug down to the bottom of the box for the prize. "Hey, flag tattoo," he said, making to hand it to her, but with her hands pulled into her cuffs, he tucked it into her jacket pocket.

"I guess I'm just imagining my father in prison. . . ."

Why was she pawing him with questions? "I'm not my father," he told her. "Maybe that's what you're asking. It took a while, because as a kid I idolized him—it was just him and me, after all. Took a while for me to get a good look at him and start working hard at being everything he's not."

She nodded, liking what she heard. Still, something in her eyes wanted more.

Doug looked down. This seemed as good a time as any. He prefaced his story with "Seems like I'm always doing this with you."

"Doing what?"

He took a breath before launching into it. "I was at this bar once. Five years ago now. Bully's, a Townie tavern. Doing my thing, bunch of us, drinking pitchers, carousing. I don't remember much of this firsthand. I know a guy came in, older than us, getting his drink on. He's looking at me, and I'm getting annoyed. Some point he comes over, asks am I Mac MacRay's son. Tells me he knew my dad years ago, worked with him close, and I'm like, whatever. Until he tells me how he recognized me. Smiles and says I look exactly the way my dad looked when he got drunk."

The wave came around, everyone jumping to their feet and throwing their hands in the air except Doug and Claire.

"And I guess I attacked the guy. I have almost no memory of this. But if they hadn't pulled me off him, it would have been bad. Hospital he went to got the law involved, and the guy fingered me. And I'm grateful now. I am."

She watched him closely. Almost like she knew this already or suspected something like it.

"I did some prison time for that. Hated it, and I will never go back. Only thing to come of it was, I started on the program while I was in there. Changed my life. Cleared probation a year ago, now I'm free and clear. And I *feel* free and clear." All of this was the truth. He'd only left out his earlier stint inside.

"Wow," she said.

"Yeah, I know. It's like a knife in my eye, every time I have to tell you these things." He ticked them off on his fingers. "Alcoholic. Broken family. Ex-con. Not much to take home to your parents, huh?"

She absorbed all this, turning back to the field. "I told my parents I quit," she said. "They want me to go see a psychiatrist. Which I actually had been considering on my own—but now, forget it."

"You don't need one."

"No?" she said, shooting him a quick, angry look she seemed to regret.

Doug felt the chill. "You're full of questions tonight."

"Am I?"

"Something on your mind?"

She shook her head, hesitant, as though easing her way into this. "Agent Frawley came to see me again and I guess it shook me up a little."

Doug stared at the mound to control his reaction. "Yeah? How so?"

She was looking at him now. Fucking *looking* at him, and Doug made a study of the Milwaukee pitcher checking the runner on first. He would not look back at her.

"He said they were sure now that the bank robbers are from Charlestown."

Doug nodded. "Yeah?"

"He said they're watching some people. Getting close."

Did she know? Would she be telling him this if she knew anything? Was she testing him? Feeling him out? Trying to *help* him?

"I guess I'm worried," she said.

Maybe she did know. Maybe she knew and she accepted it and she was only waiting for him to come clean to her. Clear the air. Put all this behind them.

A fantasy. He turned slowly, giving her plenty of time to break off her scrutiny of him. "What are you worried about?"

She shrugged inside the dugout jacket. "Testifying, I guess. Living in the same town as these people. Things like that."

She looked back at him on *Things like that,* searching him—was she?—and Doug held his expression, nearly impossible, looking into her eyes, wondering suddenly who was lying to whom.

Had Frawley put her up to questioning him? This was Jem's voice inside his head, he knew that, and it twisted his stomach.

Would she wear a wire for Frawley?

"He told me there were some developments in the case," she said. *Don't ask.*

Doug nodded, checking the game, keeping his eye on the ball. *Developments?*

Don't. Let it go.

"Must be a long process," he said, "an investigation like that." He had hardly felt the words leaving his throat. "Probably still a long ways off."

Why was she nodding? Was she waiting for more from him? Baiting him here?

Don't.

Going crazy. "Maybe if you just don't think about it," he said. Were they communicating in code now? *Don't think about me that way—think about me the way I am now.* "Put it out of your mind. Don't deal with it unless you have to."

Her eyes were on him again, and he tried to guess her emotion. Relief? Surprise? Was she hearing this other thing in his words?

Do not ask.

Developments.

He had to know. Maybe she wanted to tell him—maybe she was trying to warn him here.

Or maybe she didn't know anything. His head was pounding like his heart had traded places with his brain.

Don't.

His words caught her just as she was looking away in relief. "Why?" He shrugged it, like he didn't have a care in the world. "What are these developments?"

And she came back to look at him—they were searching each other—and he could tell by her eyes that he had made a disastrous mistake.

She turned away first, looking down at the ballcap of the boy sleeping against his father's shoulder in the seat before her. Doug had been found out.

"Fingerprints," she told him.

Doug nodded, frantic to unmake his mistake, trying to swamp her doubts with forced enthusiasm. "Fingerprints, wow." *Whose?* "I didn't even know they still solved crimes that way."

She shrugged.

"Anyway," he went on, headlong, "you definitely shouldn't worry. Not about your role in it. There's really nothing to worry about, that I can see."

The silence that came over them was charged, the game going on before their eyes and not mattering. Nothing mattered suddenly. The wave swept past and again failed to lift them. Then another sort of commotion—someone slapped Doug hard on the shoulder, and he turned fast, expecting Adam Frawley and federal badges and guns.

It was Wally the Green Monster, Fenway Park's furry green mascot, demanding a high five.

People around them pointed to the electronic scoreboard over the center-field bleachers, the seat numbers flashing there. Claire was one of four lucky winners of a free pancake breakfast at Bickford's.

The guy inside Wally said, "Jesus, man, lighten up," and Doug stuck out his hand, accepting the Green Monster's salute and watching him dance away.

Claire looked bewildered.

"Free pancakes," Doug said, riding the interruption. "Not bad."

"Sure," she said.

If he had any chance of salvaging things with her, it would have to be away from the ballpark crowd, alone. "You okay here right now, or . . . ?"

She turned and looked straight into his eyes. "Let's go back to my place."

Doug blinked. "Your place?"

Her hand came out of its sleeve and took his. "On one condition."

"Okay, sure."

"You can't stay over."

"Okay," he agreed. He would have agreed to almost anything.

Only after driving back to the Town in near silence—his hand leaving hers only to shift gears—as he neared Packard Street, did he ask:

"Why can't I stay over?"

She turned toward him. " 'Mornings after' are so excruciating, and I don't want that with you. Morning only raises questions. I'm tired of questions."

He eased down her block, pulling up outside her door, shifting into neutral. He idled there, not turning off the engine.

"You're not parking?" she said.

Doug looked over at the light shining above her front door. "Oh, man."

"What?"

He couldn't go in there. Not this way. There was no future in sleeping with her without telling her everything first.

Her hand went slack in his but he would not release it. All the cars parked up and down the block—the sleuth could have been watching from any one of them. "How about I come back first thing in the morning instead? We'll make breakfast, we'll do the whole 'morning after' thing first, get that out of the way. All those questions. What do you say?"

Disbelief in her eyes, but also concern. The dash vent fans floated the edges of her hair.

The urge was powerful, and for a moment he relented. "Oh, fuck it, no. Christ, what am I . . ."

But then he remembered the ballpark and how it had felt sitting there, thinking he had lost her. He still had a chance here. *Don't blow this too.*

"No," he made himself say. "I can't."

She yielded a little. "If it's about leaving . . ."

He saw it in her eyes then: she was afraid it was ending. All she was doing here was trying to hold on to him a little while longer.

"Look," he said, "there's plenty of time, right? Tell me there is. Because I have a long night of second-guessing ahead of me."

"What about work tomorrow morning?"

What was she asking him? Was she asking him something?

"I quit that," he said. "I told you, I'm ready for a life change. I'm committed to it. What about you?"

"Me?"

"Your if-only place. Us blowing this town. Together."

She searched his face, reaching for his eyebrow, touching the smooth scar. "I don't know."

Yet her indecision lifted Doug's heart. Whatever she knew or had figured out about him—she did not tell him no.

"Pancakes, maybe," said Doug. "You like bacon? Sausage or bacon?"

She looked at their intertwined fingers, then pulled her hand free. She opened her door, swinging one leg out, looking back for him.

"If I walk you up there," he said, "if I get anywhere near your door . . ."

With the interior light on now, he felt anxious, exposed. She read more into it than that. "Is this good night or good-bye?"

He reached for her, pulling her back inside. The kiss was deep and all-encompassing, and she surrendered to it, gripping him tight. She didn't want to let him go. Maybe never, and maybe no matter what.

"Good night," he told her, stroking her hair. "Definitely good night."

35
DUST

JEM, IN MOTION.

On foot patrol in the Town, feeling the air currents curl around him as he walked. If it had been foggy, moisture giving character to the air, then others would have witnessed the slipstream in his wake, would have stared in awe at this native son trailing a flowing cloak of smoke. Then they would have understood.

Some knew already, a respect he felt but never deigned to acknowledge. Their hesitant glances, the quick look-aways. It hurt their eyes to stare. But their esteem for him was evident in their silence, the hush that fell over people and children as he passed.

He was carrying this Town on his back. All his concentration, all his brainpower was focused on remembering the Town as it had once been, and returning it to glory.

Fucking Duggy.

Jem fingered the tea bag in his pocket, the smooth plastic packet. As he walked, he envisioned the Town in flames. Cleansing flames, flames that built, destroying the unworthy, flames that cauterized and forged. The row houses and triple-deckers burning clean and new.

At the corner of Trenton and Bunker Hill, another new dry cleaner's. Yuppies passing him unaware. In a purging fire the dry cleaners with their chemicals would be the first to go up. Then back across the bridge would go the yuppies, ants fleeing a burning log. On paper, they owned the properties, but Jem still owned the streets. In the way that animals own the forest, he owned the Town.

He felt the itchy flecks of Colonial brick flowing in his blood.

Fergie. Jem could listen to him talk about the old Town for hours, having just left the wise man sitting in his flower shop walk-in cooler. The Florist knew about tenacity, about pride. The ex-wrestler and ex-boxer wore it on his face, the defiance of a window all cracked up but unbroken. Fergie knew how to win and win ugly.

Fucking Duggy. Treason and betrayal all around Jem. Everyone weakening and succumbing to change, to *progress,* and Jem, the glue, single-handedly holding everything together. Patching up the cracks. After Fergie it would all be up to him.

On the fucked-up clock face of the Town—as off-kilter as Fergie's—Pearl Street ticked up toward midnight. The witching hour was where Jem was born, lived, and would die. He was proud of the house's disrepair, the way it taunted the refurbished triples up and down the street, houses that had gone condo like whores transformed into virgins. All the sellouts who bailed: the Kenneys, Hayeses, Phalons, O'Briens. If it had been firstborns the yuppies were paying top dollar for, these traitorous fucks would have placed their kids' school portraits in the classifieds section of *The Charlestown Patriot.* Moving out ain't moving up—it's giving up, it's pussy.

Where the sidewalk plummeted like the first drop on the old Nantasket Beach roller coaster, Jem walked in the door. He had duct-taped an old cardboard box where Duggy had busted out the glass— solved that window rattle anyway. At the bottom step, he stopped and looked at Krista's door. Thinking about the next generation produced in him a powerful urge to see Shyne. His eye fell upon the old pictures standing on the hall table: the house as it had been in the sixties; an old jalopy parked on the slant with his dad unloading something—swag, most likely—from the trunk; his parents' wedding-party photo, Kennedy/Johnson campaign buttons under each groomsman's rose boutonniere; him and Krista in rompers, sitting on a blanket out on the back lot when it was grass.

He walked in without knocking, down the dark-wood hall, finding Shyne in her high chair as usual, abandoned in front of the tube. Her hands, face, and hair were smeared with bloodlike ravioli sauce while she zoned out on the goddamn purple dinosaur hopping around on a pogo stick. Sauce in her ears too.

"Hey, kid," he said. She did not turn. He touched the back of her neck, a clean spot there, but he might just as well have been touching a Shyne doll. "Uh-oh!" sang the purple dinosaur, and she stared like she was receiving some coded message, unable to look away.

The toilet flushed and Krista came out of the bathroom wearing a Daisy Duck T-shirt and saggy-ass bikini underwear.

"You didn't cook nothing, did you?" He didn't even want dinner, only to point out one more thing at which she had failed.

"The fuck do I know when you're gonna be home anymore?" she said.

But he had neither the time for nor the interest in fighting—and this, she noticed. A weird little moment of mind reading between the calendar twins, and suddenly she knew exactly where he had come from, whom he had met, what he had in his pocket. Almost like she could see inside his shorts to the little tea bag nestled there. A look crossed her face—hunger, want—and Jem saw it. She knew he saw it.

"What?" he said, more taunting than angry—another chance to punch home his authority.

She used to say, after every slow, smoky exhale, *Don't tell him, Jem.* Every single hit. Stronger than her taste for dust was her fear that she would be found out by Duggy. Everybody needed a parent or a spouse to run around behind. Come to think of it, Jem spent a lot of his time running around behind Duggy's back too.

He stared at his sister, the failure. To be a slut was one thing, but a failed slut? That took something almost like talent.

Now he is as disgusted by you as I am.

Jem almost said this. Yet even he held out hope for a turnaround from Duggy. It had happened before. The kernel of a plan was already forming in Jem's head.

Maybe, Kris, I can save even you.

Anything was within his power. But now he was furious again, staring her down, hating the thing that he loved. He bent down and kissed the top of Shyne's stained head and tasted sauce. The kiss said, *She will not be a fuckup like you,* and at the same time, *I alone can save us all.*

"I'll be upstairs," he said—knowing that she knew what that meant, knowing that she would sit down here in her saggy-ass panties and stare up at the water-stained ceiling knowing he was up there getting high without her. *Because you couldn't hold up your end of the deal. Because you couldn't hold on to Duggy, and now it falls to me.*

Upstairs in the cramped air of his hi-fi room, he dialed up the Sox on his stolen cable, his big-ass TV, and drew the tea bag from his pocket. He got his stuff from the cabinet over the kitchen sink and set it all out on the coffee table, slicing open the tea bag with the tip of his X-Acto knife. In a shot glass nicked from Tully's years before, he mixed the milligrams of magic with an equal pinch of dry Kool-Aid powder. Then he worked up a little saliva, drooled it into the glass, and watched the dust take to the spit and fade, becoming one.

He thought of that dude at the halfway house those years ago, the four-eyed former CVS pharmacist who in his spare time made lung-busting bongs out of bicycle pumps, and who was eventually bounced back into lockup for cooking speed in his room. He had told Jem that dust was medically not a hallucinogen but in fact classified as a "deliriant." Jem had never forgotten that. A *deliriant*. That was the fucking balls.

He swirled the glass, the mix turning cherry red. Then he tapped out a Camel unfiltered and dipped the tip into the scooped bottom of the shot glass, soaking up paste. His thumb came down on his Irish-flag Zippo, the bloody tip flaring as he inhaled.

He took it all in, so deep he thought he might never send it back out again, his chest expanding like the universe.

The atmosphere in the room depressurized as his head sank back and sighed. Things changed. Sounds—the TV, his heartbeat—separated from their sources, jettisoned like escape pods from the mother ship, tumbling free. Time stopped for him and he drifted out of it, watching it slide greasily by. The play-by-play man called a home run, and minutes later Jem watched the ball sail into the bleachers.

Wind back the clock. His words, speaking about the Town. *Wind back the clock.*

A Texas voice talked to him out of the TV, Roger Clemens yelling at him from the mound between pitches. "She's the G, you stupid fucking dicksuck!"

Jem said, *Fuck, Rocket—you think I don't know that?*

"The hell is Duggy? Where *is* he?"

What do I look like, his goddamn keeper?

"Fuckin' A, man, you do. Don't shake me off here. I will plunk you in the ass."

You couldn't plunk fucking Mo Vaughn's fat ass, you washed-up has-been.

"Don't Buckner this, bitch!"

Well, fuck you, you fat fucking . . . oh, shit . . .

Clemens was now a big, soft purple dinosaur in a Red Sox cap, singing, "Uh-oh!"

Jem's jellyfish brain glowed in the room. The transformation had already begun, his blood turning into mercury. Jem stripped to boxers and flip-flops and flapped down to the basement.

He hit it hard, chest presses and forty-pound curls, heart thumping like a body falling down an endless flight of stairs. The dank basement smelled of the sea, the iron weights clanking like anchor chains.

The camo kids. His foot soldiers. It would start with them, this rebel army he was putting together. Roving bands of Townie kids taking back their streets. Patriots planning for the second Battle of Bunker Hill, winding back the clock. The red, white, and blue of their bloodshot eyes.

He finished with power squats and climbed back up the stairs, his legs and arms aching the way bent steel aches. He shut his door on the world and stood there as the hallway wavered at either end. Jem the deliriant.

He flipped on the hanging lamp over the mirror, his body so pumped that there was no longer any distinction between flexing and not flexing. Jem was flexed. Every part of him blood-tanned and tumescent.

Every part.

The shorts came off. Facing himself in the mirror under the swinging lamp, he gripped his ass with his other hand, and his third hand—had to be—pulled back on the bank manager's hair, making her want it, making her work for it. The purple dinosaur pounding at the door threw him off, the bank manager momentarily becoming Krista, but he concentrated hard, and by the time he corrected himself he was too close for Kleenex.

His acid spew scorched the vanity in the shape of a question mark, Jem finishing and stepping back, decreeing, "That shit is fucked-up."

In the hot shower, his pig's dick hung swollen and pink between his legs. He gave the nozzle his back, shutting his eyes—the water jet turning to fire on his shoulders, the nozzle like a welder's torch spewing flame. Sparks danced off his body like spray, the blue flame fashioning something of him, forging a new being, a man of iron transformed in a baptism of fire.

He knew now what he had to do. What the Man of Iron—formerly the Man of Glue—must do.

He dressed in black and returned to the basement, to his grandfather's old steamer trunk under the stairs. He worked the combination on the lock, and the hinges—arthritic from the dankness—groaned as the trunk opened its mouth. He lifted his gramps's uniform off the weapons and trophies the old man had brought back from the Pacific—his rifle, the swords, the half-dozen grenades cling-wrapped in an oversized egg carton—along with some other small arms he had tucked away, and some cash, that was the seed out of which the great rebellion would soon grow. From the bottom of this trunk, he pulled out the Foodmaster bag, then closed and relocked his treasure chest.

This was what brothers did. They watched each other's back.

In darkness he set out on his mission, soldiering through the night Town with the bag tucked under his arm. Crows and keening pterodactyls swooped down from the Heights, screaming over Bunker Hill Street. Voices spoke at him from doorways, alleys, corners. An impossibly ancient woman, older than the sidewalk, whispered to him, *Take care of her for us,* to which Jem replied telepathically, *Ma'am, I will.*

Through Monument Square under the granite spike. Night creatures sailed around it on robe wings—the spirits of altar boys loosed from church attics—drawn to the heaven finger that was a radio tower broadcasting WTOWN, all day and all night, the reception strong and clear inside Jem's head.

Doug was getting ready to fly. Jem picked up his pace, the ocean roaring in his ears.

Packard Street was the heart of the disease. The G was a cancer in the Town, Jem the fucking deliriant chemo. Jem, the sin eater, the avenging archangel.

In the alley behind Packard he saw her glazed bathroom window, pushed open a few inches for him, just enough. Jem pulled on gloves, and with a glance up and down the alley, tucked the bag into his belt.

He asked for invisibility. It was granted.

Up onto her purple car without a sound, from its roof to the top of the dividing brick wall. He found a hand grip on the brick face of the sleeping building, the window within his reach now. It was old, like those in his mother's house, hanging on clothesline pulleys, needing only a shove to rise.

He asked for, and received, stealth, night vision, and cloaking silence. For a moment he hung two-handedly from the wooden sill—then he raised himself over it, crawling inside headfirst, being born into the room, coming to rest on the cold tile floor.

The bathroom—the crotch in the body of the home. The kitchen was the heart; the bedroom the brain; the dining room the stomach; the living room the lungs. The front door its face; the garage its ass.

The crotch was dark and cool. A steady dripping inside the porcelain bowl at his shoulder. The flower smells of night creams.

His vision was good, and he untucked the paper bag from his waist, controlling the wrinkling noise. He pulled out the mask by its oval eye sockets, standing, fitting the black strap over the back of his head.

So long as you ditched the masks, she's got nothing.

Course I ditched the masks.

Well, you seemed pretty fond of your artwork, I want to be sure.

Fuck you, Duggy. So fucking clever.

In the sink mirror, the white Cheevers mask floated against the blackness of its eyes and graffiti scars.

He emerged from the crotch into the lungs. Green digits of a stereo clock pulsing against the wall. A nightlight showing him the way.

The door to the sleeping brain was closed. He gripped the knob with his gloved hand and entered.

Streetlights gave him the room. Red clock digits quivering near the bed where she awaited him.

His knee touched the side of the mattress as he stood over her, listening to her breathe.

She sensed his presence. Her legs moved beneath the sheets. Her head turned under spilled hair, first finding the opened door. She brushed the hair back off her eyes. Then she saw.

The face of the deliriant. She opened her mouth to scream.

36
WIRE

DOUG SHOWED UP ON her doorstep with a plastic Foodmaster bag of groceries, feeling pretty good. There was a peculiar morning-after pleasure in having refused immediate gratification, in resisting his craving with an eye toward a greater design. This was the bedrock of Alcoholics Anonymous, and it occurred to him that this was also how religions were born.

He found her door open a crack and felt a moment of concern, quickly mastered by rationalization. Lots of people in Town left their doors half-shut while running out for a quick errand. There would be a note on the table telling him that she had gone for more eggs, and to make himself at home.

"Hey?" he said with a knock on the open door, moving inside. "It's me."

Nothing. He moved down the hallway, telling himself it wasn't danger he was sensing.

"Claire?"

She was standing in the living room, on the other side of the sofa between the coffee table and the stereo, wearing faded blue jeans and an untucked yellow T-shirt, a cordless telephone in her hand at her side.

"Hey," Doug said, stopping, feeling something in the air. "You know your door was open?"

The way she was staring told him that she knew.

"Why?" she said.

Doug went numb. He set the grocery bag on the floor. "Why what?"

"Is this a thing you do?"

Something in him believed he could bluff his way out of this, even as it was all slipping away. "You talking about breakfast, or . . . ?"

"Tearing women down and building them back up again?"

The side of the sofa was as near to her as he dared move. His talk was pointless, but he wanted to keep on believing. "I brought bacon, I . . ."

"Or was I some sort of bet? A contest maybe?"

Something had happened since last night. Somehow she knew things now, and his instinct for self-preservation kicked in. The way she was standing at the back of the room with the phone. "Who else is here?"

Her eyes filled with tears. "No one," she snapped. "Not anymore."

Frawley. The kitchen was empty. Doug stepped to her bathroom, sweeping aside the shower curtain on the wide open window. He crossed to her bedroom, also empty.

Doug's defeat found an outlet in fury. "What did you tell him?"

She hadn't moved, watching him. "I didn't tell *him* anything."

A trap. The plan was to draw him into apologizing his way through a confession, him explaining himself right back into prison. The microphones could be anywhere.

He reached for her stereo, the CD player, turning it up loud. Smashing Pumpkins music filled her condo, all gunning guitar and bald-boy thrashing.

Her eyes went dark as he advanced. "Stay away from me," she said, backing up a step, raising the phone antenna-first. "I'll call the police."

Doug lunged for her and grabbed the phone, ripping it out of her hand, whipping it across the room at the sofa.

She froze, stunned.

With the music blasting, he pushed her up against the wall and shut his hand over her mouth, his callused palm catching her scream. He felt down both sides of her chest, her belly and her waist, groping her through her shirt.

Her voice was smothered, eyes wide. She tried to fend him off but he pinned her near arm to the wall with his elbow, working fast.

He reached beneath her shirt, sliding his fingers around the waist of her jeans. Then up her abdomen to the satin band linking the cups of her bra. Her free hand gripped his wrist, trying to stop him from going there. He pushed his fingers underneath the center strap, exploring her cleavage, finding no wires.

His hand came out of her shirt with Claire still gripping his wrist. He was too strong for her, reaching around for the small of her back, feeling nothing through her jeans there, then sliding his hand along the insides of both thighs, feeling up her inseam to her crotch.

Nothing. No battery pack, no wire.

She stared into his face, her hand still fighting his wrist. Then he eased off, realizing what he had just done. "I had to see if you were wired," he told her. "I had to—"

She jerked her knee up, hitting him in the thigh, just missing his balls. She went at him, slapping and whacking, and he let her. Her barefoot kicking didn't have much behind it, but the cracks across his face hurt. He defended himself without fighting back, eventually retreating a few steps.

She screamed, "You go to fucking *hell*!"

"It's not what you think." What could he say to her? "Whatever he told you—"

"I fucking *hate* you!"

"No." He shook that off, he refused it.

She looked for something to throw at him, found the *AM Gold* disc he had loaned her, cracked it off his elbow. Then she struck out at her blaring stereo, shoving it twice before it crashed to the floor—and even then, the music still played. Not until she ripped the plug out of the wall did the tune die.

Doug talked fast. "The robbery—whatever you know is true. But since then—I don't know what happened. All I can think about is you."

"You Townie gym-head . . . asshole . . . convict . . . fucking street *trash* . . ."

He stood up to all of this.

"What?" she said, wild-eyed, fixing her bra through her shirt. "Did you think you were going to come over here this morning and make me breakfast and *fuck me*? Tell all your *friends*?"

He shook his head, mouth closed tight.

"Making me feel sorry for you," she said.

He exploded. "*Sorry* for me?"

His rage shocked her. A long moment of brittle defiance, then she cried like she was vomiting tears into her hands. "Why would you do this to me?" she wailed. "Why would you do this to anybody?"

What could he tell her? *I am in love with you? I want to go away with you?*

"You knew last night," he said. "At the ballpark—*you knew*. Yet it was all right. You wanted me back here." He opened his hands down at his sides. "Why not now?"

She caught her breath, sniffling, bringing her hands away from her raw face. Defiant again. "I guess your friend refreshed my memory."

Doug's blood rose again. "Is that what Agent fucking Frawley calls me? His *friend*?"

She stood still, breathing. "What?"

Doug could not disguise the look of murder on his face. "What else did he say?"

"Frawley? It wasn't Frawley." She smiled crazy. "It was your friend in the hockey mask."

Hockey mask. Doug stared at her, confused. *"What?"*

Claire crossed the room to retrieve her phone from the sofa.

Doug shook his head but couldn't feel anything. He looked to her bathroom, the window she kept open. He looked at her open bedroom door. "He what?"

Hockey mask. Open window.

"I want you to go," she said.

Jem. Doug looked her up and down. "Did he touch you?"

She held the phone poised to dial. "He warned me not to go to the police, but so help me God, if you don't *get the hell out* . . ."

Doug shook his head, staving off hysteria. Jem's lips on her lemonade straw. *"Did he touch you?"*

She had tears again, and Doug stared, looming before her, fists at his side. "Out," she told him. "Of my house. Of my life."

Her words drove him back a step. "Claire. Wait—"

"Don't you *ever* fucking speak my name again." She held out the phone with her thumb over the numbers. "If you make me call, I will tell them everything."

He stepped back again, the phone like a gun in her hand. "All I ever wanted—"

She pressed her thumb down. *"Nine."*

"Don't do this."

"You better run now." She pressed again. *"One."*

He was going to stay. He was going to face whatever came.

Then she lost it, screaming at him, *"Get out!"*—backing him down the hall to the front door by the sheer force of her emotion—*"Get out!"*—shaming him down the steps and out alone onto Packard Street.

37
A BEATING AND A MEETING

THE OLD DOOR GAVE in like it had been waiting years for someone to put a good shoulder to it. Doug brushed past the cardinal's picture and the holy-water bowl to Jem's game room,
where the stereo was on, the CD long over, the volume turned way
up on nothing, speakers emitting a dry auditorium PA hum. The
couch of green leather was empty.

Seeing the plastic tea bag underneath the glass coffee table was
like finding the last piece to a jigsaw puzzle Doug didn't even know
he was working on. If he had been paying closer attention, he
wouldn't have needed that one final piece to make out the complete
image.

The late-night music. Jem's disappearances, his raccoon life. The
camo kids. His dukes to Fergie.

Doug tore back down the hall, banging open Jem's bedroom door
along the way and whipping blankets off the heap of cushions Jem
called a bed. Then into the front parlor and its bow windows with
torn screens overlooking Pearl Street. Jem's woodworking tools were
laid out on sheets of newspaper, and there, atop an old end table,
stood a nearly completed dollhouse. It was a scale replica of that very
same triple-decker, all three stories with the western wall cut away.
Doug lifted his boot to crush it, but some small voice of mercy told
him the house was a gift meant for Shyne. Instead he kicked over a
standing lamp and stomped in its head.

Then he heard the familiar revving of the overtuned engine and
went to the center window. The Flamer was pulling up curbside on
the street below. Doug was downstairs and outside in a flash.

Jem smiled his broad, Joker-faced grin as Doug strode toward him, the grin fading just as he saw Doug's fist coming around—no telegraphing it, no buddy-boy slo-mo—Doug tagging his chin with a "Fucking mother*fuck*!" and Jem banging off the trunk of his car and rolling into the gutter. A shopping bag spilled out of Jem's hand, little paintbrushes and tubes of modeling paint and wood glue tumbling into the street.

"*Chrissst!*" said Jem, getting up on his knees and touching his mouth, his fingers coming away bloody.

"You kept your mask, you fucking *psycho*—" Doug kicked him under his shoulder, high on his ribs, bouncing him against the bumper of his car.

"Wait. What?" Jem was back up on one knee. "Hold it. Duggy. Hold it."

Then Jem sprang at him from a crouch, burying his neck and shoulder in Doug's midsection and running him back across the sidewalk, slamming him hard against the clapboard siding of the house.

Doug took a fist to the hip. He hammered Jem's back, trying to throw him off, but Jem anticipated this and shifted his weight as Doug tried to muscle him around, Doug falling ass-first to the slanting sidewalk.

Jem was on top of him now, head still buried in Doug's gut, arms swinging strong. A hockey fight, Doug with Jem's shirt almost up over his head, the freckled spray of his back exposed.

"Fucking duster!" shouted Doug. "How you stayed up all night after the wedding, huh? Why you shot up the place? I pulled a job with a fuhhh—"

Jem landed a shot on Doug's kidney. He was working hard, wrestling his way up Doug's chest, a lot bigger and stronger than he used to be. With just a little more leverage, Jem would have him pinned.

Doug was losing this fight. If Jem got up onto his chest, Jem would hammer him into the sidewalk.

Doug reached under him and grabbed Jem's belt with one hand, his shoulder with another. In a burst of righteous fury, Doug used all his strength to lift Jem off his chest, the dust-head's work boots kicking in the air as Doug boosted him up and over, Jem coming down hard on his shoulders and back, Doug rolling away free.

Jem scrabbled to stand but Doug was up and running at him, grabbing shirt and shorts and ramming him headfirst into a neighbor's pickup. Dented and dazed, Jem tried to kick backward at

Doug's balls, but Doug caught the boot and spun him around, grabbing him up and teeing off, landing a good hard punch, undeflected, in Jem's face.

His nose burst its blood and Jem crashed back onto the hood of a car, sliding down off the corner headlamp and dumping onto the street in a heap.

There he lay, squirming on his belly, holding his face with both hands. Doug stood over him, head roaring from the madness of savagery and the earlier fall to the sidewalk. The wet things in his eyes: they were tears.

"Get up."

Jem rolled over, curling in pain. Blood hung in snotty ribbons from his chin and a gash had opened over his nose, street sand matted in the bloodstain on his cheek. "Did it few, man," he said.

"Get up."

"I did it few." His words came out in gobs of bloody drool. "Did it fuss. Why her, man? All udder chicks in a world. Why?"

"Get up, Jem, so as I can *knock you the fuck down again!*"

"Fuckin' who you better 'an? You better 'an me?"

Onto his knees. Far enough. Doug tagged him in the chin and Jem dropped back, sprawling.

Jem smiled now, bloody-toothed, lying there in the street. "Din't even touch'er, man. Jest a warning. I true her back. Small fiss."

"Good for you. Then you'll live."

Jem wanted to sit up but his ribs wouldn't let him. He rolled to his side but couldn't get up that way either, so he gave up and lay back, grinning up at the sky.

It wasn't enough for Doug. He bent down and grabbed Jem's bloody shirt, lifting him off the road. Jem's white eyes lolled as he smiled at Doug's fist.

"Why 'on't you hit youssell," said Jem. "Jest fucking hit yousself."

Doug wanted one more. He wanted it bad. But he feigned it first, and Jem didn't flinch, his eyes cloudy like dishwater.

Doug let him drop. Jem coughed, giggling as he bled. "'Appily ever after," he muttered.

Doug walked away unsatisfied, a dark cloud carrying a massive electrical charge, still needing release.

Krista was out on the sidewalk. She had stood there and watched her brother get the Irish kicked out of him—and remained there still as he lay muttering and giggling in the street. She looked at Doug, taking a step toward him—but Doug was already starting away up the slope, hands aching, ears roaring, half-blind with despair.

FRAWLEY'S SUBLET CAME WITH a parking space in a low-ceilinged garage just off First Avenue, the main road bisecting the decommissioned Charlestown Navy Yard. On the land side of First stood the old brick shipbuilding factories, including an obsolete ropewalk building a quarter mile long. On the water side stood the redesigned wharves, brick foundries that had been carved into waterfront two-bedrooms. The redeveloped yard was more campus than neighborhood, skewing predominantly toward successful single professionals. Frawley imagined the old dockworkers and longshoremen coming back from the grave to find their stomping grounds turned into a community of high-rent condos populated by the young, the clever, the uncallused.

The ninety-minute commute home from Lakeville had nested in Frawley's lower back, and he stood out of the dread Tempo, both hands on its roof, stretching the pain away. He was examining the car's fading blue finish—gray spots spreading across the roof like mold—when he heard footsteps coming up behind him, hard and thudding, like boots. Frawley instinctively reached inside his jacket before turning.

MacRay was empty-handed, unshaved, and hungover-looking in a faded gray T-shirt and jeans, moving fast through the sulfurous light.

Frawley gripped the butt of his SIG-Sauer 9mm but did not draw, and MacRay stopped within an arm's reach, breathing hard, homicide in his eyes.

Frawley was shocked and trying to conceal it. Pulling his gun would have been prideless. He slid his creds out of his breast pocket instead, folded them open.

"Special Agent Frawley, FB—"

MacRay swatted the billfold out of Frawley's hand. It fluttered like a wounded bird and dropped to the concrete a few feet away.

Frawley's heart fell just as fast. The rudeness of the act, its near childishness, settled on his face like a dark pair of sunglasses, helping him move past fear.

"Don't make a mistake here, MacRay," said Frawley. "I want to take you down, but not for this."

MacRay stared, more controlled than Frawley had first thought.

He looked past Frawley with expert distaste. "Upgraded to the Tempo, huh? Nice ride."

Frawley fought off questions: How long had MacRay been on him? How had MacRay known he would be here?

MacRay said, "Know what happened to me? Some fucking douche bag keyed my Vette. You believe that shit?"

Frawley saw the emerald green car parked along the wall, saw its long silver scar.

"Fucking with a man's ride, that's some cowardly-ass shit, don't you think?" MacRay went on. "I mean, what do you call someone who would do a thing like that, huh? A punk? A pussy?"

Frawley said, "I take it she dumped you."

"Hey, *fuck* you."

Frawley worked up a smile. "How long did you think that was going to last? What was your play there, MacRay?"

"You don't know nothing about it."

"Reminds me of smokehead ATM jumpers. Password thieves, they get the secret code, they think they can ride that card forever." Frawley then noticed MacRay's open, anxious hands—the crook's knuckles cut, swollen like walnuts. Frawley said, "If you laid a hand on her—"

"Fuck you," said MacRay, dismissing him with a wave. It was convincing, but Frawley would have to check on Claire Keesey himself to be sure.

MacRay backed off a little, walking in a tight, agitated circle like a dog in a cage, while Frawley stood in repose.

"Like your sponsor there," said Frawley, pushing back at him now. "Firefighter Frank Geary. The wife-beater, trying to school me. You reformed drinkers, you're the worst."

MacRay came back at him hard, pointing. "Listen to me. You stay the fuck away from him, got that? Who's this between? You want to know something about me? Here I am. What?"

Frawley held his composure. "I have nothing to say to you."

"'Course not. You'd rather go slinking around, talking to everybody else *but* me. Who had the balls to face who? Fucking little dink."

"You came here to call me names, MacRay?"

"Just thought I'd swing by, introduce myself personally."

"Damn neighborly of you."

"Strip away some of this bullshit between us. This dance."

Frawley said, "I'm not dancing."

"Yeah? Me either." MacRay looked out through the open walls of the garage to the lights along First Avenue. "What you think, you're undercover here? You think you live in Charlestown? The yard ain't Charlestown. You got no idea what's going on."

"I know plenty."

MacRay squinted, taking Frawley's measure. "So what is this? This about her?"

Frawley frowned him a *fuck you*. "This is about a bank."

"Yeah." MacRay turned away, his circular pacing again. "Sure it is."

"About a movie theater too."

"Movie theater?" MacRay cocked his head like he might not have heard that right.

"You fucked up, MacRay. You and your crew."

MacRay continued his circuit. "You lost me back at the movie theater thing."

"Surprised me, that. Armored-truck heisting with the crusts cut off. A soft job. Maybe you're gun-shy. Maybe you're a little more afraid of me catching up with you than you'd like to admit."

Frawley was inside his head with a bullhorn, MacRay walking faster, mad.

"Struck me that maybe," Frawley went on, "maybe this was a job pulled by someone thinking about getting out. Even hanging it up for good. For the love of a good woman, perhaps. I'm thinking it's fifty-fifty you came here tonight to tell me good-bye."

MacRay slowed then, denying Frawley the explosion he expected. "She doesn't want you, man," MacRay told him. "Nothing you can do will change that."

Frawley grinned away a chill. "Yeah, she's Helen of Troy. She's the Mona Lisa. I mean, she's nice, MacRay, she's all right. Got all her teeth. But why her? Careful guy like you. A vic from one of your own jobs? What made you cross that line?"

MacRay stared.

"Wait—was it love? That it, MacRay?" Frawley's taunting smile bloomed and died. "What made you think it would ever work?"

"Who's saying it's over?"

Frawley smiled wide at his bluff. "Oh, it's not?"

MacRay said, "Nothing is."

Frawley grinned, stopping himself from saying *Good*.

"What's so funny, sleuth?"

"Funny?" Frawley shrugged. "Us standing here. Chatting."

It had gone on too long, them standing there together, Frawley's anxiety building.

MacRay said, "You know how in movies, cop and robber, they spend the whole picture matching wits and end up with this grudging respect for each other? You got any grudging respect for me?"

Frawley said, "I have not one ounce."

"Good. Me fucking either. I just didn't want you to think we'd be holding hands at the end of this."

Frawley shook his head. "Not unless you count handcuffs."

MacRay took his measure once again. "If you did get a finger-print—it wasn't mine."

She had warned him. Frawley burned. "You're a dead end, MacRay. Maybe you *should* just walk away for good, you're so afraid to go up against me."

MacRay came close to a smirk then, and Frawley *knew* he had him locked in—then MacRay started back to his car, and Frawley wasn't so sure.

"I'll see you around then," Frawley called after him.

"Yeah," said MacRay, opening his car door and climbing inside. "Yeah, maybe."

PART IV
A SORT OF HOMECOMING

38
EXCALIBUR STREET

MRS. KEESEY ANSWERED THE front door in a designer running suit, the Round Table Estates' version of the 1950s house-coat. Theirs was one of the few screen doors in the world that did not squeal when opened. "Thank you, Mrs. Keesey, for letting me stop by in the middle of the day," said Frawley, stepping inside the chilly foyer.

"Quite welcome," said Mrs. Keesey, looking out at his moldy Tempo cluttering up Excalibur Street, then closing the heavy door. She stepped to the balustrade, where bank statements and investment prospectuses in sliced envelopes were filed between egg-white banister spindles. "Claire!" she sang out, then looked at Frawley with a nonsmile. "She's back with us again. I don't know what brought this on."

She eyed the manila envelope in his hand suspiciously, as though it contained information on her. The odor of whiskey on her breath was like a premonition of early death.

"Can I offer you some spring water?" she said, studied and formal, an actress bored in her long-running role as wife and housemother.

"No, thank you. I'm fine."

Claire Keesey came down the stairs in a white T-shirt and even whiter sweatpants, greeting Frawley without expression—Mrs. Keesey already withdrawing to the kitchen.

Claire took him the other way, her white socks whispering across a smooth maple floor, through French doors into her father's home office, just as before. This time Claire sat behind the desk, puffy-eyed from crying, but not bruised or battered. MacRay's swollen hands had beat up somebody, but not her.

Frawley sat in the college rocking chair, eyeing her, harboring feelings he was not proud of. Triumph. Satisfaction. Also pity.

"You made a mistake," he said, magnanimous in victory. "A misjudgment."

She picked at her fingers, ashamed, sullen.

"I wish you hadn't gone through this," he said, and meant it. "And I wish we didn't have to do this now."

Frawley opened the envelope flap and slid out four photographs, playing the mugs out on the desk blotter like a winning hand. MacRay's cocky black-and-white was top right. She locked on it, her eyes showing hurt.

"Okay," said Frawley. "Know any of the others?"

She took in each, lingering an extra moment on nasty-eyed Coughlin and his jerk smirk.

"No?" said Frawley. He pulled another photograph from his envelope and placed it down in front of her. It was a still developed from Gary George's wedding video: an off-angle image of Kristina Coughlin in a black dress, sitting next to MacRay in a tuxedo at an otherwise empty table, drinks before them. "What about her?"

Claire stared, confusion giving way to a defiant blankness. She asked no questions. She didn't even shake her head.

Frawley was just trying things here. He laid down a blurry, retouched, six-year-old surv photograph of the reclusive Fergus Coln, the Florist wearing a dark sweatshirt hood and apparently pointing out the telephoto lens. "What about this man?"

She squinted at the murky image, rejecting it immediately.

"Have you ever been inside MacRay's place?" Frawley asked.

No answer, but it didn't look like she had.

"Ever seen him handling large amounts of cash? Or talking about a particular hiding place? Ask you to hold or hide anything for him?"

Her silence answered no.

"Did he ever admit anything to you or implicate himself in any way? How did you finally find out about him?"

Now her silence seemed like something greater than mere recalcitrance.

"Look," said Frawley. Her hand was on the desk and he reached out and squeezed it reassuringly. "I'm sure your sense of trust is pretty tender right now."

She looked at his hand on hers, pulled away. "How long did you know?"

Frawley withdrew his empty hand. "Not long."

"But long enough," she said. "When you came to see me that day—you were carrying that same envelope."

Frawley shrugged. "I might have been carrying *an* envelope."

"Were you . . . punishing me?"

"Don't be ridiculous."

"Did you want me humiliated? Because I chose him and not you? Is that why you didn't tell me?"

Frawley shook his head adamantly, not in answer but in retaliation. "You don't get to do this. Don't look at me like I'm the one who seduced and betrayed you. Like I'm the one who made you a fool."

She went silent, and Frawley knew he had been too harsh. He eased off.

"You're angry," he said. "You're feeling betrayed. I understand these things. But don't take it out on me. I wanted to help you. No big deal, but I was here for you. And you chose badly. It happens, people make mistakes. And now you know."

She was looking down—not at the photos, not at him.

"What you need to do now," he went on, "is turn your anger where it belongs—on them." He knocked on the blotter of pictures. "With your help we can put these assholes away for a long time."

She went into her sweatpants pocket and brought out a business card, handing it to him. The first thing Frawley noticed was the icon of the scales of justice printed in the lower-left corner.

"This is my lawyer," Claire said. "If you want to talk to me again, you do it through her."

Claire punched the *her*. Frawley read and reread the card, the saliva in his mouth turning bitter.

"Lucky," he told her, slowly collecting his photographs from the desk blotter. "Lucky for you I don't need you much anymore, or else this would get very unpleasant." He took MacRay's mug last, reviewing the cocksure face once more himself before returning it to the envelope. "Why didn't I tell you you were being sweet-talked by the guy who kidnapped you? Because I needed to keep MacRay close. Because this is a federal criminal investigation, not fucking *Love Connection*."

"You can go now."

"Here's the deal, Ms. Keesey. MacRay is going to come back to see you again."

"No, he's not—"

"And when he does," Frawley talked over her, "and when he does—any contact you have with him, any conversation *whatsoever*, you will report it to me. Either yourself or through your *lawyer*"—he flicked at the business card—"or else you will be

looking at a criminal prosecution yourself. That is not a threat, that is a promise. This is a felony case I am investigating, and any unreported contact between yourself and the suspect will be prosecuted."

He stood, pocketing her lawyer's card, still pissed.

"You think you feel humiliated now? How about going on trial for aiding and abetting an armed felon? How about putting this whole affair out there for the entire world to see? 'Bank Manager Falls for Armed Robber'—how's that sound? You like reading tabloids? Want to be in one?"

He stopped himself there, opening the French doors.

"Yeah, it's rough, but you brought this on yourself. I can't help you if you won't let me. MacRay *will* come to you again. And when he does, you will tell me."

39
LINGER

WHAT IT FEELS LIKE, being underwater.

Krista was there, finally. Submerged. The Tap Downstairs a brick aquarium tank now, the bourbon in her system giving her gills.

Everything slower. Sounds reaching her late, stretched out so that she could mull them over or just let them pass her by. Life becoming fluid, languid. She reached her hand to the bar and met the resistance of the water, the push starting a ripple. Every movement began a current and left a wake. A twist of her head tipped the balance of the room, everything lifting then settling back into place again, the sounds lagging behind, a moment or two before finding her ears in their new position. One thing flowing beautifully into the next.

Alone at the bar in the center of the liquid universe. *Fuck you, Mrs. Joanie Magloan.* The former Joanie Lawler always used to love to say, *Shit, what you think, I'm gonna be one of those married girls who stops going out?* This was before she kissed the freckled frog prince Magloan and got turned magically into a housewife. Two nights ago Krista called her—*Sorry, Kris, can't make it.* So tonight, Krista didn't even bother trying her. She'll put in a call to her tomorrow—you bet—letting it slip out that she hit the Tap without her, because that was psychology. Making her think she's missing out was what would get her ass in gear next time. Not Krista being the single girl, begging.

The music was a pleasant warble. No U2 without the Monsignor there tonight—her Pope, her grateful Pope. His cock crowed three times—so gratefully—each crow a stab of betrayal at Duggy, and now she couldn't get him on the phone. Hiding away in the Forgotten Village, his Vatican City.

A dollar bill from her jeans pocket—her last. Undulating in her hand like a waving fern. Her shoes touched the floor, a swimmer walking across colored rocks on the bottom of the night-lit Tap aquarium, toward the wall of brick coral, the jukebox a treasure chest opening and releasing bubbles. Three bubbles for a dollar. She punched in the same code three times, The Cranberries, "Linger."

Swimming back, she pretended to snub the guy who had been checking her out all evening. *So check this out,* she thought, moving slow, giving him the full view.

Splashy was always good for one on the house, but she liked to know she still had the power, especially now as she felt it starting to fade. They say the day your baby starts living is the day you start dying, and if they were right, then she had been wasting away for twenty-one months now.

Twenty-one months was the average life span (she remembered Duggy telling her this once—she remembered everything he told her) of a one-dollar bill in circulation. Fifties and hundreds, they lasted the longest.

I am wanted. I have currency. She was a clean, firm bill, no longer quite so crisp, but still negotiable legal tender. Maybe not a C-note anymore, but definitely a fifty.

She regained her seat and waited for the ripples to subside and her vision to clear. He was stirring now. Hooking his Bud bottle by the neck and walking it over, pulled by the tide.

I am a fifty you want in your pocket.

The swell and sway of displacement as he mounted the empty stool to her right. Sitting open-legged, aggressive, waiting for her to look his way. His words swam to her.

"Seemed like we were having a bit of a staring contest over there."

"Yeah?" said Krista, the word a soft bubble escaping from her mouth. She could tell immediately he wasn't Town. She didn't trust his face. A sea horse with barracuda eyes.

"I think I was winning," he said.

She nodded. "I think you were."

"This your song?"

It took a while for the music to reach her. "It's mine. All mine."

"Kind of sad, no?"

She finished her drink in front of him. "Only if you let it be."

Like he was studying her. A little creepy, but she hung in there. The bourbon dose reached her gills and in rushed more equalizing water.

"One night at a bar," he said, leaning closer, "this guy was going around to ladies telling them he was judging a Hugging Contest, and would they like to enter. And most of the time, believe it or not, they fell for it, and he would hold them and rub their backs, all smarmy and shit. I finally got so sick of watching this guy that I took him outside. I told him I was judging a Face-Punching Contest."

Krista smiled, drifting. "Anyone tried that shit on me, I'd do the punching myself."

He toasted her with his Bud, draining it, returning it empty on the bar. "Oh, by the way," he said. "I'm here tonight judging a Fucking Contest."

Water rushing around them, the undertow of the late hour washing bodies from the bar, Krista smiling, licking her lips. *Okay, sport.* "Why don't you buy me a drink."

He produced a twenty from his pocket and laid it Jackson-up on top of the bar.

Here I am, she thought. *Here I float.*

He ordered two of what she was having and hopefully didn't catch the knowing wink Splashy gave her. The guy talked and he was all right. Cute guy, just not her type. Her type was Duggy. He was another in a long line of not-Duggys.

Something about kids, did he say? "I have a daughter."

It was an excuse for him to look her over again. "That you gave birth to?" he said. "Yourself?"

"Twenty-one months ago."

Only thing that bothered her was him not checking her hands for rings. *What, like there's no way I could catch a husband?*

Early on, he had said his name. She had missed it because it wasn't Doug. He had nice, strong hands. The nice, strong hands ordered two more drinks.

He said something about the price of real estate in the Town. "I own," she told him.

"You own your own condo?"

"My own *house,*" she said, his disbelief both annoying and flattering. "A triple. Left to me by my mother."

"Wow. Just you?"

"That's right." It was easy, as well as nice, to pretend she had no brother.

"I have to ask. A woman with her own house. Sitting here with an ass making the rest of the barstools crazy with envy. What are you doing down here alone on a weeknight?"

She nodded Indian-like, like she had the answer but wasn't telling. "Getting wet," she said, dancing her drink on the waves. "Drifting with the tide."

He toasted her. "Bon voyage."

"You live in the yard, huh?"

"Is it that obvious?"

"Always. What you doing down here? Slumming?"

"That's right."

"Looking for an easy pickup? A tasty little slice of Town pie?"

"Mostly just trying to do my job."

"Your job? Oh, right. I forgot. The Fucking Contest."

"Basically correct. I work for the FBI."

She threw back her head, laughing, starting to like him more now. "That was the first good giggle I've had in a month."

"Yeah?"

"You're awright. Doesn't mean I'm going home with you or anything. Don't think I'm looking to do you on your balcony, cooing over the view."

"I don't have a balcony."

"No? That's too bad."

"I'm in a shitty sublet, and out on my ass in like six weeks. A toast, Krista. Let's drink to balconyless me."

"Fair enough." She figured she must have told him her name when—

"I don't see your brother around tonight."

"My brother?" Who is this guy? "You know Jem?"

"We bump into each other now and then."

Thought he wasn't Town. "I had a higher opinion of you."

"You and Doug MacRay used to run around, right?"

Now she stared. "How you know Duggy?"

"We sorta work together."

"Ah," she says, feeling tested. "Demolition."

A smirk in this guy's eyes. "Nooo."

Things changing now. Water temperature falling a few degrees. She tightened up, a reflex around people she didn't know.

The guy pulled out one, two, three, four, five more twenties, stacking them on the bar. "You a pretty decent judge of size?"

"Depends," she said. "Size of what?"

He held up a single twenty. "How big would you say this is?"

"If this is a bar game, I'm not much of a—"

"How long? Six inches? In your estimation. Over or under?"

She squinted. "Under."

"Wrong. Six point one four inches exactly. Now the width."

"You're turning into kind of a weird guy."

"The girth. Some claim it's more important. Give a guess."

She just looked at him.

"Two point six one inches. I know everything there is to know about money. Thickness of a bill? Point oh oh four three inches. Not much to excite you there. Weight? About one gram. That makes a twenty almost worth its weight in, say, dust."

Staring at him now. Him staring at her. The water stopped dead.

"So how's it work?" he said. "Bartender takes a call, gives you an address? You pick up a package at Point A, deliver it to Point B, and for that the Florist pays you a C? That right? Easy as A-B-C?"

Water starting to drain, the stopper pulled and that sucking sound going.

"You're thinking about walking out on me," he said. "See, it's not that simple, though. I start waving this gold badge around"—he opened it on the bar next to the twenties, briefly—"lots of questions then, for you. So here's how we'll do. I'll buy you another drink, and you and I will repair to the back of the room there, a table away from everyone, have a little talk."

The door was near, but it was a long walk up those crooked rubber steps, and she didn't have her land legs yet. *Don't be stupid here.* "I don't want another drink."

He took her hand, gripping it, leaning in close. Smiling his government eyes. "Fine. We'll do this right here, nice and intimate. Like lovers." He pressed the five crumpled twenties into her hand like a wad of trash. "I'm paying you a C-note right now, to deliver a package to me. And that package is information."

No need to bother looking around to see who might overhear them because all she was going to tell this asshole was to go fuck himself. "I don't know—"

"You don't know anything, sure. I understand. Only one problem with that. I *know* that you do know things, okay? A-B-C. That's as simple as one two three. You and me."

So cold once the water runs out. When the dry air attacks you like your conscience. She looked for Splashy's help, but he was gone.

"I'm really not an asshole, all right?" the guy said, his hand squeezing her hand holding the cash. His humid cologne. "Lucky for you, I'm not the kind of cop who's going to come down hard, threaten you with losing your daughter, talking foster homes and all that dreadful, dreadful shit. Not me."

Her mind was shivering.

"And I don't even care about your messengering for Fergie. Drug dealing, racketeering, criminal conspiracy—you're just a cog in that machine. A go-between. But a good broom sweeps clean, and I'm riding a good broom here. A dynamite fucking broom. I'm not asking you to wear a wire. I'm not looking to *use* you like that, *endanger* you, no. I'm going totally positive on this. How many cars you own, Krista?"

"What?" His face was close enough to spit at. "None."

"Seven. You own seven vehicles. You didn't pay for any of them, but they're all registered in your name. Doug MacRay and your brother did that, to shield their assets. Ever seen Doug's Corvette, his green machine? You like that ride? That car is yours, Krista. Legally. He had you sign some papers for him once, go to the registry, right? Something happens to Doug—that car cannot be attached to any penalties he might have to pay, any restitution for, oh, let's just say, bank robbing. And I bet you don't even know where he garages it."

Say nothing. Show nothing.

"And here you are messengering dust for scratch money. *Scratch* money. For your daughter, right? Of course. But living like this? Do you have *any* idea how much money they pulled down on that movie theater thing? Every cent of it untraceable. Immediately spendable."

"I don't know what you're—"

"Talking about, sure. You're loyal, of course you're loyal. It's family. But listen. They are all going down. It's going to happen, and soon—that's a fact. That's what I'm here to tell you. Now you seem like a practical girl, resourceful. You must have considered this day would come. They go down—what happens to you? You don't want to be the one left behind. The cars are in your name—that's good and fine, that's safe. But hold on. Your house. Now I happen to know that your brother's name is on it too, you share it. And we will take that away, his half of your house. And if you don't get practical and resourceful with me here, the fact is that you could be going up for aiding and abetting—and this is above and beyond any drug charges—in which case we take *everything*, and you will move into a new home, called MCI Framingham. Your little girl?" Frawley shook his head. "But that's worst-case scenario. That's *if*. And I don't even like to talk about *if*. Not when there's so many things actually going in your favor. Primarily, this house of yours that we need to save. You know how much a stand-alone on Pearl Street is worth in today's market? A ready-to-renovate triple-decker in Charlestown? You're sitting on a small fortune—all legit—and yet, here you are, waiting for a call to deal dust, flirting with strangers for drinks. The sale of that house would set you and your daughter up pretty good. But for that, we need a working arrangement, you and I. I need a good reason to protect your *ass*et."

Only the stink remains, once the water is gone. Musty emptiness. "Bullshit, trying to scare me. I want a lawyer."

"Good, do that. Get one. Because all this is about protecting yourself. No—not even yourself. Your daughter. Think, Krista."

"You leave her out."

"I can't, and neither can you. They've been shafting you for years. Keeping you on this leash—and why? To hold you down. Keep you dependent, like a junkie for their goodwill. Keep you close. The right thing would have been to pay you generously for all the secrets you so faithfully keep." He ducked low to see up into her eyes. "And look, your brother? Hey. He's not even the one I'm really after."

"No?"

He picked up on the thing in her eyes. He watched her and absorbed it. "Unless, that is, you want me to be."

Duggy. He was after Duggy.

"This MacRay," the FBI man went on. "How long you put up with him?"

Hearing his name out of the G's mouth was like hearing that Duggy was dead, and her heart fell.

"The hoops he made you jump through? And if I heard about it, you know everybody in Town knows."

Elbow on the bar, she grabbed a handful of her own hair, twisting it.

"This sad song," he said, thumbing back at the jukebox. "You gonna listen to this over and over again, the rest of your life?"

Go right home and tell Duggy about this guy. Straight to his door. He would be so grateful.

"One more question. You were with him how long?"

Krista's nose was almost touching the bar. "All my life."

"Let me ask you this. In all those years you were together—how many diamond necklaces he buy you from Tiffany?"

All the water out of the air now, the dry world dripping loud. "What are you talking about, diamond necklaces?"

The FBI man said, "Answer my question, then I'll answer yours."

40
MAC'S LETTER

June 1996

Little Partner,

What a shock you just got. Finding this with my riteing and the Walpole return adress in your mailbox. Wish I could of seen your face. Whats the old crook up to now? Im not riteing to ask you anything. You no thats not my style. I never ask for anything from anyone in my life. What I wanted I took and what I needed done I did myself. I no your the same Duggy.

I do'nt rite much and I no I never rote you before. Hard to get you out here tho and after last time I felt like we were'nt done. Whenever it comes time to see you theres so much to say that it never all gets said. So much saved up in my mind. Then your gone and I got another year to puzzle you over.

When I get out theres no way I can make up for the things I owe you. Your a man you understand this. Misstakes take 2x as long to fix as they do to make. Thats why you never look back. OK you look back but never go back Duggy. You keep going on.

About your mothers house. I met your mother at the Monumint in November of 63. Kennedy had just died—shot in the head—and the town was in morning and Coffy and me and the rest of us were sick of moping so we went out to find trouble. We were kicking around the steps there and this little gide comes out—this little tour gide with copper red hair—she was younger but she bitched us out like somebodys mother. A little pint glass with a black band on her school uniform giving us all kinds of shit till she started crying her eyes out for Kennedy. We had our fun but next day I came back alone. I listened to her school speech to the torists and she saw me. Her name tag was Pam. I came back 6 days in a row before I got a smile. I do'nt no what she saw in me. I did'nt no what I wanted exept to take her out. 1 nite she snuck away from her frends and came bowling.

We had to get marryed Duggy. Her parents new I was Bottom Of The Hill. A Slope Kid and they never liked me but they never gave up on her ether. They gave us the downpayment for the house on Sackville when you came along. But I always payed the moregage. The house was mine.

What I promised her on that day we bowled was that Id never make her cry again and I broke that promise a thousand times. She did things because she was angry at me. I was away a lot and she left you at her mothers to much. The $$ I gave her for food she took down to the corner. I scared off all her hippy friends, but from then on she just did these things alone.

I am not telling you this because I am a prick. I am telling you this because I am not a prick.

She did'nt do it on purpose. The thing of the time in the 60s was to push bowndrys and walk on the moon and free your mind. Her mind just got to free. You were asleep in front of the tv when I came home and found her in the bathroom and the needle. I got you to the naybors 1st thing. When you woke up in the morning and started asking for her what coud I say? What do you tell a 6 year old kid? Your mother went away. Shes gone. I do'nt think shes coming back.

You wanted to go out looking for her so we looked. Her parents had a private funeral and insted I took you out walking the nayborhood looking for her until you cried so hard you coud'nt walk. You saw a tv show about a missing dog and wanted to put up posters on telephone polls so we put up posters. You wanted the light on over the front door for her so I change that bulb every month. You woud'nt sleep if you coud'nt see the light from your bed.

I said she went away and so who else in Town would say other wise. My truth was truer than truth. But what I did'nt plan for was that she would become this bigger than life thing and I would go from Daddy to no one. A lot of you you made yourself. I give you that. I always see her in you. But I did what I could. I teached you the things I new.

Bottom line is I will be out soon. Then it will be the 2 of us again. You had trouble with Gem but patch it up. Loyalty is what we need now. You cant buy that.

Maybe you always new about her or gessed or never wanted to ask. If you do'nt want to talk about this again I would not mind.

This is the longest letter Ive ever ritten.

By the way. Old Uncle G came to see me. But I did'nt see him.

Do'nt no how to end this Duggy. Do'nt even no if Ill mail it.

Mac.

PS. Your mother never came back, Duggy. I am.

41
BIRTHDAY

DOUG ROLLED DOWN A lane of tidy homes, checking addresses, coming up on a line of parked cars and an inflatable castle in a driveway. The bladder castle jerked and jiggled like a stomach full of screaming, indigestible kids. Doug slowed at the silver mailbox festooned with birthday balloons. The house number matched.

He pulled over at the end of the row of cars and stood out of the Caprice. The house was a gray Cape, kids chasing each other around the front yard with squirt guns, parents chatting in the driveway. Doug was about to get back in his car when he saw Frank G. step away from a small group near the castle's generator and wave him up. Frank wore a collared, short-sleeved shirt, long shorts, and Converse flats, walking down the driveway to meet him. "You found it."

Doug pulled off his shades, looking at the party. "Frank, man— you should have told me."

"You said you needed a few minutes, right? C'mon."

Frank walked him past the screaming castle toward an open garage full of chairs and folding tables of food. Twin girls in matching pink eyeglasses sat hip to hip on the front lawn, eating melting blocks of ice cream cake, and three plastic paratroopers came swaying down to earth out of a bedroom window, followed by a balsa wood airplane in a tailspin. Then a kid with his arm in a blue cast came racing past, nailing them each in the gut with water out of a tiny green pistol, taunting, "Ha-ha, Uncle Frank!"

Frank pulled a pastel pink Saturday night special out of his pocket and turned on the kid, blasting him, the kid running off squealing in a war-movie zigzag as Frank's piece ran dry. "Inside," he said. "Gotta reload."

He did so at the sink, the kitchen bustling with women wrapping to-go plates of ziti and lasagna and cold cuts. Frank led Doug past two dads talking business in the hallway, past a cooing woman changing a sleepy baby on the dining room floor, past the Sox game in the family room. A ruckus up on the second floor made Frank reverse direction, taking Doug to a side door, down wooden steps into a cool basement.

Half of it was finished, the paneled walls papered with Michael Jordan, Ray Bourque, and Mo Vaughn posters. There were Koosh balls everywhere, old U-Haul boxes overflowing with sporting equipment, and an elaborate Matchbox racetrack setup in the back. In the center of the room stood an air hockey table under a billiards lamp.

"So what's doing?" said Frank.

Doug shrugged. The birthday party had thrown him, he didn't know where to start. "How *you* doing?"

"Me?" Frank walked around to the other end of the table rink. "Much better. You caught me at a bad moment last time. I let that little old guy get to me, I don't know why. He doesn't stand for everybody. I know he doesn't stand for me."

"Good. Good to hear." Doug prowled back and forth, uncomfortable, as though asking for money.

Frank switched on the game table, the jets pushing air through the perforated playing surface. "I'm back at meetings, been to a few." The puck stirred, a red plastic disk drifting to the side as though by an invisible hand. Frank flicked it back to the opposite boards—just diddling, not an invitation to play. "What about you?"

Doug ran his hand briskly through his chopped hair. "Meetings? Nah. Not since before we talked."

A herd of elephants went trampling overhead. "Big mistake," said Frank. "You got crisis written all over your face, I can see it. Beeping me was the right thing to do. Listen to me now. She's not worth it."

"Who? Not worth what?"

"That drink you haven't taken yet. Your girl isn't worth it."

"Nah, Frank—"

" 'I think I met someone . . .' You remember that?" Frank pushed the wafer puck harder now, sending it clicking off the boards, coasting on the low-friction surface. "The way you first told me about her—I knew. This girl is your disease, Doug."

Doug held out his hands. "Frank—and I never said this to you before—but you're dead wrong here. This girl . . . if *anything*, she's my sobriety."

"And she's gone now."

Doug admitted, "Yeah."

"And you're thirsty. It's right there on your face. But if you can somehow get her back—that'll cure everything, right?"

"Frank, look. This other girl, my *old* girlfriend—*she's* my alcoholism. Fucking haunting me every good step I try to take. But this girl—no. She's *too* good for me. She's—"

"Everything you want but can't have. You've poured all your hopes into this person who can't be with you—am I right? *She's too good*. Can you hear it? You set up this unattainable thing."

"You're reading me wrong."

"Set it all up maybe even since the beginning. A long, slow slide into you giving yourself the okay to drink again, with her as your excuse. *With all I'm going through, who wouldn't slip just a little?*" The disk click-clanked into one of the slot goals like a coin dropping into a bank. "That's the bullshit you have to fight here. That's the demon."

Doug paced with his hands folded behind his head. "How did it get so complicated?" he said. "It's a beer. You drink it, or you don't."

"It *used* to be a beer," said Frank, switching off the table, coming out from behind it. "Face that, Doug. You got to eat what's eating you. You can't drown it. You tried that already. Didn't work."

Doug wondered what it would taste like, this thing that was eating him.

The door opened on the party above them, a woman's voice: "Frank?"

"Yeah, down here, hon."

Toeless summer sandals stopped two steps down. "Steve and Pauline just left, they couldn't find you."

"I'm sniffing glue with a friend. Hold on."

Frank trotted up the steps for a whispered conversation. Then the sandals flapped down ahead of Frank.

"I'm Nancy Geary," she said, offering her small hand for a quick, purposeful shake; not unfriendly, but not sweetly fake either. He was a guest in her house and she was presenting herself to greet him.

"You have a beautiful home here," said Doug, because he was supposed to, and because it was true.

She was small, a tough city girl. "You get anything to eat yet?"

"I'm a gate-crasher. Frank didn't tell me you were . . ." He waved at the thumping upstairs.

"Take some sandwiches home with you, okay?"

"I will. Thank you."

She was already starting back up the stairs. Probably never beautiful, but steady, no more attractive with makeup than without. A constant. Not trying to impress anybody, she had a house and a family and a birthday party to run.

The door closed, and Doug looked at Frank. "You wanted me here for this," he said. "Wanted me to see the house, the wife, the kids."

"It's not unattainable. All you gotta do is get lucky. This girl, Doug—people come and go. There're reasons. That's what life is. It doesn't mean anything about you yourself."

Doug shook his head at how wrong Frank was. "'Course it does."

Frank studied him. "What's this do to you moving on from your friends?"

Doug felt the suffocation again. "No, that's still on."

"You've been saying that."

"Frank, look, I'm committed. There's nothing left here for me now. I'm setting it up so that there's no turning back. But I gotta . . . I gotta take care of things first."

"That I don't like the sound of. You trying to save people who don't want to be saved."

"It's not that. Truly. It's knowing what will happen to them after I'm gone, and trying to give them, at least, one good last chance."

"Chance at what?"

Doug shrugged. "I guess, life."

"You really think that? Think you're the only thing kept them safe all these years? The designated driver for everyone?"

Doug considered this. "Yeah. I have to say—it's exactly that."

They went back up the stairs together. In the hallway a kid went racing past waving a plastic sword, and Frank stopped him with a shoulder squeeze. "Mikey, where's Kev?"

"Right here, Dad," said a shorter, tow-haired boy in the kitchen doorway, holding a hockey stick with a big blue bow on it.

"C'mere, Roscoe," said Frank, steering the two boys across into the dining room, past a supermarket tray of cookie crumbs. Frank stood with one hand on the swordsman's shoulder and the other on the shorter boy's blond head. "Michael, Kevin, this is the guy I was telling you about. This is Doug MacRay."

Doug looked at Frank, surprised but getting it now. Frank G. had had his number the whole time.

Frank said, "This guy was the fastest backward skater I ever saw, including pro."

Doug stood before the boys, feeling like he was the kid and they were the adults.

"Kev turned seven today," said Frank, roughing up his boy's hair, pride and love coming off him like heat.

"Yesterday," corrected Kevin.

"Right. Sorry. Birthday yesterday, party today."

Brown-haired Michael looked up at Doug with his mother's no-nonsense eyes. "You were drafted by the Bruins?"

Doug said, "I was."

They looked him over closely, this stranger in their dining room, this former hockey star, mysteriously a friend of their father's.

The birthday boy, Kevin, shrugged. "So what happened?"

Doug nodded, unable to meet their young eyes, almost unable to say the words. "I blew it."

42
THE LAST BREAKFAST

BREAKFAST AT HIS MOTHER's house, without the breakfast. He hadn't eaten anything in a couple of days, and thought he might never eat again.

My mother is a house.

Why come here now? To mourn her? Hadn't he always come here to mourn her?

My mother is dead.

No. He had always come here to mourn himself. His motherless self.

Gone now was his fantasy of her brave midnight flight from the Town, winning her freedom from his father and living reinvented and happy somewhere in the outside world, yet with a tender spot in her heart for the son she hated to leave behind.

All the baths he had taken in that porcelain tub, emerging barefoot and shivering and dripping tears of bathwater onto the tile floor where she last lay.

He wanted to believe in her sickness, her suffering. Her passionate, epic torment. Anything but the banality of a junkie fixing to self-destruct.

That night he had dreamed that the one-way streets of the Town were lined not with houses but with heads, the giant, weathered faces of old mothers talking at him as he hurried past them toward the empty lot on Sackville Street, the mouths on either side of it going *tsk-tsk*.

The Town kept its secrets close, raising them like its children. Thinking this brought on an absurd surge of panic for Krista and for Shyne, one he fought down.

Doug hadn't seen the guy exit the house. He was so lost in thought, he didn't notice the owner of the bottom-floor condo walking to his red Saab, keys in hand. Dark-haired, compact in an unbuttoned suit jacket, long tie, tasseled shoes. The guy saw Doug and slowed, and Doug couldn't even work up the energy to pretend to be doing anything other than what he was doing: sitting against this low brick hedge wall, watching the guy's house.

The guy tossed his underarm portfolio into the backseat of the car, then shut the door, considering heading over and saying something to Doug.

"Hi," the guy said, doing just that, slowly crossing the one-way street. "I notice you sit out here some mornings. Most mornings."

"Yeah?" Doug said, low-energy, off his guard. "I'm just waiting for a ride."

The guy nodded, stopping at the front bumper of the Caprice. "We—I see you out here a lot." He glanced back at the house. "You seem to be watching our house, or something. Unless I'm . . ."

"I used to live here a long time ago," said Doug, surprised by his tired candor. "That's all."

"Ah." The guy was still confused.

"It's cool, don't worry," said Doug. "After today I won't be coming around anymore."

The guy nodded, trying to think of something else to say, then turned and started back. Then he stopped, something nagging at him.

"Say—you want to step inside? I don't know, see it again, one last time?"

Doug never expected the guy to be decent. Doug could see the lady of the house now, peeking out at them from behind the parlor-window curtain. He pictured them all inside together, a pair of wary yuppies watching 210 pounds of Grade-A Townie getting misty in their bathroom.

The offer was tantalizing, but the house was his mother, and his mother was long dead.

Doug said, "You got a little girl there, huh?"

"Yes," the guy said, at first brightening, then suspicious.

"Sleeps in that corner room?"

The guy looked at the window where the faded ghost of a TOT ALERT! fire-safety sticker remained—not knowing how or whether to answer.

"Those dolphin curtains there," said Doug, pointing them out. "You want to draw those every night. Headlights come by on the street, they reflect off the ceiling and look like ghosts flying past. Scary for a kid lying there alone."

The guy nodded, mouth hanging open. "I will certainly do that."

Doug slid into the Caprice and pulled away down the steep decline.

THE KNOCK ON KRISTA'S door brought her answering it in a tank shirt, nylon workout pants, and Tweety slippers. She straightened with surprise, looking past Doug as though he might not be alone. "What's up?"

Doug shrugged, uncertain himself. "Nothing really."

She moved aside, and he entered. Shyne was trapped in her sticky high chair in the dying parlor, shredding a cord of string cheese into white threads. A crushed butt in the table ashtray was still smoking.

"I think I'm hungry," said Doug.

Krista disappeared into the kitchen and Doug dropped into a chair at the table, exhausted at 9 A.M. He watched Shyne's wormy fingers working at the cheese, the dull concentration in her close-set eyes, her lips lax along the flat line of her mouth. He heard the microwave hum for about a minute, then beep and stop.

He said, toward the kitchen, "I'm going away."

Silence, then Krista's padding slipper-steps resumed, the microwave door opened and shut. "You in some kind of trouble?"

Doug shook his head, though she couldn't see him. "No more than usual."

A drawer opened, silverware rustling. "Is it the heat in Town?"

Her insider status grated on him as she reentered the room. Jem told her too much. "What do you know about it?"

She set down a steaming plate of chicken à la king in front of him with a fork and knife. Thick cream sauce studded with chunks of white meat. Anything would have looked good to him then.

Krista lifted a strand of cheese off Shyne's tray and dangled it before her daughter's mouth like a mother bird with a white worm. When Shyne didn't bite, Krista pressed the cheese in between the girl's lips, only to have it fall back onto the tray. She gave up and sat across from him on a folded knee. "When are you coming back?"

Steam from his plate rose between them. Doug shook his head.

She studied him, doubtful. "This have to do with you and Jem?"

Behind her, Shyne almost made a word then, a sound like *Shemmm.*

Doug said, "In a way."

"Does he know?"

"Probably." Doug picked up the fork, checking that it was clean.

"I'm gonna do this one last thing he wants. You can tell him that for me."

She nodded. "And afterward?"

The thin wood handle of the knife was cracked, the blade rusted and wobbly. "You know I've always looked out for him."

"You were the only one who could."

"Well, this is it for me. He wants a chance at one big score, I'm gonna give it to him. It's up to him whether he makes it his last or not."

Her eyes tightened, seeing that he was serious now. "Where are you gonna go?"

"I don't know yet."

"Is she going with you?"

Doug had a forkful almost to his mouth. He set the fork back down and absorbed her blunt stare. As Shyne dropped the threads of cheese to the dusty floor, one by one, Krista's glare became full of violence, a scorned lover's inward scream.

43
THE FLORIST

GLOANSY REALIZED WHAT THE Florist's walk-in cooler reminded him of: a vault. The small-room-within-a-room thing, and the thick butcher door with the locking clasp, and the quiet inside. But with flowers in bunches on the shelves instead of stacks of bundled cash.

Why a flower shop? Gloansy wondered that now for the first time. Why not a smoke shop or a deli or something? The Main Street shop had always been there, with Fergie always running it. Probably he had taken the store from someone as part of a long-ago debt, and then— maybe with just the touch of his hand—transformed it into the ugliest flower shop ever. Petals had to be brown and wrinkled like bottom-of-the-bag potato chips before he would yank a $2 rose from a display pot. The vase water was never freshened, scummy and black-green like the harbor, and it was the only flower shop anywhere with plastic vines and silk plants in the display window.

Fergie did good parade business around Bunker Hill Day. He did some winner's circles on featured horse races over at Suffolk Downs, the wreaths they used for big-purse runs. It was bragged around that sometimes Fergie mailed the bill to the winning horse's owner the day before the race. Funerals, he did a lot of. Death, Fergie had a knack for. It followed him around in place of his lost conscience, his two sons gone, one of them a casualty of the dust he peddled, and his daughter gunned down in an ambush meant for the other. And always Fergie survived, coming back here to his workroom and wiring up his wreaths. Spools of ribbon hung in tongues of black and gold off his workbench: DAUGHTER; MOTHER; WIFE; SON.

They sat on small folding chairs with padded seats like mourners at a graveside burial, the four of them facing Fergie. Rare to get within spitting distance of Fergus Coln. He was mostly a recluse now, either bona fide paranoid or maybe just letting the legend that was The Florist feed on itself. The Code of Silence trials had all but wiped out every one of his contemporaries, but still he soldiered on. He lived somewhere near the old armory, but supposedly kept crash pads all over Town, constantly moving, like a fugitive king.

He was also known as Fucked-Up Fergie, because that's what his face was, totally fucked-up, thanks to early careers as both a wrestler—some of his bouts were televised in the late 1950s—and as a prizefighter on the Revere and Brockton circuits. His nose was wrong, his eyes doggy and tired, his skin waxy like fake fruit. His lips were so thin they were nonexistent, and his tiny cauliflower ears were things a child would draw in crayon. As they used to say about him, in his days as a mob enforcer: some hearts he stopped with just his reputation and his face. His hands were messed up too, crooked fingers looking like each row of knuckles had been separately slammed in a drawer, his nails flat and silver like coins.

Always there was this guy with him, keg-chested Rusty, supposedly an IRA or ex-IRA gunner who couldn't go back home. Rusty had fading white hair, pale Irish skin, and liked to wear dark running suits like he was on vacation. In other words, there was nothing red about Rusty, nothing to support the name. Unless he was "rusty" because he was a little slow. Guy never talked. A zombie following Fergie everywhere—except inside the cooler on that warm afternoon, a big nod of respect to the crew. Paranoid Fergie never met with anybody alone.

He sat before them in his little chair like a fighter in the corner between late-round bells. His legs were fanned wide, as though daring somebody to kick him in the balls. He wore a grease-stained white tank, black uniform-type pants, and a scally cap turned backward over his rearranged face.

Usually if you did see Fergie around Town, you recognized him first by the tight sweatshirts he always wore, the hood string drawn around his head, shadowing his face. It was no coincidence that Jem had cribbed Fergie's look that day. Jem also flattered Fergie in the fucked-up-face department, his nose and cheek still pasted in gauze, his left eye full of blood, lips cut and swollen.

Duggy sat on the other side of Gloansy, silent. He had been so sullen since their fight, you would have thought he had been the one who took the beating.

It was Doug's pride getting pummeled here. Gloansy knew how Doug was about the Florist. Fergie had some young muscle in the store when they came in, project kids in camo pants, and Doug had almost gotten into it with them too.

But being all together again, that was what counted. Doug and Jem had reached a sort of unspoken cease-fire. In fact, the one to watch here was Dez: sitting on the other side of Duggy, staring full-out at warlord Fergie, the guy who maybe—"maybe" in the Town sense—offed his father. Gloansy had to hand it to him. He couldn't believe that Dez had come at all.

"He looks like me now," said Fergie, nodding at Jem. His voice was clipped and raspy. "A little rumpus, eh?" He looked back and forth between Jem and Duggy, aging muscle hanging off his arms like rope. "Coupla stitches between brothers, it's good. Healthy. Clears the air."

Jem shrugged. Doug had no reaction that Gloansy could see.

"This room is clean, by the way, and that's guaranteed. Nobody comes in here without me, ever, and I got one of them mercury switch things to tell me if anyone tampers with the lock. So we can all talk free."

He reached for a cut daffodil, twirling it in his hand, then dipped the rounded pads of his fingertips into the petals and brought pollen to his nostrils, leaving a smear on his upper lip the color of sulfur. Guy was some kind of pervert of nature.

"This's been a long time coming," he said. "Wondered when you boys were finally gonna come round."

"Yeah," said Jem out of the side of his mouth. "Well, we been working hard. Sorta proving ourselves worthy."

A lift of Fergie's mangled chin passed for a smile. "I see your fathers' faces in each and every one a you." He ended with a look at Dez, Dez staring back hard. "Reminds me I'm still in the ring after all these years. Still on my feet. Gloves up, taking on all comers. And still ahead on points."

Jem said, "We're guys you want in your corner. Old enough to know the Town as it was, young enough to do something about putting it back that way."

Gloansy stayed attentive but blank-faced, the kid who didn't want to get called on.

"You're good thieves," said Fergie. "But these ten percent tributes to me." He shrugged like it pained him. "Ten percent is what you throw after a waiter you don't like. What is that? I'm not liked?"

Funny to see Jem squirm. Doug had his arms crossed now and Gloansy didn't think he was going to speak at all. He was going to let Jem do all the work.

Fergie went on, "But I been tracking you four. You've put together a good little run here. And I like your style. You're quiet, you keep your business close. Last crew I had got careless. Fucked up a good thing. You four, you're a crew that's been together awhile. What are you looking for from me?"

"We're looking to make a mark," said Jem. "We think we earned our shot at something big."

Fergie laid the stem across his lap and patted clean his hands. "Funny thing, fate. Because as long as it took you boys to hitch up your pants and come knocking at my door like men—this turns out to be good timing. Very good timing. Because I happen to be sitting on something here, something that's got to fall soon. And big it is. Big enough only for the best. I got someone on the inside, someone who owes me something."

Jem nodded. "We're interested."

"'Course you are. Who's not interested in something like that? But are you committed? Because you got to pay to play here, that is how we work. Blueprint fee just for me talking about things. That's on top of my percent of the take, and it's a big bite. But this is nothing you could get anywhere near without my inside. Do it right and there'll be plenty left over."

"What's the buy-in?"

"Normal job, average weight—between fifty and seventy-five large, up front."

Jem nodded, waiting. "And for this one?"

"This one is twice as much, easy."

Gloansy tried not to react, sitting up and mashing his hands together. One-fifty? Had he heard that right? Divided by four?

Fergie said, "Yo-yo's looking at me like you ain't got the money. Don't forget my little ten percent duke tells me what you been taking these years. And don't think I farm these out 'cause I can't do them myself. I put on guys like you because it's your specialty. I hire *professionals*. Because I'm generous, I like to spread it around Town for the good of all. You come here telling me you're ready for the big time? Well, this thing is bigger than Boozo ever saw from me, and it's all right here, right now, this moment."

Gloansy glanced at Jem, then at Doug, who hadn't moved, and then at Dez, who hadn't moved either. Then Gloansy regretted having moved himself.

"Who knows?" said Fergie to all this silence and not moving. "Maybe you're not as ready as you think you are." He picked the daffodil up off his lap again and Gloansy wondered how his touch alone hadn't shriveled the thing already. "This flower. Who owns it? Me, right? No. I don't own it. It's not *mine*, I didn't *create* it. Somebody somewhere, who knows who, pulled it outta the ground. Those who *take*. Versus those who can't *hold*. Someone tries to take this flower from me without payment, they're gonna get the ultimate lesson in this. 'Cause I will catch them and take something from them instead. A hand. A foot. Your hand, your foot—you think it *belongs* to you, think you *own* it? Your *life*?" He waited, though they all knew better than to answer. "Not if I can take it away. Not if you can't hold on to it." He twirled the flower in his fingers, then tossed it to the floor between them. "I'm a *taker*, that's my thing. Why else you come to me, right? Not cause I'm so pretty. You boys need to figure this out. Are you wanters or are you takers?"

It was Duggy who said, "We'll buy the job."

Gloansy turned to look at him, as did Dez. A shock, hearing him speak—never mind him saying yes to the Florist. Jem, Gloansy noticed, didn't look at all.

"For a hundred large, even," added Doug, cutting short Fergie's approving nod. "Twenty-five each. If it's as good as you say, and you haven't thrown it to nobody else yet, that means you got nobody else to throw it to."

Fergie's stare reminded Gloansy of his late father—God rest—and the looks the man could give, eyes that said, *Remember that you are here before me today only because I did not kill you yesterday—and that what you do right now will determine whether you will be here before me again tomorrow.*

But Fergie had met his match, or at least the first mirror he had ever faced that didn't automatically crack. No one could reach Doug now, and a shadow of nervousness flashed across Fergie's mangled face like that of a passing crow.

"With the balls of his father," Fergie said ultimately, reasserting himself with a kinglike nod. "I'm gonna make a present of this and give you your price. A onetime introductory offer."

He sat back grandly, but it was in the air now like the steam of their breath: Fergie the Florist had bent to the will of another.

"We won't let you down," said Jem.

"No, you won't," said Fergie. "Till now, you been like altar boys dipping into the Sunday collection. But this thing I'm talking about here, this ain't no parish church, boyos. This is a fucking Roman cathedral."

44
DEPOT

FRAWLEY AND DINO STALLED for time at the water bubbler until the fat black kid lugged his backpack into the classroom and the last hallway door closed. They were on the top floor of one of the buildings of Bunker Hill Community College, erected on the site of the long-closed prison.

The door at the end of the hall read: Radiation Lab Do Not Enter.

A guy dressed like a graduate student answered Frawley's knock, opening the door just wide enough to show his eyeglasses and the soul patch clinging to his bottom lip. "Hey," said Agent Grantin, recognizing Frawley, admitting him and Dino and shutting the door.

A second agent was under headphones near the windows. Dino put his fist to his own nose and said, "Whoa, Mary."

Grantin nodded. "One of you guys please tell my partner, Billy Drift, here, not to eat falafel during a surv in a room with *no working windows.*"

Agent Drift pulled his headphones down and sheepishly stood out of one of the student desks. "I *said* I was sorry, man. It just didn't agree with me."

The room was tight and empty except for scattered student desks and a blond wood table. On the table was a Nagra tape recorder, a computer and a color printer, a cell phone charging, and a video monitor wired to a tripod camera aimed out of an east-facing window. The hi-res monitor showed people crossing in front of the Florist's Main Street shop.

Frawley looked out the window, taking a moment to orient himself and locate the camera's line of sight, finding the Bunker Hill Mall and the cemetery and looking west from there. He introduced Dino to the Organized Crime agents.

"We're running twelve-hour revolving shifts here with a pair from the DEA," said Grantin, pulling off the glasses and the soul patch, his masterful disguise. "I was going through some of their cuts from the past few days—and that time you came down to ask about the Florist, those pictures you brought, your bank jackers? I think we got them."

He handed over four time-coded video captures printed on photo paper. The first one Frawley recognized immediately as Magloan, in profile, entering the front door with a second man wearing a hooded sweatshirt, his face bandaged.

"It's them," Frawley said, passing the picture to Dino.

The next image was from two minutes later: Elden wearing a ball-cap, one hand in his pocket, the other on the doorknob, turning to check the street behind him.

The last one was of MacRay, six minutes after Elden, a one-quarter profile of him entering the store. Just enough of his face was visible for grand jury identification.

"A sit with the Florist," said Frawley. "For how long?"

"Twenty minutes or so. They all left separately—it's on tape somewhere but I didn't have time to hard-copy it."

Dino handed the cuts back to Frawley. "Bandage man?" Dino said.

"Coughlin, must be," said Frawley, remembering MacRay's swollen hands, but unable to share this insight with Dino. He sorted through some other captures of unsuspecting shoppers. "How well are you guys in his shop?"

"Not good. We're there, but he runs this Irish music nonstop. Picked up nothing on your team but the bell jingling over the door and *Heyhowyadoing*. I was hoping maybe you were on them better, could help us."

Frawley nodded. "We're on their vehicles. Eyes, but not ears. This town—it's impossible."

"Yeah," said Drift, motioning to the window and their panorama of the Boston face of Charlestown. "Look at us up here."

"We got bumper beacons on all four of their cars, sparing the special-ops guys tails and survs. We did manage to wire up a T-4 in Magloan's car, but he rides alone and plays that JAM'N 94.5 crap all day."

"Worse than that," said Dino, "he sings along."

"We're on their phones, but they don't use them for anything. They're wise because one of them works for Nynex—though we did stick a transponder beacon on his phone company truck."

"Well," said Grantin, looking out over the Town, "something's up."

Frawley pulled out a cut showing Krista Coughlin in shorts, a strap-shouldered tank, and flip-flops, pushing her canopied stroller into the shop. "What's the Florist been up to recently?"

"The usual. He keeps hanging in there. The whole diva gangster thing."

"When are you guys going to take him down?"

Grantin shrugged. "When someone in his organization cracks. He's the only one of the old guard left. Guy's a full-time freak. DEA wants him even worse than we do."

Frawley held up the photos. "Can I keep these?"

"Hey, with our compliments."

FRAWLEY HAD TO GO to the Boston Field Office at One Center Plaza to find out that the judge had thrown out his second request, made through the U.S. attorney's Major Crime Unit, for Title Three taps and surv warrants on Claire Keesey's Charlestown condominium. The judge cited insufficient evidence, ruling again that she could not be reasonably considered a suspect in the Kenmore Square armed robbery.

Back inside the tech room, Frawley waited with Dino while a computer program swallowed up longitude and latitude GPS coordinates from the bumper beacon transponders and spit the information back out to them in the form of street addresses and connect-the-dots grid maps.

"What's this?" said Dino. "MacRay actually went to work two days ago?"

At least he had driven up to the Bonafide Demolition site in Billerica and parked there for eight hours. Then that night, and the next morning and again in the evening, he did circuits around the shark fin of Allston, parking for long stretches in the vicinity of Cambridge Street, near the Conrail yards. Cross-checking showed Magloan spending time in that area as well, and Elden's work truck cooping there for an hour or so at midday.

Dino said, "Cambridge Street? Christ. What is that, Dunbar?"

"Nope," said Frawley, reaching for his jacket. "Magellan."

WHERE DO ARMORED TRUCKS go at night, and where do they issue from in the morning? Unassuming buildings tucked behind high-security fences and electronic gates, deep inside industrial parks or hidden among office-building complexes—the locations of which are the most closely guarded secrets in the armored-carrier industry. Inside, under video-surveillance systems that rival those of most casinos, cashiers in pocketless smocks work in glass-walled counting rooms, tallying, sorting by denomination, stacking, and strapping hundreds of thousands of dollars each night, in currency notes and coins.

For example, on December 27, 1992, thieves looted a windowless office building in an industrial section of Brooklyn, New York, making off with $8.2 million—and leaving behind $24 million they were physically unable to carry.

Set back from the southern side of Cambridge Street before the road crossed the Charles River into Cambridge, in the shadow of the elevated Mass Turnpike, stood a two-story building with no name, surrounded by twin twelve-foot-high chain-link fences topped with concertina wire. That side of the road was barren, lacking even a sidewalk, and the building looked like a modest storage facility gone belly-up.

The electronic gate at the rear of the armored-truck depot was hidden from the street. Frawley could just see it from the dusty lot, holding down his tie as cars whipped past.

"Not one exit," said Dino, pointing his clipboard at the Pike. "Not two exits. Three big exits, all within an eighth of a mile of where we stand."

Frawley squinted, blasted by sand and grit. "Firepower needed for this. Stepping out of profile."

"So is going to the Florist though. Must have somebody on the inside."

"That's an angle for us. But I don't want to tip our hand either." Frawley looked at the cameras on the corners of the roof. "You said MacRay went to work, right?"

"You think explosives? Think they're going to blow their way in?"

"Or else put up a hell of a diversion."

Frawley had not filed a 302 summarizing his meeting with MacRay. He didn't want that part of the official record, at least not yet. He had, however, filed a Confidential Informant report, Form 209, on Krista Coughlin, getting her assigned a six-digit snitch code in order to cover himself and the investigation, in case she did come through with anything. Such as, when exactly MacRay and company were planning on taking down the Magellan Armored Depot.

A black 4X4 ran up on the shoulder, Frawley and Dino stepping back, squinting into the dust cloud as a cop-type in a security uniform climbed out. He wore a badge and an ID tag, but nothing that read Magellan.

"Guys lost?" he said, coming up on them cordial but firm. "Help you with something?"

Frawley didn't badge him. He had no way of knowing who might be the inside man. "No thanks," he said. "We were just on our way."

45
BALLPARK FIGURE

MOST PEOPLE—INCLUDING MOST bank robbers—think that getting at the money is the toughest part of heisting, when in fact it is the getaway that separates the pros from the cons.

Doug climbed inside the Nynex truck at the corner of Boylston and Park, wearing a work shirt of Dez's, rapping fists with the Monsignor.

"Got the hotel room?" said Dez.

"It's a palace."

"How long you gonna stay?"

"Long as it takes. Registered under 'Charles.'"

"'Charles?'"

"As in 'Charles Town' "

"Ah."

Doug checked the mirrors for tails. "You put in for next Tuesday off?"

"Personal day, all set. But this decoy shit's a lot of work."

"Tell that to the G. You switched trucks, I hope."

"Bleeding radiator—damn the luck. Here. Buckle this on."

Doug clasped around his waist a leather lineman's belt just like Dez's, with a red-orange plastic phone-company handset on a wire holster loop.

Dez double-parked prominently on Yawkey Way, right across from the Gate D entrance, stepping out with his work-order clipboard and yanking open the back of the truck. He loaded Doug up with a pile of equipment, then they crossed the road and commiserated with the red-shirted gate girl about the heat. She consulted her clipboard. "Are you on the work list?"

"Should be," said Dez. "I know you're on mine. I just go where I'm told."

Her red shirt meant ballpark staff, not security. "This is about the . . . ?"

"System upgrades. All I'm here for now is to check things out, save us time on job day by making sure we bring everything we need. Something about everything having to be done over the next West Coast road trip. Twenty minutes, tops."

"Could I just see your work ID?"

Dez showed her. She looked it over and filled out a work pass for him.

Doug made a show of struggling under his load as she finished. "My trainee," said Dez.

"That's okay," she said, filling out a second pass without asking for Doug's ID.

The caves and tunnels beneath the Fenway stands, the concession area, was where the oldest park in Major League Baseball showed its age. Food-service workers wheeled racks of bagged hot-dog rolls to the stalls, already loading up for that night's game. A blue shirt met them at the doors to an elevator, a recent college graduate, his security ID hanging on a shoelace around his neck, handset radio on his belt. He was short, wide with machine-pumped muscle, and Dez flashed him the passes.

"Where to, guys?"

Dez said, "Ah, press box, I'm told."

The blue shirt stepped aboard the elevator and pressed five. Doug stood between black-and-white photographs of prewar Ted Williams leaning on a bat and a beaming, Triple Crown–winning Carl Yastrzemski.

Dez said, "Guess this ain't gonna be the year, huh?"

Blue shirt said, "Nope, doesn't look like it."

When the elevator stopped, Dez said, "Anyone ever ridden in this thing with you and not said those basic words?"

Blue shirt said, "You pretty much nailed it."

The doors opened on the sunny flat of an outdoor pedestrian ramp, the blue shirt leading them inside glass doors past an unmanned security desk, past back-to-back cafeterias—one for park employees, one for media—and down along a white hallway of doors open to broadcast booths. The end of the hall doglegged wide into two tiers of long counters, both of them print-media booths, resembling nothing so much as the old grandstand at Suffolk Downs. The glass wall looked out from just left of home plate, over the infield diamond of June-green grass, the cocoa base paths and warning track, thirty-four thousand tiny-ass seats, and the city of glass and steel beyond.

"Field of screams," said Dez, unloading Doug.

They made a show of walking around and plugging things in, thumping on walls, the blue shirt lasting maybe three minutes. "Say, you guys good here for a while?"

"Yeah, sure," said Dez, busy.

"I'll be back, couple of minutes."

Dez waved without looking. "Take your time."

When the footsteps faded, Dez slipped a radio wire into his ear, scanning for ballpark security frequencies. Doug affixed his work pass to his sweat-dampened shirt and nodded to Dez, starting quickly back out to the hallway, holding down his flopping telephone handset as he returned to the outdoor ramp.

Doug walked down one floor, nodding to the white-aproned food service workers on their break, entering the first open door and finding himself inside the glass-enclosed 600 Club. He strode through it like he owned the place, passing only a carpet cleaner and a bar back, crossing behind the stadium seats and their fishbowl view of the park. An escalator brought him down one more floor to a concourse running high above the third-base seats, and he made his way down through the grandstand and loge boxes, ducking into the first ramp.

Busy red-shirted Fenway employees passed him underneath the stands without much of a look. With the ballpark quiet and the concessions shuttered, Doug felt like he was back in his demo crew days—doing a basement sweep of a condemned building ahead of the wrecking ball. The angled stone floor was a skateboarder's wet dream, the iron stanchions hoisting up the park like the corroding girders boosting the interstate over the Town.

Doug passed behind Gate D, the red-shirted gate girl sitting out on the sidewalk, drinking from a bottle of water with her back to him. He passed a broad souvenir booth locked up like an old newspaper stand, eyeing the open red door beyond it. A sign on the inside face said Employees Only. Doug passed it with a long, careful glance, seeing a short hallway inside, leading to a second door with a square, one-way window.

This was the money room. Game time always found a member of Boston's finest working a detail outside it, but right now there were only cameras. According to the Florist's inside squeal, the security work scheduled for the long road trip included surveillance upgrades, meaning the park's central monitoring network would be dark for a few days. This was the reason for the job's narrow timeline.

The money room door was protected by an electronic keypad lock. Doug had the combination, but no intention of using it. He meant to grab the haul while it was on its way from the money room to the can, all packaged and ready to go.

The snag there was that the cash pickup went down inside the closed park. The can was admitted through the ambulance bay door on Van Ness Street and loaded inside at the first aid station. That meant the job had to fall right there underneath the stands.

He walked the tunnel between the money room door and the first aid station—park-wise, it matched up parallel with the distance between home plate and the edge of the outfield grass beyond first base—a brick-walled, advertisement-filled passageway with a low, slanting roof. Along this route the couriers wheeled the cash on a motorized handcart. Once loaded, the ambulance bay door opened again and the truck departed, making no other jumps before returning to the Provident Armored depot in Kendall Square.

Doug lingered at the empty first aid area—just a kiosk inside the bay—eyeing the distance between iron girders, seeing how much floor space they'd have. Then he doubled back to the money room, checking the sight lines. He was stalling there, worrying about them becoming trapped inside the park, when the door opened.

Doug turned and started away fast, back down the low tunnel toward the first aid station, making like he'd taken a wrong turn. A voice called to him, but he did not stop, fiddling busily with the handset on his belt.

The voice called to him again, loud in the tunnel, enough to attract more attention. Doug stopped just a few paces from the first aid station, half-turning, still trying to shield his face from view.

"Help you?" said the man, coming along behind him. A blue-shirt security guy, thin-haired and well-tanned, his radio still on his belt.

"Nope, all set," said Doug, still fooling with his handset. "Little lost in here."

"Hold up a minute."

The security guy came up, looked Doug over, his pass, his line-man's belt and boots. The guy was older, in his fifties. Maybe head of security. "Come on with me."

He continued past Doug, and Doug followed, weighing his options. They turned left through the first ramp, out into the open air, walking along the field boxes in the lower stands down to the Red Sox dugout behind first base. Next to the dugout was a short door open to the field. The grounds crew was in the outfield spraying down grass and raking the warning track.

"This what you were looking for?" said the security guy.

He wore a knowing smile, and Doug realized then this guy was trying to do him a solid. Give him a thrill, one working man to another. At Doug's hesitation, the guy said, "Unless you throw a base-ball ninety miles an hour, or hit one thrown that fast, this is your only chance to get out there."

Doug started onto the foul-territory dirt with the cautious first step of a ship passenger arriving on land. He crossed the grass, avoiding the freshly laid foul line as superstitious managers do, moving onto the infield. He paused before the pitcher's mound, then walked up onto it, standing just shy of the rubber.

He looked toward home plate with a bolt of fan vertigo. He found the press box high to his right, Dez standing in the wide viewing window, watching him, smiling in tribute, probably thinking, *Duggy working the old magic, talking his way out onto the field.*

Doug looked out at the dinged tin of the Green Monster, then over it to the Citgo sign looming above Kenmore Square. The sight of that sign would forever kick him with a sense of failure, and of loss—the bank job, Claire—the city a boneyard of memories to him now, another good reason to walk away.

He crossed back to the home team's dugout like a pitcher headed for the showers. The security guy was leaning against the backs of the first row of seats, arms crossed, enjoying the gift more than the recipient had. "Still remember my first step out there."

"Hey, thanks," mumbled Doug, concerned about the guy remembering his face now. Doug watched him close the little door to the field, saw the guy's small, jeweled pinkie ring. He noticed the care the guy put into his fingernails, and the warm Florida vacation tan of his skin. *Head of security,* thought Doug, putting it together.

"You like to gamble?" Doug asked him.

The guy shrugged, a personal question but not too intrusive. "Here and there. Ponies mostly. Why?"

"How much you into the Florist for?"

The crash of the guy's face. From lighthearted generosity to dead-eyed fear. He looked around, said quietly, "You're not supposed to have any contact with me."

"Don't vary your routine next Monday morning," Doug told him. "Not one iota."

The guy glanced at the grounds crew, the empty stands behind him. "I was not to be approached."

"The cops're going to approach you. They'll be approaching everyone, after. You ready to sit for a lie detector?"

The guy stared at Doug: a proud man in a panic, in deep debt to the Florist, nothing left to bargain with except his life. He turned and walked off underneath the stands, and Doug saw, as clear as the seams on a Wakefield knuckler, that the Florist would off this guy as soon as the job was done.

ROOM 224 WAS IN the rear center of the block-deep, two-story Howard Johnson Hotel. With no direct sun and no cheerful amenities—just a humming TV, a mismatched chair and table, a stiff, yarny rug, a phone-booth shower, and a creaky double bed—the second-floor room was a suicide's dream. Doug drew open the stiff, ratty curtain on a patchwork window with one pane tinted rose—and looked out across Van Ness Street to the southern exterior brick wall of Fenway Park.

Fenway resembled a factory on that side, a long block of red brick and steel with small square windows made of glass as opaque as blocks of ice. Six old bay doors were widely spaced along the length of the wall, each painted green, all unlabeled except the one directly across the street from Doug's window, the last before the canvas-lined fence of the players' parking lot. Beneath a candle lamp with a red warning bulb, small, stenciled white letters on the green door read AMBULANCE.

Doug changed out of Dez's shirt and went right back outside again, crossing Boylston Street against the traffic, the hotel equidistant between the ballpark and the Fenway Gardens.

He walked slowly to her gate. The vitality of the summer flowers stood in stark contrast to the cut stems that littered the Florist's cooler tomb. Weeds were beginning to sprout in the neglected flower beds. Doug looked at the impatiens planted near his buried stash, ragged and thirsty and threatened by encroaching spearmint, wondering when she would return.

DOUG SPENT THE EVENING in the suicide room, watching the park's comings and goings before game time. The red bulb lit up two hours before the first pitch, the door rising and the ambulance backing carefully inside. Every bay door lifted in the eighth inning, the crowd soon flooding out onto Van Ness after a satisfying win, slow to disperse. The ambulance pulled away around the same time as the last of the players drove off in their Blazers and Infinitis, the red lamp going dark. The light towers above the park faded out a half hour later, and then it was just the homeless trawling for cans, pushing their shopping carts to nowhere.

THAT NIGHT HE DREAMED he was crushed beneath the rear wheels of an armored truck, twelve tons cutting him in half. But it was not Frank G. removing his fireman's helmet to take Doug's hand—it was the bank sleuth, Frawley, his federal eyes smiling.

A HORN BLAST FROM a passing truck woke him that morning—lying across the made bed, still wearing yesterday's clothes. He checked the clock, got up to take a piss, then pulled a chair to the window and waited.

At 9:17 the red lamp went bright. The ambulance door opened as a silver Provident Armored can with twin rear doors pulled up, turning toward Doug before stopping and backing into the narrow bay. Doug saw the two guards in the cab, and knew that, given the size of the haul, a third had to be riding the jump seat inside the locked cargo hold. He noticed one other critical detail, getting a clear look down at their faces, shoulders, and chests from his second-floor window: neither guard wore ear wires. No need, he reasoned, given that the exchange took place behind locked doors.

The can backed inside and the bay door closed. The red light above the closed door remained on.

A second car, a black Suburban, pulled up onto the curb on Van Ness, stopping just to the right of the closed door and idling there. Doug watched the driver, apparently the only occupant, speaking into a handheld radio.

A tail car. This complicated things.

At 9:31 the ambulance door lifted again and the can rolled out, turning toward Yawkey and pulling away. As the bay door started to close, the black Suburban eased off the curb, following the truck, and Doug curled farther back from the window as it passed. The red lamp over the closed bay door went dark just as the lamp inside Doug's criminal mind clicked on, suddenly illuminating the job before him.

46
THIRST

DOUG TOOK THE ORANGE line out to the Community College stop and walked up the hill toward Pearl. The dilapidated house leaning on the slant looked a hundred years older since he'd last seen it. His Caprice and Jem's blue Flamer were parked in front.

He slipped inside through the unrepaired front door. Above all else he wanted to avoid seeing Krista. Up in his apartment, he went around filling his father's old army sack with clothes. The only black shoes he owned were the pinching pair he had bought for his date with Claire, so he threw them in. When he realized he would never again return to the house, he made another quick, final pass. A convict's personal possessions—few in number, weighted with significance—took on a totemic quality, and Doug had, over time, winnowed his meaningful totems down to exactly one. From the bottom drawer of his bureau, he pulled out his original draft letter, typed on Boston Bruins letterhead stationery and pressed in a clear plastic sleeve, slipping it into the bag.

On his way back out, Doug paused on the steps below the second-floor landing. Jem's door lock and frame remained busted. Doug walked back up, set his laundry bag down in the hall, and rapped a knuckle on Jem's door.

"It's open," he heard, and stepped inside. He started toward the game room, but Jem's voice—"Down here"—turned him around, brought him into the bright front parlor.

Jem wore a pit-stained, V-neck undershirt and black-and-gold, smiley-face boxers as he worked on the triple-decker dollhouse. He was interior-decorating it now, having pasted in old wallpaper swatches and tiny curtains, furnishing it in miniature, even sitting a thin wooden Krista doll at the bottom-floor dining room table. Except for the empty third floor, the dollhouse was room-for-room an exact replica, inside and out.

Jem had just finished his stereo and speakers—meticulous, down to the brand names, equalizer bars, tiny knobs—and was at work on his entertainment-center TV. "Heard you walking around up there," he said without turning.

"Yeah," said Doug. "Clothes."

A bottle of Budweiser stood open on the table, soaking another ring into the ruined oak. "Where you been?"

"Working this thing," said Doug, pulling his eyes away from the Bud. "It's coming together."

"Good to hear. You walking the can guards home at night?"

"No," said Doug. "I don't do that anymore."

Jem put the tiny TV down to dry. "Tools are set," he said, making a gun of his thumb and forefinger. "Got our armor. No masks needed with the uniforms."

"Gloansy get Joanie to clean those yet?"

In the summer of 1993, Gloansy had worked as a driver on the set of one of the all-time worst motion pictures ever made, a Boston bomb-squad movie called *Blown Away*. The klepto had come through big time on that production, nabbing four cop uniforms out of a dressing room trailer, complete with badges, belts, and hats. Everything but the shoes. The costumes were so authentic that the theft was reported in the papers the next day, and Gloansy was questioned along with the rest of the film crew. He stashed the uniforms in his mother-in-law's attic, where they had been cooling until that week.

"I got yours here," said Jem. "He had his bride do a little tailoring on them, so make sure your pants don't have three legs. And he still needs to know what we want for a work car."

"Tell him I got that covered. Built into the gig."

Jem nodded without questioning it. They were quiet then, each pondering their uneasy truce. "Heard you're thinking about leaving."

"Maybe. Yeah."

Jem nodded. "Only asking 'cause I need to know whether I should put you in on the third floor here or not. Shyne, you know—I don't want her wondering who that guy's supposed to be up there, if there's no Uncle Duggy living upstairs anymore."

Jem had even included the roof wires he used to steal his cable. "I'm done," Doug told him. "And if this job falls the way it should, it's your time to step away too. A walk-off home run."

Jem considered this, eyeing his house. "Yeah, maybe you're right."

"Things do change, man. Nothing wrong with that."

"No, sure."

"We had a fucking amazing run. By any standard."

"Yo, we *set* the standard."

"The Florist, if you keep going back to him—kid, the guy's a pimp like that. He'll keep turning you out till you get bounced for good."

Jem scowled, and Doug saw that Jem was just shining him on.

"Other thing I have to say to you is, the weight of this take, all the variables involved—you should pack a parachute. We all should. In case things don't go smooth."

"Nah," Jem said. "It's gonna go great."

"It is. But in *case*."

Jem shook his head. "I don't see me running. If I have to stay away a little while, let things cool down, whatever—yeah, fine. But I don't see it."

Doug turned to the windows, chilled by Jem's faith in an unchanging future. He'd build the entire Town in miniature if he could, and sit in this same room, playing the pieces forever.

"Still out there?" said Jem.

Doug looked down to the gray van with twin antennas and tinted windows parked a few houses down the slope. "Still there."

"Dumb fucks," snorted Jem, reaching for his beer and taking a hard swig. "It's gonna go awesome, man. Fucking awesome."

THE AREA SURROUNDING A Major League ballpark is a minefield for a recovering alcoholic. Doug's own hotel had a baseball-themed lounge out front, and he sat there now, alone at a small table by the darkened windows, two hours before game time, watching fellow ticket-holders tanking up. On the wall near him hung an unlit Bud Man sign, the red-masked "super-beer-o" of the 1970s. When the waitress came by, Doug said, "Bud draft," and it was like flexing his muscles at the beach. *Let's see how strong I am.*

Frank G. always said, *Never walk into a tavern or a liquor store, especially alone.* But sometimes fate had to be tempted. Sometimes you had to walk right back up to the edge of that cliff, just to remind yourself what it had felt like lying at the bottom.

The beer arrived in a short glass, set upon a cocktail napkin like a supplicant on a prayer mat. Doug looked down at the thin brew, held a little powwow with it, then rejected it as unworthy. A vow was only as strong as its greatest temptation, and this was not enough. He threw three crumpled dollar bills at the table and emerged sinless into the all-knowing, all-seeing light of day.

He crossed the street again to the gardens. He walked to her gate and saw that she had still not been back. A few fallen leaves lay around her beds now, like dead thoughts in an idle mind. Something small-mouthed and busy had been chewing on her herbs.

After leaving Jem that morning, he had humped his laundry sack over the hill to the Boys and Girls Club, just to give fate a chance. But he didn't see her there and didn't go inside. Instead, he hailed a cab and directed it up Packard Street and the alley behind there one last time. The purple Saturn with the *Breathe!* bumper sticker was back in its parking space. When the cab drove out of City Square, Doug looked back one last time, determined never to return to the Town again.

FRIDAY NIGHT, THEY STROLLED the caves of iron and stone beneath the stands, Doug and Dez, now in the company of packs of hungry, bladder-heavy fans.

The bored detail cop stood inside the short hallway between the open Employees Only door and the heavier door to the money room. Doug and Dez cruised it five or six times in the anonymity of the grazing crowd, getting familiar with the layout but learning nothing new.

The ambulance sat inside the closed bay door at the first aid station, a pair of EMTs sitting on the metal backstep, chatting up two girls. Doug's eye followed the tracks the door rose on, finding the manual on/off switch for the outside red lamp.

Concession lines ran ten and twelve deep, stretching back to the relish bowls and squirt tubs, condiment droppings spotting the stone floor like bat shit. Money was changing hands everywhere and Doug should have been thrilled. Red-visored girls tissuing out pretzels and milking soft-serve vanilla into collectible batting-helmet cups, kids jumping up and down with their pennants and posters and machine-signed team pictures, hassled dads pulling green from their wallets. Yellow-shirted snack hawkers humping empty drink racks and metal hot-dog boxes to a busy side room near Gate D, emerging moments later with a full whack and marching back out to the stands. And it was hot that night, nineties and humidity predicted all weekend, what Red Sox Nation called a *scawcha*, perfect for moving ice cream bars and Cokes.

But all this chewing and spending he viewed through a filter of disgust. The swine and their swill. He sidestepped a lump of cheesy nachos on the floor that looked like someone had shat them there and kept on moving, then ducked into the men's room to take a leak at the trough. The ballpark seemed to him a factory of shit and piss and cash. At root, the business of baseball was no better or different from the movies or from church: put on a show, promise people something transcendent, and then bleed the suckers dry.

They took their seats again in the sixth, just back of the right-field pole. A foul ball arced high over their heads, slowing at the top of its ascent like a firework shell about to explode, bloom, and twinkle away, then drifted back over the roof boxes out onto Van Ness. The fans groaned and sat back down, except for Doug and Dez, who had never stood.

Doug was hunched over a bag of peanuts, shelling one after another. Some asshole had kicked over a beer two rows back, the stain spreading like urine under Doug's seat. He dropped the cracked shells down there to soak up the spill, the same way the peanuts absorbed the saliva flooding Doug's mouth. He would never give in for a Fenway beer.

Thinking about drinking now was like fantasizing about the perfect crime. How he would do it—*if* he were going to do it.

A halfhearted wave came by, fans rising and falling in a ripple around them, Dez and Doug again keeping their seats. Dez said, "And I used to think the beach-ball thing was annoying."

Doug muttered, "Fucking retards."

Dez checked him. "What's up? You been pissed all night."

Doug frowned, shook it off. "Thought I could lose myself in the prep, but it's not happening. I'm like borderline okay when I'm focused on the job."

"Otherwise?"

Doug cracked another peanut shell. "This thing can't happen fast enough for me."

"You always said, Duggy—no marquee scores."

Doug nodded. "That is what I always said."

"And never be greedy."

"Right."

Dez looked him over. "Is it the girl?"

Doug shook his head. "Girl's gone, man."

"That's what I'm talking about."

"It's the Florist, it's the G—it's fucking everything."

Dez watched him working the peanuts. "They don't bake fortunes in those things, you know."

Doug spread his hands and saw the heap of cracked shells between his work boots, kicking it over like the mound of trash that was his life. The smell of piss-water beer assailed him from all sides, but especially from the guy in the brand-new Red Sox ballcap sitting next to him.

"Dezi, man, listen. I've been thinking it over, and this one's not for you. There's no tech on this job, nothing cute. It's us walking in the front door with guns in our hands. Something goes wrong, it could get messy. I'm serious."

Dez looked at him. "You think I can't—"

"The other two, I couldn't talk them off it if I tried. Wouldn't waste my breath. I told Jem this morning to pack a bag just in case, he didn't even hear me. But you. You know better. And I'm the one who got you into this thing. Dez—you know I used you, right? I mean, in the beginning."

"I—sure."

"'Cause I'm a piece of shit that way. 'Cause it was all about the job then, and nothing else. But now you're my responsibility, and I can't have that on me, okay? Because things are ending. You don't wanna be in business with the Florist anyway. Think of your dad."

Dez looked out at the field. "I *been* thinking about him. Probably too much."

"Fuck the Florist. Guy's a relic. Once he goes down, the whole Town goes. All the old ways."

Dez said, staring out at the field, "Someone's got to get him."

"Forget about that. Hey." Doug punched him in the shoulder. "I don't even want to hear that from you."

Dez shook his head. "I'm not backing out now, Duggy. Even if I wanted to, see? Which I don't. And besides—you couldn't pull this off with just three guys."

"Easily."

"You lie. You're full of bullshit, and I don't like this, Duggy. You look desperate. And everything you taught me, everything you're about, says that's the wrong way to go into this."

"Then gimme your out. Steer clear."

"Fine, I'll walk. When you do."

"Cut that shit out now." Doug cracked his last peanut shell, then crumpled the bag and threw it to the floor. "See, I am desperate. My life right now—fuck it. Two or three weeks ago, I could have walked away, come out way ahead. Now, I need this. Makes me sick, this whole thing—Fergie, the G—fuck them all. But I'm not leaving here without nothing. I thought one big final stake would free everybody, but Jem's not gonna stop. Gloansy, neither. It was just my fantasy. But you—you got your thing going, you got your job, your ma to take care of."

"Is there something about this job you're not telling me?"

"What I'm telling you is that you should walk. You're clear right now. Me? I'm a point down, I got no choice but to pull my goalie from the net, go for a last-minute score. I gotta finance my walkaway. This is the only way I know how."

The crowd surged around them again, jumping up—then diving out of the way of a screaming foul ball.

"The fuck—!"

A splash of wet into Doug's lap. Coldness soaking his chest through his shirt, running down his arms.

The guy next to him righted himself, standing, his beer cup dripping empty in his hand.

"Oh, Christ!" he said, the MLB hologram-logo tag dangling off his ballcap. "*Shit*, I'm sorry about that. Let me get some napkins, let me buy you something—"

Doug got to his feet and slammed the guy in the face. The guy went over backward into the row behind them, his brand-new hat popping off his head.

Doug continued to whale on him until someone hooked up Doug's arms—Dez—practically climbing onto Doug's back to stop him. Everyone shouting, no one making sense, Doug ready to turn and start fighting Dez.

Only the sight of the kid made him stop. Eight years old, sitting in the next seat over, frozen in fear. Also wearing a new ballcap. The guy's son.

Doug shook off Dez and slid past the cowering kid into the aisle, ducking quickly down the ramp into the caves just as blue security shirts arrived on the scene. He walked out the first open gate he could find and started running when he hit the street—trying to escape the odor of piss-beer rising off him, the stink watering his eyes.

47
GETAWAY

AFTER THE GAME, THERE was a party two doors down from his, and Doug lay across his bed, hearing the music, the laughter in the hallway, the late-night splashing in the hotel pool. He busied his mind by cooking up a grand scheme to implicate the Florist in the heist, while at the same time cutting him out of the split—with the double cross forcing the four of them into permanent exile from the Town, thereby saving them all. It was a plan both vengeful and heroic, but he grew tired working out the particulars, falling asleep happy. When he woke up Saturday morning, the scheme's logic fell apart like wet tissue in his hands.

The one dream he remembered was him watching the lottery drawing on his hotel-room TV, Claire Keesey in a sparkling lottery-girl gown pulling four zeros in a row from the ball machine, matching the ticket in Doug's hand.

He paced, trying to keep himself holed up inside the room and away from trouble. All the time now he was thinking about that crappy baseball lounge in front of the hotel. Everything still so open-ended. The getaway he had set up for the job was a good one, maybe even a great one—but he still had no getaway plan for himself. No getaway from the Town.

He slipped out the rear hotel entrance at the end of the hall and did a circuit around the park's perimeter. He told himself it was just light recon, passing Boston Beer Works, Uno's, Bill's Bar, Jillian's. Anything could be endured, he thought, so long as it had a foreseeable end. What he needed now, and what he did not have, was a future worth being strong for. Suddenly it was obvious to him why he had been so reluctant to plan his getaway.

Doug heard the players being announced over the Fenway PA system as he returned to the gardens on his third or fourth pass in as many days. Her plot looked empty, and it was almost with relief that he turned away, only to catch a flicker of movement out of the corner of his eye. He looked back and there she was, standing in the middle of her garden.

He gave himself no time to think or chicken out. His chest was a beehive as he walked to her gate, trampling his better judgment on the way, his mind telling him not to do this, his heart telling him he must.

She turned when the latch clinked. A floppy straw sun hat veiled her shocked expression, her bare limbs glowing in the afternoon sun. White T-shirt and jeans shorts, a pair of pruning shears in her gloved hands. Her knees smudged with dirt.

"Just let me say this."

She took one step backward, the pruning shears falling from her grip. She looked pained, scared—this was what seeing him did to her now.

"I am hanging by a thread here," he said.

She looked at him as though he were a man she had murdered, returned from the grave.

"We can do this," he said. "We can, I know we can. We can make this work. If you want to. Do you want to?"

"Just please go."

"We met in a Laundromat. You were crying—"

"We met inside the bank you were robbing—"

"We met in a Laundromat. It's true if you believe it. *I* believe it. The rooftop, that first night? We are still those same two people."

"No, we're not."

"I took advantage of you. I admit that. And I would do it all over again, exactly the same, if it were my only chance to get close to you. Telling you I'm sorry for it now—that would be a lie."

She was shaking her head.

"You want control over your life. You said that. You want to be in charge. I want to give you control over both our destinies. Everything about us, all in your hands."

The words were tumbling out. She was listening. Doug pointed to the light towers above Fenway Park, behind her.

"Monday," he said. "Two days from now. An armored truck will enter the ballpark to pick up receipts from this weekend's games. I'm going to be there."

She stared. Frozen. Appalled.

"I don't care anymore," said Doug. "About anything, except you. After this job, I am done. I am gone."

"Why tell me this?" She made fists of her hands at her sides. "Why are you *doing* this to me?"

"Frawley probably told you, what—to report anything I say? Okay. What I just told you—you could send me away forever. If you hate me, if you want me gotten rid of, that's the easiest way."

She shook her head, hard. He couldn't tell whether that meant she wouldn't report him, or didn't want the choice, or didn't want to hear any more.

"But if youdon't," he said, "then come away with me. After. That's what I came here to ask you to do."

She was too shocked to speak.

"We'll ride out the statute of limitations together. Anywhere you want to go. Your 'if only.'"

A horse's snort interrupted. Doug heard hooves clopping and saw Claire's eyes track left and widen. A mounted policeman was trotting down the path toward them.

"You decide," Doug said, backing to the gate. "My future, our future—it's all up to you."

He was outside her gate now, surging with devotion, the horse hooves clopping near.

"Doug—" she started, but he cut her off.

"I'm at the Howard Johnson down the street." He told her the room number and the name. "Either turn me in or come away with me," he said, then started back toward the ballpark, back toward the job.

48
NIGHT CRAWLERS

SATURDAY NIGHT FOUND FRAWLEY in a surv van down the block from the Magellan Armored Depot with a young agent on loan from the fraud squad named Cray. Dino had knocked off after the depot went dark at seven, the turnpike traffic overhead the slowest it had been in Frawley's week of watching, Cambridge Street giving over to the night crawlers shuttling back and forth between Allston and Cambridge, from bar to party to club. Cray, single like Frawley—family men usually caught a break on weekends—ran the radio awhile, a show called *X Night,* broadcast live and commercial-free from one of the dance factories on Landsdowne Street. A taste of what they were missing.

The crew's activity around the depot had slowed to a trickle. Magloan was there yesterday for two hours with dark sunglasses on, the bug in his car picking up snoring. Coughlin had cruised the depot exactly once, though the Pearl Street detail reported a lot of activity in and out of his house. Elden was the only constant, parking there for lunch every day—even that day when he had switched work trucks, ditching their bug.

But most troubling to Frawley was that MacRay had all but fallen off the face of the earth. He hadn't been sighted near the depot in days, and his Caprice hadn't budged from its resident space on Pearl Street in a week. Frawley had raced to Charlestown when the Pearl Street surv spotted MacRay leaving the house, carrying what looked like laundry, but MacRay vanished again before Frawley arrived.

He had expected the crew to keep their distance from each other in the run-up to the heist, but he should have been seeing a lot more prep activity in and around the target—especially with Elden's day off from work just three days away.

Krista Coughlin had hung up on Frawley twice. He worried that he had overplayed his hand with her, that she had gone to MacRay after Frawley's initial contact, maybe scared him off this mark.

Cray tapped a pencil against the dash in time with the techno music, using the passenger seat as a desk upon which to read the case file. "Explosives, huh?"

"It's a theory," said Frawley.

"Three turnpike exits. This thing was made-to-order."

Frawley nodded, then sat back against the van wall, thinking. He was quiet and still so long that Cray stopped tapping and looked over. "Ever play any hockey?" Frawley asked him.

"You kidding? I grew up in northern Minnesota, closer to Winnipeg than Minneapolis. You?"

"I ran track. Played a little basketball. Not being six-six, I used to have to fake a lot. Do you fake much in hockey?"

"Sure, all the time." Cray moved his pencil over the file like a hockey stick. "You're on a breakaway, say. You and the goalie, one-on-one. You're charging in hard, he centers himself, stick down, elbows out. You draw back on a slap shot, bring the blade hard on a fake. The goalie commits. You've frozen him. You flip a little wrist shot past his skate—and the hometown crowd goes wild."

Frawley nodded, buzzing. After a moment he pushed open the back doors of the van and stood out on the dirt shoulder of the road. He looked at the double-fenced Magellan Armored Depot, and then to the turnpike overhead, the cars shooting into the city, thinking, *And the hometown crowd goes wild.*

49
THE SUICIDE ROOM

THIRTY-FOUR THOUSAND SEATS. Times three sold-out games.

Equals one hundred thousand mouths.

Saturday and Sunday matinees, loads of kids in attendance: multiple Cokes, beers, ice cream; on top of programs, T-shirts, caps, souvenirs.

Round it off. Say $25 average per mouth. Times one hundred thousand.

$2.5 million.

Adjust up for day-of-game cash ticket sales, down for coins—call it even.

Subtract Fergie's greedy 40 percent, then divide by four.

Seven minutes of work = approximately $400K.

AROUND NOON WAS THE only time he left the room on Sunday. Walking the perimeter of the park before the game was the bare minimum of what he needed to do in terms of prep, and he kept his eyes off the taverns, cutting it short at the end to hustle back to 224, convinced that Claire would be there waiting for him. At the very least, there would be a message from her flashing on his phone.

Nothing. He went through the whole lifting-the-receiver thing, making sure the telephone was working, then walked to the front desk to double-check that no messages had been left, then raced back to the room hoping the phone hadn't rung in the meantime.

Around about the third inning he started to pretend he wasn't nervous. He opened the only hinged pane on his window and listened to the crowd noise across Van Ness, the game playing on his TV with the sound down. He paced. At one point he saw a female beat cop out on the sidewalk, and Doug pulled the shades, watching out of the window edge as the cop passed under the red light over the closed ambulance door. She turned the corner and never came back, and Doug told himself that it was exactly what it had looked like: a cop walking a beat. Not a uniform scouting out his room.

Claire would never dime him out to the G. He had offered her the chance to put him away only because he knew she couldn't do it.

It was the room that doubted her. The squalid little suicide room telling him that opening himself wide to Claire had been a mistake. Doug telling the room, *Fuck you*.

Again and again he reviewed their encounter in her garden. If only she had told him to stop. *Stop, for me*. And he would have. He would have called off this job and walked away without a regret. He had come too far to risk their future together on one final score. Claire Keesey was his one final score. All she had to do was come to him now.

He clung tight to this ideal of her, but as the hours passed, his faith began to pale.

A burst of noise and movement outside his window brought him back to the sash, crouching. But it was only the game letting out. He stood like the fool that he was and walked the room, pacing back and forth past the telephone, the afternoon growing short.

AROUND SIX, DOUG TRIED on the uniform in front of the bathroom door mirror. With his size and haircut, he made a good cop. Too good—the mirror cop looking at him like this was a big mistake Doug was making.

Doug took the uniform off and walked the room in his underwear. Had Claire forgotten the name on the register? Somehow confused hotels?

The impulse to call her was strong and wrong. Not even from a phone booth; they had her tapped for sure.

He checked the view hole in his door for the umpteenth time, imagining Frawley and a SWAT team of federal agents setting up around the hotel, evacuating it room by room.

He thought food might make him feel better, but by the time the Domino's guy arrived after eight, Doug was crackling with paranoia, studying the guy for cop traits, paying him quick and getting him out of there. He set the pizza box on top of the TV and never even raised the lid.

TEN O'CLOCK, HE WAS under a burning-hot shower trying to chase the crawlies away when he thought he heard knocking. He shut off the water and stood there listening to his dripping for a few, precious seconds, then grabbed a towel and walked damp to the door, opening it to the hallway.

A woman stood in the middle of the corridor three doors down, turning fast to the sound of the opening door. It was Krista, not Claire, with Shyne a dead weight on her hip.

Doug was too empty to say anything. He didn't move from the doorway, Krista coming before him, looking past his shoulder into the room, Shyne blinking slow-eyed against her chest. "Have any juice or milk or anything?" She held up Shyne's empty bottle. "I'm out."

He backed away, moving into the bathroom to pull on pants. When he came out, Shyne was sitting straight-legged on the floor, sucking on a big, pink-handled face plug and hugging her bubba full of green Mountain Dew, staring at whatever was on HBO. Krista stood at the foot of the bed, looking at the cop uniform hanging on the door.

"Dez told me you were staying here."

"What do you want, Kris?"

"To see you before you go."

Doug raised his bare arms and let them fall again. "Seen."

"To give you one last chance."

"Kris," he said. He saw it all unfolding: Claire arriving late at his room, bags packed, only to find Krista and Shyne there.

She sat down on the end of the bed. "Do you know my prick brother wouldn't even let me use his car?"

"You can't stay. We're grouping up here in a couple of hours."

"Like I'm his slave. Him and his bullshit, I've *had* it."

"We're not using the cars, you know that. How'd you get here?"

She shrugged. "I had no other choice."

Doug moved to the window, seeing his Caprice parked at a slant in the lot below. Now the G would have his car at Fenway the night before the job. "You stole my car."

"The registration says I borrowed *my* car."

He looked back at her. "Where is this coming from?"

"I'm ready to go away too. I've decided. I need the change, like you. Away from the Town, I think I can be a different person. Away from *him*." She glanced at the mayhem on TV, people running out of a burning building. "You know he's pissed at you leaving. Thinks you're hiding from him here. I said you're hiding from me." She looked back at Doug. "Which one of us are you hiding from?"

"I'm not hiding."

"He smoked tonight. He's dusted. Thought you'd want to know that."

Doug rocked on his feet, squeezing his fists.

"You know what's going to happen to him after you leave. Without you here, he's going to fuck up, and they're gonna come after his half of the house, and then where am I?"

"They can't take the house."

"Like hell they can't. Where's my security? Why am I still asking guys for rides, and washing Jem's frigging underwear?"

"That's between you and—"

"It's not because of him that I've waited. That I've been so fucking patient all these years. I took Jem's shit only because I always believed my time was coming. My time with you. My whole *life* I've lived in terms of you, Duggy. What—have I not been *loyal*?"

"What does loyalty got to do with—"

"It has to do with *fairness*. It has to do with me being treated the way I *deserve*. I have been here since the beginning—before Dez, and *waaay* before Joanie. I've been loyal and I've been patient. But I will not be left behind. I *deserve* not to be left behind."

"Kris—" he said, but had nothing to follow it up with, having no idea where all this was coming from. "Fuck is going on here? You want to go? Then go, same as me. There is no chain on any of us, holding us to the Town. Just the same, there's no chain holding us to each other, either."

"You're wrong there." Her smile was out of place. "You're wrong."

"You gotta give this up. Every day of your life, living in that same house, walking those same streets, looking up and always seeing the same patch of sky—this is the result. Hanging on too tight, thinking that things can stay the same forever."

"Just because we've been having some trouble, and you've been going through this thing—"

"It's not a *thing*," Doug said, needing to end this. "I am leaving. Leaving with someone else."

He felt like shit saying it because he wanted so hard to believe it himself. Not because it hurt Krista. Krista had come there to be hurt. To make him hurt her, then use his pity to make him stay. That was why she came toting Shyne.

"Kris," said Doug, glancing again at the mute phone. "We grew up together, you and me. Like brother and sister—"

"Don't fucking sugar me off."

"—and it should have stayed that way. I wish it had. We were too close. It wasn't right."

She stood and came to him. She reached out to his bare stomach, and his gut rippled, but he was backed up against the window. Her hands crept around his sides and she leaned into him, holding him. There was no way out of this clinch without getting rough. He let her hold him but did not return the embrace. He felt nothing for her. He watched Shyne flashing blue-green in the light of the TV, her body casting a small, flickering shadow. Then he looked at the door that Claire was going to knock on, knowing that Krista would ruin him if she had the chance.

She released him, her earlier smugness returned to her face. "You can't wait for me to leave, can you?"

"You picked up on that."

"Why isn't she here now? If she's going with you." Krista looked at the room. "And such a trashy little fuck pad. After a Tiffany necklace, I'd've thought a room at the Ritz or something."

"What did you say?" Doug went to her, fast. "Who told you about that?"

She was smiling now, having drawn him to her. "A little bird."

Doug grabbed her arms. "Who told you?"

She smiled more fiercely in his grip. He shook her but he couldn't shake away the smile. "You always did like it rough."

"What do you know about a necklace?"

"I know I don't see one around my neck. I know you'd rather see a rope there than jewels."

"You don't know what you're talking about," he said, pushing her away to keep from smacking her.

"You better be more careful. Pushing around a pregnant woman like that."

Doug froze. She looked down at her flat belly, regarding it as though it were some new part of her body, laying a proud hand over it the way pregnant women do.

"It's Dez's," she said.

Doug's hands came up to his forehead. He mashed his eyes with the heels.

"Ah," she said. "So broken up for a friend. Most people offer congratulations."

Doug raised his face to the ceiling, eyes still covered, elbows pointing at the corners of the room. He pressed until he saw stars. *Dez.*

"You think the Monsignor will do the right thing?"

"Make an honest woman of you?" Doug said. Then he dropped his hands, his vision clearing around her defiant face. "You Coughlins."

Her eyes were fierce, teasing. "I don't think his mother likes me."

"What do you want? What is this? If I agree to stay, you'll set Dez free?"

She stepped before him, her hands resting against his pecs, fingertips light as flies. "Take me with you. I'll get an abortion—I'll go to hell for you, Duggy." Her palm settled over his heart. "But do not leave me behind."

Doug stared at her with the disgust he normally reserved for his morning mirror. "Probably we deserve each other," he said, pulling her hands off his chest and throwing them back at her. "But I'm not doing this anymore. No more fixing things, me smoothing it over for everybody. Babysitting Jem. I told Dez to stay away, I *warned* him."

He moved past Krista, scooping up Shyne and her bubba, the girl's eyes still glued to the set as he carried her away.

"The fucking problem here," he went on, "is me. I'm the enabler. I'm the guy helping everything hold together, when it's all screaming to break apart." He marched to the door with Shyne under his arm, opened it, turned. "Everybody will be better off once I'm gone."

Krista followed him only as far as the corner of the bed. "Duggy. Do not do this."

"Or what? You'll have the kid? Just like you had this one?" Sad Shyne sagged under his arm, hanging from his side. "Who's her father, Krista? Huh? Since we're letting in a little truth here. Who was it? Was it Jem?"

She recoiled in disgust. *"Jem?"*

"Who, then?"

Her "Fuck you, Duggy" seemed heartfelt, but he couldn't trust anything she said now. And anyway the point was moot.

"You know what?" he said. "If I was going to take anyone with me, it would be her." Doug set Shyne gently down on the floor of the empty hall, then stepped back into the room.

Krista was not budging. "We're coming with you."

"You're getting out of here. Now."

"Duggy. Don't you say no to me. You *think* about this, Douglas MacRay. I want you to *think* about what you're doing—"

He grabbed her arm. She fought him—*"No!"*—pounding his chest, pushing up at his chin, digging her nails into his windpipe, while inexorably he maneuvered her toward the door. With a final kicking yell, she shook herself free, then walking the few remaining steps into the hallway, as though she had some last shred of pride to preserve.

Outside, she turned, alternately cool and smiling furiously. "You don't know what you just—"

Doug closed the door, threw the lock. He expected banging, screaming, and knew that she could outlast him, this woman without shame, and that he would be forced to readmit her before guests complained and police were called.

But there was nothing. When he looked through the spyglass later, fully expecting to see her still standing there with Shyne, she was gone.

50
THE DIME

FRAWLEY'S TELEPHONE RANG AS he was sprinkling shredded cheese over his scrambled eggs. Ocean-driven rain whipped his window overlooking the toll bridge. His microwave clock read 7:45.

A Sergeant Somebody, calling from the emergency room at Mass General. "Yeah, Agent Frawley? Hey, we got a DWI here, banged up in a one-car in the Charlestown Navy Yard? Kissed a big anchor on display in front of one of the dry docks."

Frawley's first thought was Claire Keesey. "I need a name."

"Coughlin, Kristina. Got that off the auto reg. A white Caprice Classic. Had a kid with her. Little girl's fine, but the mother is banged up and belligerent. Claims she's working with you, which seems specious, but she did have your card, this phone number written on the back. DSS came already and took away the little girl. Ms. Coughlin is under arrest, but she says we need to get you involved first."

Frawley dumped his hot eggs into the garbage. "I'm leaving now."

The walk to his car, the rain, the rush hour cost him thirty minutes. He walked the halls of Mass General in wet shoes, his creds getting him thumbed inside the ER to a wide room like a voting hall under morgue light, rimmed with curtained bays.

"Hi," he said, stopping at the nurses' station, "I'm looking for . . ."

Then he heard her voice cutting across the room—"How 'bout you put on that assless smock first, Denzel, then I will"—and started in that direction. A good-looking, flustered black doctor shrugged aside a pale yellow curtain.

"Coughlin?" said Frawley, heading past him.

But the harried doctor slowed him up. "Listen. She needs to be seen by our plastic surgeon. If you have any influence over her, please stress that. Laceration's too deep for simple stitching, she'll be scarred for life."

"Yeah—okay." Frawley tried to get past, but the doctor had a hand on his arm now.

"She claims she was pregnant," he said. "But the blood test was negative, and no signs of miscarriage."

Frawley took his arm back. "Hey, I'm not family or anything, I don't need to know." He walked to her bay, pushed the curtain aside.

Krista was sitting in the padded visitor's chair, a gauze wrap around her forehead with a bright red bloom over her left eye, blood spatter on her sweatshirt and her jeans. "Here's handsome," she said.

Frawley nodded to Sergeant Somebody, the older cop rolling his eyes at her and moving to the break in the curtain. "Five minutes," Frawley told him.

Krista called after him, "I take mine milk, three sugars!" She smiled over tightly folded arms as Frawley closed the curtain. His card rested on the bed, on top of the folded johnny she had refused to wear. She flicked her fingernails and bobbed her crossed foot—a black shoe with a broken heel—restlessly. "I was on my way to see you."

"That's interesting," said Frawley. "Considering you don't have my address."

"You're in the yard." She shrugged. "I would of found you."

One look at her eyes told Frawley she was good and dusted. Recognizing this slowed him down a bit. "What happened?"

"I don't know. Guess someone left an anchor in the middle of the road." She shrugged the grin of someone for whom life was such a daily absurdity in and of itself that a car accident made for a welcome start to the week. In that grin Frawley discerned the bullying contempt of her brother.

He saw the empty car seat in the corner—blue plaid fabric crumb-dusted and milk-stained—its vacancy like a mouth opened to scream.

Krista saw him looking, sucked in her smile, swallowed it down. "She wasn't hurt," she said proudly. "Not a scratch."

"Then you could be looking at Mother of the Year here," he said, unable to help himself.

"What do you know, what I go through? Look at you." She broke the knot of her arms. "People make mistakes sometimes—and who are you, Mr. Tsk-Tsk college boy? The mistake catcher? A fucking hall monitor with a badge, what do you know about someone like me? I am a *real* person. I am a *single mother*."

"Your daughter is in the backseat of a state van, being driven by a stranger to the Department of Social Services. How long do you want to talk here?"

Krista stared, eyes dampening. Frawley was being hard, but it was working.

"What were you coming to see me about? You needed a baby-sitter? I tried to call you twice, you hung up both times."

She glowered at the waxy curtain, keeping her dusted emotions in check. "DSS only holds her for a while. There's an evaluation. Nothing happens until the evaluation."

"So maybe you want a lawyer here, then. Not the FBI."

She looked at him again, nearly amazed. "Why is it I'm always the one who gets used? Every man I know."

"Who's using you here? Who called who? Who's asking for help—me? I'm pretty sure I'm here because you want your daughter back. Because you can use me to get her."

"Real people make *real* mistakes—"

He talked over her. "This is not about you anymore, this is about your daughter. *Look* at this empty car seat."

She did, her eyes blinking wet.

Frawley went on, "You're going to need some sort of plea agreement on these charges now, in order to retain custody."

She looked up fast. "And my house. I want your guarantee."

"Whoa, hold up. I never said I could guarantee. I said I could *try*."

"You said—"

"I said I could *try*. And that is what I will do, Krista, that is my promise, provided you're straight with me here. And if that isn't good enough, maybe you want to wait for a better offer. How many more Get Out of Jail Free cards you got on you? Could your brother get you out of this jam? MacRay? Who? Fergie?"

Her eyes sparked to that.

"What, Fergie's your benefactor, is he? Why should a degenerate dust dealer help you out with your daughter?"

Nothing in her low-eyed look was telling—except the duration.

Frawley's stomach curdled. "Oh, Jesus."

She kept looking at him: defiantly, then starting to fall apart.

"You and the Florist . . ." Frawley had to stop himself from saying more. He was picturing the gangster's mashed face in a spasm of feral ecstasy, looming over her.

Krista's chin trembled. A hard woman crumbling was an awful thing to see. "Why you have to lean on me so hard? Why make me *beg* for everything I get? Treating me like I'm nothing, I don't matter. All you men."

Frawley summoned the memory of MacRay coming after him in the parking garage in order to sustain his anger, counterbalancing his sympathy for Coughlin's sister here. "You called me. That means you have something to trade."

She looked down, taking deep, shuddering breaths. "Duggy's going away with her after."

"Her?" Frawley stepped up. "What do you mean, with *her*?"

Krista looked up. She read the desire in his eyes, the anger, and said, "You too?"

He lost it. "What do you mean, *with her*?"

Krista was aghast. "What is she anyway? What does she have—Jesus Christ—to make all of you so fucking crazy over her?"

Frawley remembered himself, stepped back. "You said *after*. Going away with her *after*. *After* what?"

Krista turned to look at the clock—and Frawley's blood came crashing.

"Today?" he said, pouncing on her look. "Not Tuesday—today? Where? When?"

Her jaw quivered like mortar cracking off a facade. "My daughter. . . ."

"You need to be smart now, Krista. A life full of bad decisions, this is the one that could do you good, help turn things around. But their clock is your clock too."

"My daughter," Krista said, finally breaking. "She's retarded."

Frawley's breath was gone. He stood very still.

Krista spilled tears, her face collapsing in despair and defeat. "She's going to need things . . . special things . . . special schools . . ."

"Right," he gasped out. "Uh-huh."

She looked up, her face tired and tear-streaked. "For her I'm doing this. Not me."

"No," said Frawley, stealing another glance at the clock. 8:25. "Of course not."

"It's not for me . . . not for me . . ."

51
THE MOURNING OF

T HE FOUR OF THEM standing around the hotel room, all in cop uniforms, guns and folded black duffel bags on the bed.

Rain fell hard outside the shaded window. A punishing rain was almost as good for a job as snow. It darkened the day, obscured loud noises, kept bystanders off the streets, and gummed up the city in general. Gloansy had picked up four bright safety-orange raincoats at the army/navy store the day before. The coats covered up the armored vests that bulked out their cop uniforms.

"Rain's good," Jem was muttering, walking back and forth from the drawn window curtains. "Rain's good. Rain's good. Rain's good."

Doug looked at the phone. He was barely there, the crashing of the rain outside like the shit coming down all around his head. He answered when spoken to and moved when it was required of him, but everything felt distant and rehearsed, occurring outside himself while he watched. The four of them going through their pregame rituals. He was having trouble placing himself in time, figuring out what led to what and how he had arrived at this hotel room at the end of the world, dressed like a Boston cop.

Dez cursed the bathroom mirror, having trouble with the hard contact lenses he wore on jobs. His face looked undressed without glasses, his nearsighted eyes small and lost in his face. *What's up?* Dez had said at the door, the last to arrive. *Nothing,* said Doug, until then hoping that Dez might stay away.

Gloansy gobbled down two pancaked slices of cold Domino's, while Jem's pacing and muttering and knuckle-cracking bordered on the lunatic. Where was the prejob ragging and the goofing that used to drive Doug nuts? Gone was all that crazy joy.

Would the G even let them leave the hotel? Or wait until they were going into the ballpark and nail them there, all packed up and loaded, a headline bust? Or would agents be waiting inside, wearing can guards' uniforms—a reverse Morning Glory?

Worse than the doomed feeling of the trap was knowing that he was the only one aware of it. Asshole that he was. Falling for this creature of his imagination, this all-forgiving, all-healing girl—this magic, winning ticket. Trusting her. Needing her. What was it about him that wanted a wounded girl to vanish into? If the phone rang now, it would only be the G calling from the lobby, telling them the place was surrounded and ordering them out, hands behind their heads, one at a time.

It was not too late. He could tell the others what he'd done. They could all change back into street clothes and ditch the uniforms and guns and walk away clean—three of them heading back into Town, and Doug in a different direction. He had some money, he'd be all right. For a while.

But part of him still held out hope. Arguing that if there was going to be a takedown, it would have happened already, there at the hotel. The G didn't want them out on the streets, armed and unpredictable. Maybe Claire hadn't told them anything. Every second that ticked toward Go time, Doug's hope grew.

He went around wiping down the dresser and table with rubbing alcohol, removing his prints from the room. Krazy Glue on his hands, krazy thoughts in his mind. Glugging bleach in the bathroom sink and shower, blitzing the drains, obliterating his DNA. Erasing every trace of his existence. The bundle of cash he had buried shallow in the garden of a girl who hated him, and the clothes piled up in Mac's old army bag by the door: they were all he had in the world now. And these three guys.

Gloansy and Dez went around rapping fists, pulling on orange coats and slipping out one at a time, down the hallway stairs to the rear door. Doug watched from the window, the slapping rain providing decent cover for two bright orange cops ducking out of a hotel and into a stolen car. They were leaving early to snarl the morning city commute before returning to the ballpark. Doug watched them roll around the corner out of sight and envisioned them being pulled over just outside the parking lot, boxed in at gunpoint by a roadblock shutting down Boylston Street. He closed the curtains as though tear-gas canisters were about to come crashing through the window, smoke filling the room.

Jem stood there with his 9mm drawn on Doug. Doug froze,

losing it a moment in Jem's sight, Jem holding the pose, grinning—then returning the gun to his holster and snapping the leather catch. "You want the Tec-9?"

"Don't care," Doug said, dizzy. "Just put a gun in my hand."

Jem tossed him a loaded Beretta, Doug basket-catching it. Jem admired the Tec in his hand, an oversized pistol with a clip feed in front of the trigger. *"Yeah,"* he said, then put it down on the bed and fit his thumbs into the front of his gun belt, strutting around the room. "All those years watching *Cops* finally paying off." He smiled, enjoying himself, grinding his jaw the way dust makes you do. "I'd've made a good cop. A *rich* cop." He stopped and tried his delivery—"License and registration, ma'am"—impressing himself, continuing his cop strut around the room. "Fucking ticket to *ride,* man. How you ever gonna walk away from this?"

Doug couldn't see any way to go forward or backward. To walk or to stay. He looked at the gun in his hand. *I'm not that guy anymore.* But here he was.

"By the way," said Jem. "I put you in after all."

Doug shook his head. "Put me in what?"

"The third floor. Shyne's dollhouse. I took the chance. Maybe you'll change your mind. You walked away once before and found your way back again."

FRAWLEY WAS STALLED IN traffic downtown, grappling with his car phone, wipers slashing rain. He couldn't get any numbers for Fenway Park from information. Nobody from the Task Force was in the Lakeville office yet, so the field office was calling New York for Provident Armored's headquarters number. He did manage to catch Dino at home and stop him from heading out to Lakeville. Now Dino was calling him back.

"My captain took it straight to the commissioner. You're *sure* now."

Frawley leaned on his horn. "I got it from the sister."

"Coughlin's sister?"

"They're going in strong. Some bullshit about a 'last job,' MacRay leaving after. That's all I know."

"Any clue how security works at Fenway?"

"None, but Dean—you gotta keep patrol cops away."

"There'll be nothing on the radio."

"And no helicopters to scare them off."

"Easy now, Frawl. We got Entry and Apprehension Team suiting

up as we speak. That's our SWAT. They're on a scrambled freq. Do
we know where these tea-pissers are jumping from?"

"We know nothing but the time." Frawley looked at his radio
clock. "And it's fucking eight forty-five now! What's with this traffic?"

"That's another thing. It's the rain, but also my cap says they got
two separate major jams, one westbound on Storrow, one in
Kenmore Square."

"Kenmore Square?" said Frawley, punching the thin ceiling of the
Tempo. "That's our guys!"

"A semi stalled across the intersection. The one on Storrow is an
oversized rental van jammed under one of those height-restricted
bridges. Both vehicles were abandoned, left locked up and running."

"Fucking—it's them, Dean!"

Frawley hung up and threw his phone, unable to bear the thought
of missing these guys. Of not being there to hook up MacRay.

Screw the field office. Frawley bumped over a curb, gouging the
Tempo's undercarriage on the street corner, swinging up one of the
side streets climbing Beacon Hill, heading directly to Fenway.

DOUG SAT NEXT TO Jem in the backseat of the big Thunderbird,
parked at the corner of Yawkey and Van Ness. Gloansy sat behind the
popped ignition in front, Dez next to him. The windows were all
cracked open in the drumming rain to keep their view from fogging.
Doug saw the G everywhere, on the spilling rooftops, in surrounding
windows, in every car that passed.

The can was three minutes overdue; the news radio station was in
hysterics over the traffic tie-ups. Jem thumped his black shoes into
the floor, marching in place as he sat, the sound like a pounding
heart.

"I don't know," said Doug, going secretly crazy. "I don't know
about this."

"Can's stuck in traffic with the rest of them," said Gloansy.

"I don't know."

Dez turned his head. "What do you mean?"

Doug was trying to give them at least a chance. "Doesn't feel
right."

Jem said, "Everything's cool. We're gonna do this."

"I think something's up."

"Check this out." Jem unbuckled the clips on the front of his raincoat. In addition to the Glock in his holster and the semiauto Tec-9

strapped off his shoulder, he wore four fat pinecone grenades, World War style, affixed to his cop belt with black electrical tape. "From my gramps," Jem said. "Guy was a fuckin' war hero." He flicked at the little metal pins, still in place.

Dez said, "Those live?"

Gloansy said, "For Christ. You're gonna blow us up in here."

"Insurance, ant-dicks. You think they'd let anything happen to historic Fenway? These are our tickets out. One for each."

Dez glanced over the seatback at Doug, Doug fed up with his altar-boy disapproval.

Jem clipped up his coat again, white-blue eyes brimming with dusted confidence. "We're gonna do this. We're gonna do this."

Lightning brightened the street, Doug thinking it was a flash-bang charge, the G swooping down on them. He waited for thunder. There was none.

He couldn't sit still another moment. He opened his door and stood out of the T-bird, shutting the door before any of them could say anything, starting away through the rain.

He turned onto Boylston, the chime ringing as he pushed inside the package store. Bewildering, the lights, the colorful promotions—it had been a long time. He cut down a long aisle of wines to the back cooler. Two sixes of High Life longnecks waited for him on the rack. He grabbed both and brought them to the counter.

There was a cop waiting there: Dez, dripping on the floor. "What are you doing?"

Doug had no money in his uniform pockets. "Give me some money."

Dez said, "Put it down. Come on. Let's go—"

"Shut the fuck up." Doug turned to the cashier. "Put these on the police account." Without waiting for an acknowledgment, he walked out past Dez.

Dez caught up with him on the rainy sidewalk. "Duggy! What's happening to you? You don't need this—"

Doug shoved Dez back with an elbow. "I fucking told you not to come."

Doug returned to the car first, his wet coat crinkling as he sat. "The fuck was that?" said Jem, before seeing the twin caddies of tall boys.

Doug said, "Thought you wanted to be there for my first one back."

Jem's smile grew wide and fierce, all-encompassing. "Duggy Mac is *back*."

Doug passed one of the sixes over the seat to Gloansy as Dez returned, settling in, not removing his orange hood. Doug reached for his Leatherman, finding it missing. A twinge of panic as he pictured it sitting forgotten on his bureau—a tool he had carried with him on every job.

No matter. The trick, when you don't have an opener, is to use one beer for leverage, inverting it and hooking the cap of the beer to be popped, then twisting and pulling back the top one like snapping a stick in two. Doug cracked one for Jem and one for himself.

Genie mist escaped out of its small mouth. Doug's chest was pounding.

Jem waited for Gloansy to crack two, then said reverently, "To the Town."

Jem rapped fists with Doug, neither one spilling a drop. Doug said, "Here's how."

He brought the bottle to his lips, the beer splashing hard to the back of his throat, tasteless at first, swallowed like seawater. Then came the tang, the bite. His throat worked the brew along until the bottle was empty and weightless, the taste settling into his tongue like surf foam sinking into sand.

The first belch was an echo from a dark abyss. He popped open another and caught sight of Dez, slow to drink his first, disappointment and disapproval evident in the sag of his shoulders. Doug drank harder.

The other part of Doug was coming out now. The old Doug MacRay, the one resigned to his fate. The Jem in him who was damned and knew it. *Never prison again*. His only goal now.

No tomorrow: that was what Billy T. had been all about. No consequences, nobody to disappoint, not Dez, not Frank G., not even Doug himself. Nothing could touch him now.

Jem cracked open his third, ahead of Doug, meaning Doug was without another bottle to open his. He was working on the cap with his Krazy Glue fingers when Jem let out a war whoop.

The red light was on over the ambulance door on Van Ness.

The silver Provident truck turned off Ipswich, starting down the road, slowing at the rising door. It swung around, stopped, and began to back inside.

The black Suburban pulled up at the curb outside Fenway as the bay door closed.

Jem dropped his empty on the floor, kicking open his door to the street and the rain.

Doug stood out on the sidewalk, the downpour cracking loud against his hood. Dez got out in front of Doug, standing there, not looking at him, waiting for Gloansy. Those two started up Van Ness toward the Suburban as Doug crossed the street through blowing wet sheets, side by side with Jem, walking toward the Gate D entrance and looking for the G in every raindrop, thinking, *ambush, ambush, ambush*.

52
THE LAST JOB

JEM PULLED HARD A few times on the chained gate.

The red shirt sitting dry and comfortable on the folding chair inside looked up from his newspaper, then dropped it at the sight of the cops, hustling to the entrance.

Jem said, "Was it you who called?"

He was a young guy, cinnamon-skinned, puffy, maybe Samoan but not huge. "Huh?"

"Nine one one call, we got. Open up."

"I didn't . . . it wasn't . . ."

"Robbery call. Who else is here?"

"Robbery?" He looked around, panicked.

"There's no one else here?"

"Sure there is, but—"

"Call says you're being held up. Right now."

"Then I need to phone security."

"Phone whoever you want, but we gotta get in there first, do our jobs. Then make your call."

He nodded and unlocked the chain, admitting Doug and Jem.

Doug stiffened up to hide his jumpiness. "Go ahead, lock it back up if you have to."

As the red shirt did, Doug and Jem both unclasped the bottoms of their coats, baring their holsters. With the rain and the lack of lights, it was darker than a night game in there.

"Where's everyone else?" said Jem, starting down the ramp.

"Some around the corner there. Let me—"

"And what is your name, sir?"

"My name's Eric."

"Eric, point me in the right direction here. Let's make sure everyone's safe, then we can all sit down and make our phone calls."

Eric nodded obediently and showed them the way, moving down the slope toward the corner. Doug glimpsed the open Employees Only door, and then, wider, the tunnel.

The motorized flatbed pushcart was on its way toward the first aid station at the tunnel's end, loaded with thick bundles of plastic-wrapped cash. One gray-and-black Provident guard operated the cart's handle controls, the other backing him up with one hand on his holster. Doug double-checked their ears, seeing no wires.

Jem started after them, his voice booming inside the tunnel. "Who called 911?"

The guards stopped, turning fast, spooked.

"Who called it?" said Jem, hand at his waist, coattails flapping. Doug pushed Eric down to the floor, telling him to stay still, lie flat.

The guards looked at each other, hands on their holsters.

The anxiety in Doug's voice worked as he said, following Jem, "We got a distress call. Who made the call?"

The guards stayed between Jem and Doug and the money cart. "No call from us."

"Who called it?" said Jem, pressing closer.

"Hold on," said one guard, raising his off-hand.

"ID!" said Jem, not stopping. "Let's see some ID! Both of you!"

"Hold on, hold it, now," said the guard, half into a protective crouch.

"Whoa, *whoa!*" said Jem.

"Don't do that!" shouted Doug.

"We didn't hit it!" said one guard.

"We're on the job here!" said the other.

Two Fenway Park security blue shirts appeared at the mouth of the tunnel behind them. "What the . . . ?"

"Get down back there!" commanded Doug.

They put their arms out like this was all a big misunderstanding. "It's okay!" they yelled. "They're okay!"

Doug drew his Beretta, keeping it low at his hip, muzzle down. "Everybody on the ground, now!"

"For our safety!" said Jem, also drawing. "I want IDs from everybody!"

Twenty yards away, Doug just kept asserting himself. "Get down!"

"Wait, hey!" said the guards.

"On the floor!" yelled Jem.

The blue shirts lay facedown.

The panicky guard pulled his sidearm clear of his holster. Doug swung up his Beretta, aiming, bracing it on his opposite forearm. *"Gun!"* he yelled. *"Gun!"*

"Drop your weapon!" bellowed Jem, aiming his Glock. "Put it down *now!"*

"No, no!" said the other guard, covering his head, backing away.

Jem and Doug came at them gun-first, with legit tension: "Drop your weapon! We got a call! Put it down!"

Guard yelling, *"We did not call!"*

Doug stopped ten yards away. The four of them barking back and forth over drawn guns until the retreating guard dropped to his knee, took his hand off his holster, and laid on his belly, arms out.

"Stop resisting!" they yelled at the other one. *"Get down! Get down!"*

Cursing, the panicky second guard yielded, lying down arms-out, still holding on to his gun.

Doug and Jem came up fast, Jem stepping on the armed guard's wrist, covering both guards, Doug going to the blue shirts beyond the cash cart, gathering hands and binding them with plastic ties. The can idled just around the corner from the mouth of the tunnel, backed in—the driver unable to see or hear anything.

Doug ripped off the blue shirts' security radios and tossed them away. "Lie still," he told them, rejoining Jem, pocketing the other guard's gun and yanking his stiff hands behind his back. "Jesus *Christ,*" spat Doug's guard, red-faced, gruff. "The fuck're you two doing? We're on the goddamn job here!"

"We got a call," said Doug, binding the guard's wrists. Doug then pulled up the black bandanna knotted around his neck, covering his mouth and nose and leaving only his eyes visible. Jem did the same as Doug turned and started back for Eric.

The puffy guy was already sitting up. Incomprehension, at first—masked cop with gun raised, coming at him—then Eric got to his feet and, with one hand on the tunnel wall, began to run for his life.

Doug yelled at him to stop as the round whizzed past. The crack of the gunshot echoed in the tunnel, and Eric turned, still galloping, his cinnamon hands reaching for the hip of his jeans as though trying to catch the bullet that had just entered his side. He ran like that a few more feet before collapsing—the shock of having been shot bringing him down, not the round itself.

Doug turned, seeing Jem with his 9mm still aimed, his knee and his opposite hand on the backs of the two squirming guards.

Doug rushed to Eric, who was gripping his wide hip in horror. But all four limbs were moving, and he had plenty of padding to absorb the round. Doug hoped the rain would do the same to the gunshot report.

He wrestled one of Eric's wrists away from the tiny wound, then the other, binding them behind his back. "There'll be help here soon," said Doug, leaning on his shoulder for emphasis. "Stay down and shut up."

He ran back to where Jem was, wasting a glare at him, then yanking his guard to his feet. The guard twisted and fought, Doug finally bouncing the guy off the wall, stunning him before muscling him around the corner.

Doug got the full view of the silver can there, the Provident medallion bold beneath the rear windows. He dumped the guard down against the brick wall and walked up to the passenger side of the cab to get the driver's attention.

He hadn't expected a woman. She was frizzy-haired and long-faced, throwing Doug off his game for a second.

She went white, jerking back and fumbling with the keys in the ignition, starting up the truck, diesel smoke coughing into the cave. Doug heard the locks automatically reset and watched the yellow rooftop beacon start spinning, the can going into lockdown. With the bay door closed in front of it and the iron girders behind it, there was nowhere for the truck to go.

Jem dragged the blue shirts over to the dazed guards, dumping them along the side wall. The driver peeked out the passenger window, now talking fast into the handset of a ceiling-mounted radio. "Assholes fucked up," snarled one guard. "Sandy's locked in there. She's calling the law."

Doug moved to the switch controlling the lamp outside, turning it off. He checked Jem standing over the four captives, bandanna puffing with breath, then started back past the trapped armored truck to the next bay door, pressing the call button on the cop-style two-way Motorola clipped to his shoulder. "Ready?"

"Ready," came back Dez's voice, breathless. "All clear out here."

Doug hit the switch and the second door crawled up the wall to the ceiling, rising on the crashing rain and Dez in his orange cop coat and black bandanna, holding his Beretta on the driver of the tail car: a swarthy bodybuilder type in a collared shirt and jeans, hands bound behind him, pissed off. Dez walked him inside, and then the big black Suburban followed them into the bay, backing in trunk end first. The wet tires slid to a stop on the downward incline, Gloansy jumping out wearing his bandanna, and Doug hit the switch that closed the bay door.

Gloansy took control of the tail-car driver, walking him back to the others at the Provident truck as Dez touched the radio wire looped over his ear. He blinked and squinted as he monitored all police channels plus the security net inside the park itself, muttering something about his contact lenses. "There it is," he said. "Call just went out from dispatch."

The driver had done her job, calling in a Mayday.

They jogged back to the idling can at the first aid station, where the mouthy guard was still going at it: "I put in twenty-two years as a guard at Walpole, I have friends that'll see to it you all live out the rest of your lives in rip-ass hell."

Jem pointed his gun at him and the guy shut up.

Gloansy and Dez stayed on the five hostages—the two uniformed can guards, the two Fenway security blue shirts, and the Suburban driver—while Jem and Doug worked the pushcart, Doug thumbing buttons on the electric handle to roll it past the back of the can and down to the open rear door of the Suburban. The cash was sealed in clear, tight, shrink-wrapped bundles, roughly the size of four loaves of bread packaged side by side. Jem scattered the paperwork off the top and dumped off two heavy racks of coins, the rolls bursting nickels and dimes on the floor. They pulled folded hockey duffel bags from their coat pockets, Doug spreading them open in the back of the Suburban.

Jem played baggage handler, tossing the parcels of currency at Doug as fast as Doug could pack them, six bundles to a bag. He was five or six bags in when Dez called back, "How much longer?'

Jem kept throwing. "What's up?"

"Scrambled traffic on one of the special cop freqs."

Jem stopped. Doug turned, seeing Dez in the flashing yellow light of the can beacon, his hand at his ear.

"Too soon off the initial call," Dez said. "Can't be because of us. Maybe something else going down somewhere."

Doug's heart was in his throat. He said, "I'll check it out."

"No," said Jem, already starting away. Doug watched him break open his coat on the Tec-9, stepping inside the tunnel.

Doug returned to the loaves of money, packing up the last bag, loading it as fast as he could.

* * *

FRAWLEY PULLED UP OUTSIDE the "1912 Fenway Park" facade at the original entrance to the park, Gate A, at the other end of Yawkey Way. All he had for rain gear was the blue Nautica jacket he had grabbed rushing out to the hospital that morning. He opened his trunk and threw his nylon FBI vest over his shoulders, good for identification only—bank agents don't carry body armor—and found an old orange Syracuse ballcap for his head. He grabbed what he had in there, sliding two extra 9mm mags for his shoulder-holstered SIG-Sauer into his pants pockets, emptying a box of shotgun cartridges into his zippered coat pockets, and pulling his Remington 870 twelve-gauge from its padded sleeve.

Dino's Taurus pulled up fast on the opposite sidewalk, Dino unfolding himself out of it, buttoning his trench coat to the downpour. "I looped the block," he said, concerned. "Nothing hinky. Looks tight. No vans around, nothing parked with handicapped tags."

Frawley gripped the brim of his cap, curling it one-handedly, cursing. A bad call here would ruin him, plain and simple. Good-bye, Los Angeles. Hello, Glasgow, Montana. "Maybe we're too early, maybe too late."

They turned to the blue Boston Police Department camper that had just arrived, the Entry and Apprehension Team mobile-command center parked outside a closed souvenir shop. Two pairs of black commando-types in balaclavas, Fritz helmets, and trunk armor, with the initials EAT on their backs, walked along Yawkey Way as though it were Sniper Alley in downtown Sarajevo, one team headed toward the nearby ticket office, the other away toward Gate D.

A silver Accord came by, slowing, a blond mom watching the show, her little boy in back waving. Dino said, "We gotta close off these streets."

Frawley was soaked with rain and doubt when he saw the EAT pair start sprinting from the ticket office down Yawkey toward Van Ness. Dino leaned into the open camper. "What?"

Two tactical cops were coordinating. "Voice inside, male. Says he's been shot."

Frawley saw the tac cops going in through the far gate and started running, thinking maybe he wasn't too late after all.

DOUG LEFT THE SUBURBAN'S rear door open with the cash-stuffed duffel bags, moving past the others toward the tunnel. Jem was more than halfway through it, walking slow. Doug could see Eric lying at the end, his thick legs kicking, groaning over and over again, "I'm shot, I'm shot." Doug was about to call Jem back when Jem dropped into a half-crouch.

Doug saw it too—a glint of light beyond squirming Eric. It was a small mirror on a long pole, extending across the mouth of the tunnel.

Jem opened up on it, cracking the mirror, the pole clattering to the stone floor. The echo of his fire was tremendous inside the tunnel, Doug going half-deaf, wincing, backing off and drawing his Beretta. Jem sprayed another volley at the mouth, then turned, firing mad bursts behind him as he ran back toward Doug.

The tunnel filled with fireballs. Fiercely bright but nonlethal Starflash rounds ricocheted off the walls, a disorienting salvo. Jem outran these sparkling bees toward Doug as Doug opened up, blasting cover fire at nothing but flashlight beams. He choked the trigger too tight, the Beretta coughing and jumping in his hand, the sound like firecrackers in a drum. Then Jem ducked past him and together they folded around the corner.

Jem broke off his empty magazine and reloaded, howling curses.

"What the fuck!" said Gloansy, panicked, edging away from the guards.

"We got dimed!" said Jem, leaning out, spraying the tunnel with fire, then leaning back again, the Tec smoking. "Fucking *dimed*! "Mother*fucks*!"

Three gunshots cracked from a different direction, Gloansy shrieking and twisting, hit, falling forward to the stone floor.

Doug ducked, looking around wildly, then grabbed Gloansy's ankle and dragged him to the side of the can by the rear right tire. All five hostages were squirming and yelling and covering their heads. It hadn't come from them. Gloansy had been hit from behind, and Doug peered out behind the can, back toward the Suburban. No one he could see.

Gloansy sat up swearing, reaching for his lower back. His vest had saved him, but it still hurt like hell.

Then more cracks over their heads. Jem opened up against the hull of the can, wasting rounds, the ricochets pelting the floor near Doug. Doug howled at Jem, but at least now he knew where the shots were coming from.

The can driver. From the safety of the armored interior, she was potting them through the gun ports. Doug and Gloansy were safe where they were—crouched against its hull—yet pinned down.

Doug looked under the can and saw Dez's legs on the other side. Doug yelled but couldn't get his attention, so he ripped off his radio and threw it beneath the truck, hitting Dez's shoe.

"The door!" Doug yelled to him. "Open the door!"

Dez crawled to the front of the can and jumped up to punch the red plunger button, the bay door starting to rise.

"What the fuck!" yelled Jem from where he was trapped at the near mouth of the tunnel.

But Doug was right: the driver was panicking, and as soon as she saw the door go up, she jumped into the front seat and powered forward, scraping the side of the can against the brick doorframe, lurching over the curb and out onto Van Ness.

Doug stood in the now empty bay and hit the button, shutting the door. He pulled the guard's gun from his pocket and went next to Jem, sticking his arm around the corner of the tunnel and firing, the .32 going crack-crack-crack.

"We bail!" Doug yelled over the reports. "Now!"

"No fucking way!" said Jem. "The ride is loaded and ready to go!"

"Leave it!" Doug said, over the racket of return fire. "Bail out!"

Gloansy was on his feet again, hunched over but moving. He drew on the tunnel and fired into it blindly, then tugged down his bandanna, exposing his face. "I'm driving!"

"No!" said Doug.

But Gloansy was already hobbling to the Suburban, his tunnel fire keeping Doug from giving chase. Gloansy was hurt, he was flipping out, he wanted the presumed safety of a mobile cage of glass and metal. "Meet you at the switch!" he yelled.

Dez was closer to the Suburban, wavering, torn between staying behind or taking off with Gloansy. *"Fuck!"* he said, watching Gloansy slam the trunk door shut. Then Dez hustled back to Doug.

With a rebel yell, Jem curled out into the mouth of the tunnel and filled the passageway with fire and noise.

CLOSER, OVER THE RAIN and the sound of his own slapping footsteps, Frawley heard gunfire. He saw flashes inside Gate D and heard echoed yelling.

Then someone out on the street near him cried, "Here they come!"

He ran with Dino and the others to the corner of Van Ness. A silver armored truck came scraping out of the block-long brick wall, yellow beacon twirling, surging down the street toward them through the rain. Two sergeants who should have known better rushed to the sidewalk and wasted bullets against the can's grille and windshield.

Frawley worried about the gun ports. He tried to make out the driver but the wipers weren't going, and all he could see through the rain was a blur of frizzy hair—maybe a bad disguise. Whoever it was, the driver was running scared.

Dino yelled at the rest of them to get away as the truck wheeled past doing thirty. It turned hard right and went into a heavy skid on the wet road, the driver righting the wheels and briefly regaining control, then overcorrecting, the truck veering toward the sidewalk across from the ballpark, ramming the parked police camper head-on.

The blow was tremendous, the loudest, ugliest thing Frawley had ever heard, the camper buckling and grinding on its rims, all four tires exploding, tearing up the asphalt and taking out a hydrant before stopping some forty feet away. Cops tumbled out of the open end of the wrecked camper, falling hurt to the wet pavement and trying to crawl away from the fountain the hydrant made in the rain.

Dino and the rest of the lawmen ran to the truck, the crash bringing two tac cops charging back out of Gate D to investigate. The silver truck was unhurt, the driver grinding gears, still trying to flee. Dino warned the men back from the gun ports.

Approaching sirens drew Frawley the other way, back out onto Van Ness—just as a second vehicle, a big black Suburban, jumped from the park.

It started away in the opposite direction, but the screaming patrol cars forced it to reconsider, cutting its wheels into a controlled skid that ended with the truck facing Frawley's end of the street, then starting toward him.

Frawley couldn't see the driver at that distance. All he knew was that he had someone fleeing a shooting. He stepped left onto the curb, working the pump action and aiming low for the tires—*Blam!*—missing the first shot, kicking sparks off the asphalt, pumping again and leading the truck this time—*Blam!*—striking the right front tire, pumping again—*Blam!*—bursting the rear. The tires shredded and peeled back off the rims, and there was a spray of wet sparks in the road as the driver fought the steering wheel, losing control on the turn going the other way, jumping the curb and plowing into a Thunderbird parked at the corner.

Frawley ran wide around the rear of the Suburban, assuming all four of them were inside the tinted windows. A two-man tac team advanced with MP5 submachine guns off their shoulders, and Frawley backed away, letting them do their work.

THEY HEARD THE CRUISERS wheel past after Gloansy in the Suburban. Shotgun blasts in the rain. The sickening glass punch of the crash.

"They got him," said Dez, hands on top of his head. "Oh, fucking shit, they got Gloansy."

Jem wheeled and screamed, sending more angry spray down the tunnel. *Who the fuck dimed us?* he bellowed. *I'll fucking kill them!*

Doug swallowed hard, going after the two uniformed guards and pulling them to their feet, powering them back near the tunnel.

Jem was reloading again, gripping his weapon in anguish. "Gloansy, you fucking shithead . . ."

Dez's bandanna eyes showed dull shock, his gun hanging in his hand. Doug woke him up by thrusting the guards at him and making him hold them at gunpoint.

Doug ran down the length of the cave, hitting plungers and opening the other four doors, then running back.

One empty duffel bag remained on the floor by the pushcart, and Jem was kneeling over it, stuffing it with cash, the Tec dangling from his shoulder rig.

"What are you doing?" said Doug. Jem kept on loading. "The fuck are you doing? Leave it! Come on!"

When Doug went to grab him, Jem raised up the Tec.

It was the guilty way in which Doug backed off. Jem sensed it, standing, tasting it the way a shark tastes blood, realizing, bright-eyed.

"This is you," he said. "You fucking did this. Did you fucking do this?"

Dez shouted from behind, "Fucking *come on, assholes!*"

Jem stared in white-eyed astonishment. He kept the gun on Doug as he knelt and zipped the bag shut, then pulled the bandanna down off his bewildered face. "Why, kid?"

Dez didn't know where to point his gun, at the guards or at Jem. "Tell him you didn't, Duggy!"

More sirens now, Jem's face going grim. He hefted the bag at his side, eyes and gun never leaving Doug as he backed up the incline to the open bay door, pausing there before the rain.

Doug awaited Jem's bullet.

The Tec came down and Jem tucked it into his raincoat, dead-faced, then ducked his head and started out with his black bag into the rain.

THE DRIVER OF THE Suburban, whoever he was, was at the very least unconscious. The spotter could see his shoulders rising and falling through the windshield, but his head remained down on the blood-ied steering wheel. It was a potential medical emergency, but the spotter could not get a clear view of the backseat or of the cargo trunk. The status of the other three—their very presence—remained unknown.

A cordon of cops surrounded the crash site—the smaller of the two wrecks on Yawkey—one of them with a bullhorn, trying to coax out the occupants.

Frawley was down on his haunches behind a patrol car angled across the intersection, holding his shotgun across his knees. The boots next to him belonged to an ear-wired tac cop standing with his submachine gun braced atop the rain-popping roof of the car, trained on the Suburban. Frawley was coasting on adrenaline, not even feel-ing the rain. Fucking Special Agent Steve McQueen. *I just shot out a car's tires in the street.* He looked around for Dino. He had to tell this to someone.

More sirens coming, flashing blues arriving from everywhere. Frawley liked the cavalry's sound. But then he remembered the two cruisers that had scared off the Suburban. Those early patrol cars—who had called them?

There'll be nothing on the radio, Dino had said. *They're on a scram-bled freq.*

Frawley got up and started looking for Dino for real, finding him under a borrowed umbrella at the corner fence, talking to a police captain. Frawley stepped in between them, interrupting, jacked up on hormones though barely aware of it. "Where'd the patrol cars come from?"

The captain looked at the letters *FBI* on Frawley's chest. "Well," he said under the umbrella patter, "when a daddy patrol car and a mommy patrol car love each other very, very much . . ."

Dino rested a stop hand against the captain's chest. "This is my guy, Cap. Frawley, bank squad. Good cop."

The captain looked back at Frawley, nodding a grudging apology. "We got a 911. Radio distress call from inside the armored."

Frawley turned and looked at the silver Provident truck near the camper wreck, now empty—a distress call going out inside his mind.

"Dean," he said, and Dino registered it, completed the thought.

This crew never left things like that to chance. They went *around* alarms.

"Trip it on purpose?" reasoned Dino. "But why?"

Frawley stepped back to take in the car wrecks on Yawkey, the multitude of cops in orange coats attending. He turned and looked up Van Ness, seeing more orange coats. "They wanted police here."

He noticed one cop crossing the street carrying a loose black bag—walking away from the ballpark, moving too calmly.

DOUG STOOD WATCHING JEM go. Another arriving cruiser squealed past, and then Dez was yelling at him. Doug turned to find Dez still holding his gun on the guards. Flashlights and footsteps in the tunnel.

Doug pulled his Beretta and extracted the magazine. Only two rounds left. He pocketed that clip and pulled a full mag from his belt, reseating it, chambering a round. He took a guard from Dez and hustled them all down to the last door, the one farthest away from the tunnel, at the end of Van Ness.

Doug put his guard facedown onto the floor there, then holstered his gun and untied his bandanna from around his face. The guard was begging for his life, certain he was about to be executed, until Doug's bandanna across his mouth gagged his pleas.

Dez did the same, then stood, still wiping at his eyes, trying to blink his contacts right. "Can we do this?" he said.

Doug looked out the door at the rain. *"Fuck,"* he hissed, considering their chances, then turned to Dez. "It's life for me—I got no choice. For you it's just a couple of years. Cut a plea, give them everything you can. If I make it out, I'm gone from here anyway."

Dez stared, uncertain.

"Gloansy's already hurt," said Doug. "Give yourself up. It's what I would do."

Dez blinked, sore-eyed. "No, it's not."

Doug leaned out of the bay and saw cops coming up from both sides, almost upon them. He stepped right out into the rain and quickly waved over the nearest pair.

In orange coats they came running up the sidewalk, guns at their sides. Doug made sure they saw his empty hands, then pointed them around the corner to where Dez was standing over the bound and gagged guards.

The cops got busy immediately, one officer dropping his knee down hard on a guard's back, the other calling in their position. "Nice catch," said the kneeling cop.

The guards started to wriggle, grunting in protest, trying to talk with their eyes.

"Transport these two," said Doug. "We're going after the third."

Doug and Dez started across the street, briskly but not running. Doug glanced down the length of Yawkey to where the Suburban was bunched up at the corner, having smacked into their stolen T-bird, cops in orange all over it. A paramedic was at the driver's-side door, working on Gloansy, and a chill rippled through Doug.

To their left lay Landsdowne Street, beyond a pair of empty cruisers. Ahead was Ipswich Street, full of orange cops, the direction in which Jem had gone.

"Come on," hissed Dez, starting left, looking to slip the police perimeter.

Gunshots sounded on Ipswich up ahead. Doug felt the reports in his chest, the way you feel thunder or a woman's scream.

"Holy fucking hell," said Dez.

"Take off," Doug told him, then started alone after Jem.

THE COP HAD REACHED the end of Ipswich where it met Boylston, walking in the street along the left-hand row of parked cars. "Excuse me!" said Frawley, coming up behind him. "Officer! Hold up a minute there, please."

The cop stopped, the bag hanging heavy and low in his hand. A gas station was to his left, another one across Boylston, a Staples office supply store to his right. Traffic continued on four-lane Boylston as usual.

The cop did not turn at first, his slick orange back wrinkling as his free hand went into it. When he did turn, it was with a sweeping arm motion such that the rounds rattling out of his gun would have zippered Frawley up from feet through groin to head, dropping him dead in the street. But Frawley had spun away behind a small gold Civic hatchback, which the cop now fired into.

Two other cops nearby came under fire, dropping the blue Boston Police sawhorses they were carrying, and Frawley hazarded a look through the cracked auto glass at his assailant.

Frawley only caught a distorted flash, the wild face with its white-out eyes and upper lip ridge looking profane in cop blues, like a cannibal wearing a chef's apron. James Coughlin. He was backing away behind cover fire with the engaged smile of a teenager seeing his violent daydreams come true.

Frawley tried to get his shotgun over the roof of the car, but pedestrians scattered behind Coughlin, cars waiting for a green light. Then Coughlin swung back, turning with the shoulder-harnessed semi-auto—an illegal Intratec-9—popping window glass out of the car.

It sunk in then that Frawley was actually being shot at, and he went into a tight fetal crouch, putting his shoulder into the hindquarters of the car. Many of the rounds went through-and-through, puncturing the roof and thumping into the wooden fence behind him.

Then the firing stopped. Frawley gripped his shotgun wildly, expecting an ambush.

What he got instead was a sound like a stone skittering across the road. The thing rapped against the curb and Frawley peered down under the car, watching it spin and settle.

It looked like an old hand grenade. Frawley couldn't believe it. And then of course, he did believe it—and jumped up, racing away, yelling to the responding cops to get back—

The grenade blew, and the Civic's gas tank blew, and Frawley and his shotgun went sprawling. He turned from the wet asphalt and saw the little import on its side, undercarriage aflame. The windows of the storefront Staples were blown in, and everywhere on Boylston Street people were leaping out of their cars and running. Coughlin was gone.

Frawley got to his feet, pissed. That mangy fucker had tried to kill him. And a guy who'd open up on a federal agent would open up on anybody.

Frawley regripped his Remington and took off after him.

DOUG CAME UP ON the burning car, its stinking black smoke rising into the rain.

The grenades. Doug couldn't believe it.

"Fucking crazy," said a voice behind him.

Doug turned, found Dez still there. "Get out of here—"

"You two!" barked a voice from the side.

Two other cops ran past them. The one yelling to them had rank.

"Pick up that left flank! We're gonna sweep up Boylston and shut this end down!"

Doug nodded and did as he was told—pulling his Beretta and moving past the abandoned cars to the far sidewalk, past panicked citizens crawling away in the rain.

"What are you doing?" said Dez, coming up at his side. "What do you think you can do for him?"

"Desmond," said Doug, furious. "Get out. Leave me."

Then Doug saw Jem break from the Howard Johnson's parking lot half a block up, orange coat flapping, the bag in one hand, the Tec out in the other. Four, maybe five car lengths behind him, a plain-clothes guy with a shotgun cut across after him, wearing a nylon vest reading *FBI*.

COUGHLIN WANTED THE MCDONALD'S, running toward it, proba-bly for hostages.

Frawley could not allow that to happen. He ranged left, and as Coughlin reached the curb up the street, Frawley pulled the shotgun to his shoulder and fired wide, between Coughlin and the restau-rant—*Blam!*—shredding a Free Apartment Guide stand on the side-walk. He pumped, fired again—*Blam!*—this time killing a *Boston Herald* machine.

Coughlin jerked back from the exploding stands. He spun and fired into the street, finding Frawley, but not quickly enough. Frawley dived between parked cars, scraping up the skin on his elbows and his knees, hearing rounds pick through the side of the truck, *rap-rap-rap*, thinking, *I'm in a fucking gunfight*. He got up off the road, wor-ried about ricochets, sitting on the front bumper of the truck with his feet on the tail of the next car. He went into his jacket pockets and reloaded the shotgun, spilling some shells.

Smatterings of small-arms fire behind him, a burst here, a burst there. Then only the rain. Frawley leaned out one way, looking up the sidewalk toward McDonald's, people streaming out of the back entrance with kids in their arms. The front of the restaurant was glass, and he could see in between the painted Mayor McCheese and the Hamburglar, Coughlin was not inside.

Frawley leaned out the other way, looking up the rain-swept street cluttered with abandoned cars, their wipers still going. Not there either.

Frawley pulled back patiently, thinking Coughlin was waiting to pick him off if he moved. Somebody was going to get hurt in the cross fire. Coming up toward him were two cops on his side of the street, still half a block away. They were orange just like Coughlin, and he checked them for a split second, remembering that MacRay was likely still at large.

Shots again, *rap-rap-rap* off the side of his truck, and Frawley ducked out the other way, charging up the sidewalk, determined to keep Coughlin in the middle of Boylston and moving west.

DOUG MADE THE FBI shotgun as Frawley—the sleuth propped up on the front bumper of a UPS van, stopping to reload.

Dez was rubbing his eyes, trying to see clear. "You gonna shoot at cops?"

"Fuck away from me, Dez."

"How you gonna save him? How?"

Doug could take out Frawley. If he wanted Frawley to be dead, he could do it right now.

"You don't owe him anything, Doug. You can't do anything for him except die with him."

Then rounds cracked and pinged off the parked car next to them, popping glass, kicking rain off the street.

Jem was spraying rounds at them—at cops—from half a block away. Dez stooped low, swearing. "Duggy. We'll be pinned down here. We gotta bail *now*."

Doug watched Frawley curl out from behind the truck. Sometimes just knowing you can pull off a thing is enough. He let Dez tug on him, and together they started back down Boylston toward the black smoke of the bombed-out car.

WHETHER OUT OF PANIC or confusion or just softheadedness, Coughlin started across the intersection where Boylston met the end of Yawkey. Cops lay in wait there, the rounds pecking at Coughlin's vest, dancing him, picking at his leg and his shooting arm. Still he turned and spit rounds back, silencing the service pieces but not the submachine gunfire. Controlled double-taps staggered Coughlin, who held the money bag in front of him now as a shield, retreating back to the corner in front of Osco Drug.

Bloodied and sniggering, he hobbled up the wheelchair ramp to the drugstore, where someone inside had had the foresight to lock the doors. A wasted stutter of gunfire broke some of the glass until his Intratec clicked dry. Frawley heard it clatter to the pavement from his position in the drugstore parking lot, flat against the wall, listening to Coughlin's half-laughed cursing and the drag of his wounded foot.

Coughlin rounded the corner and Frawley was there with the Remington. Coughlin grinned like he knew him, or maybe thought the letters across Frawley's chest were funny. Frawley was yelling at

Coughlin. He didn't know what he was saying, and it was just as likely Coughlin never heard it anyway.

Coughlin laughed, the pistol in his bloodied hand starting to rise, and Frawley squeezed one blast low—*Blam!*—then pumped and—*Blam!*—squeezed one blast high.

Coughlin flew back, puppet strings of insanity keeping him on his feet, backpedaling until he fell off the wet curb and spilled hard into the road.

Frawley did not move, frozen in the shooter's pose, still feeling the jerk of recoil. A bloody pistol lay on the sidewalk where Coughlin had once stood.

Coughlin rolled over in the street and started crawling. He was dragging himself, the black bag still in his grip, reaching for the double yellow lines like they were the top ledge of a high building.

Frawley finally moved, keeping his distance behind Coughlin, knowing that he had killed him and it was just a matter of time. Tac cops came charging up alongside Frawley, guns trained on the bright wet orange target, everyone waiting.

Coughlin stopped, laughing blood, then rolled over and looked up at the sky spilling down on him, his chest bucking, his mouth smiling even as his throat groaned for air.

DOUG WATCHED JEM'S ORANGE form crawl into the middle of the wide road, stop, and roll over.

Cops were coming up near them now. "Doug," hissed Dez.

Doug backed away, turning, striding fast alongside Dez. He and Dez would go on the run together now. The switch car with their change of clothes was lost, but the Fenway Gardens were right around the corner. They'd dig up Doug's stash, hit the nearest clothing store they could find, then hop a taxi to the long-term parking lot at Logan, boost an older model car, head out of state. Then figure out what shape the rest of their lives would take.

All these things raced through Doug's mind until he realized he was alone. He turned and saw Dez wandering back into the middle of the street, looking down the length of the double yellow line at Jem. Dez was trying to see through the rain, rubbing at his contacts like a man disbelieving his eyes.

Vested Frawley and some commando cops were coming up slow on Jem. Doug didn't understand Dez's concern—until, at once, he did.

The grenades on Jem's belt.

"Hey!" Dez started to yell.

The commando cops would never hear him through the rain. *"Dez!"* said Doug, calling him back. Regular cops coming from the burning car.

Dez ran a few steps forward, waving an arm. His stand here had to do at least as much with getting some final triumph over Jem— thwarting his grand battlefield exit, Jem's plan to take a few of his enemies with him—as it did saving the cops' lives.

Dez drew his gun and fired it for the first time that morning, straight up into the rain, then a few times low at the road around Jem. It worked, the only way to back the cops away from that distance.

The blast was like a road mine exploding, Jem erupting into lumpy pieces. The bag coughed money into the air, cash fluttering like confetti shot out of cannon, drifting back down to the wet road.

The cops near the smoking Civic were drawing on Dez now, yelling. All confusion in the slapping rain, Dez trying to see, his eyes bothering him, arms rising to his face.

The first shot spun Dez around. The second jerked him the other way, his vest vulnerable at close range, Dez dropping to the asphalt with a splash.

Doug drew and started after him. But already half a dozen orange raincoats were advancing on Dez where he lay.

You gonna shoot at cops?

Doug watched Dez squirming on the ground until the encircling cops blocked his view. Dez was down. Gloansy was caught. Jem was dead.

Something washed over Doug then, with the rain. He holstered his gun and turned and walked away.

THE RINGING IN FRAWLEY'S ears was his mind screaming as he picked himself up off the wet road and stumbled back toward the pieces of Coughlin. It was snowing money now, and he moved gun-first through the flurry of cash to the double yellow line.

Coughlin's armored vest was cracked open like a bloody husk. The fucker had blown himself up and tried to take Frawley and everyone else with him.

Frawley looked down the road to where the shots had come from, his thoughts too shrill to even speculate about what had happened. Someone was in custody down there. Frawley only hoped it was MacRay.

* * *

DOUG SAT ON HER stone bench. The willow was weeping rain into her garden, and he was trying to understand what it was he was feeling, until finally he realized—he felt nothing.

He got down on his knees in the muck. Rain battered the purple impatiens as he thrust his hands wrist-deep into the soil, as though he could reach all the way down to his money, take it, and leave. As though he had anything to run to now. As though he had anything to run for.

Nothing left in him but vengeance. Sirens wailed out on Boylston as he stood and shed his orange coat, starting back toward the Town.

53
HOME

DOUG WALKED OFF THE T at the Community College stop and crossed over Rutherford Avenue on the elevated walkway, seeing the soaked Town before him, the shoulders of its twin hills shrugged against the rain.

He walked along Austin Street between the rink and the Foodmaster plaza toward Main Street, umbrella people nodding at this drenched beat cop passing them on the sidewalk, kids in slickers and rubber boots staring up at the man in blue. Doug didn't see any of it. The only thing he noticed other than the bricks at his feet was the State Police helicopter cutting through the rain over the city across the river, looking for him.

The bell over the front door giggled as he entered the flower shop. He heard harp and fiddle music, "A Little Bit of Heaven" serenading the thirsty plants and squatting stone gargoyles. Doug stood alone among the pale blooms for a few airless moments, until Rusty, the Florist's guy, pushed through the black curtain hanging over the door behind the back counter.

He wore a green tracksuit and was eating a lettuce sandwich out of tinfoil. He looked at the sodden blue cop in the store as just another customer, until he recognized the face.

For a moment it seemed that Doug wouldn't have to shoot the ex-IRA man. Rusty had nothing but a cold sandwich to defend himself with, and Doug thought the guy might just bend to the will of force and time and step aside.

But a glance at Doug's empty hands showed him that Rusty had too much pride. The Florist's guy dropped his sandwich and lunged for something under the counter.

Doug cleared his holster and fired twice, the white-haired Irishman falling back against the wall to the floor. Doug passed the counter on the way to the back, Rusty facedown and gasping for air.

Doug pushed through the black curtain gun-first. The Irish music was louder there, warbling out of an old turntable. The glass-doored walk-in cooler was empty, Fergie's workbench standing across the room.

Doug heard a toilet flush. He turned toward the latch door as it opened.

Fergie wandered out carrying a newspaper, wearing his tight, hooded sweatshirt, long work pants, and maroon suede slippers. He saw the cop there with the gun in his hand and at first just looked annoyed. Then he pulled off his reading glasses for a clear look at the cop's face. The half-glasses fell against his chest.

He said Doug's name and Doug filled the air between them with smoke. Doug did not stop firing until Fergus Coln lay beneath the workbench, barefoot among the stem clippings, condolence ribbons unspooling over him.

It was a while before the Irish music returned to Doug's ears. He never heard the bell over the front door.

Two gunshots punched him high in the back of his vest. Another round bit into his left rear thigh, a fourth skipping off his shoulder to slice into his neck.

Doug twisted and dropped to the floor, firing from there, aiming back through the curtain into the store. He heard something fall, then the giggle of the doorbell.

He pushed himself to his feet. The lead in his leg burned and blood was spilling down the front of his shirt over his fake silver-and-blue badge. He felt a warm, pulsing hole in his neck and closed it with his palm, pressing hard and hobbling to the doorway, tearing down the black curtain.

Rusty hadn't moved, dead where he had fallen. Among the floor pots in front lay a body on its side, a young guy quaking, his black boots thumping the tile. A tear in the back of his T-shirt was blooming red, just over the belt of his fatigues. Doug limped over, his left hand holding the blood into his neck, his right hand holding his gun.

One of Jem's camo kids. The giggling bell had been the other one getting away.

Doug stood over him, waiting, but the kid refused to look up, lying there shaking in the scummy pot water he had overturned.

Doug holstered his gun and started away, leaving the kid twitching on the floor.

* * *

FRAWLEY SAT INSIDE THE McDonald's, still trying to count all the shots he'd fired. There was going to be an FBI investigation as well as civil liability hearings, and he would be held accountable for each and every round. He had already surrendered his Remington for ballistics.

"I'm going to be fired," he said.

Dino was drinking a strawberry shake next to him. "Easy, now."

"Look out there." The street was filled with umbrella-toting city, state, and federal lawmen, Suffolk County coroners, city hall lawyers, and news crews pressing against BPD sawhorses. "Shots fired in Fenway Park. A goddamn grenade blowing up a car." Frawley sat up. "I killed a man in the street."

"You shot him pretty good, but technically I think it was that crazy mofo's hand grenades that cashed out his tab."

Frawley's wrinkled FBI vest lay before him. "They can't clip me right away. Wouldn't look good. Got to wait for the inquest to run its course. Transfer me somewhere cold in the meantime."

"You at all curious about that other one down the street?"

Frawley grimaced. "Okay."

"It was Elden. The one in the Suburban, that was Magloan—with what looks like the entire take in the trunk, minus whatever got blown up out there with Coughlin."

Frawley waited. "And MacRay?"

"We'll find him. Bringing in the Canine Unit to search the ballpark."

Frawley looked at the half-eaten breakfasts left on the tables by the windows, empty high chairs, open newspapers.

"Dean," he said, unable to look the older man in the eye. "I did some stupid things with this. I did some things I probably should have run by you first."

Dino looked at him, quiet, maybe counting slowly to ten.

"Nothing illegal," Frawley stressed. "But I pushed it. I put myself inside this. I got involved."

Dino took a long draw on his shake, then set the cup aside. He stood. "You're in shock, Frawl. Couple of hours, we'll talk. Rather—you'll talk."

Dino walked away, leaving Frawley staring out the window, thinking about cold weather. He still had his law degree. Maybe this McDonald's was hiring.

Outside, he watched two detectives jump into an unmarked Grand Marquis, driving fast out of the parking lot.

Frawley read excitement on the faces of the remaining patrolmen. He pulled himself together and went outside. He asked the youngest-looking uniform what was going on.

"The Florist's shop in Charlestown," said the cop. "A bloodbath, gangland style. Looks like somebody got Fergie."

Frawley's mind seized up like a fist. All that time he'd been sitting there on his ass in a McDonald's, feeling sorry for himself—

Claire Keesey.

He took off running across the street, back up Yawkey toward his car.

DOUG PRESSED THE BELL again and hung his head low so that the badge on his hat was in the spyglass.

Claire opened the door to the cop. She saw Doug's face and his bloody hand at his neck and her hand went to her mouth, eyes widening.

Doug's first step over her threshold was okay. He faltered on the second step and went down hard on the third.

Claire screamed.

He could not move his hand from his neck. Pressure was the only thing keeping him alive. This slow throb against his palm was his clock running down.

He got himself into a sitting position and used his free hand and the heels of his shoes to push back from the open door. Making it to her place was all he'd thought about in the rain. Now he just wanted to push in deeper. He got to the small table outside her kitchen and slumped back against the legs of a chair.

He went away for a little while. Then he came back.

"Made it," he said. He needed a yawn in the worst way, but couldn't get one.

Claire came toward him. Impossibly tall, her hands covering her mouth, eyes screaming tears.

Doug fought down a swallow. "Why?"

She started to kneel, hesitated, remained standing.

"In your garden." He spoke in hoarse bursts. "That last time. I wanted you . . . to tell me not to do it. I wanted you . . . to stop me."

She shook her head in horror.

"I wanted you . . . to give me a reason . . ."

"But nothing *I* could have said . . ."

She still didn't get him. "I would have done . . . anything for you. Even save myself."

She slipped to her knees, sitting on her heels at his outstretched feet, mystified. "Why? Why leave that to *me*?"

And there, in her bewilderment, he recognized his grave mistake. He had surrendered himself to Claire, just as Krista had to him. When you give someone the power to save you, you give them the power to destroy you as well. That was what Frank G. had been all about—not relinquishing that grip on yourself.

A man coming at him down the front hall, gun out. The sleuth, Frawley. Doug tightened his grip on the side of his neck.

FRAWLEY WENT IN THE open door, seeing the trail of blood and rain, his SIG-Sauer out of his armpit. MacRay was in a cop uniform, slumped against a chair on the floor, Claire kneeling before him.

MacRay's gun was in his holster. One hand was wet red and clamped over a neck wound, blood dripping from his bent elbow to the lemon yellow carpet. No grenades on his belt.

MacRay, dying, frowned at Frawley's gun, then at Frawley himself.

Frawley came up behind his SIG to MacRay's side, smelling blood, reaching across and tugging the Beretta from MacRay's cop holster while MacRay sat there and watched him take it. Frawley backed away past Claire, easing up on his aim, putting the Beretta in his back pocket. He saw a telephone on the table and circled to it, picked it up.

"Don't."

MacRay's voice was as bloodless as his face. Frawley put down the phone, moving back into MacRay's line of sight.

Claire turned her head to look up at Frawley through tears. "Did you do this?"

Her words cut him. She was asking, *Did you do this because of me?*

MacRay worked hard to breathe, harder still to speak. "She dimed me?"

He seemed to know the truth already. Frawley said, "That's right."

MacRay swallowed with difficulty. He looked at Claire until his eyes fell, then blinked back to Frawley. "Why let it go so far? Why not take us . . . at the hotel?"

"What hotel?" said Frawley. "I didn't find out anything until an hour beforehand."

MacRay looked hard at Claire again. Something was going on there.

Frawley said, "We're talking about Coughlin's sister, right?"

MacRay's eyes came back to Frawley, so still and staring that Frawley thought MacRay was gone. Then MacRay nodded. He seemed to relax.

Frawley's heart was pumping hard enough for both of them. "You got the Florist."

MacRay blinked. "Tell Dez I did it for him. For the Town."

Frawley wanted to feel nothing for the crook, but to be in a room with a dying man is to die a little yourself. "You'll have to tell him."

The only reaction was a flicker in MacRay's eyes.

"The money." said Frawley. "Where's the rest of your stash?"

MacRay was falling into himself.

"Where's the money?" pressed Frawley.

Claire said, "Leave him alone."

MacRay was going. Frawley backed away, heavy-legged. He picked up the phone and dialed 911.

SHE CAME FORWARD AND took his empty hand, holding it tenderly in her own, as though the hand itself was the thing that was dying.

Doug said, "You were never going away. With me. Were you."

She held his gaze. Her wet-eyed expression said no.

He felt love streaming out of his hand into hers like electricity.

She would find it in the spring. The money he had buried like doomed hope in her garden. Like a note he'd left for her. Maybe she could use it to fund her work at the Boys and Girls Club. Maybe in time she'd think of him differently.

His left hand fell away from his neck as he focused on her face. He wanted her to be the last earthly thing he would see.

Even if a thing is doomed—there is that moment of absurd hope that is worth the fall, that is worth everything.

CLAIRE FELT THE SHOCK of lifelessness in his limp hand. She dropped it out of fright and would only later wilt at the shame of letting him go. Right now a dead man was lying on her floor and her mind was choking on this.

Why had he come to her to die? Dragging himself into her kitchen, just as he had dragged himself into her life. She despised him for the mess he had made, the blood on her floor like the stain on her soul. And yet. And yet as she looked at him now, she could not help but feel for the motherless boy inside. For Adam Frawley too, the vengeful one whispering into the telephone—these two lovesick sons she had gotten caught between. But for the men they had become, she had only scorn.

She recalled a news story about a woman who was accidentally knocked overboard a moored cruise ship. She came up to the surface unhurt, treading water, but trapped by the tide pushing the massive ship back against the dock. She would have been crushed to death if she hadn't wriggled out of her evening dress and kicked off her heels, swimming straight down into the blackness, feeling her way blindly along the hull to the deep bottom keel, then pulling herself past it and kicking free, lungs bursting as she surfaced on the other side, naked and alive.

Had Claire made it to the other side? Was she coming up for air now?

The police were already in her foyer, and she reached for Doug's hand one last time before they were separated forever. His body had settled against the chair, his hand impossibly heavy now and wanting to fall. She noticed dirt under his fingernails and darkening his cuticles, and thought immediately of her garden. She couldn't imagine any reason why he would have gone there—nor why she felt so certain that he had.

Walk to the water until you can feel it on your toes. Then take off the blindfold.

She felt the same sensation of passing as she had watching her young brother die: of something coming to nothing, yes, but at the same time, a conferring of responsibility, a covenant passed from the dead to the living.

Claire was taking off the blindfold now. She looked deep into Doug's dimming eyes, reminded of hearth fires and how, even after the flames died, the glowing cinders were slow to cool. She wondered what it was that Doug MacRay saw as the glow of his life faded. She wondered what died last in the heart of a thief.

54
END BEGINNING

"CAN'T DO IT," SAID Jem. "I can't fucking do it. He's turning my fucking stomach with this. We ordered these sandwiches what, twelve hours ago? You couldn't get cold cuts like the rest of us, Magloan? Sitting here with your soggy-ass steak sub, these fucking limp peppers."

Dez said, "Never mind that he's been eating the thing for like, three hours."

"This isn't eating anymore," said Jem, "this is lovemaking. He's getting it on with a steak sub. Somebody cover my young, impressionable eyes."

Dez said, "Joanie does usually go around with a smile on her face."

"Oh—no question Gloansy gives primo head," Jem said. "I can vouch for that."

Doug shushed their groaning laughter, not very concerned about the audio sensors inside the vault's antitamper package, but careful just the same. The four of them sitting on the floor behind the teller counter in dusty blue jumpsuits, the bank brightening with morning light, trucks and cars rumbling outside through Kenmore Square.

"Know what we need?" said Gloansy, still munching. "Those headsets with ear wires, like in the movies. So we can talk while we're in different rooms."

"Headsets are gay," said Jem. "You'd look like a girl folding pants at the Gap. Walkie-talkies—that's a man's radio."

"I'm talking hands-free," said Gloansy. "Gun in one hand, bag of cash in the other, capeesh?"

"Do not say *capeesh*. You sound like a douche." Jem got to his feet, stretched. "See, this is too fucking relaxed here. This isn't robbing. This, we could do back at my place. Why going in on the prowl sucks. All night, cutting a hole in the fucking ceiling. Like *working* for a living."

"Prowl is smart," said Doug.

"Prowl is pussy," said Jem.

Doug checked the wall clock. "You want strong, kid, we go strong in about ten minutes. Let's pack this shit up."

Gloansy said, "But I haven't finished my snack."

Jem snatched it out of his hands and mashed it, threw it into their trash bag. "You finished now? 'Cause I got a fucking bank to rob."

Doug checked his Colt's load and dropped it back into his pocket, knowing he was much more likely to hit someone over the head with the thing than he ever was to fire it. As obsessive as Doug was about the jobs they pulled, Jem's weapons source was the one detail he preferred to know nothing about. If indeed it was the Florist or one of the dust-brained kids in the Florist's employ, that would only piss Doug off.

Gloansy got to his feet without his Mountain Dew. Doug told him, "You gonna leave your tonic there, you might as well write your name and Social Security number on the wall in blood."

"I got it, I got it," said the freckled wonder, stowing it in the open work duffel near the bleach jugs.

They went on with their bickering for a few more precious preheist minutes, and Doug took a step back and realized that this was the part of the job he liked best. The intervals of downtime when they were all just kids again, four messed-up boys from the Town, so good at being so bad. He realized he never felt more secure, more at peace, more protected, than he did then, cooping inside a bank they were about to rob. Nobody could touch them there. Nobody could hurt them except each other.

Jem said, "Bad news, Monsignor. *Rolling Stone* said U2's next album is disco."

Dez rubbed at his eyes, prodding his contact lenses. "Not true."

"It happens, kid. These things can't last forever. Got to end sometime."

"We'll see," said Dez, wiring his police radio into his ear. "We shall see."

Jem pulled a paper Foodmaster bag out of the work duffel. "Game faces," he said, handing out black ski masks.

"This is it?" said Gloansy, pulling on the knit mask. "This what you been so top-secret about?"

Jem grinned his grin and went back into the bag. "Feast your eyes, ladies."

Doug received his goalie mask and looked it over—the oval eyes, the jagged, black, hand-drawn stitches.

"Gerry Cheevers," said Gloansy, awestruck, pulling it on over his ski mask.

Jem pulled a gun into his blue-gloved hand and said, "Let's make some motherfucking *bank*."

The other masks nodded, smacked fists all around, Doug looking at the stitched-up faces of his friends. Dez went to take his position inside the shaded front windows, Gloansy remaining behind the counter.

Doug turned past the vault, following Jem down the short hallway to the back door where they faced each other in the shadows, standing silent and still on either side. Doug had no dark premonitions about the job as he pulled the black .38 into his hand. The only thing bothering him now was that the fun part was already over.

A car pulled up outside, doors opening, shutting. "Fucking clockwork," hissed Jem's empty-eyed mask.

Claire Keesey. That was the branch manager's name. She drove a plum Saturn coupe with a useless rear spoiler and a bumper sticker that said BREATHE! She was single, as far as Doug could tell, and he wondered why. Surprising, the things you could learn about a person from a distance, the impressions that you formed. Tailing her for so long, watching her from afar, had raised more questions than answers. He was curious about her now. He wondered, with the idle affection of a guy thinking about a girl, what she was going to look like up close.

ACKNOWLEDGMENTS

Debts owed to: Charlotte, for unwavering support; my father, source of strength and inspiration; my Melanie and my Declan; the uncanny NewGents; Richard Abate, Prince of Agents; Colin Harrison, who enriched this book in record time; Kevin Smith at Pocket; Sarah Knight and everybody at Scribner; and Nan Graham and Susan Moldow.

ABOUT THE AUTHOR

Chuck Hogan is the author of several acclaimed novels, including *Devils in Exile* and *The Killing Moon*. He is also the co-author, with Guillermo del Toro, of the international bestseller *The Strain*. He lives with his family outside Boston.

The History of the
Royal Commonwealth Society
1868–1968

The History of the
Royal Commonwealth Society
1868–1968

by

Trevor R. Reese

London

Oxford University Press

MELBOURNE   TORONTO   CAPE TOWN

1968

Oxford University Press, Ely House, London W. 1

GLASGOW NEW YORK TORONTO MELBOURNE WELLINGTON
CAPE TOWN SALISBURY IBADAN NAIROBI LUSAKA ADDIS ABABA
BOMBAY CALCUTTA MADRAS KARACHI LAHORE
DACCA KUALA LUMPUR HONG KONG TOKYO

Printed in Great Britain by
The Camelot Press Ltd., London and Southampton

To
G. S. G.

Table of Contents

Illustrations

Author's Preface

THIS study is designed to relate the development of the Royal Commonwealth Society to that of the British empire and commonwealth as a whole over the last hundred years. It is neither an exhaustive analysis of the internal affairs of the society nor a full account of British imperial history in this period, but rather an essay on the evolution of the empire and commonwealth as reflected in the activities of the voluntary society founded a century ago to foster imperial sentiment and promote the empire's interests.

When the council of the society invited me to produce a centenary volume, it made freely available to me its records, proceedings and minutes, and this history is based largely on them. It placed no restraint on my selection and use of material and made no attempt to influence the opinions and criticisms expressed in the book: I greatly appreciate the council's liberality in this respect.

I received much assistance from the present librarian of the society, Mr. D. H. Simpson, who was a perceptive guide to the records and placed his extensive knowledge of the society's internal history at my disposal. Sir Charles Ponsonby gave me some of his papers and in discussion elaborated on several aspects of the society's affairs. Professor Gerald S. Graham of King's College, University of London, my mentor both during my student days and throughout the years since, cast a gimlet eye over the typescript, tidied up points of style, added information drawn from his long association with the society, and made useful comments on the description of general imperial developments.

I am grateful also to the secretarial staff of the Institute of Commonwealth Studies, University of London, who have been most generous of their time and patience, and especially to Miss Anne Norris, who typed from my manuscript with her usual superb efficiency. My wife helped to correct the script, suggested improvements, and was an unfailing source of encouragement at all times.

Finally, in a book of this kind it is impossible to include the names of all who have worked, and are working, devotedly for the society: to those who have served the society well and long but who receive no mention in these pages, I offer my apologies.

T. R. R.

Institute of Commonwealth Studies,
London, January 1968

Chapter One

The British Empire, 1868

ON becoming secretary of state for the colonies in 1868, Lord Granville was assured by way of comfort that his duties required but a modicum of sense. *The Times* on the last day of the previous year had remarked upon the 'prosperous monotony' of the colonies and assumed that the problems weighing on the British government were almost exclusively domestic: the Colonial Office, it concluded, 'once the most onerous Department in the Imperial Government', was now 'in a great measure relieved of its legislative and administrative functions'. This would have suited well Granville's relaxed approach to the exercise of ministerial office, and it may be assumed that it was then that he began his avowed practice of opening all incoming letters himself, only to discover that most of them, if left alone, would answer themselves. Britain, in 1868, had evolved a propitiatory and, as it proved, flexible relationship with the settlement colonies of its extensive and growing empire.

Three centuries earlier England had been scarcely on the margin of world history. The country to whose throne Henry VII had succeeded in 1485 had been neither large nor strong. There had been momentary triumphs during the preceding 200 years, when its kings had humbled French armies and extended their sway across northern France, but by the middle of the fifteenth century England's overseas possessions had been reduced to a bare foothold on the continent. The lead in establishing European contacts in the wider and then largely unknown world had been taken not by England but by Portugal, which, with the capture of Ceuta from the Moors in 1415 had initiated European expansion into Africa. Portuguese navigators, helped by improvements in sailing vessels, had piloted their way successfully down the west coast of Africa, explored the Gulf of Guinea and, before the end of the fifteenth century, had rounded the Cape of Good Hope and reached southern India. By 1529 the Portuguese had entered the Pacific, established themselves in the valuable trade of the Spice Islands, and sighted the northern shores of New Guinea. Some Portuguese traders may have ventured beyond New Guinea through the reefs and strong currents in the seas to the south and perhaps even touched upon the north-west coast of Australia. The existence of a great southern continent, however, about which geographers had speculated since classical times, was as yet no more than a matter of conjecture, and energies which might have been devoted to exploration in the South Seas were diverted by Chrisopher Columbus's accidental discovery of America while searching for a westward route to the Orient. Columbus was in Spain's employ, and the New World upon which he chanced in 1492 was for a century the prerogative hunting-ground of Spanish treasure-seekers and adventurers: two European empires, the Spanish and the Portuguese, were erected on the ancient civilizations of the native peoples of central and south America.

Not until the seventeenth century was England a serious competitor to the continental nations in colonial expansion. The defeat of the Spanish Armada in 1588 marked the beginning of English power at sea; Drake's circumnavigation of the globe and the establishment in 1601 of the East India Company signified the advent of England as a colonial power. The first successful English settlement colony was established in 1607 at what became known as Jamestown in Virginia, which, by 1619, had over 2,000 inhabitants. In 1620 another settlement was made north of Cape Cod at a spot named Plymouth on the shores of Massachusetts, and other English colonies emerged in rapid succession during the next hundred years until, by the middle of the eighteenth century, there were thirteen settled along the eastern seaboard of America from Maine in the north to Georgia in the south.

The miscellaneous forms of government that grew up in the various colonies were all gradually reduced to an imitation of that in London. A governor represented the crown and executed the policy of the British government. He was advised by a council which was nominated by the crown and occupied a constitutional position in the colony corresponding roughly to that of the House of Lords in England. Legislation was initiated and taxes levied by a representative assembly or lower house elected on a property franchise. Although the assemblies preened themselves in the image of the House of Commons and steadily enhanced their status in colonial politics throughout the eighteenth century, they were not allowed to forget that their privileges, powers, and very existence depended on the royal prerogative and that the ultimate and decisive authority lay in London.

The principal element in colonial policy in the eighteenth century was the mercantilist notion of a self-sufficing empire, whereby the colonies produced raw materials for the mother country and consumed its manufactures in exchange. The incentive to possess an empire lay partly in the monopolization of imperial trade, which therefore had to be regulated to exclude foreign countries. A series of Navigation Acts or laws of trade enacted in 1651 and 1660 and onwards erected a commercial system which restricted to British markets alone the export of certain enumerated commodities produced in America, and obliged European imports into the colonies to be landed first in England before re-shipment to their destination. Economic oppression did not drive the colonies to revolution, but the operation of the mercantilist system was a constant reminder to them of their subordination, and it served as a useful instrument for the arguments of radical spirits in their campaign against what they regarded as British tyranny.

By the middle of the eighteenth century the colonies had begun to generate a national pride of their own and were no longer purely English. The English language and English institutions predominated, but there were Swiss, Germans, French, and Dutch who held no natal predilection for the United Kingdom; even among those of English origin were many who had left their native land because of poverty or persecution and whose affection for the mother country often declined after years in a new environment. When the British government implemented a stricter colonial policy, therefore, and made evasion of the laws of trade difficult, American thought began to turn towards the idea of independence. British policy after 1763 intensified discontent in the American colonies and in 1776 they joined in declaring their independence, which in 1783 was recognized by the British government.

American independence inevitably produced disillusionment in London about the value of settlement colonies, but overseas expansion did not cease, and within five years a new settlement colony was founded in the southern hemisphere. For years European explorers had searched the Pacific for a vast southern continent until in April 1770 James Cook sighted the sandhills of the mainland of eastern Australia, where he made the first European landing, fiercely but perfunctorily resisted by aborigines. The English colours were displayed ashore and on a tree an inscription carved to signify formal annexation, consent to which the natives were assumed to have granted by their absence. When Cook was killed at the water's edge in Hawaii in February 1779, he had sailed the Atlantic, Pacific, and Indian oceans for nearly twenty years, discovering or re-discovering continents and islands and correcting the contemporary map of the world. He had revealed the true shape of New Zealand, found and charted the east coast of Australia, and opened the way for effective imperial and commercial enterprise by Britain in the South Seas. Cook was not only the greatest explorer of the eighteenth century and the greatest navigator of all time; he was also the progenitor of British colonization in Australia.

At the time of Cook's death in the Pacific a committee of the House of Commons in London was investigating the problem of transportation. American independence had closed the most obvious and convenient destination to which unwanted sections of the population could be sent. In 1776 Parliament formally terminated the old system of transportation, euphemistically characterized as now 'attended with various inconveniences', and replaced it by a system of hard labour under supervision in England. In spite of numerous executions and the dispatch in appalling conditions of small shipments of convicts to the Gambia on the west coast of Africa, overcrowding in United Kingdom gaols had become acute. Transportation was the solution, and in the early morning of 26 January 1788 marines and convicts disembarked at Sydney cove and hoisted the Union Jack over what was to be the penal colony of New South Wales. In the generation that followed, settlements were made at other points around the Australian coast and in New Zealand, Cape Colony was acquired, and trade and war carried the British flag further in Africa, India, and South-East Asia.

The development of Britain's new settlement empire after the American Revolution was more an offshoot of domestic and social difficulties than part of an imperial design. Changes and improvements in Britain raised new problems. The decline of gin drinking and the progress in medical science reduced the death rate, while the mechanized production of cheap goods and the use of new methods in agriculture encouraged the rising birth rate, with the result that the population was increasing more rapidly. Life in Britain was undergoing a transformation, and in consequence a strain was thrown on the social structure.

A growing population intensified the need for increased domestic production, and farmers and landlords used improved methods to extract the utmost from their soil, making splendid market gardens out of heaths that were once the playground of highwaymen. The husbandmen worked in the fields from dawn till dusk, their womenfolk plaited straw and sat at the loom, spiritedly preserving domestic handicrafts doomed by machine competition, and the yeomen, though declining in numbers, kept their families nearly self-sufficient by careful nursing of their freehold or copyhold land. The landed gentry prospered as the value of farm lands soared. In contrast, the lot of the wage-earners became calamitous as the war with Napoleon persisted and the price of bread went up, and the small husbandmen found themselves unable to meet rising costs and obliged to sell their allotments to the larger land-owners. Those displaced from the land joined the population movement from the country to the town in search of employment, principally in the factories and cotton mills of the midlands and the north. In this migrating population lay one of the potential sources of free settlers for Britain's expanding territories overseas.

When Napoleon met his final defeat in 1815, Britain's naval supremacy was unchallengeable, and under its protection in the palmy days of the nineteenth century the second British empire was established without serious competition. In the flush of its leadership in the Industrial Revolution, with commercial

B

rivals reduced by the ravages of war and colonial competitors removed from the stage, Britain entered upon a period of serene economic and imperial hegemony. Trade was still mainly with Europe, North America, and the Mediterranean countries, but trade with India, China, and the countries of the Pacific Ocean was growing rapidly in importance, tilting the balance of empire away from the west and towards the east. Such world-wide traffic required command of the sea routes along which it was carried, and this was secured by possession of strategic bases at Gibraltar, Malta, the Cape of Good Hope, Mauritius, Ceylon, Tobago, and St. Helena, enabling British naval power to encompass the globe. Yet the immense territorial expansion of the empire that took place in the nineteenth century was not deliberately sought and was not necessarily in harmony with public thinking. The retention and increase of the trade with the former colonies in America after their independence indicated that territorial possession was not essential in order to dominate a country's commerce. There were domestic issues in abundance to occupy British politicians and economists, and there was no agitation for expansion overseas, but with continental Europe preoccupied with problems of German and Italian unification, and with the empires of Holland, France, Spain, and Portugal in stagnation or revolt, it was certain that European occupation and exploitation of new territories would devolve upon the United Kingdom.

Spurs to emigration were provided after the Napoleonic war by reductions in the armed forces that created some unemployment, by agricultural depressions, and by the accelerating change to mechanized processes that unsettled some of the labouring areas, particularly in Lancashire. The unprecedented increase in the population, its ten million multiplying nearly fourfold in the course of the nineteenth century, alarmed economic thinkers and provoked a substantial, and at first ill-organized, exodus to the United States, Canada, and Australia. As a new and larger empire came into existence the mother country was again faced with the problem of how to govern and keep in allegiance peoples overseas possessing an inherited consciousness of their democratic rights as Englishmen. The lessons of the American Revolution had not been immediately understood in Britain, whose colonial policy in the early nineteenth century showed a remarkable resemblance to the policy in the eighteenth, and there seemed a distinct possibility that mistakes would be made similar to those which had preceded the disruption of the old empire. That discreet statesmanship ultimately prevailed was due partly to a general indifference towards the colonies evoked by memories of the American war of independence and confirmed by the nation's global supremacy, partly to the agitation of zealots within the overseas settlements themselves, and partly, and not least, to the sound, if academic, ministration of officials in London.

After 1782 colonial affairs were the responsibility of the home secretary assisted by a committee of the Privy Council. He answered the dispatches of colonial governors with reasonable punctuality, but his department was overworked and in 1801 colonial administration was transferred to the secretary of state for war, a combination that lasted until the outbreak of the Crimean War in 1854, when the departments were separated and the Colonial Office was given the organizational framework that was to last for more than a century. In the period from 1801 to 1854 most secretaries of state for war and the colonies reckoned upon a short tenure of the office, and the consistent conduct of business was more by the permanent officials, particularly the under-secretaries, among whom Sir James Stephen earned himself a special niche. The administration by these men was genuinely disinterested: it was also academic in that they never visited the colonies nor felt the inclination to do so. The colonies, to them, denoted governors' dispatches and slightly distorted configurations on maps, places so distant as to be almost unreal.

The conservative outlook that took root at the Colonial Office in London was not radically shaken by the officials and governors sent out to the settlements overseas. They were usually men with an ingrained sense of duty but seldom with a sustained interest in imperial development. On the whole they performed their task creditably and efficiently, but they had been trained in military or naval careers and had come from established families with influential connections, and necessarily they were increasingly out of communion with the sentiments of aspiring colonists and immigrants from the British

Isles. Colonial administration in the early nineteenth century was in the hands of men who echoed the views of former generations; the political minority that was thinking afresh on imperial questions remained a peripheral influence until the 1830s.

For many of those who went out of their own volition to the colonies, the venture was a speculative one in which a quick fortune was the expected reward for risking life and capital. Those who succeeded sought to preserve their connection with the mother country; they sent their children there to be educated as American planters had been wont to do a century before, they aped the society that they had left behind in Britain, and they occasionally returned to the home country to pass their final years. At the same time, within sections of the colonial communities stirred a political consciousness based squarely on English political philosophy, particularly on that of Burke and the eighteenth-century whigs; the constitution of England was the inspiration of that which the colonists sought for themselves, and 'the rights and liberties of Englishmen' formed the principle upon which their agitation was grounded. Few of the colonial leaders were yet concerned with political democracy. There were liberal thinkers among them, but, as with the merchants and planters of the American Revolution, their reforming zeal was directed against the strong executive authority exercised from London and was not concerned with a broad franchise or popular democracy in the colonies themselves.

The colonial agitation for self-government found a response in London among the colourful band of colonial reformers that collected around Edward Gibbon Wakefield and Charles Buller. The reformers not only attacked the alleged ignorance and narrow-mindedness of the occupants of the Colonial Office but also, after the publication in 1839 of the Durham Report, advocated something akin to responsible government in the colonies at a time when it was regarded by cabinet ministers as outside the realm of practical policy. The report by Lord Durham on the vexed situation in Canada was of general imperial significance because the recommendations were eventually to affect all British settlement colonies. According to the report, one of the principal causes of unrest in the

Canadian provinces was the lack of harmony between the executive and the legislature, and the remedy was to choose executive ministers from the majority grouping in the representative assembly. The British government, however, feared the disruptive effects on the imperial relationship of Durham's recommendation. Lord John Russell denied that the English cabinet system could be properly applied in colonial territories and refused to legislate for the introduction of responsible government because, he said, it would entail an abridgement of the authority of the crown.

In the following years, colonial problems still occupied a relatively minor position on the programme of the British government, which, though badgered by colonial agents and sympathizers, was more interested in the famine in Ireland and the repeal of the corn laws and the navigation acts in 1846 and 1849. The adoption of free trade revolutionized imperial policy. The fiscal advantages to Britain of possessing an empire were now less obvious, and the demise of the colonial reformers in England was hastened. Their influence on British colonial policy was replaced by that of the advanced free traders of the Manchester school led by Richard Cobden and John Bright, whose ideas were already infiltrating the outlook of both political parties in the 1840s, although their most powerful period was in the 1860s. The Manchester school was separatist in its imperial notions, regarding the empire as unnecessary, expensive, and doomed to disruption. Hitherto, it had been possible to argue that colonies brought commercial benefits to the mother country, but by the middle of the nineteenth century this reasoning was being widely refuted. 'The time was', wrote Goldwin Smith in 1863, 'when the universal prevalence of commercial monopoly made it worth our while to hold colonies in dependence for the sake of commanding their trade. But that time has gone. Trade is everywhere free or becoming free; and this expensive and perilous connection has entirely survived its sole legitimate cause.' Britain was the world's largest manufacturer and would dominate the trade of Canadian, African, and Australasian territories whether they were colonies or not, and therefore it was extravagant and unnecessary to maintain military establishments to defend them. The separatist doctrines of the Manchester school permeated the opinions of most Members of Parliament, and in 1852 Disraeli made his reference to the 'wretched colonies' as a 'millstone round our necks'. The doctrines became increasingly characteristic of British opinion, and had it not been for the caution and devotion of the crown's servants in the Colonial Office and overseas the British empire might well have disintegrated into its several parts, connected only by commercial necessity. As it was, the leavening of thought that regarded colonial independence as both inevitable and desirable helped to engender a disinterested imperial policy which ensured that the blunders preceding the American Revolution were not repeated.

The new approach was most in evidence in relation to Canada, where the governor-general, though advised to work as far as possible in harmony with the elected representatives, remained responsible to the sovereign alone and was under no constitutional or conventional obligation to change his advisers whenever they lost the support of the elected majority. Nevertheless, Sir Charles Bagot, during a brief term in Canada in 1842 and 1843, governed in accordance with what Lord John Russell called the 'well-understood wishes' of the people to the point where responsible government in effect existed. With the arrival of Lord Elgin in 1847 responsible government in Canada was assured, for he deliberately retired from the political foreground and, in accordance with instructions, governed on the advice of ministers who commanded a majority among the elected representatives. Once the principle of responsible government had thus been accepted, its extension to New Zealand, Newfoundland, and the Australian colonies followed rapidly.

In an age when the doctrines of the Manchester school were rife and the ultimate severance of the colonies from the mother country was widely considered inevitable, the grant of responsible government might have been regarded in British political circles as a step towards complete independence. The separatist prophecies of the Manchester school were not realized, however. Colonial populations were loyal to what they still regarded as in some respects their homeland, and the grant of responsible government removed the strongest colonial objections to the imperial connection, the permanence of which was thereby assured. In transmitting the royal assent to the Australian constitutions in 1855, Lord John Russell remarked appreciatively on the bonds that still linked Britain with the colonists, who, 'by their avowed desire to assimilate their institutions as far as possible to those of the mother-country', had proved that their imperial loyalty was 'not merely the expression of a common sentiment arising from common origin, but connected with a deliberate attachment to the ancient laws of the community from which their own was sprung'. While the colonies would continue their independent course, therefore, Russell was confident that they would combine with it 'the jealous maintenance of ties thus cemented alike by feeling and principle'. In the application of responsible government, Britain had not only discovered a salve for colonial discontent but also prepared the way for the development of a wholly new concept of the imperial association.

By 1868 the separatist philosophy appeared to be in complete ascendancy. Before the end of the year Disraeli and the Conservatives were swept from power by Gladstone and a large Liberal majority that saw few virtues in British imperialism. No government since the dissolution of Lord Aberdeen's in 1856 had contained so extensive and varied a range of talent as Gladstone's at the end of 1868, when he formed his first and, as it proved, most successful ministry. It came to power at a time of economic gloom: there had been a commercial depression since the spring of 1866, regular trade was stagnating, investment had been retarded by the disclosure of irregularity and unsoundness in the affairs of the railways and other joint-stock undertakings, the Royal Bank of Liverpool had failed, and in the early days of 1869 the Lancashire cotton mills were reduced to working half time. It was a reforming administration and in six years of office it created a national system of primary education, extended the rights of trade unions, improved army organization, removed religious obstacles to entry to universities, and ensured the secrecy of voting at elections.

The government's attitude towards the empire was frankly separatist, but the cabinet was not unversed in colonial affairs. Gladstone himself had been both under-secretary and secretary of state for the colonies; Edward Cardwell, the secretary of state for war, had also been colonial secretary; Chichester Fortescue, the chief secretary for Ireland, and W. E. Forster, the minister for education, had been under-secretaries of state for the colonies and, indeed, had pronounced imperialist sympathies; Robert Lowe, the chancellor of the exchequer, and Hugh Childers, the first lord of the admiralty, had each spent some years in Australia. And notwithstanding the cabinet's alleged indifference to the imperial connection with the overseas settlements, four members, including the prime minister and the secretary of state for the colonies, were present on Wednesday evening, 10 March 1869, at the inaugural dinner of a colonial association which had been founded the previous year as a reaction to the separatist philosophy and which was to develop into what a century later had become the Royal Commonwealth Society.

Chapter Two

Foundation of the
Royal Colonial Institute (1868–1882)

THERE had been attempts before 1868 to organize a colonial society in London. One established as early as 1837 had lasted only five years, and a body known as the General Association for the Australian Colonies that began functioning in 1855 had petered out through lack of funds in 1862.[1] The Australian association, however, at one time had well over 200 members, and although it had been founded principally to promote the passage of the Australian constitution bills, it also campaigned for a federal arrangement between the Australian colonies, for colonial representation in the United Kingdom, and for harmonious relations between the mother country and the colonies. Among the leaders were James Youl, Hugh Childers, Sir Charles Clifford, F. G. Dalgety, F. A. Du Croz, F. H. Dutton, A. L. Elder, Arthur Hodgson, Sir George MacLeay, Sir Charles Nicholson, William Westgarth and Edward Wilson, all of whom were to be among the early members of the colonial society founded later. In 1857 the council of the Society of Arts had considered a proposal by Hyde Clarke emphasizing the need for 'a colonial centre in London', but the idea was one the society could not have actively entertained without sacrificing its major objectives and freedom of action.[2] During the 1860s Australian colonists living in London tried to form a colonial club, but there was anxiety lest it acquire a virtually exclusive Australian character, and the scheme was dropped when Lord Carnarvon, who had been

---

[1] Its minute book is now kept in the library of the Royal Commonwealth Society. For the establishment of the society in 1837 see *Journal of the Royal Colonial Institute*, I (1891), 255–7.

[2] D. Hudson and K. W. Luckhurst, *The Royal Society of Arts, 1754–1954* (London 1954), 344–9.

well disposed towards it, left the Colonial Office in 1867.[3]

Prominent among the Australian colonists in London was Sir Charles Nicholson, who had returned to England in 1862 after nearly thirty years in Australia, including ten as speaker of the New South Wales legislative council. Nicholson had been noted for his advocacy of popular education while in New South Wales and had been closely concerned with the foundation of the University of Sydney. In London he was active as a magistrate and chairman of an insurance company and retained an interest in matters affecting the colonies. He deplored the attitude of the Manchester school, and found indifference towards the empire prevalent among political leaders and a large proportion of the English people, who, he wrote, talked 'with the greatest complacency of abandoning the colonies altogether, looking upon them as mere burdens on the parent state'. He was in contact with other colonists, and one evening in March 1867, while dining with Canadians visiting London to discuss the terms of the proposed federation of the Canadian provinces, the idea of a colonial institution in London was resurrected.[4] It failed to mature until taken up by A. R. Roche, Hugh E. Montgomerie and Viscount Bury in 1868, when a meeting called by public advertisement to consider the formation of a colonial society was held on Friday, 26 June, at Willis's Rooms in King Street, St. James's. Present at the meeting were Nicholson and most of those who, like him, had been taking a vigorous and sympathetic interest in colonial affairs and were distressed by the influence of the separatists on parliamentary and public opinion in Britain.

Bury was voted into the chair and in his opening statement made clear that what was proposed had several times already been canvassed by various people:

I need not remind you that a great want has often been felt by gentlemen connected with our several colonies, on arriving in England, of some meeting-place, some centre of attraction where they might resort on their arrival, and where they might obtain the latest intelligence from their own part of the world, and place

[3] *Proceedings of the Royal Colonial Institute*, 1 (1870), 9–12. D. S. Macmillan, 'Australians in London, 1857–1880', *Royal Australian Historical Society Journal and Proceedings*, 44 (1958), 164.

[4] Macmillan, loc. cit., 156–7, 161–2.

themselves in communication with other gentlemen connected with their own and other colonies, and with them concert such measures as should tend to the interest of all. We want some medium by which we may form our scattered colonies into a homogeneous whole.

To accomplish this, he suggested that a colonial society should be formed:

As you are probably aware, many gentlemen have entertained the idea before this of establishing some kind of colonial association in London; but it is only now that that idea has assumed a tangible shape.

One of the principal functions of the society, according to Bury, should be the presentation of papers on colonial subjects for consideration at regular meetings. After the ensuing discussion, the formation of a colonial society was unanimously approved. It was also agreed that the society should be 'entirely non-political, and that any organization for political purposes be forbidden by the fundamental rules of the society'. Another resolution defined the projected society's objects:

To occupy as regards the colonies the position filled by the Royal Society with regard to science, or the Royal Geographical Society with regard to geography; that a lecture-hall, a library and reading-room, and a museum of science, industry, and commerce be opened as soon as the funds of the society will allow, where the natural products and resources of the colonies will be exhibited; to afford opportunities for the reading of papers, and the holding of discussions upon colonial subjects generally; and to undertake those investigations in connection with the colonies which are carried out in a more general field by the Royal Society, the Society of Arts, the Royal Geographical Society, and by similar bodies in Great Britain.

Finally, the meeting formed a provisional committee to draw up rules for the government of the society and to prepare lists of those willing to serve on the governing council.[5]

The provisional committee presented its recommendations to a general meeting on 12 August under the chairmanship of Chichester Fortescue, later chief secretary for Ireland. The committee had based the rules it suggested on those of the Royal Geographical Society and the Society of Arts, and after amendment at the general meeting they were adopted. Bury

[5] *Proceedings*, 1 (1870), 2–17.

was elected president of the new society, which appointed several vice-presidents and members of a governing council that had the power to add to its own number, to fill the offices of treasurer, secretary and trustees, and to elect fellows. The council held its first meeting the same day at the Colonial Office and appointed W. C. Sargeaunt as honorary treasurer and A. R. Roche as honorary secretary. At this stage, the society was inevitably rich in leaders and deficient in ordinary members, but applications were soon being received from enthusiasts in the overseas empire, and in October the council established a category of non-resident fellows by admitting persons living in the colonies. [6]

On Wednesday, 10 March 1869, the Colonial Society held an inaugural dinner. It was a distinguished gathering: among the more than 200 guests who sat down to dinner were Gladstone and Granville, the Duke of Manchester, the Marquis of Normanby and Lord Alfred Churchill, along with a strong contingent of persons with Australian connections, notably Hugh Childers, a cabinet minister who had experience of politics in Victoria, William Westgarth, who had experience of commercial affairs in Victoria, Captain Charles Sturt, the explorer, and W. C. Wentworth, once a considerable force in New South Wales politics. Of the many speeches during the evening, Gladstone's was, naturally, the most important. He declaimed in general terms about the spirit of brotherhood and spoke of the society 'handing down from generation to generation the great and noble tradition of the unity of the British race'. A separatist tone was detectable in some of the speeches, but the only jarring note was struck by the United States minister, Reverdy Johnson, who tactlessly alluded to colonies ultimately leaving the British empire and being absorbed into an American empire. Gladstone reported the speech to the Queen, who, it may be safely assumed, was not amused. [7]

From the beginning Bury hoped that the society would secure the royal prefix to its title and he fastened on to 'an unpremeditated opinion' that Gladstone let fall in conversation to the effect that on 'certain suppositions, the Colonial Society

[6] Council Minute Books, 1 (12 Aug. 1868), 2; (6 Oct.), 11; (16 Dec.), 21.

[7] Gladstone to Granville, 11 March 1869, P.R.O. 30/29/57, fol. 13 (Granville Papers: Public Record Office, London), *Proceedings*, 1 (1870), 22–35.

might be an institution proper to be decorated with Her Majesty's name'.[8] In May 1869 Bury reminded Gladstone of the matter, which was passed to Granville for his recommendation and put to the Queen in June by the lord president of the council.[9] With the Queen's approval the society became known as the Royal Colonial Society, but the Royal College of Surgeons protested that the initials were now the same as its own and likely to cause confusion, and at the prompting of the Colonial Office it was decided by a vote of a general meeting on 7 March 1870 to assume the title of the Royal Colonial Institute.[10]

It might have been expected that the institute's political appeal would be more to Conservatives than to Liberals, but membership was at first reasonably well balanced in this respect. At its foundation, the institute was not an advocate of a new imperialism, which would have necessarily given it strong political overtones. Its declared objects were sober, restrained and, politically, unexceptional:

to provide a place of meeting for all gentlemen connected with the colonies and British India, and others taking an interest in colonial and Indian affairs; to establish a reading-room and a library, in which recent and authentic intelligence upon colonial subjects may be constantly available, and a museum for the collection and exhibition of colonial productions; to facilitate the interchange of experiences among persons representing all the dependencies of Great Britain; to afford opportunities for reading papers, and for holding discussions upon colonial subjects generally; and to undertake scientific, literary, and statistical investigations in connection with the British empire. The rules do not permit of any paper being read, or discussion being held, tending to give to the society a political or a party character.[11]

Moreover, in its early years, at least, the institute enjoyed a distinguished leadership in which both political parties were represented.

The first president, Viscount Bury, was, at this time, a Liberal. He was married to the daughter of Sir Allan MacNab,

[8] Gladstone to Granville, 20 May 1869, P.R.O. 30/29/57, fol. 33.

[9] Bury to Gladstone, 15 May 1869, R.C.S. Archives. Granville to Grey, 7 June 1869, P.R.O. 30/29/32, fol. 38. Granville to Bury, 18 June 1869, R.C.S. Archives.

[10] Co. Mins. 1 (20 Aug. 1869), 66. Roche to Barrett, 17 Aug. 1869, Letter Books, 1 (1868–73), 121.

[11] *Proceedings*, 1 (1870), 20.

a prominent political leader in Canada, where he had served under Lord Elgin and Sir Edmund Head both as civil secretary and as superintendent of Indian affairs. He had drawn upon this Canadian experience in writing a two-volume history of North America that was published in 1865. In this work Bury hoped that Britain had 'learned the lesson taught by the war of American independence' and would not, even if it were able, prevent the colonies severing their connection with the mother country, a separation that he regarded as ultimately inevitable. The procedure and timing of this separation, he suggested, should be decided 'by statesmen and on statesman-like grounds' and should not be left to chance:

It is not argued that separation should take place now, nor in five years, nor in ten; it is not even proposed that the time of separation should be hastened by a single day; it is only urged that the certainty of eventual separation should be recognized at once, that the manner in which it is to take place, and the treaty which must be substituted for the present connection should be arranged now, while it may yet be done in peace, without reference to any immediate subject of dispute.

He even drafted in specific terms the articles of separation which he proposed should be agreed upon between Britain and North America.[12] By 1868, however, Bury was championing empire unity against the doctrines of the separatists, and in 1869 he used the occasion of the Colonial Society's inaugural dinner to attack the influence of Goldwin Smith and his disciples: 'The existence of such a school as this', he said, 'would of itself be a sufficient reason for the existence of our society.'[13]

There was clearly a possibility that Bury's role as president of the Royal Colonial Institute would conflict on some issues with his support of the Gladstone government as a Liberal Member of Parliament, and if such a conflict of loyalties should have arisen he would certainly have placed his parliamentary career first. He was ambitious and sought opportunities to serve Gladstone,[14] and in April 1870 he was happy to reply for the government to a motion by R. R. Torrens, another Liberal,

[12] Viscount Bury, *Exodus of the Western Nations* (2 vols., London 1865), I, 17–28; II, 423, 459–63.
[13] *Proceedings*, 1 (1870), 53–4.
[14] Bury to Gladstone, 26 Nov. 1868, Additional Manuscripts 44416, fol. 251 (Gladstone Papers: British Museum, London).

and argue that the emancipation of the colonies was a law of nature and that Britain 'could not successfully contend against that law'.[15] In the institute's dealings with the colonial secretary Bury was unable to use his political influence to the institute's advantage: he was, as a press critic observed, 'the last man in the world to be an efficient representative of any opinion adverse to that of "my noble friend"'.[16] Bury relinquished the presidency of the institute in 1871, and later left his party to become a Conservative and his denomination to become a Roman Catholic.

Bury's successor as the institute's president was the Duke of Manchester, whose election was received by one press commentator with the faint praise that it 'might have been worse'.[17] His principal overseas interest was New Zealand, and he was a strong believer in closer imperial union, looking forward to the creation of a representative empire council, a 'central body in the Constitution of the Empire, with effective legislative power, and a power and an influence over the destinies and the laws of the country'.[18] He had originally favoured a society with a more distinctly political complexion, and as president he was anxious to preserve its character as 'a scientific and literary association' and resisted suggestions that would turn it more into a social club.[19] Manchester discharged his duties diligently, was a prolific correspondent, presided at meetings regularly, and attempted to extend the institute's influence by his travels in the overseas empire. His leadership, supported by the honorary secretary, was to a large extent instrumental in expanding the influence and enhancing the reputation of the institute in the 1870s.

Among other important names in the founding years of the institute were those of Sir Frederic Rogers and Herman Merivale, permanent under-secretaries of state, the one for the colonies and the other for India, both of whom served on the first council. Sir George MacLeay, a companion of Sir Charles Sturt on his exploration of the River Murray in Australia, became a fellow in 1869 and one of the earliest and longest serving members of the council. The Marquis of Normanby, a vice-president, brought to the council the zeal for empire to be expected of someone seeking further employment as a colonial

[15] U.K. *Parliamentary Debates*, 200 (House of Commons, 26 April 1870), coll. 1848–62.
[16] *Standard*, 24 Dec. 1869.   [17] *European Mail*, 14 July 1871.
[18] *Proceedings*, 1 (1870), 31.   [19] Ibid., 1 (1870), 2; 17 (1886), 411.

governor, an ambition that was satisfied in 1871 when his entreaties were acknowledged by Gladstone and he was appointed to Queensland. [20] The engaging Chichester Fortescue, a more decided Liberal than Bury, played a significant role in the foundation of the Colonial Society, but as chief secretary for Ireland in Gladstone's administration he had little time after 1868 for other than Irish affairs. Australians were always prominent, and Sir Charles Nicholson, Francis P. de Labillière and Sir James Arndell Youl were especially active. Labillière had been born in Melbourne and moved to London during his childhood. He was an ardent advocate of Britain's closer association with the colonies, and at a meeting of the institute in 1870 suggested that a union between the mother country and the colonies was not only possible but should be made indissoluble. [21] He had joined the Colonial Society in 1869 and was a frequent contributor to its general meetings; he was an enthusiastic and conscientious member of the council for over twenty years, and for a time acted as assistant secretary. His son later became the Dean of Westminster and in 1944 was invited to be a vice-president and honorary chaplain to the society. [22] Youl was among the society's founders, served on the provisional committee and on the council, was chairman of its finance committee for thirty-five years, and retained a working interest in the management of its affairs until his death in 1904. Born in New South Wales, he had moved to Tasmania as a child and served that colony as its political agent in London, where for seven years he was also the secretary and treasurer of the General Association for the Australian Colonies. He continued to pay attention to Australian affairs and was a director of the Commercial Banking Company of Sydney, but the achievement for which he is usually mentioned was the introduction of salmon and trout into the rivers of Tasmania after patient experimentation, although it was to the efforts of the Acclimatization Society that the credit was given when, at the end of 1866, salmon produced from ova imported from England was first caught on the Tasmanian coast. [23]

[20] Gladstone–Normanby correspondence, 10 and 11 Dec. 1868, Add. MSS. 44417, foll. 19, 22, 84. *Proceedings*, 3 (1872), 76.
[21] *Proceedings*, 2 (1871), 48–57.   [22] Co. Mins. 22 (15 March 1944), 88.
[23] *Athenaeum*, No. 2050 (9 Feb. 1867), 193. *The Times*, 7 and 9 June 1904.

By the beginning of the 1870s the government of the institute was established and functioning smoothly. In 1878, when the Prince of Wales agreed to become president, the office assumed a largely ornamental nature, and the rules were amended to provide for a chairman of council who would preside at meetings in the president's absence. Manchester, who had been the president, was duly elected by council into the new office.[24] The council was chosen from the resident fellows and comprised twenty-four members in addition to the president, the vice-presidents, the four trustees, and the treasurer and the secretary. It formed committees on finance and housing, on the library, and on papers and publications, each of which was empowered to make recommendations to the council, whose approval was required for any action to be fully authoritative.[25] A part of the council's membership retired periodically but was eligible for re-election, and there soon appeared a tendency to re-elect the same men to council year after year, with the result that by the end of the 1870s it was already developing a gerontic and patrician character.

The council was assisted by a small number of devoted and often long-serving administrators. Initially it relied heavily on the services of Alfred R. Roche, the secretary, and Frederick F. Roche, the assistant secretary. Alfred Roche had lived in Canada, campaigned in the Montreal press for the development of the north-west territories, then under the jurisdiction of the Hudson's Bay Company, and initiated the agitation which eventually led to the transference of the territories to the Dominion of Canada.[26] Roche resigned in 1871 and was succeeded by Dr. Charles W. Eddy, who had some experience of Australia, kept sheep on his land at Putney, and used the rooms of the institute for attempts to cultivate eucalyptus shoots. Though trained for the medical profession, he never practised in England, and from 1862 until his death was secretary to the Danube and Black Sea Railway Company. His appointment as secretary to the Royal Colonial Institute was regarded in the press as auguring well for its future success and

[24] *Proceedings*, 9 (1878), 394–401.

[25] Ibid., 8 (1877), 445–54. A. Folsom, *The Royal Empire Society: Formative Years* (London 1933), 66–7.

[26] Co. Mins. 1 (31 May 1869), 55; (7 March 1870), 82. Folsom, *Royal Empire Society*, 37.

C

usefulness, and although he was somewhat unsystematic and untidy in the regular work of administration, he was indefatigable and believed in the institute concerning itself less with publicity and display than with working practically and unobtrusively to strengthen relations between the mother country and the colonies.[27] Eddy died suddenly on Glasgow railway station in 1874, and was succeeded as secretary by Frederick Young, assisted by Labillière. Young had been a fellow since 1869 and proved to be a diligent secretary for twelve years, after which he became a vice-president. He remained active in the institute far into an extended old age, when he was inclined to refer to the length of his service with wearisome frequency, but his devotion and industry were undoubtedly important factors in the institute's development in the last quarter of the nineteenth century. He was knighted in 1888.

Membership of the institute grew rapidly at the start. The first fully financial member was Edward Wilson, who had been an enthusiastic advocate of the formation of a colonial society in London.[28] As a young man Wilson had been imbued with radical ideas. After emigrating to Australia in 1841 he had purchased the Melbourne *Argus* and used it to direct his own fierce brand of journalistic criticism against the colonial government until 1854, the year of the Eureka Stockade, after which he modified his views and the paper became an organ of moderate conservatism. On his return to England he had taken up residence first near London and later at a country house in Kent, where he lived a sociable life in princely style, latterly with his cultivated sister, and where his emus and kangaroos reminded him of his Australian experience.[29] Tall, and not a little conceited, but always a welcome figure at dinners, Wilson was the richest and most colourful of the Anglo-Australians who swelled the institute's early membership. Like Sir Charles Nicholson, he had been disturbed by the popular indifference

[27] Co. Mins. 1 (27 Nov. 1871), 139; (4 Dec.), 141. *Proceedings*, 6 (1875), 1–5. J. R. Boosé, *Memory Serving: Being Reminiscences of Fifty Years of the Royal Colonial Institute* (London 1928), 5–6. Folsom, op. cit., 59–62, 243.

[28] Roche to Wilson, 15 Aug. 1868, Letter Books, 1, pp. 4–5.

[29] W. Westgarth, *Personal Recollections of Early Melbourne and Victoria* (Melbourne 1888), 98–108. A. Serle, *The Golden Age: A History of the Colony of Victoria, 1851–1861* (Melbourne 1963), 18–19. *Proceedings*, 7 (1876), 36–67.

in Britain towards the overseas settlement empire, and the newly-formed colonial society was the natural rendezvous for him, but although he became a member of council he was to play a lesser role in its activities and development than that for which his background, character, bachelorhood, and considerable private fortune appeared to fit him.

By March 1869 the society had over 200 members. The council appealed for names of persons who might be encouraged to join, and proposal forms were circulated with the annual report of 1870. The agents-general of the colonies soon overcame their distrust of the society and joined, and Eddy, while secretary, boosted membership by notifying senior officials in each colony whose names appeared on the Colonial Office list that they had been nominated as fellows and that they should forward to him the requisite fees.[30] Fellows who resided in the United Kingdom were classed as resident and paid an entrance fee of £3 and an annual subscription of £2. Those who lived in the colonies were classed as non-resident and paid an annual subscription of one guinea but no entrance fee until one of a guinea was introduced in 1883. Both resident and non-resident fellows might compound their annual subscription by a single payment that gained them life membership. A resident fellow who was away a year or more could be transferred to the non-resident category, and a non-resident who lived in London for a year or more became subject to the increased subscription of a resident. Elections to membership were made by the council on the nomination of any two fellows, and all fellows received an annual volume of the institute's proceedings.

In 1872 a new category of membership was introduced when the council began the occasional practice of electing honorary fellows: the first to be elected to this category was J. A. Froude, the historian; the second was Alfred Tennyson, the poet laureate, in 1873 in appreciation of his patriotic ode to the Queen. Ladies were not eligible to become fellows. Membership, as was to be expected, was overwhelmingly Anglo-Saxon, and no other races of the empire were significantly represented, although there were a number of Indians and Africans in the 1880s, and several wealthy Creoles contributed in December

[30] Boosé, *Memory Serving*, 7.

1881 to a meeting that discussed Sierra Leone.[31] There were perfectly sensible reasons for what was an inescapable racial imbalance, but racial consciousness was clearly an important contributory factor in the nineteenth century, as Manchester implied in his remarks to a meeting in 1876: 'We must remember', he said, 'that India is a country of very ancient civilization different from our own, whereas the Colonies, from which the bulk of our members come, are all members of our own family civilization, and our own nation.'[32]

The pace of increase in the institute's membership and income was slow for many years. In 1874 the membership was still a mere 420 and the annual income only £906. After 1878, however, following the acceptance of the presidency by the Prince of Wales, membership and income began to increase a little more rapidly, and by 1882 there were 1,613 members and income reached £3,236. By 1884 membership was well past the 2,000 mark, and by 1888 it had passed the 3,000 mark, while the annual income in those years rose to £4,539 and £6,581 respectively.

For many years the institute suffered from the lack of an adequate permanent home of its own. It had access to rooms in Victoria Street, Westminster, provided by the agent-general for Victoria until May 1869, when its funds allowed the occupation and furnishing of a suite of rooms at the Westminster Palace Hotel formerly used by the India Office. It soon moved from Westminster to the first floor of a branch of the Union Bank of London in Suffolk Street, and then again in January 1872 to three rooms on the first floor of Number 15 in the Strand; in the following year rooms on the second floor were added. It was from the rooms in the Strand that the institute's flag, a blue ensign with the inscription 'Royal Colonial Institute, United Empire' was first flown. The need for more extensive premises continued, however, and the room where meetings were held was criticized as 'a pokey hole over a shirt shop'.[33] The difficulty was the cost, which, it was assumed, would be overcome only by increased membership, which, in turn, would intensify the need for yet larger premises. In 1875 one fellow, with the council's permission, placed a book in the

---

[31] *Proceedings*, 13 (1882), 54. C. Fyfe, *A History of Sierra Leone* (London 1962), 433.
[32] *Proceedings*, 8 (1877), 2.　　　[33] Ibid., 9 (1878), 409.

rooms inviting subscriptions towards purchasing new premises, but for a long time his was the only name on the list of contributors.

In 1881 a building committee appointed by the council investigated sites suitable for the erection of the institute's own premises, and in 1883 the council obtained an eighty-year lease of a piece of ground in Northumberland Avenue, leading off Trafalgar Square, at an annual rent of £1,090 commencing in March 1884 and terminating in December 1962. The substantial outlay involved disturbed some members of the finance committee who predicted bankruptcy, but the erection of a new building was now more generally recognized among fellows as essential because, as Sir Henry Barkly told the annual general meeting in 1883, 'it was scarcely respectable that we should be carrying on our operations in the rooms over a hosiery shop in the Strand'.[34] A building fund was opened, and a contract was made with the firm of Patman and Fotheringham for the construction according to the architectural designs of W. A. Habershon of a six-storey building to be completed by March 1885. The building and furnishings required an expenditure of nearly £20,000, but arrangements to lease to the government some of the rooms enabled the institute to recoup the heavy ground rent. The new premises were occupied on 10 August 1885, and at a special general meeting the following March the council was authorized to acquire the freehold. To do this, it borrowed £35,020 at four and one-eighth per cent, the principal and interest repayable over forty years by half-yearly instalments of a little over £897.[35]

At the foundation meeting in 1868 that had led to the formation of the Colonial Society, the establishment of a library had been among the objectives mentioned. Chichester Fortescue on that occasion had urged the formation of a good public colonial library in London, pointing out that the Colonial Office library was not open to the public and, indeed, in practice was not easily accessible for members of the Colonial Office, so lamentably was it lacking in space.[36] As early as November 1868 the council resolved to ask the colonial

---

[34] Ibid., 14 (1883), 363.

[35] Ibid., 1 (1870), 210; 3 (1872), 84; 4 (1873), 211; 5 (1874), 220; 10 (1879), 379; 15 (1884) 4, 141, 222, 332;, 16 (1885), 359; 17 (1886), 210, 411; 18 (1887), 162. Boosé, *Memory Serving*, 5, 53–5. Folsom, op. cit., 72–5.

[36] *Proceedings*, 1 (1870), 6.

governments to supply parliamentary and financial papers for the society's use.[37] Early in December the president and a committee of council persuaded the colonial secretary and the secretary of state for India to invite colonial governors to support the society. The fall of the Conservative government later in the month caused some delay, but the incoming Liberal ministers kept their predecessors' promise, and the result was the acquisition from some governors of books and papers illustrating the development of their colonies. With these donations and others by fellows and well-wishers, the institute by 1873 possessed files of a wide selection of colonial newspapers and about 300 books, the nucleus of the library that was now in the process of formation. The council had appointed a library committee to which a number of fellows were nominated year after year but which never met until January 1880, when it recommended an annual grant of £25 for the purchase of books. The responsibility for managing the library devolved on the secretary and on fellows who agreed to assist in an honorary capacity, but by 1881 the library had so expanded that a full-time salaried officer had become essential and J. S. O'Halloran was appointed librarian and assistant secretary.

The catalogue of the library was first printed in the annual volume of the institute's published proceedings in 1877. A more elaborate catalogue was published in 1886, when the library contained 4,700 volumes and 1,600 pamphlets. It was the work largely of J. R. Boosé, who had entered the institute's service in 1873 at the age of fourteen as a clerk under Eddy. The council had considered the cost of publishing the catalogue as more than the institute itself could bear, and publication was made possible by financial assistance from Charles Washington Eves, a fellow with extensive and profitable West Indian interests, who for some years took a generous interest in expanding the library, especially its collection of material on the West Indies.

From 1869 to 1873 the institute published its proceedings in a new newspaper, the *European Mail*. In 1870 it issued the first of a series of annual volumes containing reports of annual general meetings, of the papers read at ordinary general meetings, and of the discussions to which the papers gave rise. These

---

[37] Co. Mins. 1 (3 Nov. 1868), 13.

volumes were distributed widely in the United Kingdom and the colonies, and after the early numbers, some of which were in paper covers, they were handsomely produced in blue binding until the end of the century, when the discovery that blue faded in tropical conditions led to later numbers appearing in red.[38]

The papers presented at the institute's meetings were generally substantial pieces of work, often of high intellectual quality, and they normally provoked discussion of an equally informed character. The avoidance of party politics was maintained with remarkable success despite the problem of deciding what was admissible and what was not. Every paper to be read before the institute was submitted first to a 'papers committee', which inevitably ran into trouble whenever it decided to reject one. It became increasingly difficult to persuade anyone to serve on this committee and it eventually ceased to function.[39] Occasionally a paper was sent in by a contributor from overseas and read for him by a resident fellow and discussed in the usual way. So far as was possible, the programme each year was arranged to allow for each area of the empire to have at least one evening devoted to it, although over the years Canadian, Australian, and South African topics were more in evidence than Indian or East and West African. For several years most of the papers were printed in pamphlet form for immediate distribution and often were published also in the *European Mail* which, after the termination of its publishing agreement with the institute in 1873, continued to devote some space to the institute's proceedings. This practice did not affect the publication of the papers in more durable form in the annual volume of proceedings, but it did ensure a more extensive circulation than would otherwise have been possible.

The society displayed an aptitude for the social occasion at the inaugural dinner in 1869, and within a few years it had successfully developed the festive side of its affairs. In November 1872 it organized a dinner at the Cannon Street Hotel to commemorate the establishment of telegraphic communication with the Australian colonies the previous month. The hotel was decorated with flags, ladies filled one gallery overlooking the

---

[38] Royal Commonwealth Society *Library Notes*, 18 (June 1958).
[39] Boosé, *Memory Serving*, 33–4.

dining hall, and the band of the Honourable Artillery Company
filled the other as it played music for dinner, during which
a large number of toasts were drunk with cumulative
enthusiasm.[40] In June 1874 the institute held a conversazione
at the South Kensington Museum (later the Victoria and
Albert Museum), the first of what became an important annual
event in the London social season.[41] The Union Jack would
always be suspended in a conspicuous position, the reception
room would be decorated with plants and flowers, and a
military band would play a selection of suitable music. The
first conversazione was attended by over 500 guests, but
by 1882 over 2,000 were attending. The institute was, indeed,
as much a club as a learned body or an imperialist pressure
group. It was a meeting place for those interested in the empire,
an address to which those arriving in England from the colonies
could have their correspondence sent, a place where they could
meet others like themselves or discover the whereabouts in the
United Kingdom of visiting colonial friends.

By 1882 the Royal Colonial Institute was firmly established
as an organization of importance to those interested in colonial
affairs. It was growing, and confidence in its future was
indicated by the decision to erect a permanent headquarters
building. It could not possess property, however, until it was
incorporated, and this, the council suggested to a special
meeting of fellows in March 1882, should be by royal charter,
notwithstanding that it would be more expensive than by an
act of incorporation. Despite some misgivings among a few fellows, the meeting empowered the council to take the steps
necessary to secure a royal charter, and on a petition from
the president, the Prince of Wales, and from the chairman, the
Duke of Manchester, the Queen granted a charter on 26
September 1882. The charter neatly defined the continuing
objects of the society as 'to promote the increase and diffusion
of knowledge respecting as well Our Colonies, Dependencies
and Possessions, as Our Indian Empire, and the preservation
of a permanent union between the Mother Country and the
various parts of the British Empire'.[42]

---

[40] 'Account of the Dinner held at the Cannon Street Hotel on Friday, 15th
November 1872', *Proceedings*, 3 (1872).

[41] Boosé, op. cit., 38–9.   [42] *Proceedings*, 14 (1883), 2. Folsom, op. cit., 79.

Chapter Three

Colonial Policy under
Gladstone and Disraeli (1868–1876)

THE Liberal government that took office in December 1868 was known to include ministers who believed that ultimate separation of the colonies from the mother country was inevitable. It was to be expected, therefore, that critics of the government should interpret the various manifestations of its colonial policy as evidence of a desire to rid the United Kingdom of imperial connections. The historian Froude wrote to John Skelton in 1870 that Gladstone and his colleagues intended deliberately 'to shake off the colonies. They are privately using their command of the situation', he surmised, 'to make the separation inevitable'.[1] Granville, the colonial secretary, was certainly inclined to view the formal links with the self-governing colonies with Laodicean detachment. The government, he told the Canadian governor-general in June 1869, had no wish to maintain the relationship with Canada 'a single year' after it had become injurious or distasteful to the Canadian people:

It has been more and more felt on both sides that Canada is part of the British Empire because she desires to be so; and under the influence of this conviction the attachment of the Colonists to Great Britain has grown with the growth of their independence.

He asked the governor-general to bring to his notice

any line of policy, or any measures which without implying on the part of Her Majesty's Government any wish to change abruptly our relations, would gradually prepare both Countries for a friendly relaxation of them.[2]

[1] J. Skelton, *The Table Talk of Shirley* (Edinburgh 1895), 142.
[2] Granville to Sir John Young, 14 June 1869, C.O. 43/156, pp. 204–5, 208 (Colonial Office Papers: Public Record Office, London).

Since the newly-formed Colonial Society had been conceived largely out of a desire to check what seemed to be a movement towards the disintegration of the empire, there was an obvious possibility that members would disagree with some of the policies of the Gladstone administration. The society, as the president declared in his inaugural address, hoped to counter the theories of those politicians who thought that colonies were 'an excrescence of our empire', an encumbrance and a source of commercial and political loss rather than gain.[3]

The society's propagation of the imperialist cause was not indiscriminate. The council refused a request in 1869 from the National Emigration and Aid Society to join a deputation to the government on state aid for emigration, a subject that Granville thanked Gladstone 'for having killed and buried' in a parliamentary debate on a resolution moved in March 1870 by Robert Torrens.[4] An issue, however, towards which the society could not be wholly indifferent was the government's determination to implement the policy of reducing British garrisons in the colonies. The reduction of the garrisons had been the aim of successive cabinets since the grant of responsible government to the colonies, but its achievement had been hampered by native wars in New Zealand and South Africa and by the need to retain large establishments in Canada during the uncertainty created by the civil war in the United States. The House of Commons had resolved in March 1862 'that where responsible government was given to a colony the primary responsibility of its military defence should also be cast upon it.' It was also moved that the house,

while it fully recognizes the claim of all portions of the British Empire on Imperial aid against perils arising from the consequences of Imperial policy, is of opinion that Colonies exercising the rights of self-government ought to undertake the main responsibility of providing for their own internal order and security.[5]

There was a strong feeling in Britain that the colonies should bear a larger share of their own defence burden, and the

[3] *Proceedings*, 1 (1869), 52.
[4] Co. Mins. 1 (19 April 1869), 49. Roche to Bate, Letter Books, 1, p. 82. Granville to Gladstone, 2 March 1870, Add. MSS. 44167, fol. 21. *Parliamentary Debates*, 199 (H.C., 1 March 1870,) coll. 1063–76.
[5] *Parl. Debs.* 165 (H.C., 4 March 1862), coll. 1035–8.

Liberals came to office at the close of 1868 pledged both to army reorganization and to retrenchment in colonial defence.

The withdrawal of overseas garrisons, however, proved to be a vulnerable feature of the new government's policy because of renewed Maori uprisings in the North Island of New Zealand and the danger of Fenian unrest in Canada. The considerable reduction of colonial garrisons in 1869 was at once resented in Canada, whose protests were ignored despite a Fenian uprising in May 1870. The sharpest reaction was in New Zealand, where only one British battalion remained following the withdrawal of troops that had begun in 1866. The New Zealand government asked for the postponement of the departure of the last British troops and for a loan for defence purposes. Granville rejected both requests. He had a low opinion of New Zealand's native policy, deplored the confiscation by the settlers of Maori lands, thought the New Zealand government had been lethargic in creating its own local military force with which to repress disaffection, and believed the Maori insurrection to be no longer really dangerous.[6] He advised the governor that, despite the agitation, there was no reason for anyone to expect the decision to be modified: 'The policy of Her Majesty's Government', he insisted, 'has been uniformly that which has been communicated to you—the policy of immediate withdrawal.'[7]

Granville's arguments against conceding the requests aroused protests in New Zealand, where the tone of his remarks was commonly regarded as indicative of a desire to sever the imperial connection with New Zealand. In the United Kingdom his decision had the full support of the prime minister: 'My minute', Gladstone assured him, 'was in decided affirmation of what you had done.'[8] Granville was aware, however, that his action had not pleased the Queen:

The Queen has said nothing to me about politics, excepting to express doubts of our Colonial policy, and strong objections against our over economy. H.M.'s principal objections to the latter were 1st that England was being reduced to the state of a second rate

[6] Granville to Bowen, 21 May 1869, C.O. 209/210, foll. 320, 438–41. Granville to Bowen, 7 Oct. 1869, *Parliamentary Papers*, 1870, Vol. 50, C.83, pp. 196–7.

[7] Granville to Bowen, 18 June 1869, C.O. 209/210, foll. 391–2.

[8] Gladstone to Granville, 21 May 1869, P.R.O. 30/29/57, fol. 35.

power, and 2nd that it would be disadvantageous to the Sovereign if all places available for old Household servants were abolished.[9]

Press comment was divided. *The Times* and *Morning Post*, for example, supported Granville's action, but elsewhere it was criticized by one editorial as a 'notable attempt to teach the colonies self-reliance *per saltum*', and was attacked by another as evidence that the government had not only accepted Goldwin Smith's separatist colonial policy but was acting on it.[10] In Parliament, Lord Carnarvon, one of Granville's Conservative predecessors at the Colonial Office, believed that there should be no retreat from the course adopted but suggested that the government should take steps to improve communications between New Zealand and the mother country and ensure that misunderstanding in the colonies about British policy should not recur.[11] Lord John Russell protested that the withdrawal of troops had been made with an unnecessary haste that made it appear part of a process of ridding the mother country of the colonies. Granville blandly recounted the protest in a letter to Gladstone:

Johnny Russell wrote a violent criticism to me on my Colonial policy in which he compared himself to Oliver Cromwell and Chatham, and me to Lord North and Geo. Grenville. I rejoined much too good-humouredly, my private Secretary thinks—and I have had a rejoinder, in which amongst other things he says
'That which I wish to see is a Colonial Representative Assembly sitting apart from our Lords and Commons voting us supplies in aid to our Navy and Army, and receiving in return assurances of support from the Queen.'
Shall we immortalize your administration by proposing this?[12]

The attempt to portray the withdrawal of the garrison in New Zealand and the intended withdrawal of that in Canada as a step towards separating the colonies from the mother country signified the development of a new imperialist movement. This development found expression in the motion introduced in the Commons in 1870 by Torrens, who sought a select committee 'to inquire into the political relations and modes of

[9] Granville to Gladstone, 21 Nov. 1869, Add. MSS. 44166, fol. 216.
[10] *Standard*, 2 Oct. 1869. *Spectator*, 24 July 1869.
[11] *Parl. Debs.* 198 (H.L., 27 July 1869), coll. 779–82.
[12] Granville to Gladstone, 2 Sept. 1869, Add. MSS. 44166, foll. 153–4.

official inter-communication between the self-governing Colonies and this Country, and to report whether any or what modifications are desirable, with a view to the maintenance of a common nationality cemented by cordial good understanding.'[13]

The most dramatic reaction, however, came from within the ranks of the Royal Colonial Society. Henry Blaine, Henry Sewell, James Youl, and Edward Wilson were the leaders of a meeting held at the society's rooms on 4 August 1869 and attended by colonists living in England who were disturbed by the government's attitude towards the colonies, and more especially towards New Zealand. The meeting decided to appoint a committee to communicate with colonial governments about the 'present state of relations between the Mother Country and her Colonies', and on 13 August Blaine, Sewell, and Youl addressed a letter to the various colonies declaring that the constitution of the Colonial Office was 'ill adapted for carrying on friendly intercourse with Colonial Governments in which Responsible Government has been established'.[14]

Granville was alarmed by the idea, and Sir Frederick Rogers at the Colonial Office drafted a dispatch for him designed, as Rogers put it, 'to turn the flank' of those who were trying to arrange what he regarded as 'an anti-Downing Street Colonial Conference'.[15] The dispatch, dated 8 September 1869 and addressed by Granville to colonial governors, deprecated the idea of 'a standing representation of the Colonial Empire in London' and maintained that the motive for suggesting it was based on a misrepresentation of the government's colonial policy. There was no cause or common ground to warrant such a conference, he argued, and the wishes of the colonies would be more effectually brought to the notice of the British government by their governors and by their recognized agents in London.[16]

The critics of the conference suggestion tended to direct their strictures not only at the originators but at the whole group of

[13] *Parl. Debs.* 200 (H.C., 26 April 1870), col. 1847.
[14] *Parl. Paps.* 1870, Vol. 49, C. 24.
[15] F. Rogers to Lady Rogers, Nov. 1869, *Letters of Frederick Lord Blachford, Under-Secretary of State for the Colonies, 1860–71*, ed. G. E. Marindin (London 1896), 279.
[16] *Parl. Paps.* 1870, Vol. 49, C. 24.

enthusiasts that formed the essential core of the colonial society. Sections of the press were particularly disdainful:

> It is always curious and interesting to observe how a few worthy and intelligent gentlemen of leisure, possessed with a laudable ambition to rise superior to prosperous obscurity and ease, and to rescue their names at least from retirement, can persuade themselves that they are an army of martyrs, and that by dint of making as large a number as possible of her Majesty's subjects discontented they can save the integrity of the Empire.[17]

Blaine, Sewell, and Youl had not acted on behalf of the society, but they were prominent members of it, they borrowed its rooms for their meeting, and they used its address for their letters. Bury, as president of the society, had written to Granville on 25 August explaining that, although the authors of the letter to the colonial governments were members, the society was 'not in any way responsible for the views advanced'. In October, however, Bury allowed himself to be nominated into the chairmanship of an enlarged committee which was attempting to organize the proposed colonial conference and which, at his suggestion, communicated with the government in the hope of being able to act as far as possible in concert with it.[18] This strengthened the impression that the proposed conference was a brainchild of the colonial society. Moreover, other members of the society, including the Duke of Manchester, Leonard Wray, Nicholson, Wilson, Labillière, Young, Eddy, Roche, and William Westgarth, joined Bury, Blaine, Sewell, and Youl in a deputation to the Colonial Office to protest that Granville, in his dispatch to colonial governors, had mis-construed the appeal for a conference, which, they insisted, had not been devised in any spirit of hostility towards the British government. Newspaper reporters were excluded from the deputation's meeting with the colonial secretary, but the Colonial Office produced for the press an authorized account of his reply that, according to Youl, was not entirely accurate.[19] According to this account, Granville told the deputation that there appeared to be confusion over the aims of the suggested

---

[17] *Daily News*, 17 Dec. 1869.

[18] *Parl. Debs.* 200 (H.C., 26 April 1870), col. 1853. *The Times*, 2 Sept. 1869. *European Mail*, 3 Dec. 1869. Bury to Granville, 17 Oct. 1869, R.C.S. Archives.

[19] *Standard*, 24 Dec. 1869.

conference, which was described variously as intended to define relations between the mother country and the colonies and to supply knowledge of local conditions in the colonies, and he questioned the value of it for either purpose:

I doubt whether any attempt to define our relations more strictly would have a strengthening effect. Many a man and wife notwithstanding occasional differences, live happily together, who could not do so if they had called in a lawyer to define how much each was to yield on every occasion, and what the terms of a possible separation should be.

He also declared that the conference committee's meetings were not being conducted in a friendly and co-operative spirit towards the Colonial Office.[20] The deputation marked the end of the society's flirtation with the colonial conference committee, whose chairmanship Bury hastily resigned with a pointed reminder to Youl that the committee had no formal connection with the society.[21] He told Parliament later that

A sort of colonial 'Cave of Adullam' came to be formed at the Eastend of the town, around which every description of colonial discontent appeared to have a tendency to crystallize itself. He could, under the circumstances, only dissociate himself as quickly as possible from what he believed to be an utterly false move.[22]

When a conference to discuss colonial questions was eventually assembled in London in July 1871, the council of the Royal Colonial Institute resolved not to be officially associated with it. Nevertheless, individual members of council and fellows of the institute were at liberty to attend the conference in a private capacity, and many did so, one of them, Labillière, acting as the secretary.[23]

The proposal for a colonial conference, as Granville and the Colonial Office had expected, was not endorsed by the colonies.

[20] *Daily News*, 17 Dec. 1869.

[21] *The Times*, 28 Dec. 1869. Carnarvon had threatened to resign from the society if it became involved in the colonial conference: Carnarvon to Bury, 25 Oct. 1869, R.C.S. Archives.

[22] *Parl. Debs.* 200 (H.C., 26 April 1870), col. 1853.

[23] Co. mins. 1 (17 July 1871), 131. C. S. Blackton, 'Australian Nationality and Nationalism: The Imperial Federationist Interlude, 1885–1901', *Historical Studies Australia and New Zealand*, 7 (Nov. 1955), 2.

Granville described it in November 1869 as 'made by a self-constituted triumvirate' and believed that few, if any, of the colonies would agree to it:

> I do not know a single thing the Australians want which we have not given or are ready to give. We wish to remain on the most friendly terms with them, but to let them govern themselves. They do not want to have our troops—although some of them retain them on payment of a small sum of money. We are on the best terms with Canada. I see at the very first meeting of the Colonists they quarrelled among themselves—one man going for the maintenance of the Established Church in Jamaica.

He could think of no colony other than New Zealand, he asserted, with which the British government had any difference.[24] Granville's dispatch to the colonial governors was effective, as Rogers, its author at the Colonial Office, noted with satisfaction:

> It seems to have answered its purpose, for I hear they complain that till that dispatch went round they got nothing but favourable answers, and now they get nothing but unfavourable answers. They are, as may be seen by the papers, agitating to the best of their powers, but I think we shall beat them.[25]

Although the promoters of the conference had strong Australian connections, the Australian colonies were its bitterest critics. Blaine, Sewell, and Youl had been warned by the agent-general for Victoria that the colonies would be jealous of any attempts to interpose a self-constituted, quasi-representative body between themselves and the British government, but the warning went unheeded.[26]

The Queensland government referred disparagingly to 'the mischievous interference of self-constituted colonial societies and other pretended representatives of the colonies in England', and elsewhere the matter was derided, both in parliaments and in the press.[27] 'At first sight the affair really seemed almost too ridiculous for belief', commented a Sydney editorial:

---

[24] Granville to Glyn, 27 Nov. 1869, P.R.O. 30/29/77.

[25] F. Rogers to Lady Rogers, Nov. 1869, *Blachford Letters*, 279.

[26] H. L. Hall, *Australia and England: A Study in Imperial Relations* (London 1934), 185.

[27] E. Fitzmaurice, *The Life of Granville George Leveson Gower, Second Earl of Granville, 1815–1891* (2 vols., London 1905), II, 21.

To think that the Australian colonies, for instance, to which responsible government and representative institutions have long been conceded, should recognize any such power of summoning a conference on the part of a few holiday-makers on the other side of the globe, scarcely any of whom would have a chance of election to our local Parliament if they offered themselves, was almost impossible. [28]

The resentment at what was regarded as patronizing interference was reflected throughout colonial comment:

Some people in London appear to have been seized with the idea that it is their special mission to provide for the future of Australia, and they seem desirous of emulating the Abbé Sieyes in the number and variety of their constitutional nostrums for what they believe to be our complaints. [29]

Press opinion was reflected in the New South Wales legislative assembly, where government and opposition were united in repudiating the idea of a colonial conference and in characterizing its proposers as presumptuous busybodies. [30] In the Victoria legislative assembly George Higinbotham introduced resolutions inspired by opposition to the colonial conference proposal that were debated on five nights during November 1869 and discussed again in committee in December. He charged the conference promoters with ignorance and gross presumption, the worse because they had made large fortunes in the colonies, their responsibilities to which they had abandoned in order to enjoy their wealth in London. [31]

It was evident that the colonial critics often equated the conference promoters with the Royal Colonial Society, which, in consequence, shared the odium for the idea and for what were suspected to be the motives behind it. This was not unjustified, for the patrons of the colonial conference campaign included a strong contingent of the society's membership, and many of the papers read before the society in these years propounded ideas about the empire that were akin to those

[28] *Sydney Examiner*, 5 Nov. 1869.

[29] *Australian and New Zealand Gazette*, 11 Dec. 1869, quoting the *Sydney Empire*.

[30] *Argus* (Melbourne), 8 Nov. 1869.

[31] Victoria *Parliamentary Debates*, 9 (L.A., 2 Nov. 1869), 2123–50; (3 Nov.), 2162–88; (10 Nov.), 2212–18; (16 Nov.), 2262–75; (24 Nov.), 2343–50. *Argus*, 8 Nov. 1869. *The Times*, 28 Dec. 1869. E. E. Morris, *A Memoir of George Higinbotham, An Australian Politician and Chief Justice of Victoria* (London 1895), 160.

D

which opinion in the colonies resented. The attacks were in many instances prejudiced, emotional, and unfair, but they had alighted on one of the society's weaknesses. The moving spirits in the society were men with a distinguished colonial past but with a dated and patronizing view of the communities in which they had once served. The society's leaders did not enjoy the *rapport* with the colonies or the understanding of their interests that they imagined they did. The ex-colonists in London, declared a Brisbane article, were in no way representative of colonial opinion, and it asked that the colonies should be left alone by 'the gentlemen who favour Colonial Institutes'.[32] It was natural that men who had enjoyed distinction in the overseas empire, and who, in most cases, found their importance much reduced when they returned to England, should have fostered the development of a society in London which sought to strengthen the imperial connection and which appeared to offer an opportunity for them to re-assert themselves by virtue of their colonial experience. Their error was to expect this experience to entitle them to colonial support when they pretended to represent colonial interests. The early activities of the zealots in the society not only failed to gain colonial support but also petered out in the United Kingdom, where they were of little immediate effect except in producing points for election speeches by Conservative candidates.

Although the society suffered in allowing itself to become associated in the public mind with the campaign for a colonial conference, it was able to feel, nevertheless, that it was participating in what was clearly becoming something close to an imperial expansionist movement in Britain. It is impossible to determine whether the society was a contributor to, or a symptom of, this movement. It was reasonable for the Royal Colonial Institute to believe that its meetings and activities had been contributory factors in the increasing attention that empire affairs were attracting in Parliament, literature, and the press. Attitudes towards the empire, however, were changing on account of a variety of factors, many of which had nothing to do with the institute or its pressure. The reduction of the burden of colonial defence on the British treasury was, in

[32] *Brisbane Courier*, reported in *The Times*, 25 July 1872. See also *The Times*, 26 July 1872.

effect, removing one of the arguments against empire and helping to clear the way for a revival of imperialist sentiment in Britain. International changes being brought about on the continent of Europe, where the problems of German and Italian unification had been settled, led to the emergence of two new powers to compete with Britain's overseas hegemony in the territories of Africa and Asia. Possession of colonies was becoming a matter of national prestige in the European power balance, and it could no longer be argued convincingly that separation was desirable.

Disraeli was impressed by the growing interest in the empire as revealed in the institute, the press, and Parliament, and in a celebrated speech at the Crystal Palace on 24 June 1872 he identified his party with it. The colonies, he pointed out, had shown that they had no wish to see the empire disintegrate, despite the actions of the Gladstone government:

Well, what has been the result of this attempt during the reign of Liberalism for the disintegration of the Empire? It has entirely failed. But how has it failed? Through the sympathy of the Colonies with the Mother Country. They have decided that the Empire shall not be destroyed, and in my opinion no minister in this country will do his duty who neglects any opportunity of reconstructing as much as possible our Colonial Empire, and of responding to those distant sympathies which may become the source of incalculable strength and happiness to this land.[33]

Hitherto, the Conservative party had been barely distinguishable from the Liberal party in its concept of the imperial relationship, but Disraeli had decided to ride with the growing tide of imperialist sentiment. He was personally fascinated more by India than by the self-governing colonies, but his association with the imperialist revival was important for the development of the Royal Colonial Institute, which now took on the appearance of a Conservative organization. Moreover, Disraeli's pronounced inclination to identify the empire with power rather than with liberty or free association accorded well with the views being expressed at the institute which were increasingly expansionist in their philosophy of the empire. After 1874, when Disraeli succeeded Gladstone, the institute

[33] *Selected Speeches of the late Earl of Beaconsfield*, ed. T. E. Kebbel (2 vols., London 1882), II, 531.

was a predominantly Conservative body, both in outlook and membership.

In the 1870s, as the institute became as interested in expanding British rule overseas as in consolidating the ties between the mother country and the self-governing colonies, no issue involving the extension of British dominion escaped its notice and no colonial request for Britain's acquisition of more territories failed to win its support. Its pressure was given weight by the challenge to Britain's imperial hegemony from other powers, notably France, Germany, and Italy, whose growing interest in overseas possessions appeared to invalidate the view that the security of empire could safely be neglected. The expansionists found a ready vehicle for their arguments at the Royal Colonial Institute, where the tenor of the regular discussions was unmistakable. A prime, if extreme, example of the institute's mood was a paper read in January 1875 by Labillière, who enraptured his audience with a vision of the Anglo-Saxon race destined providentially to accomplish the civilization of the world.[34]

Of the specific questions of annexation to which the institute addressed itself, that of Fiji was the first. French, American and British missionaries had established themselves in the Fiji group of islands, and as early as 1855 the leading chief, on the advice of Wesleyan missionaries, had requested annexation by Queen Victoria, but this and later offers had been rejected by the British government.[35] The annexation suggestion, however, gained immediate approval in the Australian colonies, which were always anxious to advance the British frontier in the Pacific. In 1870 a conference of the Australian colonial premiers in Melbourne resolved that it was of the utmost importance that the islands should not fall to any power other than Britain. The Australian pressure made no apparent impression on the government. Granville had been succeeded as colonial secretary in 1870 by Lord Kimberley, whose advice, as Gran-

[34] *Proceedings*, 6 (1875), 36–48. This paper is mentioned by C. A. Bodelsen, *Studies in Mid-Victorian Imperialism* (Copenhagen 1924), 84, and by R. Koebner and H. D. Schmidt, *Imperialism, the Story and Significance of a Political Word, 1840–1960* (London 1964), 131.

[35] The best accounts of these are by J. M. Ward, *British Policy in the South Pacific, 1786–1893* (Sydney 1948), 184–96, and by W. P. Morrell, *Britain in the Pacific Islands* (London 1960), 117–40.

ville's would have been, was against annexation. Gladstone could see no justification for acquiring further territory. Britain, he told Kimberley, should not be 'a party to any arrangement for adding Fiji and all that lies beyond it to the cares of this overdone and over-burdened Government and Empire', though he would not object to the burden being taken on by New South Wales or New Zealand if it were prepared to accept the responsibility.[36] The government, Kimberley later advised Lord Belmore,

must decline to admit that, because a certain number of British subjects proceeding for the most part from the Australian colonies, have established themselves in the Fijis, the Imperial Government is called upon to extend British Sovereignty to these Islands in order to relieve such persons and their property from the risk which they may incur.[37]

All that the government was prepared to do at this stage was to approve a code of regulations for controlling the treatment of Polynesian labourers imported into Fiji.[38]

In June 1872 a debate was initiated in the House of Commons on a motion that 'an humble Address be presented to Her Majesty praying that She will be graciously pleased to establish a British Protectorate at Fiji'. The motion was rejected, but Gladstone denied that his government was committed to not extending the colonial empire in any circumstances:

So far as it was possible to lay down an abstract and general rule with regard to annexation, he was prepared to say that Her Majesty's Government would not annex any territory, great or small, without the well-understood and expressed wish of the people to be annexed, freely and generously expressed, and authenticated by the best means the case would afford.[39]

At the end of January 1873, however, the British chief secretary in Fiji asked the British government whether it would entertain a proposition from the Fiji government to cede the Kingdom 'if

---

[36] P. Knaplund, *Gladstone and Britain's Imperial Policy* (London 1927), 133, 137. E. Drus, 'The Colonial Office and the Annexation of Fiji', *Transactions of the Royal Historical Society*, 32 (1950), 99.

[37] Kimberley to Belmore, 3 Nov. 1871, *Parl. Paps.* 1872, Vol. 43, C. 509, p. 472.

[38] Kimberley to Canterbury, 27 Oct. 1870, *Parl. Paps.* 1871, Vol. 47, No. 435, p. 58.

[39] *Parl. Debs.* 212 (H.C., 25 June 1872), coll. 192, 217.

its King and people once more, and now through the King's responsible advisers, express a desire to place themselves under Her Majesty's rule'. It seemed that there was danger of civil war between the Fijians and the British settlers, and a decision could not be completely evaded, but in June the cabinet decided upon investigation rather than action. A commission of two men was appointed to study and report on the question and to make recommendations on the course to be followed.[40]

It was at this point that the Royal Colonial Institute began to exert its influence in favour of accepting the cession. The council formed a committee for that purpose, and in May 1873 it joined the Aborigines Protection Society in a deputation to the colonial secretary with a memorial urging annexation. The deputation argued that trade followed the flag, that colonies were a source of profit, and that it was questionable whether Australia and New Zealand would submit to an American or German occupation of Fiji. Kimberley, who was now more disposed than Gladstone to appreciate the case for annexation, and, indeed, wrote privately to the prime minister suggesting assent to it, was unable officially to accept the arguments advanced by the deputation, which, if valid, were applicable to other Pacific islands. Possible commercial and humanitarian benefits, he argued, would be offset by the expense of establishing law and order and by the danger of precipitating United States action in Hawaii and other Pacific islands.[41]

By this time, according to one authority, the case for annexation was unanswerable, and the problem was whether the manifest interests of British subjects and the necessity of suppressing British misdeeds in the group 'could be held to outweigh the expense and complications of a new addition to the Empire'. The commission that had been appointed to study the question was not well qualified for the task and was inquiring into conditions already adequately reported to the British government.[42] In its report the commission recommended annexation, concluding with the reflection that it

[40] Ward, *British Policy in the South Pacific*, 243–8. Morrell, *Britain in the Pacific Islands*, 161–2.

[41] Papers left with Kimberley by deputation, 14 May 1873, C.O. 83/4, foll. 313–18. *Proceedings*, 5 (1874), 221. Drus, loc. cit., 101. Ward, op. cit., 241–2. J. I. Brookes, *International Rivalry in the Pacific Islands, 1800–1875* (Berkeley 1941), 381.

[42] Ward, op. cit., 246–55.

could 'see no prospect for these islands, should Her Majesty's Government decline to accept the offer of cession, but ruin to the English planters and confusion in the native Government.'[43] Lord Carnarvon, colonial secretary in Disraeli's administration which had replaced Gladstone's, was not in a position to reject the recommendation, though he said he did not think the calculations of the commissioners were so reliable that they could be trusted on all important points.[44] On 25 August 1874 he telegraphed the Governor of New South Wales 'that he was at liberty to accept the cession of the islands if it should be unconditional or virtually unconditional, and to make arrangements for a temporary Government'.[45] The annexation was effected in the October.

Throughout this period the Royal Colonial Institute had maintained its support for annexation, though the Fiji committee had been able to do little beyond memorialize the colonial secretary and place its views before him. The institute's annual general meeting in June 1874 had carried by acclamation a recommendation that the council should 'consider the expediency of promptly taking steps to convey to Her Majesty's Government the strong opinion of this meeting in favour of the annexation of the Fiji Islands to the British Empire.'[46] The effect of the institute's pressure is impossible to measure; certainly, by the time the council appointed a Fiji committee the eventual annexation of the islands was already regarded by the cabinet as inevitable. Kimberley reminded Gladstone of this in November 1874:

As I expected the Govt. have taken possession of Fiji. All the newspapers almost I see applauded. It is curious that John Bull is not cured of earth hunger by this time. I must say however I think it would have been very difficult to avoid taking Fiji.[47]

Nevertheless, the Conservative government, while agreeing to the annexation of Fiji, was only a whit less cautious than the previous Liberal administration towards further territorial expansion. No such caution inhibited the Royal Colonial

---

[43] *Parl. Paps.* 1874, Vol. 45, C. 1011, p. 16.
[44] *Parl. Debs.* 221 (H.L., 17 July 1874), col. 181.
[45] *Parl. Paps.* 1875, Vol. 52, C. 114, p. 2.   [46] *Proceedings*, 5 (1874), 221.
[47] Kimberley to Gladstone, 4 Nov. 1874, Add. MSS. 44225, foll. 156–7.

Institute, which promptly diverted its attention to other areas where colonial and British imperial interests might be furthered.

In 1875 the institute's protective eye fell upon the contentious question of French and British fishery rights in Newfoundland, which were being studied by an Anglo-French commission with a view to settling the differences between the two countries. In March 1875, at the suggestion of the Duke of Manchester, the council appointed a committee to collect information and draw up a report on French claims.[48] The committee, under the chairmanship of Frederick Young, first met on 12 March, and at a meeting on 21 April resolved to ask William McArthur to put a parliamentary question to the colonial under-secretary concerning the protection of the rights of British fishermen on the Newfoundland shores during the negotiations with France.[49] Carnarvon deprecated the institute's interest in the matter, but in April agreed to receive a deputation from the council. The committee continued to meet during the summer, and at its request James Whitman, a barrister from Nova Scotia, drafted a report on the fisheries for which he was sent an honorarium, one he regarded as inadequate and by virtue of firm words to that effect contrived to secure its increase from ten to twenty-five guineas.[50]

The report concluded that the French had been allowed fishery rights in Newfoundland waters concurrently with British subjects, and had no right to exclude British subjects from occupying the land on that part of the coast called the French shore.[51] The council regarded the report as 'a complete, succinct, impartial, and exhaustive exposition of the facts of a question of most vital importance to the interests, not only of the inhabitants of Newfoundland, but of the whole British Empire'. The report was used by those involved in the negotiation of the dispute, but Carnarvon protested against its publication, believing it unwise to marshal public opinion that could not have any effect on the French government.[52] The council eventually decided to proceed with publication notwithstanding

[48] Co. Mins. 1 (2 March 1875), 334.
[49] Newfoundland Fisheries Committee Minutes, 12 March and 21 April 1875.
[50] Ibid., 9 Oct. 1875.　　[51] *Proceedings*, 7 (1876), 6–35.
[52] Co. Mins. 1 (16 Nov. 1875), 378. Manchester to Young, 15 June 1875, Frederick Young Papers (Royal Commonwealth Society), File I, 57.

opposition at the Colonial Office, assuring itself that the knowledge imparted by the report 'ought to further rather than retard negotiations on the subject, and to lead to a more satisfactory settlement of the question than if the public had not been so fully informed respecting it.'[53] The report appeared in the institute's annual volume of proceedings in 1876, but by that time the question had been dropped by the French and British governments, to await final settlement in the Anglo-French *entente* of April 1904.

The institute's decision to publish the Newfoundland report had been hastened by the suspicion that the British government contemplated the cession of territory along the Gambia in West Africa in a barter arrangement with the French. It was to be expected that a body campaigning for the consolidation and expansion of the empire should be concerned when the government considered abandoning territory. In West Africa the French were established in Senegal and the British in what were no more than coastal colonies at the Gambia, the Gold Coast, and Lagos. The disappearance of the slave trade had drastically reduced European commercial interest in West Africa, and European control was largely confined to the coastal areas and had not penetrated significantly into the hinterland. British interest in West Africa was minimal, and the colonies there were apparently of such slight importance that their abandonment had been canvassed for some years. In 1865 a select committee of the House of Commons had considered that it was 'not possible to withdraw the British Government, wholly or immediately, from any settlements or engagements on the West African coast', but had recommended that settlement on the Gambia should be reduced and 'confined as much as possible to the mouth of the river' and had declared that all further extension of territory 'would be inexpedient'.[54] The recommendation by the Governor of Sierra Leone in 1869 that the Gambia colony be exchanged for French African territory had been agreeable to the Gladstone government, but in July 1870 Kimberley had informed him that, 'in consequence of the outbreak of war between France and Prussia', the government had thought it necessary 'to postpone proceeding with the intended transfer to France of the British Settlements on the

[53] *Proceedings*, 7 (1876), 332.   [54] *Parl. Paps.* 1865, Vol. 5, No. 412, p. 3.

Gambia'.[55] The French reopened the question in 1874 with the suggestion of an exchange of the Gambia for French stations in Guinea, to the east of the Gold Coast. The Disraeli government prevaricated until early in 1875, when another local conflict between the Soninke and the Marabout seemed a likely threat to the Kombo and Bathurst. Carnarvon interpreted this complication as a reason for avoiding any further delay in the negotiations with France.[56]

In the United Kingdom, however, strong opposition to the barter of British subjects arose. The Manchester Chamber of Commerce protested against the idea in October 1875, and less than a week later the council of the Royal Colonial Institute resolved to appoint a committee to collect information and draw up a report on the Gambia question.[57] The report was published in January 1876 and forwarded to the colonial secretary. In adopting it the council felt a duty

to enter an emphatic protest against the cession of the Gambia, on commercial, political, and Imperial grounds, as well as from a sense of the obligations imposed upon the British Empire not to abandon or hand over without their consent, to a Foreign power, any of its subjects, who desire to retain the privileges and benefits of its rule.

The Council therefore trusts that the project of this cession may be immediately given up, even were the advantages to be expected from it more obvious than they appear.[58]

In January 1876 the council decided to send a deputation to the colonial secretary to present its views on the Gambia issue, and in February produced a memorial submitting that there was 'no reason for Great Britain to abandon so important a possession'.[59]

The institute's campaign was a useful supplement to the pressure being applied on the government by other interested bodies. The Manchester Chamber of Commerce sent a deputation to the colonial secretary early in 1876, and a new organization, the Gambia Committee, in effect took over the leadership

[55] Kimberley to Kennedy, 23 July 1870, *Parl. Paps.* 1870, Vol. 50, No. 444, p. 70. Kennedy to Kimberley, 23 Sept. 1870, ibid., 95–6.

[56] Lady Southorn, *The Gambia: the Story of the Groundnut Colony* (London 1952), 175.

[57] *Parl. Paps.* 1876, Vol. 52, C. 1409, pp. 62, 65. Co. Mins. 1 (19 Oct. 1875), 373.

[58] *Proceedings*, 7 (1876), 68–85. *Parl. Paps.* 1876, Vol. 52, C. 1409, pp. 77–8.

[59] Co. Mins. 1 (18 Jan. 1876), 391. *Proceedings*, 7 (1876), 122–3, 332.

of the protest movement. [60] The Gambia Committee's arguments were similar to those put to Carnarvon in February in the institute's memorial, which objected that British subjects could not honourably be abandoned against their will to 'a nation of a different religion', that a transfer was 'very likely to give rise to much confusion and inconvenience, as well as to occasion native wars', and that the river was 'a valuable highway into the interior'.[61] Carnarvon put the case in Parliament for the transfer, and the House of Commons agreed to the appointment of a select committee to consider it, but the government, partly because of clumsiness and vacillation and partly because of deference to the various protests, prolonged the negotiations unduly and the French government reduced its original offer. In March 1876 Carnarvon told the House of Lords that

it now appeared that the French Government were unwilling to give up to them that entire and exclusive control of the coast which Her Majesty's Government expected, and upon which, of course, the articles of agreement were based. Under these circumstances, they had no option but to abandon the negotiations. [62]

The Gambia colony was retained.

The conclusion of the Gambia affair was, in a sense, a victory for the Royal Colonial Institute, the Manchester Chamber of Commerce, the Gambia Committee, and other interests which by public pressure at Westminster, in Whitehall, and in the press had contributed to the government's hesitancy in pursuing the offer from the French government. The institute was motivated less by the commercial and humanitarian arguments that it expertly advanced than by a deepening inner emotion that made the surrender of any portion of the existing empire seem an immoral sacrifice. Its imperial outlook was still as much expansionist as consolidatory, and its mood was illustrated by the cheers at a meeting in June 1876 when a speaker looked forward to the day when the Union Jack would be 'flying permanently in the centre of Africa'. [63] The empire was now

[60] J. F. Hutton, *The Proposed Cession of the British Colony of the Gambia to France* (Manchester 1876), C.O. 87/109. *Parl. Paps.* 1876, Vol. 52, C. 1409, p. 79.

[61] *Proceedings*, 7 (1876), 122–3. J. D. Hargreaves, *Prelude to the Partition of West Africa* (London 1963), 186–8.

[62] *Parl. Debs.* 228 (H.L., 20 March 1876), col. 265.

[63] *Proceedings*, 7 (1876), 282; mentioned by K. Goschal, *People in Colonies* (New York 1948), 31.

important, and indifference to it was coming to be regarded as unpatriotic.[64] William Westgarth, recollecting in 1888 the early days of the institute, noted that it 'had the smallest of audiences then'; it was 'marvellous', he added, 'to look back now upon that indifference.'[65] The new mood was clearly attributable to many factors, and not least to changing political and international circumstances. Nevertheless, in organizing the advocates of empire and in promoting the discussion of imperial problems, the institute had begun to play a notable part.

[64] Koebner and Schmidt, *Imperialism*, 127–34.
[65] Westgarth, *Personal Recollections*, 8.

Chapter Four

Colonial Policy under
Disraeli and Gladstone (1876–1886)

THE activities of the Royal Colonial Institute and the increased discussion of imperial problems in magazine articles and books, from Sir Charles Dilke's *Greater Britain* in 1868 to J. R. Seeley's best-seller on the *Expansion of England* in 1883, uncovered and stimulated popular interest in the overseas possessions. It was natural that working people in Britain newly enfranchised by the Reform Act of 1867 should be attracted to the most vigorous contemporary political movement before the revival of socialism in the 1880s, particularly as a substantial number had friends and relatives in the colonies with whom cheap postage enabled them to maintain contact. The steamship, the railway, and the telegraph also helped to bring nearer home parts of the empire that had previously been almost inaccessibly distant and to instil more conviction into the sense of kinship. The prognostications of the separatists had not come to pass, and the colonies showed no desire to sever their connection with the mother country. Moreover, European powers now challenged Britain's imperial predominance in Africa, Asia, and the Pacific, and produced their own advocates in colonial expansion and their own counterparts to pressure groups like the institute. Men like Dilke, Froude, and Seeley were matched by Rambaud, Leroy-Beaulieu, and Ferry in France, and by Roscher, Bücher, and Treitschke in Germany. In the changed international framework it might be unwise needlessly to lose colonies which were not only expanding markets and sources of raw material and primary produce but also a source of strength upon which Britain's position as a great power in some part rested.

The appearance of German merchants and missionaries among the Pacific islands was of particular concern to the

Australian colonies, whose assertiveness attracted the Royal Colonial Institute, with its strong and energetic Australian membership. The institute was at once aroused, therefore, when Germany showed an interest in New Guinea, only a hundred miles across the water from the northern reaches of the Australian mainland.

Although Dampier, Cook, Bligh, Flinders, and others had sailed along the coast of New Guinea, very little was known of the forests and tropical grassland of the interior. The western half of the island belonged to the Netherlands, but the remainder belonged to the indigenous cannibals, unless informal and spasmodic British interest constituted a shadowy title to it. The Union Jack had been hoisted there as early as 1846, when Lieutenant Yule had landed at Cape Possession in the Gulf of Papua, but the British government had made no attempt to pursue the matter. The New South Wales government had joined the British government in refusing to assist the colonization plans of a New Guinea company formed in 1867 by a group of Sydney businessmen, and the field had been left to the missionaries and pearl fishers until four years later, when a New Guinea prospecting association was formed and would not be deterred by governmental indifference. The promoters had purchased a brig that was suitably cheap but so decrepit and untrustworthy that the appointed captain prudently declined the command. Nevertheless, it had sailed from Sydney in 1872, and for three weeks coasted northward until fresh winds blew down some of the masts and boisterous seas dislodged the tiller, rudder, and some of the bulwarks. An attempt to reach a Queensland port through the Barrier Reef ended on the rocks, and only a few of the nearly seventy on board survived. In the following year, Captain John Moresby discovered a good land-locked harbour on the south coast of New Guinea and took formal possession of the eastern portion of the island pending confirmation from London. None of the Australian colonies was prepared to share in the cost of the administration, however, and the British government saw no cogent reason for burdening the British taxpayers with the bill.

Nevertheless, agitation in Australia for annexation was attracting a strong and articulate following, prompted by the danger to Australian security that would be posed by the extension of foreign influence in the Pacific islands, and, in some instances, by beguiling assumptions of New Guinea's economic potential and possession of treasure. The cause was taken up in Australia by Sir Henry Parkes, Sir John Robertson and, not least, Dr. John Dunmore Lang, a fiery, heavily built Presbyterian minister, who had been one of the provisional directors of the New Guinea company of 1867.[1] The annexation of Fiji in 1874, as Kimberley feared, was a spur to these advocates:

The worst is we shall have pressure for further annexations in the Pacific.

The New South Wales people are I see already calling out for annexation of the independent part of New Guinea, and I have been assured by those who know Australia that there is sure to be a rush of adventurers to that island before long.[2]

Moreover, the case being expounded in Sydney was also presented in London by former Australian colonists at the institute, especially by Labillière, who both in the council and at general meetings made the subject his special concern.

Early in 1874 Labillière called a private meeting of those interested in New Guinea, and followed this with a letter to the colonial secretary urging annexation on economic and political grounds.[3] The permanent under-secretary, R. G. W. Herbert, who had succeeded Rogers, knew Australia well and regarded New Guinea as strategically more important than Fiji. Labillière's letter, therefore, was studied at the Colonial Office and not merely acknowledged and filed. In April it was transmitted to the Admiralty and, on Herbert's advice, to the governors of the Australian colonies with a request from the colonial secretary, Carnarvon, for their observations. The governors' replies were generally cautious and did not show any pronounced enthusiasm for annexation.[4]

At an ordinary general meeting of the institute in March

[1] J. D. Legge, 'Australia and New Guinea to the Establishment of the British Protectorate, 1884', *Historical Studies Australia and New Zealand*, 4 (Nov. 1949), 35–6.
[2] Kimberley to Gladstone, 4 Nov. 1874, Add. MSS. 44225, fol. 157.
[3] Labillière to Carnarvon, 26 March 1874, *Parl. Paps.* 1876, Vol. 54, C. 1566, pp. 1–4.
[4] *Parl. Paps.* C. 1566. M. C. Jacobs, 'The Colonial Office and New Guinea, 1874–84', *Historical Studies Australia and New Zealand*, 5 (May 1952), 107–8.

1875 the agent-general for Victoria, Archibald Michie, presented a paper on Britain and New Guinea in which he emphasized the need for Britain to command both sides of the Torres Strait and forestall the acquisition of eastern New Guinea by a foreign power.[5] A fortnight later the council of the institute decided that the secretary should communicate informally with the Colonial Office to secure an audience for a deputation urging immediate annexation.[6] The deputation met the colonial secretary on 29 April, and Young read the institute's memorial calling attention to 'the important questions' arising from recent developments in New Guinea:

The nearest point in the territory in question approaches within eighty miles of the shores of Australia; and through Torres Straits flows already a large and rapidly increasing British commerce. It would, therefore, be in the highest degree undesirable that any foreign Power should, by settling on the Papuan coast, enter upon the joint occupation with us of this strait.

It was submitted that British authority should be extended without delay to the portion of the island not possessed by the Dutch:

Your memorialists submit that all that will be required to secure the objects and prevent the evils with respect to which they have the honour to address your Lordship, is the immediate occupation of such one or more positions as shall be sufficient to make good by actual possession our claim to the whole of the coast line of the eastern moiety of the island.

The expense, it was held, would not be large:

Some of the Australian colonies might, perhaps, contribute a portion of it, and one of them ultimately undertake the government of New Guinea, as South Australia has undertaken that of an exclusive part of North Australia.

Manchester, in introducing the deputation, emphasized that the annexation would facilitate and protect Britain's channels of trade, would enable the government to control the employment of natives in the pearl fisheries, and would bring to the empire an area apparently rich in minerals and ensure order and

[5] *Proceedings*, 6 (1875), 121–40.
[6] Co. Mins. 1 (30 March), 338; (15 April), 343; (27 April), 345.

justice between settlers and natives before reckless Australian goldminers arrived.

Carnarvon, in reply, refused to express a firm opinion in what he regarded as an early stage in a serious matter, but he admitted to possessing some doubts. The climate was not one in which Europeans thrived, the friendliness of the natives could not be guaranteed, the existence of mineral wealth was no more than supposition, and it was impossible to appropriate every available island and territory to police the trade in native labour. He was prepared to consider placing the waters to the south-east of New Guinea under the jurisdiction of the Fiji high commissioner, but further than that depended, he felt, on the Australian colonies, whose interests were those most directly concerned and which had not yet displayed any notable urgency.[7] The following day Manchester wrote to Carnarvon to underline a point he feared the deputation had failed to make wholly clear, namely, that the occupation of the two strategic points commanding the Torres Strait and a declaration of a protectorate over the eastern end of New Guinea would be sufficient to keep out other powers. Carnarvon was interested in the suggestion of occupying strategic positions and passed it to the Foreign Office, but there it came to a halt.[8] He was not disposed to yield on the other points, however, as he told Lord Cairns in October:

There is at this moment a very great pressure being put upon me from the Australian Colonies to annex that part of New Guinea which is not claimed by the Dutch. The story is too long a one to enter upon in a letter and complicated by too many details: but as at present advised I am prepared to resist the cry for annexation and to get over the difficulties of the case (which do exist) by other means.[9]

The council of the institute, while regretting that the government refused to annex New Guinea, refrained from pressing the matter further that year, feeling, according to the annual report in 1876, that 'the facts and arguments' it had presented the previous session remained on record 'as a warning against

---

[7] *Proceedings*, 6 (1875), 189–203. *Parl. Paps.* C. 1566, pp. 18–20, 65–7.

[8] O. W. Parnaby, *Britain and the Labor Trade in the Southwest Pacific* (Durham, N.C., 1964), 110.

[9] Carnarvon to Cairns, 30 Oct. 1875, P.R.O. 30/6/66, fol. 32 (Carnarvon Papers).

E

the danger to the interests of the Empire, of leaving a position of such commanding importance open to any foreign nation or to adventurers who may compromise and embarrass the future relations of Great Britain with the natives.'[10] The council responded firmly in June 1876 to approaches from the New Guinea Colonizing Association, whose secretary was advised that the institute declined 'to be in any way mixed up with the New Guinea Colonizing Association, or its affairs'.[11]

In 1878 Labillière was again perturbed by the activity of foreign powers in the Pacific and by the British government's indifference to it. In June he submitted to the council the draft of a letter to the colonial secretary reminding him of the arguments in favour of annexation, and after revision by a sub-committee of the council it was dispatched.[12] The importance of forestalling the foreigner was still the prime motive:

The rights asserted on behalf of the British Crown when formal possession of Eastern Papua was taken by the discoverers of its coast cannot but be impaired by the lapse of time, during which no occupation of any part of the territory has been effected with a view to make good by actual possession such formal claim.

The Council would, therefore, submit that Great Britain would now have less right of complaint were any other Power to annex the territory than at the period referred to.[13]

The Colonial Office reply on 26 July reaffirmed the decision not to consider annexation. The government refused to be pressed into action the purpose of which was doubtful and the consequences hazardous. It believed the possibility of foreign interference in New Guinea was being exaggerated, and the reluctance of the Australian colonies to share in the expense of an action from which they would derive the benefit was reason enough for the negative decision. Nevertheless, the institute was assured that instructions had been issued by the Admiralty for the dispatch of a war vessel to the New Guinea coast to assist in preserving order.[14]

Rumours of foreign activity around New Guinea in 1882 revived anxiety at the institute. Gladstone was again prime

---

[10] *Proceedings*, 7 (1876), 333.
[11] Co. Mins. 1 (20 June 1876), 431–2; (29 June), 435.
[12] Co. Mins. 2 (25 June 1878), 121.
[13] *Parl. Paps.* 1883, Vol. 47, C. 3617, p. 35.   [14] Ibid., p. 37.

minister, and his new administration began with aims as lofty as those of his successful first administration. As it happened, the Boers rose in revolt and defeated a small British force at Majuba Hill in 1881, and as a result the British government was constrained to recognize the Transvaal as the South African Republic. The Irish problem was in an especially dangerous phase, and Britain became bloodily involved in Egypt and the western Sudan. The government wished to avoid antagonizing colonial opinion, but it was also anxious to avoid entanglements with foreign powers and was wary of agreeing to territorial annexations whose consequences might be far-reaching and affect diplomatic relations in Europe. This was a delicate balance to preserve, and it resulted in governmental hesitation and uncertainty that exasperated the unequivocating pundits at the Royal Colonial Institute.

In January 1882 the council conveyed to the foreign secretary its opinion that, in view of the projected opening of the Panama Canal and the growth of trade in the Pacific, reports of French activity among the islands were cause for alarm. In a reply dated 25 February the council was assured that the government's attention had 'already been directed to the matters represented' and that the subject would 'continue to meet with careful consideration'.[15] The council reminded the foreign secretary of this correspondence when, in a letter dated 9 December 1882, it called his attention to a recent article in the Augsburg newspaper *Allgemeine Zeitung* advocating German colonization of New Guinea. The Foreign Office referred the matter to the colonial secretary, who in January 1883 replied that the government had no reason to believe that Germany contemplated annexation. The government did not regard the newspaper article as significant and would not be harassed into changing its attitude to annexation.[16] When writing to the foreign secretary in December, however, the institute's secretary had addressed similar letters to the agents-general for the various Australian colonies, where the offending German article was translated and published in the local press. The institute attached more significance to the article than was warranted, and, in stimulating anxiety among the Australian

[15] *Proceedings*, 13 (1882), 409–10.
[16] Co. Mins. 3 (5 Dec. 1882), 49; (19 Dec.), 54. *Parl. Paps*. C. 3617, pp. 119–20.

colonies, acted in an uncharacteristically irresponsible fashion. The council did not consider adequately the evidence upon which it was basing a course of action whose ramifications might be more extensive than the mere question of annexation of part of New Guinea and might impinge on the policy of the Foreign Office as well as on that of the Colonial Office. The institute's letter was taken especially seriously in Queensland,[17] whose government cabled London in February 1883 urging annexation and offering to bear the expenses of the administration of the territory. On receiving a non-committal reply, the Queensland government in April took formal possession of south eastern New Guinea in the name of the Queen.

Although the Queensland government's move was unconstitutional and, if condoned, would have established a dangerous precedent, the institute was now too committed to the annexationist cause to be able to dissociate itself from it. The wider implications of the situation were not discussed by the council, which, under Labillière's energetic pressure, appointed a committee to organize a deputation to the colonial secretary.[18] On 1 June the council presented him with a second memorial on the subject and recounted the arguments in favour of the New Guinea annexation, the most important of which remained that of keeping out foreign powers.[19] Whatever the colonial secretary, Lord Derby, may have thought about the case for annexing part of New Guinea, the government clearly could not endorse the method employed by Queensland: 'It is well understood', he wrote, 'that the officers of a Colonial Government have no power or authority to act beyond the limits of their Colony, and, if this constitutional principle is not carefully observed serious difficulties and complications must arise.' The British government doubted the German interest in New Guinea that harrowed the Australian colonies and their champions at the Royal Colonial Institute, and in any case declined to risk a war to acquire 'a large coloured population' which had evinced no desire for British rule. Britain was already beset by troubles in Ireland, the Sudan, South Africa, the Balkans, and Afghanistan, and friendly relations

[17] Queensland *Votes and Proceedings of the Legislative Assembly* (1883), 773–88.
[18] Co. Mins. 3 (8 May 1883), 104; (22 May), 109.
[19] *Proceedings*, 14 (1883), 250–63.

with Germany were important at a time when France was proving difficult in Egypt. The financial and administrative responsibility for an annexed New Guinea would have to lie with the Australian colonies, which could shoulder it only if they learned to co-operate more closely:

> I trust the time is now not distant when in respect of such questions (if not for other purposes of government), the Australian Colonies will effectively combine together, and provide the cost of carrying out any policy which after mature consideration they may unite in recommending, and which Her Majesty's Government may think it right and expedient to adopt.[20]

A meeting of delegates from the Australian colonies that met in Sydney at the end of 1883 was unanimous on the need to take the non-Dutch part of New Guinea but revealed differences on the creation of a federal government.

New Guinea at this time represented a complex political and international problem for the British cabinet involving consideration of issues that the Royal Colonial Institute was able to ignore. Granville at the Foreign Office believed that the most important objective was an understanding with Germany about Egypt, and he was aware that this would be unattainable if Britain created jealousies over colonial matters. Thus, the intimation that Germany was interested in the northern side of New Guinea affected the decision at a cabinet meeting in August 1884 to proclaim a British protectorate over the eastern half of the island. This decision was made against the wishes of Gladstone at the insistence of those within the cabinet such as Kimberley, Chamberlain, Dilke, Hartington and, latterly, Derby, who had become more amenable to the imperialist anti-German sentiments that were being propagated by the institute and in the country at large. Granville, however, persuaded Derby of the importance of not quarrelling with Germany, and the protectorate established in New Guinea in November 1884 was limited to the south-east.[21] This has been described by one authority as 'a half-hearted compromise between the Consolidationists' objection to increased responsibility, Hartington's and the Radical ministers' support of the

[20] Derby to Palmer, 11 July 1883, *Parl. Paps.* 1883, Vol. 47, C. 3691, pp. 22–3.
[21] Fitzmaurice, *Granville*, II, 354, 371–2.

colonists' claims, and Granville's fear of upsetting Bismarck.'[22]

The compromise perplexed the Australian colonies and their sympathizers in London, who were incensed when, before the end of the year, Germany established itself in north-eastern New Guinea. At the end of January 1885 the council of the Royal Colonial Institute sent the Colonial Office resolutions against conceding any part of the island to Germany. In a reply on 28 February the Colonial Office pointed out that

while Her Majesty's Government trust that there is no foundation for the apprehension that great injury to British interests is likely to result from the German occupation of a part of the Island distant from Australia, there has not been any ground on which they could claim to prohibit that occupation.[23]

Derby, indeed, was anxious not further to antagonize colonial opinion, and was supported by Childers, the chancellor of the exchequer, but action on the basis of the resolutions forwarded by the institute was impracticable, especially when Gladstone asserted himself in favour of concessions to Germany. Early in March the prime minister urged Granville to press on for a settlement of the New Guinea question with Germany:

It is really impossible to exaggerate the importance of getting out of the way the bar to the Egyptian settlement.[24]

In June concessions were made to Germany in settling the boundaries in New Guinea and the neighbouring islands, and the position was regulated the following year in a declaration signed in Berlin confirming the Germans and the British in their respective spheres in New Guinea.

The efforts of the Royal Colonial Institute on New Guinea annexation were the focal point of a wider campaign to forestall German expansion at any point where it might impinge on British imperial interests. Thus, reports of Germany's intending to establish a protectorate over settlements at Angra Pequena, a barren area north of the Orange river on the south-west coast of Africa, provoked the institute's council into writing to the

[22] R. E. Robinson, 'Imperial Problems in British Politics, 1880–1895', *Cambridge History of the British Empire*, III, *The Empire-Commonwealth, 1870–1919* (Cambridge 1959), 144.
[23] Co. Mins. 3 (3 March 1885), 348–9.
[24] Gladstone to Granville, 6 March 1885, in Fitzmaurice, *Granville*, II, 431–2.

colonial secretary on 28 May 1884 urging the government 'to exclude Foreign Powers from the occupation of this valuable harbour, and the country adjacent thereto'.[25] The letter was formally acknowledged on 3 June, but notwithstanding the views of the institute and pressure from Cape Colony the government recognized German sovereignty over Angra Pequena. The institute was pressing upon the administration a philosophy of empire abhorrent to Gladstone. 'Till the end of his days in office', it has been asserted, 'Gladstone scrutinized with the greatest care all demands for further additions to the Empire.'[26] He held so far as was possible to the principle that new territories should be taken under British protection only with the assent and at the request of the inhabitants. The principle was admirable, but in the competitive world of European colonialism in the 1880s it was the hard expansionist line favoured by the Royal Colonial Institute that was more in accord with public feeling. Gladstone's government collapsed in 1885, unpopular partly on account of its unheroic and inept handling of colonial and foreign affairs.

The institute's interest in matters affecting the colonies in these years was not confined to major territorial issues, such as New Guinea, the Gambia, or the Newfoundland fisheries, but was spread over a multitude of less conspicuous issues. That the colonies regarded the institute as a useful ally was shown by the large amount of correspondence the council received every year seeking to enlist support. The council treated all approaches from the colonies with respect, and in the great majority of cases was actively sympathetic. The institute possessed a strong following in the City, which ensured that the financial and commercial aspects of the imperial relationship were not ignored, especially in the 1880s. A coinage bill in 1884 and measures for replacing depreciated gold coinage were studied by the council in case they should affect the interests of colonists.[27] In 1885 the council protested to the government about the terms on which a stamp duty on colonial government securities was proposed in one of the taxation measures, objecting particularly to the classification with foreigners of colonial

[25] Co. Mins. 3 (27 May 1884), 258; (10 June), 262–3.
[26] Knaplund, *Gladstone and Britain's Imperial Policy*, 157–8.
[27] *Proceedings*, 15 (1884), 337.

subjects, who were 'no more Foreigners than the people of India, or the people of the Mother Country itself', none of whom bore the tax.[28] Something of the same feeling was discernible in the council's decision in 1886 to acquaint the colonial secretary with the desirability of distinguishing colonial from foreign trade in statistical reports.[29]

In February 1887 the council complained to the government of the hardships imposed by those provisions in the Companies (Colonial Registers) Act of 1883 which, it argued, compelled 'shareholders in companies in this country, resident in Colonies, though possessing no other estate or effects in the United Kingdom, to take up here Probate of Wills and Letters of Administration, and to pay Stamp Duty thereon'. The Treasury replied that it could not consent to an unconditional repeal of the offending sub-section of the act, but that it was willing to consider an amendment that would afford relief when the person entitled to the shares or stock on the colonial register died domiciled elsewhere than in the United Kingdom.[30] The institute's intercession encouraged a reconsideration of the act at the Treasury, and the amendment suggested was effected in 1889 by the provisions of Section 18 of the Revenue Act. The council was less successful in an attempt in 1888 to persuade the chancellor of the exchequer to permit the investment of trust monies in colonial government stocks. The chancellor replied peremptorily that he would not authorize such investment and he refused to receive a deputation on the subject. The council took the matter up again at the end of the year, but the chancellor would not be moved and maintained his refusal to receive a deputation.[31] Nevertheless, the principle for which the institute was contending was recognized after the Colonial Stock Act of 1900, when a large number of colonial government securities became eligible for trust investments on compliance with the provisions of the act.

The practically prohibitive duty on colonial wines occupied the council's attention for much of 1884 and 1885. It asked the government to give effect to a promise in the chancellor's

---

[28] Co. Mins. 3 (16 June 1885), 393–4.   [29] Co. Mins. 4 (26 Oct. 1886), 124.
[30] Co. Mins. 4 (15 Feb. 1887), 171; (19 April), 193.
[31] Co. Mins. 4 (8 May 1888), 345; (29 May), 350; (12 June), 357; (27 Nov.), 401; (11 Dec.), 410.

budget speech of April 1885 so that wine under a certain alcoholic strength could be admitted to the country at a duty of one shilling per gallon. The council forwarded its views to the prime minister, the colonial secretary, the chancellor of the exchequer, and some Members of Parliament, and it was gratified in 1886 by a bill in Parliament that adopted its suggestions.[32] In 1899 the council communicated with the chancellor of the exchequer deprecating a proposed increase in wine duties that it believed would impede the development of the wine industry in the colonies and their growing trade with the United Kingdom.[33] The government subsequently modified the proposal so that the wine-exporting colonies were not severely affected by the increase.

Of all the self-governing colonies the Australian were those most assured of support from the institute. The question of New Guinea in the 1880s, for example, was given far more attention than that of the Gambia or of Angra Pequena or of other areas that concerned the colonies in South Africa. The council lent support in 1887 to the unsuccessful application by the agent-general for Victoria seeking a subvention from the British government to an exploratory expedition from Australia to the Antarctic.[34] The council welcomed the meeting between the Australian colonies in Sydney in December 1883, and it shared Australian feeling against the French practice of sending convicts to New Caledonia, an island from which they might escape to Australia.[35] The council was not, however, carried away by every emotion that surged through its Australian supporters, and in 1888, when Labillière seconded by Sir Frederick Young moved a resolution sympathizing with the Australian people in their efforts to restrict Chinese immigration, the council countered with an amendment that it had no information to show that Chinese immigration had been prejudicial to Australia or was likely to make Australia unsuitable for English migrants, and that it was inadvisable and unnecessary for the institute to express any opinion or take any action in the matter.[36]

[32] Co. Mins. 3 (26 May 1885), 383–4; 4 (14 Jan. 1886), 6–7.
[33] Co. Mins. 7 (9 May 1899), 152–3.
[34] *Proceedings*, 19 (1888), 3, 152, 332–4.   [35] *Proceedings*, 15 (1884), 336.
[36] Co. Mins. 4 (17 July 1888), 369; (31 July), 375.

The council would occasionally plant questions through members in Parliament to secure information or publicize an issue, but it relied mainly on memorials, letters, and representations. Sometimes it had to be satisfied with a virtually meaningless response: for instance, a representation in 1888 of the desirability of taking a census of the whole empire at the next United Kingdom census was met with the short assurance that the colonial secretary would not lose sight of the idea and the principle involved. The institute was perhaps too often content with merely making its views known to the colonial secretary, who might, or, more usually, might not, heed them, instead of engaging in extensive publicity to influence public opinion, an activity at which, on occasion, it could be adept. This was a point made by the Marquis of Lorne in 1887, when the council joined in representations to the government for a subsidy to a new steamship line between Vancouver and Hong Kong: 'If they want to have any influence of any kind', he wrote of the members of council, 'they must speak out—A memorial sent in with a written acknowledgment received in reply is only a futile whisper.'[37]

By the 1880s the separatist philosophy was largely discredited, and the imperialist revival gathered momentum in a period when Britain was adjusting to a new international situation in which its economic ascendancy appeared to be in danger and other powers were constructing empires.[38] The nations that were challenging Britain in the colonization field were also those competing with Britain in the markets of the world, and the vast areas and growing populations of the colonies became attractive prospects for economic development and investment. The idea of the extension of the empire to counter foreign acquisitions and to safeguard the country's economic future was beginning to find more favour, but it did not, it has been pointed out, commend itself to everyone: 'There were certainly those who were cool enough to point out that trade did not necessarily follow the flag since the question of cost had something to do with it; that the trade with the colonies was only one-third of the total trade of the country; that France, Germany, and the United States, all protectionist

[37] Lorne to Young, 2 Aug. 1887, Young Papers, File I, 47.
[38] J. E. Tyler, *The Struggle for Imperial Unity, 1868–1895* (London 1938), 27–37.

and rival powers, were nevertheless still England's best customers.'[39] Nevertheless, the institute now had a common interest with a developing segment of political life that regarded imperial expansion as the answer to the threat of foreign imperialism. This school of thought included Liberals as well as Conservatives, but it had naturally a greater appeal to Conservatives, to those most devoted to the royal entourage, to army and naval officers, and to civil servants who had served in the overseas empire. These were the people who increasingly formed the reservoir of support for the institute and moulded its character, sentiment and outlook.

[39] Tyler, op. cit., 36.

Chapter Five

The Imperial Federation Movement (1870–1911)

In their annual report of 1875 the councillors of the Royal Colonial Institute gave an assurance of 'their desire to continue energetically to promote the great principle of the "Unity of the Empire", the keystone of the policy which they advocate, as being in their opinion the best bond of its permanent security, and of its power and influence among the other nations of the world.'[1] The institute was the platform for the suggestions made during the 1870s for bringing the self-governing colonies into closer association with the mother country, and by the 1880s it was at the centre of the burgeoning imperial federation movement. The new imperial consciousness of which the movement was an outcrop was powerfully expressed in 1883 when J. R. Seeley, a Cambridge historian, published a series of lectures propounding an imperial theme that contrasted with that which had been advanced earlier by the Oxford historian, Goldwin Smith.[2] Three years later J. A. Froude, a narrative historian as vigorous as Macaulay, and as capable as Macaulay of bending his historical authorities, produced an account of a tour overseas he evocatively entitled *Oceana*, and, like Seeley, added literary and scholarly authority to a new enthusiasm for Britain's colonies.

The imperial federation to the achievement of which the movement devoted itself was a term used so loosely and variously that it embraced almost any scheme for strengthening or formalizing the bonds between the United Kingdom and the self-governing colonies. The federal idea had been made more credible by improvements in international communications and more attractive by the examples set by the federation of the Canadian provinces in 1867 and of the German states in 1871. Imperial federation was certainly being thought about

[1] *Proceedings*, 6 (1875), 265.
[2] J. R. Seeley, *The Expansion of England* (London 1883).

seriously by a few individuals before the end of the 1860s. In 1870 A. J. Cattanach, a Toronto lawyer later prominent in the imperial federation movement in Canada, produced for the Royal Colonial Institute a paper on relations between the colonies and the parent state in which he expatiated on the desirability of some form of federal system for the empire.[3] In January and April 1871 two articles on the subject were published in the *Contemporary Review* by Edward Jenkins, who had resigned his membership of the institute the previous year, being unable, it would appear, to satisfy himself completely about the institute's effectiveness or value. In February 1871 R. A. MacFie read a paper proposing a representative council and uniformity of laws and coinage in the empire; the following month MacFie's projected council was dismissed as impracticable by William Westgarth, who favoured arranging the colonies into groups, each of which would send a representative to Parliament. In July imperial federation was discussed by Labillière in a paper read at a conference at the Westminster Palace Hotel.[4]

Thus, it was largely at the institute and through the work outside of individual fellows that the imperial federation movement began to take shape. The institute frequently touched on the subject at its meetings and produced the first definite proposal for the establishment of a Council of Advice. The idea was probably derived from the advisory council of the secretary of state for India and was proposed by Sir Bartle Frere, who had served in India, but it was difficult to determine what the council's composition or powers should be. The idea was regarded with suspicion in the colonies and repudiated by the agent-general for Victoria, who was perplexed by the differences of opinion among 'the amateur Constitution-Mongers of the Colonial Institute'.[5] The proposal was dropped, but imperial federation continued to fascinate large audiences. The last paper of the honorary secretary, Eddy, was concerned with the best means of drawing together the interests of the mother country and the colonies, and although it rejected as premature any scheme for imperial federation, it suggested

[3] *Proceedings*, 2 (1871), 70–1.
[4] Folsom, *Royal Empire Society*, 179–82. Tyler, *Struggle for Imperial Unity*, 100.
[5] *The Times*, 26 July 1872. Bodelsen, *Studies in Mid-Victorian Imperialism*, 142–4.

the revival of the Privy Council committee for trade and plantations, in which the colonies would be represented and which would advise on 'a few simple but grand subjects'. This suggestion found favour with the third Earl Grey, who was not associated with the institute, and with W. E. Forster and the Marquis of Lorne, both of whom were soon to become fellows.[6] Two meetings at the beginning of 1875 were devoted to imperial federation, the tireless Labillière leading the way with a paper on the permanent unity of the empire that envisaged a central parliament and executive, and over a period of two decades a year seldom went by without at least one paper being presented that was relevant to the subject.[7]

In 1876 Frederick Young edited and published a correspondence he had initiated on imperial federation at the end of the previous year in the *Colonies*, a newspaper edited by S. W. Silver, a keen member of the institute. Young's views were enthusiastic and based on the widely-held premise that ultimately the empire must federate or disintegrate.[8] J. Denistoun Wood produced a paper advocating a powerful federal assembly and a court of appeal as instruments of a federation that was essential for the preservation of peace between the members of the empire.[9] In 1880 a paper by George Bourinot, clerk of the Canadian House of Commons, historian, and the institute's corresponding secretary in Ottawa, proposed a federation between Britain and the self-governing colonies in which matters of federal concern would be the responsibility of a parliament established by the component states of the federation.[10] Another paper by Alexander Staveley Hill, a lawyer and Member of Parliament, sketched the practical steps by which a federal council for the empire could be brought into operation by legislation in the various parliaments.[11] In 1882 Labillière took the discussion further with a detailed consideration of the division of powers that would have to be established between the colonial legislatures and the imperial

---

[6] *Proceedings*, 6 (1875), 5–35. Tyler, op. cit., 97–8.

[7] F. P. de Labillière, *Federal Britain* (London 1894), 23. *Proceedings*, 6 (1875), 36–85.

[8] F. Young, *Imperial Federation of Great Britain and Her Colonies* (London 1876), xii–xiii.

[9] *Proceedings*, 8 (1877), 3–44.   [10] Ibid., 11 (1880), 90–132.

[11] Ibid., 136–77.

legislature in any form of federation that might be achieved.[12]

In 1884 the continued interest in imperial federation at the Royal Colonial Institute resulted in the foundation of the Imperial Federation League 'to secure by Federation the permanent Unity of the Empire'. The formation of a society to promote federation had been broached early in the year by Labillière and Captain J. C. R. (later Sir John) Colomb, who, with George Baden-Powell, William Westgarth, Denistoun Wood, and Young (all of the Royal Colonial Institute) formed themselves into a small committee for this purpose. On 9 April the committee interviewed W. E. Forster, a vice-president of the institute, and submitted to him a proposal that he and other leading public men should be invited to a non-party conference to consider the maintenance of the unity of the empire. The provisional committee added to its number, drawing largely on the institute's ranks, the notable exception being H. O. Arnold-Forster, who was Forster's adopted son and became the committee's joint secretary with Labillière. The committee held all its meetings at the institute's rooms in the Strand, and organized the conference held on 18 November which formally established the Imperial Federation League, the motion for its foundation being moved by the Marquis of Normanby, a vice-president of the institute.[13]

The imperial federation movement had critics within the institute who doubted the wisdom of attempting to put a constitutional form to imperial unity. Prominent among the critics were Sir Robert Torrens, a member of council, and Viscount Bury, now a vice-president, who attacked the Imperial Federation League as 'another instance of that craze for over-legislation' which could not resist 'tinkering with our Institutions'.[14] Lord Norton (formerly C. B. Adderley), who before his retirement from political office with a barony in 1878 had served as a vice-president of the institute, relinquished his membership on account of the interest in imperial federation, a subject with which he had no sympathy.[15] The critics, however, were in a small minority, and the council's attitude towards the new organization was formally expressed in its annual report of 1885:

[12] Ibid., 12 (1881), 346–91.   [13] Ibid., 24 (1893), 111–12.
[14] *Nineteenth Century* (March 1885), 382. Tyler, op. cit., 98.
[15] Folsom, op. cit., 57–8, 233–4.

The Council, without wishing to commit the Institute to any expression of opinion on the question of Imperial Federation, regard the formation of the Imperial Federation League, and the widespread and powerful support the movement has evoked both at home and in the Colonies, as a proof of the increasing interest which is felt in Colonial matters, and of the general desire to maintain and strengthen the connection between the Mother Country and the Colonies.[16]

The league held its preliminary meetings at the institute, and although its separate existence was carefully respected the institute's sympathy was assured.

The close connection between the league and the institute was illustrated in their extensive common membership. The league's first head, W. E. Forster, an ardent churchman and brother-in-law of Matthew Arnold, was a Liberal imperialist and former colonial under-secretary who had long possessed a fond interest in the idea of a vast federated empire with the United Kingdom at the centre, and he was one of the first at the institute to support the formation of a league to promote it. Among the league's founders, the ubiquitous Labillière was an active and long-serving member of the institute's council, Young was still the honorary secretary, and Colomb had been a fellow since 1872 and a frequent contributor to meetings, working for many years to arouse interest in problems of imperial defence. Among the many Conservative politicians who supported the league, Lord Carnarvon had been a fellow of the institute since 1868 and W. H. Smith, soon to become leader of the House of Commons, had been a fellow for ten years. Of the Liberals supporting the league, Lord Rosebery, who became foreign secretary in Gladstone's third and fourth administrations and prime minister on Gladstone's retirement, had become a fellow of the institute in 1881 and later was elected a vice-president. Among the colonial leaders associated with the league were Sir Alexander Galt and Sir Charles Tupper, successively Canadian high commissioners in London, both of whom had been cabinet ministers in Ottawa. Galt, a vice-president of the institute and a non-resident fellow since 1880, had noted the separatists' influence in England in the 1860s: 'I am more than ever disappointed at the tone of feeling here as to

[16] *Proceedings*, 16 (1885), 361.

Sir Frederick Young (1817–1913), Honorary
Secretary and Vice-President

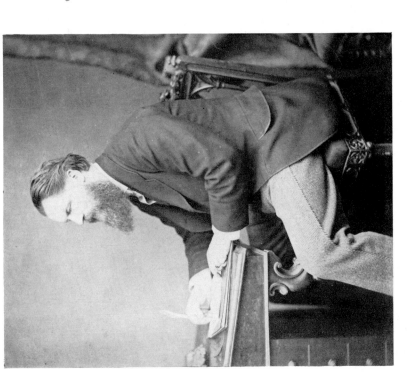

Viscount Bury, later 7th Earl of Albemarle (1832–1894),
First President

Sir Charles Lucas (1853–1931), Chairman of
Council, 1915–1920

Richard Jebb (1874–1953)

the Colonies', he had written to his wife in January 1867. 'I cannot shut my eyes to the fact that they want to get rid of us.'[17] Attitudes had changed since that time, and Galt found some satisfaction in the activities both of the institute, in which he took a sustained interest, and of the league. Tupper, who for a short time was both high commissioner and a Canadian cabinet minister, had become a resident fellow in 1883 and was soon to be elected to the council; he retained a strong interest in the empire into an extensive old age, though perhaps always inclined to exaggerate his own importance and influence in imperial affairs.[18]

It was partly because of the initiative of the Imperial Federation League that the British government summoned a colonial conference to meet in London at the celebration of Queen Victoria's jubilee in 1887. The conference had been suggested to the prime minister, Lord Salisbury, by a deputation from the league's council in August 1886, and in November the Colonial Office had dispatched invitations to the colonial governments 'to attend for the discussion of those questions which appear more particularly to demand attention at the present time'.[19] The conference was a purely consultative occasion and was attended not only by representatives of the colonies but also by many others associated in some way with imperial affairs. The Royal Colonial Institute was represented by its chairman, but several other fellows of the institute attended the conference in various capacities, notably Sir Charles Mills, the Marquesses of Normanby, Lorne, and Hartington, Sir John Rose, Sir Henry Barkly, Sir Alexander Galt, Sir William Sargeaunt, Nevile Lubbock, Hugh Childers, Captain J. C. R. Colomb, Baden-Powell, Sir Samuel Wilson, and Frederick Young. The conference met on twenty days between 4 April and 9 May 1887, and half of that time was devoted to consideration of imperial defence, whose cost Britain wished the colonies to share, particularly as it was now confronted with the prospect of serious naval competition from continental countries. The British government ruled out any discussion of political federation:

[17] O. D. Skelton, *The Life and Times of Sir Alexander Tilloch Galt* (Toronto 1920), 410.
[18] Ewart to Jebb, 9 May 1913, Richard Jebb: Letters and Documents (Institute of Commonwealth Studies, London).
[19] *Parl. Paps.* 1887, Vol. 56, C. 5091, pp. vii–viii.

F

There has been no expression of Colonial opinion in favour of any steps in that direction; and Her Majesty's Government are of opinion that there would be no advantage in the informal discussion of a very difficult problem before any basis has been accepted by the Governments concerned. It might, indeed, be detrimental to the ultimate attainment of a more developed system of united action if a question not yet ripe for practical decision were now to be brought to the test of a formal examination. [20]

The very calling of the conference, however, represented a gesture of approval towards the general idea of improved imperial relations, and it was realized that the conference would probably be a precedent and that other conferences would follow.

After the colonial conference of 1887 the Imperial Federation League ran into increasing difficulties, and was racked by internal dissension, mainly over the question of whether federation should be a matter primarily of trade or of defence. At a meeting in London on 24 November 1893 the league was dissolved because, the executive explained, it had 'reached the limits of its effective action'. [21] There was some secrecy and disagreement about the dissolution decision, which was against the wishes of many members, notably George Parkin, who at once transferred his support to the Royal Colonial Institute. [22] The league split into a number of subsidiary organizations. There was already the United Empire Trade League, founded in February 1891 with C. E. Howard Vincent, a fellow of the institute, as the secretary, which attracted those in the Imperial Federation League who supported preferential trade arrangements and a form of commercial union within the empire. An Imperial Federation Defence Committee, which demanded that the colonies should make large cash contributions to the support of the Royal Navy, absorbed those who regarded defence as the principal consideration and appropriated the office, records, addresses and crest of the defunct league. [23]

The most important group to emerge after the dissolution of the Imperial Federation League, however, was the British

[20] *Parl. Paps.* 1887, Vol. 56, C. 5091, p. viii.
[21] *Imperial Federation*, 1 Dec. 1893, p. 279.
[22] J. Willison, *Sir George Parkin* (London 1929), 84.
[23] Tyler, op. cit., 191–2, 208. G. T. Denison, *The Struggle for Imperial Unity* (London 1909), 339–40.

Empire League, which originated largely from the Royal Colonial Institute. The decision to found it was taken at a meeting on 20 July 1894 at the home of Sir John Lubbock, president of the City of London branch of the Imperial Federation League and a fellow of the institute; in April 1895 the Duke of Devonshire, a vice-president of the institute, was invited to be the new league's first president, Lubbock became chairman of the general council, and Sir Robert Herbert became chairman of the executive committee. Herbert, who had been permanent under-secretary of state for the colonies, had joined the Royal Colonial Institute on his retirement in 1892 and had immediately been elected to the council; he has been described as the first expansionist under-secretary, and was noted for his industry and patience and for possessing what *The Times* later referred to as 'a great deal of the tact which is more usually found in women than in men'.[24] The British Empire League's declared object was to strengthen the connection between the United Kingdom and the overseas empire by discussion of questions of common interest, especially those relating to trade arrangements and mutual defence. In thus promoting and organizing discussion of questions of general imperial interest, the new league dredged off some of the importance of the Royal Colonial Institute as the Imperial Federation League had done previously.

The closing years of the nineteenth century in England were a period of social and industrial progress guided largely by Lord Salisbury's Conservative administrations allied with the Liberal Unionists. The collapse of the Conservative ascendancy in December 1905, when Balfour resigned and a Liberal government was formed by Campbell-Bannerman, opened the way to a new generation for which imperial unity was not important: a Labour party appeared in Parliament in force, and social reform was the primary concern. The most significant imperial development in the period was Joseph Chamberlain's choice of the Colonial Office instead of the Treasury in the Salisbury cabinet that was formed in June 1895. Hitherto, the Colonial Office had been regarded as among the less important

[24] *The Times*, 8 May 1905. R. B. Pugh, 'The Colonial Office, 1801–1925', *Cambridge History of the British Empire*, 3 (Cambridge 1959), 744. *United Empire*, 6 (1915), 431–2. Denison, op. cit., 206–24. *The Times*, 1 June 1895.

cabinet offices. The Queen, though enjoying the role of Empress of India, was not much interested in empire affairs beyond the appointment of colonial bishops, and with a very few exceptions the permanent officials at the Colonial Office had normally thought of themselves as winding up a disintegrating partnership. Chamberlain, however, impressed by the opportunities for constructive statesmanship offered by the empire, had wanted the Colonial Office for nearly ten years. He had been impressed by Seeley's *Greater Britain* and was sympathetic to the idea of imperial unity, as he explained at the annual dinner of the Royal Colonial Institute in March 1897:

It was my earnest—I may say almost that it was my only—ambition when I took the office to which the Queen appointed me that I might during its term be able to do something to render more close the bonds of union between the Colonies and ourselves, because I have faith that upon this alliance between the nations of the British race the future of this country and of the Empire must entirely depend.[25]

He viewed the empire as an undeveloped estate which it was the government's duty to use to buttress Britain's economic prosperity and to accelerate social reform.

Chamberlain presided over the colonial conference that met in 1897 on the occasion of the Queen's diamond jubilee. It was attended by colonial premiers and was more a meeting of governments than the amorphous assembly of 1887 had been. Chamberlain opened the conference with a speech stressing the need for a council of empire to which the self-governing colonies would send representatives:

I feel that there is a real necessity for some better machinery of consultation between the self-governing Colonies and the mother country, and it has sometimes struck me—I offer it now merely as a personal suggestion—that it might be feasible to create a great council of the Empire, to which the Colonies would send representative plenipotentiaries,—not mere delegates who were unable to speak in their name, without further reference to their respective Governments, but persons who by their position in the Colonies, by their representative character, and by their close touch with Colonial feeling, would be able, upon all subjects submitted to them, to give really effective and valuable advice. If such a council were

[25] *Proceedings*, 28 (1897), 243.

to be created it would at once assume an immense importance, and it is perfectly evident that it might develop into something still greater. It might slowly grow to that Federal Council to which we must always look forward as our ultimate ideal.[26]

The conference, however, was wary of the suggestion and declared that the existing political relations between the United Kingdom and the colonies were satisfactory. The conference also agreed that periodic colonial conferences were desirable, but the aims of the imperial federationists had been virtually removed from the sphere of practical politics. At the colonial conference of 1902 Chamberlain submitted a plan for 'a real Council of the Empire to which all questions of Imperial interest might be referred', which, though advisory at first, would evolve executive and perhaps legislative functions, but it was not even discussed.[27]

Notwithstanding the fate of Chamberlain's proposal, the hope of devising a political instrument to symbolize and strengthen imperial unity was not eradicated at the Royal Colonial Institute, where it continued to be discussed in varying forms. At a meeting in June 1903 R. B. Haldane, who became secretary for war when the Liberals replaced the Conservatives in office at the end of 1905, read a paper proposing a committee of advice on imperial affairs, which would include privy councillors nominated by the crown at the request of the colonial governments, and envisaging the House of Lords as the 'Senate House of the Empire'.[28] Haldane was closely associated with a group led by Sir Frederick Pollock, a legal authority best known for his joint authorship with Frederick William Maitland of a monumental history of English law before the time of Edward I, a work which, published in 1895, transformed academic knowledge and interpretations of English legal history. Pollock found the institute a congenial platform for expounding his views, and in a paper read on 11 April 1905 suggested an imperial advisory committee based on

[26] *Parl. Paps.* 1897, Vol. 59, C. 8596, pp. 5–6.

[27] *Parl. Paps.* 1902, Vol. 66, Cd. 1299, p. 4. J. E. Tyler, 'Development of the Imperial Conference, 1887–1914', *Cambridge History of the British Empire*, 3 (Cambridge 1959), 419. See also R. H. Wilde, 'Joseph Chamberlain's Proposal of an Imperial Council in March, 1900', *Canadian Historical Review*, 37 (Sept. 1956), 225–46.

[28] *Proceedings*, 34 (1903), 328–31.

the existing premiers' conference but enlarged by the addition of all the heads of the great departments and of others specially appointed to it; the committee would have a continuous existence and be assisted by an imperial secretariat and intelligence department.[29]

Pollock's plan was taken up by Chamberlain's successor as colonial secretary, Alfred Lyttelton, who in a dispatch to the self-governing colonies on 20 April 1905 invited comments on the idea of changing the title of the colonial conference to imperial council, which might have a permanent secretarial commission in London. It met with approval except in Canada and Newfoundland and was publicized and promoted in *The Times* by the journalist, mountaineer, and future colonial secretary, L. S. Amery.[30] When the conference met in 1907, however, a Liberal government had replaced the Conservatives and Lyttelton had been succeeded at the Colonial Office by Lord Elgin, who was not impressed by the suggestion for a permanent commission. Alfred Deakin, the Australian prime minister, who had been urged by Pollock and others to give a lead on the proposals for imperial reorganization, put before the conference his own suggestion for a secretariat to act as a connecting link between conferences and between governments. The Canadian prime minister, Sir Wilfrid Laurier, opposed the suggestions, and the result was a compromise whereby a secretariat was established but the colonial conference became the imperial conference, not an imperial council.[31]

The Royal Colonial Institute remained a centre of propaganda for imperial unity, but effective leadership of the cause moved to individuals who, though in many cases fellows of the institute, conducted their campaign more outside the institute walls than within. Leopold Amery found his most influential outlet in articles on imperial affairs published in *The Times*.

[29] *Proceedings*, 36 (1905), 288–304. R. Jebb, *The Imperial Conference* (2 vols., London 1911), II, 8–10. J. E. Kendle, *The Colonial and Imperial Conferences, 1887–1911* (Univ. of London Ph.D. thesis 1965), 8–9.

[30] *Parl. Paps.* 1906, Vol. 77, Cd. 2785, pp. 1–3, 14. L. S. Amery, *My Political Life* (3 vols., London 1953–5), I, 302–4.

[31] *Parl. Paps.* 1907, Vol. 55, Cd. 3404, pp. 15–16; Cd. 3523, pp. 26–9. J. A. La Nauze, *Alfred Deakin: A Biography* (Melbourne 1965), 500–3. Jebb, *Imperial Conference*, II, 51–2, 116–18.

Richard Jebb served on the council, but became increasingly disillusioned with his colleagues. Others with an active interest in the empire were Fabian Ware, editor of the *Morning Post*, F. S. Oliver, Leo Maxse, and Lionel Curtis, none of whom was much interested in the institute, and Curtis, indeed, was suspected of discouraging his pupils from joining.[32] Many of the new imperial theorists found a more satisfactory vehicle for their activities in the Round Table movement, the creation largely of Sir Alfred Milner, whom Deakin regarded as 'the hope of the Imperial party in the U.K.'[33] Milner had served as Governor of Cape Colony and of the Transvaal and Orange River Colony, and was later to become colonial secretary. It was principally service under Lord Cromer in Egypt, however, that confirmed in him a strong nationalist and imperialist fervour:

I am a British (indeed primarily an English) Nationalist. If I am also an Imperialist, it is because the destiny of the English race, owing to its insular position and long supremacy at sea, has been to strike fresh roots in distant parts of the world. My patriotism knows no geographical but only racial limits. I am an Imperialist and not a Little Englander, because I am a British Race Patriot.[34]

Milner would have found many in sympathy with his outlook at the institute, of which he became a fellow in 1895 and a vice-president in 1909 and at whose meetings he was a prominent contributor and sometimes presided.

The Round Table movement in England was organized during a number of meetings between Milner and others during the spring and summer of 1909, and formally established at the beginning of September. It secured financial support from a variety of sources, the most important being the Rhodes Trust, which agreed to match all other contributions. The movement's main consideration in 1909 was fear of Germany, and imperial federation was one of the ways in which it believed imperial defence should be strengthened.[35] It was a propaganda organization as much as a study group, and it founded a

[32] Curtis to Jebb, 13 May 1913, Jebb Papers.
[33] La Nauze, *Alfred Deakin*, 513.
[34] *The Times*, 27 July 1925.
[35] C. Quigley, 'The Round Table Groups in Canada, 1908–38', *Canadian Historical Review*, 43 (Sept. 1962), 205, 209–11, 219.

quarterly journal on imperial affairs, the *Round Table*, with Philip Kerr as editor, to revive and promote the idea of a federal council of the empire. The first issue was published in 1910, the year in which the Royal Colonial Institute reformed its journal to give it a more journalistic and popular flavour. The journal of the Round Table was soon recognizably superior to that of the institute as a regular commentary on imperial affairs, and Jebb wished the institute to take it over,[36] but it maintained its separate identity, and eventually broadened and moderated its outlook to become the foremost regular reading matter for those with a serious interest in the empire.

The Round Table groups and the Royal Colonial Institute were the centres of the discussion on empire unity that preceded the imperial conference of 1911. Amery believed that the conference itself, rather than the creation of a federal imperial parliament, offered the best machinery for closer unity if it were to meet more regularly, and he publicized his ideas in an address to the institute in June 1910.[37] He was supported by Jebb, who influenced the decision of the council the following month to press, not for a federal parliament, but for the more general objective of closer constitutional union.[38] At the beginning of April 1911 the secretary informed Asquith's private secretary of the council's wish to send a deputation to advise the prime minister of its views on constitutional relations within the empire and, without advocating any particular proposal, to urge upon him in general terms the need for imperial union. The prime minister consented to receive the deputation in May, despite objections from other ministers, including the colonial secretary, and from permanent officials at the Colonial Office.[39]

When the imperial conference met in 1911 at the Foreign Office in London, the first two days were taken up with discussion of a resolution moved by the New Zealand prime minister, Sir Joseph Ward:

[36] Co. Mins. 9 (21 Nov. 1911), 213; (20 Feb. 1912), 237.

[37] *United Empire*, I (1910), 487–501.

[38] Jebb to Edwards, 9 July 1910; Edwards to Jebb, 14 July: Jebb Papers. Co. Mins. 9 (12 July 1910), 89.

[39] Co. Mins. 9 (14 March 1911), 154; (4 April), 161; (2 May), 170; (16 May), 174.

That the Empire has now reached a stage of Imperial development which renders it expedient that there should be an Imperial Council of State, with Representatives from all the self-governing parts of the Empire in theory, and, in fact, advisory to the Imperial Government on all questions affecting the interests of His Majesty's Dominions oversea.[40]

Ward's proposal was closer to the ideas of Milner, Curtis, and those members of the Royal Colonial Institute such as the chairman, Sir Bevan Edwards, who were less convinced than Jebb or Amery that the gradual development of the imperial conference machinery was preferable to the creation of a new parliamentary body. Most of its details had already been discussed by the Round Table and the institute, but Ward presented a muddled case and it was rejected by the other prime ministers, notably by the Canadian, Laurier, whose caustic wit played havoc with a scheme which confused 'council' and 'parliament' and which would establish a body that could spend but not raise revenue. The imperial conference, however, continued to function as a consultative assembly of the empire, providing a forum for the discussion of a wide range of common problems. At a private session of the committee of imperial defence, following a resolution moved by Andrew Fisher of Australia regretting Britain's failure to consult the dominions prior to its recent acceptance of the terms of the Declaration of London, the foreign secretary, Sir Edward Grey, gave the dominions for the first time a review of the international situation and of British foreign policy.[41]

The role of the Royal Colonial Institute in the struggle for imperial unity had been to a large extent appropriated by individuals, committees, and other organizations which drew heavily on its membership for their support. The council became less inclined than in earlier days to study as thoroughly as it should the imperial issues in which it interested itself, and consequently the more important imperial promotion tasks were increasingly undertaken elsewhere. Jebb felt that the members of council were reluctant to master complicated problems, with

[40] *Parl. Paps.* 1911, Vol. 54, Cd. 5745, pp. 36–7.
[41] *Parl. Paps.* 1911, Vol. 54, Cd. 5745, pp. 104–16. Tyler, 'Development of the Imperial Conference', loc. cit., 431–5. I. R. Hancock, 'The 1911 Imperial Conference', *Historical Studies Australia and New Zealand*, 12 (Oct. 1966), 359.

the result, he told Earl Grey, that 'their well-meant efforts' were 'apt to be misdirected'.[42] The fear of becoming involved in what might be interpreted as political matters deterred the institute from taking an active interest as a body, but its membership supplied most of the leaders of the imperial unity movement, and its meetings provided the occasions for individuals' suggestions and for discussions.

After 1912, following a lengthy period of somnolence, the institute began to show signs of reinvigoration. The remodelled monthly journal was a fair success, and the institute attempted to become more active again with a view, according to Jebb, 'to taking advantage of the next Imperialist revival'.[43] Though scrupulously non-political, it had acquired a political and social character that was unmistakable, and was in the van of an empire patriotism that had racial and jingoistic overtones. In 1897 Chamberlain had told the institute of his admiration for the faith of its founders, who had 'sowed the seeds of Imperial patriotism'.[44] Its outlook was at once both national and racial, inspired by pride in Britain's achievements and by kinship ties with the people of the self-governing colonies. The greater unity for which the institute was striving was a unity of the Anglo-Saxon settlements and was not normally envisaged as at any time embracing the tropical dependencies, whose acquisition and retention the expansionists at the institute had consistently urged upon the government. Lord Rosebery, presiding at a banquet in 1893, regarded the important feature of the empire as its predominantly Anglo-Saxon quality, and he congratulated the institute on the part it had played 'in the moulding of such sentiments'. Britain, he believed, was now pegging out claims for the future:

We have to consider what countries must be developed either by ourselves or some other nation, and we have to remember that it is part of our responsibility and heritage to take care that the world, so far as it can be moulded by us, shall receive an English-speaking complexion, and not that of another nation.[45]

The non-settlement areas of the empire were valued more for

[42] Jebb to Grey, 5 Dec. 1912, Jebb Papers.
[43] Jebb to Cahan, 3 April 1912, ibid.   [44] *Proceedings*, 28 (1897), 235.
[45] *Proceedings*, 24 (1893), 227.

the prestige and power of which they were evidence and for the opportunities they provided Englishmen for dedicated self-sacrifice and service, a form of moral exploitation that found popular exposition in the full-blooded poetry and prose of Rudyard Kipling.

Chapter Six

Education (1868–1914)

Among the original objects of the Royal Colonial Institute was the establishment of 'a Museum for the collection and exhibition of Colonial and Indian productions'. It was an ambitious aim and was not achieved, but interest in it was manifested periodically until the end of the nineteenth century. In 1871 the council supported a committee that was campaigning for a colonial museum, and at the annual general meeting in June 1875 it was asked to consider ways of forming one in association with the institute and to ascertain whether colonial governments would contribute to the cost.[1] On 7 August a deputation from the council waited upon the colonial secretary to present the view that it was 'of the utmost importance that a permanent Colonial Museum, worthy of the Nation, should be established in London, as the centre and Metropolis of the Empire'. It suggested that if the British government granted a site in central London the colonies would be induced to contribute towards the cost of erecting and maintaining a building. The advantages of a museum were described as not only commercial and educational but also scientific, ethnographic, mechanical, social, and political:

It is hardly necessary to draw your Lordship's attention to the fact, that it would be of the most inestimable advantage to all Colonists visiting this country to be able to see the productions of their own Colonies, and to have the opportunity of comparing them with those of others, while it would be no less advantageous to English capitalists as well as to the mass of the people of this country, whether they contemplate—as many of them do—becoming Colonists themselves, or remaining at home, to be practically acquainted with the vast and varied riches and resources of their own great Empire.

Carnarvon professed to be in favour of the project and had

[1] *Proceedings*, 3 (1872), 193; 6 (1875), 267.

communicated with some colonies on the subject, but the offers of support that he had received amounted to less than £10,000, only a third of the amount that would be needed. The selection of a site would also be a problem, but he promised to use his influence to support the institute's efforts.[2]

The council allied with the council of the Royal Asiatic Society in forming a committee which decided in favour of a newly-vacant site on the Thames embankment as suitable for the proposed museum and approached the Treasury and the metropolitan board of works.[3] In September 1876 the council wrote to colonial governments seeking contributions towards a museum's construction and maintenance, and the following month resolved to approach the secretary of state for India, and the viceroy, governors, and lieutenant-governors of the Indian provinces for assistance from the native princes towards what, in these instances, was diplomatically referred to as an Indian museum. The replies indicated a willingness in general terms to co-operate.[4] The council supported the distribution of publications giving information on the subject, communicated with town councils and chambers of commerce in the United Kingdom and persuaded them to memorialize the government in favour of the project, and arranged a public meeting at the Mansion House in London in March 1877. The Mansion House meeting was unanimous on the need for the museum, on the desirability of the embankment as its location, and on conveying the meeting's opinions to the government.[5]

Throughout this period the campaign was led by Dr. J. Forbes Watson, who was made an honorary fellow of the institute in 1877. Unfortunately, the enthusiasm of Forbes Watson and, spasmodically, of the institute could not secure support for the museum to the extent required, despite favourable responses from most of the colonies and the United Kingdom chambers of commerce and general approval in the colonial press. The main difficulty was financial: influenced partly by the example of the Algerian museum in Paris, the museum's advocates envisaged an institution of a style and

[2] Ibid., 7 (1876), 1–5.
[3] Co. Mins. 1 (25 May 1876), 424–5; (30 May), 428.
[4] Co. Mins. 2 (19 Sept. 1876), 5; (28 Nov.), 19. *The Times*, 2 July 1877.
[5] *Proceedings*, 8 (1877), 232–60, 426.

character that the Treasury was not prepared to subsidize. Another difficulty was the location, a strong section of opinion mainly outside the institute, and including the Prince of Wales, advocated the South Kensington area, while the institute, which hoped eventually to be accommodated in the museum buildings, insisted on a central site on the Thames embankment in the Westminster area. No further progress was made towards the establishment of the museum, but hopes were revived by the official announcement by the Prince of Wales of the decision to hold a colonial and Indian exhibition at South Kensington in 1886. In successive annual reports from 1884 to 1886 the council expressed pleasure at the possibilities opened up by the exhibition:

The opening of the Colonial and Indian Exhibition—an Exhibition illustrating exclusively for the first time the vast and varied resources of the outlying parts of the Empire—affords, in the opinion of the Council, a most favourable opportunity, which probably will never again present itself, for realizing one of the primary objects for which the Institute was founded, viz., to promote the establishment in London of a Colonial Museum. The unique collection of the products and manufactures of India and the Colonies, now brought together at the cost of so much time, thought and money, will thus find a fitting repository, and be permanently preserved and displayed for public inspection and instruction.

The Council wrote to the colonial agents-general and the Canadian high commissioner in London offering to co-operate in any plan to use the exhibition as the foundation of a museum.[6] What materialized from the exhibition, however, was not the colonial and Indian museum desired by the institute but something like it in the form of the Imperial Institute, which was granted a charter in May 1888 and given a site in South Kensington.

The establishment of the Imperial Institute had been the suggestion of the Prince of Wales in 1886 and had been given the blessing of the council of the Royal Colonial Institute in a resolution passed in October of that year. In the November, at the invitation of the Prince of Wales, the council nominated one of its members, Nevile Lubbock, to join the temporary committee which was studying the suggestion, and which, in its

[6] *Proceedings*, 15 (1884), 335; 16 (1885), 359; 17 (1886), 412.

report, recommended that provision should be made for 'the incorporation in some form into the proposed Institute of the Royal Colonial Institute, if, as is hoped, it be possible to bring about such a union'.[7] Committees of the two bodies discussed the terms of a union and the possibilities of concerted action, but there were constitutional obstacles, and in August 1889 the secretary of the Imperial Institute's organizing committee, Sir Frederick Abel, notified the Royal Colonial Institute of his committee's decision to leave the question of closer association in abeyance until the affairs of the Imperial Institute were more advanced. No formal approach on future relations was made until 1893, but there were informal discussions between individual members of the two governing bodies, and officials of the newly-founded institute freely availed themselves of permission to use the library of the older body.[8] Eleven members of the Royal Colonial Institute council were also on the governing body of the Imperial Institute as representatives of various colonies or, in the case of Rosebery, as a nominee of the Queen, but none of these was on the governing body in the capacity of a representative of the Royal Colonial Institute, although twenty-five other organizations and institutes in London were represented.

The relationship between the two institutes was a contentious subject among members of the Royal Colonial Institute, where there was some jealousy of the fine buildings with which its rival was being favoured. The new institute had objectives that overlapped those of the older body and it inevitably lured away some of the other's normal support and, with bodies such as the Imperial Federation League, was a contributory factor in the stagnation period into which the Royal Colonial Institute was now moving. Fear of being absorbed by the Imperial Institute was evident at the annual general meeting in 1887. The two main arguments against becoming entangled with the rival institution were first, that the site in Northumberland Avenue was preferable to the one in 'the dreary wastes of South Kensington', and second, that the sound financial position established over a long period of years might be jeopardized.[9]

[7] Ibid., 18 (1887), 165–6.
[8] Ibid., 21 (1890), 155; 24 (1893), 185–6, 206–7.
[9] Ibid., 18 (1887), 174–82; 24 (1893), 214.

Cries of dissent punctuated the speech of Lord Knutsford at the anniversary banquet of the institute in March 1893 when he referred to future generations celebrating 'the Silver Wedding of the Royal Colonial Institute with the Imperial Institute'.[10]

The subject had been brought into the open at the annual general meeting the previous month, when a group of members submitted a memorial to the council calling for amalgamation with the Imperial Institute and declaring that a separate existence was undesirable and that the Imperial Institute possessed 'all the requirements for the advancement of knowledge and information, for the promotion of Imperial Federation, as well as every requisite for comfort and sociability.'[11] The upshot was a special general meeting of fellows in March to consider the whole question. The feeling of members was quickly apparent, and with only three dissentients it was resolved that 'the independence of the Royal Colonial Institute should be strictly maintained in the future, as it has been in the past', and that it was 'inexpedient that any amalgamation, which might endanger the autonomy of the Royal Colonial Institute, should be entered into with the Imperial Institute'.[12] Although the council of the Imperial Institute had recently intimated that it was prepared to reopen discussions on concerted action, and special committees of the two councils conferred with this objective in mind, the separate identities of the two institutes were now assured.[13] Prompting from the Prince of Wales resurrected the issue in 1900, and Lord Grey toyed with the idea of amalgamation in 1912 as a way of altering what he regarded as the anachronistic title of the Royal Colonial Institute, but he had not thought deeply about the idea and it is doubtful whether he would have been able to carry it any further than previous efforts.[14]

In the 1880s the council of the Royal Colonial Institute was increasingly concerned with improving the younger generation's knowledge of the empire, and in February 1883 money prizes were offered to schoolchildren and university students in the United Kingdom for the best essays submitted on a set imperial

---

[10] *Proceedings*, 24 (1893), 233.   [11] Ibid., 210.   [12] Ibid., 265–86.
[13] Co. Mins. 6 (27 March 1893), 52; (11 April), 55–6; (25 April), 63.
[14] Co. Mins. 7 (10 July 1900), 242. Jebb to Grigg, 18 March 1912, Jebb Papers.

topic.[15] The response was disappointing: a total of thirty-six essays was received, seven from universities and twenty-nine from schools, and their quality was poor according to the report of the council's essay committee:

Whilst several of the essays exhibit considerable care in their preparation, it is evident that as a general rule they emanate from persons who, having little knowledge of the subject, have been led to study it with the especial object of winning the prizes offered by the Council. There are many errors in facts, even in the essays recommended for prizes, and the statistical information given is often quite out of date.[16]

The council repeated the experiment the following year in the vain expectation that the results would be more encouraging, and then abandoned it.

In 1913 the institute revived the essay competition, opening it to schools and universities not only in the United Kingdom but throughout the empire. The results were better than they had been thirty years before, although of the twenty-six entries for the school section fourteen were at once dismissed as of little merit by the assessor, Professor H. E. Egerton. Of the remaining school essays one was concerned largely with the the misdoings of motorists and another found what Egerton regarded as a 'dangerous fascination' in the figure of one thousand as the life span of the empire. Thirteen essays were submitted for the university section, and of these one was inferior to any of the school entries and another was a vision of imperialism described in a poem of heroic couplets.[17] The rest were of an acceptable standard, however, and the essay competition was retained and, except for the war years of 1939 and 1940, became a regular annual feature of the institute's educational programme.

The essay competition inaugurated in 1883 represented one aspect of a campaign to boost empire studies in the schools and universities. In February 1883 the council sent a letter to headmasters of the public schools and the better known middle-class schools urging on them the importance of including colonial history and geography as part of their courses of

[15] Co. Mins. 3 (6 Feb. 1883), 66. [16] *Proceedings*, 15 (1884), 64–6.
[17] Co. Mins. 10 (4 Nov. 1913), 23–4.

G

instruction.[18] This achieved no more than courteous replies of polite interest and desire to co-operate, but in 1892 the council returned to the issue, declaring that it considered the history, geography, climate, and resources of the colonies and India to be of sufficient importance to be a separate and specific subject in school curricula, and it again entered into correspondence with headmasters to gain their support and their advice on ways in which the institute could assist in achieving that goal. Several headmasters professed sympathy and offered suggestions.[19] Some progress was now being made, especially in the board and public elementary schools. The Education Department's code of regulations for 1892 expressly provided for instruction on the British colonies and dependencies, and the revised instructions issued to school inspectors contained a paragraph referring to the desirability in the 'examination of the Fourth and higher Standards that attention should be given to the English Colonies and their productions, government, and resources'. The Cambridge University local lectures syndicate now offered six courses of lectures on empire subjects, and at a summer school in 1893 for university extension and other students there were courses offered in imperial history. In 1896 the council supported a memorial drafted by the Geographical Association recommending secondary school examination boards to require a special study of the geography of the empire.[20] The efforts of the Royal Colonial Institute were an important factor behind the increasing attention given to the empire by educational bodies at the turn of the century, and they contributed indirectly to the Library Association's decision to demand a general knowledge of colonial literature for the library assistants' examination in 1904.

In their replies to the institute's letter of 1883 pressing the case for the study of imperial history and geography, several headmasters had alluded to the lack of trustworthy textbooks and maps. This led the council in May 1883 to write to the colonial governments for copies of recent maps and suitable books to assist the preparation and publication under the institute's authority of a suitable school book on the colonies, but the estimated expense of producing it proved to be larger

---

[18] Co. Mins. 3 (13 Feb. 1883), 70; (27 Feb.), 74–8.
[19] *Proceedings*, 24 (1893), 182, 365–70.   [20] Ibid., 28 (1897), 162.

than the institute at that time was able to shoulder.[21] The inquiries, however, had drawn public attention to the textbook situation, and in the following years several works on the colonies were published, some of them by fellows of the institute, including a series of books with maps issued from 1889 onwards under the institute's auspices for the use of students and general readers. The first publication in the series was by Charles Washington Eves on the West Indies and appeared in 1889 and in second and third editions in 1891 and 1893; this was followed by volumes on the history of the Dominion of Canada, on the geography of Canada and Newfoundland, and on the geography of Africa south of the Zambesi, all of them by W. P. Greswell and appearing in successive years between 1890 and 1892. The books on the West Indies and Canada were almost at once placed by the management committee of the School Board for London on its requisitions lists of books for use in the schools of the board.[22] Nevertheless, it was soon apparent that a self-supporting organization like the institute with only limited means lacked the resources to ensure the continuous revision necessary for maintaining adequate textbooks, and after the publication of four volumes the series ended in 1893 with the third edition of the first volume.

In 1890 the council concluded that it was desirable to produce a monthly journal during the session from December to July in advance of the annual volume of proceedings, and the first number was issued in December of that year. The contents of the monthly journal were similar to those in the proceedings, but it included additional material such as advertisements, notices of forthcoming events, comments by the librarian on new books, and, in the case of some later issues, illustrations. In 1909 the report of a committee seeking to revitalize the institute recommended that the monthly journal should be issued throughout the year, and not merely during eight months of it, and that the size and scope should be increased to make it comparable to the journal of the Royal Geographical Society. The council decided to amalgamate the existing journal with the annual volume of proceedings as a new monthly publication

[21] Ibid., 14 (1883), 387–8; 15 (1884), 6, 334.
[22] Ibid., 24 (1893), 369–70. For a selection of favourable reviews see ibid., 22 (1891), 338.

throughout the year with the title *United Empire*. A good editor was regarded as essential if the reform was to have the desired effect, and Archibald Ross Colquhoun was appointed at a salary of £200 per annum.[23]

Colquhoun was a writer of some ability and of considerable colonial experience. He had been born on board ship off the Cape of Good Hope in a violent storm. He had served in the Indian police, explored the country from Canton to Bhamo, in order to trace the best rail route between China and Burma, and been deputy commissioner in Burma, where his career prospects were ruined when his candid criticism of his superiors fell into the wrong hands. He had also visited Africa and Central America and written a book on schemes for cutting a canal through Panama. He was a good choice for editor, and the new journal possessed a lively character the institute's publications had previously lacked. It contained articles, poems, correspondence, reviews, and editorial notes and observations on imperial affairs that were sometimes contributed in part by others, notably by Richard Jebb, who had a high regard for Colquhoun and, in collusion with Earl Grey, tried to get the editor's salary increased.[24]

In April 1912 the institute published its first yearbook, a new venture that included some of the features of the former proceedings. It was largely the idea of the fertile mind of Jebb, then an active member and at the peak of his influence among imperialist thinkers. The yearbook comprised an historical sketch of the institute, accounts of the various departments of the institute's affairs and of the previous year's activities, lists of fellows and the proceedings of the annual general meeting. The world war in 1914 hampered its publication, and the issue of 1916 was the last.[25]

The institute's most successful service to education in empire affairs was its expanding library. Free public libraries were increasing rapidly in number throughout the country in the closing years of the century, when the American millionaire Andrew Carnegie and the British newspaper owner John

[23] Co. Mins. 8 (8 June 1909), 448; 9 (2 Nov. 1909), 10.
[24] Jebb to Ware, 11 April 1912; Jebb to Hawkes, 30 July; Grey to Jebb, 4 Dec.: Jebb Papers. *The Times*, 19 Dec. 1914.
[25] *United Empire*, 3 (1912), 269. *Library Notes*, 18 (June 1958).

Passmore Edwards took a beneficent interest in them. In the accelerating development of library facilities the library at the Royal Colonial Institute succeeded in establishing itself as the best in the British empire on colonial affairs. It had been largely dependent on donations from fellows, colonial governments, universities, chambers of commerce, and other societies ever since its inception, and its purchases were comparatively few, but by 1907 it was estimated to be holding about 70,000 books, certainly the most representative collection of colonial literature in the world. It specialized in works of reference, and colonial directories and handbooks (normally presented by the publishers), blue books, gazettes, and the latest official statistics of all the colonies were available for reference soon after publication. The library received regularly, as donations from the proprietors, colonial and Indian newspapers that were made readily available for consultation in the reading rooms, but problems of space compelled the council to accept an offer from the British Museum to store certain files of back numbers after the expiration of stated periods.[26] Maps and other miscellaneous items as well as books and pamphlets found their place in the library's collections. The most notable acquisition was that in 1889 of William Westall's original pencil and water-colour drawings which had been prepared as illustrations to Matthew Flinders's account of his voyage of discovery around Australia at the beginning of the nineteenth century. The majority were purchased from the artist's grandson for a nominal sum and some were the gift of a second grandson; they were ultimately edited by T. M. Perry and D. H. Simpson and published in June 1962.

Foreigners as well as British subjects browsed and pursued their researches in the reading rooms, and the library staff developed into what the secretary and librarian, J. S. O'Halloran, in 1888 likened to 'a not unimportant Intelligence Department'.[27] This educational service was taken further in 1913, when the council took up an idea suggested to it in 1911 in a letter from a J. W. Ford and organized an information bureau to answer inquiries on empire matters and to distribute

[26] *Proceedings*, 19 (1888), 149–50; 24 (1893), 184–5; 33 (1902), 138; 38 (1907), 122.

[27] Ibid., 19 (1888), 167.

information on the resources and the opportunities for trade and enterprise in the colonies.[28]

The institute's activity on the educational side of empire promotion was constant and wide-ranging. In 1882 the council attempted to enlist colonial support for the movement led by the Prince of Wales to establish a Royal College of Music 'as an Institution for the benefit of all portions of the Empire without exception'.[29] In 1889 it became interested with the Imperial Institute in the foundation of a school of modern oriental studies, and in 1912 it began to probe possible sources of finance for the establishment of a chair of empire trade at the London School of Economics.[30] In 1901, prompted by the absence of good maps for either civil or military use, the council appealed to the government to arrange a systematic survey of all British colonies and protectorates in Africa, contending 'that a comprehensive scheme should be organized such as would eventually enable a map of British Possessions in Africa to be compiled on a homogeneous plan, and on a scale that would adequately suffice for practical purposes'.[31] In 1908 the council participated in an unsuccessful deputation to the postmaster-general to seek a reduction in the postage rates for publications of scientific and learned societies, among which the institute was numbered, and in 1910 it launched an appeal for subscriptions to an empire lectures fund from which to finance talks on imperial topics at centres outside London.[32]

In 1906 the council published a resolution that in the interests of the empire as a whole colonial questions should be kept out of the arena of party politics.[33] The institute strove hard to preserve its non-party character, but in June 1914 George Parkin, a craggy Canadian with a corrugated face and untidy hair, made a provocative speech at an institute banquet, where he attacked British party politics as a threat to the foundations of the empire, an argument he repeated in a letter to *The Times*. The colonial secretary, Lewis Harcourt, a vice-

[28] Co. Mins. 9 (7 Feb. 1911), 146; (1 July 1913), 457.
[29] Co. Mins. 3 (9 May 1882), 6.
[30] Co. Mins. 5 (9 July 1889), 59; 9 (March 1912), 249–50; (2 April), 258.
[31] *Proceedings*, 33 (1902), 140.
[32] Co. Mins. 8 (7 April 1908), 359. *The Times*, 23 Sept. 1910.
[33] Co. Mins. 8 (8 May 1906), 239.

president, regarded the speech as too frank for the occasion and a protest on his behalf was sent to the council:

Mr. Harcourt feels very strongly that the speech then made by Dr. Parkin was a most serious breach of the principles which are supposed to govern the constitution of the Institute and the conduct of its functions, and that it cannot be allowed to pass unnoticed. You will readily see that Mr. Harcourt's own position as a Vice-President of the Institute and that of other Vice-Presidents and Members of the Council would be rendered impossible if it became the practice to allow speeches of this kind to be made with impunity at the dinners of the Institute. He trusts, therefore, that the Council will take such steps as they may think proper to mark in unmistakable fashion their disapproval of the course adopted by Dr. Parkin and their sense of its inconsistency with the basis on which the Institute was established and has hitherto been maintained.

Sir John Anderson, the permanent under-secretary, added his protest and assumed that the council would dissociate itself from Parkin's remarks: 'If not it will, of course, be necessary for public servants like myself to put an end to our connection with the Institute.'

The council refused to repudiate Parkin or to admit that he had infringed the non-political principle upon which the institute was founded. It declared that Parkin had referred to the mischief that party politics was doing to the cause of a united empire, a cause to which the institute was committed, and that

it would be injurious to the public interest if a speaker of his world-wide repute, and his well-known detachment from party politics, were precluded from expressing on such an occasion his own strong convictions in regard to matters of vital moment to the great cause which has been the study of his life.

Anderson resigned as a fellow, but Harcourt, after being interviewed by Sir Godfrey Lagden, the acting chairman, said he would not resign but would be unable to take further part in such functions because he could not expose himself to a repetition of such a demonstration against the government.[34] The institute, in fact, had been losing much of its non-party

[34] Willison, *Sir George Parkin*, 215–20. Co. Mins. 10 (23 June 1914), 121–2. *United Empire*, 5 (1914), 552–4.

image from the time Disraeli had made imperial consciousness an attribute of the Conservative party. An organization such as the institute which, as Jebb admitted, was compelled by circumstances to depend largely on Conservative speakers could not in practice maintain the external appearance of being genuinely non-party in character.[35]

By 1914 the institute was clearly recognizable as predominantly a social and educational body; such political influence as it might once have been able to exercise had now become minimal. It had not fulfilled the founders' original objective of establishing a colonial museum or that of undertaking 'scientific, literary, and statistical investigations in connection with the British Empire', but it had fulfilled the other objectives of providing a meeting place for those connected with, or having an interest in, the overseas empire, of establishing a reading room and library 'in which recent and authentic intelligence upon Colonial and Indian subjects' would be 'constantly available', of facilitating the 'interchange of experiences' among persons representing all the British dependencies, and of affording opportunities for reading papers and holding discussions on imperial affairs generally. Informative, and often original, papers were printed in the monthly journal after 1890 and reached a growing number of readers; they were also reported in the press and sometimes occasioned public discussion. In promoting the study and knowledge of the empire as a worthy end in itself, the institute found its best and most significant activity in the generation before the First World War.

[35] Jebb to Croft, 1 Nov. 1912, Jebb Papers.

Chapter Seven

Stagnation and Revolution (1882–1914)

AT the end of the nineteenth century the Royal Colonial Institute had the advantage of being physically established in the centre of London between the Thames embankment, the Strand, and Trafalgar Square. When the council had acquired the building site in Northumberland Avenue in 1883 on a lease terminating in 1962, it was hoped, according to the chairman, that it would be enabled in the future to offer 'influential and wealthy residents of the Colonies and those connected with the Colonies' the accommodation which they were entitled to expect and with which the institute had not provided them hitherto.[1] A loan was raised to finance the construction of the new headquarters, but by exercising the right to anticipate certain statutory payments the institute succeeded in freeing itself from debt much more rapidly than had been originally planned, thereby saving about £15,000 in interest, and in 1906 it acquired the freehold.[2] The one serious anxiety that arose was in 1900 when land promised in a bill before Parliament for use by the South Eastern Railway included part of that on which the institute stood, but a petition from the council led to the withdrawal of that section of the bill affecting the premises.[3] Although the upper part of the building was for a time leased to the Admiralty, in the early years of the twentieth century there were extensive structural alterations and when the new premises were formally opened on 19 December 1910 the council had taken over use of the whole building.

Hitherto, the building had been cramping and unattractive, but the acquisition of an adjoining block of premises facing Craven Street made expansion possible. The new structure provided the institute with accommodation for members

---

[1] *Proceedings*, 15 (1884), 4.   [2] Ibid., 38 (1907), 3. See *supra*, 25.
[3] Co. Mins. 7 (13 Feb. 1900), 204; (27 March), 215.

comparable to that of any of the other clubs and societies in London, and probably better than most. The main entrance was in Northumberland Avenue, and a reception room, a lounge and a writing room abutted the hall on the ground floor. The library occupied the whole of the first floor, the newspaper and magazine room the second, the council room and smoking room the third, and on the fourth were rooms in which students could do their research and also offices for the editorial staff of the monthly journal and for the empire lectures department, a recent addition designed to provide illustrated lectures throughout the country. Electric light had replaced gas lighting during the summer of 1891 and, somewhat belatedly, telephone communication with the metropolitan area was established in 1898. Coffee and afternoon tea, but not meals or stronger beverages, were supplied on the premises, and an attentive staff, including a page boy in the hall, provided a high standard of service.[4]

By the end of the nineteenth century death had removed from the governing body most of those who had served the institute from its foundation years. A random selection of those who died in the last decade of the nineteenth century and the opening years of the twentieth might include Sir John Coode, a councillor for eleven years and chairman of the building committee; the Earl of Albemarle (Viscount Bury), the first president; Sir Henry Barkly, who was identified with the institute for twenty-one years; William Maynard Farmer, a fellow for twenty-two years and a not inactive councillor in the 1890s; Sir Henry Jourdain, a fellow for twenty-seven years; Sir Sidney Shippard, a fellow for twenty-two years; and Admiral Sir Anthony Hoskins, a fellow for nineteen years. Sir Charles Mills, who died in 1895, had been a fellow since 1874 and a councillor since 1883 and was also a governor of the Imperial Institute. His colonial ties were with the Cape, of which he became the agent-general in London in 1882, and although he maintained an official veneer of impartiality he was personally sympathetic to the expansive policy of Cecil Rhodes. His cheerful and businesslike approach had been a considerable asset to the council's deliberations, and his portly,

---

[4] *United Empire*, 2 (1911), 46. Co. Mins. 4 (14 Jan. 1886), 6; 7 (12 July 1898), 86; 9 (4 April 1911), 165.

florid figure could normally be relied upon to energize social occasions, of which he was known to be fond.

Among the institute's senior administrative staff, the quiet unostentatious Sir William Sargeaunt was honorary treasurer from the foundation until the summer of 1888, when he resigned on account of failing health and died soon afterwards at the age of fifty-eight. He had served in Natal, St. Vincent, and the Colonial Office, and been one of the crown agents for the colonies for nearly twenty years.[5] He was succeeded as honorary treasurer by Sir Montagu Ommanney. Joseph Sylvester O'Halloran, who had been appointed librarian and assistant secretary in 1881, was made full-time secretary and librarian in 1884; he served until 1909 when ill-health obliged him to resign. He was a South Australian and had spent the early part of his working life in the South Australia audit office as clerk to the executive council and court of appeals, eventually becoming private secretary to the governor.[6] O'Halloran's original appointment as both secretary and librarian was soon modified to that of secretary only, the post of librarian falling to James R. Boosé, who had been employed at the institute since he was a boy and in practice had already been managing the library's affairs for several years. He succeeded O'Halloran as secretary in 1909, when P. Evans Lewin became librarian.[7] Boosé, the anglicized mispronunciation of whose name was a perennial irritant to him and an endless source of amusement to some of his colleagues, later became an inexhaustible traveller on the institute's behalf and was instrumental in accelerating an increase in overseas membership.

Before the appointment of O'Halloran, the institute's administrative and secretarial responsibilities had for many years been borne largely by Frederick Young, who continued for a time as honorary secretary and then became a vice-president, an office which he held until his death in 1913 at the age of ninety-six. Born two years after the battle of Waterloo, Young's memory was long and restless, and he took great pleasure in recalling events and personalities that were remote to most people by the turn of the century. His passion for

[5] *The Times*, 2 Aug. 1888.
[6] *United Empire*, 11 (1920), 136. *The Times*, 30 Jan. 1920.
[7] *United Empire*, 1 (1910), 3. Boosé, *Memory Serving*, 20.

imperial affairs had been roused by Edward Gibbon Wakefield, the apostle of systematic colonization, whose views Young maintained to the end were the soundest he had heard: 'So long as he lived', he told a meeting in 1909, 'he should maintain that that was the only right plan to be followed in our schemes of emigration, which, in his opinion, ought to be conducted on a broad and comprehensive system of national State colonization.'[8] He was a shareholder in the New Zealand Company which Wakefield founded and of which Young's father was a director, the shipping manager of the Canterbury Association established in 1850, and chairman of a society formed in 1868 to promote state organized emigration from the United Kingdom. While taking an energetic part in the activities of the institute, Young was also a magistrate for Middlesex, a leader in a campaign for the preservation of Epping Forest for public use, secretary of a movement for securing Victoria Park as an open space, and one of the first vice-chairmen of the Imperial Federation League. He published a number of lectures, letters, pamphlets, and miscellaneous writings on imperial affairs, and visited Canada at the age of eighty-four. Although he led an abstemious and disciplined life, he was generally popular, frequently chairing ordinary meetings, where he could be relied upon to contribute to the discussions even in his last years. He attended every annual general meeting from the time the institute was founded until illness finally broke his record in 1909. In his later years he was in straitened financial circumstances: on his ninetieth birthday in 1907 the institute presented him with a purse of £1,000, in 1912 the council placed a further £100 at his disposal, and in 1914, after his death, it applied unsuccessfully to the Treasury for civil list pensions for his daughters.[9]

The increase in membership of the institute was steady but modest. The armed services and the professional and landed classes naturally predominated, there was a strong contingent of clergymen, and the institute became what one member described disparagingly as 'the place of resort of a particular

---

[8] *Proceedings*, 40 (1909), 233–4.
[9] Co. Mins. 9 (5 March 1912), 242–3; 10 (26 Feb. 1914), 73–4; (25 March), 78; (5 May), 100. *The Times*, 10 Nov. 1913.

set of persons'.[10] In 1892 about 10 per cent of the resident fellows were members also of one or more of over thirty other London clubs, of which the Carlton, Oriental, Athenæum, United Service, and Conservative were the most favoured, and nearly a third of the governing body belonged to the peerage or royalty and another third were knights. Membership of the institute carried a mark of respectability that was carefully protected by the council, which ruthlessly expelled the remarkably few persons over the years who disgraced it. A fellow was called on to resign following unseemly behaviour at a banquet in July 1897, and another was advised to resign following his dismissal from the Sierra Leone civil service in 1904.[11] The council removed from the list of fellows an uncertified bankrupt sent to prison for fraud in 1904, a member sentenced in 1905 to five years' penal servitude, another from Cape Colony sentenced in 1908 to three years' hard labour for embezzlement, another convicted in 1916 of making a false statement to a police officer and of possessing a false passport, and two others imprisoned for fraud in 1923.[12] A life fellow, sentenced to imprisonment in 1906 for obtaining credit without revealing that he was an undischarged bankrupt, was struck off the list of fellows and his demand for repayment of a proportion of his life subscription studiously ignored by the council.[13]

In 1892 the total membership was 3,775, of whom 1,350 were resident fellows, 2,416 were non-resident, and nine were honorary. Increases had averaged 230 a year during the 1880s, but in the 1890s the average dropped substantially, and the 1892 membership, indeed, represented a reduction of seven since the previous year. Fewer than 800 were added to the membership in the twenty years from 1890 to 1909, a period in which the institute showed signs of decay and subsided into a passive rather than an active role in imperial affairs. Its most exhilarating achievement was the creation of Loch's Horse, a scout force of mounted men that served in the Boer War. Reverses to British arms in Natal and Cape Colony in December

[10] *Proceedings*, 11 (1880), 369.
[11] Co. Mins. 7 (13 July 1897), 4; 8 (12 April 1904), 84; (26 April), 90; (31 May), 96.
[12] Co. Mins. 8 (26 Jan. 1904), 62; (28 Dec. 1905), 210; (11 Feb. 1908), 346; 11 (7 Nov. 1916), 163–4; 14 (14 May 1923), 93; (9 July), 113, 123.
[13] Co. Mins. 8 (16 Oct. 1906), 260; (13 Nov.), 264–5; (12 March 1907), 290.

1899 gave rise to an urgent call for volunteers from Britain, and the council, on the suggestion of several fellows, formed a committee to take advantage of the presence in the United Kingdom of young men acquainted with South Africa and speaking Dutch and Kaffir. The lead was taken by one of the governing body, Lord Loch, and subsequently the force that was raised and equipped was named after him.[14] Loch's Horse, however, was merely an isolated fillip in a period when non-governmental initiative in empire matters passed to other organizations and to individuals acting outside the institute, which now lacked the dynamic enthusiasm that had been a feature of its earlier history. Its morale was low, and was not appreciably improved by the completion of its handsome new headquarters, which members tended to compare jealously with the magnificent building erected for the Imperial Institute.

By 1909 there was some dissatisfaction among the resident fellows. The council had become staid, cautious, and, it was suspected, effete. It should have done much more towards establishing branches outside London and absorbing some of what were described as the 'one-horse, single-barrelled, dot-and-carry-one Leagues' which had subducted some of the institute's support and duplicated some of its activities.[15] The council was a self-perpetuating body which for forty years had filled by its own nomination any vacancies that appeared in its increasingly unprogressive ranks. A part of the governing body retired periodically: the president every second year, and five of the twenty vice-presidents and six of the twenty-four councillors every year by rotation. They were all eligible for re-election, however, and in practice the remaining members of council and the fellows at the annual general meeting always confirmed the retiring councillors in office, naturally shunning the responsibility of rejecting men who had devoted themselves to the institute for long periods. On no occasion since the institute was founded had the nominations by the council not been ratified by the fellows at the annual general meeting. The inevitable consequence was a council composed of members virtually elected for life. Of the vice-presidents, two had served

[14] *The Times*, 21 June 1900. Co. Mins. 7 (26 June 1900), 238. *Proceedings*, 31 (1900), 123; 32 (1901), 4, 200.
[15] *Proceedings*, 40 (1909), 191, 245.

for thirty years, three for over twenty years, one for seventeen years, and seven for over ten years; of the councillors, one had served for thirty years, three for over twenty years, and seven for over ten years. Although non-resident fellows were more than two-thirds of the total membership, under the existing rules none was able to serve on the governing body either as a vice-president or as a member of council.

In October 1908 the council appointed a committee to report on means of increasing membership and making the institute better known,[16] but this faint stirring on the council was overtaken by a movement among the fellows seeking to democratize and revitalize the whole organization. At the annual general meeting in February 1909 Archibald Colquhoun, a resident fellow, and Professor William L. Grant, a non-resident fellow from Canada and son-in-law of Sir George Parkin, moved that the adoption of the council's annual report should be deferred 'pending the calling of a special general meeting to consider the advisability of making certain changes in the constitution'. The report, said Colquhoun, showed that income had been almost stationary for twenty years and its membership for over a decade:

Considering the vast improvement in communications which has taken place in that period, the much larger number of Colonials who visit us annually, and (I may add) the growth of our library and its attraction for students of Colonial subjects, I regard this stagnation in our work as a most serious matter, and one which makes it imperative for us to consider seriously what may be the causes of it.

He thought the government of the institute should be more representative and should include non-resident fellows.[17] The chairman of the meeting, Admiral Sir Nathaniel Bowden-Smith, ruled the motion out of order, but a special general meeting was called a month later in response to a requisition signed by thirty-one fellows headed by Colquhoun and Grant who wished to 'consider the revision of the constitution of the Institute with special reference to making the Council more representative'.[18]

---

[16] Co. Mins. 8 (13 Oct. 1908), 389.   [17] *Proceedings*, 40 (1909), 188–97.
[18] Co. Mins. 8 (2 March 1909), 419.

Colquhoun's opening statement on behalf of the reformers contained four main proposals: first, that retiring vice-presidents and councillors should not be eligible for re-election until after the expiration of at least one year; second, that up to one-third of the vice-presidents should be men from the colonies who would attend and preside at meetings during their visits to London; third, that a chairman of council should be elected annually who would be 'something more than a figurehead'; and fourth, that the council's nominations to fill vacant offices should be presented to the fellows at an ordinary meeting at least four months before the annual general meeting at which they would form the balloting list for the election. The resolution that the constitution should be revised to make the council more representative was adopted unanimously, and a committee of three councillors and three reforming fellows was appointed to study the rules and working of the institute and report to the council.[19] The committee consisted of Lieutenant-General Sir James Bevan Edwards, Sir Nevile Lubbock, and George Parkin from the council, and Colquhoun, Grant, and Ralph S. Bond from the general body of fellows.

The committee held its first meeting on 5 April 1909 and presented an interim report to the council on 25 May. It recommended that the number of vice-presidents should be increased from twenty to twenty-four and that measures should be taken to ensure that eventually one-third were non-resident fellows: the council approved this. The committee also recommended that retiring councillors should not be eligible for re-election until one year had expired but that the council could, on showing special reason, nominate two of the six retiring councillors for re-election: the council approved this in principle, but suggested that only three councillors should be ineligible for re-election because six would deprive it every year of too many of its most useful members whose places would be difficult to fill with new men. The committee declared that, 'with a view to making the Council more representative of the Fellows, greater facility should be given to the Fellows for having some voice in the election of the members of the Council', and proposed that voting by post should be allowed and should be open to non-resident as well as resident fellows.

[19] *Proceedings*, 40 (1909), 235–49.

The council considered the new form of voting unnecessarily complicated and disapproved of non-resident fellows having the power to nominate councillors. An important recommendation by the committee was that there should be a chairman of the council elected annually to hold office for one year and to be ineligible for re-election the succeeding year:

The Committee feel that the appointment of a regular Chairman of the Council will not only be of great assistance to the permanent staff of the Institute, who will then have some recognized member of the Council to whom to refer, but also that the prosperity of the Institute may be considerably increased thereby, and through the emulation there will naturally be among the members of the Council when holding the distinguished and important post of Chairman of the Council to make his year of office as successful as possible.

The council approved this recommendation on the understanding that the chairman should be eligible for re-election to a second year of office. The committee had much to say on the question of membership:

It is felt that there are many persons who would like to participate in the work of the Institute who cannot afford the present subscription, and also that if the Journal of the Institute be enlarged in accordance with a scheme to be dealt with in the subsequent report of the Committee, there will be many who will be glad to be able to obtain the Journal and attend meetings of the Institute, at which papers are read, at a reduced subscription, but who would hesitate to become Fellows on the present terms, feeling that, either because of their not living in London, or for other reasons, they have no need to make use of our valuable library or our Institute buildings.

Accordingly, it recommended a new category of associate membership that the council approved in principle but decided to restrict to ladies.[20]

The council approved the declaration of the committee's final report, presented on 8 June, that, 'while efforts should be made to brighten and popularize the Institute in minor ways, the status of the Institute as an intellectual body should be maintained, and that it should in no way be allowed to degenerate into a second-rate club'. It also approved the

[20] Co. Mins. 8 (25 May 1909), 443–4.

H

suggestion that local committees of the institute might be formed in leading provincial cities, that a conference on imperial questions should be held in the provinces each year, and that special efforts should be made to attract the younger generation. Among other ideas raised were the extension of educational propaganda, the offer of medals for essays on imperial topics, and the enlargement of the institute journal. The report also recommended that 'efforts should be made to establish a closer connection between the Institute and commercial and industrial interests in the City of London and other commercial centres', and it supported the idea which had been put forward at the annual general meeting in February by a new fellow, Ernest Turnbull, that the institute should follow the example of a number of empire clubs in Canada and organize businessmen's lunches at which addresses would be given by prominent colonial visitors: the council was sceptical of these ideas, wanted to know what practical steps could be taken to establish closer relations with the City, and complained that the committee should have thought more about the likely cost of the recommendations in the report.[21] Nevertheless, it welcomed the decision later in the year of the Lord Mayor of London to join the institute because it expected that he would assist any attempts to foster a more intimate association with the City.

The reform committee's two reports were considered by a special general meeting held in the afternoon of 26 October, when the discussion revealed a wide measure of agreement on the desirability of the proposed reforms. Sir Frederick Young contributed his now customary historical account of his long connection with the institute, and on a division forty-five voted for the resolution that the suggested alteration of the rules should be adopted, and only eight voted against.[22]

The revolutionary movement in 1909, while not completely shaking the institute out of its complacency, did produce important changes. The rules were revised to increase the number of vice-presidents from twenty to thirty and allow for the election of non-residents. Three of the council's twenty-four members now retired each year by rotation and were not

---

[21] Co. Mins. 8 (8 June 1909), 447–8.
[22] Co. Mins. 8 (24 June 1909), 452; (27 July), 463. *Journal of the Royal Colonial Institute* (Dec. 1909), 35–44.

eligible for re-election until a year had elapsed, and all resident fellows and non-resident fellows who were in the United Kingdom had a direct vote in the election of the council. A chairman of council held office for not more than two years consecutively, a rule that was at once broken by the first incumbent, Bevan Edwards, who served for six consecutive years from 1909 to 1915. Edwards, moreover, had served on the reform committee whose report had recommended that chairmen should serve for only one year, but he was a good choice for the period of revitalization that was expected. He was a military man and a Conservative, had been a fellow since 1890, when he returned from investigating for the British government the defence of the Australian colonies. His report on Australian defences emphasizing the weakness inherent in separate military establishments around the continent and the advantages to be derived from federation had provided the opportunity for which Henry Parkes, the New South Wales leader, had been waiting to initiate a campaign for a national convention to frame a federal constitution for the Australian colonies. Edwards had been elected to the institute's council in 1893 and was among the most regular in his attendance. He liked action and decision —he married three times—and he provided the vigorous leadership that was required and achieved results where other men might have failed. He quickly extended the system of working by committees, each of which had a permanent chairman and whose composition was not restricted to members of council but included fellows whose special knowledge or interest in the subject was considered useful; although the committees reported to the council for final decision, they acted almost independently in the routine conduct of their departments.

The idea of organizing businessmen's lunches in the City with a talk by a prominent colonial visitor was approved by the council at the end of 1909 and put into effect the following year. It was hoped that the lunch-hour meetings would promote a closer relationship with commercial and industrial interests and would assist in 'spreading the knowledge of Empire among City men'. Several companies lent halls for the occasions and the meetings were a success from the start.[23]

An important innovation was the admission of ladies to associate membership at a subscription of one pound a year. The charter, by implication, did not allow ladies to be admitted as fellows, but as associates they were entitled to receive the monthly journal, attend ordinary meetings and receive invitations to the annual conversazione. Ladies had attended meetings as guests of fellows since the early 1870s, but had been prohibited in 1885 from using the institute's rooms.[24] Female membership was considered by the council as early as 1876, and in July 1893 the question had been referred to the finance committee, which advised against the admission of ladies as members on the grounds that the accommodation was inadequate to meet the new demands that would be made on it.[25] A few months later, however, the council decided to invite Flora Shaw (later Lady Lugard) to read a paper at a meeting in January 1894, and it adhered to the practice of inviting the speaker to dinner, for which, on this occasion, it allowed other ladies to be present as guests. For a woman to be invited to address an institute meeting was a new departure, and her talk secured two columns and an editorial in *The Times*.[26] Lady Lugard, as she became, returned to give a paper in June 1904,[27] and there was a large female attendance at a meeting in March 1909, when Mrs. Douglas Cator read a paper embellishing her initial assumption 'that one Englishman is a match for seven foreigners, and that it is our heritage and our inalienable right to be first'.[28] At the end of the year ladies were admitted to associate membership, and finally, in 1922, they were admitted as fellows, Mrs. Alec Tweedie, on Lord Meath's nomination, becoming the first.[29]

The campaign after 1909 to attract membership had considerable success. Total membership rose to 10,904 in 1915 from

[24] Co. Mins. 3 (3 Nov. 1885), 435.

[25] Co. Mins. 2 (24 Oct. 1876), 11; 6 (13 June 1893), 73; (11 July) 83.

[26] *The Times*, 10 Jan. 1894. Co. Mins. 6 (12 Dec. 1893), 111. *Proceedings*, 25 (1894), 138–57. E. M. Bell, *Flora Shaw: Lady Lugard, D.B.E.* (London 1947), 168–9.

[27] *Proceedings*, 35 (1904), 300–21. M. Perham, *Lugard: the Years of Authority, 1898–1945* (London 1960), 233. Lady Lugard addressed the institute on four occasions.

[28] *Proceedings*, 40 (1909), 223–35.

[29] Co. Mins. 14 (10 Oct. 1922), 15. Mrs. Alec Tweedie, *Me and Mine: A Medley of Thoughts and Memories* (London 1932), 113.

the 4,527 of 1909, and revenue in the same period rose to £13,306 from £7,434, a sum which had included £1,450 rental from the Admiralty that ceased in 1910 when the institute took over the whole building in Northumberland Avenue for its own use.[30] The membership campaign was helped in a small way by the practice begun in 1909 of admitting all Rhodes scholars to honorary membership during their time in residence at Oxford, and by the grant of reciprocal concessions to members of other societies with which the institute agreed to affiliate, notably the Empire Club of Canada in 1911 and the Malta Association in 1912.[31] A more significant development would have been the establishment of a formal connection with the undergraduate Ralegh Club, which was inaugurated at Oxford in 1913 by Milner and James Allen and met to discuss imperial questions; Jebb and Egerton toyed with the idea of creating an institute branch out of the club, but nothing came of it.[32]

Lord Grey, who became president in 1912 and who, it was hoped, would be a working president and not, as his predecessor the Duke of Connaught had been, an ornamental figurehead, had been interested since 1902 in expanding the membership and he wished to raise it to 8,000 by the end of his first year of office. He succeeded in securing a number of South African nominations when he went to Cape Town in June 1912 to unveil the Rhodes memorial on the slopes of Table Mountain,[33] and visits to Canada and South Africa by the secretary and to South America by the editor of the journal encouraged further additions to the overseas membership. The membership campaign was also assisted by the formation in 1912 of a masonic lodge 'for the purpose of enhancing the ties of Empire and Craft and as an additional bond between the Resident and Non-Resident Fellows and Members'. The lodge had been suggested in May 1911 by Major G. T. Beeching, a meeting of those interested was held on 11 July, and the lodge was

[30] Co. Mins. 11 (30 Jan. 1917), 203.
[31] Co. Mins. 9 (16 May 1911), 174; (25 July), 192; (7 Nov.), 204; (2 July 1912), 308.
[32] Curtis to Jebb, 12 April 1913; Egerton to Jebb, 27 April: Jebb Papers. The Ralegh Club still meets to discuss commonwealth questions.
[33] Co. Mins. 7 (13 May 1902), 389. Jebb to Grigg, 18 March 1912; Jebb to C. H. Cahan, 26 Sept.; Grey to Jebb, 4 Dec.: Jebb Papers.

consecrated in the Grand Temple at Freemasons Hall on 10 January 1912, when Lord Ampthill, the pro-grand master of English masonry, was the principal officiant. The first master of the lodge was the grand master, the Duke of Connaught, Governor-General of Canada and a former president of the institute.[34]

An issue that was certain to arise out of any reform movement was that of the institute's designation. At the annual general meeting in March 1910 the chairman referred to the changing circumstances in the empire that appeared to render the existing title inappropriate, and his invitation to fellows to send the council their views on the question was taken up two days later in a press comment on the inadequacy of the existing name and the desirability of a change: 'And since', it added, 'the period has now come when the useful work of the Institute is to be largely extended, it may well consider, like the lady of uncertain age who received her first proposal of marriage, that it is high time to have a change of name.'[35] Letters from non-resident fellows in 1911 asking for an alteration that would make the name more representative of the empire as a whole led to a motion on the council in favour of becoming the Royal United Empire Society, but no immediate practical step was taken.[36] In January 1912 the council asked George Parkin to write a memorandum for the journal giving reasons for changing the name. He argued that the term 'colonial' in connection with India, Canada, Australia, South Africa and New Zealand was a misnomer

It seems likely that the work of the Institute in the future may be as much concerned in cultivating throughout the Empire sound views in regard to national responsibilities as it has hitherto been in making the Colonies understood in the Mother Country. Consequent upon the great growth of membership, the policy of the Institute may well be in the near future to establish centralized branches in each of the Dominions where its members may readily meet for discussion as now in London. The use of the term 'Colonial' would certainly be inadequate in such a case, and would indeed seem to stamp the colonial status permanently upon the country where it is used.

[34] *United Empire*, 3 (1912), 156–7; 4 (1913), 195. Boosé, *Memory Serving*, 83.
[35] *Globe*, 3 March 1910; quoted in *United Empire*, 1 (1910), 231–2.
[36] Co. Mins. 9 (7 Nov. 1911), 205; (21 Nov.), 210.

The memorandum was inserted in the April issue of the journal in order to bring the question to the notice of fellows, who were again invited to submit their views.[37]

In a referendum completed in October 1912, however, only 483 fellows voted; of these 332 were in favour of a change of name and 151 were against, and the alternative title with the largest number of supporters was British Empire Institute with seventy-two votes. On the council Jebb was the principal advocate of alteration, and he campaigned strongly on behalf of the title of Royal Britannic Institute as the correct one for an institute composed of subjects of His Britannic Majesty not only in the empire but also in foreign countries. The council itself was divided on the issue and decided to allow Jebb to put his proposal to the annual general meeting in March 1914. It was soon apparent that the majority of those attending the meeting were averse to a change, and after discussion an amendment was carried that no alteration in the title should be made without the consent of a majority of fellows indicated in a postal referendum. Jebb was disappointed but not surprised: 'the plain fact is', he wrote, 'that the London membership, including the ex-politician-of-30-years ago Australian Agents-General, is probably the most ultra-conservative section of the whole body'.[38]

By 1914 the reform movement of 1909 had run its initial course. It had succeeded in increasing the total number of fellows and attracting associates, and it had at least produced the feeling of a revitalized organization. It had reduced the influence of the hidebound London membership which for years had held the organization in its unimaginative grip. The journal had developed a popular appeal it had previously lacked, although it continued to suffer, like the institute itself, from what one of the contributors, A. Wyatt Tilby, described as a distaste for saying anything definite.[39] There was a renewed awareness of the need to extend the institute's influence and improve its reputation in the community at large, but while there was every appearance of progress and activity there

---

[37] *United Empire*, 3 (1912), 279–80.
[38] Jebb to Hawkes, 9 April 1914, Jebb Papers. Co. Mins. 14 (14 Nov. 1927), 477–8. *United Empire*, 5 (1914), 289–90.
[39] Tilby to Jebb, 18 April 1917, Jebb Papers.

was little evidence of a substantial broadening of character or liberalization of outlook. Jebb was the member of the council who was most depressed with the progress being made: 'The Colonial Institute', he told Fabian Ware, 'seems to be going ahead in members but not, really, in anything else. It is a bad policy to rake in members by tall talk of what you are about to do when you can't do it after all.'[40] There was still a pronounced Australian influence, and the Australian members in London, mainly journalists and businessmen, established what was in effect an Australian section which met periodically and conducted its own private discussions on imperial affairs.[41] Even in Australian matters, however, the institute's approach had become vague and indecisive, as Hugh Childers had complained as early as 1885, when he had been a vice-president.[42]

A continuing weakness lay in the fact that the members from whom the institute might have derived the initiative and intellectual stimulus it needed were men of multifarious activities and interests, heavily committed to a busy public life and often to other societies. Among these men the Royal Colonial Institute was seldom regarded as warranting a high priority. Amery protested that he had 'so many irons in the fire' that he found it difficult to attend council meetings,[43] and others had to squeeze their responsibilities into a tight schedule of other commitments. 'What a lot might be done with that Institute', exclaimed Jebb, 'if only it were properly run all round! But no one seems able to afford the time.'[44] The institute had lost its talent for engaging public opinion and applying pressure on the British government on behalf of colonial interests and was increasingly unable to match the requirements of a world with which it was not yet fully abreast. It tried, on occasion, to arouse public concern over imperial issues but its organization, as Jebb pointed out, was 'too elementary to do this kind of thing effectively'.[45] By 1914 the

[40] Jebb to Ware, 2 June, 1912, Jebb Papers.
[41] Jebb to Arthur Hawkes, 28 June 1913, ibid.
[42] E. S. E. Childers, *The Life and Correspondence of the Right Hon. Hugh C. E. Childers, 1827–1896* (2 vols., London 1901), II, 257.
[43] Amery to Jebb, 21 Oct. 1912, Jebb Papers.
[44] Jebb to Ware, 11 April 1912, ibid.
[45] Jebb to Hawkes, 9 April 1914, ibid.

degeneration had been checked and a valuable educational role had been evolved, but the institute was still largely an exclusive, conservative organization and had not regained the clear sense of purpose that had inspired its foundation and early years.

Chapter Eight

World War One (1914–1919)

In August 1914 the British government committed the empire to war with Germany. It made no demands for military or financial support from India and the dominions, which would have been at liberty under the constitutional conventions of the empire to refuse it, but all pledged themselves immediately to the imperial war effort. The war was in a real sense the empire's war, and it was natural that the Royal Colonial Institute should feel that it had a special obligation to contribute as fully as its resources would allow. The council at once advertised to the members Lord Kitchener's call to arms:

Fellows and Associates of the Royal Colonial Institute! The Council commends to your notice Lord Kitchener's stirring and soldierly appeal, and calls upon you, collectively and individually, to support it to the best of your ability at home and overseas.

Another 100,000 men are needed!

Help to give Lord Kitchener the men he asks for!

The call was answered enthusiastically by resident and non-resident fellows, and by the end of the war in 1918 nearly 200 fellows had been killed in action or died of wounds.[1]

Soon after the declaration of war, a special meeting of the council resolved to offer honorary membership until the end of the year to all men from the overseas empire visiting the United Kingdom and unable to return to their own country. Lack of accommodation prevented the offer being extended to women visitors, for whom accommodation was secured at the Hotel Metropole. The War Office was offered use of part of the main building, and within a few weeks took over two large rooms on the ground floor for what was known as its voluntary assistance department, which arranged speakers for military meetings to promote recruitment for special trades in the army and which

[1] *United Empire*, 5 (1914), 681, 823; 10 (1919), 188, 297.

functioned until 1916, when it dispersed, its usefulness having been reduced by a new scheme of enlistment under a group system. Institute rooms were also used either regularly or occasionally by several other wartime organizations and approved bodies dealing with overseas affairs, including the committee of the Australian Voluntary Hospital and the London sub-committee of the Child Emigration Society.

As a result of a well-attended informal meeting of fellows on 11 August 1914, just one week after the outbreak of hostilities, a war services committee was formed. It acted as a source of advice and information for personnel of the armed services and helped institute members to enlist in the forces in the capacity that they desired, which in the majority of cases was as officers in the army. Except for postage and small administrative expenses, the committee carried out the tasks without cost to the institute and was well served by its honorary secretary, Coleman P. Hyman. It conducted the negotiations that led to the institute's becoming the patron of a motor ambulance for conveying wounded soldiers between railway stations and hospitals. The ambulance bore the bold inscription that it was 'under the patronage of the Royal Colonial Institute, Northumberland Avenue', and was managed and maintained by Smetham Lee and an advisory board on which the institute was represented.

On 13 August the council asked one of its number, Harry Brittain, to chair and direct a special overseas committee created by the council to help and advise armed forces from the overseas empire while they were in England.[2] The committee quickly arranged a meeting for the beginning of September to enable women from the dominions to meet members of the *Daily Express* nursing corps, and followed by appointing a ladies sub-committee to organize a series of nursing classes for women and a sewing class to co-operate with the Red Cross. The overseas committee acted as a clearing-house in London for empire servicemen, whether or not they were members of the institute. It supplied them with information, obtained recruits for special trades in the forces, received institute members from overseas who came to enlist and recommended them for commissions, distributed magazines and newspapers to the

[2] Co. Mins. 10 (13 Aug. 1914), 137.

services, started ambulance classes for men, and generally looked after overseas citizens of the empire while they were in London.[3]

The institute's ability with a depleted staff to sustain increased responsibilities was attributable in an important degree to two men. Sir Charles Prestwood Lucas, who succeeded Bevan Edwards as chairman of council in 1915, had entered the Colonial Office in 1877 and risen rapidly to become assistant under-secretary of the newly-created emigrants information office and was unfortunate not to be appointed to the under-secretaryship of state when Sir Montagu Ommanney (the institute's honorary treasurer) retired from the post in 1907. In that year the Colonial Office was reorganized so that the business of the dominions was separated from that of the colonies, and Lucas became the first head of the dominions department, a post in which he made an exhaustive tour of Australia and New Zealand before retiring prematurely in 1911 at the age of fifty-eight. He was for a time the principal of the Working Men's College, but he devoted his retirement mainly to scholastic writing about the empire, producing several standard works on the subject, and in 1920 he was elected to a fellowship at All Souls College, Oxford.

When the council of the institute decided in 1916 to promote an authoritative six-volume history of imperial co-operation during the war and signed an agreement with Oxford University Press for its publication, Lucas was the inevitable choice for general editor, and, in the event, he was to a large extent the author. The project's scope was later reduced from six volumes to five, which were published between 1921 and 1926. Lucas was a shy and modest man, a bachelor whose house in London was for years presided over by his two unmarried sisters, and his long experience in official affairs had developed in him what he once termed 'essentially a half-way House mind'. He recognized the weaknesses in the institute's organization that the strains of war were aggravating and believed that too many committees had been created to do too many things: 'The difficulty', he complained, 'is to find time for any proposals in the direction of rearrangement and more co-ordination —which seems to me to be wanted.'[4] Nevertheless, he was an

---

[3] H. Brittain, *Happy Pilgrimage* (London 1949), 340. *The Times*, 27 Feb. 1928.
[4] Lucas to Jebb, 8 July 1916, Jebb Papers.

excellent chairman of council, perhaps the best it has ever had: gentle, kindly, moderate, reliable, and thorough.

Lucas was heavily dependent on Sir Harry Wilson, the tactful and capable secretary from 1915 to 1921. In his younger days Wilson had been a keen player of rugby football, and was largely responsible for the tablet erected in the close at Rugby School in memory of W. W. Ellis, the inventor of the game according to a report on its origins of which Wilson had been one of the authors. Wilson, like Lucas, had a long career of public service. A classics scholar, he became a barrister and entered the Colonial Office, where he was private secretary to Joseph Chamberlain, the colonial secretary, in the period of the Jameson Raid and the colonial conference of 1897. He subsequently served in South Africa as legal assistant to the high commissioner and secretary of the Orange River Colony administration, for which he acted as lieutenant-governor at various times between 1903 and 1906, retiring in 1907 when it received responsible government. He became chairman of the North Charterland Exploration Company and of British Overseas Stores, and took an active part in the public life of Hereford, where in the 1920s he was chairman both of the finance committee of the Unionist association and of the museum and art gallery committee.

Wilson had been elected to the council of the Royal Colonial Institute in 1913, and two years later was persuaded by the president, Grey, to become secretary on the retirement of Boosé. His enthusiasm and energy made him an excellent adjutant to the more reflective Lucas, and they worked together to place the institute at the service of the imperial war effort and, after the war, to popularize it at home and overseas. On the death of Colquhoun in 1914, he edited the journal for six years with the assistance successively of Colquhoun's widow (later Mrs. Tawse Jollie), H. Thurburn Montague Bell (formerly a foreign correspondent of *The Times* and editor of Shanghai's *North China Daily News and Herald*), and Edward Salmon. Despite difficulties that eventually necessitated reducing its size and printing it on inferior paper, Wilson kept the journal lively and topical, emphasizing military matters and until June 1917 including a diary of the war. In 1918, following a request from Major Evelyn Wrench of the Ministry of Information, he permitted the journal to be employed temporarily to disseminate government propaganda.[5] By 1918 Wilson, like Lucas, was feeling the strain of his extensive duties and the inability to obtain more assistance: 'At present', he wrote in the July, 'I am far too much "a maid of all work" and am getting immersed in detail.'[6] He resigned as secretary in 1921, and though he became a vice-president and served on the council until 1924 he now devoted more of his time to Hereford and indulged his love of art, literature, and gardens.

So far as was possible in war conditions, the institute maintained its normal activities. It was especially careful not to allow the educational efforts of the pre-war years to be nullified or stopped. In 1915 the council associated itself with the work of an imperial studies committee appointed in 1912 by the University of London to co-ordinate teaching on subjects that concerned the empire. The committee was the consequence of a paper read before the British Academy in November 1912, when Sidney Low advocated the establishment of a school of imperial studies in London. The university promptly prepared a syllabus showing the inter-collegiate courses on imperial subjects then being conducted in London, and appointed the imperial studies committee on which sat representatives of the university teaching and administrative staff and others with a special knowledge of the empire. A pamphlet issued by the university for the session beginning in 1914 set out the courses that were regarded as falling under the heading of imperial studies and defined the subject as a 'specialized study of the past and present conditions that govern the life and development of the communities under the British Crown, together with the study of cognate problems'.[7] Apart from tabulating and co-ordinating the lectures on imperial matters given within the university, the committee also organized a distinguished panel of speakers which provided academic lectures in various parts of the country, notably at the provincial universities and university colleges with the exception of Liverpool, which displayed some reluctance to accommodate itself to the scheme.

[5] Co. Mins. 12 (11 June 1918), 32; (30 July), 52.
[6] Wilson to Jebb, 14 July 1918, Jebb Papers.
[7] *United Empire*, 6 (1915), 665–8.

Later in the war the scope of the imperial studies committee was extended from universities and university colleges to include the schools and non-university towns, of which Hull was the first to agree to arranging a series of lectures. The committee was enlarged and three sub-committees constituted, one for universities and general education, one for secondary education and continuation schools, and one for elementary education and training colleges. The sub-committees established contact with the departments of the Board of Education, and in June 1918 the committee sent a deputation to the president of the board with a memorandum urging a proper place for empire subjects in public instruction. The memorandum set forth the committee's opinion

That properly endowed Chairs or Lectureships should be founded in every University to provide centres of research into the historical, political, and economic problems of the life of the Empire.

That an adequate study of the history and geography of the Empire should form an integral and compulsory part of the curriculum in all Training Colleges for Teachers, except such institutions as are concerned with purely technical and professional subjects.

That in all schools (Public, State-aided Secondary, Continuation and Elementary) every pupil should be taught something of the way in which the Empire has grown and is now governed, and something of the physical, economic and political features of the component parts.[8]

Subsequently, the committee sent to every education authority, all public schools and many libraries in Britain a letter suggesting that English history should be taught as the history of the British Empire and enclosing select bibliographies. Later in the year the committee took charge of the lantern slides and other material of the visual instruction committee of the Colonial Office and created a fourth sub-committee to be responsible for the proper use of the equipment for the teaching of empire subjects.

The institute's scheme of lectures on imperial topics was organized by Dr. A. P. Newton, the secretary to the university's standing committee on imperial studies. Newton had begun his university career as an assistant lecturer in physics, but, following the loss of an eye, imperial history became his con-

[8] *United Empire*, 9 (1918), 396–402.

suming interest. His particular study was of European colonization in the Caribbean in the sixteenth and seventeenth
centuries, but he preferred broad and general narrative to the
assembly of new detail. Newton virtually created the study of
imperial history in the University of London, and he was one
of the formulators of the original approach to the subject as a
projection of a British colonial policy whose development was
traced through a series of well-defined and labelled concepts.
He held the Rhodes chair of imperial history at King's College,
London, and was one of the three editors of the early volumes of
the *Cambridge History of the British Empire*. In the Royal Colonial
Institute, which he served for nearly thirty years, Newton
found an additional outlet for his considerable intellectual
energy, and in 1938 he was awarded its gold medal. Under his
direction the 'Imperial Studies' series was launched, publishing
the research work of young historians, most of whom later
headed university departments.

The institute was especially concerned by the war's possible
consequences for empire migration and land settlement. In 1910
a conference of most of the societies dealing with emigration
matters had met under the institute's auspices to consider
co-operation in encouraging emigration to the empire in
preference to foreign countries. There was some discussion in
these years of the idea of governmental control of emigration
to the dominions and there was a common impression that
the emigration department attached to the Colonial Office
was inadequate. Following the conference in 1910, a standing
committee on emigration was established and succeeded in
securing the inclusion of the subject of emigration in the terms
of reference of the dominions royal commission of 1912. The
war, however, led to the committee's suspension in 1915 and its
replacement, in response to a resolution passed at an informal
meeting in the smoking room, by an after-the-war empire
settlement and rural employment committee. The main
originator of the committee was Edward T. Scammell, but it
was based on an idea conceived by Grey, the institute's president, in the opening months of the war and was intended to
devise means for settling ex-servicemen on the land both at
home and in the overseas empire after the war.[9] The com-

[9] Co. Mins. 10 (10 Nov. 1914), 179–80.

mittee, which in November 1915 the council renamed the empire land settlement committee,[10] was, in practice, interested not so much in the overseas settlement of the non-commissioned ranks as in that of the officer class: a sub-committee formed in 1917, for example, to assist the training of servicemen in practical and theoretical farming was expressly designed for officers.[11] This bias not only reflected the character and outlook of the institute but was also the inevitable concomitant of the committee's primary interest in land settlement, for which the commissioned officers would naturally provide more candidates than would the other ranks.

The empire land settlement committee had a chequered career, partly because it was regarded without enthusiasm by government departments. In 1915 it was unsuccessful in an attempt to obtain representation on a departmental committee appointed by the president of the Board of Agriculture, Lord Selborne, to report on the settlement of ex-servicemen on the land in England and Wales. A deputation was received by Selborne and the colonial secretary, Bonar Law, in July, but Selborne refused to add to the departmental committee, though he professed a willingness to accept evidence from representatives of the institute.[12]

One of the deputation's suggestions was that a commissioner should visit the dominions to confer with their governments on the post-war land settlement of British ex-servicemen, and the council of the institute opened a fund for this purpose. The name originally mentioned in connection with the proposed commissioner's task was that of Sir Rider Haggard, the novelist, who thirty years before had found in mysterious Africa a memorable setting for his imagination and descriptive powers. He was a strong believer in the civilizing mission of the English people, and in politics was a staunch Conservative. 'I think Anglo-Saxon blood is so precious', he told a meeting in 1920, 'that every drop of it should be preserved within the Empire.' Haggard was interested in a scheme that would simultaneously decrease unemployment among returning servicemen after the war and improve British agriculture, and his plan was for the British and dominion governments to set aside land for the

[10] Co. Mins. 10 (8 Nov. 1915), 345.   [11] Co. Mins. 11 (24 July 1917), 273.
[12] Co. Mins. 10 (27 Nov. 1915), 301. *United Empire*, 6 (1915), 680–90.

I

servicemen to enable them to take up farming. His ideas were supported by the council, which asked the colonial secretary to send him on a tour of the dominions to discuss land settlement. When Bonar Law refused, the council called for donations to defray expenses and sent out Haggard on the tour as the institute's representative in a private and unofficial capacity.[13]

Haggard left England in February 1916 at the age of sixty on a journey of 20,000 miles around the overseas empire to determine what lands would be available for returning servicemen. The Colonial Office was opposed to the tour, fearing that Haggard would make trouble with the governments in the dominions; he in turn suspected that the Colonial Office wrote to the various governors cautioning them against him. He had an encouraging tour, though many of the promises made him were later found to be impossible of fulfilment, chiefly for financial reasons. He felt that he had conciliated governments which had been wary of his schemes, converted a hostile Australia to his views and brought back valuable information and propositions which the British government wasted.[14] After his return to the United Kingdom in July 1916, he spent the rest of the year explaining and publicizing his ideas and the assurances he had been given by the overseas governments. Haggard's report, which was published soon after his return, concluded that in general there were extensive opportunities for British ex-servicemen throughout the dominions except in South Africa, where the conditions arising out of the supply of black and poor-white labour were such as practically to rule out settlement by British workingmen or by ex-servicemen other than those from the commissioned ranks.[15]

The institute's empire land settlement committee maintained pressure in other ways. It organized a meeting in May 1916 with six Members of Parliament who promised to support its campaign in the House of Commons. The meeting unanimously approved 'the principle of the establishment of an Imperial

[13] Co. Mins. 11 (30 Nov. 1915), 5. *United Empire*, 11 (1920), 251.

[14] Haggard to Kipling, 2 March 1925, *Rudyard Kipling to Rider Haggard: The Record of a Friendship*, ed. M. Cohen (London 1965), 142. L. Rider Haggard, *The Cloak that I Left* (London 1951), 247–8. M. Cohen, *Rider Haggard: His Life and Works* (London 1960), 264–5.

[15] *The After-War Settlement and Employment of Ex-Service Men in the Oversea Dominions* (London 1916).

Board, representative of the Mother Country and the Dominions, to deal with the whole question of Land Settlement within the Empire.'[16] The idea of an imperial board was also pressed by a commission appointed by the Ontario government, a point put to the colonial secretary and the president of the Board of Agriculture in August, when the institute's committee sent another deputation to them to urge the establishment of such a board from which ex-servicemen would be able to ascertain what lands would be available and what the conditions for settlement were both in the United Kingdom and overseas.[17] Bonar Law replied that he hoped it would not be long before the government did 'something to set machinery to work to carry out the wishes of the Deputation'. In April 1917 the government appointed an empire settlement committee, of which Haggard was a member, and in 1919 replaced it with what became known as the oversea settlement committee under the chairmanship of the colonial secretary and served by an oversea settlement office, which functioned as a separate branch of the Colonial Office carrying out the committee's policies.[18] The establishment of the government committee and the oversea settlement office and the organization of various land settlement schemes in the dominions made the institute's empire land settlement committee superfluous. It continued for a while giving information and advice to interested settlers and supplying them with the latest relevant publications, but in May 1920 the council dissolved it.[19] Some of the work was resumed by the standing emigration committee, whose activities had been suspended during the war.

The empire land settlement committee's last major act was the publication of a report based on an overseas tour by Christopher Turnor in 1919 and 1920 to investigate progress made in land settlement.[20] The report, which appeared a few weeks after the committee's dissolution, was a controversial one and aroused protests in the dominions. Canadians were particularly incensed by Turnor's warning to British ex-

[16] *United Empire*, 7 (1916), 443.   [17] Ibid., 614–27.
[18] W. A. Carrothers, *Emigration from the British Isles* (London 1929), 258–9. Pugh, 'The Colonial Office', *Camb. Hist. Brit. Emp.* 3 (1959), 758. Cohen, *Rider Haggard*, 267–8.
[19] Co. Mins. 12 (17 Feb. 1920), 290–1; (19 May), 344.
[20] *Land Settlement for Ex-Servicemen in the Oversea Dominions* (London 1920).

servicemen against settlement on the dry belt of the prairies, and there were complaints from Canadian official sources and from Canadian members of the institute. The council was concerned at the injury the report might cause the institute and delayed the printing to enable modifications to be made. Even after the report's modification, the council insisted on a slip being inserted absolving the institute from any responsibility for the opinions expressed. The Colonial Office, too, was concerned at the character of the report, but eventually agreed that no further revision was necessary. Nevertheless, the colonial secretary later received a telegram from the Governor of Western Australia protesting against that part of the report dealing with his state. [21]

The institute continued to proclaim the slightly jaded principle of empire unity. At the end of August 1915 the council issued to the press a resolution it had sent to the prime minister and the colonial secretary:

Bearing in mind that the fundamental object of the Royal Colonial Institute is the unity of the Empire, and in the conviction that they are expressing, and that it is their duty to express, the feeling of the vast majority of their Members both at home and overseas. The Council of the Royal Colonial Institute desire to place on record their unanimous opinion that at this time of crisis it is the duty of every efficient person, male or female, between the ages of 16 and 65, to place themselves [sic] at the disposal of the Crown for the performance of such service, whether Military or Civil, as at the discretion of His Majesty's Government may be required of them in the interests of the State. [22]

What precise, practical purpose this resolution in favour of national service was intended to serve is difficult to see, though it was likely to divorce the institute further from the Labour party, where the main organized opposition to conscription was to be found. Three months later the council supplemented the resolution with another, again forwarded to the prime minister, colonial secretary, and press, expressing its 'further unanimous opinion' that the institute's 'fundamental object', the unity of the empire,

[21] Co. Mins. 13 (15 June 1920), 6–8; (21 July), 23–4; (16 Nov.), 59; (30 Dec.), 87.
[22] Co. Mins. 10 (27 Aug. 1915), 313.

would be greatly and permanently furthered if the Principle of Training for National Service which has already been put into practice in some of the Self-Governing Dominions were adopted throughout the Empire, so that it might be universally recognized that it is the duty of all adult male British subjects to be qualified to bear arms for the Defence of the Empire in time of need. [23]

This declaration may be regarded as a forceful contribution to the heated public debate on the merits and disadvantages of compulsory national service or as a harmless declaration of imperial patriotism, but its emphasis on the principle of empire unity illustrated the lingering determination to continue to work for an objective whose achievement was still the supreme hope of a majority in the governing body.

The imperial loyalty and common purpose produced in the United Kingdom and the dominions during the war revived discussion of closer empire unity and imperial federation, notably by the Round Table groups, whose studies were the basis of a number of publications by Lionel Curtis. In 1915, in considering the problem of how a British citizen in the dominions could acquire 'the same control of foreign policy as one domiciled in the British Isles', he rejected the idea of an imperial council, that of representatives of the dominions sitting in the British parliament, and that of using the imperial conference, and advocated the creation of an imperial parliament with an executive responsible to it for the conduct of imperial affairs. W. B. Worsfold even framed a draft constitution for a central or imperial legislature that would consist of the crown and two houses of parliament with power to pass laws concerning the common affairs of the empire and to vote supplies for the imperial services. Professor A. B. Keith, on the other hand, lent his authority to the view that a true union was impracticable because of the differences between the dominions in national outlook and constitutional advance, and A. F. Hattersley concluded that the only contribution to closer imperial co-operation that was yet feasible was the appointment by the dominions of resident ministers in London. [24] Among the

[23] Co. Mins. 11 (30 Nov. 1915), 3–5.
[24] L. Curtis, *The Problem of the Commonwealth* (London 1916). W. B. Worsfold, *The Empire on the Anvil* (London 1916). A. B. Keith, *Imperial Unity and the Dominions* (London 1916). A. F. Hattersley, *The Colonies and Imperial Federation* (Pietermaritzburg 1919).

politicians, Asquith referred to a refashioning of the fabric of the empire, Bonar Law to making the empire 'one in structure in all the time that is to come', and A. J. Balfour to its coming together 'with a yet closer intimacy and union, organically as well as sentimentally and patriotically'.

The evidence of renewed interest in the subject of empire unity was warmly welcomed at the Royal Colonial Institute. Further encouragement was derived from the operation of the imperial war cabinet, in which the dominion prime ministers, when they arrived in London for the imperial conference of 1917, joined the British war cabinet for confidential discussions on the aims and conduct of the war. The cabinet was distinct from the conference, whose proceedings indicated that any expectations of a form of closer empire unity emerging from the emotional bonds of war were ill-founded. The comradeship of wartime was balanced by the national pride that was flowering in the dominions, whose leaders were determined not to surrender to a new organ of imperial unity the voice in foreign policy or the growing independence that they had acquired. The conference resolved that any readjustment in the constitutional relations of the empire,

while thoroughly preserving all existing powers of self-government and complete control of domestic affairs, should be based upon a full recognition of the Dominions as autonomous nations of an Imperial Commonwealth, and of India as an important portion of the same, should recognize the right of the Dominions and India to an adequate voice in foreign policy and in foreign relations, and should provide effective arrangements for continuous consultation in all important matters of common Imperial concern, and for such necessary concerted action, founded on consultation, as the several Governments may determine.[25]

The constitutional relationship was deferred for discussion by a post-war *ad hoc* conference that was never summoned. 'The mood was gone', according to a recent authority, 'which had given heart to the Federalists.'[26]

On the collapse of Germany and the precipitation of the negotiation of peace terms, the dominion prime ministers and

[25] *Parl. Paps.* 1917–18, Vol. 23, Cd. 8566, p. 5.

[26] A. F. Madden, 'Changing Attitudes and Widening Responsibilities, 1895–1914', *Camb. Hist. Brit. Emp.* 3 (1959), 405.

representatives of the Viceroy of India 'were warned to be in readiness to come over in order to be in close touch, as members of the Imperial War Cabinet, with the whole situation, and to take part in the discussion between the Allies as to the peace settlement itself'.[27] They became the British empire delegation to the peace conference in Paris, and as such were subject to heavy pressure from the electorates in the United Kingdom and the dominions. The Royal Colonial Institute, consistent with its history and character, devoted itself principally to stressing the claims of the dominions and the importance of retaining colonial territories acquired from Germany in the war. The acquisitions had been largely by the efforts of the dominions themselves: Australia had occupied the German portion of New Guinea; New Zealand had removed the Germans from Western Samoa; and South Africa had participated in military expeditions that conquered German South-west Africa and German East Africa. All the dominions were determined that these territories should not be returned to Germany and their view was echoed by the Royal Colonial Institute.

The question was raised at the annual general meeting in May 1918, and in June the council made public its strong feeling that, 'alike in the interests of the Empire and in the interests of the Native Races concerned, no one of the former German Possessions beyond the Seas should be restored to Germany.'[28] When there were signs that the mandatory principle would be applied to the former enemy territories annexed to the British empire, the council again made its views known in a resolution forwarded in February 1919 to the British prime minister, the empire delegation in Paris, and the press:

The Council of the Royal Colonial Institute most earnestly request His Majesty's Government not to give their final consent to any agreement which will leave any opening for doubt as to the future of the late German Colonies. In particular, they venture to urge that the ownership by the Commonwealth of Australia and the Dominion of New Zealand of the Pacific Colonies occupied by their representative forces during the War, and the ownership of German South West Africa by the Union of South Africa, should be confirmed to these Dominions as an accomplished fact beyond all

[27] *Parl. Paps.* 1919, Vol. 30, Cmd. 325, pp. 10–11.
[28] Co. Mins. 12 (11 June 1918), 33.

possibility of question. They would suggest that any supervision on the part of an International body should, at most, be restricted to general rules similar to those which have been laid down from time to time at International conferences with regard to Tropical Africa, and which, so far from invalidating the exclusive claims to the respective Colonies and Protectorates by the interested Powers, have, on the contrary, been based upon full recognition of the individual Sovereignty or Protectorate of each of the Territories concerned. [29]

The resolution was superfluous, for a compromise arrangement for three classes of mandate had already been approved in Paris and became Article 22 of the League of Nations covenant. The German colonies in New Guinea, Western Samoa, and South-west Africa passed to Australia, New Zealand, and South Africa respectively as C-class mandates, or territories that could be administered as integral parts of the mandatory power. Although the League of Nations, acting through a permanent mandates commission which examined the annual reports of the mandatory powers, retained a useful and benevolent working interest in the management of the territories, the C-class mandate arrangement enabled the British dominions to operate what was, in effect, an indirect or disguised form of colonialism. The system, in practice, proved to be very close to that for which the institute had pressed.

The Paris conference and the signing of the final peace treaties in 1919 marked a new stage in the evolution of the British imperial relationship and demonstrated the international status sought by the dominions, which participated in the negotiations both individually in their own right and collectively as integral parts of the empire. The British empire functioned both as one unit and as several parts, an esoteric arrangement that other countries understandably found incomprehensible, confusing, and unpalatable. The problem of signing the treaties was resolved by the United Kingdom delegates signing for the empire, and the dominion delegates and the secretary of state for India signing for Canada, Australia, South Africa, New Zealand, and India but preserving a formal semblance of unity by indenting their signatures under the general heading of the British empire.

[29] Co. Mins. 12 (18 Feb. 1919), 121–2.

In Paris the dominions had enjoyed rather more than the consultation and 'adequate voice' in foreign policy recommended by the imperial war conference in 1917. Although there were ambiguities and uncertainties in the relationship that had now developed, it was already apparent that a new style of imperial unity was being forged in which the old doctrines and assumptions would have to be discarded and in which the intangible bonds would become predominant. In December 1918, in what he described as a hastily written 'practical suggestion' for the League of Nations, J. C. Smuts, who had exerted a statesmanlike influence in the imperial war cabinet and in the British empire delegation in Paris, likened the composite empires of the past to rudimentary leagues of nations, keeping peace among themselves by the coercive and repressive strength of the dominant member: 'These empires have all broken down', he concluded, 'and today the British Commonwealth of Nations remains the only embryo league of nations because it is based on the true principles of national freedom and political decentralization.'[30] In a farewell statement issued to the press on leaving England in July 1919, after the peace conference, Smuts envisaged the ideals which had shaped the commonwealth becoming the common heritage of Europe and the League of Nations, and he reiterated his confidence in the new commonwealth association whose foundations he believed had now been laid:

The Dominions have been well launched on their great career; their status of complete nationhood has now received international recognition, and, as members of the Britannic League, they will henceforth go forward on terms of equal brotherhood with the other nations on the great paths of the world. The successful launching of her former colonies among the nations of the world, while they remain members of an inner Britannic circle, will ever rank as one of the most outstanding achievements of British political genius. Forms and formulas may still have to be readjusted, but the real work is done.[31]

[30] D. H. Miller, *The Drafting of the Covenant* (2 vols., New York 1928), II, 23–5.
[31] *Selections from the Smuts Papers*, ed. W. K. Hancock and J. van der Poel (4 vols., London 1966), IV, 273–5.

Chapter Nine

Headquarters between the Wars (1919–1939)

THE twenty years between the First World War and the second were an eventful period for the internal development of the institute. It continued to be ably served and led by men of considerable personal distinction with a pronounced faith in the virtues of the Anglo-Saxon race and of its 'dominion over palm and pine'. The council, which managed affairs with practical good sense and keen determination, remained a somewhat autocratic body. In general, the fellows were usually indifferent to the election of the council and were not inclined to exercise their right to suggest nominations or to challenge the council's own recommendations. On one occasion when the fellows broke custom and nominated a councillor, his name was marked with a star denoting the fact that he was not a nominee of council. The finance and general purposes committee operated virtually as an executive; it met fortnightly throughout the year to consider all matters affecting the institute and reported to the council, which retained the final decision on questions of major significance. Direct management of affairs was largely in the hands of a small group of enthusiasts of whom the chairman of council, the secretary, and the treasurer were the most important.

The chairmen of council continued to be drawn from the ranks of the retired colonial service, the rich business community, and the Conservative party. Perhaps the most able in this period was Sir Godfrey Lagden, who had been deputy chairman for eleven years before he finally succeeded Lucas in 1920. Lagden's overseas experience had been in Africa. As an assistant colonial secretary in Sierra Leone he had been struck off the Colonial Office list when he took six months leave in defiance of orders, but he was reinstated as secretary and accountant to the resident commissioner of Basutoland and then as the British commissioner in Swaziland. Lagden had been commissioner of native affairs in Milner's administration in the Transvaal and chairman of the South African native affairs commission, but on the grant of self-government to the Transvaal in 1907 he retired to England to live at Weybridge. Apart from an indefatigable interest in the work of the Royal Colonial Institute, he was also a vice-president of the Bible Society and of the African Society and a director of the South African Gold Trust and other companies. He brought to the chairmanship of the council an intimate knowledge of African affairs and exceptional financial ability that was of great value to the finance and general purposes committee, of which he was chairman longer than any of his predecessors.

Lagden was succeeded in 1923 by Sir Charles Campbell McLeod, the senior partner of a business in Calcutta and of another in London. He became chairman of several tea companies, of the National Bank of India in London, of the London and Lancashire Insurance Company, and of the Ross Institute, which was eventually affiliated to the London School of Hygiene and Tropical Medicine, and he was on the governing body of the School of Oriental Studies. He was noted for his passion for sport, and in his young days had been a successful steeplechase rider, a fearless hog-hunter with the Calcutta Tent Club, and a regular member of the Calcutta polo team. Between 1923 and 1925 he was an energetic, if not especially productive, chairman of council and conducted meetings with celerity and good humour. Lord Stanley of Alderley, who was chairman from 1925 to 1928, was loyal to his family's Liberal tradition and had been a Member of Parliament for four years after the Liberal victory of 1906, but in 1931 he refused to be associated with the policy of his Liberal friends who were maintaining the Labour party in office. He had been the governor of Victoria during and after the world war, and became a director of the National Bank of Australasia and of the Australian Mercantile, Land and Finance Company and president of the British Australasian Society. During his period as chairman of council he tactfully prepared the way for the change of title in 1928 to Royal Empire Society.

Stanley was succeeded by Sir John Sandeman Allen, a prominent figure in marine insurance and in Liverpool public life. At one time or another he was a member of the Liverpool city council, chairman of the Liverpool chamber of commerce and an occasional lecturer at Liverpool University on foreign trade. He became chairman of the federation of chambers of commerce of the British empire and a member of the governing bodies of several other commercial associations. He entered politics as a Conservative in 1924, when he was annoyed at Labour's attitude towards Russia, and wrested from the Liberals a Liverpool constituency that he held until his death. He had a wide knowledge of trade conditions in the empire, some ability as a linguist, and a keen interest in the trustee savings bank movement. He was chairman of council from 1928 to 1930, a councillor for eight years, a vice-president for seven years, and a member of the finance and general purposes committee also for seven years. He was in some part responsible for the inauguration of the society's junior fellows section which started its activities shortly after his death.

Colonel Sir Alexander Weston Jarvis was chairman from 1930 to 1932. Jarvis was a soldier, sportsman, politician, businessman, and intimate friend of Cecil Rhodes, who had sought his advice on the form that the Rhodes scholarships should take. He fought in the Matabele war of 1896, the Boer war and the world war, and was nearly sixty years of age when he took the 3rd County of London Yeomanry to Gallipoli. His father had been a local Tory leader in the King's Lynn neighbourhood, a borough which the son represented in the House of Commons between 1886 and 1892 as an uncompromising Conservative. Many years later he remarked: 'I left the House as I entered it, an unregenerate Tory, an opponent to the last of Home Rule, a Diehard, a Last Ditcher, and everything else that is anathema to the Radical Socialist.'[1] As a sportsman he was a noted rider to hounds, angler, and shooter of big game. He was a fellow of the Royal Empire Society for forty-four years, a vice-president for seven, a member of council for twenty, and chairman for a short, inauspicious, and unproductive period that coincided with the world-wide economic depression.

From 1932 to 1938 the chairmanship was held by Sir Archibald Weigall, familiarly known as Archie. Weigall was an agriculturalist, land agent, justice of the peace and, like Jarvis,

[1] *Daily Telegraph*, 2 Nov. 1939.

soldier, sportsman, and politician. He had begun his career in agriculture and was a member of the council of the Royal Agricultural Society for many years and eventually its president. In 1911 he became Conservative Member of Parliament for an agricultural constituency in Lincolnshire, where he founded and presided over an efficient local newspaper. He was appointed governor of South Australia in 1920 but retired from the position in 1922, when increased taxation made it difficult for him to afford to retain it. As chairman of council he successfully launched a regular summer school on the empire, inaugurated an advisory social committee that was later transformed into what was termed the house committee, and strove hard, with the support of the dominions secretary, J. H. Thomas, to effect an amalgamation with the Overseas League. Weigall lacked the wide knowledge of Lucas, the financial acumen of Lagden, or the strength of character that Jarvis derived from a reputation as a cast-iron Tory, but he was a witty, genial, and enterprising chairman of council.

The secretaries who served the institute between the two world wars were less distinguished than most of those who had preceded them. When Sir Harry Wilson resigned in 1921 he was succeeded by George M. Boughey, who had been on probation as Wilson's assistant for six months without pay. Boughey was forty-one, and had taken an honours degree in the classical tripos at Cambridge before entering the Indian civil service, from which he had retired with a pension in 1916 on account of ill-health. That he already possessed private means was a recommendation to an organization unable to pay high salaries. The council was also impressed by the fact that he belonged to a well-known country family and would eventually inherit a baronetcy, and that he was able to hold what it termed 'a good social position'.[2] Boughey was followed in 1929 by George Pilcher, a former journalist with an interest in Indian affairs, who gave up his parliamentary career to become secretary of the society. He had been foreign editor of the *Morning Post*, joint editor of the Calcutta *Statesman*, and an elected member of the Indian legislative assembly. He worked well with Sandeman Allen, but failed to achieve a similarly smooth working relationship with Weigall, Allen's successor as chairman of council, and

[2] Co. Mins. 13 (30 Dec. 1920), 83–4; (14 June 1921), 180.

after serving two difficult years under him he resigned in 1935.[3] Robert Edward Hertwell Baily, who became secretary in 1935, had served in the Sudan political service for twenty-three years and been the governor of Kassala Province from 1926 to 1932. Baily was an efficient secretary for three years until 1938, when he decided to devote more of his time to his other major interest, the Boy Scouts, of whom he became the Herefordshire county commissioner.[4]

The honorary treasurers, though clearly vital to the satisfactory functioning of the institute, were less influential than either the chairmen of council or the secretaries. In the immediate post-war years Sir Frederick Dutton, son of a former agent-general for South Australia, was an admirable treasurer. A solicitor by profession, he had joined the institute in 1880 and became a councillor in 1888 and a vice-president in 1916. In 1922 he relinquished his task to Arthur Seymour Bull, a prominent freemason who had strong working connections with the Sudan. Bull charted the institute through financial difficulties accentuated by the effects of the nation's coal strike in 1921 and by continuing unemployment and industrial unrest in the 1920s, including the general strike. He died in 1927 and Ralph S. Bond became treasurer. Bond, who held the office for eleven years, had been an active member of the reform committee of 1909 which had stirred the institute out of a period of stagnation. As treasurer, he led the institute's successful appeal against its income tax assessment in 1930 and initiated a superannuation scheme for the staff. After the middle of the 1930s, however, he had increasing difficulty in gaining the council's support for his attempts to achieve economies, and feeling that he had los his influence he retired in 1938.[5] To these chairmen of council, secretaries, and honorary treasurers, should be added William Chamberlain, who had joined the staff in 1874 and became successively chief clerk and assistant secretary, retiring in 1923 and continuing part-time service until his death in 1927, when he left his estate to the institute's new premises fund. Joseph Farrow, who died in December 1931 at the age of sixty, had also served in a clerical capacity for forty-eight years and been

[3] *United Empire*, 20 (1929), 177; 26 (1935), 340.
[4] Co. Mins. 18 (8 April 1935), 153. *United Empire*, 29 (1938), A.G.M. report.
[5] Co. Mins. 20 (14 Feb. 1938), 40.

chief clerk since 1916, when he had succeeded Chamberlain.[6]

The problem of the institute's title, which had been much discussed in the years immediately preceding the war, was dropped after 1914 but taken up again when the war was drawing to a close. In April 1918 the council decided that an alteration should not be considered until the question of new premises had been decided, and it remained in abeyance for nine more years. The issue was brought to the fore at the annual general meeting in May 1927, when the chairman, Lord Stanley, intimated that he personally would welcome a change in the designation to indicate more accurately the institute's nature and aims: 'We are an Empire Institution—not a Colonial Institution—an Institution which people of the whole Empire may join in order to get to know, to appreciate and to love their fellow-citizens from whatever part of the Empire they may come.'[7] The council addressed itself to the problem, and at a meeting at the end of November 1927 a suggestion that the title Royal United Empire Institute should be adopted led to a discussion from which emerged the recommendation that the new title should be Royal Empire Society, a name that had been near the bottom of the list of suggestions in the referendum in 1912, when it had received only four votes compared with seventy-two favouring British Empire Institute.[8] A somewhat informal and haphazard referendum among the nearly 15,000 fellows secured a response from only 1,200, but of these only 279 objected to the change: 'The Council', the chairman coolly told the annual general meeting in May 1928, 'are, therefore, of opinion and I think you will agree, that it is reasonable to assume that we have the support of the great majority of the Fellows in making this change.' Several fellows present disliked the proposed new title, described by one as 'a petty jingle', but the requisite three-quarters majority at the meeting agreed that the existing title was inaccurate, particularly since the evolution of the self-governing colonies into dominions, and approved the resolution for a change put to it on behalf of the council.[9]

A special meeting of fellows in the smoking room in June

[6] *United Empire*, 23 (1932), 42, 348.   [7] Ibid., 18 (1927), 340–1.

[8] Co. Mins. 14 (14 Nov. 1927), 477–8; (30 Nov.), 481–2.

[9] *United Empire*, 19 (1928), 361–3. *The Times*, 24 May 1928.

1928 confirmed, by what the chairman declared to be 'a very large majority' on a show of hands, the resolution carried at the annual general meeting.[10] The change to Royal Empire Society was generally well received by interested persons and critics in the United Kingdom and the dominions, but an unrepentant minority opinion regretted it and found some support among expatriates in the colonial empire. A press critic in Malaya, for example, refused to believe that the change was a desirable improvement:

Old habitués of the Institute, especially those with Malayan connections, must feel a natural affection for the old name, which stands for a congenial meeting place in London offering unique opportunities of keeping in touch with friends and interests in the East. The old name, too, served a useful purpose in keeping the affairs and interests of the Crown Colonies and Protectorates before the Home public, whereas the great self-governing Dominions have other means of making themselves known.[11]

Most observers, however, were agreed that the alteration was a necessary and belated recognition of the fact that the empire was now an association vastly different from that which the society had originally been formed to serve.

It was evident when the war ended that the institute would have to extend its premises in Northumberland Avenue. There was no hall for meetings, no rooms for meals and no accommodation for ladies, and activities were likely to suffer from the restrictions the existing building imposed. The institute's jubilee was linked with a new premises fund inaugurated at a dinner in May 1919. The appeal for funds was followed by a meeting at the Mansion House presided over by the lord mayor with the object of enlisting the support of the citizens of London for the development of the institute. The council wanted £300,000, but the extended economic depression of the early 1920s affected the response to an appeal, which the vast majority of fellows ignored. In September 1924 the council approved a proposal by Sir Frederick Dutton for a new contributory scheme under which prominent individuals and firms promised to give certain sums of money provided that equivalent amounts were forthcoming from fellows and others.

[10] *United Empire*, 19 (1928), 424–6.   [11] *Malay Mail*, 20 Dec. 1928.

The Royal Colonial Institute Headquarters

The Royal Empire Society Headquarters, 1937

The general strike of 1926, however, and the dislocation of trade and economic conditions that followed impeded the proper development of the scheme, and the economic depression in 1930 and 1931 delayed plans for the erection of a new building. In 1934, after fifteen years of appeals, the fund amounted to nearly £100,000, and most of that sum was spent in acquiring the freehold of the site. Nevertheless, early in 1934 the council decided to proceed with the rebuilding of the premises in accordance with plans and specifications prepared by Sir Herbert Baker and A. T. Scott, and an appeal for a further £100,000 was launched. The adjoining property had been acquired, and in October 1934 the old building was dismantled to allow a new structure to be erected on the same site but extending over the whole area of which the society possessed the freehold.

The foundation stone of the new building was laid on 3 June 1935 by the Prince of Wales, who observed that it was fitting that the ceremony should take place on the King's seventieth birthday in the silver jubilee year of his reign. The prince used a special steel trowel which had been presented to him for the purpose and which had a detachable handle that could be employed for a walking-stick or umbrella. Nearly 800 persons filled the enclosure for the short ceremony of which perhaps the most portentous feature was the Nazi swastika superimposed on a Union Jack that was held aloft from a building facing the prince while the national anthem was sung.[12]

The building, which was formally opened on 12 November 1936 by the Duke and Duchess of York, exploited to a remarkable degree, according to one architectural critic, the decorative range and variety of the materials for which the society had appealed to the overseas empire.[13] Its face on Northumberland Avenue was of Portland stone, and the alternation of square-headed and round-headed openings in the window pattern was characteristic of the work of the designer, Sir Herbert Baker. The stones used also included Maltese marble and polished Ancaster and Hopton Wood stones. Among the timbers were blackwood, jarrah, New South Wales brush boxwood and Tasmanian oak from Australia; mahogany and mvule from

12 *The Times* and *Daily Telegraph*, 4 June 1935. *United Empire*, 26 (1935), 401–6.
13 *The Times*, 11 Nov. 1936. Co. Mins. 18 (11 June 1934), 45–6; (10 Dec.), 105.

K

Uganda; odum and danta from the Gold Coast; mahogany and teak from Rhodesia; sapele and opepe from Nigeria; silky yellow birch and British Columbia western red cedar from Canada; mora from Trinidad; figured rimu from New Zealand; silvergrey from India; white serayah from Borneo; stinkwood from South Africa; olive from Kenya; and English sweet chestnut from Gloucestershire. The intrinsic qualities of the timbers in some instances overpowered the architectural design of the panelling, and some of the furniture was criticized as aggressive for the setting.[14] Nevertheless, the new building represented a triumph of persistence by a number of council members who, over the years, had vigorously campaigned for funds and had never allowed disappointments and difficulties to discourage them or to reduce the ambitious, but worthwhile, objective they had set themselves.

The need to attract membership was perennial. The membership drive begun in 1909 was maintained during the war, and in 1915 the council turned to British residents in the United States as a source of recruitment to the institute.[15] Membership reached a total of over 13,700 at the end of 1918, of whom nearly 3,000 were resident fellows, 8,700 non-resident, and over 2,000 associates. In the next year it rose by another thousand to over 14,700 and by the end of 1920 it was over 15,000. In 1921, however, there was a slight decrease, attributable partly to the erasure from the membership list of a number of fellows who had been kept on it long after their membership had ceased, and partly to adverse financial conditions which led to the withdrawal of members who were unable, or unwilling, to pay the increased subscriptions introduced in 1920. Membership decreased again in 1922, as strikes in the engineering, shipbuilding, and other trades added to the financial depression and unemployment in the United Kingdom brought about by a trade slump the previous year.

By the end of 1927 membership had fallen to 14,400, and it was in these circumstances that the council decided to form a membership committee, including non-council members, in order to devise and recommend schemes for increasing membership. In 1928, the year of the institute's diamond jubilee and assumption of a new name, membership began increasing

[14] *The Times*, 11 Nov. 1936.   [15] Co. Mins. 10 (26 March 1915), 243–4.

again, and in October 1930 it reached more than 18,000, but
the economic depression of that year started another decline,
and by 1933 membership was reduced to under 15,400. The
council was at a loss how to reverse the continued decline, and
it suspected that there was a widespread habit among overseas
fellows of joining the society to enjoy its facilities during a stay
in England and of resigning as soon as they had returned
home.[16] As the economic depression lifted, however, an
upward trend in the society's total membership was resumed,
and by the beginning of 1939 it was over 20,200, of whom over
6,000 were resident fellows, over 11,000 non-resident, over
1,300 associates, and over 1,500 the new category of companions.

When the Royal Colonial Institute became the Royal Empire
Society in 1928 there were already nearly 2,000 lady members,
and that year for the first time one of them, Lady Davson,
the daughter of Elinor Glyn, was elected to the council. The
society, as the editor of its journal dared to say, welcomed lady
fellows 'with open arms'.[17] Ladies fitted well into the essentially
conservative character of the society and were an important
influence in its now noticeable process of transformation into a
more social organization. In the 1930s the society made a
further crusading effort to attract young people into its ranks:
'There was a time', reflected *The Times* in 1935, 'when the
Society seemed to cater for, or at any rate to appeal mainly to,
the middle-aged or the elderly. Of recent years it has addressed
itself more to the youth of this country and of the Empire.'[18]
When the foundation stone of the new building was laid in that
year, the establishment was announced of a new junior section
of members under twenty-four years of age to be known as the
companions. Young people were drawn into a new youth
movement, the success of which was demonstrated when it
held its first conference at the society in December 1937.

The membership campaign of the inter-war years failed to
modify significantly the society's preponderantly Anglo-Saxon
complexion. In the circumstances of the period the society

---

[16] Co. Mins. 14 (10 Oct. 1927), 467; 15 (13 Feb. 1928), 24; 18 (11 Feb. 1935),
127–8; 20 (14 March 1938), 57.
[17] *United Empire*, 16 (1925), 398; 19 (1928), 306–6.
[18] *The Times*, 3 June 1935.

could not have been anything other than a white men's organization. The opportunity to make use of the society's facilities in London, the ability to pay the subscription, the sentiment for the imperial connection and the capacity to find the empire story a source of pride and admiration as well as interest, were all inevitably the preserve of Englishmen, of white settlers and colonial civil servants. The society itself had contributed to the racial imbalance, and it was admitted in the council in 1920 that there had always been difficulty in assimilating proposed fellows from the African and Indian parts of the empire.[19] The council had discussed the admission of non-white citizens of the empire in the early years of the century, and in May 1914 it had remitted to the general purposes committee for report the question of admitting 'Asiatics and men of colour', but no progress had been made when, in the October, the council deferred the admission as a fellow of Juganauthai Iraji with the suggestion that the whole problem of admitting coloured members should be examined.[20] In 1918 the council resolved that so far as the acceptance as fellows of 'Indian gentlemen of position' was concerned, each case should be treated individually on its merits.[21] An India committee appointed by the council in that year suggested that an approach should be made to 'prominent Anglo-Indians' and those classes of Indians 'who would be desirable members' of the institute. On the committee's recommendation, the council in the following year invited six specified Indian princes to become vice-presidents of the institute.[22] No colour bar was operated, and the anxious attitude towards the election of non-white fellows was gradually relaxed, but the council remained cautious, and even in 1931 it was felt that 'it was advisable to ensure that too large a proportion of coloured persons was not elected'.[23]

The council maintained a firm, but usually generous, policy on the disciplinary problems with which it was very occasionally confronted. The ultimate disciplinary measure was the removal of the offender's name from the list of fellows. Thus, a member had his name removed in 1927 for having libelled

---

[19] Co. Mins. 12 (12 Feb. 1920), 276.
[20] Co. Mins. 10 (26 May 1914), 113–14; (13 Oct.), 161.
[21] Co. Mins. 12 (28 June 1918), 43.   [22] Co. Mins. 12 (17 June 1919), 170–1.
[23] Co. Mins. 16 (12 Jan. 1931), 158–9.

another member of the institute, and in 1930 a member's name was removed from the list after he had been sentenced to three years' penal servitude for forgery and falsification of accounts.[24] On a different level, a clergyman fellow was reprimanded in 1929 for his practice of proposing for election to membership persons whom he had known only a few hours. In the following year a member was asked by council to resign when he failed to answer satisfactorily complaints that he had helped himself to the contents of match-boxes in the smoking room and substituted an empty box for a full one, had mutilated a copy of one of the newspapers in the reading room and taken magazines from the library, and had sat in the smoking room with his hat on.[25] Such problems arose rarely, however, and in general the society's procedure for electing fellows and associates was successful in producing a respectable membership, and standards were not relaxed even during the most fervent periods of membership campaigns.

The afternoon and evening meetings in the immediate post-war years were held at Caxton Hall and the Central Hall, Westminster. The addresses at the meetings were normally of a reasonable intellectual level, though not as substantial or as detailed as they had been in the nineteenth century, but there was a recurrent complaint that they were given to audiences already converted to imperial ideas and that the institute should be spreading its faith among others.[26] A house and social committee organized fortnightly afternoon meetings at which talks were given and tea was served, and also arranged dances, excursions, recitals, billiard tournaments, and outings to major sporting and social occasions, and dealt with requests from fellows to reserve hotel accommodation. In the 1930s its responsibilities were assumed by an advisory social committee which worked in close co-operation with a social organizer and house secretary. In 1937 a house committee was formed to deal with matters concerning the administration and good order of headquarters; it met monthly and devoted itself principally to the management of the catering and house services and of the bedroom accommodation that had been made available in the

[24] Co. Mins. 14 (9 May 1927), 437; 16 (12 May 1930), 66.
[25] Co. Mins. 15 (14 Oct. 1929), 251; 16 (12 May 1930), 66.
[26] See, e.g. *United Empire*, 15 (1924), 386.

new building. The freemasons at the institute grew steadily in strength and the Royal Colonial Institute Lodge formed in 1912 was added to, until by 1924 there were a United Empire Lodge, a Mark Lodge, a Royal Arch and Rose Croix Chapters.

The most valuable and significant activity of the society between the wars was undoubtedly in the field of education. In 1919 the imperial studies committee acquired the slides, photographs, paintings, and other materials of the visual instruction committee of the Colonial Office and continued the work of providing illustrated lectures on the empire. The imperial studies committee was increasingly a co-ordinator of the activities of other agencies and it maintained close working relations with bodies such as the historical and geographical associations. At the request of an imperial education conference of directors of education held in the summer of 1923, the committee invited the historical and geographical associations to appoint representatives to a joint committee to consider the issue of an agreed syllabus for the teaching of empire history and geography. Several meetings were held, and a syllabus was prepared and forwarded to the secretary of the Board of Education and circulated to schools throughout the empire.[27]

Although the funds for the imperial studies committee were provided by the society, its membership was not confined to fellows but included schoolteachers and representatives of the Board of Education, the London County Council, and the Victoria League, and it co-operated with the Universities Bureau of the British Empire. It owed much in the early years to the inspiration of Sir Charles Lucas, who, as chairman of council, had been largely instrumental in the committee's foundation and was later adviser to the University of London in the establishment of the Rhodes chair of imperial history tenable at King's College. In concert with the society's librarian and the historical and geographical associations, the imperial studies committee prepared bibliographies and syllabuses to assist students and teachers, and in 1926 it initiated what became known as the imperial studies series: original monographs by young scholars who might otherwise have been unable to publish the results of their researches. The essay competitions were firmly established among the committee's

[27] *United Empire,* 15 (1924), 243; 16 (1925), 314.

responsibilities in the inter-war period. The competition for boys and girls gained in popularity, and in 1924 the committee began an additional competition that was open to all teachers in schools within the empire. In 1930 Mrs. Walter Frewen Lord, widow of the author of several books on imperial history, placed £500 with the society to provide in memory of her husband an annual prize of £25 for the best essay on any subject in British imperial history by an undergraduate or graduate of not more than four years standing. The prize was awarded by the society on the advice of the imperial studies committee. More advanced studies were recognized by the society's award of a gold medal for the outstanding book of the year bearing on the affairs of the empire.[28]

The Royal Empire Society organized conferences on the development of the empire and contributed to educational conferences organized by others; it campaigned with little success among the universities to promote empire subjects and worked for the creation of university posts specializing in the study of the empire; it offered assistance to colleges and institutes with interests relating to the development of the empire; it published handbooks and pamphlets for the guidance of those giving instruction in empire studies, and issued lists of the principal official publications relating to the overseas empire; it maintained a regular programme of ordinary meetings at which empire problems were discussed by experts and laymen, and after 1930 it organized summer schools at Oxford. The society's educational work was well conceived and thoroughly executed, but the feature that may be criticized was the concentration upon educational advancement in Britain, the dominions, and white expatriate colonial communities, and its comparative neglect of native education in the tropical dependencies. If this was a failing, however, it was one for which the Colonial Office also could be criticized. Indeed, the task was one primarily for the Colonial Office, and it could have been argued on the society's behalf that it was operating in the area for which it was most fitted and in which its influence was greatest and success most assured.

[28] For accounts of two of the gold medal awards see L. S. Amery, *My Political Life*, III, 138–9, and L. J. L. Dundas, *Essayez: The Memoirs of Lawrence, the Second Marquess of Zetland* (London 1956), 167–8.

The journal *United Empire* was the society's chief vehicle for canvassing public interest and spreading awareness of empire problems. In 1920 Edward Salmon, who for two years had assisted Sir Harry Wilson with the journal, became editor and filled the position for sixteen years. Salmon had been editor of *Home News for India and Australia* from 1889 to 1899 and assistant editor and managing director of the *Saturday Review* from 1899 to 1913, and was the author of several biographical works. In 1929 the journal was given a new and brighter cover designed by Ralph Bond, the honorary treasurer, and in March 1930 it was introduced to the railway bookstalls for sale to the general public. In 1937 Salmon was succeeded by A. Wyatt Tilby, who had worked on the *Saturday Review*, edited the London *Evening Standard*, and written six volumes on the English People Overseas. Tilby was not satisfied that the journal was reaching as wide a public outside the society as it deserved, and in 1938 it was given a new style and format, the size was increased, the type was made bolder, and more reading matter and better illustrations were included. Salmon had tried to make the journal more a record of the activities of the society, but the reports of these had expanded to a point where they dominated the journal, and Tilby immediately curtailed the features dealing with the society's internal affairs and extended the comments on national, imperial and international issues.

At the centre of the society's work, the library was the haunt of students and research scholars as well as of fellows. The librarian, Evans Lewin, had left in 1917 for national service at the Admiralty, where he was responsible for the preparation in 1918 of a report for the Foreign Office on German administration in Africa. He returned after the war and remained until his retirement in 1946. Lewin, a modest and genial person, published a number of books and directed the compilation of the library's printed catalogue. In 1927 the Carnegie United Kingdom Trust granted the library £3,000 payable in three annual instalments for certain defined purposes. This was the first substantial monetary donation the library had received, and it made possible the continued publication of the society's bibliographies and the preparation of a magnificent printed catalogue of the library's holdings.[29]

[29] Co. Mins. 14 (17 Jan. 1927), 405.

The catalogue was the result of nearly twenty years' work and was important because there had been very little bibliographical publication of this character, and in London the only general list of literature relating to the overseas empire was still the institute's previous catalogue which had been issued in 1901. The new catalogue was not exhaustive and did not entirely supersede that published in 1901. The first volume appeared in March 1930 and covered the empire as a whole and Africa in particular, and included an impressive section on imperial federation; the second volume appeared in 1931 and covered Australia, New Zealand, the South Pacific, and voyages and travels; the third volume appeared in 1932 and covered Canada, Newfoundland and the West Indies, and American colonial history. A fourth volume appeared in 1937.

The library was also responsible for a quarterly bulletin of all the overseas official publications it received. This was begun in 1927 and was the only publication then available concerning current official materials; a charge of five shillings a year was made to meet part of the cost of publication, but after five years the bulletin was discontinued because of financial difficulty.[30] The library continued to carry a large number of current newspapers and periodicals, most of them supplied free of charge by the various proprietors. These provided a valuable service to visitors from the empire who could continue reading their local newspapers while in London; naturally, many of the papers and periodicals could not have had a large readership and some were more in the nature of curiosities whose usefulness would be mainly to later historians. There could not have been a large demand, for instance, for the *Jacobite*, a New Zealand quarterly that supported Rupert, the ex-king of Bavaria, as the unquestionable heir to the House of Stuart. Expenditure on books was small in relation to the library's size, mainly because great reliance could be placed on the generosity of government departments, learned institutions, other societies, and private individuals. Between 1919 and 1939 the library increased its holdings of books and pamphlets from about 134,000 to over 262,000.

The character of the society was a source of anxiety to the council, which attempted to control two major disturbing

[30] *Library Notes* (Oct. 1958).

features. The first was the society's overwhelmingly Conservative loyalty. The society drew heavily on retired colonial civil servants and officers of the armed forces, and the governing body had not lost its awesome display of titles and noble lineage. It signally failed between the wars to enlist the support of organized labour, an objective whose achievement one sympathetic historian believed would revolutionize the range of the society's activities.[31] The council was aware of its own Conservative bias, and conscientiously ensured that at least one of its members, and by 1930 at least two, came from the ranks of the parliamentary Labour party.[32] Nevertheless, the trade union and working classes generally remained uninterested, and the society continued to be a middle-class organization with a strong leavening of the well-born in its governing body.

The second feature of the society's character that the council tried to control was the new tendency, under the pressure of financial difficulties, for learning and research to be subordinated to the development of social amenities and activities. Since its inception the society had operated in a double role: it was a forum for serious discussion and also a club for bringing together people from all parts of the empire. In the nineteenth century the first role had predominated, and suggestions for making the society more of a club had been rejected by the council.[33] By the end of the First World War the social side had grown in importance, and with the influx of female members threatened to become overwhelming. There was soon a luncheon room, a card room, and a dressing room, and it was possible to take part in river trips, informal concerts, afternoon teas, billiard tournaments, and bridge drives. A correspondent in a Malayan newspaper in 1929 advised everyone who visited London periodically to join the society because it was a 'comfortable club' where food and drink were 'remarkably cheap'.[34]

Sir Charles Lucas warned in 1925 that education was the essence of the institute:

[31] H. E. Egerton, *British Colonial Policy in the XXth Century* (London 1922), 169–70.

[32] Co. Mins. 13 (21 Sept. 1920), 36–7; (19 Oct.), 48; 16 (10 Feb. 1930), 24.

[33] Co. Mins. 1 (19 Feb. 1872), 151; (4 March), 154; (26 June), 174; 2 (17 April 1877), 49.

[34] *Times of Malaya*, 5 June 1929.

It was founded to be an Institute or Society, not a Club, to be an educational agency in the widest sense, to teach the Home-people about the overseas peoples of the Empire.

It was still needed, he declared, for teaching and learning,

and the provision of additional club facilities, a great and undoubted improvement, must never be allowed to obscure our main purpose or to divert us from our mission, which is to expound and insist upon the true meaning of the British Empire and the privileges and responsibilities of its citizens.[35]

Nevertheless, there was a widespread feeling that the society was changing its character, and in 1927 its income tax exemption was withdrawn by the inland revenue on the grounds that it was not a charitable organization, that its objects were political, and that among its functions was the provision of a social club for the use of members. It was only after a successful appeal to the income tax commissioners that the society in 1930 regained recognition for revenue purposes that it was a charitable organization and not a club and that the social amenities it provided were merely incidental to the main work.[36]

A *Times* editorial in 1930 compared the Royal Empire Society to 'a club to which a Museum had been bequeathed', and it advised placing more emphasis on spreading understanding of imperial questions: 'The Empire Society', it suggested, 'is the obvious body to do for the Empire what the Institute of International Affairs has been created to do for the affairs of the world.'[37] The suggestion was discussed in the council, where members expressed concern at the danger of lapsing into a club and hoped that the balance between learning and discussion on the one hand and social activities on the other would be restored.[38] The problem was understood, but little effective was done to solve it. Although the reform of the journal in 1938 was an attempt at giving a more serious guise to the society's affairs, the outbreak of war the following year put an end to further discussion of the problem.

[35] *United Empire*, 16 (1925), 383–4.
[36] Co. Mins. 14 (17 Jan. 1927), 405; 16 (8 Dec. 1930), 142.
[37] *The Times*, 24 Oct. 1930.   [38] Co. Mins. 17 (11 Jan. 1932), 4.

Chapter Ten

Relations with Other Organizations (1882–1939)

IN the twentieth century there were a number of organizations whose activities supplemented and often overlapped those of the Royal Empire Society, which was normally prepared to co-operate in matters of mutual interest. Thus, in 1914 it allied with the Overseas Club to organize public support for a uniform naturalization law for the empire.[1] During the war it maintained a working relationship with the Victoria League, the Overseas Club, and the Patriotic League of Britons Overseas through a joint committee which met twice a year and exchanged reports between the represented bodies with the aim of avoiding overlapping wherever possible. The institute was also associated with the Victoria League and the League of the Empire in the imperial studies committee. It was not unusual for the various patriotic societies to combine their efforts for special occasions, as in November 1926 when they pooled their resources to give a dinner at the Guildhall in London for the visiting prime ministers from overseas. Sometimes the desire to co-operate with other reputable organizations, particularly those in the dominions, took the institute outside its proper sphere: in 1896, for example, it agreed to a request made by the Royal Society of Canada to urge the British government to consider the unification of time at sea by harmonizing astronomical time with civil time.[2]

On the whole, the institute was cautious in its selection of other causes to support, and was wary of becoming connected with bodies which it regarded as less sophisticated than itself and of a more propagandist nature. It had little to do with the Primrose League, which avoided detailed study of imperial issues and concentrated on straightforward, emotional, and

[1] Jebb to Lord Emmott, 13 Jan. 1914, Jebb Papers.
[2] Co. Mins. 6 (29 Dec. 1896), 398.

largely uncritical enthusiasm for the empire.[3] In 1917 it refused to be associated with the newly-formed British Empire Land Settlement Propaganda League.[4] Its response to a request from the Kipling Society in 1934 for accommodation in the headquarters building in Northumberland Avenue was unenthusiastic, and the room it offered at a rent of £150 a year was rejected as being too expensive.[5] In 1937 and 1938 the council declined an invitation to establish links with the British Empire Union, which it rightly regarded as a strongly pro-capitalist and anti-socialist propagandist body. The British Empire Union, founded in 1915, had consistently campaigned on an imperial preference platform and the slogan 'Buy British', and in the 1920s had been foremost in urging the British government to 'clear out the Reds' and prosecute the 'Enemies in our Midst'.[6]

There were some responsible bodies with which the Royal Empire Society might have been expected to find much in common but with which, in fact, it had remarkably little to do. The Round Table movement had few links with the society. The movement owed most in the United Kingdom to such men as Lionel Curtis, Philip Kerr (later Lord Lothian), the first editor of its journal, Milner, Lord Selborne, Lord Lovat, Lord Robert Cecil, and Leo Amery. In Canada it owed most to Sir John Willison, Arthur James Glazebrook, and Sir Edward Peacock; in New Zealand to W. Downie Stewart, the Mayor of Dunedin, and Professor Laby; in Australia to Lord Chelmsford, the governor of New South Wales; in South Africa to Sir Patrick Duncan and the lawyer Richard Feetham; and in the United States to Whitney Shepardson, who for many years contributed the American article to the journal, and Irvine Cannon of the *Christian Science Monitor*.[7] None of these persons was much interested in the Royal Empire Society, and this indifference was reciprocated by the society's council. Nor was the council in the twentieth century as much concerned about

[3] J. H. Robb, *The Primrose League, 1883–1906* (New York 1942), 183.
[4] Co. Mins. 11 (24 July 1917), 272.
[5] Co. Mins. 18 (8 Oct. 1934), 77–8.
[6] Co. Mins. 19 (10 May 1937), 210; 20 (11 April 1938), 72. British Empire Union, *Annual Report* (1936), 24.
[7] For information on the persons involved in the movement the author is indebted to J. P. S. Daniell, honorary secretary of the Round Table Ltd.

the Imperial Institute as it had been in the nineteenth century, although the society's journal occasionally published short commendatory pieces on the Imperial Institute's work. The British (later Royal) Institute of International Affairs was in a different category in that it was the sort of body that many members of the council thought the Royal Empire Society should strive to become. It was formed in 1919 and its purpose was originally defined as 'to keep its members in touch with the International situation, and enable them to study the relation between national policies and the interests of society as a whole.' It was hoped that branches or similar institutes would develop in other states. 'The Royal Colonial Institute, which', commented *United Empire*, 'has been doing much the same thing as regards Colonial affairs for the past fifty years, with not inconsiderable success, will watch with sympathetic interest the working out of what should prove a fruitful and felicitous idea.'[8] There was little practical co-operation between the two, however, until 1936, when discussions were held on the allocation of fields of study of imperial problems so as to avoid duplication.[9]

The busiest period for assisting other causes and exploring the possibilities of association with other organizations was in the second decade of the twentieth century. In 1915 the council responded sympathetically to suggestions of co-operation made by the British Empire League, one of the residuaries of the defunct Imperial Federation League. In its twenty years of life the league had established a social centre known as the British Empire Club, published a monthly review containing notes from special correspondents overseas, and been primarily responsible for the erection of a life-sized bronze statue of Captain Cook at the Admiralty Arch end of the Mall near Trafalgar Square. The league suggested to the institute that a joint committee of the two societies should be appointed to consider a proposal for a post-war convention to devise a scheme of closer empire union. The committee was duly appointed and was reported by the institute's journal as evidence of the efforts being made to remove the risk of overlapping, which it regarded as 'the bane of philanthropic and patriotic effort in our queer old country, where well-meaning

[8] *United Empire*, 11 (1920), 406.　　　[9] Ibid., 28 (1937), 399.

individualism runs rampant to the detriment of national efficiency'.[10]

In the middle of the war an attempt to unite the institute with the National Service League nearly succeeded. The National Service League had been founded in 1902 in order to persuade the government to adopt a system of national compulsory military training. Early in 1916 the institute's chairman, Bevan Edwards, had private discussions with the league, and a joint committee was nominated to conduct more formal negotiations. The joint committee met on 15 May and agreed that an executive council should be formed by combining the two existing councils and recommended the assumption of the mutual title 'Imperial Union', or, alternatively, the 'Royal Colonial Institute and National Service League'. There were doubters on the league's council, however, and the institute's council, after studying the draft agreement for amalgamation, found some of the provisions unacceptable, especially that relating to a new title, and the amalgamation scheme was dropped.[11] The league was disbanded in 1921, when it was clear that its principal objective was unattainable.

A common form of assistance to new organizations and clubs was the provision of occasional accommodation in the institute's headquarters building. In 1914 the institute lent its rooms for the inauguration of the Society for Practical Education, which aimed to encourage manual training in elementary school education. In 1919 the council invited the committee of the Britannic Industrial Alliance to use the council room for meetings until it had acquired premises of its own. The alliance was the result of a movement launched at a dinner in the House of Commons and was designed to 'promote co-operation and industrial harmony with a view to developing the Empire's resources and furthering the cause of Empire unity', objects which strongly commended themselves to the institute's council.[12] In the following years use of institute rooms was at various times granted to a large and, at times, curious assortment of organizations, among which were the Anglo-Egyptian

---

[10] *United Empire*, 6 (1915), 573.
[11] Co. Mins. 11 (27 Jan. 1916), 34–5; (9 May), 90; (25 May), 96–7; (20 July), 128.
[12] *United Empire*, 11 (1920), 209.

Association, the Society of Comparative Legislation, the Dominion Students Athletic Union, the Royal African Society, the Worcestershire Old Elizabethan Association, the Upton Habitation of the Primrose League, the International Colonial Institute, the Australian Natives Association, the Old Melburnians, several emigration societies and committees, and a number of clubs, including the Casual, the Compatriots, and the Diggers.

Among the most important of the voluntary bodies so far as the institute was concerned was the Overseas Club, established in 1910 and largely organized and led by Evelyn Wrench, founder of the English-Speaking Union and a member of some years standing of the institute's council. Some of the club's central committee, including the first chairman, Richard Jebb, were members of the institute council and it held some of its meetings in the institute's council room. Within a few years the club had enrolled over 100,000 supporters, a rapid expansion attributable partly to the low annual subscription—a maximum of five shillings—and partly to the simple, straightforward, and evidently popular creed that it professed:

Believing the British Empire to stand for justice, freedom, order and good government, we pledge ourselves, as citizens of the greatest Empire in the world, to maintain the heritage handed down to us by our fathers.

It closed all its meetings with a rendering of the national anthem lengthened by an additional verse with a new concluding adjuration:

> One great united band,
> Pray we through every land,
> God guard our Empire grand,
>   God save the King.

In 1922 the club was amalgamated with the Patriotic League of Britons Overseas, which had been founded in 1914 with Lord Selborne, a vice-president of the institute, as chairman, and Lord Aldenham, a fellow, as vice-chairman. The new organization brought about by the amalgamation between the Overseas Club and the Patriotic League received a royal charter of incorporation as the Overseas League.[13]

[13] Overseas League *Annual Report* (1921), 2. *United Empire*, 6 (1915), 19–20, 650–5.

The Library, 1928

Lord Bruce, Australian High Commissioner, and Lord Woolton, Minister of Food at the presentation of a mobile canteen for war-time use in Britain, provided by High School girls of Sydney, July 1940. (See p. 191)

The Overseas Club was professedly committed to supporting 'any kindred societies or movements working on patriotic lines for the welfare of the British Empire'. By 1919 it was widely felt both in the club and in the Royal Colonial Institute that a closer association or even integration was desirable. The objects of the two organizations were not dissimilar, and the two councils to a significant degree consisted of the same men. The membership of the institute was over 14,000, while the club had about 170,000 supporters, most of them in the dominions, but any scheme of amalgamation would affect only the subscribing members of the Overseas Club, numbering some 26,000, so that the combined membership of an amalgamated society would have been in the region of 40,000. The advantages of amalgamation had been illustrated in 1918, when the institute issued a jubilee appeal for a new building fund and came into competition with an appeal being made by the Overseas Club. Businessmen protested against the double appeal, and one declared that he would not subscribe to either individually but would give a substantial four-figure sum if the two were amalgamated. The situation thus created led to an informal meeting of representatives of the two governing bodies in May 1919, when it was agreed that amalgamation was desirable and a joint committee was established to carry the matter further.[14] The committee, under the chairmanship of Sir Godfrey Lagden, produced a report in January 1920 favouring a scheme of amalgamation. The committee felt that 'many sections of the work of both Societies were being carried on upon much the same lines, and might readily be unified'. It made suggestions for creating a governing body of the joint society, which was to be entitled the Royal United Empire Society. The aims and objects of the new society were an amalgam of those of the institute and club, but were in general to 'work for the permanent unity of the British Empire in thought, action and ideals, and to draw its peoples together in the bond of comradeship', and also to 'promote patriotism, in no spirit of hostility to any other nation'. The committee concluded that there were 'no technical obstacles in the way of amalgamation, but much preliminary work would be necessary,

[14] Co. Mins. 12 (18 March 1919), 130; (3 June), 162–4; (17 June), 170; 13 (17 Feb. 1921), 110–11.

L

and, as in all fusions, many details would have to be explored and adjusted before any final agreement could be reached'.[15]

The exploration of the details of amalgamation, however, brought negotiations to a deadlock by the end of July 1920. The most difficult problem was the reconciliation of the various classes of membership into which the institute and the club were divided and which the joint committee had attempted to combine and reclassify. The institute had recently increased its rates of subscription, which were already well in excess of those of the club, and the wide disparity between the rates made the arrangement of a uniform subscription impossible. There was also some difficulty in reconciling the status, privileges, and voting powers of the members of the two organizations. The union of the two journals into one that would preserve the individuality of each and satisfy the requirements of all members of the combined society was impracticable. The title suggested for the amalgamated organization—Royal United Empire Society—was not acceptable to the Overseas Club, and it was impossible to assure Evelyn Wrench of the commanding position in the governing body to which he and his admirers believed he was entitled.

There were also constitutional difficulties which, though probably capable of being surmounted if necessary, contributed to the argument against attempting an amalgamation. The institute wished to use its existing charter and secure by means of a supplemental charter such powers as were required to effect the amalgamation, whereas the club, fearing this procedure would convey the impression of an absorption of one organization by the other rather than of an amalgamation, wanted an entirely new charter to be devised, and this would have involved considerable additional expense. Moreover, the club had no constitution and could not as a corporate body negotiate a binding agreement such as a union with the institute would demand. After twenty months of discussions, the attempt to amalgamate was dropped. At the beginning of 1921 the joint committee made a final declaration: 'in view of difficulties which subsequent considerations have revealed, it has been found impracticable to give effect to amalgamation as con-

[15] Co. Mins. 12 (12 Feb. 1920), 267–8. *United Empire*, 11 (1920), 330–9.

templated in the original Report of the Joint Committee dated January 28th, 1920'.[16]

Efforts to reopen negotiations were of no avail until July 1935, when the two organizations discussed closer co-operation, and early in 1936 Sir Evelyn Wrench and the chairman of the Royal Empire Society, Sir Archibald Weigall, signed a memorandum proposing a joint advisory committee to investigate means of working together.[17] On 6 February 1936 a special general meeting of the Royal Empire Society considered a resolution to put the proposal into effect:

That, in order that steps may be taken to give ultimate effect to a scheme of amalgamation or federation of the Royal Empire Society and the Over-Seas League, we propose the immediate establishment of a Joint Advisory Committee, consisting of six members of each Society with an independent Chairman and a Secretary; there to be two Deputy Chairmen, one representing each Society, who will take the chair alternately in the absence of the Chairman. The recommendations of this Joint Advisory Committee to be submitted to the Councils of the two Societies before any action can be taken.

It was expected that Lord Athlone would be chairman and Wrench the Secretary. It was soon apparent, however, that there were a number of fellows strongly opposed to an amalgamation with the league. There was some dissatisfaction with the outlook of Wrench, who was inseparably wedded to the interests of the Overseas League, the English-Speaking Union, and the All Peoples Association: 'Sir Evelyn Wrench', it was remarked, 'was perfectly entitled to his own views, he was entitled to everything except taking over the Royal Empire Society.' An amended resolution was eventually carried that approved the appointment of a joint advisory committee not, as in the original resolution, 'in order that steps may be taken to give ultimate effect to a scheme of amalgamation or federation', but 'to consider the desirability, or otherwise, of closer association'. Lord Athlone was duly elected chairman unanimously, but a resolution that Wrench should be elected secretary was lost.[18] Amalgamation was unwanted by the majority of members of the two organizations and would have been

[16] Co. Mins. 13 (17 Feb. 1921), 111–17. Overseas Club and Patriotic League *Annual Report* (1920), 4.
[17] Co. Mins. 18 (13 Jan. 1936), 252.   [18] *United Empire*, 27 (1936), 143–5.

attended by numerous difficulties, the most prominent now being the importance attached by the Overseas League to keeping its overseas subscription at ten shillings a year, while the Royal Empire Society was unable to reduce its subscription of £1. 11s. 6d. a year. Nevertheless, the joint advisory committee met on several occasions and enabled the two organizations to maintain friendly contact and combine their resources for the entertainment of visitors from overseas.[19]

Another organization with which amalgamation was periodically considered was the Victoria League, which had been founded in 1901 and to which the Imperial Order of the Daughters of the Empire was affiliated. Like the Royal Colonial Institute, the league was supposed to be strictly without party political predilections, but unlike the institute, its membership was predominantly female and the first committee was composed entirely of women, though in later years men were elected to it. The declared aims and objects of the league were of immediate relevance and concern to the institute. It held itself ready 'as far as possible, to support and assist any scheme leading to a more intimate understanding between ourselves, and our fellow subjects in our great Colonies and Dependencies'. It also endeavoured

to become a centre for receiving and distributing information regarding the British Dominions, and invites the alliance of, and offers help and co-operation to, such bodies of a similar nature as already exist, or as shall hereafter be formed throughout the Empire.

Among its activities were the provision of lectures on the empire, the operation of a newspaper and magazine scheme between people in the United Kingdom and people overseas, the welcoming of visitors to England, and the dissemination through pamphlets and leaflets of information about the dominions and the history and general conditions of the empire. By 1915 it had well over 6,000 supporters and an income derived from membership subscriptions and from grants by the Rhodes Trust.

Amalgamation with the Victoria League was considered informally at the institute as early as 1909.[20] In July 1912

[19] Overseas League *Annual Report* (1936), 16.
[20] Co. Mins. 9 (12 Oct. 1909), 5; (7 Dec.), 18.

a joint committee of an equal number of representatives of each council was established, and in 1913 this developed into a permanent committee meeting twice a year to exchange information and confer on the work of the two organizations and on future plans. In 1916 the committee was expanded by the inclusion of a representative from the Overseas Club and one from the Patriotic League of Britons Overseas.[21] Notices of lectures given by each were circulated to members of the other, and overseas branches and corresponding secretaries of both organizations were encouraged to co-operate with one another in similar ways. The question of amalgamation or union, however, was allowed to fall into abeyance.

The Royal Empire Society was the natural home for the Empire Day Movement that developed at the end of the nineteenth century and the beginning of the twentieth. The idea of observing one day in each year as a public holiday throughout the empire was first suggested to the council in 1894 and 1895 by Thomas Robinson, the institute's honorary corresponding secretary at Winnipeg in Canada.[22] Taking up Robinson's suggestion, the council addressed a petition to the Queen in July 1894 declaring that, whereas other nations had annual days for national celebration, the British empire had no such day, and proposing that the Queen's birthday should be set aside for the purpose. In a reply the prime minister, Lord Rosebery, stated that it was a matter not for the government but for the community and pointed out that government departments already kept the Queen's birthday as a holiday.[23] The idea was gaining support in Canada, however, and on the initiative of Mrs. Clementina Fessenden, the wife of a country clergyman, the Ontario minister of education, Senator George W. Ross, promoted a scheme for children to commemorate the empire on one day each year. The scheme was put to a meeting of the Canadian Education Association in 1898, passed unanimously, and subsequently presented to the various provincial educational departments and adopted first by Nova Scotia and then by Ontario and Quebec.[24]

[21] Victoria League *Annual Report* (1912–13), 17; (1914–15), 10; (1916–17), 22. Co. Mins. 9 (2 July 1912), 309; (4 March 1913), 397–8.

[22] Co. Mins. 6 (10 July 1894), 181; (31 Dec. 1895), 312; (14 Jan. 1896), 314.

[23] Co. Mins. 6 (24 July 1894), 187–8. *Proceedings*, 26 (1895), 377–9.

[24] *United Empire*, 5 (1914), 521, 667–8; 6 (1915), 154.

The news of the observance of an empire day by Canadian schoolchildren stirred the patriotic emotions of the Earl of Meath in England, and he began to campaign for its extension to the entire empire. An empire day observed by all ages in the community and not merely by children was not advocated until after the turn of the century, when the British League of Australia passed two resolutions in support of the idea as 'likely to aid in maintaining and strengthening the unity of the British race under one flag'. The president of the British League of Australia, Canon (later Archdeacon) F. B. Boyse of Sydney, wrote to Meath in February 1903 informing him of these resolutions and to *The Times*, which in April 1903 published his letter expressing the hope that Britain, in consultation with the dominions, would arrange the regular observance of one day in the year to celebrate the empire and suggesting Queen Victoria's birthday, 24 May, as the most suitable. In the same year the council of the Royal Colonial Institute produced another petition in favour of Queen Victoria's birthday being celebrated throughout the empire as a holiday, but by this time Meath had made himself the leader of the 'empire day' campaign.[25]

Meath had retired from the diplomatic service as Lord Brabazon in 1873 and settled at Sunbury-on-Thames near London, where he and his wife resolved to devote themselves to social problems and the relief of suffering. They became prominent campaigners on behalf of hospitals, parks, public gardens, and playgrounds. Meath joined the Royal Colonial Institute in 1888 and began to interest himself in fostering empire patriotism. In December 1892 he made an appeal for the teaching of patriotism in London schools and backed it with the offer of fifty pounds towards the purchase of Union Jacks. In 1893, in collaboration with H. O. Arnold-Forster, he crowned several years of work by persuading Parliament to permit the Union Jack to be flown over the Palace of Westminster. In July 1902 he wrote to the colonial secretary, Joseph Chamberlain, on the observance of an empire day, and thereafter the subject obsessed Meath, who for many years carried on the campaign largely on his own and at his own

[25] *Proceedings*, 38 (1907), 171–2. *United Empire*, 14 (1923), 118; 21 (1930), 256. *The Times*, 11 April 1903.

expense. The empire day movement tended to revolve around his reverence for the Union Jack, and under his energetic management it took on something of a chauvinistic, flag-waving character.[26]

During the world war official recognition was given to empire day in Britain, and its first national observance took place on 24 May 1916, when children in over 70,000 schools saluted the flag and even at the Stock Exchange the national anthem was sung in commemoration. Meath's Empire Day Movement had succeeded in producing a public frame of mind that enabled the United Kingdom to discard the airy indifference evident in Victoria's reign, and to follow the example that had been set in the dominions: 'The cold and haughty England of those days is gone', remarked *The Times*. 'We have come to realize that it is not unseemly to be enthusiastic.'[27] Nevertheless, the observance of empire day was not as widespread or as strong as the enthusiasts desired, particularly in Britain, where there was resistance to it in some quarters, including the trade unions, the Labour movement, and the public schools. The Empire Day Movement, therefore, continued campaigning to extend public recognition and enthusiasm. Meath remained the principal force behind the movement, but by 1920 he felt that he was unable to give to it as much time as he had been giving, and in January 1921 he formally invited the council of the Royal Colonial Institute to assume control of it. At the council's request, he agreed to continue managing the movement for that year, in view of the institute's involvement in negotiations on amalgamation with the Overseas Club, but the movement's eventual incorporation into the institute was approved in principle and duly took place in 1922.[28]

The Empire Day Movement was accommodated in the institute building and directed by a committee composed of members of the institute and of Meath's original committee, with Sir Lawrence Wallace as chairman and Meath himself choosing to occupy the position of vice-chairman. In 1927 Wallace was succeeded by Lieutenant-Colonel Sir William

[26] Earl of Meath, *Brabazon Potpourri* (London 1928), 92–3. *The Times*, 12 Oct. 1929. *United Empire*, 21 (1930), 340.

[27] *The Times*, 24 and 25 May 1916.

[28] Co. Mins. 13 (8 Feb. 1921), 102; (12 July), 198–9. Earl of Meath, *Memories of the Twentieth Century* (London 1924), 292.

Wayland, and Meath, at the committee's request, became the movement's first president. As part of the institute, the movement continued its propaganda activities, revising, reprinting, and expanding its propaganda literature, sending letters to the press, distributing thousands of posters, and supplying speakers and Union Jacks to schools. It concentrated on secondary schools in particular, and after 1926 made special, but not notably successful, efforts to spread its faith among the working classes and the ranks of the Labour party. It influenced the institute's annual dinner, which became a celebration of empire day, and inevitably tagged the institute's name to many of its activities, including the much publicized annual presentation of an empire Christmas pudding to the King. The pudding was supposed to have a symbolic significance in that the ingredients were drawn entirely from the empire and were ceremoniously stirred in the bowl by representatives of the various parts of the empire. The pudding, Meath solemnly declared at Christmas 1926, was a symbol of imperial unity and an epitome of trade within the empire: 'The King's acceptance of it was an act of real value to the Empire which would touch the imagination of every British family.' If housewives throughout the empire, it was said, followed the King's example, the foundations of empire trade would be firmly laid: 'If the whole Empire confined itself, on Christmas Day, to the use, in its puddings, of Australian currants, that fact alone would go a long way to setting the new Australian dried fruit industry on its feet.'[29]

In 1929 Meath was succeeded as president of the Empire Day Movement by Admiral Earl Jellicoe, a proud, deeply religious man, who in the twilight of his life interested himself in several voluntary organizations. The economic depression of the next few years reduced the financial support the movement had been enjoying, but its leaders, convinced of the worthiness of their cause and of the continuing necessity to enhance and propagate it, did not allow the movement's activities to be relaxed: 'It must be remembered', noted the chairman at the beginning of 1931, 'that, in spite of unremitting efforts for a number of years, there are still many dark corners in Great Britain, especially in the industrial areas, where the

[29] *United Empire*, 18 (1927), 21.

rays of our Empire sun have not yet been able to penetrate.'[30] Under the guidance of Jellicoe and Wayland an energetic educational campaign was begun among the working classes in the population, and determined attempts were made to enlist the support of the press, churches, local authorities, schools, workingmen's clubs, and women's institutes. Honorary corresponding secretaries were appointed in various parts of the British Isles and the co-operation of women's institutes was secured in organizing empire day celebrations in country districts. In 1932 the movement supported a campaign for 'empire meals on empire day' inaugurated by the women's committee of the Fellowship of the British Empire, in 1933 it authorized the compilation of an empire song sheet of representative songs of the British Isles and of the dominions, and in 1934 it issued an empire calendar.

Some education authorities criticized observance of empire day, and in 1934 the education committee of the Labour-controlled London County Council issued a circular to schools in the metropolitan area proposing that empire day should thenceforward be observed as commonwealth day. The chairman of the Empire Day Movement committee, Sir William Wayland, raised the matter in the House of Commons, where he argued that the alteration was undesirable, and asked the parliamentary secretary to the Board of Education to consider introducing a bill to make the day a general holiday in all schools, 'the day to be named Empire Day and to be celebrated by the saluting of the Union Jack and the giving of an address to the children on the greatness of the British Empire'.[31] He was told that no useful purpose would be served by such legislation, but he had succeeded in publicizing the concern felt by the movement, and three weeks later the concern felt by the council of the Royal Empire Society was also publicized by its chairman, Sir Archibald Weigall. At the annual general meeting he asserted that 'commonwealth' was not a proper or adequate substitute for 'empire' and described the action of the London County Council as a grave mistake:

Commonwealth Day assumes that the British Empire is only composed of what is known as the Commonwealth of Nations, those

[30] *United Empire*, 22 (1931), 35.
[31] *Parl. Debs.*, H.C. 289 (3 May 1934), coll. 463–4.

great self-governing Dominions, and eliminates entirely from the mind of the child the fact that he or she is the trustee of the great heritage of your Crown Colonies, Protectorates and Mandated Territories.[32]

At the empire day dinner the following evening, Weigall returned to the subject and expressed his regret that the London County Council should have implied to the people of the United Kingdom that 'empire' was a word that could be usefully discarded. In a strong, but singularly impercipient speech, he presumed to affirm the society's unswerving loyalty to the existing nomenclature: 'Whatever any authority in this country may do', he declared, 'let me say here and now that under no possible circumstances are we going to call ourselves the Royal Commonwealth Society.'[33]

In 1936, after the death of Jellicoe, the presidency of the Empire Day Movement was accepted by Admiral Earl Beatty, but he died shortly afterwards and in 1937 Viscount Bledisloe became president. The movement showed a remarkable resilience over the years, and it experienced few administrative or organizational problems. Except for the confusion in the public mind threatened in 1936 by the promotion by John S. Webb of what he chose to call an Empire Movement, it was able to conduct its propaganda activities with little serious difficulty. It owed much to the hospitality and benevolent interest of the Royal Empire Society, and it recognized this by furnishing in the society's headquarters the Earl of Meath room, which was opened in 1937 and allocated to the companions in the society.

In 1932 the chairman of the finance and general purposes committee of the Royal Empire Society discussed with the dominions secretary, J. H. Thomas, the co-ordination of the work of patriotic societies and analogous bodies and supplied him with a list of those most suitable for inclusion in any co-operative arrangement.[34] Thomas promised to raise the matter in the House of Commons, and did so in December, when he referred to the risk of confusion caused by the multiplicity of organizations operating in the field of empire migration:

[32] *United Empire*, 25 (1934), 363.   [33] Ibid., 360–1.
[34] Co. Mins. 17 (12 Dec. 1932), 128.

I do not want to say a word that would be construed as reflecting in the least upon the Imperial activity or sentiment and loyalty of these Societies, but I do say that a real effort ought to be made to bring these 33 bodies together. I believe they could do more effective and useful work under one machine than under 33.[35]

The Royal Empire Society was joined by the Victoria League in calling for a conference to consider a federation of bodies dealing with empire affairs, and they forwarded to the dominions secretary a joint resolution of their own willingness to federate their work in the hope that it would strengthen his resolve to call such a conference. Thomas felt unable to take any positive action until after the international economic conference in London in June and July 1933, but then, after eliminating from his list societies with marked political or commercial interests, he summoned a conference of representatives of patriotic societies for 20 November. Thomas suggested that closer co-operation should be examined in detail at further meetings between the societies, and it was thereupon formally resolved

That, in the opinion of this conference, it is desirable that the whole question of closer co-operation between societies engaged in various spheres of non-political work for the advancement of the interests of the British Commonwealth should be further explored at future meetings under a chairman nominated by the Secretary of State, and that such meetings should be arranged at the headquarters of the various societies, so far as possible in turn.

Two standing committees were appointed, one for hospitality, convened by the Royal Empire Society, and one for education, convened by the Victoria League, to study means of reducing overlapping.[36]

The subject of co-operation with other organizations continued to attract the attention of the council of the Royal Empire Society up to the outbreak of a second world war in 1939. The council's principal interest was in the Victoria League and the Overseas League, with which there were already close working arrangements, especially in the matter of entertaining distinguished people, and the chairman of

[35] *Parl. Debs.* H.C. 272 (7 Dec. 1932), col. 1722.
[36] Co. Mins. 17 (10 April 1933), 181; (8 May), 191; (19 June), 204; (13 Nov.), 244. *The Times*, 21 Nov. 1933.

council sat on the executive committee of the Victoria League. On certain other occasions the society also combined with the Royal African Society, the East India Association, and the dominions and colonies section of the Royal Society of Arts. Co-operation with analogous organizations had been substantially extended and improved by 1939, but despite professions of interest in co-ordination of activities and even in federation, there was never any real likelihood that the council would seriously consider surrendering the society's individuality or independence. It might have been prepared to federate with the Victoria League or the Overseas League, but only on terms that those organizations would have found unacceptable. The Royal Empire Society regarded itself as not only the senior but also as the only learned body among the voluntary, patriotic organizations, and it was not prepared at any time to endanger its unique character for the sake of extending its membership and influence by amalgamation with any other body.

Chapter Eleven

Migration and Trade (1910–1939)

Two aspects of the imperial association in which the Royal Empire Society took a consistent and constructive interest were migration and trade. It had shown an intelligent awareness of the significance of migration within the empire in the nineteenth century, and from the 1880s onwards it had sought to draw attention to the desirability of directing a larger proportion of British emigrants to the overseas empire in preference to the United States and other foreign countries.[1]

In those years no governmental financial assistance was available to migrants, who, if they lacked private means, were dependent on the more than forty voluntary societies that actively promoted emigration. In May 1910 the Royal Colonial Institute organized a conference attended by representatives from these societies in order to discuss both general emigration questions and the particular problem of diverting to the empire the stream of migrants then flowing to foreign countries. The high commissioners and agents-general of the dominions were invited to the conference but did not attend. The conference resolved that

the attention of the Governments of the Overseas Territories of the Crown, which are geographically united, should be called to the desirability of adopting some uniform arrangements as to (1) the grant of assisted passages, (2) the protection on voyage of young women going to domestic service, (3) the method of receiving emigrants on arrival oversea, (4) the receiving and placing out of lads, and (5) the guarantees that may be given for the employment of suitable settlers.

The conference went on to suggest to the British government 'the desirability of holding as soon as possible, in accordance with the first resolution of the Imperial Conference of 1907,

[1] *The Times*, 2 July 1885. G. S. Graham, 'Imperial Finance, Trade, and Communications, 1885–1914', *Camb. Hist. Brit. Emp.* 3 (1959), 478.

a Subsidiary Conference to consider the subject of emigration from the United Kingdom to the Dominions beyond the seas'. It also resolved that the institute council should be invited to appoint a representative standing committee to which the recommendations of the conference should be referred for consideration and action. This committee, composed of representatives from the institute and from the emigration societies, was designed to advise on emigration questions, to work for the diversion of British emigration more to empire countries, and to co-ordinate the activities of the emigration societies by devising a uniform policy in which the various governments in the empire could co-operate.[2]

The emigration committee issued a report in May 1911 declaring that 'the tide of satisfactory emigrants from North-Western Europe' appeared to be ebbing and that 'a less eligible class' was presenting itself from the east and south. The dominions were anxious to attract settlers from the United Kingdom, but there was a problem in that they wanted a class of people the mother country was unwilling to lose. The committee believed that a *via media* could be found, since there were many unemployed or under-employed persons who had no prospects in Britain and who would be admirable colonists if they could be transferred to the dominions before a long period of idleness had 'undermined their self-reliance and weakened their habits of industry'. It recommended 'that the Imperial Conference should give the fullest consideration to the problem of emigration within the Empire, and if, as seems probable, it cannot attend to questions of detail itself, it should summon a subsidiary Conference for the purpose'. It also suggested that 'an official committee should be constituted representative of the private emigration societies of the United Kingdom, to which the Government should nominate a chairman, representatives of the chief departments concerned, and other persons having special knowledge of the subject of emigration, and for whose staff and administrative expenses it should pay'. Such a committee might be developed out of the existing Emigrants Information Office and might include representatives of the dominion governments; its functions

<hr>

[2] *Official Report of the Emigration Conference held on May 30–31, 1910, convened by the Royal Colonial Institute* (London 1910). Co. Mins. 9 (7 June 1910), 77.

would be to advise on general questions of emigration policy, co-ordinate the work of the emigration societies, disseminate information, negotiate with labour exchanges, boards of guardians, distress committees, and similar bodies, and confer with high commisioners, agents-general, and dominion agencies. The committee stressed the importance of facilitating the emigration of women and children, and suggested grants in aid to the proposed official committee for distribution in *per capita* grants to the private emigration societies to help in the payment of passages.[3]

The imperial conference of 1911 discussed empire migration, but resolved merely that 'the present policy of encouraging British emigrants to proceed to British Dominions rather than foreign countries be continued and that full co-operation be accorded to any Dominion desiring immigrants.'[4] This was no more than a reaffirmation of a resolution passed at the 1907 imperial conference, but in April 1912 a dominions royal commission was appointed to investigate the natural resources and trade of the dominions. The Royal Colonial Institute's standing committee on emigration was aware of the opportunities provided by the appointment of the royal commission, and secured the inclusion of migration among the commission's terms of reference. In 1912 the emigration committee submitted to the commission a report supporting both the dominions' determination to exclude undesirables and the United Kingdom's unwillingness to part with its best citizens, and advocating the emigration of unemployed and those whose departure would relieve social distress at home. Three years later, the institute asked the commission to recommend the Board of Trade to offer facilities for the emigration of widows and orphans.[5]

In 1916 the institute's committee was adjourned for the duration of the war, but the results of its pressure were discernible in the royal commission's final report in 1917. The report described the successful organization of migration as lying 'at the root of the problem of Empire development' and as the factor upon which the progress of the dominions and

[3] Co. Mins. 9 (7 June 1911), 179. *The Times*, 31 May 1911.
[4] *Parl. Paps.* 1911, Vol. 54, Cd. 5745, p. 205.
[5] *The Times*, 23 Oct. 1912. Co. Mins. 10 (19 Jan. 1915), 206; (16 Feb.), 221.

the strengthening of the empire as a whole largely depended:

It is a problem which requires, in our judgment, far more sustained attention than it has hitherto received. Of all the subjects which we have investigated we have found none in which scientific study and scientific treatment are more necessary to replace the spasmodic fluctuations of opinion which have governed the discussion of emigration problems in the past.[6]

The report followed the views of the institute's emigration committee in its advocacy of deploying Britain's surplus population to increase the political and economic strength of the empire, and from its recommendations originated an overseas settlement branch of the Colonial Office.

The war of 1914–18 interrupted the stream of emigration to the dominions, and when it recommenced afterwards it was at a much reduced rate compared with the rate in the four years immediately preceding the war, despite the fact that between 1919 and 1922 the British government provided free passages for approved ex-servicemen. At a special conference on state-aided empire settlement held in January and February 1921 with Canadian, Australian, and New Zealand representatives, the British government proposed that the assistance it was giving to ex-servicemen should be extended to other classes in the community, provided the dominions contributed to an equivalent degree.[7] A meeting of prime ministers approved the proposals, which were passed through Parliament as the Empire Settlement Act authorizing the British government to make loans for a period of up to fifteen years to meet half the cost incurred in transporting settlers overseas. The act was intended to make Britain and the individual dominions equal partners in developing the empire's resources and distributing its population more equitably.[8]

Nevertheless, migration within the empire in the 1920s remained predominantly a private venture, and a majority of those who left the United Kingdom to settle in the dominions continued to do so without governmental assistance. A com-

[6] *Parl. Paps.* 1917–18, Vol. 10, Cd. 8462, p. 83.
[7] Ibid., 1921, Vol. 14, Cmd. 1474, pp. 59–61.
[8] 12 and 13 Geo. 5, c. 12, An act to make better provision for furthering British settlement in His Majesty's oversea dominions (31 May 1922). T. R. Reese, *Australia in the Twentieth Century* (London 1964), 84.

mittee appointed by the imperial economic conference in October 1923 to consider problems of overseas settlement remarked upon the disappointing results achieved by the Empire Settlement Act:

These results would seem to be incommensurate with the needs of the situation, both in the United Kingdom and in the Dominions, more especially in Australia and Canada, but it is clear that the rate at which any redistribution of the white population of the Empire can take place must be governed by the rate at which the Dominions can satisfactorily absorb these new settlers.[9]

The committee expressed confidence that the ultimate results of the act would justify the policy, but the days of teeming emigration were ended. The total number of emigrants from Britain had declined by 1923 to little more than a third of what it had been ten years before. In the 1930s the migration movement went into reverse and there was a substantial inflow of migrants into the United Kingdom, whose net gain in population by means of migration in the decade after 1930 was nearly 20 per cent more than the net loss in the preceding decade.[10]

The Empire Settlement Act embodied most of what the Royal Colonial Institute had been working for in migration policy. The institute had sought a co-ordinated policy centrally administered and directed to relieving congestion in the mother country and strengthening the Anglo-Saxon character of the empire. The sentiments upon which the institute's outlook on migration was based gave it something in common with the National Council for the Promotion of Physical and Moral Race Regeneration, which had begun to develop an interest in the opportunities afforded by migration. The institute journal referred to 'British ideals' which British emigrants to the dominions would help to maintain:

Australia wants British settlers to promote her White ideal; Western Canada wants British settlers in order that the country between the Rockies and British Columbia may not be smothered by a Babel, with nothing in common either with the Dominion or the Empire; British Columbia . . . wants British settlers for the security

[9] *Parl. Paps.* 1924, Vol. 10, Cmd. 2009, pp. 136–8.
[10] Ibid., 1929–30, Vol. 16, Cmd. 3589, pp. 5, 31. Ibid., 1948–49, Vol. 19, Cmd. 7695, pp. 9, 225.

M

of her coastal belt. British teachers, British women, British men with visions of the future bred of a full consciousness of the glory of the past are essential.[11]

It was soon apparent that the Empire Settlement Act was not as productive of these ends as had been hoped. In 1923 the institute's migration committee held meetings with the empire development committee of the House of Commons to decide upon a national scheme of propaganda on behalf of the proposals in the settlement act, and in October 1924 it addressed a memorandum to the prime minister urging amendment of the act and further financial assistance to the voluntary societies.[12] In 1925 and 1926 it brought to the government's notice the dissatisfaction of the voluntary societies with the progress of the migration and settlement policy and their conviction that an entirely new act was needed; it thought the British government should pay the whole cost of the settlement scheme because the less developed dominions had difficulty in paying an equal share. The matter was also receiving attention in the House of Commons, where the institute was able through some of its Members of Parliament to ensure that relevant questions were asked regularly.[13]

When the dominions began to reconsider their immigration policies, the migration committee protested to the governments concerned. New Canadian regulations for the selection of immigrants were criticized at a meeting in February 1928; a resolution expressing apprehension was forwarded to the dominions secretary and the new regulations were later modified. In December 1929 the committee resolved for the notice of the Australian government that it regretted 'the proposal to curtail assisted Migration to Australia, and earnestly trusts that the Australian Government will give the fullest consideration to every point of view before taking such a drastic step, which may be prejudicial to the interests of the Empire as a whole.'[14] The world economic depression brought about a restriction in the emigration activities of the voluntary societies, and early in 1931 the committee decided that since migration was stagnating meetings could be reduced from monthly to quarterly

[11] *United Empire*, 13 (1922), 127.   [12] Ibid., 14 (1923), 311; 16 (1925), 316.
[13] Co. Mins. 14 (13 July 1925), 281; (16 Nov. 1925), 315.
[14] Co. Mins. 15 (9 Dec. 1929), 282.

intervals, with an executive sub-committee continuing to meet monthly.

The imperial economic conference at Ottawa in September 1932, however, was the signal for renewed pressure on the British and dominion governments. The migration committee of the Royal Empire Society and a parliamentary migration committee combined to consider the migration issue in the light of the forthcoming Ottawa conference, and it prepared a memorandum urging a redistribution of the white population of the empire in the interests of relieving the pressure of population in the United Kingdom, of encouraging trade, and of forestalling any possibility that other races or nationalities might seek an outlet in the empty spaces of the larger dominions. The memorandum was presented to the British government but not accepted for discussion at Ottawa, where empire migration was excluded from the conference agenda, but detailed discussions were initiated there nevertheless between Lord Elibank and representatives of voluntary societies in Britain on the one hand and representatives of the Canadian immigration and colonization department on the other.[15]

The society's migration committee made little headway in the 1930s. In 1937, when the Empire Settlement Act was renewed for another fifteen years, it tried to persuade the dominions secretary that economic conditions had improved to an extent that warranted discussion of renewed migration, and it suggested that state-aided passages should be revived and that the dominions should be asked to relax regulations limiting the entry of British-born persons.[16] The legislation prolonging and amending the Empire Settlement Act, however, represented a compromise that satisfied neither the act's opponents nor its enthusiasts and was criticized by both groups in Parliament.[17] The official approach to emigration had undergone a change, and although the Royal Empire Society retained its faith in the principles it had strongly advocated for over a quarter of a century, there was a realization among members of its migration committee that some of their original ambitions would have to

---

[15] Co. Mins. 17 (14 March 1932), 37; (14 Nov.), 117; (12 Dec.), 128.

[16] Co. Mins. 19 (12 April 1937), 195.

[17] 1 Edw. 8 and 1 Geo. 6, c. 18, An act to amend the Empire Settlement Act 1922 (19 March 1937). *The Times*, 29 Jan. 1937.

be discarded. The dominions, as one authority pointed out, were beginning to find themselves in a dilemma:

On the one hand they were learning that they must look beyond Great Britain for necessary defensive reinforcements to their population; on the other hand, they feared that these foreign reinforcements might impair 'the integrity of the group' and the unity of will necessary for its defence. Therefore, not without misgiving, they began to drift towards a middle course of action, that of picking and choosing the few foreigners to whom they were ready to offer a mistrustful hospitality.[18]

It was a course that the Royal Empire Society had feared and had worked hard, but in vain, to make unnecessary.

The society viewed empire migration not only as a political, demographic, and defence issue but also as an aspect of imperial economic policy. Until the beginning of the twentieth century it had paid little attention to questions of trade, shipping, and finance, but the broadening in the character of the membership in the years leading up to the world war increased the representation of merchant, manufacturing, engineering, and shipping interests, and it had acquired the capacity to consider commercial matters usefully. In 1911 the Royal Colonial Institute formed an empire trade and industry committee that was closely identified in its formative stages with Ben H. Morgan, a member of council, who had served as trade commissioner for the Manufacturers Association in Australia, Canada, and South Africa. The new committee held its first meeting in April 1911, when it adopted a resolution drawing the attention of the Colonial Office and the Board of Trade to the necessity of appointing trade commissioners for groups of crown colonies and dependencies, as had recently been done for the dominions. The committee decided to publish regularly in the institute's monthly journal a section dealing with empire trade and describing the work done by the committee, and to arrange conferences and lectures promoting knowledge of commercial opportunities for British goods in the empire and helping to stimulate demand in the United Kingdom for empire products. Among its principal objectives were expected to be the diversion into empire securities and undertakings of some of the

---

[18] W. K. Hancock, *Problems of Economic Policy, 1918–1939* (2 parts, London 1940–2), I, 177.

British capital being invested in foreign countries, the extension of British company law to all parts of the empire as a means of encouraging British investment in empire enterprises and of improving trade relations, and co-ordination of the empire's statistical systems in order that the comparisons provided by trade reports would be of real value to those engaged in cementing trade ties. Among the reforms suggested were the fixing of a common date for the trade returns of the various parts of the empire, the co-ordination of methods by which the statistics were collected, and the use of identical forms for customs entries.[19]

The committee was active from the start and received the co-operation of the governments of the overseas empire. In its first year it concentrated on uniformity of company law, the development of British trade with India and the crown colonies, the establishment of a system of through rates for convenient carriage of products from one part of the empire to another, the reorganization of the British consular service to make it representative equally of the dominions and colonies as of the United Kingdom, and the construction of a British-owned cable to link the British Isles with Canada and Australia and New Zealand.[20] It took a special interest in the dominions royal commission appointed in 1912 in consequence of a resolution of the imperial conference the previous year.[21] The commission was supposed to be composed of 'men of the very first order', but in fact was not a particularly distinguished body. Its terms of reference had been defined by the imperial conference to include reporting upon the natural resources of each part of the empire represented at the conference, but were later revised to exclude both the United Kingdom and existing trade preferences as subjects for investigation. The commission issued a series of interim reports on imperial economic policy, and in 1917 produced its final report based on a mass of evidence and information to which the institute had made significant contributions. Moreover, Richard Jebb, who represented the institute committee before the commission at the end of October 1912, when, he said, it cross-examined him 'like a criminal', used

[19] *United Empire*, 2 (1911), 222, 301; 3 (1912), 419. *The Times*, 5 April 1911.

[20] Co. Mins. 9 (7 June 1911), 179; (2 April 1912), 259.

[21] *Parl. Paps.* 1911, Vol. 54, Cd. 5745, p. 18.

the institute journal to prepare people called before the commission on the points that would be raised.[22]

The institute's trade and industry committee took up an idea advanced at the imperial conference of 1907 by the Australian prime minister, Alfred Deakin, for a joint fund administered by a joint board to improve imperial communications. This had widened into a scheme for planned imperial economic development, and although the idea in both its original and expanded form had been rejected in 1907, it was raised again at the conference of 1911. Jebb was largely responsible for a memorial by the institute committee to the royal commission in 1912 urging consideration of 'the idea of establishing a joint fund for the general purposes of what may be described as Empire Development on the lines of the proposal discussed by the Imperial Conference in 1907', and, accompanied by Ellis T. Powell, he enlarged upon the idea in his evidence to the commission. The institute committee discounted the objections made in 1907 to the Australian scheme and argued that the case for an imperial fund had been strengthened by the disappointment expressed at the imperial conference of 1911 over the failure to make real progress with the scheme.[23] The proposal was referred to in general terms in the commission's second interim report published early in 1914, and though active promotion of the proposal was retarded by the outbreak of war, it found an important place in the royal commission's final report published in 1917.

The report declared that there was

both scope and need for a new Imperial Development Board which, without displacing any existing body, would devote its energies and experience to a continuous survey and consideration of Empire resources and opportunities, and to study of the best means of co-ordinating Empire effort for the development of these resources, for the extension of Imperial trade, and for the strengthening of Imperial lines of communication.

The proposed board, it was suggested, should be composed of seven members appointed by the British government to

[22] Jebb to Croft, 1 Nov. 1912, Jebb Papers.
[23] *United Empire*, 3 (1912), 606–10, 979–85. Jebb to G. E. Foster, 23 Oct. 1912, Jebb Papers. R. Jebb, *Empire in Eclipse* (London 1926), 118–21. *The Times*, 13 June 1912.

represent the United Kingdom, India, and the crown colonies and protectorates, and five members each representing one of the dominions. The board's headquarters were to be in London and its expenses defrayed by the various parts of the empire in proportion to their trade and revenue. It was to be 'purely advisory in its initial stage', but specific administrative functions in the future were clearly envisaged for it. [24]

The royal commission, in effect, had employed the wealth of information, argument, and evidence placed at its disposal in order to present a convincing case for imperial self-sufficiency and for a unifying trend in imperial economic policy. The fundamental weakness of the case, according to one authority, was that it was based on two assumptions for which historically there was no foundation: 'The commission assumed that the distinct self-governing communities of the Empire had the will to shape themselves as a single economic unit. It also assumed that they had the power to do so.' [25] Notwithstanding the emotional unity forged by the war, the dominions were jealous of their individual identities and were as unlikely to consider seriously anything smacking of a unified economic system as they had been to consider seriously a unified political system. The proposal for an imperial development board was criticized the following year as over-ambitious and impracticable by a committee appointed by the British government to report on commercial and industrial policy after the war:

We think that it would be possible to make more rapid progress by dealing separately with a number of special commodities or groups of commodities. It would no doubt be possible at a later stage to bring organizations set up for these special purposes into one single organization should that course be deemed expedient. A subsidiary argument telling in the same direction is that the conditions in respect of particular commodities or groups of commodities and the problems arising therefrom differ so much that no single Board of limited members could possibly deal with them adequately without the assistance of a number of specialized Committees composed of technical and commercial experts. [26]

For the Royal Colonial Institute, however, the struggle for imperial unity was not yet over, and it was heartened by the

[24] Cd. 8462, pp. 160-3.　　[25] Hancock, *Problems of Economic Policy*, I, 103-4.
[26] *Parl. Paps.* 1918, Vol. 13, Cd. 9035, p. 28.

fact that the philosophy underlying the report of the dominions royal commission was its own.

The respect in which the royal commission held the institute was apparent from the paragraphs in the report suggesting that the Royal Colonial Institute should replace the Imperial Institute as the body responsible for maintaining exhibits of the empire's resources. No impartial critic, according to the report, could say that the display in the Imperial Institute's galleries was adequate, complete, or up-to-date:

The revivification which is needed can, in our opinion, be secured only by handing over the management of the exhibits to some organization which will not confine its energies to receiving specimens supplied at intervals by Government departments, but will be in daily touch with visitors from overseas who will keep it in contact with the latest developments in each part of the Empire. An unofficial body is much more likely to take care of exhibits and maintain them at a high level than even the best of official bodies.

In these circumstances we recommend that an endeavour should be made to arrange that the responsibility for the exhibits now under the care and control of the Imperial Institute should be handed over to the Royal Colonial Institute, whose splendid enthusiasm and close connection with all parts of the Empire overseas make it eminently fitted for work of this character. The Charter of the Royal Colonial Institute provides for the maintenance of a museum, but it has so far been found impossible to give effect to this provision. [27]

The suggestion was not acted upon, but it was indicative of the growing feeling that the promotion of empire trade and 'friendly intercourse' was a function of the Royal Colonial Institute rather than of the Imperial Institute, which appeared to have outlived its usefulness in its existing form. The Imperial Institute had lost the support of the government of India and of both the federal and state governments of Australia, while it received only small sums from the other dominion governments, and even these contributions were offered against a chorus of protests from their parliaments. [28]

The Royal Colonial Institute's trade and industry committee was active throughout the 1914–18 war. It collected information

[27] Cd. 8462, pp. 80–1.
[28] *Parl. Paps.* 1923, Vol. 12, Pt. 1, Cmd. 1997, pp. 11–15, 41–3.

that would assist British manufacturers and traders to capture German and Austrian markets, and tried to persuade empire manufacturers to impress upon their governments the desirability of placing all orders with British firms employing British labour and using raw materials from predominantly British and empire sources. It continued to foster commercial and industrial interests by forwarding resolutions and sending deputations to the governments or bodies concerned, by conducting propaganda campaigns, by arranging lectures, and by organizing conferences with the object of co-ordinating conditions affecting trade and industry in the various parts of the empire. It also helped in training students from the empire in the methods of major industries, and acted as an information bureau, using the library resources and its own registers and files as a reservoir of information on empire trade and industry from which to answer queries from manufacturers and traders.

The committee felt strongly about the nationality status of British persons in foreign countries, and after Jebb's prompting in 1913 and 1914 it campaigned for revision of the law on the acquisition of British nationality by persons born outside the empire. By means of personal approaches to the Home Office, it gained the inclusion of the subject on the agenda of the imperial conference in 1921, and it welcomed the legislation passed through Parliament in 1922 removing anomalies from the British Nationality and Status of Aliens Act of 1914 and 1918.[29] In 1925 the committee was relieved of the work of the information bureau and was reconstituted in order to concentrate on the broader problems of empire trade. Its duties were mainly to arrange city luncheons and talks for businessmen, organize lectures in London and the provinces, and recommend to the council views on commercial matters for representation to government departments.

The society's attention to economic affairs in the inter-war period was not confined to suggestions by the committee, but found expression also in numerous other ways. In 1929 the

---

[29] 12 and 13 Geo. 5, c. 44, An act to amend the British Nationality and Status of Aliens Act, 1914 and 1918, as respects the acquisition of British nationality by persons born out of His Majesty's dominions (4 Aug. 1922). Co. Mins. 10 (8 Jan. 1914), 54; (20 Jan.), 57–8; (3 Feb.), 65; 13 (14 June 1921), 184.

council joined representatives of commerce, industrial organizations, the press, and other patriotic societies in urging upon the
chancellor of the exchequer the case for a reversion to the
imperial penny postage in order to stimulate commerce,
improve communications, and facilitate closer union in the
empire.[30] A few weeks later the society decided to encourage
soya cultivation in the empire, and it set up a soya cultivation
committee to advise on the culture of soya seed and bacteria
and the production of soya chocolate and oil.[31] Early in 1930
the society supported protests against the blending of foreign
with empire dairy products, especially butter, and the sale of
the resulting product under misleading names suggestive of
English origin. There was abundant evidence, it was alleged,
that a large proportion of the butter imported in bulk from
foreign countries was sent to blending factories in the south-
east and south-west of England, and emerged in wrappers
bearing rural addresses, and, in many cases, county brand
names such as Devon Blend, thus deceiving the consumer.[32]
In 1931 the society decided to form an empire dairy council
whose main object was 'to co-ordinate the interests of the dairy
industry throughout the homeland and overseas Empire, with a
view to promoting the prosperity of all its branches, and all
Empire trade as a whole, including production, distribution
and consumption'. It was expected that the dairy council
would seek to protect British and empire producers from
competition by foreign producers, especially when the hygienic
and industrial conditions of production in foreign countries
were to the disadvantage of the British consumer or British
labour.[33]

At the time of the imperial conference in 1930 the society
supported the recommendation of the British preparatory
commission that a permanent imperial economic secretariat
should be established, and it offered to place at the disposal of
any such secretariat its library and store of economic information.[34] It was not greatly interested in the imperial economic
conference at Ottawa in 1932 except in the matter of migration,

[30] Co. Mins. 15 (14 Jan. 1929), 160, 174.
[31] *United Empire*, 20 (1929), 257–9. *The Times*, 6 May 1929.
[32] Co. Mins. 16 (10 Feb. 1930), 23; (10 March), 32.
[33] *The Times*, 21 Jan. 1931.　　[34] Co. Mins. 16 (14 July 1930), 96.

but it joined the Victoria League, British Empire League, and British Empire Union in pressing for the negotiation at Ottawa of preferential customs tariffs in the dominions for British-produced films.[35] The society was especially concerned about the future of the Empire Marketing Board, created in 1926 to subsidize scientific research and prepare and publish surveys of trade and production. The board had operated successfully, but in 1931 its future was put in doubt by a report produced by a committee on national expenditure under the chairmanship of Sir George May. Although the report was regarded by some critics as exaggerating the seriousness of the budgetary crisis and described by the economist J. M. Keynes as the most foolish document he had ever had the misfortune to read, the government appointed an economy committee of the cabinet to study the proposals in the report.[36] Among the economies suggested was the abolition of the Empire Marketing Board, and when it became clear that the government intended to accept the recommendation the Royal Empire Society made its views known.

The society's council in 1933 forwarded a resolution to the prime minister appealing for the Empire Marketing Board to be allowed to continue. In a memorandum accompanying the resolution, reference was made to 'the growing Empire consciousness' of the British consumers:

The Council of the Royal Empire Society are satisfied that the publicity and market promotion work done by the Empire Marketing Board has been a continuous and growing factor in the increase of such consciousness, and that the cessation of such work would be a disaster altogether incommensurate with the savings expected to accrue therefrom.[37]

The society was naturally a proponent of the existence of a body which had nurtured the idea that trade within the empire was preferable to trade with foreign countries, but though its appeal was supported by similar appeals from the Federation of British Industry and the Trades Unions Congress, it was of

[35] Co. Mins. 17 (23 May 1932), 76; (11 July), 87.
[36] *Parl. Paps.* 1930–1, Vol. 16, Cmd. 3920, p. 132. *Economist*, 8 Aug. 1931. A. J. P. Taylor, *English History, 1914–1945* (London 1965), 288.
[37] *United Empire*, 24 (1933), 440, 659–61.

no avail. The dominions secretary explained the government's attitude in the House of Commons in July 1933:

No words can adequately express the value of the work of the board, but it was instituted as a substitute for preferences to the Dominions, and the British taxpayer found all the money. We are anxious to continue the work, but we are not prepared to continue to feed the baby.

The dominions were unwilling to share in the cost of maintaining the board, and it would be unfair, said Thomas, for the British government to foot the bill for something 'designed for Imperial purposes and not necessarily for British purposes only'.[38] Before the end of the year the board had ceased to function.

By 1939 the hopes that the Royal Empire Society had held of intra-imperial trade reinforcing the British connection with the overseas empire had been largely dashed. The preference agreements made at Ottawa became a source of discord, and the dominions found them increasingly an impediment to their desire for a wider trade with the world. The retreat from the Ottawa arrangements was manifested at the imperial conference of 1937, when the dominions demanded that international trade should be stimulated as 'an essential step to political appeasement'. The element of empire jingoism that had frequently influenced the society's earlier outlook on economic affairs had been modified, and a more moderate note was now apparent.

The society was obliged to accept the fact that the empire would not be fashioned into a nearly self-sufficient economic system separated from the trade of the rest of the world. More than 60 per cent of Britain's import trade and more than 50 per cent of its export trade were still with countries outside the empire. The yearning for an economic system that would underpin a consolidated empire had been disappointed, and the society had to recognize that Britain and the dominions could not sacrifice their international trade for the sake of exclusive opportunities within their own family association. 'By 1938', concluded a commonwealth historian writing in 1940, 'the nations of the British Commonwealth had begun a new attempt to shape and adjust the imperial pattern of their trade policies to a wider world order.'[39]

[38] *Parl. Debs.*, H.C. 280 (24 July 1933), col. 2211.   [39] Hancock, op. cit., 267.

Chapter Twelve

The British Commonwealth
and Empire (1919–1939)

WHEN Winston Churchill was prime minister in the 1940s he was wont to talk of the 'British Commonwealth and Empire', a nomenclature to which most conservatives at that time subscribed. The term 'British Empire' had still been employed by many ultra-conservatives in England in the 1920s and 1930s, and was favoured by the majority of those who attended general meetings of the Royal Empire Society, but the term 'British Commonwealth of Nations' had grown substantially in usage. As colonies had become self-governing their inclusion under the title of the British Empire was increasingly regarded as objectionable, and the need for a different designation was recognized.

The term 'commonwealth' in relation to Britain and the dominions had been used as early as January 1884, when Lord Rosebery, in a farewell address at Adelaide at the close of a tour of Australia, described the empire as a commonwealth of nations.[1] The premier of Cape Colony, John Merriman, suggested the substitution of 'commonwealth' for 'empire' and was in the habit of referring to the British commonwealth rather than the British empire.[2] Milner, Ellis T. Powell, Jebb, and Ben H. Morgan of the Royal Colonial Institute argued that the word 'empire' had become inaccurate and misleading and suggested alternatives to it, but it was Lionel Curtis who popularized 'commonwealth', which was used with increasing frequency during the war years after 1914. The word was first mentioned officially in 1917, when the imperial war conference

---

[1] R. R. James, *Rosebery: A Biography of Archibald Philip, Fifth Earl of Rosebery* (London 1963), 156.
[2] S. R. Mehrotra, 'On the Use of the Term "Commonwealth"', *Journal of Commonwealth Political Studies*, 2 (1963), 4–5. W. K. Hancock, *Smuts; The Sanguine Years, 1870–1919* (Cambridge 1962), 203–4, 430.

resolved that any readjustment of the empire's constitutional relations should be based on recognition of the dominions as autonomous nations of 'an Imperial Commonwealth, and of India as an important portion of the same'.[3] This resolution had been drafted largely by Smuts, who, at the imperial war conference in June of the following year, spoke of 'the British Commonwealth of Nations' standing firm amid the upheaval in Europe. He went on, however, to speak also of 'the solid core of the British Empire, that great League of Nations, based on freedom, linked together on high ideals of government, and standing together as a bulwark against the onrush of despotism, militarism, and anarchy.'[4] The same juxtaposition of terms was used in 1922 in the Irish Free State Act, which referred in Article 1 to 'the Community of Nations known as the British Empire' and in Article 4 to 'the group of nations form-ing the British Commonwealth of Nations'.[5] The Balfour report of 1926 similarly referred to both the British Empire and the British Commonwealth of Nations, and the confusing use of the various terms continued throughout the inter-war period.

In 1937 Professor W. K. Hancock concluded that it depended 'upon a speaker's mood and temperament and train of thought, upon conditions of time and place, upon the character of his audience', whether he spoke of the British empire or the British commonwealth: 'The two names jostle each other in a competition which is perhaps symbolical of the struggle between liberty and necessity, ideal and fact, aspiration and limiting condition—a struggle which is fought continuously in every creative society.'[6] It cannot pass unnoticed, however, that in the 1920s, when the word 'empire' was coming to be regarded as incompatible with the independence and national aspirations of the dominions and a formula was being evolved to replace it, the Royal Colonial Institute, against the wishes of many of its less progressive members, took the appellation of 'empire' in the belief that it was thereby adequately adjusting itself to the contemporary situation.

A new international status for the dominions appeared to

---

[3] *Parl. Paps.* 1917–18, Vol. 23, Cd. 8566, p. 5.

[4] Ibid., 1918, Vol. 16, Cd. 9177, p. 18.

[5] 12 and 13 Geo. 5, c. 4, An act to give force of law to certain articles of agree-ment for a treaty between Great Britain and Ireland (31 March 1922).

[6] W. K. Hancock, *Problems of Nationality, 1918–1936* (London 1937), 61.

have been assured at the signing of the peace treaties after the 1914–18 war. While the dominions lacked diplomatic staffs of their own, however, the initiative in shaping the commonwealth's approach to world affairs remained with Britain, the most important and powerful member and the only one situated in Europe, still the focal point of international relations. The dominions now expected to be consulted on foreign affairs, and each government, while accepting a responsibility to co-operate with the other member governments, possessed the liberty to pursue its own independent foreign policy. The imperial conference of 1923 attempted to lay down principles by which Britain and the dominions should conduct their external policies, and declared that the negotiation of international treaties should be based on the procedure adopted at Versailles; 'that no treaty should be negotiated by any of the governments of the Empire without due consideration of its possible effect on other parts of the Empire, or, if circumstances so demand, on the Empire as a whole'; that bilateral treaties affecting more than one part of the commonwealth should be based on 'the fullest possible exchange of views' between all members; and that bilateral treaties affecting only one part of the commonwealth might be concluded solely by the government concerned, care being taken to make clear that the treaties applied to that part of the commonwealth alone.[7]

The precise status of the dominions, however, continued to lack definition, and at the imperial conference of 1926 a committee was appointed under Lord Balfour to consider the question. In its report Balfour performed what has been described as 'his last and most successful jugglery with high-sounding words'.[8] The committee did not attempt to frame a constitution for the commonwealth, and declared that nothing would be gained by attempting to do so, but limited itself to defining the existing constitutional position. The committee's report described the position and mutual relation of Britain and the dominions in an italicized statement that became the most celebrated in the constitutional history of the British commonwealth and empire:

They are autonomous Communities within the British Empire,

[7] *Parl. Paps.* 1923, Vol. 12, Pt. 1, Cmd. 1987, pp. 13–15.
[8] Taylor, *English History, 1914–1945,* 253.

equal in status, in no way subordinate one to another in any aspect of their domestic or external affairs, though united by a common allegiance to the Crown, and freely associated as members of the British Commonwealth of Nations.[9]

It was not certain what this cumbersome declaration meant. The terms 'empire' and 'commonwealth' were employed in confusing proximity, and although the report mentioned dominions it did not define dominion status, which continued to carry an implication of subordination.

The full significance of the Balfour declaration was not immediately appreciated, but conferences in 1929 and 1930 endeavoured to clarify obscure points, and in December 1931 the Statute of Westminster gave some legal definition to the changes that had been taking place in the imperial relationship. It gave the dominions power to repeal or amend United Kingdom legislation applying to them and to make laws having extra-territorial application, and it declared that no future act of the British parliament should extend to any of the dominions unless the act stated that they had requested and agreed that it should do so. The dominions were enumerated as Canada, Australia, New Zealand, South Africa, the Irish Free State, and Newfoundland, and they were 'united by a common allegiance to the Crown', which was 'the symbol of the free association of the members of the British Commonwealth of Nations'.[10] The word 'dominion' appeared in the statute and was generally used in the period between 1919 and 1939, but it dropped out of commonwealth parlance in the 1940s.

India was not directly concerned in these commonwealth developments, and throughout the inter-war period it retained its peculiar and special status. The imperial war conference of 1917 had recognized India as 'an important portion' of the 'Imperial Commonwealth' with the same right as the dominions to 'an adequate voice in foreign policy and in foreign relations'. The Indian government participated in imperial conferences, but it was not a government properly representative of the

[9] *Parl. Paps.* 1926, Vol. 11, Cmd. 2768, p. 14.

[10] 22 Geo. 5, c. 4, An act to give effect to certain resolutions passed by Imperial Conferences held in the years 1926 and 1930 (11 Dec. 1931). For an introduction to the history of dominion status see R. M. Dawson, *The Development of Dominion Status, 1900–1936* (London 1937), and K. C. Wheare, *The Statute of Westminster and Dominion Status* (Oxford 1953).

Indian people and at the conferences its interests were the responsibility of the secretary of state for India, who was a member of the British cabinet. India's position in the British commonwealth and empire was anomalous, and its future, according to a scholar writing in 1952, posed a question of outstanding importance:

Could the peoples of India, the heirs of two of the ancient civilizations of the East, find a congenial and satisfying realization of their political ideals within the hitherto almost exclusively European circle of the self-governing countries of the Commonwealth? Or would they, as much perhaps by the logic of history as by their own volition, be compelled to seek it without?[11]

The movement of India towards responsible self-government and, perhaps, independence within the commonwealth seemed bound to awake dormant racial problems and test the colour consciousness that was implied in the Anglo-Saxon nationalism of the descendants of the old imperial expansionists.

Indian nationalism had found its first political expression after 1885 in a new organization that became known as the Indian National Congress. In 1906, the Muslims, who had tended to remain aloof from the predominantly Hindu Congress, founded the Muslim League to protect and advance Muslim political rights. It is not possible in a narrative of this kind to explore the communal, religious, economic, and social problems with which the British government in India was beset in the twentieth century, or the special difficulties that arose from the influence of Mahatma Gandhi and his technique of passive resistance, or *satyagraha*. Gandhi at first welcomed the constitutional reforms proposed by the Montagu–Chelmsford commission in 1918 and enacted the following year, but changed his mind and Congress condemned the legislation as inadequate. The act of 1919 instituted a system known as 'dyarchy' in the provinces and admitted elected Indian members to a new central legislature. Under dyarchy certain matters such as law and order, finance, irrigation, land revenue, famine relief, control of the press, and labour disputes were 'reserved' to the governor and his executive council, while others such as education, public health, agriculture, and the

---

[11] N. Mansergh, *Problems of External Policy, 1931–1939* (London 1952), 335.

N

extension of local government were 'transferred' to Indian ministers who were elected members of the legislative council and therefore responsible to an Indian electorate.

The act of 1919 provided that at the expiration of ten years a commission should be appointed to examine the working of the governmental system, the growth of education, and the development of representative institutions in India, and to report on the desirability of establishing the principle of responsible government or of modifying the degree of responsible government already existing. The British government advanced the date of the investigation, however, and in 1927, before the expiration of the ten years, the Baldwin administration appointed an exclusively British commission under the chairmanship of Sir John Simon. The commission presented its report in May 1930 and made proposals touching nearly every part of the existing constitution.[12] It recommended that the dyarchy system should be abolished and that, subject to emergency powers being vested in the governors, full responsible government should be established in the provinces. The commission suggested that the central legislature should remain unaltered, but it envisaged a federal constitution for an Indian federation ultimately growing out of the development of responsible government in the provinces. At the same time, the commission was not unduly sanguine:

The introduction into an oriental country, with a long history of autocracy, of methods of self-government evolved during centuries of experiment by a Western nation for its own conditions and its own people was a momentous and even hazardous enterprise which should be studied with sympathy and understanding.[13]

It doubted the appropriateness of British institutions to Indian conditions and was unwilling to assume that the only form of parliamentary government which could emerge was one closely resembling the British model.

In Britain the Simon report was an unusually widely read public document. It was generally well received, but was not popular among the politicians, who disliked its pessimism on the application of the Westminster model of parliamentary

[12] *Parl. Paps.* 1929–30, Vol. 11, Cmd. 2568 and Cmd. 3569.
[13] Cmd. 3569, p. 47.

democracy to India, and was disliked by officials and nationalists in India. In the public debate that ensued the Royal Empire Society could not be aloof. At the annual general meeting of the society in the same month as the Simon report was issued, the chairman of the council, Sir John Sandeman Allen, said that too much attention had been paid to the agitation in India, which was not truly representative of the Indian population:

The loyalty and devotion of the Native Princes to the King-Emperor and the British Raj is very striking, but this same spirit is shown by the large majority of the leading people throughout the various Provinces of British India, while the vast majority of the inhabitants are only anxious to be left in peace under the just and beneficent régime of the British Raj.[14]

As was common, however, the opinionated image presented by spokesmen at the society's public meetings was not necessarily an accurate reflection of the approach of the council, where more rational views were apparent.

In 1918 the council had attempted to give prominence to Indian interests by the appointment of an Indian committee, but it was not a success. In April 1930, however, the council accepted a suggestion by the secretary and formed a special committee to consider the Simon report.[15] To preside over the committee the council selected Sir John Kerr, who had been governor of Assam and a member of council and acting governor of Bengal, and had been a strong supporter of decentralization at the time of the Montagu–Chelmsford reforms. He was advised that the committee's function was to examine the proposals in the Simon report point by point and assess their workability and their advantages and disadvantages:

The Council held that it would be undesirable to have on the Committee any former administrator who had already become associated in the public mind with a definite point of view regarding Indian development. All were inclined to hold that it should be no part of the Committee's function to go behind the Simon Commission's Report and discuss what was or was not the British ideal in India in 1857 or 1914.[16]

---

[14] *United Empire*, 21 (1930), 391.   [15] Co. Mins. 16 (14 April 1930), 52.
[16] Royal Empire Society India Committee, *Report to the Council of the Society on the Probable Working of the Simon Commission's Proposals* (1930), 3.

The committee sat fourteen times, in addition to sub-committee meetings, and presented its report to the council at the end of October 1930. It refrained from making predictions, but was unable to find much to approve.

The committee concluded by expressing its disapproval of the constitutional reforms that had been introduced in 1919 and its misgivings following the experience of the last decade:

We feel that grave risks were, and are, being incurred by the premature introduction of the principle of responsible Government, in anticipation of the evolution of a popular electorate, adequate not merely in numbers, but also in education and intelligence, to discharge its essential function in a political system of that character. We recognize that, as matters stand, there is no alternative to a further advance on the lines that have been adopted, but we are anxious that our willing participation in the constructive criticism of the Commission's scheme should not be understood to imply approval of the particular type of constitutional advance which has been imposed on India.

Copies of the report were sent to the prime minister, secretary of state for India, the press, and all members of the Round Table conference which was meeting in London and which decided in favour of the principle of an all-India federation and at least a measure of responsible government.[17]

The report of the society's India committee was extensively used and quoted both in the Round Table conferences in London and in discussions in India. The committee considered the provincial and central parliaments proposed in the Simon report to be too large and the electorates too small, and regarded the representation of the mass of the people in the provincial councils as essential if the parliamentary government envisaged in the Simon report was to be put into effect. The committee therefore recommended the 'group system' with village electoral colleges in dealing with any further extension of the franchise. It emphasized the question of the franchise, it declared, because it believed it to be fundamental:

In our judgement there can be no successful advance in responsible Government, unless it can be arranged for all interests in the country to be represented in reasonable and vigilant electorates,

[17] Co. Mins. 16 (29 Oct. 1930), 125–9. *Parl. Paps.* 1930–1, Vol. 12, Cmd. 3778.

capable of exercising a real freedom of choice upon a discrimination between policies rather than a preference for individuals.

The special representation of great landholders, it added, should not be abolished. As a direct outcome of the committee's study of the franchise question the chairman, Sir John Kerr, was appointed to a fact-finding Indian franchise committee.

The British government published its proposals for Indian constitutional reform in March 1933,[18] and after they had been examined by a select joint committee of both houses of Parliament and further amended in the protracted parliamentary debate that followed, they became the Government of India Act in 1935.[19] The act abolished dyarchy and gave responsible government to the provinces subject to safeguards reserved to the governors and the governor-general. Federation, however, depended on the voluntary surrender by the princely states of certain of their powers to the central authority in return for representation in the federal legislature, and since the states were unwilling to do this the federal arrangement never came into operation. In the matter of the franchise the act was clearly influenced by the suggestions made by the committee of the Royal Empire Society in its provision for a system of indirect election by way of groups and electoral colleges.

During the debates on the Government of India Act, Lord Lothian remarked that the lack of enthusiasm was a good omen that the act would endure. A strong section of Conservative opinion in the United Kingdom viewed the various constitutional changes proposed for India not only as unnecessary but as positively dangerous. These die-hards found their most eloquent advocate in Winston Churchill, who in 1931 had resigned from the Conservative party shadow cabinet on this issue and whose son, Randolph, intervened in a by-election as a protest against the India bill and succeeded in dividing the Conservative vote and facilitating the return of the Labour candidate. Winston Churchill expressed the feelings of former British officials and army officers in India that Britain was yielding to agitators and betraying its imperial mission. At the other end of the political spectrum, and especially in the Labour party, were those who felt that Britain's concessions to

[18] *Parl. Paps.* 1932–3, Vol. 20, Cmd. 4268.
[19] Ibid., 1933–4, Vol. 6, H.L. 6 and H.C. 5 (1 Part I). 26 Geo. 5, c. 2.

Indian opinion were inadequate. 'Even a Horace', commented the Royal Empire Society's journal, 'might find it difficult to maintain a middle course through the whirlpools, the rocks and the sand-banks of these political seas.'[20] So far as it is possible to deduce the prevailing opinion in the society, it would not be unjust to place it more towards the conservative than towards the reformist end of these two extremes, but it would be wrong to place it with the conservative die-hards. The India committee appointed by the council studiously attempted to avoid partisan influences and made a useful and reasonably objective contribution to the Round Table conferences and the general discussion of the form that the government of India should take. The society made a determined effort to assist in the production of what most responsible and fair-minded Englishmen hoped would be a wise and constructive policy for India.

India had always inspired the strongest emotions in the hearts of imperially-minded patriots in England. The Royal Empire Society was not immune from this emotionalism, but it appreciated the importance of statesmanship and generosity in dealing with the non-white races of the commonwealth and empire and recognized Britain's obligations towards the native peoples of Asia. The society's interest in the future of India was accompanied by a growing awareness of the problems confronting British rule in Africa. It is difficult to form a proper assessment of the tenor of feeling in the society towards African issues, for they were normally such that the society saw no reason to produce detailed studies or attempt to apply pressure on the government in connection with them, but a committee appointed by the council in 1930 did investigate the position in the East African dependencies as set forth in reports by the Hilton Young commission and Sir Samuel Wilson.[21]

For some years there had been a view that a union between Kenya, Uganda, and Tanganyika was practicable, but the idea was complicated by demands from the European settlers for an increased share in the government. In 1922 Churchill, then colonial secretary in Lloyd George's coalition cabinet, looked forward to the time when Kenya, Uganda, Tanganyika, and Zanzibar would form an East African federation, but declared

---

[20] *United Empire*, 25 (1934), 387.   [21] Co. Mins. 16 (12 May 1930), 70.

that the British government was pledged to reserve the highlands of East Africa exclusively for European settlers. In 1923 Bonar Law's Conservative government issued a memorandum summarizing the history of the Indians in Kenya and setting out the general policy laid down by Britain and the principles on which it was based:

Primarily, Kenya is an African territory, and His Majesty's Government think it necessary definitely to record their considered opinion that the interests of the African natives must be paramount, and that if, and when, those interests and the interests of the immigrant races should conflict, the former should prevail.

In the administration of Kenya, it asserted,

His Majesty's Government regard themselves as exercising a trust on behalf of the African population, and they are unable to delegate or share this trust, the object of which may be defined as the protection and advancement of the native races.

There were objections to the grant of responsible government which would be based necessarily on European dominance: 'His Majesty's Government cannot but regard the grant of responsible self-government as out of the question within any period of time which need now be taken into consideration.' Hasty action, it declared, was to be strongly deprecated:

Meanwhile, the administration of the Colony will follow the British traditions and principles which have been successful in other Colonies, and progress towards self-government must be left to take the lines which the passage of time and the growth of experience may indicate as being best for the country. [22]

The memorandum represented a significant modification in the assumption which had prevailed hitherto that the central point of concern in Kenya was the European community.

The British government later appointed a commission under the chairmanship of Sir Hilton Young to examine the question of union in East Africa. The commission was well served by a number of distinguished witnesses who came before it, among them the Royal Empire Society's chairman of council, Sandeman Allen, who appeared as a representative of the Joint East

[22] *Parl. Paps.* 1923, Vol. 18, Cmd. 1922, pp. 10–11.

African Board. The commission's report in 1929 concluded that any drastic changes would be premature: 'Communications are not yet fully developed,' it declared, 'public opinion is not yet fully prepared, and the dangers of over-centralization must be avoided.' Nevertheless, co-ordination of policy was desirable, especially of native policy, and the commission recommended the appointment of a governor-general for East Africa to act as a link between the Colonial Office and the dependency governments and 'to hold the position as it were of a permanent Chairman, with full executive powers, of a standing conference of the three Governments'. The commission believed, however, that a much closer association between the East African territories would develop, and that it 'ought to take the form of the establishment of a strong unified central government directing all affairs of common interest for three provinces, rather than a federation of quasi-independent states'.

The commission reaffirmed the doctrine of the paramountcy of native interests expressed in the memorandum of 1923, but added that a policy 'that for all time and in every respect, in any case of conflict, native interests must prevail, can hardly stand without at least some qualification'. It suggested, therefore, that native interests were not intended to prevail 'to the extent of destroying the interests of immigrant communities already established, and that their "paramountcy" must be subject to this limiting condition'. It also reaffirmed that there could be no question of responsible government being granted

until the natives themselves can share in the responsibility, because, until that stage is reached, the Imperial Government will be under obligations of trusteeship which cannot be discharged without reserving a right to intervene in all the business of government.

Responsible government, it pointed out, was dependent upon representative institutions.[23]

The report of the Hilton Young commission divided opinion both in the United Kingdom and in Kenya, where the settlers were opposed to any scheme that might retard development towards complete autonomy. It has been thoughtfully argued that the policy enunciated for Kenya was inconsistent with that pursued towards Southern Rhodesia, where responsible govern-

[23] *Parl. Paps.* 1928–9, Vol. 5, Cmd. 3234, pp. 40, 83–4, 236–7, 312.

ment was granted to a European minority in 1923.[24] The two cases, however, were dissimilar in some significant respects. British policy towards Rhodesia, a more recent authority has pointed out, had been influenced by the assumption that the territory would ultimately become part of a South African federation and would therefore follow the pattern established by the dominions:

Indeed the major institutions, the instruments of administration, and legislative policies, most of which were to endure until the present day, were at an early stage established on this view of Southern Rhodesia's future, and the structure of Southern Rhodesian institutions is even today almost entirely a reflection of European politics.

As a result, British policy in Rhodesia differed from that elsewhere, and the early delegation of power to the settlers precluded Britain from subsequently treating it as a territory inhabited mainly by Africans whose interests should be paramount.[25]

The colonial secretary, L. S. Amery, was perplexed by the findings of the Hilton Young commission. 'Unfortunately', he wrote afterwards, 'the Commission's report, admirable and comprehensive as it was, embodied detailed conclusions which put in the forefront, not the urgent and feasible economic union of the territories, but the much more theoretical and disputable aim of unifying native policy.'[26] In 1929 Amery sent to East Africa the permanent under secretary of state for the colonies, Sir Samuel Wilson, to assess the extent to which the Hilton Young recommendations were acceptable locally and to ascertain the lines along which a scheme for union would be administratively workable.[27] Wilson's report further complicated the issue. He found alarm at the Hilton Young proposals on native policy and on the development of self-government in Kenya. Whereas the Young commission had suggested that native policy should be settled by the British government in advance and a governor-general or high commissioner should execute it, Wilson favoured the high commissioner, assisted by

[24] Hancock, *Problems of Nationality*, 489.
[25] C. Palley, *The Constitutional History and Law of Southern Rhodesia 1888–1965* (London 1966), xviii.
[26] L. S. Amery, *The Forward View* (London 1935), 257.
[27] *Parl. Paps.* 1929–30, Vol. 8, Cmd. 3378, p. 14.

a central council, consulting with the governments of the territories and making policy recommendations to the Colonial Office. On the need for a form of union there was agreement, and the Royal Empire Society devoted some meetings to the subject and appointed a committee to study it, but before either the Colonial Office or the society was able to apply itself to the union idea a Labour government under Ramsay MacDonald took office in June 1929.

In 1930 the British government issued a statement of its conclusions in the matter of union in East Africa which, for the most part, followed the Hilton Young report. A high commissioner for the three territories would be the chief adviser to the colonial and dominions secretary and would administer the 'transferred' services such as railways, ports, customs, and defence; the composition of the Kenya legislative council was to remain 'substantially unchanged and to retain the official majority'; and an assurance was given that the government had no intention of modifying or surrendering the Tanganyika mandate.[28] The proposals regarding union were referred to a joint committee of both houses of Parliament which reported in October 1931 that there had been a reaction against the whole idea. The members of the joint committee decided that the time was inopportune for taking steps towards a formal union:

In fact, they consider that for a considerable time to come the progress of East Africa as a whole can best be assured by each of the three territories continuing to develop upon its own lines, lines which they consider to be still experimental. It is of no use ignoring the fact that there is considerable diversity between the central and significant features of each of these territories, and that the evolution which has taken place in the last thirty years and is still taking place today, is not on identical lines.[29]

In July 1932 the colonial secretary advised the officers administering the governments of Kenya, Tanganyika, and Uganda that he had accepted the views of the joint committee, and the idea of union was dropped.[30]

[28] *Parl. Paps.* 1929–30, Vol. 23, Cmd. 3574.
[29] Ibid. *Paps.* 1930–1, Vol. 7, No. 156, pp. 14–15.
[30] Ibid., 1931–2, Vol. 18, Cmd. 4141, p. 47.

If the Royal Empire Society was less involved in African issues than in Indian, the attitudes that emerged at its meetings and discussions indicated that its nineteenth-century conception of the inherent superiority of European over tropical peoples had been diluted. Under the influence of the League of Nations mandates philosophy and Sir Frederick Lugard's exposition of the *Dual Mandate in British Tropical Africa* (1922), there was a growing awareness that the possession of colonies in under-developed parts of the world carried duties and responsibilities to the native populations, whose interests should be paramount, and it should not be regarded merely as a vehicle for uplifting British racial pride or for extending British territorial and economic power. There was certainly an assumption at the society, and, for that matter, elsewhere, that British colonialism in Africa had a long future ahead of it. Few Africans held positions of responsibility, and the initiative lay overwhelm-ingly with the Europeans, upon whom, it has been pointed out, depended even the defence of African interests against those of the immigrant communities. European missionaries and liberal zealots in England, including a few at the Royal Empire Society, believed that the Africans were as capable as the inhabitants of other continents of being trained and educated to a western level; 'During this period,' it has been suggested, 'a new genera-tion of Africans was putting itself to school, and from it a few were to emerge equipped not merely for participation but for leadership in the new Africa'.[31]

The problems of the British commonwealth and empire were dwarfed in the 1930s, however, by a series of international crises that culminated in the outbreak of the world war of 1939–45. In 1931 Japan attacked Manchuria and successfully defied the League of Nations. In 1935 Italy attacked Abyssinia and successfully resisted the economic sanctions applied against it by the League of Nations. The imperial conference of 1937 was necessarily concerned principally with defence and assumed that in the event of war there would be co-operation, especially in such matters as the free interchange of information about the state of the armed forces. At the same time, the conference recognized that it was 'the sole responsibility of the several Parliaments of the British Commonwealth to decide the nature

[31] R. Oliver and J. D. Fage, *A Short History of Africa* (London 1962), 215.

and scope of their own defence policy'.[32] The dominions supported the efforts of the British prime minister, Neville Chamberlain, to prevent war with Germany, and it was only after the Munich arrangement of 1938 that their faith in the policy of appeasement dwindled.

The reaction of the dominions to Britain's declaration of war on Germany on 3 September 1939 was not uniform, but it was probably more unequivocal than it would have been if war had come the previous year. Australia, a country with a population of seven million in 1939, and New Zealand, with 1,500,000, adhered to the principle of undivided sovereignty and regarded Britain's declaration as binding upon them as members of a commonwealth united by a common allegiance to the crown; India, with nearly 380,000,000 people, was committed to the war by the viceroy without consulting Indian representatives; South Africa, with a population of two million Europeans and over seven million Africans, overcame a division of opinion within its government and by a small majority in Parliament entered the war on 5 September; and Canada, with more than eleven million people, joined its commonwealth partners one week after the British declaration. Only the Irish Free State decided to be neutral.

In 1939, according to Professor Mansergh, the transformation from empire to commonwealth had been carried through with 'an ease, an assurance, and a farsightedness which could be truly appreciated only in later years when equality of status was progressively matched with a growing equality of function.'[33] The dominion governments, preoccupied with questions of status and lacking independent sources of information on international affairs, committed errors of judgement in foreign policy in the 1930s, but 'they remained true to the principles which were at once the indispensable foundation of their society of free and equal states and the condition of its future growth. Because they kept faith in the great essentials they were able, when the final crisis came, to astonish the world by their capacity for united and resolute action.'[34]

[32] *Parl. Paps.* 1936–7, Vol. 12, Cmd. 5482, p. 20.
[33] Mansergh, *Problems of External Policy*, 447.　　[34] Ibid., 449.

Chapter Thirteen

World War Two (1939–1945)

On 5 September 1939, two days after the British government had declared war on Germany, the council of the Royal Empire Society passed a resolution affirming its faith in the intention and ability of the British Commonwealth to resist the spread of Nazi tyranny:

United Empire is the watchword of our Society, and never did it express more truly than at the present time the spirit that moves the countless millions that enjoy the protection of the British Flag.

That the Members of our great Society will be amongst the first to give the lead in National Service the Council have not any doubt, and they sent to all who may be so engaged a message of greeting and good wishes.[1]

The society energetically bent its efforts to meet the requirements of war, notwithstanding the difficulties it was already trying to surmount. There was a need for reorganization and for increased revenue and reduced expenditure in order to balance its accounts. The war aggravated the problems and postponed indefinitely the possibility of devising a solution to them. Some of the society's normal activities were at once suspended or modified, and the ordinary evening meetings were abandoned in favour of tea-time discussions which, as travel facilities deteriorated, black-out observance improved, and air-raid warnings multiplied, were in their turn abandoned in favour of lunch-hour meetings.

A programme of war service was begun immediately and in general followed the pattern evolved in the 1914–18 war. As in the previous war, the society's building became a rendezvous for troops from the overseas commonwealth, and a war services committee was established to advise fellows and provide them with a letter of introduction to the government authority

[1] *United Empire,* 30 (1939), clxi.

most likely to require their services during the war. General Sir Alexander Godley was chairman of the committee, and D. Hope Johnston, who had been a member of the 1914–18 committee, the honorary organizing secretary. By 1943 the compulsory entry of men into the services had reduced the scope of the committee's work, but it continued until the end of the war to give advice when asked. A women's war committee under Lady Sykes, wife of the chairman of council, organized entertainment for troops from overseas visiting London, produced knitted articles, and collected books and gifts for distribution among the armed services. A particularly active women war workers unit of the New South Wales branch of the society frequently sent gifts, and made and collected garments for women and children in England.[2] It was through the New South Wales branch that high schools in Sydney offered to pay for the purchase and part of the upkeep of a mobile canteen for victims of bombing in London, and at the request of the society the Ministry of Food agreed to assume full responsibility for the canteen's maintenance and operation.[3]

After a meeting at the Dominions Office on 5 September 1939 between representatives of the Royal Empire Society and other non-political patriotic movements, a joint war hospitality committee was established to co-ordinate hospitality in the United Kingdom for men and women from overseas in the armed forces or ancillary services. The committee comprised representatives of the various societies, the high commissions, the War Office, the Air Ministry, and the Colonial Office, with a chairman (Field-Marshal Lord Milne) and secretary nominated by the Dominions Office. Its offices were in the Royal Empire Society building and it used the society's council room for its meetings.[4]

A circular from the Ministry of Information in September 1939 emphasized the importance of maintaining a vigorous programme of activities, and the society sought to comply as far as practicable. The journal continued publication, and the Ministry of Information agreed to contribute a regular article[5].

[2] Co. Mins. 21 (20 Feb. 1940), 3.   [3] Co. Mins. 21 (18 Sept. 1941), 179.
[4] Co. Mins. 20 (5 Sept. 1939), 248–9; (27 Sept.), 257.
[5] Co. Mins. 20 (20 Sept. 1939), 254–5.

At the end of 1940 Wyatt Tilby resigned as editor, and Edward Salmon returned as honorary editor. Salmon had been elected a fellow over half a century before and was among the oldest members of the society; he had been editor for most of the inter-war period until 1937, when he had been nominated to the council. Under his direction the nature of the journal changed. Like newspapers and other journals it was reduced in size and printed on inferior paper, and after April 1941 it was issued every two months instead of monthly. At the same time, several overseas branches of the society began publishing their own journals, the Victoria branch its *Notes and News*, the New South Wales branch its *Royal Empire Society Bulletin*, and the Auckland branch its *Gazette*.

In 1942 three study groups were formed in response to a representation to the council that the society should consider the commonwealth's future and renew its efforts to be in close touch with the industrial and economic life of the United Kingdom and the commonwealth. A political group chaired by Sir Drummond Shiels discussed the political future of the commonwealth and empire, an agricultural group chaired by Sir Harry Lindsay discussed the future of agriculture, and an industrial group chaired by Lieutenant-Colonel Allan Monkhouse discussed the future of industry. The chairman of each group selected his own group committee, vice-chairman, and honorary secretary. It was difficult, however, to sustain the groups under wartime disabilities, and although regular discussion meetings were held, attendance fell off to such an extent that it was an embarrassment to invite outside speakers. This was especially the case with the agricultural and industrial groups, and no meetings of the industrial group were held in 1944 or 1945. The agricultural group had substantially the same membership as the planters group, and in 1944 they were amalgamated. In 1946 the industrial and agricultural groups were discontinued and an empire economic development committee was formed.[6] In 1944, when the ultimate victory of the allies seemed assured and post-war problems were under discussion, the society revived its committee on empire migration under the chairmanship of Sir Archibald Weigall. The migration committee remained in existence until 1950,

[6] Co. Mins. 22 (19 Jan. 1944), 68–9; (9 Jan. 1946), 252.

when it was ended formally on the grounds that migration matters were now beyond the control of the voluntary societies.[7]

When war began the chairman of the council was Sir Frederick Sykes, perhaps best known as a pioneer of wartime aviation in 1914. During his varied career of military and public service he had been a prisoner of the Boers, Conservative Member of Parliament, first in 1922 and for a second time in 1940 when he was returned unopposed for Nottingham Central, governor of Bombay for five years from 1928, an office in which he was twice responsible for arresting Gandhi, and a very active chairman of the Mines Welfare Committee from 1934 to 1946. His personal contacts were excellent, as was to be expected of a high-ranking military officer and administrator and the husband of the elder daughter of Bonar Law. Sykes was a gentle, but brisk chairman, not given to unnecessary talk, who brushed aside superfluities and concentrated on the business at hand. The society was fortunate in having a person of his qualities in the early years of the war, for as staff left on military service, he was obliged to assume additional duties, including those of the secretary.[8] He was responsible for an attempt to give the society a new purpose and for the introduction of a group scheme designed to help increase membership. He resigned in 1941 after three years as chairman of council and became a vice-president and, between 1943 and 1951, deputy chairman of council.

In 1941 the council elected Sir William Clark to succeed Sykes. Clark, too, had had a long career in public service in England, India, Canada, and South Africa. He had served at the Board of Trade, was the first comptroller-general of the Department of Overseas Trade, and was one of the principal advisers to the British delegation at the Ottawa conference in 1932. He had been a member of the executive council of the viceroy in India, and high commissioner in Canada and in Basutoland, Bechuanaland Protectorate, and Swaziland. Unfortunately, Clark had not long been chairman when the council released him from his duties for four months in order that he might accede to a request by Lord Swinton to become

---

[7] Co. Mins. 22 (8 Nov. 1944), 140; 23 (21 Dec. 1950), 250.
[8] F. Sykes, *From Many Angles: An Autobiography* (London 1942), 502–3.

head of the Lisbon branch of the United Kingdom Commercial Corporation. While in Lisbon he negotiated the gift to the society of a collection of books on the Portuguese empire, but his prolonged absence from London compelled him in 1942 to write to the council resigning the chairmanship, and he was succeeded by General Sir Alexander Godley, with Ralph Bond as deputy-chairman.[9] Godley, who, in a distinguished military career, had served at the siege of Mafeking, commanded the New Zealand forces in the 1914–18 war, and been governor of Gibraltar, had been deputy chairman since 1935 and acting chairman during Clark's absence. He was a tall, spare man, prone to illness at this time, and after a year he stepped down to deputy chairman again and was succeeded as chairman by the Earl of Clarendon, the lord chamberlain. Clarendon had been parliamentary under-secretary for dominion affairs in the 1920s and governor-general of South Africa in the 1930s, and had been a vice-president of the society since 1931. He became chairman of council on the understanding that he would have the support of deputy chairmen, and Godley, Clark, Sykes, and Weigall, all of whom were former chairmen, were appointed. Clarendon remained chairman until 1948, but his main duty was to preside at functions, matters of policy being largely delegated to the deputy chairmen.

The departure of the secretary, assistant secretary, and head clerk on military service, and the difficulties experienced by the chairman of council in carrying out additional responsibilities, led to the decision in 1941 to appoint an honorary secretary-general to relieve the chairman of some of his routine duties. The position had been allowed for in the society's charter, and under the terms of the constitution the holder was *ex-officio* a member of council. The first incumbent was Sir Walter Buchanan-Smith, who had been a popular lieutenant-governor in Nigeria, and in his retirement had undertaken several public offices, including that of acting governor of the Seychelles in 1939. He was honorary secretary-general for nearly four years until his death in November 1944 following a long illness.[10]

[9] Co. Mins. 21 (10 Dec. 1941), 193; (10 June 1942), 237.
[10] Co. Mins. 22 (13 Dec. 1944), 149. A. Burns, *Colonial Civil Servant* (London 1949), 119.

o

The council was not greatly altered by the problems of wartime, and nominations for membership continued to be distributed as judiciously as possible among people in positions of influence that might make them especially useful to the society. In 1943, for example, recommendations included Geoffrey Dawson, who was expected as a former editor of *The Times* to be valuable for publicity purposes, and as a member of the council of the Rhodes Trust to assist the society's efforts in securing money. Other recommendations included Frank Freeman, who was influential in the theatrical world; George Gibson, a trade union leader interested in the question of empire and commonwealth settlement; and Sir Thomas Southorn, who was expected to facilitate relations with the Colonial Office.[11] Many councillors inevitably experienced difficulty in interrupting their war work to attend council meetings regularly, and in consequence the council created an executive committee of doubtful constitutional propriety to manage affairs between meetings of the full council, to which it reported 'as and when it seemed desirable'. The executive committee absorbed the finance and general purposes committees, and although there were some objections to it as a clear infringement of the charter, it proved to be an efficient and effective arrangement and was retained after the war.

Situated in the heart of London, the Royal Empire Society headquarters would have been fortunate to have escaped without damage from the German bombing raids on the capital. In October 1940 many of its window panes were shattered and one end of the roof was cracked. Inconveniences arising from the raids were the intermittent disappearance of electric lighting and the temporary loss of gas, which affected the kitchens most and resulted in an emphasis on cold meals rather than hot until alternative means of cooking were installed. On the night of 16 April 1941 the building was hit by a two-ton high-explosive bomb, and on the night of 10 May it was severely damaged again. Casualties were remarkably light: one member was killed by blast on the second floor and another injured, and two members of the service staff, a receptionist and a wine-waiter, were seriously injured. The destruction and damage embraced six bedrooms on the fifth floor; most of the

[11] Co. Mins. 22 (16 March 1943), 2.

offices and the council room on the fourth floor; the ladies room, lounge, drawing, smoking and card rooms on the third floor; and the law library, newspaper room, and two rooms off the library gallery. An estimated 35,000 volumes and 5,000 pamphlets and documents were lost, and many others were charred or damaged by water.[12] The building was temporarily closed with consequent loss of revenue, but was reopened within a few weeks when repairs had made some of the damaged rooms habitable again. Claims were submitted under the War Damage Act to the War Damage Commission, and were approved, but it was not until 1957 that the work of restoration, structural alteration, and refurnishing was completed. In a gesture which a newspaper columnist described as 'in the true spirit of British sportsmanship',[13] the nose of the bomb that had done the damage was placed in a prominent position in the building.

The library had great difficulty in recovering from the losses it sustained in the war. Evans Lewin, who had been the librarian for thirty-two years, retired in April 1941 but agreed to remain until the end of the war and help the society to restore its depleted library. Collecting centres were established in various parts of the dominions to replenish the library's holdings, and a letter to the press by the chairman of council, Sir William Clark, and the chairman of the library committee, Dr. W. P. Morrell, advertised the library's needs. Books damaged by water had to be dried, those damaged beyond repair had to be disposed of, and the disorganized shelves had to be tidied. The War Damage Commission eventually assigned for the restoration of the library the sum of nearly £22,000, the amount originally claimed by the society under the War Damage Act. In 1949, however, the council, against the wishes of the library committee, devoted a portion of this sum to the purchase of new books instead of to the replacement of volumes lost in the war, and in 1953, in view of the decision not to replace the law library in its original form, it substantially reduced the total amount available for all purchases. The law library was now devoted more to statute law and the social

[12] Co. Mins 21 (30 April 1941), 140; (20 May), 141. Sykes, *From Many Angles*, 504. *The Times*, 15 May 1941.
[13] *Sunday Times*, 14 April 1957 ('Atticus').

aspect of law than to law reports and material which had been of value chiefly to practising lawyers.[14]

Towards the end of the war there was pessimism on the council about the society's future. The competition from other organizations was a matter that caused considerable anxiety among some members. In October 1944, for instance, the council concluded that the society had little prospect of success in Edinburgh because the Overseas League there possessed a fine building.[15] An air of resignation was apparent in the decision a fortnight later to agree to proposals by the Empire Day Movement that the arrangement with the society should be annulled and that the movement should become an independent body again.[16] Negotiations to renew the association were reopened in 1949 but they broke down when the idea was explored in detail.[17] The Empire Day Movement joined the Royal African Society, the Royal Central Asian Society, the Victoria League, the League of Empire, the Overseas League, and other kindred societies whose functions overlapped some of the functions of the Royal Empire Society.

There was a tendency on the council to contrast the development of the society with that of the Royal Institute of International Affairs, which, it was thought, had taken over much of the study and research into commonwealth affairs that the society should have been doing.[18] The Canadian Institute of International Affairs formed in 1928 was regarded as a particularly strong obstacle to the extension of activities in Canada. One of the declared objects of the Canadian institute was

To provide, through study, discussion lectures and public addresses, and such other means as may be approved by the National Council, an understanding of international questions and problems, particularly in so far as they may relate to Canada and the British Empire, and to promote through the like means an understanding of questions and problems which affect the relations of the United Kingdom with any other of His Majesty's Dominions, or of those Dominions with one another.

[14] *Librarian's memorandum on war damage funds* (Feb. 1967).
[15] Co. Mins. 22 (25 Oct. 1944), 136.   [16] Co. Mins. 22 (8 Nov. 1944), 138.
[17] Executive Committee Minutes, 1 (9 March 1950), 154; (20 April), 161. Co. Mins. 23 (20 Oct. 1949), 197; (26 April 1950), 217.
[18] Co. Mins. 22 (19 April 1944), 97–9.

The activities of the Canadian institute, combined with the demands of expediency which impelled Canada towards an international rather than a commonwealth outlook, presented, in the view of the Royal Empire Society council, a bleak prospect for the society's future in that part of the commonwealth. While the decline of a commonwealth outlook was less evident in England than in Canada, it was clear that the Royal Empire Society suffered in comparison with the Royal Institute of International Affairs, which, unlike the society, possessed a research staff and which, again unlike the society, had gained a growing reputation as a learned and dispassionate body with a serious and responsible purpose.

Concerned about the society's future after the war, the council in January 1945 appointed a planning committee to 'review the position of the Society in the light of conditions arising out of the war; to consider means of promoting the objects of the Society as laid down in its Charter, and of increasing its membership and revenue; and to make recommendations'. The recommendations were set out in the committee's report later in the year and touched on most aspects of the society's organization and work.[19] The council agreed with its recommendation that there should be no modification of the title despite the current practice of referring to the British commonwealth as well as the British empire. It suggested that the post of deputy secretary-general should be revived and that the executive committee of council established to deal with wartime conditions should be continued. As regards the journal, the committee felt that as wartime restrictions eased it should contain fuller reports of important addresses and more comprehensive reviews of relevant books; it also felt that space should be found at the head of each issue for the words taken from the supplemental charter describing the society's objects:

> To promote the preservation of a permanent union between the Mother Country and all other parts of the Empire; and to maintain the power and best traditions of the Empire.

In order to involve young people in the administrative work of the society, the committee suggested that the leader of the

[19] *United Empire*, 36 (1945), 40, 247–8.

companions should attend meetings of the council, though he would not have the right to vote because full membership of the council was open only to fellows. It was not discouraged by the wartime fall in membership, a decline from 20,500 in 1939 to under 17,400 in 1943, largely compensated for in 1945 by a gain of more than 2,000. Nevertheless, if the society was going to expand its membership it was clear that the social and amenity side should be stressed even at the expense of the cultural side. The council agreed.

By 1945 the Royal Empire Society was uncertain of itself, partly because so many of its functions were being poached by other organizations and partly because it was perplexed by the development of the commonwealth and empire it was supposed to serve. The society's political study group under Drummond Shiels produced a report on the political future of the British commonwealth and empire.[20] The report suggested that the imperial conferences should be held more frequently, some of them in overseas capitals of the commonwealth in order to demonstrate that the British peoples had 'chosen to form not a single, octopus-like State but a multi-national, many-centred Commonwealth'. In a section on the colonial empire it warned that the British government should listen to what was described as 'the under-tones of the masses' as well as to the vociferous sections which might be self-seeking and unrepresentative of the colonial populations. It was an optimistic and reasonable document, finding no conflict between the interests of the commonwealth and those of the world and basing its argument on the premise that the British empire was unique among the empires of history in the attempt it had made 'to reconcile Empire with liberty'.

The authors of this comparatively liberal formulary in 1945 could scarcely have been expected to foresee the rapidity or the drastic nature of the changes that were to take place in the British commonwealth in the post-war era. It was fully appreciated that the world had considerably altered and that there would be changes in the commonwealth. The challenge, reported the council, was now to the future:

[20] *The Political Future of the British Commonwealth and Empire* (1945). See also the rejoinder, *The Royal Empire Society and 'The Political Future of the British Commonwealth and Empire': a comment addressed by Lionel Curtis to the Society* (1945).

It may be that Europe can never recover the leadership of the world it has held since the days of the Caesars; to that extent Hitler, the most destructive agency of all times, may have succeeded. If that be so, in the new world, the leadership of the British Empire must be assured by the young and virile daughter countries no less than by the old Mother Country. Thus the Royal Empire Society has its marching orders, and the Council is keenly alive to its responsibilities. [21]

Notwithstanding the proposals of its planning committee, the society was not equipped in organization or character to cope with a new world in which, as a modern English historian of the period concluded, traditional values were being replaced by others and 'Land of Hope and Glory' was a refrain of declining relevance: 'Imperial greatness was on the way out; the welfare state was on the way in. The British empire declined; the condition of the people improved.' [22] When the war ended in 1945 the Royal Empire Society was still searching for a distinct and worthwhile role in the service of a rapidly changing Britain, commonwealth, and empire.

[21] *United Empire*, 37 (1946), 138.   [22] Taylor, *English History, 1914–1945*, 600.

Chapter Fourteen

The Branches (1910–1968)

I N the late nineteenth century the Royal Colonial Institute had had a large non-resident membership in the overseas empire, and of its resident members about a quarter had lived outside the London area. It was inevitable that as the numbers grew of those who lived beyond the reach of the facilities provided in London there should arise the question of forming branches both in the provinces and in the dominions. The idea had been broached as early as 1869, but the council at that time had preferred to establish in each colony a representative who would communicate with the institute in London and supply it with local information.[1] The council rejected suggestions that local committees should be appointed in the colonies to work for the institute's interests, and adhered to the view that a single corresponding secretary would provide a more satisfactory and practical channel through which to operate.

By the early twentieth century a network of honorary corresponding secretaries had been created and was the institute's only machinery outside London. The secretaries were often diligent and resourceful in their duty of keeping the council informed of local developments, but some did virtually nothing and retained their position long after their usefulness and effectiveness had disappeared. The council, however, was reluctant to replace men who had offered their service willingly and who, in many cases, had given it over a very long period. As late as 1935 it was admitted on the council that some of the corresponding secretaries were useless or unsuitable, those in Western Australia and New Guinea, for example, but there was no easy way of removing them. It was not always possible to gauge a man's character and worth before his appointment, and once he had accepted the invitation to become a corresponding secretary his tenure of the position was, in practice, for as long

[1] Co. Mins. 1 (2 May 1870), 88.

as he wished to remain. The council failed to take any action to solve the problem until April 1935, when it resolved that thenceforward the appointments should be for three years only.[2]

In 1910 the council sanctioned the idea of forming local centres or branches in the large cities of the United Kingdom, the West Indies, Ceylon, and India. The motive for this decision was the urgent need to increase membership, and it was hoped that in the new centres fellows would be able to meet for the presentation and discussion of papers. The local centres were to be established in the United Kingdom in the first instance, and corresponding secretaries in the cities were expected to initiate the organization of branches of the institute if the local support warranted. Some members of the council led by Ralph Bond, Richard Jebb, and Sir Harry Wilson thought that an *ad hoc* organizer should manage this extension movement into the provinces, and the names of Lionel Curtis and Fabian Ware were mentioned for the job, but Sir Godfrey Lagden in the chair insisted that the already over-worked secretary should assume the responsibility in addition to his regular routine duties.[3]

The first branch of the Royal Colonial Institute was opened in Bristol. On 10 April 1912 the sheriff of the city and county of Bristol, Thomas J. Lennard, wrote to the institute's corresponding secretary offering the freehold of a prominent site in Bristol for the erection of a building if a local branch of at least 500 members could be organized within two years. Lennard, who had unsuccessfully contested the parliamentary seat of Bristol West as a Liberal in 1906, was a fellow of long standing with a passionate enthusiasm for the empire born largely of a voyage round the world he had undertaken in the 1880s. He became a vice-president of the Navy League as well as of the Royal Colonial Institute, and in 1920 was knighted. Under the institute's royal charter the council had the power to authorize by resolution the formation of branches which would carry on the institute's activities locally but would have no independent or corporate existence of their own. Accordingly, a special meeting of the council in October 1913 approved a draft

[2] Co. Mins. 18 (8 April 1935), 156.
[3] Jebb to Milner, 22 Feb. 1912; Jebb to Grigg, 18 March: Jebb Papers.

constitution and set of rules for a Bristol branch, whose premises were formally opened in May 1915. Lennard was chairman of the Bristol council until 1922, when he resigned and became the branch president, but he continued to display an extra-ordinarily generous interest in the branch, and his nephew, Colonel E. W. Lennard, later became its chairman. The branch was an immediate success and was fulsomely praised in the institute council's report for 1919:

It has worked consistently since its formation in 1915 in promoting the great cause for which the Institute was founded. Its activities have been as marked as usual. Its members on all occasions show an enthusiasm in its work, and set an example which might with advantage be followed in other parts of the United Kingdom.[4]

The branch introduced special privileges for junior members or 'companions' in 1918, became intimately associated in the 1920s with the Bristol Migration Committee and in the 1930s with the newly-formed Bristol Canadian Club, both of which used its building, and by 1938 it had over a thousand members.

Other centres rapidly followed the example set at Bristol. A meeting of businessmen in Leicester in October 1916 led to the formation of a branch with accommodation in the building of the Leicestershire Club and Admiral Sir David Beatty as its first president. At a meeting in Bournemouth addressed by Sir Charles Lucas, chairman of council, in November 1917, it was resolved to establish a branch for the Hampshire and Dorset area. Other branches were established at Birmingham, Manchester, Sheffield, and Liverpool in 1918 and 1919. A Sussex branch formed at Brighton in 1918 was to have a more difficult history than the others, despite the fact that Lady Boyle presented it with a freehold property as a memorial to the empire work of her husband, Sir Cavendish Boyle. It soon ran into membership and financial problems, and in 1930 the society's council wrote off the branch's debts to headquarters and authorized an additional local levy of one guinea a year, the entire proceeds of which were retained by the branch. A Cambridgeshire branch formed in 1919 was unique in that it eventually functioned along the lines of a university society and had a fluid membership of students arriving and leaving

[4] *United Empire*, 11 (1920), 195.

the university. The Cambridgeshire branch maintained a special interest in the colleges, and among its presidents were the Vere Harmsworth professor of naval history, J. Holland Rose, and the master of Peterhouse, Field-Marshal Sir William Birdwood.[5] After an address in May 1932 by the parliamentary under-secretary for the colonies, Sir Robert Hamilton, who commented on the university's pitiful contribution to the study of the empire, the branch at its annual general meeting in October decided to submit a resolution to the vice-chancellor urging the establishment of a chair of imperial history, and the following year the naval chair which Lord Rothermere had established was broadened to include imperial history.[6]

Several of the branches began as local committees. That at Bath, for example, was formed as a local committee in 1930, largely by the inspiration of R. T. Bodey who, during the Second World War, carried on its work and acted as both its chairman and secretary, though well into his seventies by that time.[7] In 1947, when Bath had acquired the one hundred fellows required under the society's regulations for the constitution of a branch, it was duly promoted to that status.

All the United Kingdom branches had their difficulties, and for most of them the principal one was the acquisition of suitable premises. A fortunate few had premises given to them, but the majority were obliged to seek accommodation in the buildings of business firms or other societies. In 1921 the council suspended its campaign to foster the creation of new branches owing to the nation-wide shortage of offices and houses and the general economic condition of the country, and in 1923 it decided to vary the amount of rebate granted to each branch according to the branch's circumstances, which in many instances were straitened. The Jersey branch formed in 1937 suffered from German occupation during the war when it ceased activity and its records were either destroyed or sent to London, but after the war it became one of the most prosperous and energetic of the branches. Not all the branches were a success, and there was a tendency in some cases to emphasize the club and social side at the expense of study and discussion,

[5] Lord Birdwood, *Khaki and Gown: An Autobiography* (London 1941), 411.
[6] Co. Mins. 17 (11 April 1933), 49. *United Empire*, 23 (1932), 315.
[7] Co. Mins. 24 (23 July 1952), 21.

but many commendably attempted to put the accent on youth, sought to attract young people into the society, and organized and administered essay prizes in imperial subjects. Periodically, the branches held conferences at which their representatives would meet to discuss issues of common interest.

The council in London actively encouraged the formation of branches overseas. In 1912 it agreed to allow the secretary, James R. Boosé, to tour Canadian cities to enlist new members and organize branches. Boosé had entered the service of the Royal Colonial Institute in 1873 as a clerk at the age of fourteen, and he became successively librarian and secretary. In 1915 he relinquished the post of secretary to Sir Harry Wilson and became the institute's travelling commissioner, a newly created office the duties of which were to recruit new members and extend the activities of the institute outside London. When he died in retirement in New Zealand in 1936 at the age of seventy-seven, he had visited almost every part of the empire on the institute's behalf. Boosé's health was never good after 1914, and his numerous overseas tours were approved by the council partly because his doctor had advised him not to winter in England and his long service to the institute seemed to call for a generous attitude to his situation.[8] He was a kindly, cheerful person, but not inspiring or intellectually stimulating, and he was not particularly well fitted for the role he chose to play in the institute's extension movement. Jebb was to some extent justified in regarding 'poor little Boosé' as 'quite the wrong stamp of man' for the task, but Boosé's trips were not useless, as Jebb believed they would be, and in fact proved to be instrumental in adding significantly to the institute's membership and in initiating branches both in the United Kingdom and overseas.[9] After Boosé's retirement the post of travelling commissioner was held by Commander R. M. Reynolds, who had become a fellow of the institute at the beginning of the 1914–18 war and who in the late 1920s and early 1930s visited much of Africa, India, Burma, Malaya, Ceylon, Palestine, and South America in order to enrol members and organize branches.[10]

The first overseas branch was created at Christchurch, New

[8] Co. Mins. 13 (19 Oct. 1920), 49–50; 19 (20 April 1936), 1.
[9] Jebb to Ware, 30 July 1912, Jebb Papers.   [10] *The Times*, 4 Nov. 1931.

Zealand, in 1913, at the same time as the branch at Bristol was being formed. This was a significant achievement in view of the fact that for a long time the institute's following in New Zealand had been small compared with that in the other dominions, and was certainly smaller than might have been expected from a people with strong loyalties to the imperial connection.[11] The outbreak of war prevented the branch doing much except distribute literature supplied by head office in London, but later it declared its objectives to include the reduction of freight charges between the ports of the empire, the improvement of arrangements for exchange within the empire of professors of chemistry and the newer sciences, and the expansion of parcel post facilities. In 1930 the branch protested to the government that an increasing quota of British films should be shown in New Zealand and that censorship should be tightened to exclude films of what it regarded as an undesirable nature. The Canterbury branch at Christchurch remained the only branch in New Zealand for many years, although the corresponding secretaries in the country were requested by the institute council to foster the establishment of a branch in each of the main cities. The local committee at Auckland was not constituted a branch until April 1935, when the membership was nearing 200, but it ran a successful essay competition for schools, encouraged a junior section, and co-operated with the Overseas League; its first president was Boosé, who was elected to the office shortly before his death.

At the end of October 1913, the month in which the decision was made to form the Canterbury branch in New Zealand, Tasmanian members of the institute dined with L. S. Amery in Hobart, and during the evening resolved to organize a Tasmania branch. Institute fellows residing in other Australian capitals were urged to organize themselves similarly into branches or local committees in their respective states so that it might eventually be possible to create a united Australian section in the institute. The war delayed development along these lines, but by 1922 there were branches in Victoria, New

[11] K. Sinclair, *Imperial Federation: A Study of New Zealand Policy and Opinion, 1880–1914*; University of London Institute of Commonwealth Studies, Commonwealth Papers no. 11 (1955), 14–15.

South Wales, South Australia, and Queensland in addition to the branch in Tasmania, with a total membership of nearly 1,600. The Victoria branch, though initially outpaced by the New South Wales branch, was ultimately to be the most successful in expanding its membership. In 1934 the Victoria branch took the lead in acting upon the new youth policy of the council in London with the formation of a junior section under the sponsorship of Lady Huntingfield, wife of the state governor. At a meeting called for the purpose at Government House, she said that since she and her husband had arrived in Melbourne they had noticed the absence of young people from the activities of the patriotic societies. They had discussed the matter with Mrs. Herbert Brookes, eldest daughter of the former Australian prime minister, Alfred Deakin, and accepted her suggestion of a 'Junior Empire Society' in Victoria, the lady mayoress consenting to be its president for the first year.[12]

The decision in 1921 to form a New South Wales branch was the result largely of the interest taken in the idea by H. R. (later Sir Hugh) Denison, chairman and managing director of Associated Newspapers Limited in Sydney and a breeder of racehorses. Denison was well known for his enthusiasm for the empire, and he had been among the most tireless of those who had sought to promote its unity. He was a generous benefactor, and in 1919 had donated £25,000 to the institute's jubilee building fund. In view of this gift to the headquarters in England it was a surprise when, in 1922, he promised the prospective New South Wales branch a building in Bligh Street, centrally located in Sydney. The value of Denison's gesture, described by the state governor, Sir Walter Davidson, as the most noble act of citizenship during his term of office, was demonstrated within a few years by the complaints from other branches in Australia that they were able to do little because they had no premises.[13] Nevertheless, the branch had its financial problems, and, like other overseas branches, suffered from the financial arrangements with headquarters in London.

[12] *Argus* (Melbourne), 7 July 1934. Co. Mins. 18 (8 Oct. 1934), 75.
[13] N.S.W. Branch *Annual Report* (1922), 8. Co. Mins. 14 (16 June 1924), 185. *The Times*, 25 Nov. and 3 Dec. 1940. In 1967 the N.S.W. branch entered into an arrangement exchanging its premises for a strata title ownership of two floors in a new building to be erected in its place on the same site.

The subscriptions of members of overseas branches were subject to the operation by the institute of a rebate system which resulted in only one-third of the money subscribed being available for the overseas branches' own use. Moreover, the branches sometimes included non-resident fellows who had previously taken out life membership and were therefore a constant charge to the branches and made no contribution to their funds. The New South Wales branch, though fortunate in possessing a building, was in a special position among the Australian branches and incurred expenses that did not fall on others. In 1923, despite receiving about £600 in rental payments for the use of its building, it showed a loss of £86 on the year after remitting £1,000 to London. In June 1924 Denison, the branch president, raised the problem at a meeting of the London council, which at the end of the year suspended the rules relating to the proportion of the subscriptions payable to headquarters by the New South Wales branch. The branch was permitted to make a flat annual payment of £750 and, at Denison's request, it was agreed that its council should have the power to elect branch associate fellows.[14] Thereafter, the branch prospered, except during the depression years between 1929 and 1933, and by 1938 its membership had passed the thousand mark. It was associated with the formation of the Geographical Society of New South Wales, on whose council it was represented, and in the 1930s it campaigned to draw the attention of the Australian government to the inadequacy of the country's defences.

Unlike Australia, Canada never developed much enthusiasm for creating branches. Whereas the Australian membership was regularly increasing in the 1920s, the Canadian membership had reached its highest point in 1914 and was falling sharply.[15] A branch was constituted at Vancouver Island in February 1919 at the request of fellows residing in the vicinity of Victoria, the capital and seaport of British Columbia and a bastion of Britishness. A local committee functioned in Montreal until 1930, when it was promoted to branch status. The most lively branch activity in the Western Hemisphere before the 1950s was not in Canada but in the West Indies and South America.

[14] Co. Mins. 14 (16 June 1924), 185–6; (8 Dec.), 224.
[15] Co. Mins. 14 (10 Oct. 1927), 467; 15 (13 Feb. 1928), 24.

During the 1914–18 war local committees were formed in Guatemala and the Argentine, and in the closing years of the 1930s there were committees in Jamaica, Trinidad, and British Guiana. Other local committees or branches established in the 1930s included two in Southern Rhodesia, the one at Bulawayo for the Matabeleland area and the other at Salisbury for the Mashonaland area, which opened in May 1936 and at once celebrated empire day with a well-attended conversazione and an address by Mrs. Tawse Jollie on patriotism.

The establishment of branches and local committees in the United Kingdom and overseas was a desirable development if the institute was to achieve its purposes satisfactorily. The existence of overseas branches, as nearly as possible autonomous, became especially necessary as the empire evolved into a commonwealth of nations which emphasized its centrifugal tendencies. In the birth and growth of its branches, therefore, the institute reflected the changing character of the commonwealth and empire that it tried to serve. The formation of branches helped to popularize the institute outside London, but for a long time they were not as useful as had been hoped in adding to its membership and its funds. Local enthusiasm was apt to wane within a few years of the creation of a branch, and the council in London was not as energetic or resourceful as it should have been in strengthening and retaining local interest.

The branches grew substantially in number and independence in the post-war period after 1945. A supplemental charter for the society towards the end of 1964 provided for the establishment of autonomous branches in independent commonwealth countries and the creation of a commonwealth council to deal with them, the existing council at the headquarters in London becoming a central council. Most of the branches in Canada, Australia, and New Zealand applied to the council for autonomy, which was granted to the branches in Montreal, Ottawa, Nova Scotia, Toronto, Vancouver Island, and the mainland of British Columbia; to the branches in the Australian Capital Territory, New South Wales, Tasmania, Northern Tasmania, Queensland, South Australia, Victoria, and Western Australia; and to the branches in Canterbury, Otago, and Wellington.

In the United Kingdom the branches had a chequered existence and several were embarrassing to the central council at one time or another. In the 1940s the Cambridgeshire branch was reported to be suffering from the monopolistic enthusiasm of a mettlesome, peppery woman who made her home the headquarters and tended to dominate the branch's affairs herself, inevitably associating the society in the public mind with her own numerous activities and with her somewhat reactionary *obiter dicta* at branch meetings.[16] In the same period the Liverpool branch became moribund after the departure of Sir Robert Rankin, upon whom it had relied heavily; its membership was less than 200, but eventually it extended its activities by collaborating with the Royal Overseas League, and a joint committee of the two bodies met regularly. The Bristol branch prospered, and in the early post-war period its membership continued to increase in spite of the retention in office of an inefficient secretary who was almost an institution in the local community and therefore could not be easily removed.[17] From 1952 it was led by the blind but spirited professor emeritus, C. M. MacInnes, and in 1967 it had a membership of over 700. The Sussex branch was a source of anxiety on the council in the post-war period, and an investigation into its account in 1947 revealed deficiencies that were attributed to misappropriation by the branch secretary.[18] The Sussex members were unable to meet the expenses of the premises at Boyle House, but the conversion of the upper floor into flats contributed to an improvement in the financial position in the 1950s.[19] The membership of the Sussex branch declined in the 1960s, but was still over 600 in 1967. Of the other United Kingdom branches Bath had a membership of 170, Edinburgh 225, Hampshire and Dorset 604, and Oxford 176. In the Channel Islands the branch on Jersey had a membership of 454 and that on Guernsey 297.

Australia remained the most prolific source of branch membership, and it was a convention of the Australian branches in February 1948 that effectively objected to the use of the term 'non-resident fellow'.[20] The New South Wales branch was

[16] Co. Mins. 23 (15 Jan. 1947), 70.   [17] Co. Mins. 23 (23 April 1947), 102.
[18] Ex. Co. Mins. 1 (12 Nov. 1947), 28.   [19] Ex. Co. Mins. 2 (10 Feb. 1954), 165.
[20] Co. Mins. 23 (20 Oct. 1948), 159–60.

P

composed of nearly 2,000 fellows in 1967, and apart from the main office in Sydney it had units in Newcastle, Orange, and Wagga Wagga. Among its committees organizing activities was a 'Bring out a Briton' committee which had been formed in 1958 and which met and welcomed British immigrants, advising and assisting them on accommodation and employment problems. The branch was having little success in retaining young members, however, and its companions section was on the point of dissolution. The monthly journal it had begun publishing in 1944 was succeeded in 1950 by *Empire Outlook* (later *Commonwealth Outlook*), a larger product founded and edited by W. E. Stanton-Hope, a writer for whom the British Isles had hitherto been the principal market.[21] The Victoria branch had a sub-branch at Geelong and was composed of 3,000 fellows. It was an active branch, it had the advantage over Sydney of possessing a liquor licence and residential facilities, and its work in the community was raised in the state parliament in 1965 as meriting it special consideration in the matter of payment of land tax on its premises in Melbourne.[22] There were small branches at Brisbane in Queensland, Adelaide in South Australia, and at both Hobart and Launceston in Tasmania. A Western Australia branch established at Perth in 1954 had over a thousand members in 1967, and included among its activities a migration committee that sponsored young immigrants from the British Isles. In 1957 a branch was established at Darwin in the Northern Territory, and in 1958 another at Canberra in the Australian Capital Territory.

In New Zealand there were branches at Canterbury, Auckland, Wellington, and Otago. In Canada there were seven branches in 1967, all of them except Manitoba autonomous. The Montreal branch, which had deteriorated during the 1940s when it had been headed by elderly men with no initiative,[23] was in a satisfactory condition and membership, which had been static, was increasing in 1966 and 1967. The Ottawa branch, established in 1954, had about 250 members and co-operated frequently with the English-Speaking Union. Other branches were at Vancouver Island, Toronto, the

[21] W. E. Stanton-Hope, *One Only Lives Twice* (London 1955), 210.
[22] Victoria *Parliamentary Debates*, 280 (Assembly, 2 Dec. 1965), 2320.
[23] Co. Mins. 22 (24 Nov. 1943), 56.

mainland of British Columbia, and Nova Scotia. In South Africa the branches of Port Elizabeth, Cape Town, and Western Province continued in the 1960s, notwithstanding South Africa's withdrawal from the commonwealth in 1961, and in Southern Rhodesia the branches at Bulawayo and Salisbury maintained a precarious existence in the difficult circumstances that followed the government's unilateral declaration of independence from Britain in November 1965. Elsewhere in Africa there were branches at Nairobi in Kenya and at Lagos in Nigeria. The branches in Bermuda, Ceylon, Fiji, and Malaysia completed the list of overseas branches in 1967.

Branch representation among the newer members of the commonwealth was small, and the reasons were easy to guess. The absence of any branches in India or Pakistan was especially unfortunate, although the society had a few members in those countries and honorary representatives in Bihar, Bombay, Calcutta, and Madras. At the annual general meeting in June 1966 the chairman of council, Lord Glendevon, remarked upon the paucity of membership in the Indian sub-continent, which he had recently toured. He had gallantly attempted to publicize the society and hoped that as a result of his visit its work would be revived in the sub-continent. Obviously, it would be difficult to create a system of branches there, and another arrangement was provided for by a new rule enabling the council to 'grant the privilege of affiliation with the Society to any other society or body' whose aims it regarded as satisfactory and acceptable.[24] In 1967 the only affiliated body was the Commonwealth Society of Singapore.

By the close of 1967 the society possessed a total of forty-one branches, of which eight were in the United Kingdom, two in the Channel Islands, nine in Australia, seven in Canada, four in New Zealand, three in South Africa, and two in Rhodesia, while Bermuda, Ceylon, Fiji, Kenya, Nigeria, and Malaysia each had one. The Commonwealth Society of Singapore was an affiliated organization, and there were forty-six honorary representatives, four of them in United Kingdom cities and forty-two overseas, both within the commonwealth and outside it in such places as Nepal, Sweden, the United States, and the South American countries. About 70 per cent of the society's

[24] *Commonwealth Journal*, 9 (Aug. 1966), 177–80.

total number of fellows resided outside the United Kingdom, and the majority of these were from among the Anglo-Saxon peoples overseas. It was difficult to imagine how this situation could be modified and a greater proportion of non-settler peoples persuaded to join, but it was clear that unless the attempt to do this was made, and made soon, the society would not measure up to the future of the evolving multi-racial community of nations whose cause it professed to espouse.

Chapter Fifteen

The Latest Phase (1945–1968)

BY 1945 it was apparent that the society's title had again become an anachronism. In 1943 the council had considered a suggestion for a modification to 'British Commonwealth and Royal Empire Society' but had postponed a decision until after the war.[1] In 1945, when the importance of altering the name was recognized in view of the widespread adoption of the terminology 'British Commonwealth and Empire', the council felt that it would be undesirable to abandon the word Empire altogether, particularly as the branches in Australia and New Zealand were averse to change.[2] It was not until 1954 that the branches were invited to consider as alternatives to the title 'Royal Society of the Commonwealth and Empire' and 'Royal Society of the Commonwealth'. These ideas were dropped, however, when the Royal Society made clear that it would object to either of these alternatives being adopted, and the Privy Council intimated that it would uphold any such objection lodged by the Royal Society.[3] At the annual general meeting in 1955 the new chairman of council, Sir Charles Ponsonby, indicated that he was determined to effect a change in the title and he was strengthened in his resolve by discussions during travels in commonwealth countries, notably when he attended a meeting of the Victoria Branch in Melbourne in July 1956 at which the Australian external affairs minister, R. G. Casey, suggested that the words 'empire' and 'colonialism' were virtually synonymous in the minds of the peoples of Asia and that the society should substitute Commonwealth for Empire in its title.[4]

In 1957 a questionnaire was circulated among fellows both in the United Kingdom and overseas, and although the response, as usual, was small, a large majority of the answers

---

[1] Co. Mins. 22 (17 Nov. 1943), 50.   [2] Co. Mins. 22 (24 Oct. 1945), 225.
[3] Co. Mins. 24 (21 Dec. 1954), 121; (22 Feb. 1955), 128.
[4] *Age* (Melbourne), 31 July 1956.

favoured an alteration in the society's name. At special general meetings in London on 27 November and 17 December 1957 there was some expression of regret by older members that the term 'empire' should be abandoned, but the need to conform to current practice was generally appreciated, and a recommendation by the council for a change to 'Royal Commonwealth Society' was endorsed. A petition to the Queen in Council was submitted in December, and, after some delay caused by the submission of a counter-petition by two fellows of the society, the Royal Empire Society formally became the Royal Commonwealth Society on 7 May 1958. As a condition of the change, the Privy Council required an undertaking that the society's rules would be extended to prohibit the use by fellows of the initials F.R.C.S.[5] At the same time, the society's objects were re-stated in amendments to the charter as 'to promote the increase and diffusion of knowledge respecting the peoples and countries of the Commonwealth; to maintain the best traditions of the Commonwealth; and to foster unity of thought and action in relation to matters of common interest'. These objects were to be pursued by the society working as 'a non-sectarian and non-party organization'.

The central administrative machinery of the society operated adequately in the post-war period, but the need for overhaul was recognized. In 1950 an attempt was made to broaden the composition of the council and reinvigorate the committees, but there was no substantial modification until the grant in 1964 of a supplemental charter which revoked the provisions of the charters of 1882 and 1922 and the amendments of 1928 and 1958 with the exception of the original incorporation of the society. The supplemental charter provided for a commonwealth council to deal with the affairs of the branches and for the existing council to become the central council consisting 'of the Grand President, the President, such of the Vice-Presidents as may be elected annually thereto by the Central Council, the Treasurer, the Secretary-General (if honorary) and not less than twenty Councillors'. In 1967 the central council had forty-five members. Provision was made for the central council to appoint an executive committee which, following an amendment passed at the annual general meeting

[5] Co. Mins. 24 (28 April 1958), 242.

in 1965, exercised, subject to the authority of the council, 'general control over all matters affecting the Society and especially over its finances for which purpose the Central Council may from time to time by resolution delegate such of the powers conferred on the Central Council by these rules as the Central Council may deem proper to facilitate the conduct of the Society's affairs'.

The new charter provided for the election of vice-presidents to serve on the central council. Since the beginning of the century the list of vice-presidents had been lengthening steadily: some were elected to it on account of special services to the society, others on account of their office, such as that of a governor-general or of a high commissioner in London. Under the original charter all vice-presidents were *ex officio* members of the council, but under the rules they had to be elected annually: in practice they were re-elected *en bloc* at the annual general meetings and were, in effect, vice-presidents for life. In 1958 a committee studying the society's rules scrutinized the role of the vice-presidents, who now heavily outnumbered the elected members of the council. A new category was created of honorary vice-presidents who were not *ex officio* members of the council, and into it were placed governors-general and high commissioners. The other vice-presidents remained *ex officio* members of the council, though many of them ignored the honour, and since their annual re-election had become a formality it was decided that in future their election should be for life or until resignation.[6] The charter of 1964 provided that the central council might elect as vice-presidents any fellows who had rendered special service to the society or whose services as vice-presidents would be advantageous to it, and as honorary vice-presidents any fellows who held, or had held, high public office in the commonwealth; it did not provide for vice-presidents to be *ex officio* members of the council, but allowed the council to elect to itself a number of them annually. In 1967 there were thirty-three honorary vice-presidents and thirty-six vice-presidents, of whom eight were elected to the central council.

The society was well served in the post-war period by distinguished and capable chairmen of council. Lord Clarendon,

[6] *Confidential supplementary report to council by Sir Charles Ponsonby* (Dec. 1962).

who had filled the position since 1943, retired in 1948 but became one of the society's deputy presidents and until 1954 continued to be chairman of the Joint Empire Societies Conference. He was succeeded by Admiral of the Fleet Lord Chatfield, whose long and distinguished naval career had culminated as first sea lord. At the beginning of the war he had been minister for the co-ordination of defence in Chamberlain's war cabinet; he had been a friend of Churchill since 1914 and had been mildly admonished by him in 1940 for not stirring local authorities to submit more recommendations for the award of George Medals.[7] Chatfield was chairman of council until 1951, when there was considerable difficulty in finding a suitable successor, but eventually Sir Lancelot Graham, who was a vice-president and one of the deputy chairmen, was prevailed upon to accept the office. A man of candour, Graham had extensive experience of the Indian civil service and had been the first governor of Sind on its separation from the Bombay presidency in 1936. After his service in India he had settled in London, and at the Royal Empire Society became a member of council in 1945 and an able, idealistic, and hard-working chairman from 1951 to 1954.

In 1954 Colonel Charles E. Ponsonby, who had been deputy chairman under Graham, became chairman. He had joined the society in 1927, become a member of council in 1938, a vice-president in 1943, and deputy chairman in 1951. Now nearing the age of seventy-five, Ponsonby belied by his energy and progressiveness not only his years but also his background as a Conservative Member of Parliament. Largely because of his initiative and determination, the society's title was at last altered in 1958. He had had administrative experience in several parts of Africa, notably with the Uganda Company and the Central Africa Company in Nyasaland, had been chairman of the Royal African Society, and was more interested in African affairs than in the affairs of the older commonwealth members. 'When I took over', he said later, 'I was determined to modernize the outlook of the Society and to reorganize the work of the Council.' He found an ally in the dynamic Elizabeth Owen, who in 1957 was put in charge of public relations

---

[7] W. S. Churchill, *The Second World War* (6 vols., London 1948–54), I, 124; II, 625.

and who in 1961 became chairman of the newly-formed speakers department. Ponsonby regarded his main achievements as the alteration in the title and the extension of the cultural side of the society's activities, including the initiation of a commonwealth studies foundation, for whose endowment he launched an appeal that he continued to direct after his retirement as council chairman.[8] In 1968 he was still a member of the executive committee of the council. His initiative was an important spur to the society's development at a critical stage in its history, and his reports on the government and management of the society influenced later measures of reorganization.

Ponsonby was succeeded in 1957 by Earl De La Warr, who had been parliamentary under-secretary for war and for agriculture in the Labour government of 1929, left the Labour party and joined the National government of Ramsay MacDonald in 1931, joined the Conservative party in 1945, and was postmaster-general in the Conservative administration after 1951. He had extensive interests in Africa and was a director of the Standard Bank of South Africa and of two ranching companies in Southern Rhodesia. De La Warr, unlike Ponsonby, was more interested in the social than in the educational side of the society, and was remarkably successful in raising money to finance the repair, decoration, reorganization, and maintenance of the headquarters building. He brought in expert catering advisers, started plans for a buttery, and opened a modern bar on the ground floor. De La Warr, like Ponsonby, travelled widely in the commonwealth and was ably assisted by his wife, who was a vice-president of the society and a leading campaigner in the attempt to dispel the senescent atmosphere of fading memories that seemed to hang over the building.

In 1961 De La Warr was succeeded by Viscount Boyd, formerly Alan Lennox-Boyd, secretary of state for the colonies in the Conservative government between 1954 and 1959. Boyd was a dynamic chairman of council with great administrative capacity, but unfortunately he had numerous outside commitments and he surrendered the chairmanship in 1963, later becoming president when the Duke of Gloucester became

[8] Sir Charles Ponsonby, *Ponsonby Remembers* (Oxford 1965), 139. *Confidential report to council by Sir Charles Ponsonby* (Oct. 1962). Co. Mins. 24 (27 July 1954), 106.

grand president.[9] Boyd was replaced by Lord John Hope (Lord Glendevon), a Conservative Member of Parliament who from 1959 to 1962 had been the minister of works. He was an excellent chairman and played a significant part in launching the society's successful commonwealth interchange study group scheme in 1965. He retired in 1966, and was succeeded by the Duke of Devonshire. Devonshire was a man of impressive lineage and commonwealth connections; in the Conservative government he had become parliamentary under-secretary for commonwealth relations in 1960 and minister of state in the Commonwealth Relations Office in 1962. He had travelled widely in the commonwealth, and at forty-six was the youngest chairman in the society's history.[10] Although there may have been reason to believe that it was time to interrupt the peerage's near-monopoly of the council's chair—of the eight chairmen who had held office since 1945, six had been peers —the approach of the society's centenary year was a factor supporting the appointment of a person with extensive contacts and with the breeding and experience it was assumed were required to shoulder successfully the special duties that would inevitably fall upon him during the centenary celebrations.

The deputy chairmen of council also had an important role and were normally selected for their capacity and willingness to perform a particular task. Sir Gerald Campbell, for example, deputy chairman to Graham, controlled the meetings department, Sir John Macpherson under Boyd was chairman of the commonwealth studies foundation, Sir Ralph Hone under De La Warr was adviser on legal matters relating to the alteration of the charter and the rules, and Sir Hilary Blood under Ponsonby and De La Warr was closely concerned with the commonwealth studies foundation, eventually becoming chairman of the commonwealth studies committee. During the 1950s L. J. Wilmoth was chairman of the library committee for six years, and Sir Harry Batterbee, a former United Kingdom high commissioner in New Zealand, assumed responsibility for the meetings department. In 1967 the deputy chairmen under Devonshire were Sir Arthur Kirby, F. H. Tate, and Sir Ralph Hone.

[9] Co. Mins 25 (14 Dec. 1960), 52; (25 July 1963), 166.
[10] Co. Mins. 25 (28 July 1966), 269.

The most important figure in the daily administration of affairs was the secretary-general. The term had come into use in place of that of secretary during the war, and in 1945 the council decided to retain it. The charter postulated that the society should have a secretary, but the council assumed that the modification to secretary-general was a case of *de minimis* with which the law would not be concerned. It was also resolved that the secretary-general should have a deputy, but the decision was not acted upon until 1964.[11] From 1945 to 1958 the position was held by Archer Cust, who had originally entered the society's service as assistant secretary in 1935, when the council had advised him that the appointment did not mean he had a reversion to the secretaryship when it fell vacant. Nevertheless, when R. E. H. Baily retired in 1938 Cust was duly appointed to succeed him. On the outbreak of the war the following year he had left for military duties, but at the end of the war the council invited him to resume his post on his release from the forces provided he gave up an outside directorship that he had been allowed to retain when originally appointed in 1938.[12]

Cust was forty-nine when he returned to the society as secretary-general in 1945. He had served in both the world wars and had been in the Palestine civil service for fifteen years. His grandfather on his mother's side had been Lord Lyttelton, a founder of New Zealand, and his father had been a member of the royal household under King Edward VII. Cust grappled with the innumerable problems of the society's post-war rehabilitation, and achieved marked success in the laborious task of restoring the damaged headquarters building, for which he secured renewals of the timbers for panelling from the countries of the overseas commonwealth. These were vexatious years for the society's administration, but Cust, with a wide range of contacts to help him, coped manfully with the difficulties that beset him. He had been created an O.B.E. in 1939, and his services to the society were recognized by a C.B.E. in 1954 and a knighthood in 1959. Unfortunately, Cust

[11] Co. Mins. 22 (24 Oct, 1945), 226.
[12] Co. Mins. 19 (8 March 1937), 178; 20 (23 May 1938), 99; 22 (20 June 1945), 200.

gave the appearance of being pompous, his energetic supervision of the society won him critics and enemies, and in the
1950s there were factions which repeatedly attacked him at
annual general meetings. He generally maintained good relations with the chairmen, however, and he worked especially
well with Ponsonby to secure the alteration in the society's title.

In December 1958 Cust retired and was succeeded by D. K.
Daniels. Daniels, who had been a fellow of the society since
1933, had entered the colonial service between the wars and
been a district officer, magistrate, and private secretary to the
governor in Tanganyika. He had been involved in military
government in Africa during the war, after which he served
in a series of capacities in Malaya until retirement from the
Malayan civil service in 1955. David Daniels was secretary-
general for nearly eight years and played a vital part in the
society's development during that period. He was much less
forceful than Cust had been, but was a more genial, popular,
and sympathetic person, one who regarded his office as a way
of life as much as a job: 'He was in the building not just on the
requisite or critical occasions, but apparently all the time. He
was always available, always ready with help, advice or wise
counsel.'[13] He was succeeded by A. S. H. Kemp, who had been
his deputy since March 1964 and who similarly had considerable experience of Malaya, not only as a civil servant but also
as a prisoner of the Japanese after the fall of Singapore. Stephen
Kemp's promotion to secretary-general in 1967 was at a time
when the society was greatly occupied with plans for celebrating its centenary, and his coolness, good sense, and reliability
were especially valuable at the centre of an administration
that was becoming overburdened and strained. The secretary-
general's administrative duties were clearly going to increase
considerably in the ensuing two years, and therefore it was
decided that he should have two deputies, the one (Colonel
R. C. Laughton) to be concerned primarily with membership
and general house management, and the other (Brigadier
G. H. W. Goode) with educational activities and the centenary
programme.

The society maintained an impressive list of activities, and
various committees industriously organized hospitality, enter-

[13] *Commonwealth Journal*, 9 (1966), 244 (Sir Hilary Blood).

tainment, and a wide range of meetings, talks and social events. The society provided the secretariat for the Joint Commonwealth Societies Council established in 1947 to facilitate co-operation between the various voluntary organizations concerned with commonwealth friendship. This council's most important function was the promotion of commonwealth day celebrations in London and the world-wide distribution of a commonwealth day message. Among the more interesting developments during the later post-war period were the evolution of the Voluntary Service Overseas (V.S.O.) and the revival of the trade and industry committee. The foundation of V.S.O. in 1958 was due largely to Alec Dickson working through the Inter-Church Aid Society. Dickson was for a time secretary to the Royal Commonwealth Society's commonwealth studies committee, but neglected this responsibility for his greater interest in V.S.O., which began to operate in the society's building in 1958 and of which he became the director. The first volunteers to go overseas under the auspices of V.S.O. did so by virtue of donations from the society, the Nuffield Foundation, oil companies, and trusts. The society provided V.S.O. with accommodation at an economic rent, and for a few years V.S.O. occupied a small office on the fourth floor of the society's premises.[14] As its activities increased it occupied additional office space, but by 1964 it had outgrown the accommodation available at the society and moved out of the building to a headquarters of its own.

The society's trade and industry committee was revived in 1963 under the chairmanship of Lord Spens and was composed of representatives from eleven organizations concerned with commonwealth trade. Describing the committee's role in 1966, the current chairman, F. H. Tate, saw its main functions as first, 'to bring together at regular intervals the representatives of many of the bodies concerned with commonwealth trade', and second, to organize seminars and conferences at which company representatives could 'hear expert speakers and engage in questions and discussion on various aspects of Commonwealth trade and development', and from which might be acquired 'an expert up-to-date assessment of the

[14] Co. Mins. 25 (27 April 1961), 65. D. Wainwright, *The Volunteers: The Story of the Overseas Voluntary Service* (London 1965), 33, 105.

political and economic situation in the country or region under study, together with practical information on current trends in industrial development and import and export trade'.[15] The committee also administered the society's corporate member- ship scheme which entitled the London nominees and overseas representatives of business houses and organizations to make use of the society's facilities.

In 1946, when the council, and notably Sir Frederick Sykes, was anxious that the learned side of the society's work should not decline in comparison with its social side, an information bureau was created within the library organization. By 1949 the bureau was well established, and the council decided that it should become an independent department with its own com- mittee, an arrangement which offended the library com- mittee.[16] In 1954, however, the bureau was again placed under the general supervision of the library. The bureau answered queries about commonwealth countries, especially for persons contemplating settlement overseas, and compiled information papers on individual territories that were issued regularly and were revised periodically to allow for changing conditions and new developments. The papers were issued gratis, though it was possible for subscriptions to be made voluntarily, as was done by the Bank of Brussels after 1952.[17] Extensive use was made of the bureau's willingness to answer all manner of queries, especially as knowledge of its existence spread, and a short paragraph about it in a London evening newspaper brought nearly a hundred inquiries.[18] Some inquiries continued to be dealt with by the council, such as the highly-charged one made in a letter from the Argentine embassy in 1949 asking for 'a chronological summary of the dates of the revolutions and civil strifes in the Commonwealth, and also of the international wars in which they have intervened since the year 1900 up to date': this information was understandably refused.[19] In 1950 the bureau began a loan service of visual aids enabling schools to borrow picture sets, film strips, charts, maps, and posters to illustrate lessons that touched upon the commonwealth.

[15] *Commonwealth Journal*, 9 (1966), 86, 98.
[16] Co. Mins. 22 (20 March 1946), 279, 284; 23 (16 Feb. 1949), 172. Ex. Co. Mins. 1 (9 Feb. 1949), 90; (9 March), 96.
[17] Co. Mins. 24 (25 June 1952), 16.　　[18] Co. Mins. (23 April 1952), 8.
[19] Ex. Co. Mins. 1 (11 May 1949), 106.

In the 1960s, however, the bureau's future was put in doubt by the society's need to make economies, and in 1967 the visual aids loan service was abandoned. A decision by the council to abolish the bureau was deferred at the request of the library committee, and the reprieve was used successfully to investigate the possibility of the bureau's being able to meet its expenses by charging for its information papers.

In 1957 the council announced the creation of a commonwealth studies foundation to co-ordinate and direct the education work of the society. An appeal was launched for funds to endow the foundation, and it was hoped optimistically to raise £200,000, but less than a quarter of that amount was forthcoming. The commonwealth relations secretary, Lord Home, and the colonial secretary, Lennox Boyd, issued a joint statement commending the appeal:

It is, we feel, vital that the world should be continually informed of what the Commonwealth stands for, of its past activity and its future aims. It is equally important that our young people in schools and universities should learn all that is possible about the Commonwealth. [20]

The annual income from the foundation's invested capital enabled publication to be renewed in the society's 'Imperial Studies' series and assisted the revision of the library catalogue and the organization of summer schools.

The commonwealth studies committee was under the chairmanship of Professor Vincent Harlow until 1957, when his duties as Beit professor of colonial (later British commonwealth) history at Oxford University compelled him to resign. The council persuaded A. D. C. Peterson to take the position, but almost at once he became director of education at Oxford University and, like Harlow before him, was unable to pay much attention to the committee and he resigned as chairman in 1960. Thereafter, the practice of having academics as chairmen was dropped, against the wishes of some members of the committee. Sir John Macpherson succeeded Peterson, and was followed in 1963 by Sir Hilary Blood, who in 1966 made way for Dr. L. Farrer Brown. The committee was responsible for the production between 1947 and 1955 of a

[20] *The Times*, 24 Oct. 1957.

series of pamphlets on the commonwealth, for running the essay and group project competitions, for organizing the annual summer school at one of the older universities and, beginning in 1966, the spring school at one of the younger universities, and for arranging conferences for teachers and sixth-formers. The committee was loyally served by a number of hard-working persons, notably Lady Davson, a zealous committee member, Miss Gladys Buhler (later Lady Shiels), the secretary until 1958, and F. W. Wilkinson, retired headmaster of Latymer Upper School, Hammersmith. Nevertheless, the committee, half of whose members were nominated by outside bodies, was extravagantly managed, and Ponsonby felt in 1962 that it should be 'looking for work'.[21]

When the commonwealth studies foundation was established, the scope of the commonwealth studies committee was considered. Gerald S. Graham, the Rhodes professor of imperial history in the University of London, suggested the creation of a separate committee to manage the publications in the Imperial Studies series, which had ceased in 1942 owing to the war and had not recommenced until 1953 owing to lack of funds. An academic committee was formed, and under the chairmanship of Professor Graham it revived the Imperial Studies series, which by 1967 had been increased to twenty-seven volumes.

The school essay competition, which had been stopped for a short time at the beginning of the war, had an unbroken and successful history after 1941. It owed much to the devoted service of F. W. Wilkinson, who had joined the commonwealth studies committee in 1939 and was the chief examiner of the essay competition from 1957 onwards. By 1967, according to the chairman of the commonwealth studies committee, which had charge of it, the competition received 'over 800 entries a year from more than 140 schools in seventeen Commonwealth countries, from the Seychelles and Hong Kong to Canada and Britain'.[22] The examiners in their reports on the essays were perhaps too ready to rhapsodize on the unanimity among candidates on the value of the commonwealth, an assessment which, in the context and nature of the competition, was almost

[21] *Confidential report by Ponsonby* (Oct. 1962).
[22] *Commonwealth Journal*, 10 (1967), 110.

worthless. A more legitimate cause for encouragement was the improvement in the quality of the writing and the increase in the amount of reading upon which the entries were based. In 1964 the essay competition was joined by a group project competition designed to foster partnership both within and between schools in the production of entries. Schools were invited to enter one or more teams each, and any school might, if it wished, combine in a group with another school anywhere in the commonwealth, and each team was required to compose a report in essay form on a piece of research concerned with the commonwealth and carried out co-operatively. In 1966 groups from thirty-seven schools in ten countries of the commonwealth entered for the competition. For university postgraduate students the Walter Frewen Lord prize continued to be offered annually for an essay in imperial history, and was managed and judged by the academic committee under Professor Graham. The list of past winners of the prize included the names of several scholars who had achieved eminence in the academic world, among them Professor C. H. Philips, director of the School of Oriental and African Studies in London, and J. A. Gallagher, Harlow's successor at Oxford as Beit professor of the history of the British commonwealth.

The library remained the distinguished core of the educational services. Evans Lewin, the librarian for nearly thirty-six years, retired in 1946, but the society was fortunate in finding successors to him as capable and devoted to the library as he had been. The first was James Packman, who came from the British Library of Political Science and remained until the beginning of 1956, when he resigned and took the post of deputy librarian at the University College of Ibadan in Nigeria. The second was Donald Simpson, who had been Packman's deputy. Simpson, who possessed extensive library experience, was the author of histories of Anglican churches in the Mediterranean area, an interest arising from wartime service in Malta, and he soon developed a comprehensive knowledge of the society's past. Lewin, Packman, and Simpson, who between them had been responsible for fifty-eight years of the library's development by 1968, were all increasingly harassed in their management of the library by difficulties that were aggravated by shortages of space and finance.

Q

In January 1950 the library began publication in roneoed form of a monthly list of accessions that was distributed among a large number of libraries in the United Kingdom and overseas. In 1956 and 1957 the monthly accessions list was expanded to include bibliographical notes, descriptions of items and collections in the library, and accounts of the library's activities and work. In 1958 the librarian began organizing periodic meetings at which guest experts spoke on matters of library and bibliographical interest in general. The library became a refuge for the libraries of other societies, such as that of the Royal African Society in 1949 and that of the Kipling Society in 1967, but it was itself in difficulties by centenary year. It needed more space for shelves and storage and more money for books, both old and new, in order to maintain its position as a commonwealth library of reference, research, and general reading. Rising costs, commented the librarian in a memorandum in 1967, made the existing annual allocation for books inadequate for new purchases, and the exhaustion of the war damage funds meant that virtually no older books could be purchased: 'This', he concluded, 'is a deplorable situation.'[23]

The journal during the post-war period underwent several changes and introduced some new features. Its title was altered in 1958 from *United Empire* to *Journal of the Royal Commonwealth Society* and in 1961 to *Commonwealth Journal*. After Edward Salmon retired as honorary editor at the end of 1946, the journal was edited successively by H. W. Elliott Bailey (1947–53), G. D. Wood (1953–7), Percy Arnold (1957–60), Patrick Lacey (1960–3), and, since 1964, Harry Miller; R. A. Eccleston, D. E. Dean, and R. E. H. Challis were also editors for short periods. The hope that the journal would revert in the post-war years from a bi-monthly to a monthly publication never materialized, and in the early 1950s it was in financial difficulties on account of increasing costs. These were partly overcome by increased revenue from advertising after the journal's advertising space was placed with a professional agent and its appearance was improved by the continued use of 'cotine' paper introduced for the coronation issue in 1953. Successive editors performed an exacting and delicate task in producing a combin-

---

[23] *Librarian's memorandum on war damage funds* (Feb. 1967).

ation of features in the journal that met the requirements of the maximum number of fellows of the society without permitting it to become a mere social magazine. It contained accounts of the society's internal affairs, short reviews of new books of commonwealth interest, and articles, or reports of talks given at the London headquarters, on important commonwealth topics. Unhappily, the articles or talks were less weighty than those produced at the institute in the nineteenth century, but were often useful reflections on commonwealth affairs. Nevertheless, the talks given at the society were inevitably of a variable quality, often of an official or a general character, and while they might be easy lunch-time listening they were not always good reading when translated into print. By 1968 the journal needed to show more confidence in the intellectual capacity of its readers, to raise its cultural level with articles of a more critical, thoughtful, and analytical character, and to strengthen its impact by the reintroduction of an authoritative and searching editorial commentary.

The only serious disruption in the journal's management was in 1963, when Lacey's appointment as editor was terminated by the council. Lacey had become editor in September 1960 and had been entrusted with putting into effect reforms recommended by a committee which had been created by the council to report on the journal. Under him the journal was more racy and provocative than before or since, but following a disagreement with the council on a matter of policy, Lacey, who was evidently under some strain at this time, embarked on a somewhat brusque and personal correspondence with the secretary-general that the council refused to tolerate.[24] The council replaced Lacey as editor and removed his name from the register of fellows, the first important case of removal for misconduct since 1953.

In the 1960s the main organizational problems of the Royal Commonwealth Society were to improve the financial position, to increase membership, to extend influence and support among the newer commonwealth countries, and to win greater acceptance among the non-Conservative parties and the labour sections of the community. The society was racked by financial difficulties throughout the post-war period, and sub-committees

[24] Co. Mins. 25 (25 April 1963), 149–57.

of council periodically studied means by which they might be overcome. Although the society's total assets, including its freehold sites, exceeded £325,000, its annual expenditure by 1968 was exceeding revenue by about £16,000 and its overdraft had reached approximately £37,000. The deficit in 1966 was attributed to a shortfall in revenue from annual subscriptions and entrance fees following the grant of autonomy to branches, and 'the fairly widespread apathy towards the Commonwealth in Britain' was assumed to have adversely affected support for the society. There was no inclination at the society to regard the poor financial condition as merely a reflection of the economic condition of the United Kingdom, and the council devised a programme to improve the society's position 'by raising subscription rates in the London area, by launching a Centenary Membership Campaign in Britain, by putting in hand a reorganization for greater efficiency and economy, and by starting the exploration of all possible sources of external support consistent with the Society's independence'.[25] The centenary membership campaign was not as successful as had been hoped, however, and at the annual general meeting in 1967 the chairman of council admitted that, while the rate of recruitment had increased, the society was not securing the extra support it needed if it was to solve its financial problems.[26] Total membership of the society, including fellows, associates, companions, honorary fellows, and corporate and affiliate members, remained around the figure of 30,000.

The expanding commonwealth's emphasis on its multi-racial quality presented an urgent problem to the Royal Commonwealth Society. Very few Africans frequented the society before the end of the 1950s: they were often accustomed to segregation or discrimination in their own countries and would seem to have automatically regarded the society as a white men's organization. The annual subscription was based on white men's incomes and living standards and was one that few among the African, Asian, and Caribbean populations of the commonwealth would be easily able to afford even if they had wished to join. There was no African among the society's

---

[25] *Commonwealth Journal*, 10 (1967), Central Council Report, i–ii.
[26] Ibid., 197.

honorary corresponding secretaries until 1948, when Sir Henley Coussey was appointed in Accra.

In 1951, before the Labour government left office in England, the commonwealth relations secretary, Patrick Gordon-Walker, invited the society's chairman to discuss with him the affairs both of the society and of the commonwealth in general. One of Gordon-Walker's suggestions was that the society should develop its interest in India, Pakistan, and Ceylon and encourage a strengthening of the ties between them and the older commonwealth members. [27] In 1952 the council approved a visit to East and Central Africa by the secretary-general, who had served in Northern Rhodesia in the early 1930s and some of whose family still lived in Kenya: the object of his tour was professedly to promote the affairs of the society and recruit new members, but he admitted (to the concern of at least two persons on the council) that he intended to address himself principally to the colonial service and white residents. [28] The council recognized the society's difficult racial problem but had no idea how to solve it and made little serious attempt to do so in the 1950s.

The racial imbalance in the society remained throughout the post-war period, and although the transference of the Royal African Society from the Commonwealth Institute brought more Africans into the building, the society was unable to attract the non-white support most of its council desired. In an attempt to attack the problem the society in 1961 joined the Victoria League, the Royal Overseas League, and the English-Speaking Union in an agreement on joint action among the indigenous inhabitants of the new commonwealth countries, it being felt that competition between the societies would lead to chaos and misunderstanding. [29] In the 1960s the society had greater success in reducing the barriers that had seemed to lie between it and the commonwealth peoples in Africa, Asia, and the West Indies, and an increasing number of their inhabitants frequented the society when in London. Nevertheless, a real danger remained that the work in the new member countries of the commonwealth would become completely moribund following the exodus of British personnel.

[27] Co. Mins. 23 (28 June 1951), 265.   [28] Co. Mins. 24 (23 April 1952), 5–6.
[29] Co. Mins. 25 (29 June 1961), 71; (26 Oct.), 85.

The fourth main organizational problem was that, notwithstanding its non-party principle, it was still regarded by many people as a Conservative body. In October 1949 a member of council remarked on the large majority of Conservatives over Socialists and Liberals on the society's list of vice-presidents,[30] and although it was impossible to attach a party label to every vice-president, it was a fair assumption in 1967 that this Conservative majority remained. In his meeting with Chatfield, the chairman of council in 1951, Gordon-Walker suggested that the society should seek closer contact with the trade unions in the United Kingdom, and the council formed an *ad hoc* committee to consider the idea. Chatfield emphasized that trade unionists who became associated with the society should do so as individuals who supported its aims and not merely as trade unionists, since that would introduce a political bias that was undesirable. Nevertheless, an attempt was made to carry out the proposal of the commonwealth relations secretary, and temporary honorary membership of the society was offered colonial government labour officers undergoing courses of instruction in the United Kingdom.[31] Arthur Creech-Jones, a Labour member of council with ministerial experience as colonial secretary, approached leading trade unionists on the society's behalf, and later submitted to the council a list of trade union secretaries to whom letters were sent inviting them to join the society's group membership scheme, but their replies were discouraging.[32]

The society was unable to escape the essentially Conservative mould in which it had existed since the end of the nineteenth century. There were Labour members on the central council and the list of vice-presidents, but even when, in the early 1960s, the Labour party usurped the Conservative party's role as defender of the commonwealth connection, the Royal Commonwealth Society retained the appearance of a Conservative organization. This was probably unavoidable for a body of this kind, and there was nothing necessarily reprehensible about the fact itself (assuming it to be true), but there was

[30] Co. Mins. 23 (20 Oct. 1949), 198.
[31] Co. Mins. 23 (28 June 1951), 265; (26 July), 269–70; (1 Nov.), 277–8.
[32] Co. Mins. 23 (20 Oct. 1951), 293–4; 24 (25 June 1952), 15; (23 July), 18; (29 Oct.), 23.

certainly a possibility that the society's 'image' deterred some elements in the community whom the society sorely needed if it was to meet the challenge of the modern commonwealth. In its hundredth year the Royal Commonwealth Society was harassed by problems of finance, membership, leadership, and character, but overshadowing all was the supreme problem raised by the decline of public confidence in the commonwealth of nations itself.

Chapter Sixteen

The Commonwealth, 1968

THE commonwealth, observed the former Australian prime minister, Sir Robert Menzies, in 1967, was in danger of being converted into an association 'which no longer expresses unity but exists chiefly to ventilate differences, even to advertise conflicts, and to develop pressures upon individual members, frequently without reason and not infrequently for bad reasons'.[1] The commonwealth had become the object of widespread disenchantment in Britain, where it had even been described prominently as a 'gigantic farce',[2] and sceptics ridiculed the well-meaning claquers who indulged in platitudes and abstractions. Menzies admitted that the 'elements of cohesion' in the commonwealth, about which it used to be customary to make lyrical after-dinner speeches, now required 'prosaic attention'.[3] The Statute of Westminster, which little more than a generation before had attempted to formulize the relationship between the members of the old commonwealth, had used terms such as dominions, a common allegiance to the crown, imperial conferences, and the British commonwealth, none of which were acceptable in 1968, when the membership had grown to twenty-six, representing a total population of 700 million.

The first significant development in the post-war period was the grant of independence to India, Pakistan, and Ceylon and their subsequent decision to remain in the commonwealth. Britain's Labour prime minister, Clement (later Earl) Attlee, who had served on the Simon commission on India in 1927, was determined that independence for India should be arranged with the minimum of delay and should not be deferred indefinitely by the communal differences between the Hindus and

---

[1] R. G. Menzies, *Afternoon Light: Some Memories of Men and Events* (London 1967), 189.
[2] *The Times*, 2 April 1964 ('A Conservative').   [3] Menzies, op. cit., 228.

Muslims. In February 1947 the British government announced its 'definite intention' to transfer power in India by June 1948 and appointed Lord Louis (later Earl) Mountbatten as viceroy to put the policy into effect.

Mountbatten arrived in Delhi on 22 March 1947 and soon decided that a single government for the entire Indian sub-continent was impracticable and that there would have to be a partition. After years of indecision and wrangling the final transfer of power was carried through in India's hottest summer for a decade with almost unseemly haste and indifference to some inflammatory issues, such as Kashmir. Mountbatten, indeed, decided that Britain's declared timetable for the transfer was not too short but too long, especially as communal trouble had already begun in Calcutta, East Bengal, Bihar, Punjab, and the North-West Provinces. 'It was necessary', he told a meeting of the Royal Empire Society in October 1948, 'to carry out the transfer of power at the greatest possible speed. I have no doubt that history in ten or twenty years' time will prove that that was right.'[4] The independence bill was introduced in July 1947 and power was formally transferred on 15 August to the two 'independent dominions' of India and Pakistan before proper measures had been taken to maintain order in the likely event of unrest and violence. In November an independence bill for Ceylon was introduced and in February 1948 became law.

There were people in Britain and other commonwealth countries who had misgivings about the partition of India and there were some who regretted the grant of independence. At the Royal Empire Society the issue was treated cautiously but not pessimistically, and discussion was largely confined to two public meetings, the one addressed by L. S. Amery in June 1947 and the other by Mountbatten sixteen months later. The society was criticized afterwards for not studying the Indian problem more closely at this time and for having failed, amid the prolonged public debate on partition, to produce for consideration any constructive alternative suggestions.[5] This was unfair; the society was just beginning to recover from

[4] *United Empire*, 39 (1948), 273. See also L. F. Fischer, *The Life of Mahatma Gandhi* (London 1951), 497–8, 507.
[5] K. K. Aziz, *Britain and Muslim India* (London 1963), 208.

wartime difficulties and was not well equipped to investigate a problem that was urgent and sensitive and had rapidly passed into the charge of negotiators in Delhi. Members were inclined to welcome the transfer of power and wish the new dominions well, although the council's annual report for 1947 expressed regret at 'the passing of those two great humanizing and stabilizing factors in the lives of Eastern millions, the Indian Civil Service and the Indian Army. They will ever hold a proud place', it declared, 'in the annals of the British people.'[6]

The acceptance of dominion status by India, Pakistan, and Ceylon was surprising in view of earlier objections by nationalist leaders, who had believed that it implied something less than complete independence. By agreeing to become dominions, their leaders were, in effect, recognizing that the status was indistinguishable from complete independence and setting a precedent for successful nationalist movements in other British territories later.[7] The force of the Asian dominions' decision was strengthened by the coincidental decision of Burma and the Irish Free State in 1948–9 to secede from the commonwealth, demonstrating that members were independent to a degree that permitted them to leave the association if they desired. In October 1948 the prime ministers of India, Pakistan, and Ceylon attended the conference of commonwealth prime ministers in London, where they were able 'to see at first hand how the Commonwealth worked before taking any final decisions about their own position, for it was felt that only by participation in the councils of the Commonwealth at the highest level might a full understanding of its working be acquired'.[8] Commenting on the conference and the need for the new members to decide upon their national relations with the commonwealth, the journal of the Royal Empire Society was comforted by the fact that

their representatives at the Conference will at least have gone back with a full assurance of the goodwill of Britain and their fellow-Dominions towards them, and it is to be hoped that both they

[6] *United Empire*, 39 (1948), 141.

[7] M. S. Rajan, *The Post-War Transformation of the Commonwealth* (London 1963), 9.

[8] N. Mansergh, 'Commonwealth Membership', *Commonwealth Perspectives*, by Mansergh et al. (Durham, N.C. 1958), 27.

and their respective countries may decide that their true destiny lies in remaining members of our Commonwealth of free and independent nations.[9]

All three countries chose freely to remain within the commonwealth because, despite the fact that they lacked the ethnic and common historical origins of Britain and the older dominions, they evidently believed that membership might bring economic and diplomatic benefits and enhance their international influence. The Indian prime minister later defended the decision to remain in the commonwealth on the grounds that it opened 'avenues' which might otherwise have been closed to India and that it had assisted India directly and indirectly to affect world policies: 'Anyhow', he submitted, 'I cannot see how any valid reason can be advanced for our cutting away from a relationship which is the best form of relationship in the sense that there is no obligation on us or on the other party, except the obligation of occasional friendly approach and friendly talk.'[10]

Under its new constitution India became a sovereign independent republic, setting a problem for the other commonwealth members which, according to the Statute of Westminster, were united by a common allegiance to the crown. The crown did not possess for the new members the special, almost mystical, significance which the older members attached to it, and at the prime ministers conference in 1949 India was allowed to retain its membership as a republic accepting the King as the symbol of the free association of the members and, as such, the head of the commonwealth. India duly became a republic within the commonwealth in 1950, and republican status was similarly acquired by Pakistan in 1956 and by newly-independent African members in 1960 and after. The modification in the constitutional doctrine of the commonwealth disturbed some people, who feared that to reduce the role of the monarchy in this fashion meant weakening the essential bonds of the commonwealth; Menzies felt that a relationship which had been 'organic and internal' had

[9] *United Empire*, 39 (1948), 270.
[10] Nehru in the Lok Sabha, 17 March 1953, *Documents and Speeches on Commonwealth Affairs, 1952–1962*, ed. N. Mansergh (London 1963), 754–5.

become 'in a sense functional and certainly external'.[11] The principle of common allegiance to the crown, however, was what a contemporary constitutional lawyer has described as 'an already enfeebled constitutional dogma' and was not worth preserving at the risk of 'squandering the benefits of Indian membership'.[12] Moreover, as another authority has pointed out, 'it was evident that the divisibility of the Crown could be carried only so far, and that, since there was the possibility that India might take sharply different international action from other Commonwealth members, it might be better in the long run if the King were released from even token responsibility for Indian laws and policy'.[13]

The advent of India, Pakistan, and Ceylon and later of Ghana and other independent territories in Africa raised the commonwealth's multi-racial quality to supreme importance. Whereas commonwealth statesmen had been wont previously to speak of the rule of law, freedom of the individual, and parliamentary democracy as among the significant qualities possessed by commonwealth members in common, new members often discovered that these western ideals were not easily applicable in the special conditions in which they were required to establish governments and begin building nations. The commonwealth became, above all else, an association embracing diverse races and creeds, and multi-racialism became its highest principle and object. One of the dangers of elevating this highly-charged, emotional principle above all others was that it shaped the commonwealth conferences and emphasized and publicized differences and antagonisms. Sometimes the heads of member governments conducted themselves on this issue at the conferences in a manner designed partly to impress their public opinion at home, but commonwealth traditions were affected by the practice and it was arguable that the association lost rather than benefited.[14] The most dramatic consequence was the withdrawal of South Africa from the commonwealth in 1961.

In a curious address to the Royal Empire Society in October

---

[11] Menzies, *Afternoon Light*, 188.

[12] S. A. de Smith, *The New Commonwealth and its Constitutions* (London 1964), 14.

[13] J. D. B. Miller, *The Commonwealth in the World* (London 1965), 53–4.

[14] T. R. Reese, 'Keeping Calm about the Commonwealth', *International Affairs*, 41 (1965), 453.

1945, the South African deputy prime minister, J. H. Hofmeyr, had referred to the value to the entire commonwealth of the experiments in racial contact then in progress in South Africa:

I think of the diversity of the British Empire, the diversity of race, language, and economic circumstances, and the development of a common purpose, the evolution of common ideals, as an essential of continued existence. I think also of the responsibilities of the British Commonwealth. The United Kingdom and the Dominions cannot dissociate themselves from that responsibility—the responsibility of the British Commonwealth for world problems which in so many cases resolve themselves into a problem of how men of different races and languages and religions can live together in peace and harmony and effective co-operation as citizens of a common country.[15]

The racial policy of *apartheid* as practised by the government of South Africa in the 1950s, however, was abhorrent to other commonwealth countries, and when the Afrikaaner administration in 1961 paid the commonwealth the compliment of wishing to retain its membership after becoming a republic, the issue became explosive.

In March 1961 the commonwealth heads of government considered South Africa's application to remain a commonwealth member after becoming a republic, but instead of formally agreeing to it, as in the previous cases of India, Pakistan, and Ghana, the conference, with the South African government's consent, took the opportunity to question the *apartheid* policy. At the same time, the chief minister in Tanganyika, Julius Nyerere, made it known that when his country became independent later in the year it would not seek to remain in a commonwealth of which South Africa was a member.[16] Writing in the journal of the Royal Commonwealth Society on the achievement of independence, Nyerere insisted that he had no wish to interfere in the internal affairs of another state, but he refused to appear 'to countenance declared principles which are the antithesis of our own—which are, in other words, in conflict with our belief in equality of human beings'.[17]

At the commonwealth conference in 1961 the South African

---

[15] *United Empire*, 36 (1945), 231. A. Paton, *Hofmeyr* (London 1964), 411.
[16] *Observer*, 21 March 1961.   [17] *Commonwealth Journal*, 4 (1961), 253.

prime minister, Dr. Verwoerd, vigorously defended his country's racial policies. He could, no doubt, have made some interesting play with references to the position of Tamils in Ceylon, Aborigines in Australia, Eskimoes and Red Indians in Canada, or even the remains of the caste system in India, but it was soon evident that all the members, except Britain, Australia, and New Zealand were trying to outdo each other in the intensity of their attacks upon the South African government and that they would continue to attack it afterwards at every available opportunity. Verwoerd indicated that his government had no intention of changing its policies, and according to a communiqué issued on 15 March he informed the conference 'that in the light of the views expressed on behalf of other member Governments and the indications of their future intentions regarding the racial policy of the Union Government, he had decided to withdraw his application for South Africa's continuing membership of the commonwealth as a republic.'[18]

Menzies described the conference proceedings as deplorable and was deeply troubled about their implications for the commonwealth's future. Harold Macmillan, the British prime minister, who had a better understanding of the 'the wind of change' in Africa, was similarly regretful but less pessimistic and more readily disposed to recognize that the whole concept of the commonwealth had already changed and that its interests would not be served by South African membership: 'This association must depend', he told Parliament, 'not on the old concept of a common allegiance but upon the new principle of a common idealism.'[19] Menzies was concerned about the fracture of the principle that the commonwealth should not intervene in the domestic affairs of any member, but most responsible observers appreciated that *apartheid* aroused such strong feelings in the world it could not be treated with legal punctiliousness as a purely domestic issue. Summarizing this viewpoint, an Australian legal authority argued that there were limits to the principle of non-interference: 'The association

[18] *Documents and Speeches on Commonwealth Affairs, 1952-62*, 365.
[19] *Parl. Debs.* H.C. 637 (22 March 1961), coll. 448-9. See also Macmillan in the South African Parliament, 3 Feb. 1960, *Documents and Speeches on Commonwealth Affairs*, 347-51, and at the Royal Commonwealth Society, 13 April 1960, *Journal of the Royal Commonwealth Society*, 3 (1960), 77-82.

does not sit in judgement on Pakistan for abandoning parliamentary institutions, nor on Ghana for what many regarded as departures from accepted democratic standards. But in the multi-racial Commonwealth, a member state like South Africa which rejects racial equality denies the fundamental principle on which the Commonwealth is now based.'[20]

At the Royal Commonwealth Society the departure of South Africa from the commonwealth was not the subject of much public discussion, but the future of the South African fellows of the society was put in doubt. Citizens of South Africa remained British subjects in United Kingdom law until Parliament amended the British Nationality Act of 1948. The council's initial reaction was that it would be unwise to tamper with the membership of South African citizens before the amendments to the act were known, but in July 1961 it resolved that, if the amendments deprived South Africans of their commonwealth citizenship, South African fellows of the society should be offered affiliated membership, which would assure them of the same privileges as fellows excepting the right to vote.[21] This device was essential if the society was not to lose all its nearly 900 members in South Africa, since by the terms of the society's charter only fellows who were British subjects, British protected persons, or citizens of the Irish republic were eligible to form part of the corporate body of the society. The policy of offering affiliated membership was duly followed when a provision of the South Africa Act in 1962 provided that any person who was a British subject by virtue only of being a citizen of the South African republic should cease to be a British subject.

This was a sensible solution to the membership problem, but the subject of South Africa remained a sensitive one, and the society continued to have difficulty in determining how it could be discussed without causing embarrassment or giving the impression of partisanship. The editor of the journal, Patrick Lacey, felt strongly on the issue, and it was owing partly to protests by a few members who thought like him that an arrangement for the South African ambassador to address a

[20] Z. Cowen, *The British Commonwealth of Nations in a Changing World* (Evanston, Illinois, 1965), 60.
[21] Co. Mins. 25 (27 April 1961), 63; (27 July 1961), 79.

lunch-time meeting in the autumn of 1962 on *apartheid* was postponed for several weeks. When the executive committee of council ordered that the ambassador's address must be reported in the journal, Lacey managed to relegate it from the journal's major contents to the fine typography in the section devoted to the society's notes and news.[22]

The commonwealth's multi-racial quality was again tested by the problem of Southern Rhodesia, which accounted for most of the discussion and the publicity at the heads of government conferences in 1964 and 1965. In April 1964 the white minority government in Salisbury had turned to a new leader, Ian Smith, to guide the country to full independence, but discussions with Britain over the next eighteen months, both with the Conservative administration of Sir Alec Douglas-Home and with its successor, the Labour administration of Harold Wilson, failed to produce agreement. The main obstacle was Britain's insistence that independence should be granted only on a basis which was acceptable to all Rhodesians, white and non-white, and which allowed for guaranteed unimpeded progress to majority rule. Smith had stated his attitude in an address to the Royal Commonwealth Society in November 1963 when he had been deputy premier:

If there is any logic, any justice, if commitments are going to mean anything, if the word we give is to be as strong as our bond, if we believe in any moral standards at all, surely Southern Rhodesia is entitled to its independence. We have earned it, we have proved our case, we have been promised it, we have brought up our country knowing that this was something that was coming to us.

He declared that the Rhodesian government would persevere 'desperately' to reach agreement with Britain:

The thought of a head-on collision between ourselves and the British Government is something we turn our backs on. But I suppose if one is going to be realistic, it has to be conceded that eventually you have to face up to unpalatable things.[23]

---

[22] *Commonwealth Journal*, 6 (1963), 44. Co. Mins. 25 (25 April 1963), 149–51. See *supra*, 231.

[23] *Commonwealth Journal*, 6 (1963), 287.

The political philosophy of the Rhodesian government was elaborated further in an address to the society in April 1965 by the Rhodesia high commissioner in London:

Our political philosophy holds that fully democratic government cannot work without certain essential conditions: voters must have some minimum of formal education, the country requires a strong and stable middle class, and the nation must have some degree of homogeneity resting on a common economic interest, a common language or historical tradition.

These conditions, he admitted, did not yet exist:

Until they come into being, and taking into account the generally low calibre of our African nationalist leaders, 'one man one vote' would be more likely to result in some kind of dictatorship resting either on a party machine or on military force. We believe that our present system of political power whilst not ideal, is the best compromise achievable under present circumstances.[24]

This was an assessment which none of the commonwealth leaders could accept, though Menzies of Australia was close to subscribing to it.[25]

An African view of the Rhodesia problem was put to the society in June 1965 by Kenneth Kaunda, president of the republic of Zambia, the commonwealth country that would be most directly affected by ructions in Rhodesia. His thesis was that the British government had a responsibility to prevent a situation similar to that obtaining in South Africa developing in Rhodesia, and he closed with a reference to the society's interest in a just solution to the Rhodesia problem:

The Royal Commonwealth Society is an old and honourable organization, and has, over the years, concerned itself with many problems, the solution of which was desired by all the peoples of that great organization known as the Commonwealth. It would, in my view, be one of the tragedies of the twentieth century if the Commonwealth, which we all hold important, was weakened or destroyed at this time.[26]

Kaunda was speaking to the society at the close of a commonwealth heads of government conference which had opened at

[24] Ibid., 8 (1965), 95–6.   [25] See Menzies, *Afternoon Light*, 190–1.
[26] *Commonwealth Journal*, 9 (1965), 180.

R

Marlborough House a week before on Thursday, 17 June, and, like the conference of 1964, had been dominated by the Rhodesia issue, though the war in Vietnam also occupied much of the conference's attention in 1965. At both conferences it was affirmed that the sole authority for granting independence rested with Britain, but the African governments, with no constitutional responsibility for Rhodesia, used the conference as a convenient forum in which to air opinions and offer advice on the Rhodesia situation in a way that threatened to aggravate rather than assist the task of the commonwealth member whose business it was to deal with the problem. The position of Wilson, the British prime minister, was especially difficult in 1965 because the African representatives were not only in a less accommodating mood than they had been a year before but also expected more sympathy from the Labour government than they had received from its Conservative predecessor. Moreover, the Afro-Asian leaders, with the prospect of an Afro-Asian summit meeting to follow in Algiers at the end of the month, dared not appear subservient to a western colonial power and in consequence had a strong motive for emphasizing their anti-colonialism.[27]

With Menzies of Australia keeping to his customary brief that Rhodesia was the business of Britain alone, there was a strong possibility that the conference might divide itself along racial lines. The heads of government reaffirmed their opposition to any unilateral declaration of independence by the Rhodesian government and insisted on the principle of majority rule, although there were differences among them on the timing of the measures leading up to it.[28] In the final communiqué the section on Rhodesia was vague and ambiguous. Nonetheless, Nyerere of Tanzania dissociated himself from it, and informed observers were convinced that Britain would not be able to make concessions to Rhodesia in the months ahead without risking a rupture with the African countries. The commonwealth conference of 1965 had been used by the politicians mainly for their own ends, Dr. Williams of Trinidad and Tobago declaring that the British prime minister had been

[27] T. R. Reese, 'The Commonwealth Heads of Government Conference, 1965', *World Review*, 5 (1966), 21–2.

[28] Canada, *Parl. Debs.* 110 (H.C., 29 June 1965), 2988.

particularly guilty in this respect on the question of Vietnam.[29]
Notwithstanding the British prime minister's claim that the
conference had given the commonwealth 'a new sense of
direction, a new sense of purpose and a new sense of unity in
diversity',[30] it seemed rather to mark a further deterioration
in the prospects for the commonwealth's future. The tendency
to act as though the commonwealth were an inspired moral
influence in the world could no longer be maintained without
inviting universal ridicule. Two members, India and Pakistan,
had recently been at war when the conference met and were
soon to be fighting again, Tanzania was conducting a campaign
to undermine the government of another commonwealth
country—Rhodesia—and Ghana was believed to be encouraging
subversion in other African territories. It was also difficult to
see what was gained by repeating sentiments ventilated at the
previous conference and calling for the application to Portuguese territories of the principle of self-determination that India
seemed to be denying to Kashmir.

On 11 November 1965, when all attempts by the British and
Rhodesian governments to negotiate a mutually acceptable
basis for independence had failed, Rhodesia unilaterally
declared its independence in defiance of Britain and the whole
commonwealth. The British government had already rejected
the idea of using force to restore legality in Rhodesia and
instead embarked upon a policy of retaliatory sanctions. Any
hope that the sanctions would bring an early return to legality
soon disappeared and Tanzania and Ghana broke off diplomatic relations with the United Kingdom. The Rhodesia
problem remained an irritant in the commonwealth system and
a danger to its now clouded future.

At the conclusion of their discussion about international
affairs on the first day of the conference in June 1965, the
heads of government announced, with a touch of righteous
bravado, that a commonwealth mission would explore the
possibilities for promoting a negotiated peace in Vietnam. The
initiative for the mission had come from the British prime minister, who put forward his plan with a sense of urgency: 'We did
this', he told the House of Commons, 'because it had to be done

---

[29] *Nation* (Trinidad and Tobago), 27 Aug. 1965.
[30] *Parl. Debs.* H.C. 715 (29 June 1965), col. 310.

and because there was no one else to do it.'[31] He believed that he had asserted an international role on behalf of the commonwealth, and he could not resist remarking on the fact that the commonwealth was acting at a time when the United Nations was paralysed. Nevertheless, many commonwealth leaders resented what appeared to be a stratagem by Wilson to strengthen his domestic political position. Certainly, he cannot have been uninfluenced by the fact that he was governing on a tenuous majority of three and that a successful flourish in international affairs would improve his standing with the left wing of the Labour party, which was disappointed by the government's support for the United States, postponement of steel nationalization, and unpromising performance in housing and mortgages. No Asian would serve on the commonwealth's Vietnam mission: President Ayub Khan of Pakistan sceptically endorsed it but refused to become a member of it.[32] Several commonwealth leaders felt that they had been manœuvred into an anti-communist position by agreeing to the mission, and Nyerere of Tanzania publicly dissociated himself from it.

The projected commonwealth mission (which never visited Vietnam) illustrated the futility of commonwealth efforts to play a positive role in world affairs. There had always been a few enthusiasts who were impatient with the commonwealth acting merely as an inter-racial bridge, a launching-pad for aid schemes, or an international pressure group, and wished it to take a stand in the world, even to the extent of becoming, if possible, a power bloc in its own right.[33] This intriguing, but fanciful, idea was not widely held, however, and there was little disposition in the 1960s to pretend that the commonwealth could have a truly collective, common foreign policy. A study conference in Oxfordshire in April 1963 on the commonwealth's future concluded that the commonwealth was unlikely to react to world events as a unity:

Yet it has shown a remarkable ability to adapt itself to the modern world; its members have developed a habit of intimacy and retain a unique relationship with one another. There is something special

[31] *Parl. Debs.* H.C. (715, 29 June 1965), col. 309.
[32] *Dawn* (Karachi), 14 July 1965.
[33] See, e.g. G. Arnold, *Towards Peace and a Multiracial Commonwealth* (London 1964), 160–71.

which is common to all members of the Commonwealth, but which they do not share with foreign countries.[34]

This was as much as could reasonably be expected of an association which contained members intimately connected with the United States and Western Europe, and a large number of newcomers professedly non-aligned or uncommitted in the international division between the great power blocs of East and West.

The non-alignment policy had been popularized in India in the 1950s. 'It is all very well', Nehru told the Indian parliament in 1953, 'for some countries to divide up the world into the co-called Western bloc and the Eastern bloc, and the Communist world and the non-Communist world, and try to label everybody by these labels. We have refused to be labelled, and what is more, we refuse to consider these questions in terms of those labels, whether it is a racial issue in Africa or whether it is a national issue, a question of national freedom anywhere.'[35] The policy was somewhat discredited when China attacked India in 1962 and the Indian government hastily sought military aid, expanded its armed forces, and, perforce, discovered more merit than previously in the western nations and much less in its Chinese neighbour. The non-alignment policy had clearly been a failure so far as China was concerned, but India continued to believe that it was a viable policy so far as the United States and the Soviet Union were concerned.[36] Whatever the degree of non-alignment maintained by the new commonwealth members, the policy set them apart from the old members and prevented the multi-racial commonwealth from working together as a unit in international affairs. The practice of consultation could reduce differences and improve understanding between members, but the commonwealth was no longer a force in world politics, nor was it likely to become one.

The centrifugal tendencies within the commonwealth were the concomitant of an expanding and varied membership and

[34] T. P. Soper (*rapporteur*), *The Future of the Commonwealth: A British View* (London 1963), 4.
[35] Nehru in the House of the People, 17 March 1953, *Documents and Speeches on Commonwealth Affairs*, 458.
[36] Miller, *Commonwealth in the World*, 150.

the decline of Britain as a global power. The old bonds appeared to have been slackened by the greater interest of members in alliance structures such as NATO, ANZUS, SEATO, and CENTO, and in regional commitments that attracted African nations more to pan-Africanism than to the commonwealth, Canada more to the United States, and Australia and New Zealand more to the Western Pacific and North America.[37] When Britain succumbed to the regional pull in the 1960s and attempted to enter the European Economic Community (E.E.C.), it was accused of putting the whole commonwealth in jeopardy. In June 1961 the British prime minister told the House of Commons that three senior ministers would visit commonwealth capitals to confer on a British application to join the E.E.C. The commonwealth response was not encouraging, but negotiations for British entry were allowed to proceed.[38] The exchanges that accompanied the negotiations over the succeeding eighteen months were not elevating, and, an Australian lawyer has commented, 'the cloth of Commonwealth was exposed as pretty threadbare'.[39]

At the commonwealth conference in September 1962, Macmillan's opening statement that Britain was committed to a policy of seeking admission to E.E.C. was strongly attacked by Diefenbaker of Canada and other heads of government, and the existence of ill-feeling between Britain and the other members was made unusually obvious. The British government felt that the commonwealth countries were adopting a myopic and parochial attitude and was irritated to have its grand concept of Britain in a united, 'outward-looking' Europe reduced to detailed argument about lowly matters such as markets for kangaroo meat. 'The priority which Commonwealth Prime Ministers gave to the concerns of their own countries', according to an authority on the Australian attitude, 'aroused the resentment of some British Ministers. The Commonwealth system, it was argued, ought to imply two-way obligations, not merely British obligations to others but the obligations of others to Britain. There was exasperation in

[37] D. Austin, 'Regional Associations and the Commonwealth', *A Decade of the Commonwealth, 1955–1964*, ed. W. B. Hamilton, Kenneth Robinson, and C. D. W. Goodwin (Durham, N.C., 1966), 325–48.

[38] *Documents and Speeches on Commonwealth Affairs*, 628–50.

[39] Cowen, *The British Commonwealth of Nations in a Changing World*, 98.

London at the disposition to regard Britain as an almost automatic provider of aid, political recognition, and military assistance, while begrudging her the kind of freedom of movement claimed by every new arrival in the Commonwealth circle.' The necessity for continuous consultation, it was suggested, helped to slow down the negotiations in Brussels: 'The multiplicity of Commonwealth interests was an important negotiating liability for the British. So was the fact that while all Commonwealth countries, including Australia, felt free to complain about the British, none of them were obliged to offer constructive contributions.'[40]

The Royal Commonwealth Society was much exercised by the possible effects on the commonwealth of British membership of E.E.C., and its journal and weekly meetings encouraged a wide-ranging discussion of the issue. It sought to preserve its non-political principle, and all points of view were freely ventilated, although the journal, under Patrick Lacey, detected some virtue in Britain's exclusion from E.E.C. early in 1963, when it published a peculiar 'in memoriam' notice on the Brussels negotiations that upset the council.[41] Britain's application to join E.E.C. was vetoed in January 1963 by President de Gaulle of France, formerly an honorary fellow of the Royal Empire Society, a distinction he had accepted in 1940 for the duration of the war.[42] The failure of the Brussels negotiations revived interest in the commonwealth economic relationship. There were advocates of an amendment to the General Agreement on Tariffs and Trade to facilitate preferential trading within the commonwealth, and there were suggestions for a commonwealth economic development council to examine national development plans and co-ordinate policies towards currency problems and security of investment. The Royal Commonwealth Society reached an agreement in 1962 with the Federation of Commonwealth Chambers of Commerce by which companies under the cover of one subscription could become associate members of the federation and corporate members of the society. The object of the agreement

---

[40] H. G. Gelber, *Australia, Britain and the EEC 1961 to 1963* (Melbourne 1966), 202, 246, 249.

[41] *Commonwealth Journal*, 6 (1963), 10. Co. Mins. 25 (25 April 1963), 151.

[42] Co. Mins. 21 (2 Oct. 1940), 80.

was to plan co-operation in promoting industry and commerce in the commonwealth: 'We believe', the two bodies declared, 'that the Commonwealth from the business standpoint has a rewarding future.'[43]

For two years after Britain's abortive attempt to join E.E.C. the two major political parties vied with each other in demonstrating their devotion to the commonwealth connection, and the books, conferences, articles, speeches, lectures, and editorials that had been denigrating the commonwealth were balanced by others defending it. The Conservative party, with its imperial loyalties shaken by the emergence of African, leftward-looking states, and its hopes of taking Britain into the European Economic Community frustrated, was compelled, *faute de mieux*, to make a conscious effort to retrieve its reputation as the party of the commonwealth, an image which the Labour party had been sedulously pirating. At the heads of government conference in 1964, the Conservative government took the initiative in calling for development projects to be implemented in individual commonwealth countries by various members acting in collaboration, the aim being to increase the economic strength of the countries concerned and strengthen commonwealth ties. The Labour party, too, thought primarily in terms of the promotion of trade, economic aid, and development as a means of forging stronger commonwealth links, and after taking office it established a Ministry of Overseas Development to handle Britain's economic relations with developing areas, and particularly with those in the commonwealth. None of the parties, however, regarded a commonwealth trading unit as a serious alternative to the Common Market. It had become obvious that the British government, from whatever party it was formed, was dedicated to the eventual co-operation of the United Kingdom in a closer European political and economic system, and all commonwealth leaders were aware that this would necessarily entail a further relaxation of commonwealth bonds.[44]

In June 1964 representatives of forty organizations concerned with commonwealth affairs assembled at the Royal Common-

[43] *Commonwealth Journal*, 6 (1963), 61.
[44] Reese, 'Keeping Calm about the Commonwealth', *International Affairs*, 41 (1965). 455–6.

wealth Society in order to discuss ways in which co-operation in the commonwealth might be improved. The society was anxious to emphasize to the forthcoming heads of government conference in July that there existed in the United Kingdom extensive support for the commonwealth's ideals and aims, and at the meeting a statement of faith in the commonwealth was drafted and copies sent to the British prime minister and the high commissions in London. It had a disappointing press coverage but was genially welcomed by the heads of government.[45] The statement's message was well expressed in the opening paragraph:

Now is the moment for a determined effort by governments and by organizations outside of government to employ the resources and spirit of the Commonwealth for bridging the gap between the developed and the developing countries, to prove by example how different races can respect one another's views and can work together in friendship, and to show what the Commonwealth could do as a power for world peace within the framework of the United Nations.[46]

The statement of faith was designed to herald efforts to regain for the commonwealth relationship some of the sympathy and support it was clearly losing. The heads of government conference considered the establishment of a commonwealth foundation to assist and stimulate professional contacts within the commonwealth. The idea was encouraged by the Royal Commonwealth Society, which helped to create a favourable climate of opinion towards it and, at the suggestion of the Commonwealth Relations Office, in December 1964 called a meeting with representatives of professional organizations to discuss the proposed foundation and make suggestions on its scope and operation.[47] The disillusionment with the commonwealth was not confined to Britain, for it was evident also in other members as widely different as Australia and New Zealand on the one hand and Zambia and Tanzania on the other, but it was in Britain that the disillusionment was most pandemic and the most serious for the commonwealth as a

---

[45] Co. Mins. 25 (25 June 1964), 197; (23 July), 202.
[46] *Commonwealth Journal*, 7 (1964), 161.
[47] Glendevon to Bottomley, commonwealth relations secretary, 22 Dec. 1964; Bottomley to Glendevon, 1 Jan. 1965: R.C.S. Archives.

whole. British public opinion was disillusioned with a common-wealth which apparently brought Britain liabilities and few rewards, which for other members seemed to be largely a vehicle for securing aid, putting pressure on Britain and influencing its policies, and to the preservation of which the British government sacrificed its own freedom of manœuvre while other members criticized Britain in international affairs, and even severed diplomatic relations. An English editorial after the 1965 heads of government conference expressed this feeling in moderate language:

> As the Commonwealth evolves into an association of equal partners, Britain will more and more have the right to insist on its own equality, reduce the liabilities it has inherited from the past, and point out that it can help others most in the long run if it puts its own economic interests first. Part of our future will lie with the Commonwealth, it is to be hoped, for many years to come: but it will be a part of diminishing importance.[48]

In January 1966 the British government was represented at a commonwealth emergency conference in Lagos, where it was called upon to defend its policy towards Rhodesia, and later in the year Britain was described by a Zambian minister as a toothless bulldog and its prime minister as a racialist. In Britain confidence in the commonwealth naturally declined still further.

Britain had been able earlier to use commonwealth support in order to strengthen the impression of its power in the world, but it could no longer depend upon unqualified backing, except in times of crisis by Australia, New Zealand, and, per-haps, Canada. It was possible to argue that the existence of the commonwealth had been a pernicious influence on British policy, which had been distorted by the illusion of power based on the commonwealth relationship, and a case could be made out for Britain reappraising its attitude and treating its relation-ship with each individual member purely on its merits. There was both a greater willingness to question the assumption that anything with a commonwealth connotation was, *ipso facto*, laudable and good, and also a growing belief that disregard of commonwealth ties would allow Britain more flexibility in

[48] *Financial Times*, 28 June 1965.

its approach to international issues. Commonwealth idealogues continued to maintain that there was something special, if often intangible, in the nature of the commonwealth relationship, but it had now become possible to question whether it was necessarily wise or right to foster the idea that in its external relations a commonwealth member consciously differentiated between commonwealth and non-commonwealth countries. A parallel between the attitude of the sceptics and critics in Britain in 1968 and that of the Manchester school and separatists in 1868 was apparent, and although the parallel could not be carried far, a similarity could be detected in the challenge faced by the original Colonial Society and that faced by the Royal Commonwealth Society a century later.

The Royal Commonwealth Society's central problem in 1968 was to determine what it wished to be and what it wished to do. Its *raison d'être* was to serve and nourish an association of peoples which was itself in a parlous condition and whose future was uncertain. For many years the society had appeared *passé* and static; in 1956 an Australian federal minister had refused to join because he regarded its objects as out of date.[49] In the late 1950s and in the 1960s it attempted to adapt itself more to contemporary needs, but its credibility and efficacy were reduced by the widespread disenchantment with the commonwealth in general. In the nineteenth century the society had applied pressure to governments, and in the middle of the twentieth century there were sympathizers who thought that this role could be revived. Lord Casey, an Australian with long experience of political life and of commonwealth affairs, suggested somewhat rashly in 1962 that it should become 'a militant fighting body' to prevent the commonwealth fading as an active force:

You are a great institution, long established, with high prestige, with entry into the highest quarters in this country. You are, I believe, ideally situated by your membership and your prestige to take a much more militant attitude in respect of the Commonwealth: asking awkward questions, making a nuisance of yourselves, pointing out in simple, understandable language what is at stake and what might be done. That is what I would like to see. Not that you are not an active body now, but I would like to see more militancy,

[49] Co. Mins. 24 (23 Oct. 1956), 184.

facing up to the hard facts of our Commonwealth situation, and making proposals for its betterment, so that we could look forward over the years ahead to a greater degree of unity and cohesion in the Commonwealth.

He hoped that the society would become 'the spearpoint' of a movement 'to re-create a noticeable degree of unity in the Commonwealth so that we can again become a great force for good in the world'.[50] Casey returned to this theme the next year in a brisk, graceless, but constructive book on the future of the commonwealth:

There are many non-governmental associations with a Common-wealth-wide function which I am sure do good, individually and collectively, but which I do not believe have an important influence on the cohesion of the Commonwealth as a whole. I will not speak of them individually, except in one instance. The Royal Common-wealth Society is an old established institution of high prestige and large membership, with a great many branches in all the 'old' and many of the 'new' Commonwealth countries. Its description has been changed from time to time to keep pace with the evolution from the Empire to the Commonwealth. Many of its branches produce regular, well-published monthly reports of their activities, including the texts of lectures and papers on matters of Commonwealth importance by individuals of consequence. However, many of its social and other activities—and of the addresses made under its auspices—represent nostalgic recollections of the glories of the past, not anxious constructive looking-forward into the future of the Commonwealth. If the Society should decide to change direction, to look forward and not back, to become a militant body, hammer-ing day in and day out at Governments and all concerned to get imaginative things done, designed to create cohesion amongst the Commonwealth countries, it could have a substantial influence on the future health and welfare of the Commonwealth.[51]

Casey's strictures were not entirely just, and much of his argu-ment was absurd, but his suggestions were noted by the central council, which began to encourage closer co-operation between the leading voluntary societies to strengthen their response.[52]

It was doubtful whether the society was either qualified or

[50] *Commonwealth Journal*, 5 (1962), 168.

[51] Lord Casey, *The Future of the Commonwealth* (London 1963), 38. See also D. Ingram, *Commonwealth for a Colour-Blind World* (London 1965), 114.

[52] Ex. Co. Mins. 3 (14 Nov. 1963), 202. Co. Mins. 25 (28 July 1966), 267.

well advised to attempt to become what Casey desired it to be. If it was to be a propagandist body applying pressure to governments, it would have to decide what kind of commonwealth it wanted and could realistically work for. In February 1967 a 'Nudge Committee' of six members was formed under the society's sponsorship to combat public apathy towards the commonwealth and attempt to influence governments and official bodies on matters affecting the commonwealth relationship. Nevertheless, it was difficult to believe that the society could be an effective significant influence on member governments in the commonwealth of the late twentieth century, and it had little to gain from following the advice of critics who would have it advocate a positive role for what was now an essentially negative association.

The society contributed handsomely to social intercourse between the various peoples of the commonwealth. An authority on the commonwealth's non-governmental associations linked the Royal Commonwealth Society with the Royal Overseas League, Victoria League for Commonwealth Friendship, and the English-Speaking Union of the Commonwealth among bodies encouraging intra-commonwealth activity and understanding:

Their value lies as much in the fact that they have branches and committees in many parts of the Commonwealth as in the work they perform in London in promoting knowledge of the Commonwealth and in their reception of visitors from overseas.[53]

This summary description correctly interpreted the society as primarily a social and educational body, not a propagandist one. The social activity was important, but could not alone form a durable and worthwhile basis for a society that wished to be taken seriously.

For a century the society had been the champion of imperial and commonwealth causes; it had a proud record of achievement in the furtherance of study and knowledge of the old empire and of the modern commonwealth; and it had been a valuable instrument of friendship between the peoples of the various member nations and colonies. It would continue to

[53] J. Chadwick, 'Intra-Commonwealth Relations: Non-governmental Associations', *A Decade of the Commonwealth*, 141.

contribute to the late twentieth-century commonwealth in these ways, but something more was now required. Whatever course was followed would be attended by difficulties, especially of finance, but there could be no better policy than respecting the objective enunciated in the royal charter: 'to promote within Our United Kingdom and overseas the increase and spread of knowledge respecting the peoples and countries of the Commonwealth'. The Royal Commonwealth Society possessed an outstanding library that was already a cradle of learning, and if it discarded the assumption that it had an obligation to defend and glorify a commonwealth about whose nature and future there was doubt, it might raise its academic standards and become an international centre of study and research into commonwealth subjects. This would not be an easy task, but it was one that might provide the society with a challenge and a purpose that would sustain a constructive future.

Appendix A

To provide a place of meeting for all Gentlemen connected with the Colonies and British India, and others taking an interest in Colonial and Indian affairs; to establish a Reading Room and Library, in which recent and authentic intelligence upon Colonial and Indian subjects may be constantly available, and a Museum for the collection and exhibition of Colonial and Indian productions; to facilitate interchange of experiences amongst persons representing all the Dependencies of Great Britain; to afford opportunities for the reading of Papers, and for holding Discussions upon Colonial and Indian subjects generally; and to undertake scientific, literary, and statistical investigations in connection with the British Empire. But no Paper shall be read, or any Discussion be permitted to take place, tending to give to the Institute a party character.

Appendix B

OBJECTS OF THE ROYAL COMMONWEALTH SOCIETY (SUPPLEMENTAL CHARTER, 13 OCTOBER 1964)

THE objects of the Society shall be to promote within Our United Kingdom and overseas the increase and spread of knowledge respecting the peoples and countries of the Commonwealth.

These objects shall be pursued by the Society working as a non-sectarian and non-party organization by the following methods:

(1) providing a central meeting place in London and meeting places in Commonwealth countries and elsewhere,

(2) maintaining libraries and newspaper rooms,

(3) holding meetings in Commonwealth countries and elsewhere for the discussion of subjects of Commonwealth interest,

(4) producing and publishing journals and other publications,

(5) encouraging the study of the geography, ethnology, history, literature, art, natural resources and economics of Commonwealth

countries, especially in universities and schools by providing lectures and prizes for essays,

(6) undertaking scientific and other enquiries,

(7) promoting or assisting the establishment of professorships and lectureships and research Fellowships and Scholarships,

(8) promoting the Trade and Industry of the Commonwealth especially by collecting and distributing information regarding its natural resources and openings for trade and by forming or supporting the formation of organizations which are concerned with the promotion of the Trade and Industry in the Commonwealth,

(9) maintaining information services for Members of the Society and others,

(10) providing information on opportunities for and encouraging settlement in Commonwealth countries,

(11) promoting the comparative study of the ways of life in Commonwealth countries and encouraging interchange of ideas,

(12) providing facilities for the study of foreign countries as far as this may be of interest to the peoples of the Commonwealth,

(13) encouraging the formation of Branches of the Society in Commonwealth countries and elsewhere,

(14) encouraging mutual interest in Commonwealth countries among young people,

(15) co-operating with other charitable organizations,

(16) using any other charitable method proper to the carrying out of the objects of the Society,

provided that the Society shall exist only for purposes which are exclusively charitable and none of the funds of the Society shall be paid or applied for other purposes.

Appendix C

PRESIDENTS OF THE SOCIETY

1868–1871: Viscount Bury (afterwards Lord Albemarle).

1871–1878: The Duke of Manchester.

1878–1901: H.R.H. the Prince of Wales (afterwards King Edward VII).

1901–1910: H.R.H. the Prince of Wales (afterwards King George V).

1910–1912: H.R.H. the Duke of Connaught.

1912–1917: Earl Grey.

1918–1942: H.R.H. the Duke of Connaught.
1942–1964: H.R.H. the Duke of Gloucester.*
1965–   : Viscount Boyd of Merton.

Appendix D

CHAIRMEN OF COUNCIL

1878–1890: The Duke of Manchester.
1909–1915: Lieut-.Gen. Sir J. Bevan Edwards.
1915–1920: Sir Charles Lucas.
1920–1923: Sir Godfrey Lagden.
1923–1925: Sir Charles McLeod.
1925–1928: Lord Stanley of Alderley.
1928–1930: Sir John Sandeman Allen.
1930–1932: Col. Sir A. Weston Jarvis.
1932–1938: Sir Archibald Weigall.
1938–1941: Maj.-Gen. Sir Frederick Sykes.
1941–1942: Sir William Clark.
1942–1943: Gen. Sir Alexander Godley.
1943–1948: The Earl of Clarendon.
1948–1951: Admiral of the Fleet Lord Chatfield.
1951–1954: Sir Lancelot Graham.
1954–1957: Col. Sir Charles Ponsonby.
1957–1960: Earl De La Warr.
1961–1963: Viscount Boyd of Merton.
1963–1966: Lord John Hope (Lord Glendevon)
1966–   : The Duke of Devonshire.

Appendix E

SECRETARIES AND SECRETARIES-GENERAL

1869–1871: A. R. Roche (Honorary).
1871–1874: C. W. Eddy (Honorary).
1874–1886: Frederick Young (Honorary).
1884–1909: J. S. O'Halloran.

* Under the supplemental charter of 1964 H.R.H. the Duke of Gloucester became the Grand President.

S

1909–1915: J. R. Boosé.
1915–1921: Sir Harry Wilson.
1921–1929: Sir George Boughey.
1929–1935: G. P. Pilcher.
1935–1938: R. E. H. Baily.
1938–1958: L. G. Archer Cust (on war service 1939–45).
1958–1967: D. K. Daniels.
1967–　　 : A. S. H. Kemp.

Appendix F

LIBRARIANS

1881–1889: J. S. O'Halloran.
1889–1909: J. R. Boosé.
1910–1946: P. Evans Lewin.
1946–1956: J. Packman.
1956–　　 : D. H. Simpson.

List of Works Cited

ROYAL COLONIAL INSTITUTE

Council Minute Books.

Letter Books.

Newfoundland Fisheries Committee Minutes (1875).

Proceedings (40 vols., 1869–1909).

United Empire (49 vols., 1910–58); Royal Colonial Institute Journal, 1910–27.

Official Report of the Emigration Conference held on May 30–31, 1910, convened by the Royal Colonial Institute (1910).

The After-War Settlement and Employment of Ex-Service Men in the Oversea Dominions (1916); Report to the Royal Colonial Institute by Sir Rider Haggard.

Land Settlement for Ex-Service Men in the Oversea Dominions (1920); Report to the Royal Colonial Institute by Christopher Turnor.

New South Wales Branch, *Annual Reports*.

ROYAL EMPIRE SOCIETY

Council Minute Books.

General Purposes Committee Minutes (1939).

Executive Committee Minute Books (1947–68).

United Empire (49 vols., 1910–58); Journal of the Royal Empire Society, 1928–58.

India Committee, *Report to the Council of the Society on the Probable Working of the Simon Commission's Proposals* (1930).

The Political Future of the British Commonwealth and Empire (1945); Report of a Political Study Group of the Royal Empire Society.

ROYAL COMMONWEALTH SOCIETY

Council Minute Books.

Executive Committee Minute Books.

Journal of the Royal Commonwealth Society (1958–60).

Commonwealth Journal (1961–8).

Library Notes.

Confidential Report to Council by Sir Charles Ponsonby (Oct. 1962).

Confidential Supplementary Report to Council by Sir Charles Ponsonby (Dec. 1962).

Librarian's Memorandum on War Damage Funds (Feb. 1967).

PUBLIC RECORD OFFICE

Granville Papers: P.R.O. 30/29; vols. 32, 57, 77.

Carnarvon Papers: P.R.O. 30/6; vol. 6.

Colonial Office Papers:

C.O. 43/156; Canada—secretary of state letters (1868–70).
C.O. 83/4; Fiji—original correspondence (1873).
C.O. 87/109; Gambia—original correspondence (1876).
C.O. 209/210; New Zealand—original correspondence, secretary of state despatches (1869).

BRITISH MUSEUM

Gladstone Papers: Additional Manuscripts.

PARLIAMENTARY DEBATES

Canada, *Parliamentary Debates.*
Queensland, *Votes and Proceedings of the Legislative Assembly.*
United Kingdom, *Parliamentary Debates.*
Colony and State of Victoria, *Parliamentary Debates.*

PARLIAMENTARY PAPERS

1865: Vol. 5, No. 412 (June), Report from the select committee appointed to consider the state of the British establishments on the western coast of Africa.

1870: Vol. 49, C. 24 (Feb.) and C. 51 (March), Correspondence respecting a proposed conference of colonial representatives in London.

1870: Vol. 50, C. 83 (April), Further papers relative to the affairs of New Zealand.

1870: Vol. 50, No. 444 (Aug.), Petitions and dispatches relating to the proposed cession of the Gambia.

1871: Vol. 47, No. 435 (Aug.), Correspondence and documents relating to the Fiji Islands.

1872: Vol. 43, C. 509 (March), Further correspondence relating to the Fiji Islands.

1874: Vol. 45, C. 1011 (July), Report of Commodore Goodenough and Mr. Consul Layard on the offer of the cession of the Fiji Islands to the British crown.

1875: Vol. 52, C. 114 (Feb.), Correspondence respecting the cession of Fiji.

1876: Vol. 52, C. 1409 (Feb.), Correspondence respecting the affairs of the Gambia and the proposed exchange with France of possessions on the west coast of Africa.

1876: Vol. 54, C. 1566 (July), Correspondence respecting New Guinea.

1883: Vol. 47, C. 3617 (May) and C. 3691 (July), Further correspondence respecting New Guinea.

1887: Vol. 56, C. 5091 (July), Proceedings of the colonial conference 1887, Vol. I.

1897: Vol. 59, C. 8596 (July), Proceedings of a colonial conference at the Colonial Office, London, 1897.

1902: Vol. 66, Cd. 1299 (Oct.), Papers relating to a colonial conference 1902.

1906: Vol. 77, Cd. 2785 (Nov.), Correspondence relating to the future organization of colonial conferences.

1907: Vol. 55, Cd. 3404 (April), Published proceedings and précis of the colonial conference 1907.

1907: Vol. 55, Cd. 3523 (May), Minutes of proceedings of the colonial conference 1907.

1911: Vol. 54, Cd. 5745 (July), Minutes of proceedings of the imperial conference 1911.

1917–18: Vol. 10, Cd. 8462 (March 1917), Final report of the royal commission on the natural resources, trade, and legislation of certain portions of His Majesty's dominions.

1917–18: Vol. 23, Cd. 8566 (May 1917), Extracts from minutes of proceedings and papers laid before the imperial war conference, 1917.

1918: Vol. 13, Cd. 9035, Final report of the committee on commercial and industrial policy after the war.

1918: Vol. 16, Cd. 9177 (Oct.), Imperial war conference, 1918: extracts from minutes of proceedings and papers laid before the conference.

1919: Vol. 30, Cmd. 325, Report of the war cabinet for the year 1918.

1921: Vol. 14, Cmd. 1474 (Aug.), Conference of prime ministers and representatives of the United Kingdom, the dominions, and India, held in June, July, and August 1921: summary of proceedings and documents.

1923: Vol. 18, Cmd. 1922 (July), Indians in Kenya: memorandum.

1923: Vol. 12, Pt. 1, Cmd. 1987 (Nov.), Imperial conference, 1923: summary of proceedings.

1923: Vol. 12, Pt. 1, Cmd. 1997 (Nov.), Report of the Imperial Institute committee of enquiry 1923 together with resolutions of the imperial economic conference on the subject.

1924: Vol. 10, Cmd. 2009 (Jan.), Imperial economic conference of representatives of Great Britain, the dominions, India, and the colonies and protectorates, held in October and November 1923: record of proceedings and documents.

1926: Vol. 11, Cmd. 2768 (Nov.), Imperial conference, 1926: summary of proceedings.

1928–9: Vol. 5, Cmd. 3234 (Jan. 1929), Report of the commission on closer union of the dependencies in Eastern and Central Africa.

1929–30: Vol. 8, Cmd. 3378 (Sept. 1929), Report of Sir Samuel Wilson on his visit to East Africa, 1929.

1929–30: Vol. 11, Cmd. 3568 and 3569 (May 1930), Report of the Indian statutory commission: Vol. I, survey; Vol. II, recommendations.

1929–30: Vol. 23, Cmd. 3574 (June 1930), Statement of the conclusions of His Majesty's Government in the United Kingdom as regards closer union in East Africa.

1929–30: Vol. 16, Cmd. 3589 (June 1930), Report of the oversea settlement committee for the year ended 31st December 1929.

1930–1: Vol. 12, Cmd. 3778 (Jan. 1931), Indian round table conference 12th November 1930–19th January 1931: proceedings.

1930–1: Vol. 16, Cmd. 3920 (July 1931), Committee on national expenditure: report.

1930–1: Vol. 7, No. 156 (Oct. 1931), Joint committee on closer union in East Africa: Vol. I, report, together with the proceedings of the committee.

1931–2: Vol. 18, Cmd. 4141 (Aug. 1932), Correspondence (1931–2) arising from the report of the joint select committee on closer union in East Africa.

1932–3: Vol. 20, Cmd. 4268 (March 1933), Proposals for Indian constitutional reform.

1933–4: Vol. 6, H.L. 6 and H.C. 5 (Oct. 1934), Joint committee on Indian constitutional reform: Vol. I (Part 1), report.

1936–7: Vol. 12, Cmd. 5482 (June 1937), Imperial conference, 1937: summary of proceedings.

1948–9: Vol. 19, Cmd. 7695 (June 1949), Royal commission on population: report.

DOCUMENTARY COLLECTIONS

BLACHFORD: *Letters of Frederick Lord Blachford, Under-Secretary of State for the Colonies, 1860–1871*, ed. George E. Marindin (London 1896).

COMMONWEALTH: *Documents and Speeches on Commonwealth Affairs, 1952–1962*, ed. Nicholas Mansergh (London 1963).

DISRAELI: *Selected Speeches of the late Earl of Beaconsfield*, ed. T. E. Kebbel (2 vols., London 1882).

HAGGARD: *Rudyard Kipling to Rider Haggard: The Record of a Friendship*, ed. Morton Cohen (London 1965).

JEBB: Letters and Documents of Richard Jebb (Original Papers at the Institute of Commonwealth Studies, University of London).

SMUTS: *Selections from the Smuts Papers*, ed. W. K. Hancock and Jean van der Poel (4 vols., London 1966).

YOUNG: Original papers of Frederick Young at the Royal Commonwealth Society.

NEWSPAPERS AND PERIODICALS

Age (Melbourne).
Argus (Melbourne).
Australian and New Zealand Gazette.
Daily News.
Daily Telegraph.
Dawn (Karachi).
European Mail.
Malay Mail.
Nation (Trinidad and Tobago).
Observer.
Spectator.
Standard.
Sunday Times.
Sydney Examiner.
The Times.
Times of Malaya.
Athenæum.
Canadian Historical Review.
Historical Studies Australia and New Zealand.
Imperial Federation; journal of the Imperial Federation League.
International Affairs.
Journal of Commonwealth Political Studies.
Nineteenth Century.
Royal Australian Historical Society Journal and Proceedings.
Transactions of the Royal Historical Society.
World Review.
British Empire Union: *Annual Reports.*
Overseas League: *Annual Reports.*
Victoria League: *Annual Reports.*

BOOKS, THESES, AND ARTICLES

AMERY, L. S., *The Forward View* (London 1935).
— *My Political Life* (3 vols., London 1953–5).
ARNOLD, Guy, *Towards Peace and a Multiracial Commonwealth* (London 1964).
AUSTIN, Dennis, 'Regional Associations and the Commonwealth', *A Decade of the Commonwealth, 1955–1964*, ed. W. B. Hamilton, Kenneth Robinson, and C. D. W. Goodwin (1966), 325–48.

Aziz, K. K., *Britain and Muslim India: A Study of British Public Opinion vis-à-vis the Development of Muslim Nationalism in India, 1857–1947* (London 1963).

Bell, E. Moberly, *Flora Shaw (Lady Lugard, D.B.E.)* (London 1947).

Birdwood, Lord, *Khaki and Gown: An Autobiography* (London 1941).

Blackton, C. S., 'Australian Nationality and Nationalism: The Imperial Federationist Interlude, 1885–1901', *Historical Studies Australia and New Zealand*, 7 (1955), 1–16.

Bodelsen, C. A., *Studies in Mid-Victorian Imperialism* (Copenhagen 1924).

Boosé, James R., *Memory Serving: Being Reminiscences of Fifty Years of the Royal Colonial Institute* (London 1928).

Brittain, Sir Harry, *Happy Pilgrimage* (London 1949).

Brookes, Jean Ingram, *International Rivalry in the Pacific Islands, 1800–1875* (Berkeley 1941).

Burns, Alan, *Colonial Civil Servant* (London 1949).

Bury, Viscount, *Exodus of the Western Nations* (2 vols., London 1865).

Cambridge History of the British Empire: Vol. 3, *The Empire-Commonwealth, 1870–1919*, ed. E. A. Benians, Sir James Butler, and C. E. Carrington (1959).

Carrothers, W. A., *Emigration from the British Isles, with special reference to the development of the overseas dominions* (London 1929).

Casey, Lord, *The Future of the Commonwealth* (London 1963).

Chadwick, John, 'Intra-Commonwealth Relations: Non-governmental Associations', *A Decade of the Commonwealth*, ed. W. B. Hamilton, Kenneth Robinson, and C. D. W. Goodwin (1966), 124–47.

Childers, Edmund S. E., *The Life and Correspondence of the Right Hon. Hugh C. E. Childers, 1827–1896* (2 vols., London 1901).

Churchill, Winston S., *The Second World War* (6 vols., London 1948–54).

Cohen, Morton, *Rider Haggard: His Life and Works* (London 1960).

Cowen, Zelman, *The British Commonwealth of Nations in a Changing World: Law, Politics, and Prospects* (Evanston, Illinois, 1965); The Julius Rosenthal Lectures, Northwestern University School of Law, 1964.

Curtis, Lionel, *The Problem of the Commonwealth* (London 1916).

— *The Royal Empire Society and 'The Political Future of the British Commonwealth and Empire': A Comment addressed by L. C. to the Society* (1945).

Dawson, Robert MacGregor, *The Development of Dominion Status, 1900–1936* (London 1937).

Denison, George T., *The Struggle for Imperial Unity: Recollections and Experiences* (London 1909).

DRUS, Ethel, 'The Colonial Office and the Annexation of Fiji', *Transactions of the Royal Historical Society*, 32 (1950), 87–110.

DUNDAS, Lawrence J. L., *Essayez: The Memoirs of Lawrence, the Second Marquess of Zetland* (London 1956).

EGERTON, Hugh E., *British Colonial Policy in the XXth Century* (London 1922).

FISCHER, Louis, *The Life of Mahatma Gandhi* (London 1951).

FITZMAURICE, Lord Edmond, *The Life of Granville George Leveson Gower Second Earl Granville, 1815–1891* (2 vols., London 1905).

FOLSOM, Avaline, *The Royal Empire Society: Formative Years* (London 1933).

FYFE, Christopher, *A History of Sierra Leone* (London 1962).

GELBER, H. G., *Australia, Britain and the EEC, 1961* (Melbourne 1966).

GOSHAL, Kumar, *People in Colonies* (New York 1948).

GRAHAM, Gerald S., 'Imperial Finance, Trade, and Communications, 1885–1914', *Cambridge History of the British Empire*, 3 (1959), 438–89.

HAGGARD, Lilias Rider, *The Cloak that I Left: A Biography of the Author Henry Rider Haggard* (London 1951).

HALL, Henry L., *Australia and England: A Study in Imperial Relations* (London 1934).

HAMILTON, W. B., Kenneth ROBINSON, and C. D. W. GOODWIN (editors), *A Decade of the Commonwealth, 1955–1964* (Durham, N.C., 1966).

HANCOCK, I. R., 'The 1911 Imperial Conference', *Historical Studies Australia and New Zealand*, 12 (1966), 356–72.

HANCOCK, W. K., *Problems of Nationality, 1918–1936* (London 1937); Survey of British Commonwealth Affairs (Royal Institute of International Affairs), Vol. I.

— *Problems of Economic Policy, 1918–1939*, Part 1 (London 1940), Part 2 (London 1942); Survey of British Commonwealth Affairs, Vol. II.

— *Smuts: The Sanguine Years, 1870–1919* (Cambridge 1962).

HARGREAVES, John D., *Prelude to the Partition of West Africa* (London 1963).

HATTERSLEY, Alan F., *The Colonies and Imperial Federation: An Historical Sketch, 1754–1919* (Pietermaritzburg 1919).

HUDSON, Derek, and Kenneth W. LUCKHURST, *The Royal Society of Arts, 1754–1954* (London 1954).

INGRAM, Derek, *Commonwealth for a Colour-Blind World* (London 1965).

JACOBS, Marjorie C., 'The Colonial Office and New Guinea, 1874–84', *Historical Studies Australia and New Zealand*, 5 (1952), 106–18.

JAMES, Robert Rhodes, *Rosebery: A Biography of Archibald Philip, Fifth Earl of Rosebery* (London 1963).

JEBB, Richard, *The Imperial Conference* (2 vols., London 1911).

— *The Empire in Eclipse* (London 1926).

KEITH, Arthur Berriedale, *Imperial Unity and the Dominions* (London 1916).

KENDLE, John E., *The Colonial and Imperial Conferences, 1887–1911: A Study in Imperial Organisation and Politics* (Ph.D. thesis, University of London 1965).

KNAPLUND, Paul, *Gladstone and Britain's Imperial Policy* (London 1927).

KOEBNER, Richard, and Helmut Dan SCHMIDT, *Imperialism: The Story and Significance of a Political Word, 1840–1960* (London 1964).

LABILLIÈRE, F. P. de, *Federal Britain; or, Unity and Federation of the Empire* (London 1894).

LA NAUZE, J. A., *Alfred Deakin: A Biography* (Melbourne 1965).

LEGGE, J. D., 'Australia and New Guinea to the Establishment of the British Protectorate, 1884', *Historical Studies Australia and New Zealand*, 4 (1949), 34–47.

MACMILLAN, D. S., 'The Australians in London, 1857–1880', *Royal Australian Historical Society Journal and Proceedings*, 44 (1958), 155–81.

MADDEN, A. F., 'Changing Attitudes and Widening Responsibilities, 1895–1914', *Cambridge History of the British Empire*, 3 (1959), 338–405.

MANSERGH, Nicholas, *Problems of External Policy, 1931–1939* (London 1952); Survey of British Commonwealth Affairs.

— (et. al.), *Commonwealth Perspectives* (Durham, N.C., 1958).

MEATH, Earl of, *Memories of the Twentieth Century* (London 1924).

— *Brabazon Potpourri* (London 1928).

MEHROTRA, S. R., 'On the Use of the Term "Commonwealth"', *Journal of Commonwealth Political Studies*, 2 (1963), 1–16.

MENZIES, Sir Robert Gordon, *Afternoon Light: Some Memories of Men and Events* (London 1967).

MILLER, David H., *The Drafting of the Covenant* (2 vols., New York 1928).

MILLER, J. D. B., *The Commonwealth in the World* (3rd edn., London 1965).

MORRELL, W. P., *Britain in the Pacific Islands* (London 1960).

MORRIS, Edward E., *A Memoir of George Higinbotham, an Australian Politician and Chief Justice of Victoria* (London 1895).

OLIVER, Roland, and J. D. FAGE, *A Short History of Africa* (London 1962); Penguin Books African Library, ed. Ronald Segal.

PALLEY, Claire, *The Constitutional History and Law of Southern Rhodesia,*

1888–1965, with special reference to Imperial Control (London 1966).

PARNABY, O. W., *Britain and the Labor Trade in the Southwest Pacific* (Durham, N.C., 1964).

PATON, Alan, *Hofmeyr* (London 1964).

PERHAM, Margery, *Lugard: The Years of Authority, 1898–1945* (London 1960).

PONSONBY, Sir Charles, *Ponsonby Remembers* (Oxford 1965).

PUGH, R. B., 'The Colonial Office, 1801–1925', *Cambridge History of the British Empire*, 3 (1959), 711–68.

QUIGLEY, Carroll, 'The Round Table Groups in Canada, 1908–38', *Canadian Historical Review*, 43 (1962), 204–24.

RAJAN, M. S., *The Post-War Transformation of the Commonwealth* (London 1964).

REESE, Trevor R., *Australia in the Twentieth Century* (London 1964).

— 'Keeping Calm about the Commonwealth', *International Affairs*, 41 (1965), 451–62.

— 'The Commonwealth Heads of Government Conference, 1965', *World Review*, 5 (1966), 21–30.

ROBB, Janet H., *The Primrose League, 1883–1906* (New York 1942).

ROBINSON, R. E., 'Imperial Problems in British Politics, 1880–1895', *Cambridge History of the British Empire*, 3 (1959), 127–80.

SEELEY, John R., *The Expansion of England: Two Courses of Lectures* (London 1883).

SERLE, Geoffrey, *The Golden Age: A History of the Colony of Victoria, 1851–1861* (Melbourne 1963).

SINCLAIR, Keith, *Imperial Federation: A Study of New Zealand Policy and Opinion, 1880–1914* (1955); University of London Institute of Commonwealth Studies, Commonwealth Papers, No. 11.

SKELTON, John, *The Table Talk of Shirley* (Edinburgh 1895).

SKELTON, Oscar D., *The Life and Times of Sir Alexander Tilloch Galt* (Toronto 1920).

SMITH, S. A. de, *The New Commonwealth and its Constitutions* (London 1964).

SOPER, T. P. (*rapporteur*), *The Future of the Commonwealth: A British View* (H.M.S.O., London 1963).

SOUTHORN, Lady, *The Gambia: The Story of the Groundnut Colony* (London 1952).

STANTON-HOPE, W. E., *One Only Lives Twice* (London 1955).

SYKES, Sir Frederick, *From Many Angles: An Autobiography* (London 1942).

TAYLOR, A. J. P., *English History, 1914–1945* (London 1965).

TWEEDIE, Mrs. Alec, *Me and Mine: A Medley of Thoughts and Memories* (London 1932).

TYLER, J. E., *The Struggle for Imperial Unity, 1868–1895* (London 1938).

— 'Development of the Imperial Conference, 1887–1914', *Cambridge History of the British Empire*, 3 (1959), 406–37.

WAINWRIGHT, David, *The Volunteers: The Story of the Overseas Voluntary Service* (London 1965).

WARD, John M., *British Policy in the South Pacific, 1786–1893*, (Sydney 1948).

WESTGARTH, William, *Personal Recollections of Early Melbourne and Victoria* (Melbourne 1888).

WHEARE, Kenneth, C., *The Statute of Westminster and Dominion Status* (Oxford 1953).

WILDE, Richard H., 'Joseph Chamberlain's Proposal for an Imperial Council in March, 1900', *Canadian Historical Review*, 37 (1956), 225–46.

WILLISON, John, *Sir George Parkin* (London 1929).

WORSFOLD, W. Basil, *The Empire on the Anvil* (London 1916).

YOUNG, Frederick, *Imperial Federation of Great Britain and the Colonies* (London 1876).

ZETLAND, Marquess of: *see* DUNDAS.

Index

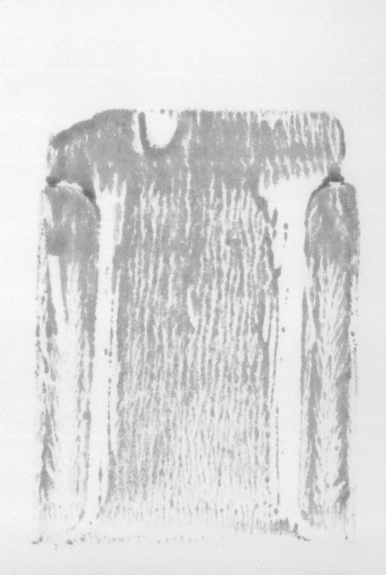